About the Cover

The idyllic garden illustration entitled, *"Call to Eden,"* was printed on holographic foil to portray the beauty of marriage as God intended it from the beginning— and *as it can be again* when He is welcomed into the relationship between husband and wife.

Design concept and art direction: HeartLight

Creative execution in Adobe Photoshop, Aldus Freehand, and QuarkXpress: D.H. Gornick

Tender Journey

*A Continuing Story
For Our Troubled Times*

James P. Gills, M.D.
and
HeartLight

TENDER JOURNEY: A Continuing Story For Our Troubled Times
© 1997 by James P. Gills, M.D. and HeartLight
Produced by HeartLight

Published by LOVE PRESS
An international outreach of St. Luke's Cataract and Laser Institute
Tarpon Springs, Florida
Printed in the United States of America
First printing: 100,000

ISBN 1-879938-17-0

Other Books & Materials by

James P. Gills, M.D.
and HeartLight

The Unseen Essential: A Story for Our Troubled Times
ISBN 1-879938-05-7
A compelling, contemporary novel about one man's struggle to grow into God's kind of love (sequel—*Tender Journey)*

Love: Fulfilling the Ultimate Quest
ISBN 1-879938-02-2
A quick refresher course on the meaning and method of God's great gift

The Dynamics of Worship
ISBN 1-879938-03-0
Designed to rekindle the heart with a passionate love for God. Gives the *who, what, when, where, why,* and *how* of worship

Temple Maintenance: Excellence With Love
ISBN 1-879938-01-4
A how-to book for achieving lifelong total fitness of body, mind, and spirit

Come Unto Me
ISBN 1-879938-00-6
Inspired by Dr. Gills' trip to the Holy Land, it explores God's eternal desire for mankind to get to know Him intimately

The Missing Link
ISBN 1-879938-07-3
In a colorful, 4"x 8.5" pamphlet, gives the key to a joyous, faith-filled life

Transform Your Marriage
ISBN 1-879938-11-1
An elegant 4"x 8.5" booklet to help couples develop new closeness with each other and with the Lord

The Prayerful Spirit
ISBN 1-879938-10-3
(by Dr. Gills with Saunders and Krueger)
Tells how prayer has changed Dr. Gills' life, the lives of patients, and other doctors

Believe and Rejoice
ISBN 1-879938-13-7
(by Dr. Gills with Victoria Krueger)
How faith in God can let us see His heart of joy

To my beautiful wife, Heather . . .

*Your precious love
and the love of God
we share together
have transformed **my** life
into a sweet, tender journey.*

*To Him and to you,
I'm forever grateful.*

J.P.G.

Most Like an Arch This Marriage

by John Ciardi

Most like an arch—an entrance which upholds
and shores the stone-crush up the air like lace.
Mass made idea, and idea held in place.
A lock in time. Inside half-heaven unfolds.

Most like an arch—two weaknesses that lean
into a strength. Two fallings become firm.
Two joined abeyances become a term
naming the fact that teaches fact to mean.

Not quite that? Not much less. World as it is,
what's strong and separate falters. All I do
at piling stone on stone apart from you
is roofless around nothing. Till we kiss

I am no more than upright and unset.
It is by falling in and in we make
the all-bearing point, for one another's sake,
in faultless falling, raised by our own weight[1]

Acknowledgments

HeartLight of Clearwater, Florida, for concept, design, co-authorship, and publishing management of LOVE PRESS since 1986

Bud and Pat Hamm, Distribution Managers of LOVE PRESS, for encouragement, wisdom, and diligence in sending books to those in need around the world

Moonlight Gowns of Schaumburg, Illinois, for the original transparency of a bridal couple. With permission, it was modified in Photoshop to better fit the application in *Tender Journey*

D.H. Gornick, "of parts unknown," for cover design expertise, overall technical consulting beyond the call of duty, and a quick sense of humor to lighten the load

Laura Watson and Tanya Dean, for keen-eyed proofreading and editorial consultation

Nebraska Printing, of Tampa, Florida, for tremendous attention to detail in quotations, pre-press refinements, film output, and printing, but most of all, for being a super family of professionals to have on our team during a complex project of this magnitude

Letterhead Press, of Waukesha, Wisconsin, for utmost patience in helping us to find just the right creative medium for the *Tender Journey* cover, then foil-stamping and embossing with excellence

Eva-tone, of Clearwater, Florida, for customer service from one end of the plant to the other, cheerful willingness to fulfill rush orders for dummy copies, and for top-notch perfect binding

Prayer support: staff and members of Countryside Christian Center, Breakthrough Intercessors, Bud and Pat Hamm, Allen and Linda Rooks, Dr. Norma Neal Gause, Prison Chaplains, and Christian inmates from around the country

Countless others, including, but not limited to: staff of St. Luke's Cataract and Laser Institute and Jireh, Inc., Pinellas County Library Cooperative, New York Convention and Visitor's Bureau, The Mayflower Hotel, The Raddison Empire Hotel, New York Public Library, New York Department of Corrections, Amtrak, National Center for Missing and Exploited Children, Centers for Disease Control, Florida Gulfcoast Chapter of the National Multiple Sclerosis Society, Sunstar Ambulance Service, The University of Illinois Department of Nuclear Engineering, Focus on the Family, In Touch Ministries, Angel Ministries, Insight for Living, Promise Keepers, Chaplains Carl Fortner, Paul Lanagan, William "Jumpin' J" Johnson, and Chris Athey, Dr. Tim Daley, family and friends of the authors

We marvel at the silence
that separates the living
from the dead.
Yet more apart are they
who all life long
live side by side,
And never heart to heart.

Author Unknown

Why a Tender Journey?

tender (adjective) [2]

a) delicate
b) gentle
c) soft

d) compassionate
e) kind
f) loving
g) responsive
h) sympathetic

i) sensitive
j) ticklish
k) touchy

l) aching
m) painful
n) raw
o) sore

Love never fails—
never fades out
or becomes obsolete
or comes to an end.

I Corinthians 13:8a
Amplified Bible

Special Note to Readers:

Have you have ever visited a nature trail
with workout posts along the way?
There you can enjoy the scenery
and derive positive health benefits,
all in one trip.

LOVE PRESS HAS CREATED *Tender Journey*
TO DO THE SAME FOR YOU.

Wherever you see this logo in the margin:

you'll find an S.O.S.—
"Spiritual Optim-Exercise Station."

Pause for a few minutes from the
entertaining imagery of the storyline.
The characters will stay right beside you,
working just as hard to strengthen
those flabby faith muscles.
And before you know it,
you'll be back on your way
to see what will happen next!

*P.S. If you ever want to return for a
quick exercise break,
just follow the signs . . .*

❧ *One* ❧

Get back, all of you! *Coming through—now!"* Fierce border guards, barking commands, charged through the dense crowd with water cannons ready to fire. They shoved aside a white-haired man and his petite wife, knocking her to the ground. In an instant, the man stooped low to lift her to her feet. Gently brushing the dirt from her face, he drew her close to him.

Who-o-osh! Water blasted from the mouths of the cannons, soaking the overcoats and shoes of those nearby. The dampness sent them into violent shivers in the November night air. But the guards' brash attempts at intimidation were losing power. Jubilant onlookers continued to cheer as, over and over, the shrill ring of metal against concrete echoed from the free side of the detestable Berlin Wall. Was there hope?

Far away in America, shimmering light from the television bathed the couple lying in bed. The handsome, dark-haired man, hands folded beneath his head, paid more attention to the shifting

1

shadows on the ceiling than to the late-night news brief flickering on the screen. His thoughts drifted—to memories of an earlier time. A happier time.

He stole a glimpse at the other side of the bed. He beheld the silhouette of a beautiful woman lying there. She was absorbed in another romance novel. Her head and shoulders were propped up by two large pillows, and her streaked-blond hair formed a striking contrast to the dark green pillowcases and brass headboard. He sighed. Seeing his wife like that added more fuel to the frustration stirring within him.

Michael Nastasis once took such pleasure in running his fingers through her hair. He loved to watch the sparkle in Stephanie's eyes as they shared secret joy. Her lips were so tender. So sweet. Yielding . . .

But that was then. Now, he shook his head to chase away the memories, angry at the effect they still had on him. They only made his bruised ego hurt worse. *What happened between him and his wife? How could something so special become a source of dread?*

To distract himself, he glanced at the TV. Although the sound was muted, the sight of a milling crowd grabbed his attention. "Hey, Steph, did you catch that?" he asked, as he leaned on his elbow toward her and tried to break the ice.

"What?"

"On TV."

"Who cares?"

Michael winced inside at the sarcasm lacing her response. "No, really, this is amazing. History in the making."

He shifted his weight to sit up. "Something to do with the Berlin Wall. Here, wait a minute." He crawled to the foot of the bed and grabbed the remote control. He aimed it at the set and pressed the volume button. Nothing happened.

"Oh, *great* . . ." he growled, shaking the gadget and slapping it on the palm of his other hand. He sat up, threw the covers off his legs, and swung out of bed. He turned back to her. "Can you believe this? Just when you need it!"

"Sure you hit the right button? It's a new one."

He glared. "What do you think I am? Stupid?" Disgusted, he tried the remote control again from the end of the bed—just to humor her. Sound blared from the set. Still mad, but now with a sheepish scowl replacing his angry mask, he adjusted the volume to a tolerable level and laid back to hear the special report.

Once it was finished, Michael grabbed the remote and lowered the volume. He looked at his wife. "Who would've thought? I've read how the Germans had found a back-door escape route to the West, but I never dreamed the Wall might open up in our lifetime. What an opportunity!" He climbed out of bed and headed for the bathroom.

Stephanie went back to reading her novel. She was just getting to a good part when she heard a light thump. She cocked her head and looked over in the direction of the noise. The shadowy outline of a figure stood in the bedroom doorway. It didn't move. She gasped and waited. Not a sound. Finally, she dared to half-whisper, "Who is it?"

A quiet voice emanated from the darkness. "Mo-om. Just me." Michelle took a couple steps into the bedroom.

"Oh, honey, you scared me! How long were you standing there?"

"I don't know. A while, I guess . . ."

"What are you doing up?"

"I can't sleep."

"You didn't have a soda before bed, did you?"

"No . . ."

3

Stephanie turned on the nightstand light. "Get all your home-work done?"

"*Yes,* Mom." Her tone ended with a tinge of annoyance.

"Do you want me to fix you some warm milk?"

"Nah."

"Well, try to get some sleep. You know how quick morning comes." Michelle nodded slowly and hesitated in the darkness. When Stephanie looked up ten minutes later, she disappeared.

Michael returned to the bed, even more enthused about the topic he had embarked on a few minutes earlier. "Steph, do you have any idea what the fall of the Wall could mean to international trade? No doubt, they'll need plenty of American consultants, which would help us . . ." Michael continued on, his thoughts filled with visions of new and expanded business markets.

Stephanie sighed, her disgust plainly evident. She flopped onto her side with her back to him.

Michael rubbed a hand across his eyes. He couldn't pin down the exact moment when the awful transformation occurred in their relationship. He just went to bed one evening and everything was fine. The next morning, he woke up beside a stranger. Or so it seemed. *Stephanie* was the one who had changed from the loving woman he married. She didn't act like she respected him much. And she couldn't care less about his advances. He rolled onto his side, away from *her,* and made himself comfortable. He could manage without her for another night, thank you.

❦ ❦ ❦

In free West Berlin, a huge crowd had also gathered at the Wall. Young men dressed in blue jeans, work shirts, and heavy jackets, armed with sledge hammers and chisels, were slamming blows against the graffiti-covered concrete. They gritted their teeth. They shouted. They cheered. And worked with all their might. Feverishly. Joyfully. One fragment at a time, they each dared to carve out their own mark in the hated barrier. Others came to gather souvenir pieces. Most seemed to want to play a small part in emancipating their fellow countrymen, held captive by a Marxist regime for nearly a third of a century.

True, the weakening government had declared the gate "open" since midnight and the exodus had begun. But there was no sense taking chances with capricious statements of a communist politburo. For too long, it had proved untrustworthy. The young men labored on, more determined than ever to break through.

❧ ❧ ❧

Stephanie felt Michael shifting. She held her breath, waiting to see if he might reach over to her. But no. Just as well. She didn't want to risk being close to him, anyway. Not since he . . . After a moment, she exhaled softly and laid the novel, pages open to mark her place, across her chest. Michael considered her books "nonsense." *She* enjoyed them. She reveled when the heroines fell in love, cried when they struggled, danced when they won happy endings. Each romantic episode stirred a chord deep within her that Michael would never understand. The books filled a void she'd forgotten existed.

She cast a furtive glance toward her husband. His back and broad shoulders faced her. He was still rather handsome, she decided, closing her eyes. A little older, but that enhanced his good looks. Olive skin, tanned brown by hours spent outdoors. High cheekbones. Strong chin. Chiseled jaw line. Wavy, gray-flecked black hair. Strong but gentle fingers that used to caress her . . .

5

 Tender Journey

Stephanie's eyes threatened to fill with tears. She remembered that special afternoon in the woods after they were newly engaged. They'd been out hiking and she fell and twisted her ankle. "Sweetheart, you okay?" he asked with alarm. In those days, he didn't make her feel like a klutz. He knelt down to her, his hand cupping the side of her cheek, his fingers tracing the sensitive skin below her ear while his thumb brushed away her tears. She could never forget the tender way he'd treated her, how he helped her up, kissed her tears away, then nipped her nose to make her laugh.

A razor-tipped arrow of intense longing pierced her heart. How she missed those caring moments! Memories, unbidden, surfaced, clenching her in their grasp. Life with Michael held such promise when they first met. They had both been full of youthful dreams. He was brilliant and motivated. Their future knew no bounds. But the years came and flew by in the wake of constant demands.

Pleasant dreams—where had they gone? She felt an overwhelming sense of loss. Of betrayal.

She had to admit, though, things did take a turn for the better after their separation and reconciliation—could it be three years ago already? That Caleb-guy Michael met while he was away must have been an extraordinary person. The change he kindled in her husband astounded her. She sighed as she thought of their first night back together. And the next morning when he brought her breakfast in bed, with a love note and a rose on the tray . . .

The second honeymoon lasted maybe six months, she guessed; his new-found spiritual zeal, not much longer. He did finally decide to leave the pressure of Eagle Aeronautics, which helped a *little*. But the long-term damage of his workaholism had cut deep. Special projects always kept him so tied up, he never had quality time for her and the kids. His career as an engineer and now private consultant meant everything to him. A passion to "be the best" kept him either away or preoccupied more often than not.

How tired she had grown of staring at his empty seat across the dinner table! Of having to play "the heavy" with Michelle and Stephen whenever they needed discipline. And of trying to reassure the kids that their father really loved them. She could only hope they believed her. Especially after she'd stopped believing it herself. Sheer frustration came to a head at the Golden Eagle Awards Banquet. Her set-up went off without a hitch. Vengeance tasted sweet at the time, but it bore a heavy price. For quite a few months afterward, during their separation, she wavered between smug satisfaction and terrible guilt. It surprised even her that she could have grown so cold-hearted toward the man she had promised to love until death. As if he deserved her love.

Michael, oblivious of her thoughts, now propped himself up on his other elbow, turned on the lamp and grabbed his favorite hi-tech magazine from the night stand. Maybe it would be better than the TV. For some reason, he couldn't concentrate. Memories kept tumbling around in his mind. Yes, she had hurt him, all right. *Plenty*. First, her no-show next to him at the head table . . . a deputy to serve him divorce papers with a restraining order right after the big awards celebration . . . and a reporter to capture it in living color, no less. She had thoroughly humiliated him. But he forgave *her*, didn't he? What more did she want?

Okay, so he fouled up. Big-time. A couple years after they had reconciled, he got caught up in the moment. Found himself in a hotel room with a pretty young woman he met at a conference and gave in. He never meant for it to get that far, he really didn't, even if things were strained at home. Guilt ate him up over it! But he decided not to tell Stephanie. She later found the girl's name and phone number in his pocket. In a fit of tears, she confronted

7

him. He confessed the whole thing. Tried his best to convince her that the girl meant nothing to him, but she cried every time he brought up the subject. No amount of repentance or promises on his part carried much weight. She spurned him for months. And whenever he would get ready to go out of town on business, she grew morose and irritable. That all started almost a year ago.

Michael tapped his thumbs on the page of the magazine. He felt sure he wasn't overworking. She better not complain about his lack of effort in *that* department. As a self-employed consultant, he was trying to fit relaxation into his schedule and still make ends meet. He really thought their "new start" with each other would bring a measure of happiness. Time would mend their frayed emotions. Though far from recovered, they were making progress. At least of late, the topic of divorce wasn't coming up in regular conversations. But the specter of Stephen's illness always loomed ahead as a dark cloud, shrouding the horizon in threatening shadows.

Hope, though held in check by so many impossibilities, still raised its timid head from time to time. It was seldom enough to wipe away the dismal reality. Could a child's mere innocence curb the relentless tread of fate? What chance that a little boy's cute smile could halt the deadly AIDS guillotine, with light glinting already from the edge of its blade? They could almost hear harsh, mocking laughter whenever they dared to believe that God might have a miracle in store for Stephen. Michael knew that's when Stephanie's battle with despair would escalate. She fought against it every waking minute, or at least, she tried to.

He, on the other hand, contended with anger. Hidden rage over the injustice of life threatened to storm his soul at a moment's notice and destroy his fragile sense of peace. Once in a while, when he floundered in an icy river of fear, he thought he heard hope calling his name from shore, but he couldn't—no, wouldn't—allow that. It carried too high a price: disappointment. He kept busy instead.

Their only son, now nine years old, was infected with HIV. Not young Stephen's fault, of course. He didn't choose to be born a hemophiliac. He couldn't pick what source the hospital used for one of his critical transfusions. "Bad blood," the doctors had told them when they explained how he had contracted the virus. Such a thing was unthinkable. "Before stringent testing regulations," they announced. As if that eased the torment of the news.

Their son's future—forfeited at age six. "Always fatal," the doctors said. "Just a matter of time . . ." Michael cleared his throat to chase away the black clouds forming in his mind. *Get back to the article or the TV,* he commanded himself. *No sense brooding.*

Stephanie set her book in her lap, leaned forward and fluffed the feather pillows behind her. When she sat up, she gazed at the portrait of Michelle and Stephen over the dresser. She loved it, a smaller version of the twenty-by-thirty in the living room. How adorable the kids were together!

Both Michelle and Stephen dressed all in white, with tanned skin and bare feet peeking out. Brown-haired, brown-eyed Michelle, in a long, Victorian dress trimmed in lace, and holding a straw hat encircled with dried flowers and ribbons. She was twelve then, petite and willowy, and radiant with pre-teen beauty. Blond-haired, blue-eyed Stephen at six, looking quite the miniature gentleman as he stood, legs slightly apart, in his short jumpsuit and bow tie. She'd hired the best children's photographer in Florida. At the time, she and Michael were still separated and she felt guilty about spending so much money. Neither of them had regretted the investment. The man produced an heirloom they would treasure for years to come. And even more so now. Where Stephen was concerned, time had become their enemy.

Ironically, she had that portrait taken just before the news came that would change their family forever. Stephanie still heard those awful words as if she had heard them only yesterday. Over and over they catapulted to the forefront of her thoughts. She had few quiet times anymore. Relax her guard for an instant and the tragic prognosis invaded. The threat of AIDS consumed her, though Stephen showed no major symptoms yet. But like an approaching hurricane, the closer and stronger it grew, the more it swallowed what little light of hope remained.

She needed someone she could reach out to for comfort, someone who knew how to listen, offer an encouraging word and a warm hug. Why wasn't Michael there when she needed him most? She couldn't talk about her feelings with him if she wanted to. He would just tell her to quit dwelling on the negative. She was suffering through it alone. He seemed able to block it out. An ache, dull and full of loneliness, throbbed in sympathetic rhythm to her heartbeat. She wrapped her arms tight around her knees and shivered. At least Michelle was doing great. That helped. She sensed Michael moving around on the bed again, but to her, he may as well have been in another world. All that existed for her at that moment she held in her heart. She laid down and pulled up the covers. If only she could find the mercy of sleep . . .

Michael let his own thoughts ramble until he recognized the sound of her slow, deep breathing. "There she goes again—out in a matter of minutes," he complained aloud. He felt irked by her lack of interest. It was getting to be a habit. He turned off the television with the remote, cast one more hopeful look at his wife, shrugged, and slid down under the covers himself.

The soft light of the moon shining through the slats in the mini-blinds revealed the outline of Stephanie's bare shoulder. How beautiful she was! He toyed with the idea of trying to nuzzle her awake, but decided not to bother. If she had been interested, she would have shown it. Might as well go to sleep. Within a short time, he, too, dozed off.

🐾 🐾 🐾

Just after daybreak, a restless crowd of thousands thronged Potsdamer Platz in communist East Berlin. It was Thursday, November 9, 1989. Chilly morning temperatures forced the onlookers to keep their coats bundled tightly around them. One handsome older couple stood off to the side, away from the crowd. The white-haired man blew out their candles and gazed at his wife. His eyes, a startling crystalline blue, sparkled with life. He reached down, encircled her thin shoulders, and hugged her with the tenderness of a young man newly in love.

She was a rather pretty woman in her sixties, with graying hair, gathered into a bun at the crown of her head, green eyes and smooth, light skin that gave her a delicate, doll-like appearance. She smiled at him and snuggled in. Joshua Lieben released his embrace long enough to point to his left, where an East German soldier was stooping to lay down his rifle. Anna nodded. They resumed their embrace, cheek to wrinkled cheek. Tears mingled.

Anna turned her head and squinted into the distance. For a long moment, she scanned the length of the Wall as far as she could see. Her tone hushed, voice quivering, she finally spoke. "Bittersweet, this long-awaited moment, my love. For so many—as for us." She blinked hard, then sighed deeply. "Our Anja's death grieves me afresh today. How much fuller would life have been . . ."

Joshua took a handkerchief from his pocket and dabbed her eyes, then his own. "Ja, my heart aches, too. Oh, that she could see

11

us, how we have grown to understand one another." Still embracing, they fell silent. Could it be twenty-eight years since the barbed-wire barricade was set in place? Forty thousand security police had worked all night to complete the job. The Wall's terrible presence would change families forever. Among them, their own.

Almost three decades had passed since tragedy invaded Joshua and Anna's home. One Sunday morning in August of 1961, a border guard shot and killed their only child, a daughter. From what they could gather from pieces of witness reports, the guard had observed her helping a feeble old man under the fence—to his wife—and to safety on the Western side. Just in time for them.

Only after several minutes did Joshua break the hush that had enveloped them. "Let us pray, my love. We would do well to talk to our God now." They bowed their heads, as they had many times a day for years. "Thank you, Father, for reuniting our homeland. You have answered the prayers of countless saints who have cried out to you from around the world . . ." His voice faltered. He paused again to wipe his eyes. "Help us to forgive our enemies, with the same grace you have bestowed on us. We pray, Lord God, that You would grant mercy on the soul of him who killed our beloved Anja. Surely, he knew not what he was doing . . ."

If the people in the crowd noticed Joshua and Anna's painful memories, they acted indifferent. And if they heard any fervent prayer, they chose to ignore it. Nothing could quench the festive mood. They were celebrating the climactic event of the century. A few East Berliners up front peered through the newly-exposed web of rusty steel reinforcement bars—to freedom. Dazed at the incredible turn of events, they gasped and stood, frozen in place. One of them clutched at his shirt.

Suddenly, chaos. More guards rushed up from behind with water cannons. *"You must get back!"* they shouted again in their most menacing tone. At first, the captives stood by, helpless, as the guards aimed blasts of water through the jagged holes—into the faces of their liberators, already soaked with sweat and grime. But they refused to tolerate the hated regime's agenda any longer. Twenty-eight years was long enough.

Something so inspired and emboldened them, that they, *themselves,* forced their captors to bulldoze many more openings in the Wall. By the thousands now, they surged through the breaks into West Berlin. To their countrymen, to their kinsmen, to *freedom!*

Some of the celebrants waved newspapers. Others held up bouquets of fresh flowers as they ran. Some popped corks on bottles of champagne and twirled around arm-in-arm. Many wept openly or, at the very least, wiped their eyes with handkerchiefs and embraced one another. A beautiful, clear chant echoed against the grotesque concrete, "Die wand ist jetz runter. Dadurch sind wier einst bekommen! *The Wall has come down. We are one!"*

Joshua hugged Anna again and whispered, "At last, my love, God has brought victory."

She nodded. "What shall we do? We, too, can cross over." They both wondered, now that the Iron Curtain was melting before their eyes, what a retired scientist and hausfrau—turned Bible smugglers—would do with the rest of their lives.

Perhaps situations would so arrange themselves that they could embark on their lifelong dream of going to America. For the moment, they could only stand, awestruck, and watch the framework of their former existence come tumbling down. What new shape would rise from the rubble of these bloodstained ruins?

So softly at first they scarcely knew when it started, a tenor voice began singing the halting strains of a hymn by Martin Luther. The shouting subsided. A hush took its place. A second voice, then a third joined in singing, *A Mighty Fortress Is Our God.*

Soon the charged atmosphere around the Brandenburg Gate reverberated with the sound of hundreds of voices. Men, women, and children, relishing the first taste of freedom in over twenty-eight years, sang out loud and clear. Joshua and Anna wiped tears from their eyes as they sang along, Joshua slightly off-key. When the singing died down, he hugged her again. "Come, my sweet," he urged, "our work here is complete."

Suddenly, a little blond-haired girl they had never seen before ran up to them. She thrust a large bouquet of fresh flowers into Anna's arms and dashed off before they could thank her. Standing nearby, watching the scenario, was a border guard—one of the brutes who had knocked her down earlier. Anna caught his eye. Her breath caught. Joshua gave her a comforting pat. She gazed at the flowers, held them up to her nose and took a deep breath. The delicious, sweet scent made her close her eyes in delight. She rubbed one of the velvety petals between her fingers and sighed long and deep. Then, before she had time to change her mind, she gently released her arm from her husband's hand and walked over to the guard. Her eyes filled with tears again. She offered him the flowers as she whispered, "May God bless you, sir."

He frowned and stepped back, making a firm, negative gesture with his hands. Then he met Anna's kind eyes.

"Your sweetheart would enjoy these, would she not?" she asked, louder, taking another step toward him. He looked away and looked back. Finally his face softened. His erect shoulders relaxed. He reached out his hand to receive the bouquet, gave an abrupt nod and hurried away into the crowd. Only Anna saw him brush a tear from the corner of his eye.

She walked back to her husband, who hugged her long and hard. "How proud of you I am! You respond when the Spirit nudges you." He held her at arm's length to look into her eyes.

"Angel choirs in heaven rejoice today, beloved! Only our God knows if that was the man . . ."

"Yes, only He." She exhaled deeply. Together, they took one final, lingering look down the Wall to the south where Anja had died and they paid their last respects. Joshua turned to lead the way home. Anna followed, huddled at his side, seeking shelter from the crisp November wind.

๙ *Two* ๒

The holidays flew by in a blur, but that still was not fast enough for Michael. He loathed the endless trips to the mall to shop for presents nobody liked, the polite social gatherings to chat with people he had no interest in, the religious productions that made him feel more alienated than ever. At home, the family tried hard to pretend everything was normal. They avoided talk about feelings and the future.

He was glad to get back to work after the first of the year. For the next several months, he travelled from coast to coast every week and overseas twice. He loved the freedom, the challenges. His client list grew steadily. At least with the arrival of spring, the weather had improved. A cold, rainy winter, by Florida standards, could make a person feel gloomier than usual.

The Monday after Easter, he was planted in front of his computer at five-thirty in the morning. A steaming cup of Swiss chocolate almond coffee filled the air with a tantalizing aroma. He took a bite of a toasted blueberry bagel covered with fruit spread and licked his lips. How he loved those early hours before anybody else was awake. He could get so much done.

After he left Eagle Aeronautics several years earlier, Michael opened his own consulting practice. He set up a complete office at the back of the house, overlooking the best view of the pond and vineyard. The rolling hills would do his mind good, whenever he needed to regroup. His investment in the latest equipment—a lightning-fast PC, plotter, laser printer, fax machine, copier, and plenty of software—would allow him to fill any client's technical design needs and at the same time, lend a professional appearance to his proposals. His favorite gadget was the modem. Within a matter of seconds, it tapped him into the Internet®, a huge world-wide information superhighway. And when he wanted to relax, he would practice piloting skills on his flight simulator program.

For most self-employed people, a rural location in Lake County, Florida, would not have been the wisest choice for a new business. But Michael felt confident he could draw national clients who needed the expertise he had gained at Eagle. His credentials included numerous awards, the most prestigious being the Golden Eagle. No, a man of his caliber wouldn't have to depend on walk-in traffic. So far, he was right. He had landed a major client from Alabama and another from Texas.

Private-consultant status proved to be a good move in many ways. For one thing, he enjoyed his work more than ever before. And living closer to the land the last few years had given him another interest—concern for the environment. He always knew problems existed, but when he lived in the city he never considered them important enough to spend any time on. It was too far removed from the pressure of company deadlines. For the first time, he began considering the tremendous toll the century's technical advances had taken on the fragile ecosystem. Now, with Caleb's beautiful property willed to him, he gained a first-hand desire to get involved. Although his relationship with Caleb had

meant far more to him than anything else, his mentor had taught him so much that he'd never have learned as an engineer. The art of cultivating grapes was a prime example. Some of the plants growing along the hillsides would outlive him. He wanted his children and grandchildren to know the sweet taste of those grapes for years to come, long after he passed on. Of course, he didn't want to become an extremist, either. Ecology had to be weighed against economic and scientific common sense. It was a delicate balance, for sure . . .

A soft cough interrupted his reverie. He twirled around in his swivel chair to face the doorway leading into the house. Michelle was standing there, dressed, and ready for school.

"Hi, honey," he said. "I'm busy—whatcha need?"

She hesitated before answering, then folded her arms across her chest and leaned against the door frame. "Just wanted to know if we can get a dog."

He frowned. "Michelle, we already talked about that several times. No, we can't."

"But *why?* I miss Ebony so much."

"We all miss her."

"Not like I do . . ."

"Well, the answer is still 'no.' We're too busy to train and take care of a dog."

She shifted her weight onto one foot. *"Please,* Dad, I'll do it, I promise." Her tone was whiny, pleading.

"No, and that's final." He turned back around to his computer. "You don't have any more time than the rest of us. You're always with your boyfriend." His fingers clicked away on the keys.

She uncrossed her arms and placed her hands on her hips. "I can see you're *real* observant about what goes on in my life. Chris and I broke up last week!"

"Oh, that's right," he replied, as he punched in the command to print his document. He rotated around to face her. "Sorry. Why don't you join an after-school club if you want something to do?"

She let out an exasperated sigh and threw up her hands. "Just *never mind!*" With that, she was gone.

He shook his head. "Teenagers," he muttered under his breath, and went back to work. Now, where was he? That's right. Ecology, energy and his latest project.

He had began paying close attention to the energy debates but would have to study even more. He would read everything he could get his hands on. Oil. Coal. Solar. Nuclear. There were good and bad points to each. And the cleanest, most efficient source, if not handled properly, had the farthest-reaching consequences. Nuclear waste—an unavoidable by-product with the potential to devastate for years to come—had to be stored. Somewhere. *Safely.* Both the federal government and private industry had spent billions of dollars on research, without coming up with a workable, long-term solution the public would accept.

Almost without realizing it, he had accepted the mental challenge. Setting a problem of such magnitude before him was like setting an old blue tick hound dog on a trail. He might zig and zag until he picked up the scent, but as soon as that sensitive nose locked in, he'd be off and running.

One day, while mentioning to his wife his grave concern about the ever-increasing number of nuclear waste sites on the earth, Stephanie had asked, "Since you're so smart, what would *you* do about it?" He had one of those "aha-type" experiences. The seed of an idea sprang forth from his lips.

He hadn't thought about his answer. Just blurted out the first thing that came to mind: "Send it to the sun."

"The *sun?* What kind of nonsense are you talking about?"

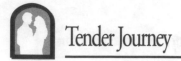

"Well, it's nothing more than an enormous nuclear reactor. Be the equivalent of throwing a bug into an electric bug-zapper." The idea sounded so absurd, he laughed at it himself. But then, why not? Every invention sounded pretty crazy when first conceived. Brainstorming couldn't hurt. The U.S. government had spent a fortune trying to design deep underground storage tunnels in the Nevada desert. That hadn't worked out, the last he'd heard. Citizens didn't want radioactive waste buried in *their* state. Of course, who would?

Thus began his latest pet hobby. The potential for worldwide impact intrigued him. Via modem, he even went so far as to communicate with several nuclear engineering professors at major universities, one of whom expressed equal concern about the waste problem. The send-it-into-space-idea had been considered by nuclear physicists decades before, but abandoned. "Fear of public opinion," the prof said.

Dixy Lee Ray's best-selling book, *Trashing the Planet,* opened his eyes further on various aspects of the waste debate. As former chairman of the Atomic Energy Commission, she advocated *reprocessing*—the nuclear term for recycling—followed by burying the remainder deep into the remotest parts of the ocean floor. She made some good points.

Who could tell? Maybe one day, he, Michael Nastasis, would play a role in assembling governmental and commercial sponsors of a major task force. If all went according to plan, the team would form the foundation for future solutions. Misinformed hysteria would only do more harm. But somebody had to do something. Clearly, the problem was not going away by itself.

He went back to pecking away at his computer and before he knew it, five o'clock rolled around. He had been sitting in front of that screen for almost twelve hours, with only a couple of short breaks. His stomach was growling. His wrists ached, his neck was stiff, and he had a good start on a headache. He decided to take a stroll outside for some fresh air and further brainstorming.

Two hours later, he stepped back into his office. The sun had already dropped lower in the sky. He couldn't believe that he had fallen asleep in the grass at the far side of the pond for that long.

As he started tidying up the office before closing for the day, he paused to glance at the large, framed poster Stephanie had hung above his desk when he first started as a consultant. The verse was entitled, *"The Secrets of Success."* He referred to it often and read it over again now:

S tart by determining your ultimate goals in life
E stablish your priorities to reflect those goals
C reate a plan that includes room for flexibility
R esearch and practice to reduce risks and errors
E fforts lead to rewards, excuses lead to failure
T ime used wisely is an investment for the future
S trength is achieved by confronting difficulties

O rganization, focus and persistence gain results
F aith in Jesus frees you from fear and doubts

S elf-control is the truest test of human mastery
U se your talents and skills as natural resources
C hallenges always offer opportunities for growth
C hange is the only constant you should depend on
E xperience exceeds all other methods of learning
S ociety never owes you more than you have earned
S uccess is a way of life, found moment by moment [3]
　　　　　　　　　　　　　　—*Wanda Hope Carter*

21

Michael smiled at the phrase, *"Faith in Jesus,"* printed in gold metallic letters. With utmost care, Stephanie had created a special patch to cover the original wording which read, "Faith in yourself."

"I like the rest of the message, but not that part," she explained, as she showed him her handiwork. "It landed us in a real mess before." He half-agreed with her perspective at the time. Caleb would have been pleased. Lately, though, neither of them seemed too concerned about such minor nuances. Getting through the day demanded all the energy they could muster. Well, maybe he'd make special effort to be sweet to her tonight, just to show he appreciated her occasional acts of thoughtfulness.

Michael took one last satisfied look around the office, closed the door behind him and headed to the main part of the house. "Hi, hon, I'm done for the day," he called down the hallway. He slid his jacket off his shoulder and laid it over a chair in the corner.

"Where have you been?" Stephanie answered him from the bedroom. "I've been back to that office of yours a dozen times in the past two hours and paged you in-between." Her voice grew sharper as she approached. "It's almost seven-thirty. Michelle's not home yet. And your dinner'll be getting cold."

He looked at her out of eyes grown wary. His voice, though, remained warm, cajoling. He teased, "Aren't *we* the sweetheart tonight? I just fell asleep outside for a couple hours—must have been exhausted."

She rounded the hall corner, but stopped in the doorway. The corners of her mouth drooped. Tension lines in her forehead were evident to him from where he stood.

"Com'ere and let me give you a hug," he offered.

"Didn't you hear what I said?" Caught between frustration and resignation, she continued. "Why don't you listen when I talk to you?" She leaned against the door frame and laid her head against the cool woodwork. Her voice softened somewhat. "Michelle isn't home yet, and it's getting late. She *never* stays out without saying something first." She paused a moment. "I'm worried."

He took two steps to where she stood and reached out to hold her left hand. Clasping it between his two larger ones, he led her to the loveseat in the living room. "Let's sit here a minute." Stephanie sighed, but sat down. She squirmed deeper into the cushions.

"Hon," he said, "do you remember how uptight I was about pursuing that latest client?" He waited until she looked at him and nodded before going on. "All my worrying turned out to be for nothing." He paused again. In truth, he hadn't been expecting any great show of excitement from her, but a little spark would have been nice.

Stephanie carried on as if he hadn't said a word. "Did Michelle mention anything to you about doing something after school?"

"No, not that I remember." Now he began to recognize his wife's agitation as fear. He hid his own hurt feelings, and answered, "I thought Charlie was bringing her home. Isn't it her week to drive?"

"Her name is Char-*maine.*" Stephanie emphasized the second syllable. "You know she hates being called Charlie."

His jaw clenched at the sound of her quite teacherly tone. "Whatever."

Stephanie gripped Michael's arm. She sat up straight and nodded. "That must be it. Michelle's still over there." To quell the nameless dread stirring in the pit of her stomach, she reached for the telephone and dialed the number. While it was ringing, she said to him, "You didn't have to be so snippy, you know." He frowned and walked out of the room.

"Hello," a polite voice answered on the third ring, "Harrington residence, Charmaine speaking."

23

"Hi, hon, this is Steph. Would you mind sending Michelle home?"

"What do you mean? She's not here."

"Wait a second. You didn't pick her up from school?"

"Well, no. Cindy said Michelle told her she had to go someplace and wouldn't need a ride."

"Had to go someplace? Where?"

"I have no idea, but Cindy's upstairs. Let me see if she knows. Hang on."

Stephanie doodled on the scratch pad by the phone and then twirled a lock of her streaked blond hair around the pen. She took a deep breath, trying to curb minor twinges of anxiety.

Charmaine came back to the phone and spoke with reluctance, "Cindy said she doesn't have a clue. Michelle's been acting quiet and standoffish, so she just minded her own business."

Minded her own business? They're best friends. Maybe something's wrong . . . Michelle didn't say anything else?"

"No, that's it."

"Oh." She paused, not knowing what else to say and not wanting her friend to sense how worried she felt. "Well, I'm sure she'll be home soon. Thanks, Charmaine. Talk to you later."

"Bye. Let me know if we can help."

"I will." She slowly replaced the receiver in its cradle and walked into the den where Michael was stretched out in the recliner. He didn't look up from the *Wall Street Journal.*

"Can we talk a minute? It's important."

He peered at her over the top of his reading glasses. "Sure."

"Michelle didn't ride home from school with the Harringtons. She told Cindy she had to go someplace, but Cindy doesn't know where. Michelle acted 'quiet and standoffish,' to quote Charmaine, as if she didn't want to talk, so Cindy didn't press her."

24

"Now Steph, please don't start worrying already. You know our daughter is independent at heart. And getting more so every day. Part of being a teenager."

"But she left school almost four hours ago and we haven't heard a word. That's not like her."

"Let's give her a little more time before we get worked up. Maybe she stopped at another friend's house."

"Maybe." She stared out the window. "She's had a lot going on the past few months."

"Like what?"

"Tons of homework . . . and her boyfriend just broke up with her last week."

Michael nodded, remembering their conversation that morning. He sure hadn't won any points with Michelle on that front.

She went on. "The tension between us doesn't help, either. It's got to be hard on the kids when we don't get along. Here we are, Christians, no less." She paused and dropped her gaze to floor level. "We can act pretty spiritual when we want to."

He shrugged, shook the folds out of his newspaper, and went back to reading. Stephanie sighed. He was so concerned about everything but the family. It was driving her crazy. She turned from him and got up to go to the kitchen.

On her way, she called up the stairs, "Come on, Stephen. Get ready for dinner." She finished setting the table and checked the orange-glazed chicken baking in the oven. When she glanced up, his curly-blond-headed frame was already seated in front of his place at the table. He hadn't made a sound. He was leaning his cheek on his hands and toying with his spoon, spinning it around on the tablecloth. Dark circles rimmed his big blue eyes. They no longer had the sparkle of a mountain lake in the sunshine. The sight tugged at her heart.

"Hi, honey," she said to him. "Thanks for being a good boy and coming when I called you."

"Welcome, Mom."

"Supper'll be ready in a few minutes."

"I'm not hungry."

"I know, sweetie. It's the medication. Eat what you can."

"Where's Daddy and Michelle?"

"Daddy's in the den. Want to go get him for me?"

"Yeah, I guess . . . Where's Michelle?" he asked again.

"She's not home from school yet. We'll warm up her supper later."

He wasn't about to be sidetracked. "Where is she? She never said she was goin' anywhere . . ."

"Does she usually advise you of her schedule?" Stephanie winked at him.

"No, but I been watchin' her since that yukky boyfriend dumped her. She won't even say 'hi' to me anymore hardly—just goes in her room and shuts the door." He sighed and slid out of his chair. "I'll go get Dad."

"Thanks, honey." The knot in Stephanie's stomach tightened. Charmaine and now Stephen were painting pretty scary pictures of Michelle's behavior. Had she really been acting so different?

He came back a few minutes later with Michael in tow. "Here's Dad. I got him for you."

Stephanie smiled halfheartedly and set their plates on the table. Stephen said grace. "Dear Lord, thank You for this food. Please bless it. Jesus, be with Mom and Dad and bring Michelle home safe. Amen."

Twenty-five minutes later, Stephanie went to put in a load of laundry and Stephen went upstairs to his room. Michael set the supper dishes on the counter by the sink. He stared out the kitchen window. Brilliant orange fingers of fading sunlight streaked the horizon before giving way to subtle waves of purple twilight sky. Night was coming on. Surely, Michelle would show up soon. He decided to be a nice guy and load the dishwasher for Stephanie. When he was done, he gathered the bills, checkbook, and calculator and settled down at the dining room table. Might as well do something constructive. It had to be done sometime.

He berated himself for procrastinating. Two months had gone by since he had last balanced the checkbook to the penny. As he flipped pages of the ledger to the right spot, a small piece of paper dropped out onto the table. He turned it over. Something Stephanie must have stuck in there, along with two deposit slips, three coupons, a grocery receipt, and a doctor's appointment card. He let out an exasperated sigh. Her messiness could scare a hobo. Tempted to toss the scrap into the garbage, he stopped and scanned it first.

> *In the worship of security, we fling our lives beneath the wheels of routine—and before we know it our lives are gone. What does a man need—really need? A few pounds of food each day, heat and shelter, six feet to lie down in—and some form of working activity that will yield a sense of accomplishment. That's all— in the material sense. And we know it. But we are brainwashed by our economic system until we end up in a tomb beneath a pyramid of time payments, mort- gages, preposterous gadgetry and playthings that divert our attention from the sheer idiocy of the charade. The years thunder by. The dreams of youth grow dim where they lie caked on the shelves of patience. Before we know it, the tomb is sealed. Jessica Mitford writes*

27

about the American way of death, but the American way of death isn't the burial ritual (silly as that is), but the way the average man lives. When you consider the beauty there is in this world, the rapture that can be known, the honest relationships, the excitement and exaltation there is for the taking—the real things to look at and feel and read—where, then, lies the answer? In choice. What shall it be: bankruptcy of purse or bankruptcy of life?[4]

—Sterling Hayden

He frowned, crumpled the paper into a small wad and aimed it at the wastebasket in the corner. Bingo. Still had his touch.

Stephanie tucked Stephen in bed at 8:45. He had fallen asleep right after dinner. She leaned over and brushed her lips across his forehead. "Good night, darling. Sleep tight. Mommy loves you." He didn't stir. For several minutes she studied his slow, deep breathing and the outline of his brown eyelashes on his caramel-colored cheeks. She brushed his blond curls off his forehead. "Lord, please heal him," she whispered. "He's such a blessing."

Wiping a tear from the corner of her eye, she got up and tiptoed out of the room, turning the lights out as she went. She passed Michelle's room on the way downstairs. Icy tendrils of fear clenched into knots deep in the pit of her stomach. She could control the anxiety no longer. Her heart raced. One thought clamored for attention. Something happened to *Michelle*. She raced headlong down the stairs. "Michael, do something *now!*"

Michael set down his pen and rubbed his forehead. The checkbook wasn't even close to balancing. He looked toward the stairs. "What? I didn't hear you."

She stumbled on a step and caught herself. "I said, 'Please call the police.'"

"What time is it?"

"After nine."

"Yeah, I guess we should, just to be on the safe side."

"Do you think she ran away?" A soft gasp escaped. She placed her hand across her chest.

He grimaced. "She would never do that."

"Maybe somebody kidnapped her. My God, you read about so much awful stuff these days . . ."

"Stop jumping to conclusions!" Michael barked. "It's only been a few hours." He picked up the phone and dialed anyway.

"911. What is your emergency?" answered a clear female voice on the other end.

"Hello. I need to report a missing teenager. My daughter."

"What is your name, address, and phone number, sir?"

He cleared his throat and recited the information.

The dispatcher continued. "Her name and age?"

"Michelle Renée Nastasis." His voice cracked. "She's fifteen."

"Give me a detailed description, please."

"Well, she's got thick, wavy dark hair, about shoulder length, brown eyes, fairly dark complexion. Most people say she's a very pretty girl."

"Race?"

"Caucasian."

"Height and weight?"

"I'm not sure. Let me ask my wife." He cupped his hand over the receiver. "Steph, the woman wants to know Michelle's height and weight."

She wrinkled her brow and thought a moment. "Let's see . . . her last physical was a year and a half ago . . . she was five-feet-two

29

and weighed ninety-five, I think. But she's grown some . . ." She sighed. "I guess about five-feet-three, one hundred pounds. Slim and well-built for her age." She shivered at the thought.

He returned to the phone. "My wife says she's about five foot three and one hundred pounds." He left off the reference to her shape. "She looks older than fifteen," he added.

"Any distinguishing characteristics—birthmarks, scars, handicaps, tattoos—"

"She's an ordinary teenager, not some biker woman."

"Sir, any unique features can be critical for identification."

Michael fell silent for a few seconds. "I'm sorry. Guess I'm a bit edgy . . . Let me ask my wife." He covered the mouthpiece again. "Steph, does Michelle have any distinguishing birthmarks or scars? I can't remember."

"Yes . . . she's got that scar on her right leg, just below her knee from when she ran into a barbed wire fence on her bike when she was seven . . . a birthmark behind her left ear . . . and a tiny chip in her bottom front tooth."

Amazed, Michael repeated the description to the woman at the other end, who typed it into a computer. He could hear the rapid click of the keys.

"When and where was your daughter last seen, sir?"

"At Lakemont High School, about three-thirty this afternoon."

"What was she wearing?"

"How would I know? Let me ask my wife. Steph, you should be talking to this woman, not me. What was Michelle wearing?"

"Let me think." She stared at the ceiling, then closed her eyes. "Oh yes, now I remember. A faded denim mini-skirt—not too short—high-topped leather tennis shoes, light pink socks—the bulky kind—and a pastel print, cotton shirt over a light pink tank top. Her hair was pulled back in a big multicolored barrette."

Again, shaking his head, Michael repeated the incredible list of details. Stephanie had a good memory when she wanted one.

"Who saw her last?"

"Her best friend, Cindy Harrington. Cindy's mother went to pick the girls up from school, but Michelle had told Cindy she had somewhere to go and wouldn't need a ride."

"Did she indicate *where* she might be going, or with whom?"

"No. My wife asked."

"Does she have a boyfriend?"

"They broke up last week."

"His name and address?"

Once more, Michael consulted Stephanie. This was getting embarrassing. Without the slightest hesitation, she provided the needed information. He passed it on.

"Okay, let me see if I have this right, sir . . ." She restated the vital statistics back to Michael. He confirmed them, and she continued. "Has she ever been in trouble?" She went on without waiting for his response. "Did anyone have anything against her? Were you and she getting along?"

"She's not the least bit of a troublemaker. No one had it out for her, that I can think of, and, yes, we were getting along fine."

"Did she take prescription medication? Any medical problems or allergies that might cause her to black out?"

"No."

"One more thing, Mr. Nastasis. Did your daughter ever use illegal dru—"

Michael cut in, "Don't be ridiculous. No child of mine is a druggie."

"Just a routine question that could provide a lead." She paused a second. "That's all I need for now, sir."

"What's the next step?"

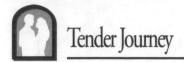

"An officer will stop by your home right away to fill out a police report, and a team will search the neighborhood around the high school tonight. If she's not back within twenty-four hours, bulletins will go out to law enforcement offices in the surrounding areas. A detective will be assigned to the case as soon as possible after that. Notify us with any updates. I do have another call coming in. Any questions?"

"I guess not."

"All right then. Good night, sir." She hung up and left Michael holding the phone.

A *detective?* He gulped. The color drained from his face. "Yeah, I guess you would need one . . ."

Stephanie overheard. "Need one what? Are they going to do something?"

"Yes, honey. They're getting right on it." He hesitated, not wanting to confirm the fear written all over her face. "They're sending officers over to where she was last seen. Within twenty-four hours, they'll reach out to the surrounding areas."

She gasped. "You mean they hardly do anything until *tomorrow* night?" Her voice climbed in tone with each word. "Good grief, she could be long gone by then."

❧ Three ❧

own the road and around the bend, thirteen-year-old
Sandy Hawkins lived with his invalid mother, Maggie.
Their small, wood-frame house made a stark contrast to
the elegant sprawling property that Michael and Stephanie
enjoyed. This house sat back from the dirt road, in the middle of
patchy brown grass and sand. At least the paint was no longer peel-
ing from the weather-worn siding. Michael and Caleb had seen to
that a few years earlier. But the roof was now in dire need of repair.
It leaked in several places.

Work had recently been done on the front stairs, thanks to
some well-meaning volunteers. The wood used to shore up the
right side called attention to itself by its very newness, and for
some reason, the steps were left slanting at a strong angle. A faded,
but cheery, welcome mat lay on the landing. Just to the right of
the torn screen door, about eye level, hung a hand-made sign with
JESUS LOVES YOU in rough-hewn letters.

Inside the Hawkins's house, a few pieces of mismatched,
donated furniture provided meager decoration. Three dented
kitchen pans sat in their usual places in the middle of the floor,

33

strategically situated beneath stained areas on the ceiling. Bare bulbs supplied most of the dim light.

Sandy sat at the 1950s-style dinette table in the kitchen with his school books spread out in front of him. His eyebrows were furrowed in concentration. Occasionally, he would sigh and lean his chin on his hands. Maggie sat across from him in her wheelchair. Although she could do nothing to help, her eyes reflected a mixture of maternal love and concern.

Multiple sclerosis had paralyzed her, a little bit at a time. She was still very alert mentally and felt deep compassion for her only son. Life had not been gentle with him. He had missed a lot of school after his dad died. Then Caleb had taken him under his wing, as a kind of grandfather figure. But he ended up dying, as well. At far too tender an age, Sandy had become the man of the house and had taken his responsibility very much to heart. Such devotion carried a high price. He'd fallen further behind in his studies and had to repeat fourth grade. English gave him the most trouble. All in all, seventh grade was pretty tough on him. The worst part was, he tried so hard.

Sandy sighed again and drew on his notebook. "Ma, I don' understand this grammar stuff. I hate it! These nouns and verbs and junk are drivin' me crazy. If Michelle wasn't hepin' me twice a week, I'd flunk for sure. She's so good at English. But you know what? She didn' show up today for my tutorin' session. That ain't—I mean isn't—like her."

Maggie could only make a slight bob of her head. Sandy went on talking, as if he were accustomed to no response. "I saw her at lunch, but not hide nor hair of her after school. Now, ain't that weird? Unless she went home sick. Maybe that's it. Wish we had a phone . . ." He looked up at his mom and cocked his head. "Could I ride my bike over and see what's up?"

She blinked a quick couple of times to indicate her permission.

"You need anything before I go—water, medicine? Need me t'bring somethin' home?"

One long, slow blink meant, "No, I'm fine."

"Okay, be right back." He straightened his papers on the table, kissed her on both cheeks, and hurried out into the night.

&a. &a. &a.

The Nastasis house was quiet. Stephanie had gone upstairs and Michael sat at the dining room table, still so engrossed in the bills, he nearly missed the soft knocking at the front door. He made his way to answer it. "Who is it?" he called, grasping the doorknob.

"Me, Mr. Michael," a deepening, cracking voice said from the other side. "Sandy."

His hopes fell. For a split second, he thought it might be someone bringing Michelle home. He opened the door. A simple, good-natured smile grinned back at him. At least the kid had all his front teeth now, which made a vast improvement in his appearance. A dentist from church had done the work pro bono. On second glance, Michael's eyebrows went up. Could that be the start of facial hair on Sandy's upper lip? Somebody would have to discuss shaving with him soon. They'd have to cover awkward topics, as well. Michael dreaded the moment. If Pastor Chip wasn't available, the job would probably fall in *his* lap.

It had been over three years since they met. The passage of time had done nothing to curtail the lad's unruly red hair, especially after he'd been out riding his bike in the humidity. Sandy saw the direction of Michael's gaze and used both hands to try to smooth out the wayward locks. He only succeeded in sending them scattering in another direction.

35

Michael couldn't stifle a slight smile at his effort and quirky mannerisms. "Hey, partner. Little dark to be riding your bike, wouldn't you say?"

"Nope. The fella at the garage gave me a light he had layin' around. Little rusty, but it works great." He cocked his head. "I come over to see if Michelle's sick or somethin'—"

Michael grasped Sandy's left shoulder. "Have you seen her?" His words faded when he saw the confusion on the boy's face.

Sandy shook his head. "That's why I come—I mean *came*—over." He hesitated. When he continued, his words spilled out in a rush. "She was s'pposed to hep me with English after school, but she didn' show up. That ain't like her."

"Oh." He let his hand fall from Sandy's shoulder. "I was hoping you might know something." His tone of voice was starting to sound as anxious as Stephanie's, which annoyed him. He added a lukewarm, "Come on in. No sense standing out here."

Sandy paused, his shoe on the threshold, as if he were deciding whether or not it was okay to enter. Curiosity about Michelle swayed him. "Thanks," he added as he walked past Michael and into the foyer.

"Let's go in the kitchen. Want something to drink?"

"That white grape juice'd be awesome. With the bubbly stuff you put in, please."

Michael grabbed a glass, walked to the refrigerator and pressed it against the ice dispenser, then opened the door and took out the fresh-pressed juice and a bottle of imported sparkling water. With his back to Sandy, he said, "We haven't heard from her. School got out hours ago and her mom's getting worried." He set a glass of juice on the counter in front of the boy.

"She's not home *yet?*" Sandy asked. "Where could she be?"

"Don't have a clue."

"Mebbe at Cindy Harriggingson's. They're super bes' friends."

"We tried the *Harringtons*. Cindy last saw her at school."

"That don't make no sense. Where could she go?" He looked up from the glass to meet Michael's gaze.

Michael expelled a loud breath to release some frustration, then shrugged. "Evidently Michelle told Cindy she had something to do and wouldn't need a ride. I guess Cindy's mom drove off and left her without asking questions."

"Gosh." He frowned. "Y'want me to hep you? I can round up some kids from church." But Michael was only half-listening. Sandy recognized the far-away look in his eyes as that of someone deep in thought. He did not want to interrupt him in case he was planning his next move, but he could only wait so long. "Got 'ny ideas, yet?"

"Huh?" Michael grunted. He jerked his head up to look at Sandy.

"Y'know . . . 'bout whatcha gonna do?"

"Right now there isn't a lot we *can* do. Her mother and I have already called the police. They've got her description and they're looking near the school tonight with the searchlights. We did some driving around ourselves, as much good as it did in the dark. By tomorrow night, if we don't hear from her, they'll start an official search with bulletins throughout the area."

Sandy listened to all this, wide-eyed. "Man! Police?" All the while they'd been speaking, his juice sat forgotten on the counter-top. He spied it and reached out for a drink. In a few long gulps he drained the glass. "Mmm," he murmured, licking his lips, then stroked his chin as he pondered the situation. "Don' worry yet. I bet she's with some other friends and fergot t'call."

Michael responded with a tense smile. "I'll tell you what— she's in major trouble when she gets home."

37

"Ooh, boy. Glad *I'm* not her." Struck with the notion that he ought to be on his way, Sandy got up from the stool. He made a halfhearted attempt at smoothing his hair back in place before venturing a question. "Mr. Michael, ya wanna pray?"

"I, uh . . . you go ahead. I've gotta make some calls before it gets too late." He spoke quickly, knowing that wasn't quite true. He didn't want to admit it, either.

Eyebrows raised, Sandy studied him for a second. "Ya sure?"

"Yes. But don't let me stop you," he added as an afterthought.

"No way."

"Good. Now, you better be gettin' home. Shouldn't leave your mom alone too long."

"Yeah, I know."

Sandy followed Michael to the door. As soon as it was open, he started to step through, then turned around. He shoved his hands in his pockets, glanced down at his dirty high-tops and back at his host. "Know somethin', Mr. Michael?"

"What?"

"I don' know how t'splain it, but . . . you kinda changed on me."

"What do you mean?"

"Well, back when Mr. Caleb was alive, you guys was *always* prayin' 'bout stuff. Now ya never want to."

Shock crossed Michael's features. His response was clipped. "Sandy, I still pray plenty, believe me—just not at this moment with you."

"Okay. Sorry I mentioned it."

"No harm done." He patted him on the head. "Night, son."

"G'night. I'll ask aroun' at school 'bout Michelle and keep checkin' in with ya." A slight nod was the only response he got. Sandy took the hint that Michael was ready for him to leave. He stepped onto the well-lit porch and hurried down the stairs to his bike, which was still leaning against the white picket fence where he had left it.

Michael cringed at the sight. "Sandy," he called, "I really wish you wouldn't leave your bike there. It leaves dirt marks on the paint."

He sighed. "I'm sorry. M'kickstand busted a while back."

"Don't worry about it. Just park against the tree next time." Sandy waved over his shoulder as he climbed onto his bicycle and started peddling down the road. Michael wiped his feet on the mat, then went back into the house. The timer turned off the porch light.

Had Michael still been standing on the landing, he might have heard the beginning of the Sandy's prayer. "Boy, Lord, I wish Caleb hadn' fell off the ladder. I miss him. He'd be prayin'—that's for sure." He pedaled harder and spoke almost in rhythm with each downstroke, "Well, he ain't here an' I am. So I guess yer countin' on me. You know what's goin' on with Michelle. Could you bring her back home real quick? She can't be stayin' out all night. And please hep Mr. Michael get back his old self." His voice faded as he turned the corner at the end of the road.

🐜 🐜 🐜

The sun had long since set. Gone were the faint traces of orange that lingered after the sun dropped out of sight. The moon had not yet risen and clouds obscured the stars. Aside from the headlights of an occasional passing car, it was dark. Pitch dark. And quiet. A single owl hooted from his perch in a dry, bare tree.

On this lonely stretch of highway, the girl walked alone. One could travel for miles here without encountering another soul.

39

Fine with her. She had chosen that road to avoid traffic, at least until she could hitch a ride at the truck stop on Route 27. She thought she could make out the distant lights already, even though she was still a good way off.

If only her feet didn't hurt! Without that, she could have almost lost herself in dreamy thoughts of a future on her own. Every time her soles hit the ground, sharp pain reminded her how far she had come. Spying a guard rail up ahead, she picked up her pace. As soon as she reached it, she sat down, pulled off her right leather high-top sneaker and began massaging the soreness out of the ball of her foot. The blisters would take more than rubbing. They would have to wait until she could find shelter. She was in good shape, but had little experience with walking so many miles at one time. She hoped it wouldn't be too much farther. Still, she breathed a sigh of relief. It felt so good to sit for a few minutes.

Try as she might, she could not stop her thoughts from wandering to her brother. Her parents? Another matter. She considered herself perfectly capable of blotting them from her mind. Stephen sure wasn't to blame for her decision. Even if his illness made her feel so unimportant, he didn't make her run away. He hadn't chosen his problems any more than she had. And yet, if he hadn't gotten sick, maybe her parents would have loved her as much as they loved him. They never had time left over for her.

Little did they care that she had earned a spot as cheerleader on a nationally-ranked squad. They hadn't come to a game in two years. Student Council officers' installation, Honor Society ceremony, French Club Annual Banquet, a school drama she played the lead in—they had missed them all. Either Stephen had needed treatment or Dad had important business and Mom didn't want to go alone. Of course, nothing new about Dad's "important business." He was hardly ever *not* busy. She felt she was interrupting him with the simplest question. If he did answer her, she could tell she merited very little of his attention—like that morning when she brought up a dog. Worse yet, he didn't even remember that she had gone through the heartbreak of a lifetime. Just a week ago! How could he forget? Chris, her boyfriend of almost three years, had ditched her—for a tall blond, no less.

Yes, Dad could be such a creep. But only to her. And so sweet to Stephen. It was sickening! Whenever he found a few minutes to spare, he usually spent time with him. Made sense. You wanna be with people you care about. Well, after years of living with rejection, she couldn't take it anymore. If she wanted to be lonely and miserable, she could do that fine on her own.

The situation deteriorated so much that she found herself secretly wishing her brother would just die and get it over with. Enough of this long, drawn-out stuff. Maybe life would get back to normal. She could have her parents back again. At first, these thoughts came only during fits of anger. Lately, they persisted in the back of her mind.

Guilt nibbled at the edges of her conscience. Here she was, jealous of her could-be-dying brother. She knew it was wrong. She hated herself for feeling that way. Sweet, unselfish Stephen, who never said a mean word about anybody. She feared the moment when the horrid emotions inside her would swallow her up or come bursting out for all the world to see. That's why she had to get away. Deep down, she knew there was something wrong with her. There *had* to be.

How often over the past months she had wanted to talk to somebody, but who? Mom and Dad? Fat chance, there. Her friends? They'd think she was a real psycho. To them, Stephen was nothing short of "adorable"—crush material if he had been older. They didn't know about the AIDS thing, though. She almost con-

41

fessed her feelings to her boyfriend one night. Was she glad she hadn't! After breaking up with her, he'd probably spread it all over school. No, she was doing the best thing. Quietly disappear. Just go away and never be heard from again.

So there she was, sitting alongside a country road at a quarter of ten at night. Lost in her thoughts, she failed to notice the approaching car until it had almost come to a stop a few feet in front of her. It started to back up toward her.

"Hey, pretty ba-by. Don't we look *good* tonight!" called a male voice from the front passenger window.

"Check out them legs," a gruff voice growled from the rear.

Startled, Michelle bolted from her sitting position. She tried to smooth down her miniskirt and put her shoe back on at the same time. It almost worked, but she lost her balance and had to grab the guard rail to keep from falling.

"You ain't gonna run, are ya little girl?" the first voice asked. "We just wanna talk."

She couldn't respond. Her heart had leaped into her throat at their first remark and lodged there. Instead, she started walking along the side of the road. Fast. As fast as her legs would carry her. If not for the guard rail, she might even have tried bolting for the woods, but climbing over the rail in front of them was out of the question. She did the only thing she could—broke into a run.

Perhaps the guys were only playing some weird joke, but what if they weren't? Time stood still for her. She felt as if she were moving in slow motion. Her legs wouldn't go fast enough. The car was gaining on her. "Don't let them get out, please!" she whispered. She didn't want to look, but her head turned anyway, as if it had a mind of its own. What she saw made her hair stand on end.

The passenger door was half open. A guy hung through the window from the chest up. His feet and legs were still in the car, hidden from sight, but his right arm snaked out, grasping. It was only a few feet from her. Without thinking, she jumped back.

Everything resumed its normal speed. The car swerved toward her. She opened her mouth. A scream of pure terror exploded. Nothing she'd dreamed of in her plans for escape had prepared her for this. She turned and darted back down the road in the opposite direction.

Too scared to even breathe, she could hear the screech of tires somewhere behind her. They were turning around. She ran faster. Already her sides hurt.

She made it to the beginning of the little bridge she'd just crossed. Her pulse roared in her ears. She couldn't tell if she was hearing her own footsteps or if someone was gaining from behind. What if one of them was following her? Should she turn around? She was too afraid. She couldn't risk losing her footing. A fall could be her last mistake.

The guys in the car called out now from somewhere across the road, "Hey, baby, come on. Let's have some fun." Their taunting laughter spurred her to even greater effort. Her chest was on fire. Her lungs felt ready to burst, her legs, like lead. She was losing ground. The next thing she knew, they turned around and drove away, squealing the tires.

But the footsteps sounded closer than ever.

The roaring in her ears grew louder.

Two more steps would put her around the widest part of the curve in the road. She'd be out of sight of anyone following, at least for a few seconds—maybe long enough to find a hiding place—if she could just make it. She had to. She couldn't maintain this pace.

One step. Another. Headlights from an approaching semi-truck turned the night into day. "Hey!" she shouted, waving her

arms in a frantic gesture. Bathed in the brilliance of the lights, she stood motionless. But only for an instant.

"Help me!" she shouted in the loudest voice she could muster. New energy flowed into her weary limbs. She jumped up and down and waved her arms high over her head.

The truck didn't seem to be slowing.

She turned to look behind her. Off the road, in the shadows, something caught her eye. A silhouette? Oh, no. Something shiny, about waist level. There and gone. She stifled a gasp.

Then it came to her—the pepper spray! She had it with her. In her purse. Hanging on her key chain. *Oh, thank God.* She fished around inside the purse and ran faster. Yes—there it was! Her trembling fingers locked around the smooth leather holster. She managed to flip open the top and place her index finger on the trigger. Not a split second too soon. She heard three footsteps just before a man's hand grabbed her shirt from behind. In an instant, she let out a blood-curdling scream and twisted her body enough to face him head-on. *Close your eyes and press the button,* she told herself. *Press the button. Just press the stupid button!*

She did, then ducked.

A hissing sound.

Screams.

This time, they were his.

He choked and gasped for breath and uttered a string of curse words about his burning eyes. When he stumbled against her and the guard rail, the force made her drop the spray.

How long did she have to get away? She had no idea. The guys in the car would really be after her now. Frantic, she ran toward the approaching truck. What if it passed her by? The car had turned around again behind her. Just when she thought she'd be left to their mercy, the pitch of the truck's engine changed. It rose and then slowly fell as the driver downshifted. He stopped a few feet from where she stood on shaking, rubbery legs.

"Oh, thank you," she repeated over and over into the night. Tears spilled over her bottom eyelashes and coursed down her face. Tremors racked her body. Now that the immediate threat of danger was past, the physical reactions were setting in.

"What's the trouble, young lady?" a woman's rather deep voice called down from the elevated passenger window.

Michelle could only see the silhouette of a head and bulky torso from where she stood. "Please, you've gotta help me." Her eyes darted up the road. "Some guys tried to . . . p-pull me into their car. One almost got me."

The woman turned to say something to the driver. He flashed on his brights, illuminating the roadway and shoulders. Empty.

"I'm telling you, they were there," she blurted between breaths.

"Well, they're gone now," the woman replied. "Nothing to worry about."

Michelle couldn't believe her ears. Were they going to drive off? And she thought she'd been rescued. She strained to see what the woman looked like, but her head only formed a dark outline against the night.

Suddenly, the passenger door swung open and a cab light came on. "Well, what are you standing out there for?" the voice called. "Don't you know how to get in one of these rigs?"

Her heart leaped with relief. "No, but I'll try!" At least, she thought she could. If only she could find that first step. The tank was too high. No, that couldn't be it.

"Over on the front of the fuel tank, near the bottom, there's a two-rung ladder," the woman called. "That'll get you started."

It was still no easy climb, but she made it up and in and perched herself on the right corner of the front seat. The woman

was already sliding off the other side to make room for her. "Name's Dot," came right afterward. "And my husband, Hank." With that, Dot ducked into the sleeping area of the cab and assumed a crouched position between the seats. A light from the dash struck Michelle's face as she settled herself more comfortably.

Hank adjusted the bill of his hat. "Miss, please put on your seat belt," he said from the driver's side. "Better to be safe."

"Here, honey," Dot offered, "let me help. That one's a bugger." She leaned forward and struggled to snap the large belt in place. "Whatever were you doing on that road alone?"

Michelle mumbled something unintelligible.

"Well, don't you pay any attention," came the reply. "You're safe here."

Michelle jumped like a scalded cat at the whoosh of air when Hank released the break and put the rig in gear. Dot patted her shoulder and murmured a few reassuring words, which made her relax a little.

Dot poked her husband in the waist and made a motion with her head toward Michelle. They both sized up her distressed state and disheveled appearance. Neither had any trouble believing something had happened on the road that had scared her good.

The truck slowly gathered momentum, inching around the sweeping curve. Without letting on to his young passenger that he was doing so, Hank scoured the roadside for evidence of her pursuers. To help, he kept his speed down. His headlights turned even the shadows into brightly lit areas, but he saw nothing suspicious.

"What in the world!" Hank yelled out all of a sudden. He pumped his brakes hard. Michelle screamed. Dot tightened her grip on the girl's shoulder. Out from behind a large clump of shrubbery, a beat-up black Pontiac hurtled onto the road. It cut straight across the road in front of them, careened around the truck, missing it by a hand's breadth, and screeched off in the other direction. Hank shook his index finger at the windshield. "If I'd been going a mite faster, you guys would've been wrapped around the front of this rig!"

Hank's quick reactions avoided an accident, but kept him from getting a look at either the car, its license plate, or the occupants. He heard a few shouted obscenities as they drove past. And someone on the driver's side had his arm, nearly up to the shoulder, out the rear window, his hand clenched into a defiant fist.

Hank turned on the overhead cab light and glanced at Michelle. She sat frozen in her seat. Her eyes were clamped shut; her right hand clutched the armrest on the door and her left was braced against the dashboard. Her mouth was quivering.

He fixed his eyes back on the road. "I take it those were the guys." For a minute, she didn't answer.

"Don't you worry anymore," Dot soothed her. "You're with us now. They're gone."

Michelle let out her breath and visibly relaxed. "That was them." She shook her head, trying to repel the vision of the black car and the man who had grabbed at her.

Hank picked up the mouthpiece of his CB and reported the car's description to Highway Patrol. "The law'll be after 'em, but I wouldn't go back out on that road if I were you."

Michelle shuddered. "No way."

"Well, we're headin' for the truck stop coming up on the right." He turned on his signal and eased toward the entrance.

"G-good," she stammered. "I need to make a call."

Dot added, "There's a row of phone booths alongside the convenience store, but if you'd feel more comfortable, there's one in the café for local calls." Her sigh of relief indicated which she'd use.

"Someone gonna pick you up?" Hank asked.

"Maybe." Her voice was firm and guarded, as if to say, *No more questions. It's none of your business.*

He took the hint and focused his attention on the job of getting parked in among the rows of tractor trailers. Before Michelle could wonder how he could ever get that huge truck in such a narrow slot, they were backing up. In just a minute, they were parked.

"Here we are," Hank said. "Hang on and I'll give you a hand." He eased himself down onto the parking lot. By the time he reached her side, she'd already gotten out. Without trying to find the rung to step down, she had jumped off the fuel tank and walked around to the front of the truck to meet him. "The scare didn't steal your spunk, I see," he teased. He reached in to help his wife. She slid off the seat and stepped onto the fuel tank. From there, Hank hugged her to him and guided her out onto the pavement. He let her go, but not before they'd exchanged a quick kiss. Michelle made a sour face, which went unnoticed.

"Come on, honey," Dot said to her, as she stepped forward and released her husband's hand, "I'll show you where the phone is." She pointed in that direction. "And the ladies' room is just down the hall, in case you wanna freshen up."

"When you girls are done, we'll get a quick bite to eat," Hank offered. "I'm starved." His suggestion met with enthusiastic approval. Michelle ran on ahead toward the building, followed by Dot, who took her time. Her gait revealed a slight limp. Hank watched them both cross the parking lot for a moment to see they made it all right. Satisfied, he strode off in the other direction, toward a trailer situated at the edge of the parking lot.

Inside the café, Dot pointed out the phone to Michelle. "Go ahead and make your call. I'll be over at the counter if you need me." She looked puzzled at the girl's tentative nod, then watched her walk away.

Michelle swallowed hard. She could do it. Nothing to be afraid of. They'd be madder than hornets, though.

A wave of nausea came over her. She rushed into the bathroom, barely making it to the sink. After cleaning up and wiping off her face with a damp paper towel, she trudged back to the phone. Her fingers trembled as she punched the numbers on the key pad. She steeled herself against the outburst she knew would follow. The connection made, she bit her lip and waited.

Tender Journey

❧ *Four* ❧

Neither Michael nor Stephanie had been able to sleep. Too distracted to relax, he was using the time to polish his burgundy loafers. They hadn't been done in a couple weeks. Stephanie was washing her hair. When he could no longer hear the soft pattering of the water against the shower stall, he called, "You finished?"

"Almost."

"Hurry up, will ya? I've been thinking . . ."

"Can you please hold on 'til I'm out? I can hardly hear you."

"Yeah, I—" Michael jumped as the phone's shrill ring cut off his words in mid-sentence.

"Get it quick," she called out from the shower. It rang again as he was putting away the buffing brush. "Michael, *for Pete's sake!* It might be Michelle."

Annoyed, he shook his head. Steph could get so uptight over nothing. He crossed the room to the nightstand, picked up the receiver, said an abrupt "hello." He listened. The blood drained from his face and came back in a rush. His brows contracted. "Young lady, *where* have you been? Your mother is worried sick."

She twisted the phone cord. "Sorry. I had to go someplace."

"Is that all the consideration you have?" He paused to take a couple of breaths. "It's nearly 11:00 at night! Where *are* you?"

She held her breath. "I'm all right."

"I didn't ask how you're doing. I asked where you are." He paused, but only for the space of a heartbeat. "Well, *answer me!*"

Stephanie wandered out of the bathroom, towel-drying her hair. His flushed face and demanding tone revealed the truth. "It's her, isn't it?" She started to sound frantic. "Let me talk to her. Where is she? Why isn't she home?" The questions tumbled out one after another.

Michael glared and tried to silence her eruption with a brisk, downward wave of his hand.

"She's *my* daughter, too, you know," she whispered through clenched teeth.

He gave her one more stern look before turning away and putting his hand to his forehead, half-covering his eyes. "Michelle, I don't have time for games. Now, tell me—where are you?"

"I said I'm all right. Isn't *that* what's important, *Dad-dy?*" Sarcasm dripped from her words.

The corners of his mouth grew taut. "Young lady, don't get smart with me. You get yourself home right now." He heard Stephanie sniffling behind him and turned. She was sitting in the bed with a towel wrapped around her head, the sheet pulled up to her chin. Tears trickling down her cheeks, she glared at him.

He put his hand over the mouthpiece to address his wife. "This is all I need. What are *you* crying about?" He asked, but he knew the answer. Even he disliked the way he was acting. The last thing he wanted to do was get angry.

Michelle's voice came back through the receiver. "Will you listen to me for once?" He turned away from his wife to focus on his

daughter's words. The scene had taken on the nightmarish quali-
ties of an old horror movie. Odd, late-night phone call. Hysterical
wife. Missing daughter.

Michelle spoke again. "I wanted to see if maybe things were
different with you. But obviously, they aren't."

Michael groped for the meaning behind her statement. The
phone cut out for a second and clicked back on.

" . . . only fooling myself."

He missed the first part of her sentence. Not enough, though,
to mistake what she was telling him. Still, he wanted to clarify.
"Would you mind expl—"

Her words shot back. "Face it, Dad. The only time you really
pay attention to me is when you're mad about something. Like
now." She huffed loudly. "Well, you won't have me around to be
mad at anymore!"

Michael's heart started to race. He swallowed hard to stem the
rising tide of panic he felt. He glanced at Stephanie. She must have
been able to tell from his expression that something awful was
happening. She bit the middle knuckle on her right hand. He
squinted hard at her, then went back to Michelle. Most of his
anger had vanished like the wind. Only a slight trace still tinged
his voice. "Michelle, what are you talking about?"

"You're the genius in the family—*you* figure it out. I won't
bother you again."

He sensed a measure of her pain. How to deal with it, he had
no idea. Easier to cover everything with his usual layer of irritation.
But that would only make things worse. He calmed his voice as
best he could, tried to reach out. "Honey, don't be silly." He
cleared his throat. "We . . . we love you."

"Right. If you do, *I* sure can't tell. Well, maybe you'll listen to
this—I won't be coming home *ever again!*"

It dawned on him how serious she sounded. "Michelle, wait. Why don't you talk to your moth—!" The click of the receiver punctuated his desperate cry. She had hung up.

He turned to Stephanie, who looked so vulnerable. Tears ran freely from eyes wide as saucers. He stared in horror at the receiver still clutched in his right hand. *What had he done?*

🙎 🙎 🙎

Michelle set the phone back in place. She could hear her dad's plea right up until the moment she cut the connection. For several seconds she stood and stared at the phone. The conversation had progressed just as she assumed it would. He never listened to her. Not really. She could be losing it and he wouldn't have a clue. He was so caught up in his own little world. Mom wasn't much better. Truthfully, nothing mattered to either of them but Stephen. AIDS was a big enough intrusion; they couldn't ignore it for very long. Despite her resolve not to cry, Michelle felt the tears coming. She blinked several times.

Why didn't she have somebody to talk to? Somebody who would do more than shove a list of demands down her throat. Her father's harshness cut deep. Tears blurred her vision. Thoughts careened through her mind, bouncing off each other like bumper cars in an amusement park. She gave up trying to stop them and just let them have their way.

From the midst of the confusion, one emotion clamored for attention louder than any other. Anger surpassed disappointment, hurt, and fear. She embraced the familiar, hardened feeling as if it were her lifeline to sanity.

No way was she going home now. How could she have even considered it a few moments before? *They* didn't love her. Did she

actually think they might change because she'd been gone a few hours? *Get real,* she told herself.

She wiped the tears off her cheeks with the back of her right hand and grabbed her purse. She turned around, ready to march back out to the highway, then remembered—she couldn't. Those guys—just the thought of them sent a shudder through her. But she had to do something. She couldn't stay at a truck stop forever. No. She had to think of a plan, quick.

When she looked up, Michelle caught the woman at the cash register watching her. Plump, middle-aged and homely, the woman probably had nothing better to do. Michelle walked over to her, ready to give her a piece of her mind.

"Evenin' Missy," the woman said sweetly. "I couldn't help but notice you're upset." She leaned across the counter and lowered her voice. "Forgive me for not minding my own business. Anything I can do?" She turned an expectant ear in Michelle's direction.

Irked that the woman had been eavesdropping, but not angry enough to turn outright rude, Michelle put on one of those plastic smiles she had learned from her mother. She'd watched her often enough. Even as she wondered what to do, a story began taking shape in her mind. Nonchalantly she asked, "Ma'am, did you see that lady who came in right after me?"

"Uh-huh. Dot—Hank's wife." The cashier raised a flabby arm and pointed down the hall toward the ladies' room. "She was here a minute ago. Probably gettin' herself prettied up for that special husband of hers."

"Right," Michelle muttered. *That'll take a few hours,* she wanted to reply. She caught herself. When she continued, it was in a softer, but more confident voice. "Well, you see, ma'am, I've been trying to get back to my folks' place up north for a while now—until something weird happened down the road. That's when the trucker couple picked me up." At least that part was true. "Some friends and I came down here on break and they didn't show up to take me back. I'm stranded." She didn't have to fake misery *too* hard. Not after what she'd been through in the last two hours.

The woman behind the counter folded her arms across her chest and studied her. For a moment, Michelle feared she could see straight through her story. She sighed with relief when the woman finally let down her arms and spoke.

"I'd say you've got yourself in a real pickle. With friends like that, who needs enemies?" She shook her head. "Leaving a young girl stranded at night in a place like this. That's disgraceful."

"Yeah, that's what I thought. I don't know what to do."

"Well, I tell you one thing. You came in with one of the best options a body could hope for." Michelle knit her eyebrows. "Look, honey. Folks just call me Ma, I've been here so long. Ain't a trucker travelin' these roads I haven't seen one time or another, and you came in with one of the finest couples I know. Not to say one of the handsomest," she added with a chuckle.

"Wouldn't go that far."

"Seriously, hon, Hank's one of the best. And Dot's a real sweetheart, too. A young lady couldn't pick a more trustworthy pair of traveling companions."

"Who said I was going with them? They didn't even ask me."

"Don't go gettin' in a tizzy. I was just tryin' to help you out. If they're headin' north, they'd probably take you along . . . "

Michelle let the seconds tick by. She was mad enough at her parents that she couldn't care less who she took it out on. Of course, the cashier who called herself "Ma" might come in handy at some point. Better be nice.

Ma looked out the front window of the café into the well-lit parking lot. "There's Hank, now," she said. "See what I mean?"

 Tender Journey

Michelle's eyes followed Ma's pointing finger. She made out an old trailer, of sorts, with a plain wooden cross on the roof. Hank was coming down the steps and heading in their direction.

"What's that? Some kind of church?"

"You guessed it. A trucker's chapel. Hank always pays his respects before he takes care of himself or his truck. Never seen him break his routine."

"You're kidding."

"Nope. Hasn't since I've been here, anyway. That's one very devout man."

She made a sour face. "Great. Just what I need."

&. &. &.

Michael had let the receiver fall into its cradle with a clatter. When he turned back to Stephanie, his face reflected some of the distress he felt. Not for long, though. He composed himself and walked over to her, placing his hand on her shoulder. An apology might help. She shivered at his touch, then jerked away.

"Don't touch me," she hissed. "I'm sick of your proud attitude. It's always your way or nothing. Now look what you've done!" She jumped up and met Michael face-to-face.

He stood his ground, but barely. The guilt she was heaping on him amounted to a fraction of what he'd been piling on himself.

Stephanie stood, hands on her hips, shoulders squared and eyes blazing. To him, she looked like a loaded shotgun with the safety off and ready to fire. She unloaded. "Are you satisfied yet, Mr. Know-It-All? Come on, tell me. Have you done enough damage? Or maybe you have *another* brilliant plan up your sleeve to bring our daughter home." She paused, not to give him a single moment's respite, but to catch her breath.

56

"I bet Michelle said she wasn't coming back," she spit out. "And of course, *you* don't have a clue where she is. You didn't have time, amid lecturing her, to find out. Go on. Admit it! I can see it written all over you." Her face crumpled. The tears came. She jerked her hands up in front of her. They clenched into fists. She pounded them once against Michael's chest. "She's running away and it's *your fault!*"

Michael stood silent against her tirade, but the inner struggle raged. One part of him fought a valiant fight to restrain the fury building behind a thin veneer of self-control. Another part of him, distant and detached, analyzed the confrontation and wondered if he would win.

He never could understand why anger, volatile and ominous, lurked so near the surface of his emotional reservoir. Regardless of the trigger, sooner or later, he would give way to anger. And always, always, with regret. Of course, Stephanie was just as bad. How he wanted to slap her! She deserved it. Instead, he walked out of the bedroom without saying a word.

☙ ☙ ☙

Hamburg, West Germany, an eleven-hundred-year-old gem set on the banks of the Elbe River, was the port of embarkation for a transatlantic voyage to America. As far as Anna knew, she and her husband were to vacation there in Hamburg before travelling on board a freighter that accepted a few economy passengers. She knew nothing about the treat awaiting her. Joshua had kept this part secret. He'd been saving for years. He also received a special price break from a man he had met who worked for the cruise line. That he had to dip into his emergency fund mattered little compared to the joy it would bring his wife.

Tender Journey

They journeyed one hundred and eighty-four miles northwest of Berlin via the scenic German Rail and arrived in Hamburg three days before the ship's scheduled departure. That gave them an opportunity to do some sight-seeing in the "Venice of the North," where Joshua had spent time as a boy. He'd reserved a spacious room at the grand old hotel, Vier Jahreszeiten (Four Seasons). Many considered it the finest hotel in all of Germany. Its impressive view of Binnenalster Lake, coupled with an Edwardian decor of wood carvings, tapestries, paintings, and antiques charmed Anna completely. And that was just the beginning.

They enjoyed a boat ride on the Hamburg canals, rode a streetcar around upper and lower Alster Lake, viewed elegant parks and majestic buildings, both old and ultra modern. Hand-in-hand, they strolled past manicured gardens, private mansions, boutiques, and art galleries. They window-shopped along the famous Colonnaden, ate in quaint sidewalk cafes, took in a Wagnerian opera and visited the Museum of History—the archive that registered the names of thousands of immigrants who had passed through Hamburg on their way to America. That afternoon, Joshua surprised her with fresh flowers from a street vendor. She rewarded him with a huge hug and kiss on the spot.

At one medieval English restaurant, they were provided with complete costumes for a traditional madrigal dinner and a keepsake portrait. She wore a dark green velvet and gold brocade gown with a lace-up bodice, cinched waist and crinoline-lined skirt. He called her "stunning" the moment he laid eyes on her. She assured him of his unequaled knight-in-shining-armor-status, even before he put on the mock suit of armor he sported as her escort. The food was delicious and the company, delightful.

Afterwards, a cab driver drove them through quaint, narrow streets back to their hotel. They promised to heed his stern advice not to venture near the Reeperbahn in the St. Pauli district. Assuredly, they had no interest in the live erotic performances devised for bored married couples and unsavory characters.

One of the most enthralling of all their adventures was a worship chorale played from the baroque tower of St. Michel's church. The pure, haunting sound of a trumpet echoing off seventeenth-century buildings created a treasured memory for both of them, especially after they learned the daily tradition had endured for over 250 years.

Just before noon on the fourth day, they checked out of the Vier Jahreszeiten. While they waited on a sofa in the lobby for a taxi to take them to the pier, Anna turned to Joshua. Her face glowed. "My dear one," she said, "in our whole married life, this has been the most glorious time of all. I feel like a new bride."

"Wait for what comes next, love," he hinted.

"Already you have made our anniversary most special. How could anything surpass the last three days?"

He winked and gave her a hug. "Soon you will know. I have kept a secret for so long, I cannot possibly reveal it yet." Rather than press him for the details, she let him steer the conversation. They reminisced about the sights they had seen and laughed again over the portrait of the two of them in medieval garb. When Joshua saw himself in the coat of armor, it triggered an idea he had been pondering. His brow furrowed. "Anna, I must remember this analogy. Would you jot it down, in case I may use it someday?" Always prepared for his musings, she reached into her handbag for a notebook and pen.

He cocked his head. "A knight wants to guard his castle and kingdom—yes? Thus, he wears a coat of armor when dueling with his enemies. A businessman, on the other hand, desires to succeed in a demanding marketplace. The coat of armor would be quite a

hindrance there. His suit and tie gives him the look of authority he needs. And a runner who seeks to win races wears lightweight athletic clothes to give him the advantage. In other words, my love, each one's outfit fits the task at hand quite nicely.

"But, Anna," he continued, "what if any one of those same men saw his house burning down, with his family inside? His outfit would do him no good at all! He would need firefighter's equipment—an asbestos suit, a mask, a hatchet, and a hose attached to a water supply . . . Do you follow my line of thinking?"

"I cannot be sure. Go on."

He smiled. She was always willing to listen to his ideas-in-progress, which endeared her to him even more. He continued, "For all of humanity, life's road ends at a 'burning building.' The Bible cautions us of that fact and gives us one way to escape destruction. Jesus Christ is our 'fireproof suit,' so to speak. If we depend on our own attire, however seemingly useful in this life, we will die. If we *put on Christ,* we will be saved!" Anna waited for him to bring his thoughts to a brilliant conclusion.

"The question from that point forward is, do we keep His suit on at all times, in preparation for the fiery trials to come? Or did we hang it up after a single wearing? One day all will know the choice we have made."

Anna looked away. She stared long at the elegant furnishings in the hotel lobby and back at Joshua. Her eyes grew moist.

He frowned. "My dear, what have I done?" he asked. "That was nothing more than one of my unpolished ideas."

"You make me remember the millions of souls who will certainly perish if we fail to warn them. How can we waste this time on a vacation for ourselves, while they race toward eternity without our Savior?" She stuffed the paper and pen into her bag and stood up. "We must get on about our Father's business."

Gently, he pulled her down beside him. "No, my love. I, too, struggled with this question before I made arrangements for our voyage. But I believe He has granted us a needed rest. He is not a merciless slave driver. Did he not tell His disciples to come apart for a while? This is our time to rejoice in one another and seek His direction for the future. Furthermore, you know very well that, no matter where we go, we will tell someone about Him. If He so prompts us." He patted her hand and spoke in a soothing tone. "Now dry your eyes. We have something wonderful awaiting us."

Their taxi pulled up in front of the lobby. Joshua hailed a bell-man to transfer their luggage while they settled in for the ride to the port on the twenty-five-mile-long harbor. "The fifth largest harbor in the world," Joshua told her. "Port of call for more than fifteen hundred ships a month!" It was obvious that he felt honored to be able to inform Anna about the maritime prowess of Hamburg.

Her eyes opened wide. "You never cease to amaze me with the facts stored in your mind. Were I not your wife, I would wander through life wearing a dunce cap."

He hugged her. "Not true. God made us to complement one another. Without you, I would be . . ." He paused a moment, then pointed at the portrait on her lap, ". . . like a coat of armor—minus the knight." She laughed at him and shook her head.

They settled in for the rest of the taxi ride and arrived at the pier the recommended three hours before sailing. When Anna saw the enormous, gleaming Deutschland-Amerika, she gasped. "Joshua, this ship. It is magnificent!"

"Yes, look at her—a snow-white, floating hotel." Their eyes scanned the multiple stories and a length of over one thousand feet, festooned from end to end with colored flags from every nation. It was a stunning sight, indeed.

Tender Journey

"Herr Lieben, you told me we would go by freighter! How, pray tell, have you been scheming this arrangement?"

He winked. "My secret." A longshoreman took their baggage from the taxi driver and stacked it on the cart with the other baggage to be loaded onto the ship. Already, an enthusiastic crowd had gathered in anticipation of the maiden voyage. Joshua presented their tickets and embarkation forms to the clerk at the check-in counter. They waited in line to climb aboard the enormous vessel.

❧ *Five* ❧

n the other side of the world, Hank helped Dot and Michelle climb the steps into his eighteen-wheeler. Then he set about cleaning the windshield while the women got themselves situated for travelling. When he finished, he lifted his cap to scratch his forehead. He and Dot weren't sure they bought the girl's story about friends abandoning her during a semester break trip to Florida. But they couldn't very well leave her at a truck stop. And she did say her family lived up north. Maybe the best way to get her together with them'd be to let her ride along as far as D.C. At least she'd be safe until then.

Hank climbed in and started the diesel engine. They would head east on Route 50 to Orlando, take I-4 to Daytona Beach and then head north on I-95 the rest of the way. It would be daylight by the time they reached Charleston, South Carolina, which was ideal. He might take a quick sightseeing jaunt around the city for the girl's sake. Like most women, she'd love it. He looked over to his right. Instead of Dot's robust frame at his side, he saw what looked like a toddler, by comparison. She was sitting cross-legged in the passenger seat. Dot had claimed the bed.

Whereas Dot seemed right at home in a truck cab, Michelle appeared a bit fragile—until she opened her mouth. "You got enough Jesus signs in here?" she demanded, placing her hands on her narrow hips.

"Nope, I don't, as a matter of fact."

"You're kidding."

"Not at all. I could never say enough about my Savior."

"Well, to tell you the truth, all this stuff kinda bugs me. But it's your truck, I guess."

"Right. And if I were you, I'd be mighty thankful to be ridin' with a couple of folks who love the Lord. You could have been kidnapped back there. Or worse."

"Nah! I defended myself with the pepper spray. The guy was history. And I learned in a self-defense class where to kick, too."

"Young lady, let me remind you—when we picked you up, you were scared spitless. You wouldn't have been strong enough to handle *one* guy lookin' for real trouble, much less a carload. All you could've done was make 'em mad."

"Think so, huh?"

"I know so. I'd say you're a tad naive."

"Now, Hank," Dot cautioned with a smile, "don't you be givin' her a hard time. She's been through enough for one evening."

"Guess you're right." He put his truck through the paces and brought it up to speed. "I'll go easy on the teasin', hon. I promise."

She patted him on the shoulder. "Good. I'm too tired to sit up and keep the likes of you in line." She winked at him and addressed Michelle. "If you'll forgive me, Missy, I've gotta get some shut-eye. Might not wake up until it's my turn to drive." Pointing back to Hank, she added, "Talk his ear off as much as you like. He loves it. Keeps him from gettin' sleepy at the wheel." Michelle gave her a nod.

Dot leaned up and pecked her husband on the cheek. "Night, sugar," she added. "Love you."

"Love you too, babe." She pulled the curtain shut across the sleeper and disappeared. Within minutes, she was snoring softly.

"Sorry I gave you a hard time, kid," Hank said, smiling.

"No problem. But I'm not naive or stupid. I'm an A student. I even tutor a dumb country kid in English . . ." Sandy came to mind for the first time that day.

"Do you, now?"

"Yes, I do. You would not *believe* this kid's grammar. His reading comprehension is horrible and spelling—the absolute worst."

"Well, I wouldn't act too uppity. From my experience, brains like yours often get in the way of common sense." He lifted his cap and readjusted it over his lengthening hair.

"I thought you promised Dot you wouldn't tease me."

"Oops, you're right. Sorry." He pulled a cassette tape out of the carrying case he had lying on a shelf behind him. "If our Jesus stickers bug you, this will *really* do the trick. We listen to Christian tapes almost nonstop when we're on the road."

She folded her arms and sighed loudly. "Great. Just my luck."

"Don't think luck has anything to do with it."

"Well . . . listen away. I'm gonna get some sleep."

"Fine with me. Nobody's forcing you. But you might hear something that could make a difference in your life."

"I doubt it."

He tapped the tape on the dash to loosen up the rollers. "This message is by a doctor who did surgery on my mom. It has to do with people accusing others."

"Boy, I wish my parents could hear that. Oh, they act real nicey-nice around their friends, but at home it's a different story. Makes me sick!"

"Do I detect resentment in that tender, young heart of yours? Not good." He set the tape on his lap.

She jerked her gaze around to see if he might be mocking her, but his features showed only a genuine concern. "Well, it's hard, ya know, living with hypocrites. Especially when they preach at you all the time." She smirked. "I learned a new word that describes our house perfectly—humdudgeon. Isn't that a super neat word? Humdudgeon. Bet you don't know what it means."

"Can't say as I do."

"It sounds like curmudgeon. Do you know what *that* means?"

"Nope," Hank admitted. "Don't know that one either."

She sighed. "Didn't think you would. A curmudgeon is a miser. A cantankerous, ornery fellow. Humdudgeon is a Scottish slang word for a complaint about trifles. You know, trivial stuff."

"Humdudgeon. Curmudgeon. Those are some strange words there. One of my less cultured buddies has his own pet term for curmudgeon types. He calls 'em, 'hemorrhoidal personalities'—because they irritate everybody around them. I should know. I used to be one."

"You were?"

"Yep. W.C. Fields was my hero. He said, 'I am free of all prejudices. I hate everyone equally.'"

Michelle chuckled. Hank went on, "As far as humdudgeon is concerned, I know about that, too. My wife and I used to complain about everything—especially each other. One of us was always upset."

"Really?"

"Uh-huh. We're less critical and selfish today, that's for sure. Guess we're more realistic, too. We don't expect perfection—from life, each other, or our kids—so we're not frustrated all the time."

"You mean your kids can mess up?"

It was his turn to chuckle. "Sure, they mess up, even though they're grown. We've taught 'em right from wrong and they know all wrong has consequences, some, serious. I guess one thing we've tried to do is set a good example. Give 'em high standards to shoot for, but allow 'em to make their own decisions. No matter what, they know we love them."

"You don't get hopping mad and start yelling?" She paused, her head cocked at an angle, toward the driver's seat. When Hank didn't respond, she hunched herself around and faced the front again. "Must be nice."

After a brief silence, Hank coughed to clear his throat. "We've had our moments, believe me. Just ask Dot. Loud arguments, screaming back and forth, followed by days or weeks of cold silence. Used to be standard operating procedure in our family."

Michelle groaned. "Sounds like our house. I get so sick of it, I could die." She waited, but curiosity got the best of her. "So what'd you do different?"

He held himself back, not wanting to sound too eager, then declared softly, "Jesus."

"I should have known."

"Well, you *did* ask. My wife and I pray together a lot now. Since we made that a part of our daily routine, the whole nature of our home has changed big-time . . ."

"I'm sure," she interrupted.

"It's true. We're better able to love each other, warts and all."

Michelle slid a quarter of the way around in her seat to face Hank. She wanted to see the expression on his face as he talked. "Coincidence," she replied.

"Not a chance. We tried for years. Things just got worse. We couldn't stand each other. Dot and I used to have an amazing ability to take an ice cube . . . and make a whole winter out of it."

In spite of herself, Michelle smiled. "Sounds familiar. At that rate, *I* live in the Arctic Circle."

He shook his head at her cleverness, then continued, "Well, it was pretty awful for us back in those days, too. We never considered that there might be a different way to live. We fell into an awful trap and assumed it was normal. But once we both got on our knees, received the deep-down grace of God . . . and started acting on it, boy, did we ever see a change in our family."

He stopped and glanced over at his young passenger. She was sitting on the corner of her seat, up against the door. She'd folded her arms across her chest sometime during the course of their conversation. Although she didn't show much interest, he took a chance and went on. "You know, kid, the gospel is really simple. I made it hard and tried to go about life in my own strength. That left me flat on my face."

"What do you mean?"

"I got hooked on alcohol and drugs. Fell back into 'em several times way back wh—."

"I'm riding with a druggie?" she cut in. "That's disgusting!"

"Don't worry. It was more than twenty years ago."

"Ever have to go to *prison* and work on the *chain gang?*" She burst out laughing.

He raised his eyebrows at her, then grew serious. "Somehow, by the grace of God, I never did. Now I'm a new man."

"Yeah. That's what all repeat offenders say."

"It took me a while to get it right, I have to admit. Most of my friends and family gave up hope."

"I know—don't tell me. *Jesus* dropped out the sky one day and zapped you. Then, you lived happily ever after."

"Not quite. He took me on the scenic route. I spent over a year at a rehab farm called Dunklin Memorial Camp, and with

Dot's encouragement, Overcomer's groups, the Word, prayer, tapes . . ." He pointed to the cassette player, " . . . they all help me stay in line. So, whether or not you approve, I *will* play my tapes during this trip." He met Michelle's defiant gaze with his own.

"You sayin' I have to put up with your Jesus stuff or hitch another ride?"

"You could wear earplugs."

"Thanks."

"You're welcome. But a good message wouldn't hurt you a bit. I once heard someone say, 'Listen to the world and you'll limp with the world. Listen to the Spirit and you'll soar with the Spirit.'" He pointed upward. "I decided to take the high road."

"Talk English, will you?"

"I am. It's simple. A person becomes what he focuses on most. For example, if he hangs around with ne'er-do-wells, listens to raunchy music, and watches suggestive movies, that's the kind of thing he'll want out of life. You've gotta be so careful these days. Lots of stuff looks appealing on the outside. Turn it over, though, and it's rotten underneath. Not like God's gifts—good clear through."

Michelle snorted her impatience. "Guess I haven't seen any of those lately. If ever."

"Of course, you haven't. Not until you accept His first and *best* gift—the love of the Savior! Sometimes that's the hardest part."

"Like hugging air. I'd rather love someone I can see, thanks."

"Understandable. Only one problem. That someone can't love you too good."

"What are you talking about?"

"None of us knows how to love. We have selfish motives that clash with other people's selfish motives. But the more we learn to love the Lord, the more we learn about real love."

Uncomfortable with the way the conversation was going, she tried another tactic. "Hank, you must be totally bored. What do you do besides go to church?"

"Who said anything about church?"

"All you talk about is God-type stuff.

"Church is only a part of the whole picture. I'm talking about a relationship, a way of life. Everything changed when I started asking the Holy Spirit to direct me every step of the way."

Michelle straightened herself in the seat. She grew taller. Cockier. She exuded the air of those who realize they're out of their league, but are too proud to admit it. "Nobody can do what you're saying," she began. "Even I know that. I've heard the verse enough over the past couple years." She recited from memory, in a sing-songy voice, *'All have sinned and fallen short of the glory of God.'*"

"That's true. All but one. Jesus Christ *is* the glory of God!"

"Right. *Him* again." She fell quiet and turned to stare out the window. The corners of her lips took a glum curve downward.

Hank spoke softly, just above a whisper. "Without Him, we could just go about our merry way, drinking, partying, doing whatever. But He is there, and I, for one, don't wanna hurt Him." He stopped talking. Michelle thought he'd finished and she was just about to change the subject when he spoke again.

"Not everyone feels the way I do. Lotsa folks—churchgoers included—do whatever they want, whenever they want to do it. They turn their backs on the Savior . . . but He keeps loving 'em, hoping they'll wake up before it's too late. Like He did with me." He paused, then shook his head. "His heart must break, kid, knowing the road they're headed down . . ."

"Sounds sweet and syrupy enough. Sorry, your theory doesn't do much for me."

"I can tell."

They sat in silence for the next ten miles. Michelle wanted to speak, but never got past a tentative cough or two. She didn't want to risk getting him started again. Nor did she want to deal with the thoughts he stirred up. After about ten minutes, Hank chuckled softly. The tension fled. She breathed a sigh of relief.

"Okay, I'm gonna put in the tape now," he informed her. "Go ahead and take a nap if you want."

"Thanks for the warning." She paused. "Say, you're pretty smart. You're trying to use reverse psychology on me. It won't work, though."

"Aren't you the suspicious one?" he teased. "Well, cheer up. You could have it worse." He winked at her, inserted the cassette, and punched the "play" button. Michelle closed her eyes tight, pretending to sleep. In truth, she listened closely, looking for some "ammunition" she might fire back later. A warm, deep voice flowed into the cabin from the speakers:

Several years ago, I travelled to the Sinai Desert in Israel with twelve men, all of whom were professing Christians. We planned to study the Jews' plight in the wilderness and compare it with our own spiritual journey. To my surprise, I learned as much from interacting with the men as I did from the tour.

Two guys in the group formed a lesson in contrasts. They personified the struggle we all face between our high calling as *intercessors* and our human tendency as *accusers*. One response is natural, the other, supernatural. The intercessor uplifts those around him; the accuser tears them down. I'll call the accuser on our trip, "Sam." (Please be assured that I'm not pointing a finger at any specific person. I've got as much Sam in me as Sam.)

71

This Ivy League gentleman joined our group in New York for the long flight to Israel. Almost immediately, he declared in a rather condescending manner, "I don't want this to be just another outing with the boys." Next, he accused one of the men—a pastor and popular writer of humor—of making fun of everything. In reality, this writer simply had a quick, dry wit. Sam kept scolding him with comments such as, "Now this isn't very spiritual. You shouldn't do that." He also accused another man of having a hang-up with the young bedouin girls because he gave them goodies as we passed by. Finally, his critique targeted me. "Jim, you have a 'running demon,'" he informed me. (That was his interpretation of my desire one day to run ahead of the group along the International Highway. Incidentally, I had a super time alone with the Lord.)

Sam had one main problem. He wasn't genuine. He excelled at pointing out faults in others, but failed to see his own sin: he had been cheating on his wife for some time! As the old song goes, he was "looking for love in all the wrong places." Yet, he was a great guy, despite his faults. He had been hurt by many things in his life. Old wounds held him captive, and he had been unable to break free to come into a real relationship with the Lord. I suppose that's why he chose the path he did.

Our group was blessed with the company of another man named "Mickey." Over the years, he had been a farmer, a country preacher and yes, an alcoholic. He now has a rehabilitation center in Florida, considered one of the premier centers of its kind. He knew the Bible as well as anyone I've ever met. He prayed for three and four hours at a time, constantly interceding for those around him.

Mickey, too, has been crushed by heartaches, but he gave them up to the Lord. The pain he endured molded him into a tough-as-nails prayer warrior. It was Mickey who brought the refreshing spirit of intercession into our Sinai group. He knew how to draw near to the throne of God. He understood not only how to "act" Christian but how to "be" Christian. I admired him. He was patterning his life after the Apostle Paul, who wrote,

First of all, then, I admonish and urge that petitions, prayers, intercessions, and thanksgivings be offered on behalf of all men.
(1 Timothy 2:1 AMP)

Sam and Mickey—each an example of the lifelong, minute-by-minute struggle we face between being *accusers* or *intercessors*. Do you realize that we make our choice the first thing every morning? If we start out determined to accomplish our own agendas, pursue our own ambitions, and do so in our own strength, we've already made our choice. Just pile on a host of inevitable hostilities throughout the day, and we'll be assured of a front-line spot in the ranks of the accusers.

Most people go through certain rituals to get ready for the day. You know, a cup of coffee, the newspaper . . . I like to exercise. After I've read some thought-provoking things from Scripture with my wife and committed a verse to memory, I'll climb on a stepping machine to get my blood circulating. While I'm there, I pray. I need to spend time with the Lord so the Holy Spirit can help me absorb a little truth through my thick head. Only then can I possibly

hope to become the type of guy who lifts others up instead of tears them down. It's not my first instinct, believe me.

You see, I'm an obsessive-compulsive. My wife, on the other hand, is a lovely-messy. We're different. We both have our faults—I more than she—and we sometimes get on each other's nerves. When I don't put on the mind-set of an intercessor, I will launch right into an early-morning litany of comments like, "Why can't you put *anything* away?" (She appreciates that at the break of dawn.)

Most of us face a similar challenge in our workplaces. We expect others to behave like divine clones. When they display their humanness, we put them down. What if we interceded instead? Yes, it's the hardest thing in the world and I often fall short myself, but it's the only right th—

Michelle broke in with a loud huff. "Hank," she said, "can you *please* give it a break?"

He stopped the tape. "What's up, kid?"

"I can't sleep with that thing playing. How does Dot do it?"

"Oh, the speakers in the sleeper are off. Besides, she knows she has to be ready to drive. Only supposed to log ten hours at a time at the wheel."

"You mean we have to listen to that preaching for ten hours straight?" A soft moan followed.

"Maybe. But he's teaching more than preaching."

"Same thing in my book."

"Not really. You have to admit, he's got some good points."

"Maybe not."

"Aw, come on, admit it."

"Well . . . I *can* see how my parents accuse more than intercess, that's for sure."

"The doctor is talking to more than just parents, I would venture to say." He looked over at her. "By the way, I think the word you want is 'intercede.'" He shook his head. "Never thought a dunce like me'd be correcting a grammar expert."

She gave him a combination of a smirk and a scowl, then tapped her balled fist on the armrest. "I don't know *why* I said something so moronic! It's one of those weird words where the verb form changes from the noun." She took a breath. "You get a kick out of that, don't you?"

"Would you?" He cocked his head, waiting for an answer. Silence. He went on, "The old human ego loves to be right— more than anything in the world. Sorry if it came off as a put-down. I didn't mean it that way." He paused and sighed. "Lord, help me with my teasin'. I don't want to hurt people."

Michelle cleared her throat. "Nice of you, but it really didn't bother me a bit."

"Well, let's call it a 'just-in-case-it-did prayer.'"

She frowned at him.

He nodded. "I'd say you probably have a good reason for being so touchy about your academic ability. Could it be that's what you depend on to feel good about yourself?"

She ignored him.

Without further delay, he pressed the play button again and the voice resumed:

From beginning to end, Scripture abounds with the call to "stand in the gap." This plea emanates from the very heart of God. No one knows better than He that there will always be a disparity between what *is* . . . and what *should be*. If you've got your Bibles with you, turn with me to the fifty-ninth chapter of the book of Isaiah. It tells of a time in

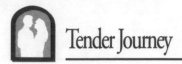

Israel's history when their sin had created a huge gulf between them and God's blessings. In verses one and two, King James version, we read,

> *Behold, the Lord's hand is not shortened, that it cannot save; neither his ear heavy, that it cannot hear: but your iniquities have separated between you and your God, and your sins have hid his face from you, that he will not hear.*

As we read through the rest of the chapter, we find that sin had become the norm among God's chosen people. Lying—accepted. Justice and truth—traits of the past. Citizens plotted and schemed against others, like poisonous spiders spinning webs for prey. To settle disputes, they resorted to bloodshed. And where could they find peace? Nowhere. It says they walked around as blind men, feeling their way along the walls. They stumbled at noon, as if it were the dark of night. Those few who tried to do right made themselves open targets for the wicked. Sounds almost too familiar, doesn't it? The situation bears striking resemblance to the twentieth century.

The Lord knew exactly what was going on, of course. His response may surprise us. In the first part of verse sixteen, we read, *And he saw that there was no man, and wondered that there was no intercessor.* God was astonished, not so much at the pervading sin throughout the land, but at the shortage of faithful to cry out for Him to turn things around!

Now, if we turn back a few chapters to the fifty-third chapter of Isaiah, we'll see how God planned to deal with the age-old sin problem. He would send the Savior to stand in the gap once and for all. Beginning in verses three through five, then verse twelve, we see the cost to Jesus,

> *He is despised and rejected of men; a man of sorrows, and acquainted with grief: and we hid as it were our faces from him; he was despised, and we esteemed him not.*
>
> *Surely he hath borne our griefs, and carried our sorrows: yet we did esteem him stricken, smitten of God, and afflicted. But he was wounded for our transgressions, he was bruised for our iniquities: the chastisement of our peace was upon him; and with his stripes we are healed . . . Therefore will I divide him a portion with the great, and he shall divide the spoil with the strong; because he hath poured out his soul unto death: and he was numbered with the transgressors; and he bare the sin of many, and made intercession for the transgressors.*

What a beautiful Savior! What a Redeemer! What an *Intercessor!* On that last point, He calls us to follow in His footsteps. We can add nothing to the saving or redeeming work He did on Calvary. When He said, "It is finished," He meant it. He had paid the price for sin. We don't earn our way to heaven; we receive our way by faith. After we have believed, however, our faith becomes evident through our actions. And standing in the prayer gap is probably the most meaningful, least popular action around.

Intercession demands sacrifice, whether in the prayer closet or in the public arena. A man shows the greatest love

when he willingly lays down his life for others (John 15:13). God may never ask us to put our physical lives on the line, as Jesus did, or as martyrs have done throughout history. We will have to risk that which we hold equally dear: our resources and reputation. Interceding for those who have fallen short will no doubt bring us scorn.

Imagine the scene in John eight when the Pharisees dragged the woman caught in adultery before Jesus. "She should be stoned!" they urged. After all, the law of Moses demanded it. Their accusations were accurate, the punishment, appropriate. "What will Jesus have to say about the matter?" they wondered. Did they value His insight? No. Scripture says, *And they were saying this, testing Him, in order that they might have grounds for accusing Him* (John 8:6a). So eager to find fault, they even sought to accuse the Son of God! That takes nerve.

Jesus quietly bent down, wrote in the sand with His finger. They kept on prodding Him for an answer. Finally, He stood up and said, *He who is without sin among you, let him be the first to throw a stone at her.* With that, He wrote further in the sand. One by one, the accusers left without saying another word. They realized they didn't have a leg to stand on.

Jesus—the only one holy enough to condemn her—refused to do so. He must have looked into her heart. Notice He didn't cloak the truth about her immoral behavior. He simply told her to quit it and to go her way. We see in His style the indelible handprint of genuine intercession: the beneficiary leaves feeling *convicted,* but *forgiven; changed,* but *uplifted; challenged,* but *motivated* to do better in the future. To quote an old saying, "A friend is one who, when you mess up, doesn't act like you've done a permanent job." Oh, what a Friend we have in Jesus . . . No one makes a better role model, throughout His life and in His death. Even in heaven, He's still going strong!

> *What then shall we say to these things? If God is for us, who is against us? He who did not spare His own Son, but gave him up for us all, how will he not also with Him freely give us all things? Who will bring a charge against God's elect? God is the one who justifies; who is the one who condemns? Christ Jesus is He who died, yes, rather who was raised, who is at the right hand of God,* **who also intercedes for us.**
> (Romans 8:31-34 NASB)

If intercession is divinely inspired from first to last, who, then, gave birth to accusation? Revelation twelve, nine and ten (NASB), leaves no room for doubt:

> *And the great dragon was thrown down, the serpent of old who is called the devil and Satan, who deceives the whole world; he was thrown down to the earth, and his angels were thrown down with him. And I heard a loud voice in heaven, saying, Now the salvation, and the power, and the kingdom of our God and the authority of His Christ have come, for the accuser of our brethren has been thrown down, who accuses them before our God day and night . . . ..*

Oh-oh. Have we accusers been siding with the adversary instead of our Ally? That's like running a touchdown

across an opponent's goal line in the championship play-offs. Not very smart. In a sense, we do that whenever we try to remove the speck of sawdust from our brother's eyes before dealing with the log cabin in our own. The Holy Spirit wants to whittle us down to size first. In the wood-shed of prayer He does His best work. By the time He's done quietly pointing out all the areas where we need improvement, we'll sound a whole lot less "holier-than-thou" when we have to set another person straight. So, how about if we quit hanging around with Satan and the Gang in Accusation Alley? Let's set up permanent camp on *Intercession Isle* with *Heaven and Friends* . . . as *fault-menders* instead of *fault-finders*.

I'd like to close with a quotation from a notecard my wife found somewhere. Unfortunately, it lists no author or credits, but we extend our thanks. The verse is called,

The Imperishable Gift
Praying for Others

Penetrates the hearts we cannot open,
Shields those whom we cannot guard,
Teaches where we cannot speak,
Comforts where our hearts
have no power to soothe,
Follows our best beloved
through the trials and
perplexities of the day,
Lifting off their blindness
with an unseen hand.

The tape player clicked off. Michelle stretched and yawned out loud, making sure that Hank heard her.

"That bad?" he asked.

"It was okay."

"Just okay, huh?"

"Well, it's kind of like believing in Utopia. Nice to dream about, but you can't really go there."

"You can sure come a far cry from the pit, though. And prayin' did it for us." Hank fell silent.

Michelle frowned. She pursued a thought as relentlessly as a kitten chasing a string. "You know, I used to see my Mom and Dad pray after they first got back together. That was a few years ago. Dad talked a lot about some old guy named 'Caleb.' I never met him. Supposedly, he helped my dad know God."

Hank spoke into the sudden silence. "Supposedly? Wouldn't you have met him if it was only a few years a—"

"He died just before dad came home," Michelle cut in. "See, mom and dad were separated for quite a few months. She even took out a restraining order against him. That means, if he would have come to the house, he'd be breaking the law."

"Must have been hard on you."

She retreated into the tough girl act. "Nah, I handled it fine. But talk about conflict. *Man!*"

Hank glanced at her. She sat staring out at the lonely stretch of road, not really seeing where they were going. Her mind's eye saw another setting, another scenario. When she spoke again, her words had become crisp, hard. "Get this—Mom had sent me and my brother off to camp and one day, out of the clear blue, the two of them came to pick us up. Early, before camp was over. They were all lovey-dovey, no less. Just like nothing ever happened. They could have warned us, but no. I couldn't believe it. Right away,

they each nagged at me to talk to the other one with respect. Give me a break! They hadn't been civil to each other for months."

She shook her head. "Well, the honeymoon didn't last long. I knew it wouldn't. They started arguing almost every day again. That's why I'm so glad I'm away at college." Her face flushed at the lie. Did it sound casual enough? She hoped so. He seemed oblivious, so she added, "I usually took the brunt of their frustration because my little brother's sick."

"Oh?"

"Yeah, HIV."

"He's got AIDS? How in the world . . .?"

"Blood transfusion. He's a hemophiliac—you know, his blood doesn't clot right. He got infected back in '85, before all the mandatory screening tests. He doesn't have any bad symptoms yet, besides being tired a lot, so they don't call it 'AIDS.' But once the symptoms start, it won't take long. He could die of complications before he's a teenager."

"Oh, man, I'm sorry."

"Yeah, it's tough. He's the lovable one in the family. Looks kinda like a little blond angel. Acts like one, too, most of the time. I can be real moody a lot. Reminds me of the book, *Little Women.* The sweet one of the four March sisters had to be the one to die. The ornery one wrote the story." She heaved a big sigh. "I think my mom and dad wish it were me instead of Stephen. They haven't said so, but deep down, I know it's true."

Hank's mouth dropped open. A lame-sounding, "I can't imagine that," was all he could muster. He felt pulled in two directions. He wanted to reach out and reassure the girl—tell her it was nonsense, that no parents would ever think such a thing. But what if they did? And part of him feared that if he dismissed her viewpoint, he'd jeopardize any further chance of getting her to open up.

She'd just turn him off and go on her merry way. So he sat there and prayed under his breath.

Finally, Michelle yawned again, long and hard. "Oh, I'm so sleepy. Hank, I've got to take a nap."

"Go right ahead. Promise I'll wait until you're asleep to play my tapes again."

"Thanks. Talk to you later."

"Night." With that, she leaned her head back against the seat and dozed off. The only sounds left in the cab were the rumble of the diesel engine and the highway slipping beneath them at sixty-five miles per hour as they sped along on their way to the nation's capital.

❧ *Six* ❧

That afternoon, Michael stared, unseeing, at the million-dollar warriors waging battle over a football on the big-screen TV in the den. The videotape had been a Christmas present to Stephen, and he had been promising his son they would watch it together "sometime soon." He couldn't put it off any longer. Stephen was insistent.

Two unchallenged Miami Dolphin touchdowns came and went while he sat, slouched, in the plush sofa. His thoughts clung to another battle, one far more deadly and closer to home. Fear and anger double-teamed the shred of faith he had left. His heart felt like the football looked—with a half-ton of brutes piled on it.

As the Chicago Bears' left cornerback leaped high and intercepted a pass meant for the Dolphins' wide receiver, he fell to his knees from the momentum. Michael found himself wondering how long had it been since he had been on his knees. He couldn't remember. Prayer felt awkward, stilted. It just didn't have the same draw it used to.

An invisible enemy seemed to be having a heyday with his family. Why? Answers eluded him. He let that question go, not liking the direction it was taking. After all, he was an engineer. Trained to correlate reactions to actions. Things didn't just happen. There were reasons. There had to be. He just didn't want to be one of them.

"Who's winnin', Dad?" He hadn't noticed Stephen back in the room. "Miami do it to 'em yet?"

"I don't know. Sorry, guess you caught me daydreaming." Michael reached out his right arm and his son came to him. He ran his fingers through his blond hair. Then, with his hand still resting on the back of Stephen's neck, he said, "Come on, sit down. We'll get it together."

"*O-kay!*" Stephen exclaimed. A smile lighting up his face, he turned around and plopped down next to his dad. "Do ya think they can pull it off, Dad?"

"Wha . . . ? Oh, sure—sure." He looked over at his son, who gazed back at him, eyebrows raised. A pang of guilt jarred Michael out of his daze. He draped his arm across his son's shoulder and pulled him closer. "Let's you and I find out. Okay?"

Stephen nodded his enthusiastic agreement, and cuddled in closer. For both of them, the moment was sufficient to ease the dim prospects of the future. Only minutes had passed when the sound of shattering glass startled both of them. *"Mi-chael!"* Stephanie called from the kitchen, a second later.

"What is it? Are you all right?" he replied. She didn't answer. He looked at Stephen, gave his shoulder a reassuring pat and called out, "Hang on, I'm coming." Then, to Stephen, he added, "Be right back. Get ready to fill me in." He slid forward off the sofa and walked toward the kitchen.

Stephanie stood with her back to the sink. Her arms were stretched out behind her, hands gripping the edge of the counter. She stared, horrified, at the shards of glass scattered on the floor—

all that remained of a large crystal bowl. Soapy water still drained from the half-full sink and a towel lay across the few dishes drying in the rack. "I was cleaning out some cupboards. Just to keep my mind occupied . . ." Her eyes locked onto Michael's the instant he came into view. "I think I'm going crazy," she half sobbed, half gasped. "Really, I'm losing it."

Michael crossed the room in two strides. Glass crunched with each footfall. "Hon, it's just a bowl. We can buy another one."

"No we can't. That was the Waterford crystal compote my parents gave us as a wedding present." Her voice broke. "It was an heirloom I was going to pass on to Michelle . . ." He stopped in front of her and slid his arms around her waist, trying to embrace her. She remained rigid, her hands glued to the countertop. "I hope it's not an omen."

"Of what?"

She stared at the calendar, eyes glazed over. "That she won't be around long enough to *get* married."

As he stood at arm's length, he watched the tears surface. Her lips stretched taut. She screwed her eyes shut to stem the rising tide, but that merely delayed the inevitable. When they opened, the dam let loose. Only then, with tears streaming down her cheeks, did she relinquish her grip on the countertop and lean into the security of Michael's embrace. "Shh, hon," he whispered. "I believe everything's going be all right."

"How can you stand there and say that? You don't know any more than I do!" she demanded. She tensed in his arms, muscles stiff and unyielding. "Or don't you care? Incredibly, you're sitting out there . . ." she nodded her head toward the den, " . . . watching a *stupid* football game, like nothing bothers you in the least, while I'm falling apart! I can't sleep. I can't eat. I'm a nervous wreck." She pointed to the broken glass on the floor.

"Wait a minute. You're the one who's always nagging me about spending more time with the kids. Stephen's been asking me to watch that video with him since Christmas."

Her shoulders shook. She leaned back and crossed her arms, hugging herself to quell the shaking. The tears continued their trek, collecting on her jaw until their numbers were sufficient to jump the span between cheek and blouse. There, they made two broadening, damp spots.

Michael gave her space. He'd learned long ago that a push at volatile times like these was like holding a lighted match over the open spout of a full gas can. It wasn't a question of whether or not there would be an explosion, but of how much damage the blow-up would cause. So, he waited.

To his surprise, the tension drained away after a minute or two. Stephanie relaxed her grip on herself, but kept her arms crossed. She looked up at him. "Sorry. I'm just *worried.* What can we do? There must be something more."

"I don't know," he admitted.

"Well, dang it, we certainly can't just sit here and watch television and clean out cupboards while our daughter is out there . . . somewhere."

"Then suppose you tell me. We've knocked on hundreds of doors and notified everybody we can think of. What can we do that the police can't, except worry ourselves to death?" Michael paused. An expressionless mask settled across his features. It gave no hint of the emotions boiling just beneath the surface. "And *you're* doing enough of that for both of us!" He dropped his arms from her waist. His eyes took on a hard, wary look.

Stephanie recognized the look. She glanced away, not wanting another confrontation now. He sensed her reluctance, but that did nothing to appease his rising frustration. Still angry about her

accusation of his lack of concern, he stormed out of the kitchen. He strode over to the couch, grabbed a pillow, and resumed his place next to Stephen. A warm smile greeted him there.

"Boy, Dad, you should've seen that last play. Miami ran a punt all the way to the five-yard line. You're just in time to watch 'em score." Stephen rubbed his hands together in a burst of energy.

He put his arm back around his son's shoulders. "Okay, big guy, let's see what they can do."

Hank pulled his rig alongside the bus station in Washington D.C., took it out of gear, and threw on the air brake. Eighteen hours since they left Florida—longer than usual—but Charleston was worth a couple of hours layover. Good thing Dot could share the driving. They kept things legal that way. Before she went back to sleep, they'd had a chance to talk about Michelle's situation. The girl didn't even stir. Their hearts ached, wanting to see her somewhere safe, yet knowing there was little they could do. She insisted she was going to "visit family" and D.C. was the best place to catch the bus. Without forcing themselves on her, they could only give her a few dollars for the road and pray. If her story wasn't true, they hoped she'd come to her senses before it was too late.

He looked over at her now where she dozed, her head and right shoulder against the window. He sighed, leaning back into his seat. Sometimes you just had to let 'em learn. He reached over to shake her. "Okay, ladies, we're in D.C."

Michelle moved around in her seat, and he could hear rustling from the sleeping compartment. A moment later, the curtain slid back. Dot's head poked through the opening. "Hey, kid," Dot asked, rubbing her eyes, "Somebody pickin' you up in New York?"

Michelle sat up and glanced back at Hank's wife. "No, I'll be all right. They're working." Hank leaned toward her, his features firm. "No hitchhiking, okay? It's dangerous, 'specially for a young lady your age."

"That's right, honey," Dot agreed. "The Lord was watchin' out for you when you ran into us on that road."

Michelle's eyes narrowed. "It was just luck. I told you I don't believe that religious junk. But I won't hitchhike. Gives me the creeps. I'm getting on the bus right here—remember?"

"We remember, honey. It's just that . . ." Dot's voice faded, leaving her final thoughts unsaid.

Dot met her husband's gaze for a moment. He nodded and looked back at Michelle. "We'll be praying for you. And for your family." While he spoke, he dug around in his travelling pouch. "Our preacher told us to put feet to our prayers. Here. You might need this." He handed her a couple of well-worn twenty-dollar bills and a ten, along with a scrap of paper with their names and home phone number. "Be careful on the bus."

"That's right. Some pretty rough characters in there." Dot reached over and closed the girl's fingers around the bills, then patted her hand. "Please don't throw caution to the wind."

Bristling slightly, Michelle replied, "You guys sound like my parents, trying to scare me into doing things their way." She squeezed the bills in her small fist. "I brought plenty of money, but I'll keep this, just in case." She pulled the door handle, grabbed her purse and backpack and hopped out with a bounce. "See ya." She took a couple steps, then turned and added a clipped, "Thanks."

"You're welcome. Take care, kid." He tipped his cap as she pushed the door shut with a bang.

Dot slid into the passenger seat and waved out the window. "Call if you need us. We check the answering machine at home

once a day. God bless you, dear!" Hank echoed her last phrase with a broad wave, but Michelle already had her back to them.

They watched her walk into the station, past the buses lined up in their stalls. Hank shook his head and closed his eyes. Dot followed suit, automatically. His voice lowered. "Lord, she's in Your hands. We know that you have plans for good and not evil for her. Draw her to You, we pray. Protect her. In Jesus' name. Amen." Dot squeezed his hand. He slipped off the air brake and pulled away from the station. A few blocks later, he looked over at his wife. "You know what? Maybe we oughta notify the police . . . just in case."

Dot nodded. "I was thinking the very same thing." She turned the CB dial to channel nine, took the mouthpiece out of its holder and started to hand it to him.

"Let me get through this intersection first," he said, as he pushed in the clutch and down shifted. "Gotta keep my clean record." He was always so careful, a trait which had earned him a "safe driver" status for the last fifteen years.

His light was green. Still, he looked to his right to be sure.

Before he could glance all the way left, Dot let out a scream. *"Babe!" she shouted. "A cement rig comin' on your si—!"* Too late.

Within a split second, the air resonated with the high-pitched wail of brakes and tires.

Then, metal against metal, a deafening crash. Shards of glass went sailing through the cab like miniature missiles.

His door had taken a direct hit, forcing his seat several inches to the right. He slumped toward her, unconscious, restrained only by his seat belt.

Dot felt around for the CB with a trembling, bloodied hand. As best she could, she radioed for help, then laid her head on the back of his shoulder and said a prayer.

❧ ❧ ❧

Michelle grimaced as she looked around the inside of the bus station. She couldn't believe how dingy it was. Of course, she had never been in one before. But it sure didn't compare to the Orlando airport. She sneezed several times, her nostrils full of the acrid smell of diesel exhaust. Her ears were ringing from the hiss of air brakes. At least half a dozen buses were lined up in their lanes outside.

She glanced around at the other travelers. An old man with a stubbly-bearded face, wearing a stocking cap with holes in it pulled halfway over his eyes, sat slouched on a nearby bench. His dark brown woolen overcoat, much too big for him, hung down over his legs almost to his filthy, laceless tennis shoes. They bulged open, showing bare feet underneath.

A few feet away sat a withered old woman with stringy, yellow-gray hair, wearing a gray cardigan sweater. Her skinny legs were crossed at the knees. She puffed intently on a cigarette, inhaling so deeply that her cheeks sank in like caverns. The woman's ragged, brownish nails protruded from stained fingers that clenched her cigarette. Michelle shivered. To her taste, it was a sorry-looking bunch.

She ambled up behind the last person in the shortest line at the ticket counter. A gray-haired lady wearing a hat and gloves was being waited on. Next was a pretty young mother with a baby on one hip. To pass the time, Michelle studied the huge woman right in front of her. She had short, straw-like bleached-blond hair with dark brown roots grown out almost halfway. Her cotton print house dress drew taut around hips that ballooned out below a non-existent waist. At her side cowered a blond toddler who stood on her canvas slip-on shoes and peered around her thick legs. His

91

cute face reminded Michelle of Stephen's when he was little, except more pitiful. His nose ran continually. He alternated between snuffing it and wiping it on his bruised, scabbed forearm.

He let out a whimper. The woman snarled at him, "I told ya, brat, t'quit yer sniveling. It gets on my nerves. Now if ya know what's good for ya, shut up!" She bent forward, slapped him across the legs and came up breathing heavily.

Michelle winced. She wanted to grab the nasty woman by the hair and whack her silly. The boy started crying. His mother yanked him by the arm and dragged him into the ladies' room. That left Michelle standing, with her mouth open, right in front of the ticket counter.

"Good afternoon, young lady. May I help you?" the cheerful clerk asked, as though nothing out of the ordinary had happened. Michelle, speechless, stared first at him, over at the bathroom door, then back at him. He repeated his question. "Miss, people are waiting. May I help you?"

Michelle swallowed hard. Her large, moist brown eyes looked like a fawn's whose mother had just been shot. "Yes, sir," she said, "I'd like a ticket to New York City."

"Which station? It's a big place."

"Um . . . I don't know the name of it. The one closest to the theaters. I'm meeting my cousin who's in drama college near there," she lied.

"One-way or round-trip?"

"One-way."

He looked up the fare in the computer and punched the right keys. Michelle paid him in cash, took the change and receipt, and tucked the ticket in her bag. "Next bus leaves in thirty minutes from Gate Three. Be ready to board fifteen minutes before departure. Seats are first come, first served, so you better get in line."

"Yes, sir." Michelle backed away from the counter a few steps and turned around. She had to go to the bathroom. Had the fat woman come out with her little boy? No sign of them. She walked reluctantly over to the door covered with black scuff marks and fingerprints, marked "Ladies," and pushed it open.

Dirty sinks, used paper towels, and other debris strewn on the damp floor, and a hole in the pale green plaster walls first greeted her, then a sickening odor. The place reeked. She gagged as she opened one of the stall doors. Stopped up. The next one seemed okay, but no paper. It would have to do. She stepped inside the stall and shut the door. Then it happened—she heard a whine. That little boy. "Please, Mommy, *no,*" he cried. "I be good . . ."

Michelle threw open the latch, splashed some water on her hands and dashed out into the lobby. She rushed toward the nearest bench. Her body was trembling. She wrapped her arms across her stomach and leaned forward to squelch a wave of nausea. A few deep breaths helped. Finally, she sat up, stretched her torso, and looked around.

Her eyes caught the stare of a nice-looking young guy. No. Nice-looking was an understatement. Gorgeous was more like it. She looked away, then pretended to dig in her purse. He walked in her direction, set his backpack on the bench she was sitting on, and introduced himself with a friendly, "Hi, I'm Matt."

"Hello," she answered, still fishing in her bag.

"What's up? You look like you saw a real ghost." He smiled a warm, casual smile.

Michelle hesitated, heart pounding. Her parents had taught her never to talk to strangers. But she was on her own now. She studied Matt for a brief moment and decided he was okay—clean-cut, actually. His pleated jeans and knit shirt did not escape her notice, nor did his nice build underneath. She answered, "The

bathroom was super gross. And that woman with her little boy!" Thinking about it, she shivered.

"The fat one?"

She shook her head. "The *dietarily challenged* one, as they say."

Smiling, he pointed to the bench. "Mind if I sit down?"

"Guess not." She shrugged her shoulders.

"I agree with you. Saw her standing in line, acting like a drill sergeant with her kid. Probably beatin' him at home. Or worse. Don't let it bother you. Happens all the time. I should know."

Michelle glanced at him but did not ask the question she sensed he wanted her to. Better to drop it.

Matt hesitated only a second before carrying on. "Guess you haven't been around much. Things like that don't happen at your house, huh?" He grinned at her shocked expression. "My stepdad beat the tar out of me every time he got to drinkin'. Been that way as far back as I can remember."

Michelle's eyes widened. "Didn't somebody protect you?"

He shook his head. "Mom was afraid herself. He pounded her good, too."

"What'd you do?"

"Got mad and fought back. That just made things worse. I couldn't take it anymore, so I left. Been on my own for a year "

"You *have?*"

He nodded.

"Do you like it?"

"Oh, yeah. Money gets tight sometimes—but I can do what I want. And I don't have to put up with *them.* How 'bout you?"

Michelle cleared her throat and folded her arms across her chest. She stared at the floor.

Matt continued as if she had answered him. "You know what? I don't even know your name."

94

Again, she hesitated. Was it safe to divulge? Her first name couldn't hurt. Finally she whispered, "Michelle."

"Michelle. My favorite name! So what brings a nice girl like you to a place like this?"

"I'm going to New York—to visit my cousin. She lives near the theater district." She blushed.

"You're a wanna-be actress?"

"Nah. Just visiting my cousin who is."

"Well, I think you're on the run, like me. Come on, you can tell me. I'm not gonna turn you in. Why'd you leave, anyway?"

"I'm *not* a runaway."

"Sure you are. It's all right. Maybe I can show you the ropes."

Michelle thought about that for a moment. Might be better to know somebody. "Okay, so I am. What's the big deal?"

"You need a friend. You're pretty young to be wandering in New York City by yourself. Lots can happen to a pretty girl there." He smiled. "Why'd you run? You don't look like you had it bad."

"Well, I didn't get beat up, if that's what you mean."

"What, then?"

She heaved a sigh. "Nothin' specific, but we had our differences. They argue a lot and my dad yells at me about everything."

"That's *all?*"

"My boyfriend and I broke up. Not much to hang around for."

"If you told your parents you were buggin' up, wouldn't they listen?"

"Nah . . . why bother? I don't fit into their schedule—not that I want to." She sighed again. "They have my brother to worry about. They don't need me and my problems."

"What's wrong with him?" His concerned expression surprised her, and encouraged her to talk more.

She paused, took a deep breath. "He's a hemophiliac, plus

HIV-positive. No bad symptoms yet, but he has tests all the time. I'm healthy. I kinda fade into the background."

"Bet you feel left out, huh?"

"Sort of."

"Like it doesn't matter whether you're alive or dead?"

"Sometimes."

"You know what? I think you believe they wish it was *you* instead of him."

She squinted at him. "How'd you know that?"

"I guessed. Met lotsa kids like you and me."

Michelle didn't like what she'd just heard. She turned a probing gaze on Matt. He was lumping her together with a bunch of misfits she didn't even know. She didn't consider herself one of them. But he did seem to understand her feelings. "You're pretty sure of yourself," she replied. "Talk like you have all the answers."

"Nah. Just been in the real world. And you know what else?" He stared straight ahead at the ticket counter as he spoke. "I've seen a lot of pretty girls, but you sure are the prettiest."

She smiled in spite of herself. Blood rushed to her face and she grabbed a quick breath. He was too cute for words. No way could she let him know.

Just then, a nasal voice over the loudspeaker roused her from her daydream. "Last call for #37 to New York, with stops in . . ."

She jumped up. "That's my bus. I gotta go." She paused for several seconds. "Guess I'll see ya around."

He held up the ticket in his hand. "We're in luck, kid. It's my bus, too." She stifled a sigh of delight and picked up her things. Together, they headed toward the door.

❧ *Seven* ❧

Michael and Stephanie faced each other across the dining room table later that evening. Thankfully, Stephen was tucked away safe-and-sound in his bed. Tension charged the atmosphere. Their untouched cups of herb tea sat cooling in front of them.

"Steph, what are we doing to each other?" he demanded. "I'm tired of fighting."

"We don't fight," she returned, not raising her eyes from her tea cup. "We *stay* mad."

"Now, that's an encouraging word before bedtime."

"It's true. We hardly ever talk."

Michael looked at her, his eyes wide with amazement. "What do you mean? We talk all the time."

"Not about anything important."

He knit his eyebrows. "I'm too busy to waste my time discussing trivia, Stephanie."

"Well, trivia or not, I need to talk about things that concern us—our family and our relationship. Not the entire universe!"

He pondered her response for a moment. "Oh, I suppose

you're referring to the Space Waste project . . . or maybe to my general interest in international affairs." He tisked. "You seem to think we live in a vacuum. I couldn't believe you fell asleep right in the middle of a news item on the fall of the Berlin Wall."

"I was not asleep. I was reading."

"Yeah, one of your mindless novels."

"They're not mindless! At least they make me feel human." Her eyes filled with tears.

"Hey, what's with the waterworks already? I'm sorry." Michael stretched an open palm across the table. He didn't touch her, though. He waited for her to meet him halfway. After a moment, he could see she wouldn't. Part of him wanted to walk around the table and wrap his arms around her anyway, to love away all her hurts and fears. Part of him didn't. He withdrew his hand.

Seconds passed. Neither seemed willing to break the uncomfortable silence. More time passed, then Stephanie sniffed and cleared her throat. "Michael . . ." She waited until his eyes met hers before continuing. "It's the same old story. I've never felt really important to y——."

"How can——" he interrupted.

"Let me finish, will you?" she cut right back before he could launch into another soliloquy. "You don't value me. Not as a woman or for my opinions. I need to know I'm the single most important thing in life to you. Besides God, of course." She paused just long enough for her words to register, and to gather courage to go on. "Something's missing. There's got to be more to life than what we have . . ." She saw a stubborn look gaining ground again in Michael's eyes, but she couldn't stop now. Hurt couched in anger spewed out. "I haven't felt happy in a couple of years. Why pretend anymore? You have all your projects. I've got our children. And now *both* of them are being taken from me!

Stephanie crumpled like a rag doll. She seemed to fold in on herself, as if the torrent of angry words had played some vital role in supporting her. Her shoulders slumped. Her entire body began to shake with wracking sobs.

He softened his tone of voice. "Honey, Michelle will turn up soon. It's only been a day."

"An afternoon, a night, a day and an evening. She's in trouble—or about to be. I can sense it. And all you do is sit there, placating me, like I'm a three-year-old."

"What do you mean? We have bothered every neighbor within miles, talked to every friend we can think of, and driven down almost every street in the county looking for her."

"Yes, but you make me feel stupid for wanting to. It's as if you're *humoring* me so you can get on to your projects. I hate it!"

Michael sat back, dazed. For a minute, the woman in front of him was gone. In her place stood another, slightly younger version. Stephanie, long before Michelle's disappearance . . . before the threat of AIDS . . . before Caleb. He remembered standing in the main hallway of their old home, hearing her holler at him, "I want a husband, not just a provider . . . I'm tired of being married to an egotistical success machine . . . you don't need us at all!"

The blood drained from his face. That memory still haunted him. It was one of the worst nights of his life—banished from his own home in a matter of hours. "I can't believe it," he mumbled half to himself, half aloud. We came so far . . ."

Stephanie raised her head from the tabletop and looked at him with eyes reddened from crying.

"How did we get back to this?" he asked, throwing his hands up in the air.

"Back to what?" She saw the faraway look in his eyes. "There you go again." Her voice grew stern, less timid. "I just told you

how rotten I feel about our marriage and life in general. You sit there talking to yourself, staring off into space. Don't you care at all?" Those words penetrated Michael's memory-fogged brain. He saw the corners of her mouth start quivering just before she cried again and dropped her head back onto her folded arms.

"Of course I care!" he shouted. "Why can't you see that?"

"Because you never *act* like it."

"How do you want me to act? Like I'm falling apart? That won't do us or the kids a bit of good."

"What a stupid thing to say!"

"Thanks a lot!"

"Of course I don't want you to *pretend* to feel any certain way."

"Okay, so I'm not showing enough concern about the kids to suit you. Where else do I not measure up to your expectations?"

She stopped short. For a long moment, she studied her nails. The tech had done a French manicure for the first time. Finally, she said, "You haven't acted sweet to me in so long, I can hardly remember."

Michael shook his head. "What does that have to do with this conversation? I thought you were worried about the kids."

"I *am*. See? That's what I mean. You have no idea what a woman needs. If you loved me, you'd take the time to find out what really matters and do something about it." Stephanie glared at him across the table.

He met her gaze, but his thoughts wandered. He remembered lying in bed just the other night, longing to make love to her. Was that what she was talking about? Stephanie's voice brought him back from his musing. ". . . a friend at church, and she—"

"I'm sorry," he interrupted. "I didn't hear the first part."

"I said . . . I was talking to a friend who mentioned she and her husband had been seeing a counselor."

"Why?" Already, the wheels were turning. Next thing, she'd want them to go. He could just hear it.

"To give them a neutral sounding board, to help them understand each oth—"

"Forget it. Our marriage isn't that bad."

"Please, Michael. Just let me finish." She waited, with her eyebrows raised.

He half-nodded his assent.

She continued, "He's not on staff, but he goes to our church and the pastors refer clients to him. He happens to have a Ph.D. in a medical field and one in biblical studies."

"So?"

"I just thought you might relate to somebody who's educated."

"That doesn't guarantee he's any good."

"I know that. But he specializes in marriage and family counseling. The girls said he's been able to help some couples a lot."

"I told you, I'm not going to any counselor—in church or out. If you want to, that's fine." His eyes narrowed. *"You* could use it, the way you get hysterical lately. By the way, thanks for insinuating to your friends that we're having marriage trouble."

She reached across the table and laid her right hand on his forearm. "I didn't do any such thing. They were talking about this counselor named Eric Marcos and I just listened."

He scowled, knowing what was coming.

"Can we please go together and talk to him a couple times? Maybe there's nothing he can do, but can we at least try?"

He'd been waiting for the big question, even had a clever comeback ready about the absurdity of such a suggestion. He opened his mouth. That was as far as he got. The words wouldn't come. Something about the pleading look in her eyes—helpless, frightened, hopeful—made him curb his biting comment.

The last thing he needed was a stranger poking around in his psyche. Maybe he could tolerate a session or two with the pastor. But a professional shrink? Yet, he couldn't quite bring himself to dismiss her request as foolishness. He wanted to, of course, which was why his next words came as such a surprise. "All right, all *right*. You want counseling? We'll get it," he heard himself say. "Not that I put much stock in that mumbo-jumbo, but I will go along. We need advice about Michelle, anyway."

Stephanie stood up and walked around the table to where he was sitting. She placed her arms around his neck and hugged him. "You mean it?" She leaned back to look him in the eyes.

"Yeah, we can go talk to the guy. No commitment, though."

"That's okay. Better than nothing—thanks." She leaned forward and gave him a quick kiss on the forehead before scooting away to do the dishes.

Sleep eluded Michael that evening. He tried reading. That usually helped, but not this time. In the first place, he had trouble concentrating on what he read. Images spawned in his too-fertile imagination painted one nightmarish picture after another. Newspaper headlines, like the "Fame to Shame" one-liner the night of the awards banquet, taunted him. What would it be this time? He could envision the worst:

"Lousy Husband Seeks Shrink."

"Last-Ditch Effort of Fame-to-Shamer to Save Family."

He shuddered. Shadows of doubt hounded him further:

"He's a terrible husband."

"A pitiful father-figure."

"A poor excuse for a man."

But the more he thought about his last conversation with Stephanie, the more he felt trapped into the counseling routine.

And the more trapped he felt, the madder he got. A walk in the evening air might chase away the phantoms. It was worth a try.

Outside, walking along the path up to the gently sloping hill-side, he rehearsed the events immediately after their little talk. Stephanie was very animated. She obviously wanted to chat more, once she'd done the dishes and checked on Stephen, but he was too preoccupied to carry on a decent conversation. Exasperated, she'd given up and gone to bed. There was a brief moment—she turned to look back at him from halfway up the stairs—when he'd almost gone with her. The "look" she gave him held a hint of promise. Her lips, with just a slight upturning at the corners, wooed him across a gulf of hurt. Desire, too long suppressed, stirred in him. Then, he caught himself.

No way, baby! It wasn't because he didn't want to be with her. She was certainly beautiful enough. No, not the problem. What, then? Yes, definitely—the ease with which she'd manipulated him into agreeing to something he had no intention of doing. That soured any chance of their seeking pleasure from one another *that* night. Perhaps she'd read the look on his face. She turned and went upstairs to their room. And here he was, wandering outside again. To get to the open hillsides where he now walked, he had to pass through the grape arbors. As usual, this triggered memories of Caleb.

Everything had felt brand-new after he first gave his life to Christ. He couldn't get enough of the Word. He loved studying and discussing passages with his old friend and mentor. Church services became a looked-forward-to event. But something had happened since then. What?

It wasn't that he loathed reading the Bible. He felt mild urges to reach up and pull it down from the shelf. But *doing* it . . . He had so little time to read in-depth. From the moment his feet hit

the floor until he finally fell asleep at night, he rushed headlong from one project or crisis to another.

"Where does all the time go?" he asked the darkness. Silence mocked him. "At least it's quiet out here," he said as he bent down and plucked a blade of grass. His eyes searched the land in front of him. He saw the silhouette of trees and hills against the backdrop of the starlit sky. Something nagged him, peering back from just within the fringes of conscious thought, but he couldn't quite put his finger on it.

He turned around and faced the house. Nestled behind the hillside, it looked cozy and protected. Light shone from the upstairs bedroom like the beacon of some seaside lighthouse. He almost expected to hear the sound of waves crashing against a craggy seashore. Instead, he heard the soft but shrill song of the katydids and a dog barking in the distance. A gentle breeze stirred the leaves on the trees.

He walked to a nearby tree and dropped into a sitting position with his back against the trunk. Letting the sounds lull him, his head rested on the cool bark. And that's when it happened. With such strength it left him almost dizzy, a scene from several years earlier once again filled his mind's eye.

They were all out on this very hill for a family picnic—he, Stephanie, Stephen, and Michelle. He and Steph had chosen the setting to break the news to the kids about AIDS. Neither of them had a clue how to go about it, so they prayed for wisdom.

His eyes grew misty recalling that moment. The kids seemed so happy to have their parents back together. Well, at least *Stephen* was delighted. He told them he had prayed every day to "be a fam'bly again." Seeing his prayers answered had almost been too much for the little guy. He jumped up and started running around in a circle, barely able to restrain himself, while Ebony chased him, barking his head off. Michael could still see Stephen cheering, *"Yay, Jesus! Yay, Jesus!"* That had broken his old father-heart.

For one of the few times in his adult life, he had cried openly, unashamed. He couldn't have stopped—even if he had wanted to. And that was the strangest thing. He felt okay baring his soul that way. Amazing. So much had changed. He didn't know it would be so easy to crawl back into his hard shell.

Of course, he was angry about Michelle skipping out without telling them where she was going. He didn't deal well with helplessness. There were times during the last twenty-four hours when he wanted to cry, out of sheer frustration, but he held himself in close check. Something inside him that wasn't there during that momentous picnic had somehow resurrected itself. Now, he would rather die than display the weakness of tears.

Suddenly, his son's words from that day started to come to mind. Moments after they told him about the AIDS virus . . . what did he say, exactly?

"Yeah, that's it," Michael murmured into the starry sky, "'Dying won't be so bad 'cause I'll be with Jesus. I have Him in my heart.'" Incredible. Straight from the mouth of a six-year-old!

That memory triggered others—how he had tried desperately to be a leader and lift his family's spirits. He talked to them about his beloved Caleb, saying:

> He spent a lot of time teaching me about an important ingredient in life called, "the unseen essential." With faith in Jesus Christ and His Word, he said we can face anything. Guess that even means *AIDS,* as scary as it is . . .

"Or runaway daughters," Michael said now to no one in particular. Somehow, it seemed a whole lot easier to believe back then.

 Tender Journey

And this counseling kick Stephanie was on. He may have half-agreed to go, but that was all. No long-term commitment. Nothing said he had to like the idea. That wasn't fair, either, though. His wife deserved more consideration. They may not have always seen eye-to-eye, but he couldn't deny his affection for her.

He remembered feeling so full of love at the picnic with the kids. He longed to hold her close, to shield her from the harsh reality they had to face. What had happened? Why didn't he feel that way anymore? Maybe what she said was true. It was his fault.

He squirmed. That kind of reasoning just didn't sit well. Even if it was true, he'd rather blame somebody else. Then he could cross counseling off her to-do list. Her *never-ending* to-do list.

There he was, sarcastic again. She wasn't even around to notice. Well, what if he *had* clammed up first? That didn't give her any excuse for losing herself in a private little romance-novel world. It sure didn't seem to matter whether he was around or not—except when she wanted to blow off steam. And she blamed him for withdrawing from *her!* Not the way it happened.

He thought back to when he left Eagle. He had every intention of spending more time at home. As a consultant, he'd have the flexibility to set his own schedule. He did manage, for a short while, to keep things under control. But lately, clients' last-minute deadlines often cut into their plans. He realized the two of them hadn't found quality time just to be with each other for months. Or was it a year? He couldn't remember how long it had been. His fault they had stopped? Probably, like everything else.

He sat, wide-eyed and wondering, beneath the night sky. The stars glimmered and the white crescent moon gave just enough light to illuminate all but the deepest of shadows. His gaze fell back on the house. He sighed. Just as he thought, the upstairs light had been turned off. Mixed feelings accompanied the realization.

Remembering some high points in their relationship had him wanting to spend some time with his wife. If only she hadn't finagled her own way about the counseling bit.

Did they really need outside help to solve their problems? A coward's way out, in his estimation. He'd stumbled onto a couple of answers himself, sitting out there alone in the moonlight. Or, maybe he just wanted answers so badly, he would grasp at straws. But quality time together had taken a major nosedive. No doubt about it. So many unexpected responsibilities with their son's condition. And the strain, the fear of the future. It never let up.

All of a sudden, he sensed a brand-new awareness enveloping him. When he was away on business, the constant reminder of impending doom disappeared. He could almost forget. But at home, no escape! He'd see Stephanie and think of Stephen. He'd overhear her crying or watch her sadly staring out the window and a red-hot poker of pain would sear his heart. His son—his only son—would never grow up to be a man. Not once had he talked to Steph about any of those desperate feelings. She was suffering enough already. He would keep his emotions in and her out.

Michael leaned forward. He pulled his legs up, wrapped his arms around his shins and dropped his head onto his knees. The weather wasn't cool enough to cause a shiver, yet a shudder ran through him just the same. He lifted his head to gaze at the millions of stars. Compared to the expanse of the universe, he felt as insignificant as a gnat. He rocked back and forth, keeping his arms locked around his knees. Tough guy, huh? *Right.*

His thoughts grew more mocking. *Real men can handle anything, and you're not one of them . . .*

He blinked, but too late to block the tears already streaming down his face. He lay down in the damp grass and sobbed.

❧ *Eight* ❧

ichael and Stephanie stood outside of a taupe-colored door in a small, professional office complex. Tasteful old Southern-style architecture gave the setting a classic, yet cozy, atmosphere. Well-manicured grass, flowers and pineapple palms completed a restful picture. "I like this place," she commented, looking around.

Michael shrugged. "It's all right." He read the nameplate: Center for Marriage and Family Counseling, Eric Marcos, Ph.D. "Guess we're here," he mumbled. He put his right hand on the curved brass handle and turned it. A musical door chime sounded as he stepped inside and held the door for her to follow.

Even before the door closed, a tall, slender man with a receding hairline entered the reception area. He was wearing navy pleated slacks and a crisp, navy and white pin-striped shirt with the sleeves rolled up. A gold tie chain highlighted a bright graphic print tie. The combination softened his otherwise conservative appearance.

He approached them, smiled, and extended his right hand to Michael. With his left, he squeezed his guest's left arm just below the shoulder and looked him straight in the eyes. "Eric Marcos. Welcome. It's great to meet you." Giving Michael's hand one more pump, he turned to Stephanie, who had made the appointment. "Hi, come on in," he urged. "There's coffee or soft drinks if you'd care for any." They both declined. He poured himself a cup of coffee, half turned to Michael, and with a brief motion of his right arm, pointed the way.

Dr. Marcos's office brought a hint of a grin to Michael's face. Maybe he'd watched too much television or read too many books, but he had been expecting something more . . . *clinical.* Or was it theatrical? He almost felt silly. No Sherlock Holmes pipe, monocle, or "shrink's couch." Certainly no sterile examining room with padded walls.

Instead, he studied the homelike atmosphere of a well-furnished den. Burgundy, navy and green plaid accents, a couple of brass lamps and several attractive paintings. Without a doubt, all a calculated effort to make him relax and open up. Well, no matter what, he refused to spill his guts to this guy. As he scanned the diplomas and awards arranged in neat groupings, a framed quotation caught his eye:

> Recovery is not here just to make you feel better or live a happier life. It's here to destroy your idols and make you God's child.   —Tanya Dean

Interesting concept, that one. Idols, to him, had always evoked images of gaudy pagan relics in faraway lands. So what harm in wanting a happy life, anyway? It'd be nice if there were some payoff for the pain. He read the quote again. Of course, it did say, "Recovery is not *just* here to make you feel better." More palatable that way, he had to admit.

He chose to shift his focus on the couch, which felt quite comfortable, actually, as he sank down into the cushions alongside Stephanie. He sneaked a quick glance at her. He couldn't detect anything in particular. She was wearing her poker face, the one *he* usually wore. He shook his head and breathed a tentative sigh of relief—tentative, because "the session" still loomed ahead.

Dr. Marcos, appearing quite at ease with the situation, sat in a leather swivel chair in front of them. He broke the silence with the question: "Have you heard from your daughter?"

"No," Stephanie blurted out, "not another word."

Michael only shook his head. Then, to her, "Go ahead. You're dying to tell him."

She shot him a quick glare, but said nothing. After their non-verbal exchange, Dr. Marcos made a note on a paper on his clipboard. "Well, we haven't heard from her since she called that first night to say she was running away. Michael was the only one to talk to her and she hung up on him." Her voice trembled. "The police don't have a clue. None of her friends, either."

He looked first at Stephanie, then Michael. "I'm really sorry to hear that. So, how are you doing?"

"How do you *think* we're doing?" Michael retorted. He thought the question was stupid and didn't mind if the doctor knew it.

Stephanie's face reddened at his outburst. She spoke softly, "I feel scared to death. Lost. Alone, like an orphan wandering down a deserted street. No one knows how terrified I am. Or cares, for that matter." She hesitated an instant.

"Go on . . ."

"I feel so incredibly *helpless.*" She lowered her eyes and stared at her hands while she pondered her next words. "Like I'm stuck in the middle of this huge, rusty trap. Only it hasn't snapped shut yet.

I'm fighting to hold back these enormous, spring-loaded jaws, but my strength's about gone. Any second, it'll be all over." She raised her gaze to meet the doctor's own. Her lips were quivering.

Michael blushed at her utter transparency. In front of a total stranger! He was tempted to comment about the dramatics of the female sex. He held back.

"How about you, Michael?" Dr. Marcos asked.

He hadn't expected that so soon.

"Your wife's done a good job describing her feelings. Want to give it a go?"

No doubt about it, his turn on the hot seat. Not sure how he got there, but certain he disliked the spot, Michael charged ahead. "I really don't care to be here. It was my wife's idea. Nothing against you, doctor . . ."

"I know." He jotted a note on the paper in front of him. "Most men react to counseling the same way, at first. We hate feeling out of control or in need." He nodded at Stephanie. "It's one of those macho things we males are born with, if you know what I mean." She managed a weak smile. Michael tried to resist and reluctantly followed suit. Dr. Marcos continued, focusing on him, "But everybody could use some candid feedback now and then. You don't have to tell me anything unless you're ready." His eyes and calm manner invited trust.

"So go ahead and get comfortable," he said. "Since this is our first session, I might talk a bit more than usual. That way, you won't feel pressured to open up before you're ready. If I share something of value you think you can benefit from, great. If not, that's okay, too. Right now I'd like to lay a foundation for any future work we might do together."

Michael marveled at the man's confidence. Whether they'd be back or not remained to be seen. So far, he wasn't too impressed.

"I'll make every effort not to mislead you in any way. Honesty is essential between us. Confidentiality, a must. However, I am required by law to report specific cases of abuse. Aside from that, you have my word—I will not discuss what you tell me in here with anyone. It's best if you do the same, unless we all agree to the contrary. How does that set with you?"

"Sounds okay," Michael answered. Dr. Marcos remained silent, looking at Stephanie.

"Yes, I'd prefer that," she responded once she realized he was waiting for her answer.

"Now, I want to encourage you. You *can* make it through these crises. With God's help, you will come out stronger in the end. I've seen it happen many times over the years."

Stephanie breathed a sigh and nodded. Dr. Marcos continued, but with a more cautious tone, "However, you're facing high odds against you."

Michael squinted at him and crossed his arms.

"So many couples wind up either divorced or miserably married within a short time after tragedy strikes. From what I understand, you two have encountered a couple of setbacks in the last few years." He waited to gauge their reactions. Stephanie remained expressionless, though some color drained from her face.

Michael, his shoulders slouching, gave him a mild scowl. "Sounds like you're implying that our marriage is doomed."

"Quite the contrary! God breaks the odds. With Him, all things are possible, as He says in His Word. We'll discuss ways to enhance your ability to weather life's storms—*and* stay in love. I just want you to know one thing: you will both have to apply disciplined effort to your relationship to overcome the obstacles. And here's why. First, marriage partners tend to neglect quality time together during a painful crisis. Eventually, they end up as strangers. Furthermore, they attack each other instead of the problem. They forget they belong on the same team. They both have strong feelings—helplessness, anger, fear, sorrow—at the unforeseen twists of life. But they fail to admit this to each other. Instead, they criticize and blame and alienate."

Stephanie squirmed. Michael cleared his throat. Almost in spite of himself, he exclaimed, "If you want to know the *truth,* I'm mad at the world right now. And I'm especially furious with Michelle. She's putting her family through you-know-what." He waited for some reaction from Dr. Marcos, a raised eyebrow, at least. All he got was an encouraging nod. The rest about Stephen spewed out in a stream. "That's it. I'm just ticked off in general," he added. After a few seconds, "Don't I have a *right* to be?" He inwardly chastised himself for opening up, when he had no intention of doing so. The counselor's "trap" had worked.

Dr. Marcos set his pen down and folded his hands. "I would agree that anger is a *natural* emotion for someone who's going through the uncertainty you are—"

"But?"

"Well, some therapists believe anger is—"

"And what about you? Hope you don't agree with them."

"I'm not dogmatic on the issue. While anger is expected, and even acceptable on occasion, venting it at will is rarely the best approach."

Michael leaned forward, ready for a standoff. "How about when Jesus threw over tables in the temple? Even *He* got mad."

"Yes, He did. Why, though?" Dr. Marcos unfolded his hands and wrote on his paper while he was waiting.

Michael stared at the books in the bookcase, then at the porcelain eagle statue on the coffee table. "I guess He didn't like what they were doing. Other than that, I don't know."

Dr. Marcos looked up. "Could it be because the money lenders were showing disrespect to His Father's house? What should have been a place of prayer had become a den of thieves. In Jesus' case, a righteous man had a *righteous* motive."

"We don't?"

"Seldom, from my experience. Victims of abuse may be one exception. Those who have experienced it begin to heal when they can release—in the safety of another's presence—buried feelings about their past. No question about it. They're very angry on the inside, and understandably so. Abuse has been called 'murder to the soul.' However, they do have to progress beyond that point if they ever hope to recover.

"More often than not, I've found, we human beings have self-ish motives for being angry. We get mad, for example . . . when we're inconvenienced, when our plans don't work out, when our egos get hurt . . . when our desires aren't met, when our reputations are threatened . . . and especially when someone has wronged us. Those last two are biggies."

"So what do you suggest?" Stephanie asked.

"In the book, *Incompatibility: Grounds for a Great Marriage,* Chuck and Barb Snyder end a chapter on anger with a quote from a book they enjoyed called, *Is It Worth Dying For?* The sage advice goes like this: *1) Don't sweat the small stuff. 2) It's all small stuff.*"

Michael couldn't help commenting, "Clever and profound, but how about something practical?"

"Own up to the anger, first of all," Dr. Marcos obliged him, "instead of just 'letting 'er rip,' as they say. Admit when your motives are sinful. Ask forgiveness and learn to diffuse negative emotions in a harmless way. Ephesians four, twenty-six gives sound advice: *Be angry and yet do not sin; do not let the sun go down on your anger.* In other words, don't lash out at others when you're upset. And conversely, don't harbor hostility in your heart, letting it fester until it becomes a cancer of bitterness." He paused.

Michael let out a loud sigh. Stephanie picked lint off her skirt. Dr. Marcos played with his pen, rotating it between his fingers. "For instance," he ventured, "it would be easy for one parent of a runaway to resent the other parent she happened to hang up on."

A slight smirk passed across Michael's lips as he remembered Stephanie's tirade against him that night. He stole a glance at her to make sure she was listening. She was staring at the diplomas and certificates displayed on the wall. Just like her. She never wanted to hear when *she* was wrong.

"On the other hand," Dr. Marcos added, "it would be equally tempting for the one who got hung up on to project blame, in order to avoid guilt. Kind of a vicious cycle, this anger business."

Michael straightened his shirt collar and studied the magazine titles on the end table. He could feel Stephanie's eyes burning a hole through him.

Dr. Marcos wrote more notes on his paper. "I'd like to ask you both a question, but you don't have to respond right now. Just think about it." To Stephanie, "Had your husband verbalized the extent of his anger about the situations you face?" He switched his gaze to Michael, "Did you have any idea how lost and alone your wife was feeling?"

They stared straight ahead. Neither dared look at the other. Michael hitched himself into a straighter position and crossed his legs. Stephanie shifted her weight from one side to the other and put her left elbow on the arm of the sofa. Dr. Marcos broke the tension by clearing his throat, then leaned back in his chair.

"To illustrate my point, here's a little anecdote. Back a century or so ago, the bloody War of 1812 was declared officially over. Commanding generals of both sides had signed a peace treaty.

However, the message failed to reach all the troops for some time. They continued to fight in hand-to-hand combat and many more lives werc lost. Why? *Poor communication.* The same takes place in homes, needlessly. That's why I asked whether or not you two had kept each other informed. Unless I missed my hunch, you haven't been the world's best in this department."

"Sure we have," Michael insisted. "We talk all the time." He glanced at her and back at Dr. Marcos. "I don't see why we should pay a near fortune to re-learn how to talk." He risked a peek at his watch.

Dr. Marcos ignored the cutting reference to his clinical fee, which fell in the midrange for counselors in the area. "I hear your frustration, Michael," he said. "Real communication, though, involves far more than talking. Remember the war illustration? The message was sent, but not received. In marriage, you need *active* listening, often between the lines, with the intent of understanding. That doesn't come naturally to us self-centered humans.

"Communication, then, in addition to being a two-way street of give-and-take, should be *frequent* and *thorough.* You see, most marriages have certain 'locked rooms in the cellar,' so to speak, piled high with unpleasant issues avoided for years. As spouses try to dig through the stored-up junk to find out where they got off-track, they strike out to avenge their own hurts. It happens on both sides. And either party may try to take unfair advantage when the other is down, I'm sorry to say. Rather like a pack of wolves, snarling threats over its prey. But our goal is *productive* communication. A marriage counselor acts as a kind of referee or overseer, so husbands and wives can begin to express pent-up stuff without causing undue injury. Truthfulness precedes renewed closeness."

He picked up the cup of coffee he had set on the end table and took a swallow. "Neither of you really knew the depth of the other's thoughts and feelings of late, I gathered. There's hope. Communication skills can be learned. And you have something going for you that far too many couples don't." He stopped short.

Michael waited. Finally, he asked, "Which is?"

"You're both believers. You can depend on more than thoughts and feelings, as important as they are. You have on your side a Power quite capable of helping you handle everything that comes down the pike. That is, if you can only learn to trust Him and do it His way." As he spoke, both parties on the sofa relaxed. "How long have you been a Christian, Michael?" he asked.

"Let's see . . . I met dear old Caleb in 1986. That makes it over three years."

"And you, Stephanie?"

"About the same. When he and I got back together after a short separation, he showed me how to give my heart to Jesus." Thinking about that time brought a smile to her face, the first real one in days. "The world came to life. I remember feeling so content, so peaceful. It was just before we found out about Stephen." Her smile slipped, along with the volume of her voice. "Even that blow was softened, somehow. It still hurt. But I guess I assumed he would be healed miraculously . . . or the Lord would return first. So far, neither has happened. His T-cell count drops a little all the time." She wiped a tear from the corner of her eyes, then accepted, with a soft "thank you," the tissue Dr. Marcos offered.

"It's been tough, huh?"

Her head moved slowly up and down.

"Anything you'd like me to do?"

"Not right now, thanks. Except maybe avoid the subject."

"I'll respect that." He leaned to one side and took a deep breath. "Michael, you mentioned Caleb. As in Johannsen?"

A brief nod.

"He was a great man. I remember many people felt a loss when he died suddenly. How long did you know him?"

"A few months, I guess. Not nearly long enough." The muscles in his abdomen tensed up.

"So you grew to appreciate him then?"

"We got real close."

Dr. Marcos said nothing, just waited, with his pen ready.

"He was the father-figure I always wanted." Talking about Caleb reminded Michael of how much he missed his old mentor. What would he have to say about everything that was going on?

"How did you two meet?" Dr. Marcos asked.

"Just a fluke. I took a trip for some 'R & R' and wound up at his place way out in the middle of nowhere. He was the one who threw me the lifeline when everything was going haywire."

"Oh?"

"Yeah, if it weren't for him, I would never have become a Christian. Steph and I probably wouldn't have made it this far." Michael paused a moment as the memories flooded his thoughts. "I owe the guy a lot."

Stephanie piped in, "But it was the Holy Spirit who really drew you to Jesus. Caleb was just a willing vessel . . ."

"Well, yeah, that's what I meant." He frowned at her and rubbed his nose.

Dr. Marcos wrote on his paper. "I can understand your affection for him. He was a great guy. And I assure you he gave his heart and soul with no strings attached. If he were here, he'd tell you himself."

"You're right. Like I said, I owe him." His voice trailed off into silence. His thoughts churned.

"What about you, Stephanie? Ever meet him?"

"No. I used to feel as if I had, as much as Michael talked about him. When we first got back together, it was 'Caleb this' and 'Caleb that.'" A half-smile escaped her lips. "Silly, but I was a little jealous. Eventually, I wished *I'd* had a chance to get to know him."

"Yes," Dr. Marcos agreed, "he was the most selfless person I've ever had the privilege of meeting. And possessed of a tremendous faith. What he preached, he practiced. I remember hearing him say one day, 'If it isn't worth doing myself, I'm not going to confuse someone else by moralizing about it!'"

Against his will, Michael felt himself warming to this Dr. Eric Marcos. His admiration of Caleb had touched a soft spot. Maybe they had some common ground after all.

"Of anybody I've known," Dr. Marcos continued, "Caleb sure had the right outlook on life." Here, he turned to Michael. "Say, you're a professional guy. Have you ever read a book called, *The Seven Habits of Highly Successful People,* by Stephen Covey?"

Michael nodded. "A number of years ago."

"I don't agree with everything in the book, certainly, but he makes some valid points. Remember the phrase, 'paradigm shift'?"

"Sure."

"What does a business term have to do with our marriage?" Stephanie wanted to know.

"Good question. A paradigm shift is simply a change in a model or pattern. In other words, a brand-new way of thinking or looking at an existing situation—to make it better. The principle has helped countless failing organizations get back on their feet. Most marriages could use a similar approach."

Michael squirmed in his seat. With a smirk, he replied, "So, you're suggesting we not only have to relearn how to *talk*, we have learn how to *think*. Sounds like we're going back to school."

Dr. Marcos chuckled. "In a manner of speaking, yes. But we all struggle to talk and think anew with the mind of Christ. Before

119

Him, we had no choice; we had only our human perspective to depend on. Now, we're citizens of heaven. We have God's eternal perspective available to us. As such, we recognize that unseen elements play a key role in every situation, especially in marri—."

"Caleb really emphasized living by *'the unseen essential,'*" Michael interrupted. "I guess I do know that much."

"Good." Dr. Marcos's tone lowered and slowed down. "Does this knowledge affect your daily life?" He raised his hand. "You don't have to tell me. Just think it over." They both remained quiet for a minute. Stephanie bit a hangnail on her ring finger.

He waited for several more seconds. "You see, you have a choice facing you right now in the midst of the chaos over which you have no control."

"It sure doesn't seem like we have any choices left," Stephanie said, her tone discouraged.

"You do, though. You still have at least one."

"Which is?" Michael's curiosity got him this time.

"Surrender to the Lord completely."

Michael pondered his statement. "I thought we did that when we accepted Him."

"Well, the process begins at conversion. To the degree that we surrender from then on, we *continue* to change, to mature and grow stronger, no matter what life hands us."

"I'm so tired of maturing and growing stronger, if you want to know the truth." Stephanie sighed. "I've had all the challenges—rather, catastrophes—I can handle, thank you."

"I understand," Dr. Marcos replied. "My wife and I have gone through those awful periods."

"You have?"

"Yes. Our first two children were stillborn. We were afraid to try again. A few months after the second child died, our house burned to the ground. We escaped with nothing more than the clothes on our backs."

Stephanie's eyes widened. "Oh, my goodness! I'm sorry."

Michael piped right in with, "Man, I had no idea." He leaned toward Dr. Marcos, resting his forearms on his knees. Maybe the guy did have something to offer.

"Do you have children now?" she asked timidly.

"Oh yes. We adopted a little brother and sister from Brazil. They were just two out of thousands of street urchins over there."

She gave him an approving nod. "That's really nice of you. Not many people would take that risk."

"Why, they've been far more of a blessing to us than we have to them! We love 'em to pieces. Mindy and I finally came to the realization that gut-wrenching crises look a whole lot different to God than they do to us. Our Father in heaven cares for us very much; He simply sees everything from a higher, all-encompassing vantage point."

Michael stroked his chin. "Sort of like planet earth to the astronauts."

"*Exactly!* Seeing everything through His eyes makes a tremendous difference in our ability to cope."

"Caleb used to tell me that, too."

"I bet he did. Romans eight, twenty-eight is my favorite verse in the entire Bible, one that I've clung to for dear life. It goes, *And we know that God causes all things to work together for good to those who love God, to those who are called according to His purpose.*" He paused a moment.

"What good has come out of your misery?" Michael asked. "Besides some orphans finding a home, I mean."

"For one, our faith is much stronger. Mindy and I can comfort others with the same comfort we have received. They know we're

genuine. And we've certainly grown less selfish, more appreciative of each other, the Lord . . . and of life."

Michael and Stephanie sat, silent, looking at the floor. Michael ran his fingers through his hair. He reminded himself that it needed to be cut and styled at the first opportunity.

"You both still with me?" Dr. Marcos asked.

They nodded.

"Good. I didn't intend to bring up my trials. That's not why you came, by any means."

"But it helps to see we're not alone." Stephanie crossed her legs.

He smiled. "Good, because you do have plenty of company. Over the next few sessions, if you come back, we'll explore ways to forge ahead in your marriage, no matter what the circumstances. In fact, I've got some homework for you before we meet again."

"What?" Michael countered. "It'll be hard enough to find time to get here once a week." He stretched his arms over his head.

Dr. Marcos countered with, "I want to be sure you get your money's worth." That grabbed Michael's attention. "Unapplied knowledge does little but clutter up the brain. Remember Caleb's example of practicing what he preached."

"What do you have in mind?" Stephanie asked.

"Easy. I'd like you to begin reading the Scriptures together, for at least fifteen minutes, every day. Can you do that?" He looked first at Michael, then at Stephanie. "Or, rather, will you?" Michael's tentative agreement echoed his wife's heartier one.

"Great. That commitment will plant your feet on firm, common ground. Once you've managed to fit in a regular fifteen minutes, try to progress to a half hour. But I'd rather have you read a little every day than a whole heap once a year."

Stephanie ventured another question. "Could you suggest what to read first?"

"There's no 'right answer,' certainly. Many of the Psalms emanated from the heart of King David when he was hurting. You can gain a great deal from his experiences. My wife and I have been reading five Psalms a day—the whole book every month—since shortly after we became Christians. Whatever the current date, we read that numbered psalm, plus thirty, sixty, ninety, etc, until we have read five. For example, on the first day of the month, we read Psalm one, thirty-one, sixty-one, ninety-one, and one hundred twenty-one. I can't begin to tell you how often they've strengthened and encouraged us. You could start there."

Michael nodded. Uncanny. Caleb had advised him to read the Psalms that way. Dr. Marcos saw his silent assent.

"Reading is only the first part. When you're finished, discuss the meaning you each gleaned from the passages. Try hard to avoid an argument over nuances in interpretation. Just discuss what you believe God is saying to you. Third, help each other find ways of applying the truth to your lives. Definitely avoid finger-pointing. Instead of focusing on where the *other* person is falling short, meditate on where you could improve. Then, do your best to pray together for at least fifteen minutes."

"Where to find the time . . ." Michael murmured.

"It's a big challenge, I know. But how about early morning? Before the demands of earning a living and raising a family set in. That's when Jesus spent time with His Father." Once again, Dr. Marcos paused to gauge the couple's reaction. Stephanie's expression reflected a cautious hope. Michael remained straight-faced, but attentive.

"All right. That's part one of your assignment. Part two comes at night, unless one of you must work odd hours, of course. Read a few more verses of the Bible together. Say, James, chapter three for instance."

Frowning, Michael cocked his head. "Hardly hear much about James. Why that one?"

"Here, let's read it aloud right now. I think you'll see. By the way, James was Jesus' brother. He didn't believe Jesus was anyone special until He rose from the dead." Dr. Marcos grabbed a burgundy leather Bible from the end table, opened it, and handed it to Michael. "New American Standard version. Sir, would you do the honors?"

Michael licked his lips. He cleared his throat, sighed, and shifted on the sofa. *"Let not many of you become teachers, my brethren, knowing that as such we shall incur a stricter judgment . . ."* The Bible fell back onto his lap. "Are you sure this is right?"

"Trust me. Go a little further."

Michael brought the Bible back up to arm's length where he could see it without his reading glasses and continued in a subdued tone,

For we all stumble in many ways. If anyone does not stumble in what he says, he is a perfect man, able to bridle the whole body as well. Now if we put the bits into the horses' mouths so that they may obey us, we direct their entire body as well. Behold, the ships also, though they are so great and are driven by strong winds, are still directed by a very small rudder, wherever the inclination of the pilot desires. So also the tongue is a small part of the body, and yet it boasts of great things. Behold, how great a forest is set aflame by such a small fire! And the tongue is a fire, the very world of iniquity; the tongue is set among our members as that which defiles the entire body, and sets on fire the course of our life, and is set on fire by hell. For every species of beasts and birds, of reptiles and creatures of the sea, is tamed, and has been tamed by the human race. But no one came tame the tongue; it is a restless evil and full of deadly poison.

Brows raised, Michael took a deep breath. He handed the Bible to Stephanie. "Here, you finish from verse nine. My throat's drying up."

Without meeting his eyes, she laid it across her lap. "How far do I read, Dr. Marcos?"

"If you can, to the end of the chapter three," he replied.

With it we bless our Lord and Father; and with it we curse men, who have been made in the likeness of God; from the same mouth come both blessing and cursing. My brethren, these things ought not to be this way. Does a fountain send out from the same opening both fresh and bitter water? Can a fig tree, my brethren, produce olives, or a vine produce figs? Neither can salt water produce fresh. Who among you is wise and understanding? Let him show by his good behavior his deeds in the gentleness of wisdom. But if you have bitter jealousy and selfish ambition in your heart, do not be arrogant and so lie against the truth. This wisdom is not that which comes down from above, but is earthly, natural, demonic. For where jealousy and selfish ambition exist, there is disorder and every evil thing. But the wisdom from above is first pure, then peaceable, gentle, reasonable, full of mercy and good fruits, unwavering, without hypocrisy. And the seed whose fruit is righteousness is sown in peace by those who make peace.

Dr. Marcos took the Bible back from Stephanie, saying, "Those words, if applied, would change the course of thousands of marriages. Can you see why I chose James?"

125

Michael nodded, his brow furrowed, then scratched behind his ear. "I don't remember reading that passage before."

"Me, either." She bit her lower lip.

"Powerful, huh?" He patted the Bible. "The Word can accomplish more in five minutes than I can in five hours. So, after you're done reading it at night, exercise those communication muscles again. Discuss the passage, if you'd like, and then spend some time learning about each other. Share dreams for the future the way you did when you first met. Find out how each other's day went. Now, do more than just relate the facts, please. Express genuine feelings about what happened.

"Stephanie, you women find this much easier than we men do, so be patient. If an event brought joy or sorrow, express it to your husband. On the other hand, Michael, if discouragement or anger caught you by surprise, make an effort to tell Stephanie how you felt and why. And to both of you, instead of just talking, focus on listening. Finally, when you're done, take time to gaze into each other's eyes for a minimum of sixty seconds. Don't say anything. Just hold hands and gaze into your partner's eyes."

Dr. Marcos looked again for signs of uneasiness. He noticed some fidgeting on both parts, but nothing overly suspicious. He chuckled. "Don't be surprised if the last thirty seconds are the hardest. Hang in there, though. They may prove to be the best. Our goal is to prevent the current crises from driving a wedge between you and turn them into a bridge before you." He paused. "Any questions?"

Stephanie shook her head. Michael glanced at his watch, stood up, and tucked his shirt in his pants.

"Before you leave, here are my phone numbers—office and pager." He handed a couple of business cards to Michael, then two to Stephanie. "Call me anytime. I promise to return the call as soon as I can. I want to see you guys come through this, stronger than ever before."

Michael sensed the doctor's sincerity. He believed him, despite his pre-session vows to half-cooperate. From the look of rapt interest on Stephanie's face, he could see she believed, too.

They closed in prayer and as he escorted them to the door, Dr. Marcos added, "In case you're interested, I'm starting a support group called, 'MarriageMaker.' Of course, the same confidentiality standards will apply. Several couples have signed up already, plus one single guy who wants to be married in the near future. I believe we all have insight to help others. Talk about it. Pray about it. You can call me if you decide to give it a try and I'll hold a spot for you. I'm keeping the first one small."

"When will you meet?" Stephanie asked.

"From seven to nine on three Thursday evenings, starting this week. If it turns out to be something people enjoy, we'll expand the number of sessions later."

They nodded and said nothing. Michael's stomach churned at the thought of airing their dirty laundry in front of a roomful of strangers. *No way,* he decided. *Not even up for discussion.*

After writing out a check and offering a polite thanks, he urged Stephanie out the door to the car.

"What do you think?" she asked on the way.

"About?"

"Michael . . . about Dr. Marcos. Did you like him?"

It irked him to admit he'd been wrong. "Yeah, he was okay."

"Just okay. That's all?"

"No, he was pretty good."

"Well, what did you like about him? Did you feel at ease? Think he gave any advice we can use?"

An exasperated sigh crept out. He hated it when she pumped

him for information. "I guess he had some good points. At least he didn't seem to manipulate us into his opinions."

She nodded. "No. I liked his relaxed style. Not like he was force-feeding or pulling teeth. When I asked him to avoid a subject, he did. And he's sure come through a lot himself, huh?"

"Yeah, he has. That alone gives him credibility." He stopped to look at her. "Steph, are you trying to get at something in particular, by any chance?"

She reached for his hand. "Oh . . . maybe. Why do you ask?"

"I'd rather you just speak your mind instead of beating around the bush. The class, I suppose. You want me to agree to go."

"Sort of. It might be nice with other couples in the same boat."

He glanced at her and shook his head with the hint of a wink. *"You* are a little weasel. I'll consider it. Okay?"

"Okay." Her eyes met his. "Good enough for now, I guess."

"Thanks," he replied, giving her hand a little squeeze.

❧ *Nine* ❧

A t a rest stop in rural North Carolina, Michelle climbed back into the bus and tugged at her miniskirt to keep it from riding up. Matt stayed on the first step until she was standing on the platform by the driver's seat. She glanced back and noticed the direction of his gaze. A half-indignant hand went on her hip. "What are you staring at?"

He smiled and shrugged his shoulders. "Just enjoying the view. Those pretty legs have this old bus beat by a mile."

"Yeah, well, take a picture—it'll last longer."

"You know, I might do that when we get to New York. Got a great camera here." He patted the leather bag and hopped up the stairs in one leap. Single file, they inched their way down the narrow aisle. He pointed straight to the back of the bus. "Hey, there's a good seat."

Michelle sensed a split-second caution, but dismissed it as silly. It would be so fun with Matt. Her friend Cindy and she had shared some wild stories about bus trips, though. She remembered one time in late fall when she had spent the night at Cindy's house. As they were sitting cross-legged on the bed, Cindy had

129

whispered, "You wouldn't *believe* what kids were doin' on the way home from the game . . ." and proceeded to relate the details as another girl had told them to her.

Michelle remembered stifling a gasp. She hadn't seen a thing. "You're kidding!" was all she could muster. They talked and giggled far into the night.

Now, she tossed her head to scatter the memories with her best friend. Those days were over. She knew she'd given her the brush-off the afternoon she left—didn't tell her where she was going or why, and she was probably miffed. They had shared many secrets. But this one secret she couldn't tell *anybody.* She wanted her running-away-plan to go off without a hitch. Well, she had already told *one* person. Matt. He seemed like a nice guy. And since he was in the same predicament, he sure wouldn't turn her in. Besides, he liked her company. Why would he want to give that up?

She had been so lost in her thoughts, she bumped into the seat that stretched across the rear of the bus and started to tumble forward into it. Matt grabbed her around the waist to pull her back. She let out a surprised squeak and turned around, only to find herself staring directly into the most awesome pair of brown eyes she had ever seen. A rush of warmth spread throughout her, flushing her face with a pink glow. She felt like jelly all over. "Better watch where you're going, kiddo," he quipped, breaking the spell. "Don't wanna bruise those pretty legs."

Michelle grimaced at him. She whirled around, backed into the seat, and plopped down with all her ninety-eight pounds. She sighed, realizing how completely exhausted she felt.

Matt squeezed in beside her and grinned again. "We're back on our way to 'the Big Apple.'" He turned to her and stuck out his hand in the latest fad handshake, and she responded with gusto. Wow, she couldn't wait. This was going to be exciting.

"You'll love the city. I know this is kinda sudden, but . . . we friends?" he asked, arching his eyebrows over those incredible eyes. His voice was sincere, pleading.

He was *so* cute! She cocked her head to the side and said with a confident air, "I'll think about it. Let you know later."

"Okay, Miss Priss, but I need a better answer than that!" He pinched her playfully in the ribs.

"All right, you got a deal. Friends." She laughed with what little energy she had left, loosened up and leaned back. Matt was nice. She didn't resist when he put his arm around her. For the first time in months, she felt wanted. No, more than that—important.

Looking around at her surroundings, she caught a glimpse of a flyer on the floor just ahead. The few words she could make out, *"Just in case . . ."* piqued her curiosity. Matt drew her attention away when he squeezed her shoulder and whispered in her ear, "Hey, you sure look cute in that outfit of yours." He nuzzled her neck with his nose and took a deep breath. "Mmm, smell good, too." She couldn't remember putting on perfume, but guessed she must have. She shivered and squirmed out of his grasp. He didn't force her back, just patted her arm. That put her more at ease. Soon, she fell asleep with her head on his shoulder. He leaned his cheek on her head and nodded off.

About ten minutes later, she awoke with a start to a strong lurch forward and the sound of squealing tires. The bus driver had braked hard. For what, she couldn't tell. She hoped he hadn't hit an animal. Not much made her cry, but that got to her every time. Matt didn't budge. He was leaning back against the seat, sound asleep, with his mouth slightly open.

She sighed and looked around at rows and rows of heads. The backs of heads, to be exact. A couple of hats. A baseball cap. Long, greasy hair. A bald head or two. One shaved with a punk mohawk

strip of hair down the middle. Nothing appealing. She glanced down. The flyer with its *"Just in Case"* title drew her attention again. She squinted and made out a sketch of a teenage girl on the front. What could it be?

She leaned forward on the seat to get a better look. The white paper had a dirty shoeprint running across it. Disgusting. But she couldn't resist picking it up. Using the tips of two fingers made it seem less icky. She read the subtitle aloud, slowly, *"Parental Guidelines in Case Your Child Might Someday Be a Runaway."* Her eyes widened. Heartbeat and breath quickened at the coincidence. She read the inside flap.

> The National Center for Missing and Exploited Children (NCMEC) serves as a clearinghouse of information on missing and exploited children; provides technical assistance to citizens and law-enforcement agencies; offers training programs to law-enforcement; distributes photographs and descriptions of missing children nationwide; coordinates child protection efforts with the private sector; networks with nonprofit service providers and state clearinghouses; and provides information and advice on the effective state legislation to ensure the safety and protection of children. A 24-hour toll-free telephone line is open for those who have information on missing and exploited children: 1-800-843-5678 . . .

With each line, Michelle felt worse. Trapped like a rat! She swallowed hard and chewed on the inside of her lip. How could she disappear if that group got on her tail? Maybe Matt would know. He must have some experience in such matters. She poked him in the side with her elbow. "Hey, wake up." He mumbled something and shifted his position. "Matt, please wake up. It's important!" She rustled the flyer in her hand. "Check this out."

He rubbed his eyes, blinked several times, and sat up straight. "What? What is it?"

"Look, a place with a free phone number, no less—where anybody can call. They do all kinds of stuff to help find kids who don't even want to be found. We don't stand a chance!"

"What's the name of the place?"

"Um . . . here it is: National Center For Missing and Exploited Children."

"Oh, yeah." He paused. "What's 'exploited' mean, anyway?"

"Somebody who's taken advantage of."

"That's us. Well, not to worry. Lotsa kids never get found. And besides, somebody has to notify them. In my case, if my parents ever bothered, it hasn't worked. I've been gone for a year now. So no problem, okay?"

"Maybe you're right." But she didn't feel any better. She held her stomach, then folded up the brochure and tucked it into the side pocket of her bag. "I could always cut my hair short and dye it blond, just to be safe."

"Nah. Looks good the way it is. You think your parents would really try to find you?"

"'Course."

"Not mine. Stepdad's too drunk to care, and my mom . . . she'd rather keep peace."

Michelle, her eyes narrowing, replied with sarcasm, "If anybody'd take up a wild pursuit, my dad would. He loves a challenge. He'd come after me just to prove I couldn't outsmart him. If he ever succeeded, he'd ground me for the rest of my life."

Matt smiled. "Come on, kid. You're getting paranoid."

"You don't know my dad. He's super-demanding. If I don't get

a perfect report card, I'm the failure of the century." She pretended to place a pair of reading glasses on the end of her nose, held the flyer way out at arm's length, and mimicked in a husky male voice, 'Why on earth did you get a B in math? You know you're capable of straight As without cracking a book!'"

Her dramatics elicited the sought-after grin in Matt. She continued, "I'm serious. This man gets major upset over the smallest stuff. Goes easy on my little brother, though, 'cause he's sick."

"Yeah, AIDS. You told me."

"Well, he doesn't seem sick yet. That's the hard part. And they don't actually call it AIDS until his immune system really breaks down. Then he'll start getting lots of infections like pneumonia and other bad stuff pretty fast."

"How'd he get it again?"

"He's a hemophiliac."

"Where the blood doesn't clot right?"

"Uh-huh. I guess there are thousands of kids who got it from transfusions."

"That's rough."

"Yeah, I was telling this truck-driving couple who dropped me off at the bus station about what it's like at home. And wouldn't you know it—they turned out to be religious nuts. 'Course, I was safe with them. Hank and Dot. Real down-home folks. They were pretty nice. But he kept up this Jesus bit non-stop and even made me listen to a tape."

"He made you?"

"Well, I didn't have much choice. It was either that or walk. He said prayer changed him and Dot big-time. Isn't that wild? Talking into thin air and believing it solves problems!"

Matt grew quiet. He tapped his fingers on his camera bag, then patted it. "Whatcha thinkin' about?" she asked him.

He stared out the window. "Oh . . . nothin', I guess. Nothin' worth talkin' about."

"Come on. You can't fool me."

He tucked his foot under him and stared at the floor. "Well . . . home." He paused and sighed. With a touch of sadness he said, "If there *is* a God, I wonder if He could've helped my family."

Michelle retorted, "Don't bet on it. Not for long, anyway."

"How do you know?"

"See, my parents were separated about three years ago. My dad got real close to some guy named Caleb, and supposedly 'got *saved*,' as he put it. Accepted Jesus into his heart, or something like that. Sounds stupid to me. Anyway, he got religion, but I think he's still upset because he didn't have enough time with Caleb."

"Why not?"

"The old man fell off a ladder while he was painting a friend's house. This kid named Sandy—that's whose house he was painting—ran down the road for help, but too late. Caleb was dead by the time he got back."

"Why didn't the airhead call 911?"

"They don't have a phone. He and his mom are real poor. His dad's dead and she's got MS."

"Man, you're full of good news. But what does that have to do with God helping my family?"

"Guess I got off-track. Sorry. You *were* asking me the questions, if you remember."

"Okay, so I was. Go on with what happened to the religion stuff, will you?"

"Well, when my parents first got back together, they started reading the Bible and doing this talking-into-thin-air-routine. My dad did seem kinda different in some ways. He didn't get mad as quick as before he left home. The bad part was, we had to go to

church on Sunday morning and Sunday night and again on Wednesday night. Good grief, I almost turned into the shape of a church pew! For a few weeks, we even had 'family devotions' at home. He would make us listen to him read the Bible and then he would tell us what it supposedly meant. Maybe if he'd asked my opinion once in awhile, it would have been okay. I had to endure that awful half hour almost every night, if you can believe it. I wanted to scream, 'Aren't we just the *cozy* ones?' Fortunately, he dropped the issue and got back to business as usual. What a relief!" She smirked and shook her head. "But now he's the same old grouch he always was—probably worse."

They clasped hands. Matt tilted his head, pausing for some deep thought. "Maybe devotions wouldn't be so bad. At least you'd be together as a half-sane family."

"Easy for you to say. You didn't have to go through it."

"True. My stepdad was never sober enough to be able to *see* a Bible, much less read it! In fact, I never laid eyes on one until a couple years ago. Some religious kids in my class who hung around together carried big fancy leather ones with gold writing on the front. Even had gold on the edges of the pages, from what I could see. They went to secret meetings after school. One morning—get this—during some national deal goin' on, a whole bunch of 'em stood around the flagpole holding hands and praying."

"Not out loud, I hope. That's *weird!*"

"I thought so, too. Said they were praying that America would stop sinning and turn back to God."

Michelle shook her head vehemently. "Yeah, I bet the kids talking the loudest were sinning *big-time,* just like the rest of the world. Some of 'em in the church youth group I went to slept around. I know that for a fact. And they'd pretend to be such 'goody-two-shoes' in front of all the pastors. *Hypocrites!*"

"At least the Bible-toters I saw didn't call me names or any-thing—'white trash' and stuff—like a lot of kids, but they still acted snooty, dressed up so perfect in their designer clothes. 'Course, everybody at school knew my dad was a drunk, and that we were poor. It was obvious they didn't want me or my friends in their tight little clique. Wouldn't give us the time of day. They just talked and laughed with each other."

"So who needs the likes of them?"

"Not me."

"Me, either."

Matt cocked his head. "To tell you the truth, I found better friends on the street. They'd give you their last meal if you needed it more than they did."

"Really?"

"Yep."

"So tell me everything I need to know."

"About what?"

"Life on the run."

Matt stroked his chin. "First, you gotta have a fake ID. That way, you can't be traced."

"Where do I get one?"

"I'll take you to a place I know in the city."

"You *will?*"

"Sure. No problem. It's a little hole-in-the-wall joint, so don't be expecting anything fancy. But they get the job done. In a few minutes, you'll have a perfect card with your color picture and a whole new name."

Michelle twirled her hair around her index finger for a moment. "I wonder which name I should use . . ."

"You can be anyone you wanna be. What's your favorite ?"

Sighing, she thought for a long moment. "Ashley Nicole."

"Wow. What an imagination! And I thought I liked Michelle."

"No way. Too blah. Ashley Nicole is much better."

"So how about a last name? That's the most important one to change from your real one."

Another long pause. "Witherton. *Ashley Nicole Witherton,"* she half-whispered. Doesn't that remind you of the heroine of a nineteenth-century novel?"

"If you say so. It's been a while since I read one of those."

"'Fess up. You never have."

"You're right. Don't intend to, either. But I know a lot of valuable information you're gonna need." For the next several miles, he proceeded to fill her in. Finally, he took a loud breath, indicating he'd done enough coaching. He reached over to the camera bag he had been guarding under his arm and opened four latches.

On the inside of the lid, in neat rows underneath little elastic bands, were stored rolls of film, brushes, bottles and circular things encased in plastic. "Every kind of lens filter you can imagine," he proudly informed her. From one of the numerous padded compartments in the bottom of bag, he pulled out a small bundle, wrapped in a soft white cloth. With utmost care, he opened it and unveiled a black camera with all kinds of buttons and windows. The name Nikon was written across the front. "Look at this baby," he said, barely breathing. "Isn't it *awesome?"* He placed the strap, with Nikon embroidered in gold letters around his neck and turned the camera over and over.

"So what's the big deal?" she asked, shrugging her shoulders. "Just a camera."

"You obviously have no idea what I'm holding in my hands. This is a Nikon F-4, the 35mm used by lots of pros. Of course, it's got auto-focus and automatic light metering, not to mention 1/8000th-of-a-second shutter speed and a high-speed motor drive that'll take up to *fifteen frames per second!*" He removed a circular piece of plastic from the front of the camera, which left a large open space. Then he proceeded to unzip a separate compartment of the bag and pulled out a long, black leather cylinder.

By now, he had piqued Michelle's curiosity. "What's that thing?" she asked.

"This, my dear Ashley Nicole, contains an 80-200mm zoom lens." He removed the coveted piece of equipment from its case and attached it over the opening on the front of the camera. It stuck out well over half a foot in front of his chest, dwarfing the camera suspended from the strap around his neck. The sight looked hilarious, so much so that she burst out laughing.

He smiled. "Go ahead and laugh. This outfit's worth over ten thousand dollars. I'm gonna be a famous photographer some day. Can't decide if I want to specialize in wildlife or sports or . . ."

Suddenly, Michelle pursed her lips and knit her eyebrows. She looked over at Matt out of the corner of her eye. "Wait a minute. You told me your family was poor. You've been a runaway for a year. How did you ever get a camera like that?"

He tugged on her arm to get her to face him, then looked her straight in the eyes. "Depends if you're good at keeping secrets."

Her eyes widened. She covered her mouth. "Don't tell me you *stole* the thing!"

He poked her with his elbow and shook his head. "Not me. Bought it for some cash and traded for the rest."

"So where'd you get so much money? Rob a bank?"

"Wrong again. I earned it. Worked long hours, took a few business risks and hit the jackpot."

"Selling what?"

"I'll show you when we get to the Big Apple."

"You know, I've always wanted a gold 280ZX with T-tops, ever

since I saw one at an old car show . . . Maybe I could help you. I'm a real hard worker."

"We'll see. First, I have one important question and I need a straight answer."

"What?" She frowned at his directness.

"How old are you?"

Without the slightest hesitation, she said, "Nineteen." She hoped he didn't notice her cheeks burning or her heart thumping.

"Nineteen, huh? That's great." He studied her for a moment and knit his brows. "You don't look quite that old, though."

"What do you mean? I was in college. I'm just *petite*."

"And put-together very well, I might add."

She returned a coy smile.

"I'd say nineteen's perfect, kid—I'm twenty-three. We could make a pretty good team." He put his arm back around her, pulling her closer.

"So, what kind of work are we going to do together?"

"Depends on what's available at the time. You have to get creative to live on your own."

"Oh, I can be very creative. I've never had a real job, yet, but I'd like to be able to support myself." She gave him an inquiring look. "Give me a hint."

He patted her arm. "Don't worry your pretty little head. We've got plenty of time to talk about serious matters. Let's just enjoy the rest of the trip, okay?"

"Guess you're right. She let out a soft, contented sigh and relaxed against his arm. How lucky could a girl get?

❧ *Ten* ❧

oshua awoke long before dawn. Disoriented at first, he took a moment to recognize his close surroundings—their berth aboard the Deutschland-Amerika. The transatlantic journey was nearing an end. They were almost in New York. *The United States of America!*

He rolled onto his right side, eased his left arm around Anna's waist and snuggled up to her. Her bare skin felt warm against his chest. He cherished the cozy feeling. He brushed her thinning, gray hair away from her soft face with his fingers, then planted a gentle kiss behind her ear. She shivered, still deep asleep, and drew closer. Her utter trust and tenderness never failed to impress him. Now, thinking back to the previous evening's shared intimacies, he felt a mounting protectiveness for his wife. He hugged her tighter.

Even today, after so many years, she had the power to stir him. And judging from the night before, she still found him desirable, too. He shook his head at the thought. Then softly, in the breath of a whisper, he prayed. "Oh, thank You, Lord, for my beloved Anna!" Tears of joy welled up as the memories came. He held her and laid his head on the pillow, just inches from her.

Through the memories, he sensed a subtle prompting. He recognized the gentle, insistent voice of the Holy Spirit. *Reassure your wife this morning. New beginnings are seldom easy for her.*

"You know her well, Lord. Better than I."

I formed you both in the womb. Before you were created, yet I knew you. Lo, I am with you always, even to the end of the age. Yesterday . . . today . . . forever.

"What would you have me do?" he dared to ask.

Another nudging inside. *Bless her. Be swift to tell her how very much you love her.*

He sighed as a sly smile played at the corners of his mouth. "Still the eternal romantic, are You not, Lord? But of course—You invented love."

Without further thought or word, Joshua agreed. "I will do as You say, for I treasure her so. If only I could love her as You do."

Taking care not to disturb Anna, he slipped out from between the covers, tiptoed around the side of the bed and knelt beside her. As he had done for many years, he laid his hand on his sleeping wife. Several minutes passed. He thanked God for every trait about her he could think of. He closed his prayer with, "Lord, help me be the best husband I can be for her. In Jesus' name, Amen."

He pushed himself up from his kneeling position, which had grown harder and more uncomfortable over the years, and tiptoed to the tiny bathroom. He took plenty of time to perform his morning ritual—teeth, mouth rinse, fresh shave. Prickly would not do for Anna's delicate skin.

Then, for the pièce de résistance. Humming softly, he opened the bottle of cologne she liked best on him. Not too much. Just enough. The pungent, masculine fragrance enveloped him as he splashed the cool liquid on his face and neck. He began to turn away from the mirror, but froze, midway. Ah, yes. With his left hand raised and index finger pointing straight up, he remembered Anna's peppermint. She always asked for one when he kissed her good morning. Instead of going back to bed, he crouched down at the closet and dug in their travel bag for the stash of mints. With two of them in hand, he retrieved the letter he had prepared the night they left Germany and tiptoed back to bed.

Settling himself on the edge of the mattress, he lifted the covers—as gently as a mother eagle lifts her wings over the eaglets huddled in her nest. He slipped in between the sheets and edged over beside Anna. Her skin felt like warm velvet against his own, now grown chilly from his morning hygiene routine. He propped himself on his elbow and placed some gentle kisses and nibbles along the side of her neck.

"Anna, dear, wake up. We will reach New York harbor this day." He let out a jubilant sigh. "Do you hear me, my precious? *America!* Today our feet will walk at last upon the glorious land of the free."

She turned her head a little toward him and mumbled in a sleepy voice. "As soon as this—*America?*"

"Soon? This is the morning of the seventh day."

She opened her eyes to meet her husband's tender gaze. His clear, light blue eyes drew her like twin pools beckoning a swimmer on a hot afternoon. She smiled and raised her eyebrows.

"What is it, love?" he asked.

"Would you bring me a peppermint?"

He winked. "Already at your service, my lady." The cellophane rustled as he held up the red-and-white striped sweet and removed it from its wrapper. She opened her mouth for him to pop in the candy. While she savored its sweetness, Joshua held her in his arms and ran his fingertips along her spine, alternating between caresses and a gentle massage.

"So thoughtful you are, love. Thank you." She inhaled deeply. "And you smell good, too!"

He leaned forward and brushed his lips against the tip of her nose. He had not forgotten that she loved such affection.

A twinkle in her eyes complemented the smile playing at the corners of his mouth. She traced the outline of his lips with her finger. "You have mischief on your mind, I see."

"How can you tell?"

"After all these years, do I not know you?"

"I must admit, I did entertain the thought. But cuddling is enough." He tightened his arm and gave her another hug. "Ummhmm. More than enough."

Anna yielded to his embrace and molded her body to match his. He smiled, adding, "We can postpone our celebration until later. Morning is seldom your favorite time." She tried to convince him otherwise, but he silenced her with a quick kiss.

She shivered and breathed out a contented sigh. His fingertips felt like silk feathers brushing across her skin, so gently did he touch her. He gave no indication that he noticed any of the wrinkles or age spots she found so unattractive.

As he had done earlier before she awoke, Joshua closed his eyes and prayed. "Lord, thank You for my precious bride, my Anna. Forty-five years as her husband have been as the passing of a night. And now here we are, standing on the brink of a new dawn." He paused, leaned forward to brush the hair from Anna's shoulder, then placed there a gentle kiss. His feathery touch brought forth another shiver.

"Thank You, Father, for this treasure You have entrusted into my care. Protect her, strengthen her, encourage her, as we begin this adventure, I pray." He paused to give her another squeeze. "Anna, I love you so!"

She leaned her head back on his chest and lifted her gaze up until their eyes met. "And I you, my dear."

His right hand reached over to the night stand for the letter. "I wrote this to you the night we left." He unfolded the paper, saying, "Would you rather I read it to you?"

His question summoned an enthusiastic nod and a pat on his chest. Again he leaned forward to kiss her, this time a tender butterfly across her eyelids. He began reading,

My beloved Anna,

A major chapter of our life together is drawing to a close. Do you realize that? Yes, of course, you do. No one knows better than you the depth of sorrow and joy we leave behind. And yet, these years of imprisonment in a hostile land have only served to make our relationship deeper, stronger, more resilient.

Our God has proven Himself faithful!

How can I possibly express to you all that you mean to me? Words would fail me were I to try. So, I shall borrow the words penned by another, perhaps many years ago. His are far more adequate than my own. He writes,

If you are for pleasure, marry; if you prize rosy health, marry. A good wife is heaven's last best gift to a man; his angel of mercy; minister of graces innumerable; his gem of many virtues; his box of jewels; her voice, his brightest day, her kiss, the guardian of innocence; her arms, the pale of his safety; the balm of his health; the balsam of his life; her industry, his

145

surest wealth; her economy, his safest steward; her
lips, his faithful counsellors; her bosom, the softest
pillow of his cares; and her prayers, the ablest advo-
cates of Heaven's blessing on his head.[5]
                                    —*Bishop Taylor*

It seems the wise bishop had you—my little Anna—in
mind. For you have been all of those, and far more. Thank
you, sweetheart. May the Lord God Himself reward you
now and forever.

                              All my love,

                              Your devoted Joshua

When he finished reading, he gazed back into her eyes. Large
tears had gathered and threatened to spill out over her eyelids.
"Already He has rewarded me, dearest one. He gave to me you."
She fell silent, then added, "Would you get me my Bible so I may
read something to you?" He retrieved it in short order. She took
out from between the pages a colorful paper she was using for a
bookmark. "'Tis my favorite verse by St. Francis of Assisi that an
American friend gave me years ago. It suits you most admirably.

Lord, make me an instrument of your peace . . .
Where there is hatred let me sow love
Where there is injury, pardon
Where there is doubt, faith
Where there is despair, hope
Where there is darkness, light
And where there is sadness, joy.

146

Grant that I may not so much seek
To be consoled as to console
To be understood as to understand
To be loved as to love
For it is in giving that we receive
It is in pardoning that we are pardoned
It is in dying that we are born to eternal life.

And so, dear husband, if I have been a suitable wife at all, it has been largely your doing—and His." They said no more, but rested in an embrace for a good long while.

Finally, he reminded her they were due to arrive at the port at 8:00 a.m. "It must be after 6:00 now. Shall we go up on deck and enjoy the view?"

"Only because of you, my sweet, would I get up from this cozy bed to shiver in damp morning air. For a man your age, you have the boundless curiosity of a child,"

"You think so, eh?"

She giggled and nodded.

"What do you find so funny?"

Another, more contagious giggle.

Joshua started laughing. "If we had more time, I would find out what you're thinking. But we must be about our business."

"It is too early to be up." She sighed and burrowed deeper beneath the covers.

"Suit yourself, my sleepy one. You will regret missing the first glimpse of our new home at sunrise. As for me . . ." He slid out of bed and stood on the soft carpet.

Anna rolled over to face him, but kept the sheets pulled up to her chin. "Oh, not yet," she moaned.

"Come," he coaxed, then leaned forward and placed his hands conveniently near the edge of the bedcovers. "Must I help you?"

Anna's head bobbed up. The mischievous glint in his eyes was unmistakable. Her fingers clutched harder at the blankets beneath her chin. "No! If you dare, I shall . . ."

He grinned and leaned closer. "Shall what?"

She kicked her legs under the covers. *"No-o-o . . .* I am too old for such a shock in the morning . . ." Her frantic protests failed to erase his playful grin. She tried another tactic. "If you love me, you will not touch these covers without my permission."

"You know I adore you." He kissed her forehead, then grasped the edge nearest him, tugged, and lifted it a few inches.

"Please, no. Just a few more minutes. We could cuddle . . ." She smiled her most captivating smile.

Joshua relaxed his grip. Then he moved. He couldn't resist. His hands and arms dived beneath the covers. Before Anna could react, his fingers had reached her most ticklish spot, under her arms. Wriggling to free herself, she let her grip go. That was all the opportunity he needed.

One hand reached back to the covers and jerked. He stepped away from the bed. The covers followed.

"A-i-e-e-e," she wailed. She made a grab for them, but missed. "You rascal!" Her arms flailed, missed again. This time Joshua scooped her up and wrapped her in a bear hug. She yielded. He kissed her tenderly on the mouth. Her arms encircled his neck. When their lips parted, she leaned back. "Maybe not a rascal . . ."

He hugged her tighter and rocked her back and forth. "Have I told you yet today that I love you?"

"Umm, in many ways," she sighed. "But never will I understand one thing."

"That is?"

"How such delightful hugs and such horrible treachery can come from the same man!" Catching him off-guard, she delivered a strong pay-back tickle under his ribs that made him burst out in hearty laughter.

"Oh," he said, holding his stomach, "I thank God to have a wife who can play. It has kept us both young."

"Without a doubt." She crawled out of bed and grabbed her fluffy down pillow. She threw it against his chest as hard as her tiny arms could muster. "My personal greetings to the official rooster. You watch, I will be dressed before you anyway. But you must promise to get me some hot tea if you insist on taking me up there to freeze."

Joshua reached for his pillow, then in another fit of hearty laughter, tossed it at her. "Hot tea you shall have." With that, he grabbed his underwear, trousers, plaid shirt, and cardigan sweater from the chair and put them on before she had half the buttons buttoned on her bathrobe. He stood there, bare feet peering out from below his pant legs and a smug expression on his face.

Anna proceeded to look through the suitcase in search of her own things. When she was ready, complete with a large fringed scarf tied beneath her chin, they headed for the deck. Joshua locked the berth door with care, offered his arm, and led the way.

It was still quite dark outside when they climbed onto the deck, except for the ship's own lights.

"Joshua . . . 6:00 a.m.? Tell me the truth."

He pulled back the cuff of his sweater, looked at his watch and then at Anna out of the corner of his eye. "Sorry, I misread the time." His sheepish grin gave him away. "'Tis five. But look over there, my love. That vast sea of lights on the horizon is New York City. See, a few other passengers have already come up to catch a glimpse, too."

Tender Journey

Within the hour, they enjoyed the first hint of dawn. The silhouette of a robed form in the distance made a dark outline against the pinkish glow of morning light. Instantly, they recognized the timeless figure. Joshua grabbed the pair of binoculars he'd hastily hung around his neck and peered through them. Even the points on her crown and her fingers wrapped around her tablet became visible through the powerful lenses. A bright golden light emanating from the torch in her upraised right hand lent her a regal appearance. "Anna, look! It's her!" He stared in awe at the famous statue and then handed the binoculars to Anna. His fingers shook as he placed the strap over her head.

She held the binoculars to her eyes. *"Oh . . . Joshua . . ."* Her voice became a faint whisper. *"Freedom!"* She squinted to see better, then let the binoculars return to a dangling position. "We lost that gift in our homeland for almost thirty years." Words memorized as a young girl came, unbidden, to mind. With a dramatic flair, she recited the inscription on the distant statue's pedestal,

> *Give me your tired, your poor, your huddled masses yearning to breathe free, the wretched refuse of your teeming shore. Send these, the homeless, tempest-tost to me; I lift my lamp beside the golden door.*

She finished and turned to Joshua. Leaning her head against his shoulder, she wiped a tear from her misty eyes.

He pulled her close. "Most inspiring, my sweet," he praised her. "Had you not married me, I fear, you could have become a famous actress. A wealthy one, as well."

"And been sad all my days."

His own eyes grew watery as he rested his head on top of hers. "You are content, then, to come to America with an old man?"

"You are young in heart. And yes, I am very happy just to be at your side. Nowhere else on this wide earth would I rather be."

"I treasure your vote of confidence. Few women would leave so many memories behind and start over at your age. I hope you are not doing it merely for my benefit."

"Fret not. All my life I have dreamed of coming here. Even as a girl, before I met you, I dreamed. I used to imagine how I would feel, knowing that the next step I took would place me in this grand country." She fell silent. Her tiny hands clenched the rail as she turned her gaze once more toward the Statue of Liberty. "Think of what she has meant to millions of immigrants. Let us never take freedom for granted, Joshua. Never."

"We will not, with God's help. Of course, it is He who gives true liberty—yes? *Whom the Son sets free is free indeed.*"

She nodded slowly. "Do you suppose He will make us useful in America, as well?"

Joshua folded his hands and pressed them to his chest. "I believe so. I want Him to, but I must be honest. I also long to find my father. I *pray* it is not too late!"

"And I pray the same. Were we to meet with success, what a delightful reunion it would be."

He paused, opened his mouth to speak, then thought better of it. They listened to the low hum of the engine, the insistent screeching of hungry gulls and the lapping of the waves against the ship.

"Such peace, my love," Anna whispered.

"Yes, glorious peace." He looked down at his wife. "Thank you for standing beside me, no matter where God may lead us. I would not want to do this alone."

"Do you mean that?"

"Every word. I have only one regret—that I do not have another forty, fifty, a hundred years to be your husband."

"I feel the same." She rubbed the joints of his hands. "Do you know what I have grown to appreciate most in you?"

"No, tell me."

"Your deep commitment to God. I admire that so. When I see your surrender to Him, I feel protected and safe, like a baby in her mother's arms . . . or like a ship in a harbor."

"You do?"

"Most assuredly. To trust your leadership has become natural to me. As natural as breathing."

He winked at her. "It was not always so, I recall . . ."

Smiling, she paused and looked into his eyes. "I remember. I resisted you and Him at every turn."

His mood grew more serious. "You thought you loved someone else . . ."

She put her finger to his lips. "Only for a brief moment. You were often away from home and I was lonely. Not since those first few difficult years have I longed for another man."

He looked into her eyes. "How happy it makes me to hear you say that! Countless women want new husbands when hard times come along."

Anna raised an eyebrow. "You must be fair. Many men look for new loves quicker than the eye blinks."

A soft chuckle escaped from his throat. "True. More than new partners, they need new hearts."

She nodded. "Softened with the sweet Spirit of Jesus."

"He alone deserves credit for keeping our love alive. How many years has it been? The number escapes me at the moment."

"Forty-five."

"Goodness! Time passes so quickly."

"We are nearing the autumn of life, my love."

His voice dropped to a whisper. "How well I know."

She sighed. "Every moment counts for so much. We cannot tell how many of them we have left together . . ."

They stood, arm-in-arm, at the railing until an old tugboat came to usher the enormous Deutschland-Amerika II into New York harbor. Every few minutes, the pudgy black and red boat sounded a blast from its well-worn horn, seeming to exude pride in its role as escort. Other boats in the area returned the salute. To one elderly couple, the greeting felt sweeter than the most royal of welcomes.

He gave her one more hug, kissed her on the forehead, and swatted her tenderly on her backside. "Come," he encouraged, as he led her back down the stairs to their berth. Once she was in bed beside him, he pulled her close and wrapped the covers around her, just long enough to stop the shivers. "Better than hot tea?" he asked, stroking her hair.

"Far better." And with a contented murmur, she snuggled in.

❧ *Eleven* ❧

The MarriageMaker class members began gathering in the reception area of Dr. Eric Marcos' counseling office at about ten till seven that Thursday evening. They mingled with one another, but it was obvious to Michael that socializing came easier for some and he wasn't among them. Stephanie was whispering something to Charmaine. A few feet away, a platinum blond seemed to enjoy herself immensely as she chatted with two men. Her husband stood quietly, hands in his pockets, at her side.

At seven o'clock sharp, Eric handed out nametags and escorted the small group into the meeting room adjacent to his private office. He had arranged padded folding chairs in a neat semi-circle. Sean Owens, the only single person in the class, went in first and sat on the end. Colette and Paul Chartier sat next to him, followed by Sid and Barbara Brenner, José and Maria Juarez, Charmaine and Bob Harrington. Michael and Stephanie sat on the end opposite Sean. That way, they could scoot out early, if need be.

Eric set down his briefcase and stood in front of the group. He opened with a sincere prayer, then spoke in an exuberant tone, "Welcome, everyone, to the very first MarriageMaker class. I heard a joke about a man whose favorite hobby was playing old movies of his wedding—backwards. That's right. *Backwards.* The guy loved seeing himself walk out of the church a free man."

Almost everybody laughed. Sid guffawed while his wife Barbara frowned at him and tapped him on the leg. Michael allowed himself a slight upturn at the corners of his mouth. Stephanie giggled.

Eric continued with a grin. "Just kidding, folks. Actually, marriage is very serious business. Half of the people who try it, fail. Some statistics say two-thirds fail. Most of the rest of the folks daydream about walking out, like the man who played his wedding movies backwards. Only one marriage in ten achieves optimum satisfaction. I don't know about you, but that sends shivers down my spine."

He scanned the group sitting in front of him and rubbed his chin. "Did any of you see that wonderful old musical, *"Fiddler on the Roof?"* Maybe you remember the song with the bouncy tune, *"Matchmaker, matchmaker, make me a match . . ."* Several in the group nodded as he sang in a lilting tenor. He finished the chorus and continued, "That could be our theme song when we're searching for a mate. 'Go matchmaker, get me one!' we cheer. Trouble is, once we've snagged a perfect catch and marry it, we haven't the foggiest notion what to do next. Sooner rather than later, we're ready to toss it overboard!" Knowing smiles sprang up on a few faces. Clearly, they had ridden in that boat.

"That's why we're here. Great marriages do not just happen. We—husbands and wives—have to make them happen. But here comes the clincher: we cannot do it, no matter how hard we try." He stopped short. He had their attention, as evidenced by the many raised eyebrows in the room.

Sid blurted out, "So why bother?"

"I'm glad you asked, Sid," Eric replied. "We need the MarriageMaker. He wrote The Book on marriage. And on every other human relationship, for that matter. Left to our own devices, we might as well hang it up. We're standing on the edge of a cliff, with nothing between us and disaster. The slightest nudge could send us reeling head over heels into oblivion."

Eric's gaze swept the room. He paused at each couple and then at Sean, the handsome African-American bachelor. "God didn't intend for marriage to end up that way. Unfortunately, for some couples in our church, it could." The sound of bodies shifting on the chairs seemed loud in the suddenly-silent room.

"So . . . in case any of you or your loved ones have considered dissolving your union, let me read to you one of the most powerful descriptions of divorce I have ever encountered. It's from the Prologue of the book, *Crazy Time* by Abigail Trafford. Please listen carefully. I hope I can get through this without getting choked up.

From what you see on television and in the movies, you'd think that getting a divorce was some yellow brick road to personal growth and happiness; all those stories of personal freedom, the joys of being single, the good sex out there; the jokes about falling off the marriage merry-go-round and having fun. The Great New Life.

But ask someone who's been through it. There is nothing funny or easy about divorce. It is a savage emotional journey. Where it ends, you don't know for a long time. In the process, you ricochet between the failure of the past and the uncertainty of the future. You struggle to understand what went wrong with your marriage, to apportion the blame and inventory the emotional resources of the present. The one thing you are sure of almost immediately:

you know that life will never be the same again. "Divorce is a death," says counselor Sharon Baker of the Los Angeles Divorce Warm Line. "Divorce is the death of a relationship. It is the death of your dreams. You have to start all over."

Most people go a little crazy. You are rarely prepared for the practical or emotional turmoil that lies ahead. You swing between euphoria, violent rage and depression. You may be promiscuous and drink too much; you may withdraw from people and not answer the phone. Health statistics tell you that you're prone to getting sick and having car accidents. Reports of triangle assaults and murders of estranged spouses make regular newspaper headlines. In the dark hours of loneliness, you think about suicide. At some point, almost everyone coming out of a marriage mutters to what was once the other half: "I could kill you."

You soon discover that cutting the legal bond with your ex-spouse is a relatively small part of the whole divorce experience. Even though the law says your marriage is finished and you're dividing up the pots and pans, the memories and friends . . . still it's not over.

You get frightened. What if you never pull out of this?

. . . It's not so long ago that my marriage cracked open on a gray Christmas afternoon. The confrontation scene began, typically, over something inconsequential—in this case, a crate of grapefruit, a present from friends in Texas, where we had been living before moving to Washington, D.C. That night, we raged at each other like bruised animals, filled our glasses again and bellowed into the dawn, stripping away a past of deception and pain. The next morning, the house was quiet. My husband had left early

157

for work. The children were upstairs in their room, playing with Christmas toys . . .

I was overwhelmed and totally unprepared for what followed. There was no Dr. Spock for getting divorced, no helpful guidelines on adult equivalents of bed-wetting and thumb-sucking; no official protocols for dividing assets or memories; no training manuals on how to decipher the past and build up new emotional skills.

At first I felt like Alice in the wrong Wonderland; I'd eaten this mushroom by mistake. My world was turned upside down. I wanted to protest to the management, I wanted to throw up, get a doctor, drink a magic potion —anything to get back on track, to get back to a universe where things go right, to get back to my dream of falling in love, getting married and living happily ever after. But the mushroom of reality stuck in my throat. Indeed, I began to realize it had been a dream—not reality—I was trying to live.

When I got back [from a weekend with my parents], it was cold in the house and the rooms were hollow. My six-year-old daughter refused to say her prayers anymore. The sink in the kitchen stopped up. I knew I had been unhappy in the marriage for a number of years—getting sick those times, repressing relief when my husband had to go away on business, wanting someone else. When we finally con-fronted each other, the betrayals were too deep on both sides. We had stunned each other by our double lives. The wedding pictures hung in the hall, but we had both "left" each other in a basic way long ago.

And then again, we hadn't. That was the agony of it. Somehow we were still glued to each other. It wasn't just the children. We both still wanted something from each other. We had started out so much in love. That's what everybody said. Ours was a beautiful wedding on an island in Maine, with bridesmaids in straw hats and the blessing of Great-grandmother's veil. "I have just one piece of advice that my mother-in-law gave me," said my Aunt Melinda on the eve of the wedding: "Never go to sleep on a grudge."

Alone now, I hated the king-size bed and got rid of it. I put away the wedding pictures and took off my ring. The children wanted a puppy. I said I couldn't handle it. The house was always cold. We lived off eggs and granola. At night in bed came the pain in my chest. As I lay there, awake and afraid, my mind racing over the past and back to the future, I tried to bring logic to my despair. In the end, I was haunted by three disturbing thoughts that wouldn't go away: I didn't really know the person I had been married to for twelve years. I wasn't too sure what kind of person I was, either; I certainly didn't like myself or some of the things I had done.

Most of all, I realized that the official issues that broke us up were not the real ones. Something else was at work, something deeper that neither of us was able to explain. It was tantalizing, this chimera, this hint that understanding was there somewhere. I felt that if I could just understand what it was—this mysterious something between us—I would not only understand what had gone wrong in the marriage; I could get over the marriage and on to a new life. I also sensed that this mysterious something might be a key to why relationships generally don't work—and why they do.[6]

159

His voice quivering, Eric finished reading and then expelled a deep sigh. He did not look at anyone. The silence in the room was answer enough. A falling feather would have made more noise. He closed the book and seated himself in the one vacant chair, facing the group.

Stephanie used a tissue to dab her eyes. After a long moment, she dared to look around.

Charmaine's misty eyes had a faraway look about them. Bob was solemnly playing with his gold pen.

José and Maria kept glancing at each other, then away again.

Paul Chartier coughed, clearing his throat. Collette stared at her hands folded in her lap. The Brenners appeared the most relaxed, both with each other and with the emotions stirred by the story. They sat, he with an arm comfortingly around her and she, leaning her head into his shoulder.

Sean was also moved. His dark, moist eyes darted the length of the row of chairs, from one couple to the next. Finally, he settled on Eric himself as the safest resting place.

The story had shaken Michael more than he wanted to admit. He swallowed hard, stared at his hands, then at Eric's shoes. To distract himself from the disturbing feelings mounting in his gut, he let his thoughts drift to the other members of the group. He wondered what type of problems each faced. Were they worse than those he and his family were going through? No. He couldn't believe that. His most surely topped the list.

What about the Mexican-Americans? José and his wife looked pretty worn out and weathered. His fingernails were filthy. Maybe they were migrant workers. From what Michael had heard, those camps could be pretty tough.

He shifted a discreet gaze to the couple sitting almost directly across from him. The guy looked to be in his late thirties. A flashy dresser, with diamond rings, gold neck chains, bracelets, and a Montblanc pen in his hand. Probably engraved, to boot. He couldn't remember his name. The wife, Collette or something, was just as flashy, but different. A bubbly blonde who spoke with an exaggerated Southern drawl, she didn't need any artificial frills to attract attention. She displayed her own natural attributes quite well. Short, tight skirt and heels too high for his taste. He sure wouldn't want Stephanie running around in public like that.

He wondered what kind of problems they had. The husband trying to keep up with his wife, Michael decided. A gentle poke in the ribs snapped him out of his reverie. "Huh?" he grumbled.

She whispered, "Michael, please listen."

"I was. You didn't have to knock the wind out of me . . ." He shook his head from side to side, then returned his gaze to Eric, but not before he gave her a sheepish look. "Sometimes," he muttered out of the side of his mouth, "you bug me. What do you *think* I was doing?"

"Sightseeing," she shot right back. Her answer brought a slight grimace to Michael's face.

"Excuse me, Dr. Marcos," the skinny guy with dark hair and thick black-framed glasses interrupted, "Do you have any extra copies of that quote? I'd like to give it to a friend who's thinking about leaving his wife and kids."

"No, Sid, I don't have permission to do that, but it's a great idea. You could try to contact HarperCollins Publishers in New York City. And by the way, from here on, let's drop the "doctor" title. Just call me Eric."

"Okay—Eric." Sid repeated the name with a bit of hesitation.

"In this class, we're all equal. I like to think of myself as more of a facilitator than an instructor. Our group will follow a simple format. We'll try to focus on a main topic per session, but I'm sure

161

we'll deviate somewhat. I'd like everyone to have the opportunity to provide input because you all have many helpful ideas to share. Most important, we'll allow the Holy Spirit to be our Guide. Now, does anyone have any questions?"

Eric's gaze moved across the faces of those gathered around him. Nearly everyone met his look. Thoughtful expressions settled on the majority as the seconds ticked away. Charmaine opened up her notebook and started writing.

Michael cleared his throat. He sat forward on the edge of his seat, with one foot back as if he were ready to leap out of it. Eric turned his head in his direction. "Eric, I can't sit still any longer and pretend that I'm convinced we need to be here. I mean, I don't believe a group can solve marriage problems." Steph slumped back into her seat and lowered her gaze to the floor. Her features were fraught with anxiety. She could hear it coming already.

Bob Harrington stepped in. "I know what you mean, Michael. Charmaine and I . . ., " he reached out with his right hand and gave her left knee an affirming squeeze, ". . . haven't been fighting a lot or anything, so I refused to entertain the thought of attending a marriage class. In fact, when she first mentioned it, I thought she was kidding. I said something to the effect that I would never become a 'headshrinking groupie.'" He grinned, then caught himself. "Sorry, Eric, but I did say it. Kind of ironic. Shrinking my swollen head—alias ego—was exactly what I needed."

Bob paused. He cast a glance around at the other members. Charmaine turned toward him. Pleasant surprise brightened her features, but it was there and gone in an instant. Only her eyes held a tell-tale, lingering spark.

"What I'm trying to say," and here he looked at Charmaine, "I haven't been very considerate these past few months—especially since my business took a beating . . ." His voice faded. "We love each other, but we could use some renewing." He shifted his gaze toward Eric Marcos. "If you can give us some tips, I'm all for it. In more ways than one, we've grown cold." He stopped speaking and lowered his gaze to the carpet. With the fingers of his right hand, he massaged his temples. He looked up and added, "I'd like to change that."

A thick silence descended as he spoke, as if the others were thinking the same, but were overwhelmed by his openness.

"Thank you, Michael and Bob, for being honest," Eric concluded. "You both have valid points. Very few of us do handsprings at the thought of exposing our inner selves to anybody, yet James five, sixteen urges believers to confess faults to one another so we can be healed. Why wait until the brink of divorce to benefit from an enrichment class? I hope MarriageMaker will help all of you—even those doing well—to kindle your love brighter than it has ever been."

Although Michael gave no response, murmurs of agreement from several people encouraged Eric to continue. "I'm thrilled to know that you care enough about your relationships to work on them. The time you invest will reap rich dividends." He clapped his hands together once. "Okay, we've addressed the painful reality of splitting up. Let's move on to a lighter side of the topic—staying together! Suppose you're planning a project that involves joining two blocks of wood. What could you use to do that? Anybody?"

José raised his hand. "That's easy. Nails."

"Good. Any other ways?"

"Special glue for wood," said his wife, Maria, also with a pronounced Mexican accent.

"How about rope?" Stephanie volunteered.

One by one, other answers popped up from around the semicircle. "A hinge with screws."

"'Tongue in groove,' I think you call it. The way they assemble good furniture."

"You could use dowels."

"A sturdy clamp."

"Wire."

After a pause indicating they had run out of ideas, Eric threw in, "What a creative bunch! I hadn't thought of half of those."

"I've got one more," Michael ventured.

"Great, let's hear it."

"Grind up the wood, wet the particles with a particular solution, then press them together with just the right amount of heat and pressure—as in particle board."

"Yes. Very original." Eric nodded and glanced around, smiling.

Sean's white teeth gleamed in contrast to his dark mahogany-colored skin. He added in a kidding tone, "Good thing *we* aren't blocks of wood. Man alive—ground to dust, hosed down and smooshed flat, just to get hitched—I mean, *married!*" Several in the group chuckled.

Michael sat up straight. A guarded look began to creep over his features. Before he could respond, Eric said, "Michael, your illustration provides an excellent way to express what I was going to say in a moment." Then he turned to Sean. "You know, we humans do resemble two blocks of wood more than we'd care to admit—'blockheads,' to quote Lucy's pet name for Charlie Brown. And if you guys don't believe it . . . just ask your wives!"

"Yes, get 'em, Eric!" cheered Colette. The women clapped, buoyed on by her boldness.

José jumped up and waved his hands back and forth. "No, no, ladies. We men will pay you back."

Eric let the fun continue a few moments before pursuing his point. "Think about this: of all the ways you mentioned to join two pieces of wood together, Michael's would be the most permanent. You can pull out nails, unscrew screws, pry apart glued pieces (or saw them apart if necessary). You can untwist wire, untie rope and unclamp clamps. But in marriage, we want to avoid the easy undos. God would have His children's marriages more like sawdust—so carefully and finely blended, that nothing could separate the original elements."

Bob Harrington's, "Not asking much, are you?" brought forth a chorus of sympathetic agreement.

Undaunted, Eric came right back. "You will never hear me call it an easy process. Worthwhile? Yes. Rewarding. Absolutely. Painful. Usually. The Lord does use heat and pressure to accomplish His goal. We don't like that one bit." He checked the group's reaction and then went on.

"By the way, did you know that this joining together has been a part of God's plan for couples from the beginning? In fact, on that momentous occasion when God presented Eve to Adam . . ." He dug into his back pocket and brought out a slim leather Bible. "Let me read it for you from the King James,

And Adam said, This is now bone of my bones, and flesh of my flesh: she shall be called Woman, because she was taken out of Man. Therefore shall a man leave his father and his mother, and shall cleave unto his wife: and they shall be one flesh.
Genesis 2:23,24

When he had finished reading, he continued, "Incidently, a guy I know loves to personalize the *first* part of that Scripture during tender moments with his wife. He says it's quite the romantic thing to do, and it makes him feel closer to her than ever. For our purposes tonight, though, let's focus on the *last* few lines. As usual,

there's more here than meets the eye. Take the word, 'cleave.' How does a man cleave to his wife?"

Collette raised her hand. "I've heard of a cleaver, a big butcher knife like the Japanese use. In fact, we have one. But I'm sure that's not what you have in mind."

"Well, strangely enough, the verb 'cleave' is one of the few words that has opposite meanings in the dictionary." Among the rest of the group, equally blank expressions met his gaze.

"I only had a vague idea myself until I did a little research. The way I figured, God doesn't tell us to do something, then leave us hanging. Cleave can mean to divide or sever as well as to adhere, cling to or support. We can easily see which meaning He intends for marriage. In the original language, the word is 'dabaq.' Any Hebrew scholars in here?"

"Not lately," Michael quipped.

"It means 'to impinge.' Don't know about you, but that helped me very little. Then I read further in Strong's Hebrew Dictionary. Even made some notes." He flipped through the pages of his Bible. "Here we are. When I looked up these definitions, I put myself in the first person, active role. I, Eric Marcos, will *abide fast* to my wife. I will *follow close* to my wife. I will *be joined together, overtake, pursue hard* and *stick to* my wife. And one of my favorites—what Strong's calls the figurative definition—I will *catch by pursuit* my wife."

He closed his Bible. "Ladies, how do you like the idea of getting 'caught by pursuit'?"

Stephanie bit her top lip. Maria and Colette smiled. "I would feel good," said Maria. "Important and special." José sat up a little straighter at her side.

"Exactly. I'd venture a guess that you speak for every lady here. God knows what He's doing." Eric grinned. His friendly gaze danced from couple to couple. "For the catching as well as the keeping, don't forget."

Paul, Collette's husband, fiddled with the gold chain around his neck. "Unfortunately, Eric, it doesn't always work that way. My sister left my brother-in-law a couple weeks ago. He 'pursued' her until she couldn't stand the sight of him. In fact, she was afraid of him. Frankly, I don't blame her."

"Very good qualifying point, Paul. There's a big difference between *cleaving* in the biblical sense and *controlling*. Nobody desires a mate who is so offensive. And certainly not one who is abusive in any way. God forbid. That's a very delicate subject requiring more individual care than we can devote in this brief class, so please forgive me if we move on.

"Back to the task of togetherness. Once the honeymoon ends—and we wake up one morning with the frightening realization that we aren't *quite* as compatible as we imagined in our fuzzy-headed, pre-nuptial bliss—we're tempted to resort to all sorts of quick-fix remedies to maintain the marriage.

"Maybe we would focus on common goals, a fatter bank account, a new home, a good sex life, or cute children. Even emotional co-dependency or bad habits keep some people married. None of these work. Not over the long haul, in sickness and in health, for better or for worse. Anybody can come sneaking in with just the right tools and split a marriage to smithereens. Only one thing creates a permanent bond. You'll have to stay tuned to find out more about this special concoction; I'm going to keep you guessing for a while.

"Those of you who brought your Bibles, read along with me. Let's see how Paul the Apostle addresses the subject of marriage in Ephesians, chapter five, verses thirty and thirty-one. That's in the New Testament, right after the book of Galatians and before

Philippians." Knowing that all members differed in their spiritual comfort zones, Eric waited while everyone who was looking, found the verse. When the soft rustle of pages stopped, he began reading from the King James Version,

> *For we are members of his body, of his flesh, and of his bones. For this cause shall a man leave his father and mother, and shall be joined unto his wife, and they two shall be one flesh.*

Barbara Brenner raised her hand. "That's amazing, Eric. The same thing you just read in Genesis."

"Yes, New Testament writers often quoted the Old Testament, as did Jesus. Where the Hebrew word was translated 'cleave,' the word here is translated *'to be joined.'* In the original Greek, it's 'proskollao.' According to Strong's Dictionary, it means *'to glue to, to adhere, cleave or join.'* Sound familiar?"

He surveyed the faces seated before him. "So, assuming we've followed the first two commands—left our parents and tried to be glued to our wives, the final question is, 'Are we one yet? To the extent that God would have us?'" His pleasant smile took away a measure of the prodding from his words.

"Eric," Sid began with a wink, "If 'one flesh' can travel in different universes most of the time, Barbara and I qualify. If not . . ." He left the sentence hanging.

Sean laughed out loud. "That reminds me of a book title I heard the other day: *Men Are from Mars; Women Are from Venus.*"

"Not so fast, buddy," Paul said, shaking his finger at Sean, with his face a mixture of playful seriousness. "Let's see if you're still laughing when *you're* married to one of those aliens!" That did it for the guys. They hooted and howled and slapped their thighs. Even Michael found himself chuckling.

Collette leaned forward, conspiratorially, and half-whispered, but loud enough for all to hear, "Don't listen to him, Sean. My husband does a good job running in opposite directions all by himself." She cast a coy smile and tilted her head. "Of course, come to think of it, so do most men." More claps from the wives in the group, along with a hearty "That's right" from Barbara.

Once the laughter subsided, Eric added, "I agree with the near-aliens theory. The Creator ordained countless differences between men and women. Why, I'm not sure. At the very least, those differences keep us on our toes. Often, they drive us crazy. And—they drive us to *Him!*

"Now, back to our word study. I have good news. The tense of the verb, 'to glue to' is called 'future passive tense.' It will happen 1) at some point in the future 2) because of an outside force acting upon it. In other words, folks, we cannot do it ourselves. Someone else has to bond us together."

"With divine super glue," Charmaine interjected.

Eric nodded, smiling. "Good analogy, Charmaine. In God's eyes, I believe it happens in the Spirit the moment we make our vows and are pronounced man and wife. Living out that reality takes a lifetime. Sometimes it requires a lot of heat and pressure to make the bond stick.

He checked the time on his watch. "We have just enough time left. Now comes the good part. Put away your Bibles. Stretch a bit and shake out some of the kinks." He stood and took his own advice, then sat back down. The others followed suit.

"All right. Here's what we're going to do. Turn your chairs so you sit facing your mate. Hold hands and look into each others' eyes. Refrain from conversation for at least five minutes."

One of the men groaned and another gave a nervous chuckle. Sean exclaimed in a teasing tone, "Man, what's wrong with you

guys? I can't wait to gaze into the eyes of my special woman. Forever won't be long enough."

The men teasingly attributed his romantic zeal to his bachelorhood status. Eric broke up the fun by saying with a smile, "Okay, I'll let you know when the time is up. Then discuss the following questions, if you would: 1) *Do we have oneness in our marriage?* 2) *Do we believe oneness is possible?* 3) *Do we want it?* 4) *What thoughts and feelings does this concept bring up?*"

The couples rearranged their chairs and got comfortable. That left the lone bachelor looking quite lost. "Sean, guess it's you and me, pal," Eric said. "We can discuss the questions as they apply to our relationships with the Lord, if you'd like, or talk about your plans with your future mate. Just promise me one thing."

Sean cocked his head, waiting. "Sure."

"No holding hands and no eye-gazing. Deal?" He winked.

Sean flashed a broad, dimpled smile. "A *definite* deal."

Several members of the class laughed outright. Michael and Stephanie finished getting situated in their chairs. He glanced at her large, blue eyes and looked away. Eric had told them to do this at home. They hadn't. He felt *more* awkward sitting in the middle of a room with a bunch of near-strangers, while he stared at his wife. She looked hesitant, confused. He ignored the observation and fixed his own eyes on the floor again.

She glanced around at the other couples who had already started. It was disturbingly quiet. A soft sigh escaped her lips. "Seems like we're the only ones struggling with this," she whispered. She put her hand on his knee and shook it slightly. "Shouldn't we at least try the exercise? It might do us some good."

"Yeah, I guess we should." He looked up. Their eyes met and locked. Part of him wanted to take the plunge into the depths of those beautiful baby blues and never come up for air. Something else inside tugged at him. He wanted to look away after less than a minute, but fought the urge and kept on. He failed to muster the least bit of tenderness. Her eyes contained such sorrow, he couldn't stand it. Why did she have to look depressed all the time? He couldn't make her happy, so why bother trying?

Stephanie searched Michael's dark brown eyes for a reflection of the pain she was feeling over the huge losses in their life—Michelle, Stephen, their dry-as-a-desert marriage. She saw no sign of response and it crushed her. She assumed that business plans consumed his thoughts—probably pondering the next candidate to meet with about the Space Waste project.

He cleared his throat and looked away. After adjusting his position in his chair, running his fingers through his hair, and looking at his watch, he spoke. "Five minutes is almost up, Steph." Relief tinged his voice. "Maybe we should start discussing the questions."

She nodded. Eric announced the end of the first segment.

Michael began, "Let's skip the first question. We both know we don't have it. Maybe number two will be easier. Do we believe oneness is possible?" He thought a moment. "I suppose it's possible. Probable—no. We're so different."

Stephanie nodded again. "I believe it's possible, even though we're opposites."

"Maybe. Eric says it can happen."

"And the Bible says so." She looked down at her notes. "How about number three—do we want oneness?" She hesitated. "I *think* I do."

"What do you mean?"

"Well, it seems like it might be a comforting place to be, though it sounds kind of scary, too. If you get really close to somebody, and that person leaves or dies, it would be much harder."

Michael shrugged his shoulders and feigned nonchalance. "I haven't thought much about the concept. Since I don't know what it involves on a practical level, I can't say whether I want it or not." Not true, a voice inside said. A twinge pricked his conscience. A memory of Caleb's tape on oneness crowded to the surface. He remembered the day he found it, shortly after Caleb died. The morning after he and Stephanie had enjoyed a consummate reconciliation. He brushed all that aside now and continued talking in a matter-of-fact tone. "Truthfully, I think we'd have to give up our own identities. A couple shouldn't get so close that they become an amorphous blob." He shuddered. "Makes my skin crawl." His words hurt her. He could see it in her face, but he felt reluctant to take back his statement.

She swallowed and bit her lower lip. "Michael, remember, right after we got back together, how we listened to Caleb's tape?"

He frowned to hide his shock and leaned back further in his chair. "What made you bring that up?"

"I don't know. Remember how it touched us, though? We cried together. We agreed we wanted that kind of relationship with the Lord. And with each other." Her voice lowered to an intense whisper. "What happened?"

Why'd she have to bring up Caleb's tape? He didn't want to think about it—or him. He missed his old mentor too much, especially now. Since the crises with the kids, his heart had turned into a hardened, parched wasteland. He had little desire to read the Bible, much less pray with Stephanie . . .

"Michael, are you listening? What happened to the closeness we both wanted? Why have we shut each other out?" Her eyes filled with tears.

"I don't know, and I don't want to talk about it right now," he replied, his mouth taut.

She could tell by his tone of voice that he meant "case closed." She grabbed her purse and hurried off to the ladies' room. By the time she returned to the class and sat down, Eric was encouraging group discussion on how everyone felt about "the eyes exercise."

In general, the ladies found it endearing, but wanted more time; the men couldn't wait to move on to something more specific. At least, that was what they said. Bob got honest and admitted that he felt like his soul had stood, stark naked, in front of his wife. He wished for something to wrap up in.

"Let me give you a few parting thoughts that you can mull over until we meet again. The first is a quote by author and pastor, Jack Taylor. He said, "If you want to know the true character of a man, look into his wife's eyes. Everything he has invested and everything he has withheld will show in her expression." The room grew instantly quiet. Men fidgeted with pens, tapped their feet, stared at the floor. Michael cleared his throat. How could their fearless leader have turned traitor so fast?

Eric surprised him by adding, "In my opinion, the same holds true for a woman, although perhaps to a lesser degree. Her husband's eyes speak volumes about what she has given or withheld, as well. And 'the eyes exercise' not only reveals where we've been in our relationships, it acts as a good barometer of where we're going. It gets us right down to the core of a thorny issue—how do we feel about genuine intimacy? Simply put, either we want to love and be loved more deeply, or we'd rather run and hide.

"According to authors David and Vera Mace, marriage resembles a large, cozy home that we inherit from our Father on our wedding day. We can either explore each room together, or resign ourselves to living in a small corner—in relative isolation, I might add. What a shame to keep so many rooms locked with a *Do Not Enter* sign nailed to the door! The MarriageMaker carries a master

key, if we'll let Him use it. So, my friends, in summary, tonight we examined one major point: God's *plan,* His goal, for marriage. Which is?"

"Oneness," answered Sid, without hesitation.

"Very good. We'll continue on in our second session to cover the *purpose* for marriage and finally, third, the *power* for marriage. Or stated another way, the *what,* the *why,* and the *how.* God bless you all. See you next week, everybody!"

The group broke up amid boisterous chatter and clanging of chairs. Several talked about going out together for coffee and dessert. Stephanie gave Michael a pleading look of, "Can we go?" but he said their polite goodbyes and scooted her out to the car. After they were both seated inside, he paused, then leaned over to give her a quick peck on the cheek. "Hon, this isn't easy for me. Just want you to know I am trying."

With a sigh, she squeezed his hand. "Me, too."

❧ *Twelve* ❧

ointing to the map spread out on the hotel room bed Anna said, "We have come this far. Why do we not ask someone how we might begin to look for him?"

"We must. I have resigned myself." He bowed his head, rested his forearms on his thighs and formed a steeple with his forefingers. "But I have doubts now. What chance have we? This country is so vast. We tried the address our German contact gave us. Those people never heard of such a person as Caleb Johannsen."

"To our God in heaven, even America looks as tiny as a grain of sand! If He knows the number of hairs on every head, does He not know where is your father?"

He glanced up and nodded. "He knows."

"Of course He does. We have prayed and we need only to continue to ask Him to show us the way."

"For so long, I believed with all my heart that He would do that, or I never would have brought you across the world. But now, the idea seems preposterous! If we tell a soul what we, two old foreigners, have in mind to do, they will think we have in the head more than loose screws."

175

"'Twill not be the first time!" She laughed and patted his knee.

He smiled, then nodded. "That is very true." He chuckled. "You always make me to see the funny side, Anna. I do so love that about you." His wrapped his arm around her in a hug.

"Thank you, my dear." She snuggled closer. "I love to encourage you." She paused, tilted her head and placed her forefinger on her cheek. "Do you remember the miracle years ago when we needed one hundred Bibles? So many families were begging us for a single copy to share among all their relatives."

He nodded. "To get them through the Wall seemed an impossible task. But I had to try."

"And what did you tell your friend Hans?"

"That somehow, God would help us bring His Word to His people."

"How did he respond?"

Joshua paused, remembering. "He said he believed in God, but he considered me an idiot to risk my life. No matter who it was for."

"And then?"

"I reminded him how God had blinded the Old Testament prophet Elisha's enemies to protect him from harm. 'God can do the same for us,' I told him boldly, 'if He feels so inclined.'"

"What did he do?"

"He laughed at me in a very loud voice, then went his way, shaking his head. But remember—you and I continued to pray that God would send someone to us with enough Bibles for His little lambs." Joshua squinted into the distance. A smile crossed his lips. "I'll never forget that night, Anna, just a few weeks later. As I was sweeping our walk . . . it was nearly dark . . . I came upon a satchel and thought it odd of you to leave our bag outside. Do you know what first entered my mind?"

She shook her head. "I have not an inkling. What could it—"

Looking into her eyes, he lowered his voice. "We had just had a slight quarrel. I wondered if perhaps you intended to leave me and had hidden the evidence outside!"

Her fine, gray eyebrows drew together as she laughed. "How silly! Not for all these years have you told me."

"Oh, it was only a fleeting thought. I soon realized that you had nowhere to go." He winked.

"I should fuss at you, Herr Lieben, but you assumed quite right, in fact."

He continued, gesturing along with his words, "So, I picked up the satchel and carried it into the house."

"Yes . . . I remember. You called me into the kitchen," Anna said. "I assured you that I had not left any such thing outside. At any rate, the one you found was in far better condition than ours. I noticed that immediately."

"Do you recall when we looked inside? We could scarcely believe our eyes!" He shook his head. "We were like the believers in Acts who were praying for Peter to be released from prison. When the servant girl told them he was standing at the door, they thought she was insane!"

Anna smiled. "Neither did it occur to us that God might be answering our prayers. Of course, we expected in the satchel a few Bibles. Certainly not a uniform of a border guard, folded neatly!"

Joshua broke in, "Left there on our walk . . ."

" . . . in a size to fit you—complete with official identification. We cannot forget that."

His eyes grew more intense. He took a deep breath. "Instantly, I knew what such a miracle must mean. God had no intention of bringing Bibles to us. I would have to go get them myself in that very uniform."

"I was so frightened for your safety, but bless the Lord, you lived to tell about it!"

"That one morning, however, I did not think I would."

"Oh, tell me the story again, dear one . . . I have not heard it for so long."

Joshua looked up, his eyes half-closed. "The border guard looked at my papers, then back at me. It seemed as if he started to smile, but quickly began to scowl and ordered me to follow him. 'Bring your satchel with you,' he snarled. My heart beat so hard, Anna, I feared it would leap out of my chest. The bag was filled to bursting with Bibles! They have detected me, I thought. I will be executed. At that moment, you came to mind. As I walked beside the guard, I prayed that someone would take care of you. I knew that you had not yet overcome the sorrow of Anja's death. Surely, you could not bear any more . . ."

"Even then, you were thinking of me?"

"Of course, my love." He looked at her. "If flowers were thoughts of you, I would have plenty enough to live forever in a beautiful garden."

Misty-eyed, she patted his cheek and added, "You are romantic beyond words. Oh, please continue."

He took a breath. "The guard escorted me about ten meters from Checkpoint Charlie. He turned his back to the crowd and announced loud enough for those standing nearby to hear, 'Produce your papers at once. I must verify their legitimacy.'

"My heart pounded harder. My mouth became dry as a desert. He took one step toward me, then another. In a low monotone, he said, 'Do nothing to arouse suspicion. I am also a believer. It was I who placed the uniform into your care.'

"I wanted to throw my arms around him in a display of Christian love! But I remembered his careful instructions: 'Do nothing to arouse suspicion.' I restrained myself. He made a good show of examining my papers, then gave a quick nod of his head and waved me through. As I left, he whispered, 'My brother in Christ, may our Lord and His holy angels go before you!'"

Anna clapped her hand over her heart. "Oh, Joshua, God showed us His sovereignty, did He not?"

"No doubt! It floods me with joy to think about it."

"Well, then, if He is all-powerful and sovereign . . . can He not do a miracle for us again?"

"Of course, He can. But, my love, this time I am not asking Him to do something which I feel certain He wants done."

"Whatever do you mean?"

"Giving His Word to hungry souls has been his desire since time began! Every beat of His heart cries out to the lost and weary and desperate, '*Come unto Me.*' My request now is far more selfish. And you know how I despise selfish prayers."

"I do. Many people confess Christ for personal gain. Seldom do I see you as distressed. But I am not convinced that your wish to find your father fits into the category of 'selfish.' How could the Lord possibly not want you united with your own flesh and blood? God calls Himself a Father! Would that not delight His paternal heart?"

He smiled, studied his weathered hands and nodded. "I suppose it would."

"So then, shall we dare to pray again for guidance?"

Joshua clasped Anna's hand and bowed his head. "Father, I thank You for my beloved wife. Just when I felt so discouraged, she reminded me of a mighty answer to prayer. I know my present request cannot compare in importance . . . but Lord, I would so love to see my father at last. We have no idea how to do that. Your Word says You give wisdom to all who ask. Would You show us

how to find him? Let us be sensitive to help those we meet along the way. Thank You for Your bountiful grace that sustains us each day. No matter what happens, Lord—if we never find him—we love You. And we know You love us. In Jesus' name, Amen."

He stood up and sighed, then stretched his arms over his head. "Shall we take a walk? We need to get these old bodies moving before they start to creak."

"Yes, it looks beautiful outside."

They each gathered a few personal belongings and headed for the street, stopping only for a newspaper at the reception desk. At a brisk pace, and hand in hand, they walked down Fifth Avenue. A well-stocked bookstore window caught their attention, but they simply studied the titles and moved on. Considering their fondness for anything that resembled a book, passing by without a purchase took more than a small measure of self-control.

They were both quiet for several minutes as they strolled along until Joshua declared, "Anna, I have an impetuous notion to find a library. For ne'er a penny, we can browse to our heart's content."

"A very worthwhile idea, indeed. Where you lead, I will follow, so be sure you know where you are going."

They stopped at a sidewalk café for coffee and decided to ask the waiter for directions to the library. To their surprise, he turned out to be a student at New York University and knew just how to get to there on foot. "Thank you kindly, sir," Joshua said and shook his hand. "You have been most helpful." The young man gave a curt nod and disappeared into the café crowd.

They resumed their pace—quick for Anna's petite frame—to Fifth Avenue and Forty-Second Street. She didn't mind, she said. She loved walking hand-in-hand with him. They stopped short at the first sight of the massive columns and regal lion sculptures. They read the engraved inscription, "New York Public Library."

"Anna, look! Two whole city blocks filled with books!" Joshua whistled like a young boy in a toy store, and, as fast as his senior frame would go, he mounted the steps to the entrance. Anna smiled. Little in life delighted her husband as much as reading. He had been that way since long before she met him. To see him now so happy made her sigh with contentment.

He waited for her at the landing for a couple of seconds, then descended the steps to escort her to the top. "Anna, do you remember Helen Keller, the woman who was born deaf, dumb and blind?"

"And a teacher went to live with her family?"

"Yes. Until then, she was like a wild animal. Due to Miss Annie Sullivan's devotion, Helen went down in history as a great author and speaker. I will never forget what she said about the treasures that reside within walls such as the ones we behold at this moment." He reached out and patted the cool stone. 'Truly,' she said, 'Each book is as a ship that bears us away from the fixity of our limitations into the movement and splendor of life's infinite ocean.'"

"Joshua, how lovely! How could you ever acquire such information, much less remember it?"

"A British teacher granted me access to his private book collection when I was an adolescent. He encouraged me to read and commit to memory whatever inspired me. So, I did!"

"Yes, you must have told me that before."

"I am certain I did. Of course, I have since learned to be more careful which books I choose. Some, though entertaining, may take us further from God instead of closer." He gave her cheek a playful squeeze.

They entered the grand lobby, climbed to the second floor and strolled around the row after row of shelves. They leafed through

magazines and newspapers. With great care, they picked up dozens of books that caught their eye. The Reader's Digest Book of Facts intrigued Joshua. After scanning a few different selections under "Science and Technology," he paused to read on the "Arts" page. When he lifted his eyes, he noted, "I have forgotten so much. Listen to this. The Bible was the first work completed on Johann Gutenburg's printing press in 1455! Was our God not ingenious to make sure of that? Imagine, Anna. It does not say so here, but until that time, scribes hand-copied every manuscript."

"Think of it!" she exclaimed. "An invention by a German changed the course of history."

"Yes. And best of all, it made the precious Word affordable to the masses." He waved a dramatic hand back and forth. "God certainly had a plan. But hear this, love. Old Gutenberg's Bible left him bankrupt, unable to pay back the money he had borrowed for the press. He died penniless and forgotten."

Anna's brows furrowed. "After such a grand contribution . . . Oh, Joshua, how sad!"

"From our perspective, yes. From heaven's perspective, he died a wealthy man. And listen to this bit of irony. An original copy of his Bible—there are less than fifty still around—is worth over a million dollars! Is that not remarkable?"

"It is. But even a million dollars cannot equal its value. Surely, no book compares."

"None, my dear. Not in beauty, longevity, or power."

"Of course, we must consider the Author!"

Suddenly, Joshua turned his head slightly to the right and froze for several seconds. "Anna, perhaps right here we could learn how to look for my father."

"A wonderful idea. And why not? There must be more information in this building than anywhere in the world."

"Except the Library of Congress in Washington, D.C. I believe that is the most complete collection, but I could be wrong. What did it say on the fact sheet about this library—millions of items?"

She unfolded the paper in her hand. "Thirty-eight million in the research libraries. And almost twelve million of those are books! That does not include what they call 'branch libraries.'"

"Goodness. We had better ask an assistant where to start." He gently guided Anna to the nearest information desk.

A middle-aged woman peered at them over her reading glasses. "May I help you?" she offered.

Joshua cleared his throat. "Madam, yes, you may. We have recently arrived from East Berlin and would like to locate my father." He steadied his voice. "I have never met him. Could you tell us how to proceed with such an endeavor?"

She frowned. "You have never seen your father?"

"No, ma'am. He and my mother separated before I was born. I learned only a short while ago that he was living in America."

"Do you know his name?"

"Yes I do—Caleb Johannsen."

"How about the city and state where he lives? Or his social security number?"

"A man in Germany gave me an address, but it must be either outdated or incorrect. The party there now had never heard of Caleb Johannsen. His security number I do not know."

The woman smiled at his abbreviated reference to the social security number and took off her glasses, letting them hang by the decorative cord around her neck. "You have taken on a monumental task." She raised her eyebrows and took a deep breath. "Well, the first place I would check is the list of associations for missing persons. They help people do exactly what you need. As a matter of fact, one of them is based here in the city."

"Can it be true?" His light blue eyes brightened at the thought. He glanced at Anna, who smiled at him.

"I'm sure they charge a fee—how much I don't know—but they might be able to help you. Would you like me to show you where you can find that information?"

"Oh, yes, we would appreciate that very much." She led the way to the reference area, pulled out the directory of associations, and opened to the section on missing persons. She pointed out a listing with her finger. "Here's the one in New York. If you would like to call, the pay phones are located by the bookstore."

"Thank you very much, ma'am. We will do that without delay."

Joshua slowly hung up the phone. He had lost six quarters trying to get through to the Missing Person's Network. The answering service operator would place him on "hold," and by the time she returned, he had been cut off. "Anna, I simply cannot reach these people." He sounded weary and a bit frustrated. "Perhaps the Lord has delayed this for a reason."

Anna rubbed his arm and gave it a pat. "Shall we try again later? Maybe we could walk around the block to get a fresh start."

"That sounds wonderful."

They were just getting ready to go down the stairs when they saw the information specialist hurrying over to them. They looked at one another, then waited for her. "Folks, I spoke to a reference librarian about your search for your father. We have another option you could try." She waited for a response.

"Oh, that would most welcome!" Joshua exclaimed. "I have made no progress with the number in the directory. An answering service disconnects me repeatedly."

"I know how annoying that can be at a pay phone. Listen. You will need to go across Fifth Avenue to the branch library where they store the CD-ROM programs. Someone will help you search for him there."

"What is that, DC-Ron?"

She suppressed a smile and enunciated, "CD-ROM is a special drive on the computer that reads CDs. They have a much larger storage capacity than regular disks."

"I see . . ."

"The particular program I mentioned contains the phone number of every person in the country. Those who have phones, of course."

"Of course," Joshua replied without thinking. "I suppose, as most Americans, my father would have one . . ." He glanced at Anna, who squeezed his hand. The realization hit him that he could be minutes away from fulfilling his dream. What if the answer turned out to be as simple as punching a few buttons and waiting for his voice to come on the line? What would he say? He had no idea. His heart beat faster at the thought.

They quickly expressed their thanks for her helpfulness and made their way across the busy avenue to the building she had mentioned. After a brief explanation of their assignment and a few questions, they soon found themselves in the proper department. All the computers were in use. They tried to occupy themselves with looking around. Every few minutes, they checked in with the clerk at the information desk. At last, she said, "Yes, sir, I see one available."

She led the way to the computer and waited for him to sit down.

He looked at Anna. Smiling, she raised her eyebrows at him.

"Sir, would you like me to help you?" the woman asked.

"Oh . . . yes, ma'am. I was just trying to adjust myself to the new possibilities."

"I understand." She sat down in front of the screen. Her fingers punched several keys until a prompt asked her a question she couldn't answer. "How do you spell your father's name—last name first?"

"I believe it is J-o-h-a-n-n-s-e-n."

She typed very fast. "First name?"

"Caleb. C-a-l-e-b."

"Middle name or initial?"

"Regrettably, I do not know. Will that hinder our search?"

"Not if there are not too many with the same first and last name." She tapped away at the keyboard and after what seemed like no time at all, an entry appeared on the screen. Joshua's eyes widened. Anna gasped. "This I cannot believe," he exclaimed. There he is. Caleb Johannsen!"

"It certainly looks that way. And only one," she replied. "Is this number different from the one you tried before?"

"Oh, yes," Joshua replied. "All the numerals." He and Anna stood, dumfounded, staring at the screen.

Several seconds passed. They didn't move a muscle. The woman asked, "Would you care to make note of the information?" She handed Joshua a piece of scratch paper. Anna fumbled in her small purse for a pen and gave it to him. His hands trembled as he wrote.

"Ma'am, we cannot thank you enough. This means so much to us."

"That's why we're here." She pressed a few more keys, then stood. "I wish you the best in your search."

Anna smiled. Joshua extended his hand. "Thank you. If we do reach him, we will notify you."

"That would be nice. For now, I'd better get back to my other projects."

"Yes, ma'am. Good day." Joshua bowed a little at the waist. Anna smiled and said, "Thank you."

They watched her walk away, then looked at each other.

Anna patted his cheek. "How are you feeling?"

He squeezed her hand and sighed, gazing out the window. "I cannot say for certain. I have this longing, this pulling deep inside me. I have hope. And many fears, too." He turned again toward her. "It is presumable that my father never heard about a son. If he did, maybe he is too old to remember. Or perhaps—he died long ago." His words dropped with a thud.

Anna pursed her lips, then raised her shoulders. "My love, we do not know. We can only trust."

He leaned over and brushed his lips in a tender kiss across her forehead. "'Tis the last great unanswered question in my life."

Anna pressed her head against his chest. She patted his hand. Her every gesture exuded tender compassion.

"Frederick, the man who told me about him, said he knew my mother from the time she was a little girl. He believes Caleb never realized he fathered a child. They were both quite young. He simply remembers a brief visitor, not too tall, slender, but handsome, with astonishing light blue eyes . . ."

"Like yours."

"He did mention that. He saw them together, but only for a short while. About a year later, Caleb returned, asking about her. Nobody in the town would tell him her whereabouts. They blamed him."

"Why?"

"She almost died in childbirth and then, of a broken heart. She was very sad to give me up when I was born, but she knew she could never care for me. She cried and asked him to tell no one."

"She must have felt deep shame to make such a request."

187

"Oh, yes, and I wish she had not." He stared at the ceiling. "If I find him, what shall I say? 'I am your son, the reason you could not find your sweetheart.'" His voice cracked.

Anna's fingers tightened on his hands. She looked into his eyes. They were veiled, as if clouded somehow by his intense struggle to peer into the specter of a lost past.

"What will he say to me, Anna? I fear to know the answer; yet, something still compels me forward." He brushed a tear from his eye. "If he did know he was a father, do you suppose he has longed to meet me?"

Anna pursed her lips, then nodded emphatically. "My dear Joshua, of one thing I feel certain." She waited.

"And what is that?"

"When your father meets you, he will adore you as much as I. If he does not, he will be the one with loose screws!"

Joshua laughed. "How kind you are, my love. But you are prejudiced, I fear."

"Not so. Everyone thinks you are a wonderful man of God." She planted an affectionate kiss on the end of his nose.

"Ah, my Savior and I are well acquainted with the real Joshua inside. But I do love Him with all my heart. I pray that makes up for my many deficiencies."

"Where are all these 'deficiencies?' I do not see so many."

"You do, but you overlook them. You simply focus on my good points. If you did not, you would be a woman most miserable, I assure you."

"And likewise, you would be a malcontent of the first order. Thank you for cherishing me over the years, in spite of myself."

"The pleasure has been all mine." He pinched her chin in a playful gesture. "We could chat the day away and enjoy every minute, but I had better not procrastinate any longer." He paused.

"Truthfully, Anna . . . I feel like a coward admitting this . . . it would be easier to just continue to hope for the best rather than to discover the worst."

She nodded and whispered, "I understand."

He led the way to the pay phone, dug deep into his pockets, and pulled out a large handful of coins. Placing them on the shelf, he punched in the number. A computerized operator came on, instructing him how much to deposit for three minutes. He used up more than half of the money he had set aside. They listened to the coins clatter as they dropped inside the phone. At last, it was ringing. Once . . . twice . . . three times . . . four times.

An answering machine came on with a female voice—something about being sorry they were unavailable to take the call. Before she had finished two sentences, Joshua hung up, then grimaced when he realized he'd lost all the money he had deposited. "That was a recording of a woman." He rechecked the number he had written down, then dialed again and dropped in the coins, plus a few extra from his other pocket.

The same recorded voice came on. He frowned and shook his head. The woman did not give her name. How could he know whom he had reached? He decided to take a chance. "Hello, madam. My name is Joshua Lieben. My wife, Anna, and I are trying to locate my father. According to our understanding, he lives here in the States."

He paused for a couple seconds as he took a breath and tried to think of what to say next. "Caleb is his name." A soft click on the line went unnoticed. "Caleb Johannsen. We are staying at a hotel in the City of New York, if you would be so kind as to return our call—at your convenience. We will reimburse you for any expenses you incur, as we would so much like to hear whether you have any information about my father." He gave the hotel's phone

number and their extension, then added a cheery, "We do appreciate your time, madam. May the Lord bless you and your family. Good day." He gently placed the receiver back in the cradle.

Anna patted his back. "That was a fine message."

"Thank you, my love." The right side of his mouth turned up in a faint smile.

She shook her head. "I would surely have stumbled over my words and embarrassed both of us."

"Not so. I think you handle yourself quite well."

"I manage, yes, but not on the telephone with strangers. The person on the recording, what was her name?"

"I have not the slightest clue. She merely repeated the number I had dialed."

"Why, I wonder?"

He shrugged and shook his head. "Perhaps for safety reasons."

"That makes good sense. But what shall we do now?"

"We can only go about our business . . . and *wait*."

❧ *Thirteen* ❧

astor Chip Hendry and the church's youth group drama troupe met Saturday afternoon at 5:00 o'clock for a last-minute run-through of the skits they were going to perform that night. Chip, Sandy and a few of the guys had already made one trip to Peace Convalescent Home in the morning to set up the portable staging, sound, and lighting equipment in the recreation room. With everybody working hard, they managed to finish in just five hours.

Everything was on schedule. The junior actors all said their lines without prompting, eliciting profuse praise from Pastor Chip. They, in turn, tried to act nonchalant about his comments, but couldn't hide their satisfaction—or their pre-performance jitters—from him. Talking nervously among themselves, they made their way outside to get ready to leave.

At the last minute, Sandy remembered he wanted to ask Pastor something. He dashed back inside. Chip was closing his office door behind him. "Pastor," Sandy asked, "okay if I take some flyers 'bout Michelle? Maybe I can put some up. And could we announce it at the end?"

191

Chip patted him on the shoulder as they made their way toward the parking lot. "Great idea. Always thinking about ways to help her, aren't you?"

"Well, I was jes' thinkin' that lotsa people work there 'n stuff. An' since we're goin' anyway . . ."

"I agree. We need kids like you to keep us on our toes." He grinned and tweaked Sandy's chin. "She's special to you, huh?"

He blushed. "Well, yeah, she's my frien'. He'ped me with my readin' 'n stuff. I haven't been doin' as good in school since she's been gone." A frown crossed his face. "Hope I don' flunk."

Chip empathized with his concern, then gave him a gentle mock punch in the arm. "Hey, big guy, God can help you. Have you asked Him?"

He shrugged, then nodded.

"Good. You just keep on. He'll help you overcome that learning disability. He will."

"Think so?"

"I know so. He created you. In fact, as weird as this sounds, you might even try thanking Him for it."

"You kiddin'?"

"Not at all. Remember, His strength is perfected in our weakness. He loves to use those very things about ourselves we look down on so the world will look up to Him. He wants to demonstrate who He is and what He can do when we give Him a chance."

Sandy scratched his head. "If you say so." He grabbed the roll of tape and a few flyers, then pulled on Chip's arm. "Come on, boss. Don't wanna be late for the big performance."

"Right. Can't have that." He turned out the lights and locked the outside door, then herded the kids into the bus. They chattered and laughed on the way to the center, even sang a couple of songs.

Fifteen minutes later, they pulled into the parking lot. The young actors piled into the bathrooms to change into their costumes. Sandy did double-duty as a stagehand and audio assistant, so he, along with a buddy and Pastor Chip, got busy making final adjustments to the set, props, and sound wiring. When Mrs. Oliver, the Activities Director, came in and introduced herself to the Pastor, Sandy stood at his side. Chip introduced him in turn and mentioned to her that he had a special request.

Sandy licked his lips. He shifted from one foot to the other, then showed her the "Missing Child" flyer with the picture on it. "Most everybody in our youth group knows Michelle," he stated in the most proper-sounding manner he knew. "Do you think maybe we could put up a flyer here?"

Mrs. Oliver took the paper in her hand and studied it carefully, shaking her head. "What a shame!" She looked into Sandy's eyes. "I'll do better than that. I'll get permission from the administrator to make copies and post them around the buildings. Families and friends come here from out of town to visit loved ones. Even from out of state. You never know who might see it."

Sandy grinned broadly. The idea of informing visitors from far away hadn't occurred to him. "Thank you, ma'am!"

She nodded, and added in a serious tone, "A missing child deserves every bit of help we can give. In fact, you may announce it tonight if you want to." Sandy looked visibly relieved. She shook his hand and Pastor Chip's, then excused herself to check on the refreshments.

Sandy noticed the first guest, a man dressed in blue jeans, cowboy boots and a red plaid shirt, guiding himself into the room in a wheelchair. A slightly heavy-set woman followed close behind him. Sandy went up with Chip to welcome them and to introduce themselves.

"Pleased to meet you. My name's Hank," the man replied and smiled. "This here's my wife, Dot. We sure appreciate you guys coming out tonight."

"Our pleasure." Chip extended his hand in a hearty greeting.

"We just happened to be here late," Hank added, "so we thought we'd stay on for the program. Gettin' physical therapy on my leg and shoulder." He rubbed his left knee. "I'm fortunate enough to come on an out-patient basis. A lot of folks have been here awhile and they get so depressed. No visits . . . not getting better fast enough . . . money problems, you name it. They have plenty that brings 'em down in the dumps."

Chip nodded. "I can imagine. That's why we're here—to share the love of Jesus."

Hank cupped his hands together. "Great! We're Christians, too. Haven't been able to get to church as often since my accident. I sure miss it." He looked up at his wife. "But she's been readin' the Bible to me, and we can still pray together. Done that for a long time, so we can't stop now. Can we, Sugar?" She leaned down to plant a kiss on the top of his head. With her right hand, she smoothed his thick brown hair, now in need of a haircut.

Sandy blushed and shifted from one foot to the other. He had not been around many married couples. Definitely not any who showed affection in front of strangers. He decided he'd better change the subject. He stammered, "Ya know, I like to pray, too. An' I'm workin' on bein' able to read better. I think I wanna be a missionary someday."

"Wonderful, son!" Hank exclaimed. "I'm a missionary myself."

Sandy's eyebrows popped up. "You *are?* Where?"

"Take a guess."

"Africa? Naw, that's not right. India?"

"Nope. You're real cold."

194

"Real cold . . ." He stopped to think. "Mexico?"

"Gettin' warmer. Much warmer."

"Hmmm . . . Brazil?"

"Gettin' colder."

"I give up. Tell me."

"America!"

"America? I thought missionaries get to go far away, like to another country 'n stuff."

"Many of them do. But not all. You know, son, one time I read a big sign as I was leaving a church parking lot. That sign set me to thinkin'. It said, *'You are now entering the mission field.'* Ever since then, I've considered m'self a missionary."

"So ya don' hafta work at a regular job?"

Hank laughed. "Of course I work. Been takin' it easy since the accident, but I'll be back in the saddle soon. My wife and I own an eighteen-wheeler."

"A semi!"

"Yep. Dot has her Class A CDL just like I do."

"I never heard of a CDL."

"Sorry. Commercial Drivers License. Together we've covered 49 states—all except Hawaii. We tell people about Jesus everywhere we go. Dot goes about it a little different, but we both figure our life is the only Bible some people ever read."

"Gee, that's a real neat sayin'," Sandy replied. He paused and frowned. "But kinda scary, too."

"Scary?"

"Well, yeah. The Bible makes folks wanna know Jesus. What if they meet me and decide they don' *wanna* know Him?"

"You needn't worry about that. Just keep on lovin' Him and spendin' time in His Word."

"I do, much as I can."

"Good man. Keep it up." Hank gave a quick nod of his head and extended his hand. "Guess I better let you go get ready. Great talkin' to you."

"I sure liked it, too." Sandy glanced around and noticed that a number of other patients and guests had wandered into the room. "Yeah, looks like we're almost ready to start." He walked around, shaking a few hands, on his way to the backstage area.

The members of the drama troupe were waiting, in costume, out in the hallway. Chip motioned to Sandy to move into position, then walked over to the microphone to give a welcome. "Hi, everyone. I'm Pastor Chip Hendry, youth minister at Crestville Christian Center. With me tonight is a fantastic group of teens. Together, they wrote and produced what you're about to see. We're so happy to have you as our audience tonight and we hope you enjoy our presentation." He paused.

"Almost all of you, at some time in your lives, have probably asked God for something. That means you have prayed. Have you ever felt that God doesn't hear your prayers? Or if He does, that He never bothers to answer? You're not alone. We've all felt spiritually 'let down.' The kids would like to present to you a series of short skits that demonstrate important prerequisites for answered prayer. See if you can figure out what they are. We'll talk about them later. Now, on with the show!"

Chip moved to the back of the room to the sound and light board. Sandy took his place against the wall backstage for quick access to the set. The first two actors stepped to center stage.

A girl offstage, as narrator, spoke first. "Would you step back in time with us—back to the age when Jesus still walked the earth? One day, the disciple Peter approached Him with an important question. It was obvious that Peter had something on his mind. In response, Jesus told him a story—a parable—recorded for us in the

196

eighteenth chapter of Matthew. We have transformed the story Jesus told into a conversation, as it might have occurred. First, His encounter with Peter."

Chip brought up the spotlight, stage left, on two bearded men in the middle of a marketplace scene. The one playing Peter was wearing a tan robe with a multi-colored tie at the waist, the other, Jesus, had on a white robe with a burgundy cloth draped from his left shoulder over to his right side. Both were wearing brown leather sandals.

Peter slapped his hands against his thighs and exclaimed, "Lord, how often shall my brother sin against me and I forgive him? Up to seven times?"

The white-robed figure shook His head. In a clear, calm voice, he said, "I do not say to you, up to seven times, but up to *seventy times seven*. For this reason the kingdom of heaven may be compared to a certain king who wished to settle accounts with his slaves." The actor playing Jesus made a wide gesture with his hand. The spotlight followed Him and gradually faded.

At the same time, another spot picked up at center stage and highlighted the inside of a palace. There, a king dressed in a purple royal robe, with a crown on his head and a scepter in his hand, sat on his throne. Guards dragged in a barefoot man dressed in tattered, dirty clothes. The man was trembling.

"What do you have to say for yourself?" asked the king.

"Your Honor," replied the slave, "I-I know I owe you a whole lot of money."

"Yes, you do. According to official records, you owe me an utter fortune. Bring me the books, Horace." With a dramatic flair, the royal assistant picked up a huge book, opened it to the correct page and set it on the king's lap. The king examined the figures with care. "Oh, my. Ten thousand talents!" He peered down at the

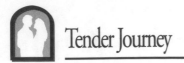
slave. "You owe so much to the royal treasury of this delightful land that, at your current wages, it will take you, let me see—"

"I knew it was quite a bit, your Honor."

"An understatement, sir. Do you know what I, the king, must do to those who cannot pay their debts? The punishment is written in the royal laws."

"N-no, your honor, I don't know."

"Quite serious. You leave me no choice. I must sell you to cover the debt. You, your wife and children, and every item in your household."

The slave fell to his knees before the king. He wept aloud. "Oh, please, no, your Honor. Have patience with me. If you give me more time, I will repay every penny to you!"

"Rise to your feet. I am a kind man at heart and you have stirred my compassion. You could not repay this debt if you were to live forever." He spread out his fingers in the air. "I release you from it. You need not be burdened anymore."

The slave nodded, bowed and quickly backed away. "Thanks. I think I should be going, your Honor." He slinked off the stage.

The lights dimmed long enough for new actors to tiptoe on. Chip raised the lights, this time on a marketplace setting, stage right, where the same slave swaggered up to another man dressed more shabbily than himself. "Have you forgotten something?" the forgiven one growled, grabbing the other fellow by the throat.

"W-what?" He started to tremble.

"You have a short memory. You owe me a hundred denarii."

"I know, sir. I-I've been trying, but—

"I don't want to hear it. Pay up, and *fast.*" He put his nose right up to the man's nose, glared at him, then shook him.

The other slave fell down before him and begged, "Please have patience with me. I promise I will repay you."

"Not a chance. I've waited too long already." He steepled his fingers and whistled. "Guards! Come and bind up this bum. Throw him in prison. He's worthless." They dragged the man off.

The other slaves stood by, watching and weeping, at their friend's plight. They pointed at the mean slave, shook their heads, and whispered among themselves as the lights dimmed.

When the lights went up, the king was back sitting on his throne, surrounded by a very animated group of slaves. They had been granted permission to speak to the king, and were all talking at once. Finally, their leader quieted them down. "Your Highness," he said, "do you remember the slave who owed you so much money?"

"Oh, yes. I remember him well—the one for whom I cancelled the debt."

"That's the guy. We're very upset with him. He went right out and had one of our buddies thrown in prison for owing him only a hundred denarii."

"He did *what?!*" The king called his guards. "Go find that scoundrel and bring him here immediately."

They dragged him in, fighting and shouting, "Let me go! I didn't do anything wrong!"

The king bellowed, "Quiet, you wicked slave!"

Silence.

"I forgave you that huge debt because I have a kind heart. Certainly not because you deserved it. How dare you refuse to show the same mercy to your fellow man!"

"B-but your Honor . . ."

"No excuses. I am furious with you." He turned to his guards. "Take him to the tormentors until the debt is repaid in full."

The spotlight picked up on the white-robed Jesus, who stretched out his arms across the room, *"As it is written, 'So shall*

Tender Journey

My heavenly Father also do to you, if each of you does not forgive his brother from your heart."

Chip dimmed the lights and brought up some worship music. The actors filed out while Sandy and Adam replaced the set on one side with a backdrop that looked like the outskirts of a Hebrew village surrounded by hilly countryside. Without making a sound, ten actors positioned themselves on one side of the stage and froze. One lone figure in white stood at a distance from them. Music faded out as the lights came up on perfect cue.

The ten, dressed in very ragged clothing and leaning on crutches made of tree branches, pretended to hobble along the road. Their skin looked surprisingly realistic, full of white leprous ulcers and scabs. The kids had wrapped rags around their extremities—some on their hands, some on a foot—and bound the rags with rope.

Reaching for Jesus, they called out, "Master, have pity on us!"

The figure in the white robe turned toward them and said simply, "Go show yourselves to the priests." They walked away, as if toward the city.

Suddenly, one of the lepers in the group ran back to Jesus. He was leaping and shouting, "Praise be to God, I'm healed! The leprosy is *gone!*" He fell down at Jesus' feet and cried, "Oh, thank You, thank You, my Lord!"

A white-robed arm extended slowly and deliberately toward the place where his friends had exited. "Were not all ten cleansed? Where are the other nine?" Jesus' arm lowered. His hands reached out to the man in front of him as he spoke. "Was no one found to return and give praise to God except this foreigner? Rise and go; your faith has made you well."

Chip dimmed the lights and put on soft worship music while the cast filed out. A hush settled over the audience. The next group of actors stood waiting, in costume, just outside the door for the third skit. Sandy and Adam removed the props and set up what looked to be the front of an old house with a small wooden door above the main door. Then they tiptoed off the stage.

The narrator's clear voice came through the speakers, "One of Jesus' disciples approached Him with a critical request—'Lord, teach us to pray.' Jesus responded by giving him some of the most famous words in the entire Bible,

> *Our Father, who art in heaven, hallowed be thy name. Thy kingdom come. Thy will be done, in earth, as it is in heaven. Give us this day our daily bread. And forgive us our trespasses as we forgive those who have trespassed against us. And lead us not into temptation; but deliver us from evil . . .*

"Immediately after Jesus taught what has become known the world over as 'The Lord's Prayer,' He told a parable. You may not know this story as well, so we will dramatize it for you now."

Once the new cast of three had taken their places, up came the spotlight on a pudgy male figure dressed in pajamas and holding an old-fashioned lantern. He was knocking hard and then placing his ear to the wood.

Finally, a man in a stocking cap opened the little trap door from the inside. In a grouchy voice, he called, "Who's out there?"

"It's me—your friend."

"Do you realize what time it is?"

"I know it's midnight. But I really need three loaves of bread."

"What! You woke me up at this hour for bread?"

The neighbor rubbed his forehead. "It sounds strange, I know, but a friend of mine dropped in on me. He's hungry and I don't have a thing to feed him."

"Quit bothering me! The door is locked up for the night and everybody is asleep."

The actor playing Jesus walked into the spotlight. Again, with a sweeping motion of his white-robed arm, he proclaimed,

"I tell you, though he will not get up and give him the bread because he is his friend, yet because of the man's boldness he will get up and give him as much as he needs. So I say to you: Ask and it will be given to you; seek and you will find; knock and the door will be opened to you. For everyone who asks receives; he who seeks finds; and to him who knocks, the door will be opened. Which of you fathers, if your son asks for a fish, will give him a snake instead? Or if he asks for an egg, will give him a scorpion? If you then, though you are evil, know how to give good gifts to your children, how much more will your Father in heaven give the Holy Spirit to those who ask him?"

Chip once again dimmed the lights and brought up the worship music. The actors filed out while Sandy and Adam stepped forward in the dim light and replaced the set on one side with a backdrop that looked like the outskirts of a village surrounded by hilly countryside. At the far side of the stage, they placed the semblance of a cave with a large stone in front of the opening. The lights came up and the music faded out on cue. The next team filed in amidst the shadows.

The narrator offstage began reading, "In the presence of His disciples, Jesus received word from two sisters named Mary and Martha that their brother, Lazarus, was sick. Jesus was close to that family; He loved them very much. He assured His disciples that Lazarus' illness would not end in death, but that it would provide an opportunity to reveal the glory of God. Immediately afterward, He told them what seemed to be a contradiction: Lazarus was not just sleeping. He had, indeed, died. Yet, Jesus purposely waited two days before starting the journey to Bethany. By the time He arrived, four days had passed. Our drama opens with one of the sisters, Martha, running out to meet Him. Try to imagine how Lazarus's family must have felt at that moment. What would *you* have said to Jesus?"

Chip raised the spotlight on the two characters. Martha cried out, "Lord, if you had been here, my brother would not have died!" She stopped and lowered her head. "But I know that even now God will give you whatever you ask."

"Your brother will rise again," Jesus replied.

"I know he will rise again in the resurrection on the last day."

"I am the resurrection and the life. He who believes in me will live, even though he dies; and whoever lives and believes in me will never die. Do you believe this?"

"Yes, Lord, I believe that you are the Christ, the Son of God, who was to come into the world." With that, Martha walked to the side of the stage, and called to her sister, "Mary, the Teacher is here and is asking for you."

Mary came running out to Him with a crowd of mourners following her. Crying, she fell on her knees before Him. "Lord, if you had been here, my brother would not have died."

Jesus' face took on a pained expression. He looked at Mary, the crowd and heaved a heavy sigh. "Where have you laid him?"

"Come and see, Lord."

Jesus groaned and cried.

Some onlookers exclaimed, "See how he loved him!"

Others murmured, "Couldn't He who opened the eyes of the blind man have kept this man from dying?"

They all followed Jesus over to the tomb and looked at each other in shock when He charged them, "Take away the stone."

This time Martha spoke up. "But Lord, by this time there is a bad odor, for he has been there four days."

"Did I not tell you that if you believed, you would see the glory of God?"

They did as they were told. Jesus looked up to heaven and said, "Father, I thank you that you have heard me. I know that you always hear me, but I said this for the benefit of the people standing here, that they may believe that you sent me." Then he called in a loud voice, "Lazarus, come out!"

Seconds passed. Several in the stage crowd covered their eyes. Others screamed. A few turned away. Finally, a mummy-like figure emerged, his hands and feet wrapped with strips of linen and a cloth around his face. In a triumphant voice, Jesus charged the people, "Take off the grave clothes and *let him go!*"

Immediately, Chip brought up the rousing strains of the "Hallelujah Chorus" and raised the lights. One by one, each of the teen players and technical assistants moved to the front of the stage. When they were all standing in a row, they held hands and took a brief bow.

The audience, composed of frail elderly folks and adults in various stages of recovery, clapped to the best of their ability. Some just nodded their heads. Few could stir up a whole lot of noise, but their broad smiles showed sincere appreciation. Hank ignored the reserved quietness of the group. He let out a quick whistle and exclaimed, "Bravo, kids! Way to go!" His wife patted him on the arm as if to say, "Easy, sweetheart, we're not at a ball game." He winked at her and clapped even more.

Pastor Chip made his way from the sound board to the front of the room. After adjusting his lapel mike and looking around, he asked with enthusiasm, "Didn't they do a great job? I'm so honored to be able to work with such a fine group of kids." He gave a few claps himself, then waited for the smattering of applause to subside. "Believe me, they spend a lot of time practicing and they enjoy it. Most importantly, they want to convey to you a powerful message of hope: *1) there is a God in heaven* and *2) He does answer prayer.*

"However, He has set up some prerequisites, some conditions we must meet for that to happen. Let's take a short break for refreshments and delve deeper when we come back."

Along the side wall of the room, Mrs. Oliver had set up a long table. It was covered now with several trays of hors d'oeuvres and a large glass bowl of sherbet-laden punch. She and her assistants had gone the extra mile to arrange beautiful decorations. Pastel peach paper tablecloths and napkins, with petite silk flower and ribbon arrangements in a peach, purple and green color scheme lent a festive appearance to the whole affair. The youth group members were urged to go first since they were guests of honor. This they did with no prompting. After patients and guests alike enjoyed their fill of treats, they settled into their places for the rest of the message. Pastor Chip stood at the podium, waiting.

"How many of you," he asked, "would like to know more about how to receive answers to your prayers?"

Most of the heads bobbed in affirmation. A number of hands went up.

"Good. Well, I mentioned earlier that God has ordained certain conditions for prayer. Do you think that's unfair of Him? Think back, those of you who have children. Chances are, even though you may have encouraged them to come to you with legitimate requests, you did not grant their every wish and whim. You, too, had conditions. For example, perhaps you made them do

their homework before they could go out and play, or finish certain chores to earn an allowance. If they asked for a car, maybe you insisted they get a part-time job. Maybe you decided to simply delay answering a request until they were older and more responsible, or until their attitude improved in a certain area. You may have even denied their request altogether because of some potential jeopardy to them. Why? Out of *love*.

"God—the all-powerful, all-wise Creator—does the same with us! Tonight's skits demonstrated several conditions for answered prayer. Let's look at each one again. The first is *forgiveness*. Mark eleven, twenty-five says, 'And when you stand praying, if you hold anything against anyone, forgive him, so that your Father in heaven may forgive you your sins.'" He stepped out from behind the podium and slipped his hands in his pockets.

"The story of the king and the servant with the large debt is our story. Each of us owes the King of Kings more than we could ever dream of repaying. We will never 'work off' this bill. We have one hope—that He release us. In turn, He commands that we forgive others. Whether their obligations are financial, physical, emotional or spiritual, they pale in comparison to what God has erased from our accounts.

"Now, I'm not saying that if we lend someone money in a business-like agreement, we should never expect it back. That's another matter, taking into consideration their personal means and ours. Nor am I saying that, if we have been the victim of a crime, the perpetrator should 'get off the hook' without consequence.

"I am talking about showing no mercy. I am talking about demanding, with relish, the highest possible penalty for offenses against us. And especially, I'm talking about holding onto bitterness toward those who have done us wrong. Biblical forgiveness does none of the above. In fact, it goes far beyond getting over a grudge. I believe it was Mark Twain who expressed the concept in a rather artistic way. He said, 'Forgiveness is the fragrance the violet sheds . . . on the heel that has crushed it.'"

Chip paused to take a drink of water and then continued, "Maybe some of you tonight ended up in a convalescent home due to the negligence, or worse yet, the maliciousness of another human being. If so, the truth we're dealing with probably hits a very tender spot in your heart. God understands your anguish. You know firsthand that some wrongs inflict life-altering trauma. In those cases, forgiveness seems to be a mockery of justice—at best, a sheer impossibility. Without God's help, it *is* impossible. But what happens if we refuse to forgive? According to the parable the kids dramatized, we're given over to a life of torment. So which is better? The choice is ours.

"Hebrews twelve, fifteen reminds us, *See to it that no one comes short of the grace of God; that no root of bitterness springing up causes trouble, and by it many be defiled.* And Ephesians four, thirty-one, *Let all bitterness and wrath and anger and clamor and slander be put away from you, along with all malice. Be kind to one another, tender-hearted, forgiving each other, just as God in Christ also has forgiven you.*

"Finally, since we've been looking at forgiveness as an important condition for answered prayer, consider Psalm sixty-six, sixteen through twenty. I'll read this one for you from the New International Version." He opened his Bible and held it up with his right hand.

Come and listen, all you who fear God; let me tell you what he has done for me. I cried out to him with my tongue. If I had cherished sin in my heart, the Lord would not have listened; but God has surely listened and heard my voice in

prayer. Praise be to God who has not rejected my prayer or withheld his love from me!

"A second condition for answered prayer stands out as the main theme in the story of ten lepers in Luke seventeen. It is *thankfulness.* Why then, if this trait is so important, would Jesus heal all ten anyway? Only one came back to thank Him. First, the lepers obeyed His command. They headed immediately for the city to 'show the priests' and, along the way, their leprosy disappeared. Another explanation for their healing may simply rest in God's mercy, which reaches to the heavens.

"However, let's not gloss over the fact that Jesus did bring up the issue when He asked, 'Was no one found to return and give praise to God except this foreigner?' He highlighted how much God values a thankful heart. You may have also noticed that the nine lepers were 'cleansed,' but Jesus told the thankful one he was made 'well', or 'whole.' That distinction could have meant a dramatic difference. We can't say for sure, but perhaps God restored fingers or toes the man had lost to the disease. At the very least, God filled his heart with great joy and peace.

"If Jesus so emphasized thankfulness, and we see that He did, can we assume the opposite—that a whiny, ungrateful attitude adversely affects the results of our prayer life? Of course it does. We human parents are no different. When our children get caught up in an unappreciative mode, we're much less likely to give them the special gift or privilege they've been wanting.

"One of my favorite Scriptures, Philippians four, six helps me keep in line in this department, *Do not be anxious about anything, but in everything, by prayer and petition, with thanksgiving, present your requests to God.* Instead of saving up all my appreciation for the annual holiday, I'm trying to practice day-by-day thanks-*living.*

"I heard a super message on this subject by pastor and author Dr. Charles Stanley. He based his sermon on First Thessalonians five, eighteen, *In everything give thanks, for this is God's will for you in Christ Jesus.* Ponder that concept—in *everything.* When we learn to thank God, no matter what, instead of trying to escape difficult situations, we not only grow through them, we please God. Dr. Stanley lists ten benefits of this approach to life." Chip fished a small notebook from his shirt pocket. "If I may, I'd like to share them with you." He began to read,

Thankfulness . . .

1) *Constantly reminds us that God is always with us. His Presence becomes more and more real to us.*

2) *Encourages us to search for God's purpose even in the midst of our pain.*

3) *Helps us submit our human will to God's divine will so we have a change of attitude.*

4) *Reminds us how helpless we are without God in every situation so that our weakness can become His strength.*

5) *Forms a stronger trust in God in our hearts while we're walking through the valley of dark circumstances.*

6) *Lends a key to finding joy—that means peace and contentment, not necessarily giddiness.*

7) *Makes a powerful impact on others when they see us triumphing over very difficult circumstances.*

8) *Directs our thoughts back to God instead of on ourselves or our situation*

9) *Gives us new spiritual energy, like getting our batteries recharged*

10) *Removes anxiety and replaces it with indescribable peace.*[7]

"Let's move on to another prerequisite for answered prayer—*boldness*—portrayed in the third parable the drama troupe performed. Remember the man asking his friend for bread at midnight? It took courage for him to go to a friend's house, knock on his door at a very impractical moment and ask for help. You notice that when the man had a genuine need, he didn't approach a total stranger. He probably believed his friend would meet it. I wonder if he was prepared for the gruff response he received. It must have felt like an ice-cold shower first thing in the morning.

"Guess what! God never gets grouchy or tells us to come back later. He neither slumbers nor sleeps, the Bible says. He knows all our needs and truly longs to meet them. He does so beyond our expectations—and occasion, without so much as a peep out of us. For some reason, however, He usually expects us to ask, seek and knock in persistent prayer.

"Does God need us to pray in order to get things done in His universe? Hardly. But we could say He allows us to participate. In the distant past, He established a 'law of prayer' and chooses to operate within that law. I suspect one reason He wants us to pray has to do with the benefits of a regular dose of humility. The medicine may taste bitter, but it does wonders for what ails us.

"Now, it's one thing to have the nerve to ask a friend for bread and quite another to ask the Eternal God for help. Yet, as the late F.B. Myer said, 'The great tragedy of life is not unanswered prayer, but unoffered prayer.' We've got to ask. God wants us to ask. How do we acquire that kind of boldness? To be sure, we don't strut into the court of heaven, throw our hands on our hips and start demanding, any more than we would barge into the Oval Office of the President of the United States with such a demeanor.

"First of all, no one gets into either place without proper I.D. Only then can we be granted permission to enter, much less, to state our case. Making requests of God—often called petition—isn't the only facet of prayer, of course, but it is an important one, and our focus tonight. In a moment, we'll look at gaining the right to petition God as we review the last skit.

"The kids re-enacted a real-life drama in which Jesus played a crucial part. You heard how Lazarus became ill and died. He and his sisters, Mary and Martha, were close friends of Jesus. Don't you suppose they prayed that he would get well? Of course they did. As did many others who loved Lazarus.

"They sent word to Jesus, 'Lord, the one you love is sick.' Mary and Martha believed with all their hearts that He could and would heal Lazarus. They both proclaimed their faith through their later plea, 'If You had been here, my brother would not have died.' Imagine how they must have felt when He didn't show up in time. They had seen Him heal so many others. Talk about disappointment! Little did they know He had an even bigger blessing in store for them.

"Martha moved beyond disillusionment. She stated the very foundation of her faith in clear terms, 'Yes, Lord, I believe that you are the Christ, the Son of God, who was to come into the world.' Folks, that solid foundation for answered prayer is the same today as it was two thousand years ago. Martha's faith was far from perfect—just perfectly placed—in Jesus Christ.

"Let me put it another way. If you were stranded out in the middle of a frozen lake, would you rather find yourself with a whole lot of faith on a thin piece of ice . . . or a little bit of faith on a thick piece of ice? I'd have to choose the latter. In essence, that's what we do when we place our trust in the Lord instead of ourselves. He's a rock-solid place to stand.

"He gives us not only the boldness we need to ask the Father for help, but the authority behind the boldness. Through His

211

painful death on the cross, He restored our right to fellowship with God. Ephesians chapter three, verse twelve, tells us, *In him and through faith in him we may approach God with freedom and confidence.* The author of Hebrews goes further when he declares in the tenth chapter, verses nineteen and parts of twenty through twenty-two (New American Standard Bible):

> *Since therefore, brethren, we have confidence to enter the holy place by the blood of Jesus, by a new and living way which He inaugurated for us . . . let us draw near with a sincere heart in full assurance of faith . . . let us hold fast the confession of our hope without wavering, for He who promised is faithful . . .*

"Mary and Martha believed Jesus was the long-awaited Savior, in spite of all appearances to the contrary. They grieved over Lazarus's death, but they didn't give Jesus the third-degree or question His motives for the delay. They surrendered to what He thought was best. They just couldn't comprehend Jesus' claims about Himself. Maybe that's why He cried out in exasperation.

"You see, His followers had a hard time understanding Him. What had He meant by, 'I am the resurrection and the life'? What relevance did His statement have to their friend? They didn't understand until their four-days-dead Lazarus stepped out of that tomb! In an instant, they saw the power . . . the glory . . . the radiance of God in action, as they had never seen it before. 'He who believes in me will live, even though he dies,' Jesus had reassured them. Without a doubt, He proved He was everything He said He was, and more.

"Folks, we can know the same Jesus Christ today. No, we can't see His physical body as they did two thousand years ago. But what does that matter? He said it was *better* that He go away, so

He could fill all believers with the very essence of Himself—His Holy Spirit. God loves to bestow that gift if we will only ask Him.

"In light of such truth, consider the following: whether or not He answers our prayers for healing or deliverance today takes on far less importance than where we will spend eternity. We don't ever have to die in the spiritual sense. I still believe He performs miracles; I have seen Him do so many times. But how can a relatively short-lived experience compare with incredible closeness with Him forever and ever, amen?

"Surely, we cannot always understand God. Isaiah fifty-five, eight and nine remind us,

> *For My thoughts are not your thoughts, Neither are your ways My ways," declares the Lord. For as the heavens are higher than the earth, So are My ways higher than your ways, And My thoughts than your thoughts (NASB).*

"Do you realize what that means? We don't *have* to understand Him! We can trust Him. We can 'give Him the benefit of the doubt,' so to speak. When tragedy strikes, when things don't make sense, when He doesn't seem to be listening, remember this: He is never early or late. He is never wrong. And He is never cruel. He loves us—each and every one of us—with an everlasting love. Nothing can separate us from that love.

"In summary, the kids' skits addressed four prerequisites for answered prayer: *forgiveness, thankfulness, boldness* and *faith in Jesus Christ*—the most important condition of all. Our list is far from complete, however. Ten reasons for *unanswered* prayer appeared in a newsletter from Bible teacher, Anne Graham Lotz. You may have heard of her father, the Reverend Billy Graham, who has preached the gospel to more people than anyone in history.

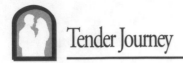
Reasons for Unanswered Prayer:
1. *Lack of expectant faith* (Matthew 21:22)
2. *Selfishness* (James 4:2-3)
3. *Unconfessed sin* (Psalm 66:18)
4. *Lack of compassion* (Proverbs 21:13)
5. *Lack of tranquility in marriage* (1 Peter 3:7)
6. *Pride* (Job 35:12-13)
7. *Lack of obedience* (1 John 3:22)
8. *Asking out of the will of God* (1 John 5:14)
9. *Lack of fellowship with other believers* (Matthew 18:19)
10. *Not praying in Jesus' name* (John 16:23)[8]

"In closing, I'd like to invite any of you who don't feel confident of your relationship with the Lord to talk with me. I'll be happy to answer your questions and to pray with you, if you wish. And remember—prayer needs more than proof. It needs practice. Thank you so much for having the kids and me over tonight. God bless you!"

Sandy watched Pastor Chip start to move away from the front of the room to mingle among the guests, and suddenly realized that he was closing the program. He hadn't had a chance to pass out the flyer about Michelle! He grabbed the stack of papers from a chair along the wall and stood ready to rush up front. He could see the opportunity passing as people moved toward the door. A few had gathered around Chip to ask questions.

Sandy's eyes narrowed. His breathing picked up its pace. How could Pastor Chip forget? He'd promised. Even that lady from the hospital had agreed! Now they would miss a great chance. He started to get upset. His shoulders slumped. He blinked, his eyes full of tears, and dropped the flyers back down on the chair. Under his breath, he whispered, "Lord, I don't wanna be a pest. Help!"

He felt a tap on his arm. He turned around to see the man in the wheelchair he'd met earlier, with his wife standing behind him.

Hank held out his hand. "Very good. All you guys did terrif—" He cut his sentence short. "Hey, what's up, pardner?" he asked, when he noticed Sandy's damp eyes.

Sandy's face reddened like it always did when he got embarrassed. His mouth flopped open and he stood, speechless, for several seconds until, "Oh, nothin'" crept out.

"Now, son, it's all right if a man feels touched in his heart. Jesus was many times."

"This is kinda stupid, though. I was jes' discouraged 'cuz we had permission t'pass out some papers, an' now it's too late."

Hank furrowed his eyebrows. "What could be so important?"

Sandy bent down, picked up a flyer and handed it to him. "This. She's my friend who's lost."

Hank studied the photo. He squinted, trying to read the print. "Dot, would you please get my glasses?" She pulled them from the pouch behind his wheelchair and handed them to him. He smiled. "Thanks, hon." Slowly, he digested the material, while Dot looked over his shoulder. "This little lady looks sorta familiar," he said, raising an eyebrow.

"She *does?*" Sandy's mouth popped open again.

"Can't place her for sure, but maybe before the accident . . ." He stopped. "The accident—Dot where were we before the accident?" He glanced up at his wife.

"I'd been sleeping," she replied, "and we just dropped off the— here, let me have a better look." She accepted the flyer from Hank and continued talking. "Remember, hon, we rescued a girl from some punk kids who were harassing her. She talked us into taking her as far north as we were going." She paused. "We notified the police after we dropped her off, but we've never heard a thing."

Hank squinted and rubbed his forehead. "Yeah, that's right. We wondered if she had told us the truth." He stared at the flyer again. "Name's Michelle, huh? Maybe I'm just dreaming . . . they tell me I had a pretty bad concussion. Lucky I have a brain left that works. But gosh, I could swear the girl who rode with us said her name was Michelle."

Dot nodded. "She did. She looked older, though." She rustled the flyer, "But this is her. I'm positive."

"Really?" Sandy's eyes widened. "This is too awesome. At the last minute, I bring flyers along. Jes' when I'm ready to give up, *you* come an' talk to me. Man, this is *unbelievable!"*

Hank held up his palm. "Whoa, boy, not so fast. We don't know anything definite at this point."

"I know, but it's still awesome."

By then, the other patients had returned to their rooms. The actors had wandered off to change clothes and remove stage make-up. Aside from Chip, who was starting to break down the sound equipment in the back of the activities center, they were alone. Sandy glanced in his direction. "Pastor Chip, please com'ere—*quick!"* His pressing tone brought Chip's eyes up and his legs moving toward the three of them.

"What?" he called, still hurrying. "Sir, are you okay?" Concern for the man in the wheelchair showed visibly on his face.

"Oh, he's fine," Sandy replied, "but listen to this! Hank and his wife here might've saw Michelle." He proceeded to relate the story without pausing for a breath.

Chip looked at Sandy and listened for a moment, then crossed his arms across his chest and put his head down to catch the rest. He raised his eyebrows and cocked his head. "Have to admit . . ."

Hank added, "I just remembered something else. The girl said she was goin' to New York."

With a nod, Dot said, "We dropped her off at the bus station in D.C. That was a few weeks ago now, though."

"Did she say why she was goin' there?"

"Said she had family." Dot looked down at Hank.

Sandy scratched his head. "Wait a minute. The Michelle I know, her fam'ly is here, right down the road from me."

Hank was quick to reply. "She could have made that part up, you know."

Sandy could barely stand still. "Well, what do we do next?"

"I guess they should contact the detective," Chip replied.

Hank nodded vigorously. "Yeah, that sounds good. We'll call from the first pay phone we see, instead of waitin' 'til we get home. The quicker, the better."

"Will ya call the church an' leave a message?" Sandy asked. His brows were furrowed.

"Of course," Dot reassured him. "We'll keep you posted."

"Thanks, guys." Chip offered his hand and his business card. Sandy nodded, then made a "way to go" circle with his thumb and index finger. They watched as Hank backed up the wheelchair, maneuvered a three-point turn, and headed out the door to his room. Dot had to walk fast beside him to keep up.

Sandy sighed. "Now I really won't be able t'sleep— wonderin'."

Chip squeezed his shoulder. "Gotta keep your strength up. It could be a long battle. Even if she is the one who rode with them, New York is a very big place."

Worry crossed Sandy's expectant face. He understood a lot more than he wished he did.

The church bus dropped Sandy and his bicycle off last. Chip insisted that he shouldn't ride on the country roads by himself at night. Once they were parked in front of the house, Sandy jumped

out and pulled his old bike out the back door with as much care as if it were an expensive racer. "Thanks for the ride, Pastor," he called.

"You're always welcome. You know that."

Sandy turned around and waved at Chip as he wheeled toward the house. Chip waved back. They had grown quite fond of each other since he had joined the youth group. Good thing the neighbor lady would take care of his mom while he was gone. Otherwise, he'd have to quit. He reminded himself to thank her.

It was already dark and the laundry was still blowing on the line. He had forgotten to take it down before zipping off to church. The basket was sitting right on the lawn where he had left it and the clothespin bag was hanging on the line. He shook his head. "Oh, boy. Could've all blowed away . . ."

He hurried to park his bike alongside the house, then set about pulling off the wooden pins from each garment, tossing them into the bag and piling the clothes in the basket. He'd fold them in the house. He grimaced at their slight dampness from the night air, then sighed. Every laundry day, he wished again for an electric dryer. Out of the question, of course. At least it'd be nice if he had the newer type clothespins, but there never seemed to be extra money to even get those. He was stuck with the plain kind—probably his grandma's from 1920.

He thought of Michelle. Maybe that nice man and his wife could at least lead them in the right direction. That was something to be excited about. He pulled open the screen door with his foot and set the laundry basket in front of it while he turned the doorknob. Locked. His spine prickled. Something didn't feel right. Mrs. Olson never locked it while she was there. Why would she have left early? He dug his key out of his pocket, stuck it in the keyhole and called out as he pushed the door open, "Ma, it's me.

I'm home . . ." Dark inside. That was weird. He was accustomed to hearing no response, but he liked to let her know it was him so she didn't get afraid. He looked forward to seeing her smile. She always smiled, if only a little bit.

Sandy set the basket by the front door and walked into her bedroom where the light was on. He took one look at the empty bed and gasped. His feet froze. He squeezed his eyes shut, hoping to see her tentative smile when he opened them back up. *"Ma!"* he shouted, to no avail. She was gone.

Horror gripped him. All the fear he had forced away suddenly overwhelmed him. "No, no, no," was all he could say. And that was more an unconscious denial of what his eyes told him could only be the truth. He just knew his mom had died and that they had already taken her away.

While he was off having a grand old time, his world had shattered. Shaking his head from side to side, he backed away from the bed. How could it have happened? He didn't want to believe it. Nobody even left a note to explain. They let him come home to find—nothing.

The door jam struck him squarely between the shoulder blades. He could back up no further. With a last desperate cry of *"No!"* he turned and bolted from the bedroom. In a few hasty strides he reached the front door. Tear-stained vision caused him to miss the handle on his first try. His second met with success. He jerked the door open, made his way across the porch and jumped down the slanted steps. He stumbled to his knees, but that hardly slowed his headlong rush.

It mattered little that he had no idea where he was going. He ran, blindly, never thinking, down the path and onto the road. He turned left and ran as fast as he could go. The stars overhead shed little enough light, but he'd been down this road enough times on

his bike to have memorized every pothole, large and small. A good thing, too. He wasn't paying the least bit of attention. Nothing touched him. He'd closed out everything except his need to escape.

An approaching vehicle came and passed by him, then squealed the brakes. He didn't bother to slow down, did not look back to see who it was. *Just keep going,* he told himself. He had to get away, had to see where they had taken her!

"Sandy, hold on!" he vaguely heard someone say. Between the monologue of disbelief and the pounding of his heart, a man called his name. He never gave him a chance. He kept on running.

The chase lasted about thirty seconds. Longer legs, plus a fresh start combined for an easy win. Sandy only slowed when the man caught him by the shoulder, jerking him to a standstill. He turned a haunted stare on his pursuer.

"Sandy, Sandy, hold on a minute." They were both gasping.

"Oh, P-Pastor Chip. My ma . . ."

"I'm sorry. Someone left word at the church. I happened to check the voice-mail from my cellular phone. If I had done that sooner, you would have known before I left."

That was as far as he got. Sandy jumped up and cut in, "But *how'd* she die?" He burst into tears.

Only then did Chip realize what the youth must have been imagining. Moved by Sandy's pain, he stepped forward and embraced him. "Son, settle down. Your mother's just at the hospital. She had a bad spell, but she's going to be all right. I checked with them before coming back here. The nurse told me they'd be looking forward to meeting you tomorrow during visiting hours."

Still sniffling, Sandy stopped crying. He wrapped his arms around himself and studied Chip with squinted eyes. "You sure? She's alive?"

"Yes, I'm quite sure."

"An' I can see her tomorrow?" His brows scrunched up. "But how will I get there? It's far."

"Don't worry about that. I'll take you." He reached out to him and mussed his already-abused hair. When Sandy nodded, he continued, "What do you want to do now?"

"Gee, I don't know. Usually, I jes' do chores, then talk to Ma and do my homework." His voice grew softer.

"Well, why don't you come spend the night? My wife always keeps the guest room ready." The youth's countenance brightened and clouded. Chip went on. "I know you can take care of yourself, but we could pray for your mom."

"That'd be good. Firs' I gotta get some stuff to take, though." He hung his head to hide the embarrassment he couldn't prevent. "I got all sweaty from running. An' I need my toothbrush 'n stuff."

Satisfied that a crisis had passed, Chip agreed. "Lead on, then. The bus is over there." They made their way to where Chip had hastily parked. Every so often, Chip risked a glance at Sandy, who started to say something and hesitated. "Pastor, I don't have a suitcase. I'd hafta bring my stuff in a grocery bag. And my PJs are pretty awful. Will Mrs. Hendry think I'm a weirdo? I mean, she's a real fancy lady . . ." Chip reassured him that she would think no such thing. She would be delighted to have him as a houseguest.

"Before Ma got sick," Sandy added, "she always tol' me to hold my head up high. God loves poor folks 'much as the rest," she'd say. "Guess I fergot for a minute."

Chip hugged him again. The boy'd had to grow up so fast, and it was far from over.

"Pastor, one more thing. I owe you a 'pology. I got so flustered, I never tol' you how much I learnt from your teachin' tonight."

"Son, you just tell the Lord. It was His doing, not mine."

He nodded. "Okay. *Thank you, Jesus,* for my Pastor Chip . . ."

❧ *Fourteen* ❧

In mid-afternoon the next day, Stephanie stepped outside to water the plants. She had just finished her Community Bible Study lesson. For the last year, she had been involved in the weekly gathering of ladies from different area churches, and she enjoyed the hour and a half very much. Given the family crises of late, though, her attendance had dropped off to almost nothing. She just couldn't get it together enough to make the trip.

A couple of ladies in her Core Group had written her thoughtful notes to say how much they missed her, and to remind her they were praying for the family. Her leader even went to the trouble to make sure she had her lessons every week, in case she would be able to attend the next time—or, just in case she felt up to doing the homework on her own. She appreciated their concern, she really did. It helped to ease the intense feelings of isolation. But still, the very thought that her peers knew her daughter had run away from home made her shrivel inside. What kind of mother did they think she was?

In some respects, it would have been easier if Michelle had been kidnapped! Her family wouldn't have such shame to bear, on top of everything else. Oh well, the session would soon adjourn for the summer, anyway. She wouldn't have to face the puzzled looks of pity in their eyes, nor her own guilt for abandoning a commitment in mid-stream.

Michael was back in his office working on a research grant proposal for the Space Waste program. For no explained reason, all of a sudden she felt a sense of peace that she hadn't felt since the day Michelle disappeared. Maybe something good would turn up. They would hear from her soon, and life would return to normal. Whatever normal was.

She saw the mailman pull away from the house next door, so she set down the watering can and walked out to meet him. He parked the mini truck, fished around in one of the plastic mail crates and stepped out. Fred and his wife attended their church. They were always cheerful, friendly to everybody, and seemed to get along so well together. Unlike Michael and her, she thought, biting her lip. She sighed and put on a smile. "Hi, Fred. Anything for us?" She tried to sound casual.

Fred waved the small bundle of mail up in the air. "Sure do, but probably not what you're looking for. A bunch of us in the men's group have been praying for Michelle. Any word yet?"

"No. I feel good about it, though. I've been studying about the omnipotence of God."

"Atta girl. Keep your eyes on the Lord. Everything'll work out." He rechecked the banded mail to be delivered to the next address. "Gotta run, Stephanie. I'm a little behind today. Had to fill in for a guy whose wife is having their first baby. Say hi to Michael for me."

"Okay." She turned to go back toward the house, then stopped to add, "Fred . . . thank the fellas for their prayers. Please ask them to keep it up."

223

"Sure will. We meet every Monday morning at 6:00 a.m. Gets the week started out right." He paused. "You know what? We've got a men's retreat coming up. Think Michael'd come?"

"I wish he would. He probably wouldn't if the request came from me. He'd think I was implying that he needed it."

"Yeah, see what you mean. The old male ego gets in the way every time. Tell ya what. I'll call him later this week and invite him."

Stephanie's eyes lit up. "Will you? Thank you so much."

Fred tipped his cap and smiled. "My pleasure. And keep the faith. Jesus loves you guys. He really does."

"I know, but it doesn't seem like it sometimes."

He had turned to head for the house next door, then stopped. "Wait a minute. I just remembered. My wife copied a quote for you from a book she was reading. Let me get it in the truck." He hurried over and back within seconds, carrying a rolled-up piece of ivory parchment paper tied with a rose-colored ribbon. "It's from the book, *Disappointment With God,*" he added.

She smiled. "Gee, thanks, Fred. Be sure to thank Christine for me. It was really sweet of her."

"No problem. We both want to help any way we can." He glanced at his watch. "Now I do have to run. Catch ya later."

She nodded, humming a song she had learned at the Bible study. With the mail and the gift clutched in her left hand, she wiped her feet on the mat and stepped inside. She stopped at the fridge, poured herself a glass of iced tea, and sat down at the kitchen table. Stephen would be due home from school shortly, so she would have only a few more minutes to herself.

She untied the satin-ribboned parchment paper and unrolled it. Inspired by the beautiful handwritten calligraphy bordered by a floral design, she read on:

Is God unfair? Silent? Hidden?

Such questions must have troubled the Hebrews until, in Moses' lifetime, God took off the wraps. He punished evil and rewarded good. He spoke audibly. And he made himself visible, first to Moses in a burning bush and then to the Israelites in a pillar of cloud and fire.

The response of the Israelites to such direct intervention offers an important insight into the inherent limits of all power. Power can do everything but the most important thing: it cannot control love. The ten plagues in Exodus show the power of God over a pharaoh. But the ten major rebellions recorded in Numbers show the impotence of power to bring about what God desired most, the love and faithfulness of his people. No pyrotechnic displays of omnipotence could make them trust and follow him . . .

The fact that love does not operate according to the rules of power may help explain why God sometimes seems shy to use his power. He created us to love him, but his most impressive displays of miracle—the kind we may secretly long for—do nothing to foster that love. As Douglas John Hall has put it, "God's problem is not that God is not able to do certain things. God's problem is that God loves. Love complicates the life of God as it complicates every life."

And when his own love is spurned, even the Lord of the Universe feels in some way helpless, like a parent who has lost what he values most.[9]

—Philip Yancey

225

For several minutes, she sat, dazed, holding the paper. How could Christine have known what she had been studying? Or about her secret doubts? They hadn't talked at all. She'd have to write her a little note as soon as she could.

One by one, Stephanie flipped through the mail. Four bills, no, five, several advertising flyers, a couple of envelopes from non-profit groups—both wanting money. Nothing from Michelle. She sighed. Until a few minutes ago, she had been positive she would see her neat handwriting on one of the envelopes, with a letter inside saying how much she missed them and was coming home soon. No such luck.

Instead, a long, thin post card fell out from between the advertising pieces. "Guaranteed approval for a VISA card," it boasted, along with a phone number to an out-of-state bank. Just what they needed. Another charge card. She felt a twinge of temptation. Hers were all near the credit limit, but she had promised Michael she would cut back.

Ever since setting out as a self-employed consultant, he was much more anxious about money. Probably because he'd had to dip into their savings to get started. Stephanie remembered, with a trace of longing, the days of regular, fat paychecks from Eagle Aeronautics.

They'd had arguments aplenty at first, but she got nowhere with him. He just didn't, or wouldn't, understand her insecurity about his going out on his own. And she resented not being included in the early stages of the decision-making process. She'd never admitted that to him. His remark, "I plan to do this while I'm still young enough to make a decent go of it," left no room for discussion. These days, though, he was focusing more and more on that harebrained Space Waste project, instead of on solid, high-paying clients who needed his consulting services right now.

Someday soon she'd have to talk to him. That settled, she turned her attention to the remaining junk mail.

She came close to tossing the advertising card into the "throw away" pile, but at the last second, flipped it over. Two photographs of young girls and a caption in bold, dark blue letters. The words, "HAVE YOU SEEN ME?" held her gaze. The pretty brunette on the left bore a striking resemblance to the older girl on the right. That wasn't what threatened to send her into a tailspin. It was the other, slightly smaller description, "Age progression."

What was this about? Stephanie took another deep breath and scanned the fine print. "How long, how long?" she wondered aloud. With every word she read, her face grew a chalkier shade of white. "Date missing . . ." There it was. "Oh, no. It can't be." But it was. Over ten years. The girl on the right was not an older sister, but an artist's rendering of how the missing girl might look today. A decade later. For a moment, Stephanie hung, poised on the brink of an abyss. If she let go, she might never stop falling. Getting a grip on herself, she gulped in great lungfuls of air.

She felt paralyzed, as if she'd been struck by a bolt of lightning. The shock had pinned her to the kitchen chair. Finally, she managed to pry herself up, and, holding the card to her chest, paced the floor. She ran her right hand through her hair. Then, she rubbed her arms to ease the goose bumps. "Dear, Lord, it can't be. This poor child has been missing for ten years. Ten years . . . My God, *ten years!* Her parents! How can they stand not knowing? How can they function? How can they go on? How can they ever laugh again? Oh my God, my God . . ."

A flood of compassion welled up. She sat back at the table and wept, her head face down on her hands. Her tears turned to sobs. For a several minutes, she let herself go. She could picture the grief-stricken mother, sitting on her child's empty canopy bed and

clutching a worn teddy bear to her heart as she rocked back and forth. Stephanie's sobs became a groaning, a wailing, from so deep inside her, she ached. She had never experienced anything like it before. Words faltered, but her heart cried out, "Oh, dear Lord, please find this child. Please. Send her home, I pray, to her parents—alive." Her voice became a faint squeak, then a whisper. "If she is already dead, Lord, be merciful, I pray . . . Please let them know. Gently." After a long while, Stephanie got up and half-stumbled to the counter to start making dinner. First, she set down the postcard and splashed a good douse of cold water on her face.

Michael wandered into the kitchen for a cup of coffee. He had been pecking away at the computer for hours. When he saw Stephanie, her hair in a damp disarray and her eyes red and puffy, he asked, "So what's with you?"

She stared at him, her expression blank. "I was just reading a notice that came in the mail."

"You look like *that* from a notice in the mail? What? We didn't pay our taxes or something?"

"No. It's from some place that helps find ki—" She glanced at the card. ". . . The National Center for Missing and Exploited Children. This little girl has been missing for ten years. I started feeling awful for her parents." She picked up the card and handed it to him. "Can you imagine?"

He passed a quick glance, then handed it back to her. "They must have simulated the second picture on a computer. It's amazing what technology can do today." He caught himself. "Please get a grip, Steph. You don't even know the kid. Or her parents. Our *own* daughter is missing. That's what we should be concerned about."

Michelle . . . The fog in Stephanie's head lifted, leaving a fresh stab of pain. Yes, Michelle was missing, too. Not just some stranger, but their own flesh and blood. It had only been weeks. She could now imagine a wait stretching into months. Or years. "Michael, what if—?" Stephanie couldn't finish the sentence before he erupted with harsh words that cut her to the quick.

"Now just *stop* it! You've got to quit conjuring up worst-case scenarios. That won't do us a bit of good. We have to maintain a modicum of sanity around here."

He poured a cup of coffee, stirred in his favorite flavored creamer, grabbed two cookies and huffed past her. In the middle of the doorway, he turned around and snapped, "Stephen is due at the bus stop any minute. He *is* in the family, and he needs you." Michael disappeared into the hall, leaving Stephanie standing open-mouthed and crimson-cheeked.

Furious at his callous attitude, and not about to let him have the last word, she stormed after him. "Well, Mr. Compassion-of-the-Year, even you can't be that selfish. So what if something does not affect your private little world? Those people are grieving parents, just like us. Aren't believers supposed to bear another's burdens?"

"We have enough burdens of our own right now! We can't handle any more. And the way you worry, you make the ones we've got ten times as bad. You have an amazing ability to make Mt. Everest out of an ant mound."

"Aren't you the clever one! Well . . . you have an incredible ability . . . to turn a down pillow into a block of cement. Your insensitivity makes life a *real pain!*"

His index finger pointed at her in a threatening manner. "Listen, you oughta feel what it's like in *my* shoes. I don't have the luxury of breaking down all the time. Have you considered that? I have to try to keep focused on work so we can pay for these crises life doles out to us!" They continued to hurl razor-edged accusa-

tions back and forth across the room, each louder and more cutting than the one before. Unbeknownst to them, Stephen was
down the road, stepping off the school bus a few minutes early.

He glanced around. With no ride in sight, he shrugged his
shoulders and trudged towards home, almost dragging himself the
last hundred feet. By the time he reached the door, he was so
exhausted, he could barely lift his legs up the steps and stretch his
hand to the brass doorbell. His dark green and tan back pack—the
one he'd picked out for his last birthday—drooped to one side of
his back, tugging his jacket almost off his shoulder. His left
shoelace had come untied. He rang the bell several times. In
between rings, the sound of his parents shouting at each other
punctuated the silence. He sighed.

Stephanie finally heard the doorbell and hurried to answer it.
When she saw the downcast expression on her son's face, her
breath caught. He stood leaning back against the house with his
head against the door frame. He half-stumbled through the door.
She reached for his arm. "Honey, you look beat. School okay?"

"Fine, Mom," came the firm, but quiet, reply. He put his head
down. She gave him a questioning gaze and lifted his chin gently
with her hand. "You don't look like it was fine."

"I'm just tired." Stephen rarely complained. He tried to cheer
them up, especially since they'd been worried about Michelle.
Tonight was different. Stephanie knew she couldn't pry the truth
out of him. He was like his father in that respect. She would have to
wait until he was ready. That moment came sooner than expected.

"I feel like somebody hit me with a ball bat," he moaned.

"Aches like the flu?"

"Sort of, I guess. But more in certain spots."

"Sounds like we need to see the doctor again." She relieved
him of his book bag and led him to the couch in the den.

"I'm *sick* of doctors. I'm sick of being sick!"

"I know, honey." She patted his leg.

"Mom, why can't my body just do what it's supposed to? Nobody else has to go get their blood out of a bag."

"Stephen, millions of people need transfusions," she replied matter-of-factly, masking her concern. He rarely referred to that aspect of his medical condition. Considering the HIV infection, hemophilia treatments posed the least problem. Of course, he was still in the second stage of HIV, with few symptoms, aside from fatigue. That could last for years, the doctors had told them.

He frowned. "Mom, other people get to put blood into a bag. It can save somebody's life. And they get to wear a neat sticker."

She raised her eyebrows. "What brought up this topic today?"

"Oh, nothin'."

"Something did."

"I just saw a poster about the bloodmobile coming to church. But I'll be the one left out. *Again.*"

"Honey, I'm sure you have to be seventeen to donate blood."

"Well, it's still not fair. They'll *never* want my blood if I live to be a hundred! You know it. Everybody wears rubber gloves to even come near me." He kicked a toy out of the way with his foot.

He flopped down on the couch and stretched out on his belly. His left arm hung off the side. She followed him and sat in the rocker across from him. "Honey, you're upset about something else. Want to talk about it? You'll feel better . . ."

He kicked his feet up in the air, then dropped them back on the cushions for a minute or so, not saying a word. It was clear from the extra force of his gesture that something was bugging him. Stephanie leaned toward him. "Come on. What's up?"

At last, he spoke. "Kids were mean at recess."

"Mean? How?"

"They made fun of me. Started laughin' and yellin' that I had 'homo cooties.' Said they didn't want to hang around me anymore. They were afraid they'd catch my cooties and 'turn queer.' They made all these yukky faces 'n stuff and ran away!" He pounded his foot on the arm of the couch to accentuate each word.

She had never heard the kids' phrase, but she understood it immediately. So the word was out. She blinked her eyes slowly. She wondered how long people had known. Michael and she had hoped to keep his condition private for as long as possible—to protect Stephen. Only a couple of their friends knew, their pastor, plus their doctor and the lab . . . She went through a brief mental checklist of everyone they had told—only people they thought would keep it to themselves. People who would pray instead of gossip. So much for confidentiality.

Teary-eyed, Stephanie got up from the rocking chair and knelt by her son. For the moment, she forgot about Michelle and the argument she and Michael had been having. Her maternal instincts took over completely. She put her arm around Stephen's waist and gave him a strong squeeze. He winced when she hit a tender spot. "Honey, I'm sorry. Just wanted to tell you I love you. Those were very mean things the kids said. It's not your fault; you needed the transfusion."

"I know all that, Mom. But it doesn't help. They don't care."

"No, they don't. And the kids aren't the only ones. They were just more blatant about it. More crude. 'Homo cooties!'" She shook her head in disgust. "Jesus wouldn't want us to attack anybody like that."

"I know, Mom." He paused, deep in thought. "Well, *was* it because of those people that I'm sick? I wanna know!"

Stephanie bit her lip. How could she explain? The topic was so complex and sensitive, even for adults. She took a deep breath before taking the plunge. "Son, according to experts in AIDS research, everyday contact does not spread the AIDS virus at all. Those kids acted out of ignorance. For the most part, sexual contact spreads the virus through body fluids." She swallowed hard. "And in many cases, yes, the contact happens between two people of the same sex." The images evoked by her words made her queasy. "But homosexuals are not the only ones who pass it around. Men give it to women and women to men. A few doctors have given it to their patients by mistake, or have gotten infected by their patients. People who shoot drugs into their veins with dirty needles also spread it. Mommies can give the virus to their newborn babies. So, honey, we have no way of knowing whose blood infected you."

"But don't they know what they're doing kills people—including kids like me? We won't ever get to grow up! Why would anybody want to do those bad things, Mom? *Why?*"

She felt helpless to answer his questions. *Lord, help me say the right words,* she prayed silently. After a long pause, she hugged him and began, "Honey, you know how good it feels to be loved?"

He nodded halfheartedly.

"Well . . . everybody on earth wants to be loved, just as much as you and me." She stroked his curly blond hair. "They want so much to be close to other people because they're very lonely inside. They're trying to fill big empty holes in their hearts, but they're going about it in a very wrong way. Only God can fill up those holes and make them feel complete—"

"Then why don't they go to Him?"

"Some are too angry. Some don't know they *can* go to Him. If they did, they would never do the dangerous things they do."

"Yeah, but if the Bible says that God hates men going with men and stuff like that, why do we have to love 'em?"

"Because God loves them. He wants them to come home to Him—even more than we want Michelle to come home to us. But He hates what they're doing. No question about that. It has serious consequences, as far as He's concerned."

"How do you know?"

"I read it during our Bible study of the book of Romans. It's somewhere in the Old Testament, too . . ."

He shrugged his shoulders, then voiced a quiet response, "I don't get it. Why does God still love 'em if they do stuff He hates?"

"I know it's hard to understand. But, honey, we can't forget that *all* of us were born wanting to do things our own way. Whether or not God dislikes our behavior, and whether or not it hurts anyone else. The Bible tells us so. If we let that old nasty nature be the boss over us instead of God, we'll do wrong every time—maybe not in the same area as another person, but we do plenty wrong. Does that make sense?"

"Yeah, I guess so." Stephen closed his eyes and didn't say a word. Just as she thought he had fallen asleep, he asked in a soft voice, "Does God like it . . . when moms and dads talk mean to each other?"

Startled, she slowly got up off her knees and sat back in the rocking chair. The muscles in her chest tightened, making her short of breath. She crossed her legs, leaned her head back and rocked. Her cheeks burned with fresh shame. Kids could be so direct sometimes. It was scary. She could only respond with a weak, "No, honey, I'm sure it hurts Him."

He rolled over onto his side, leaned up on one elbow and propped his head on his hand. His eyes glistened in the dim light. "Boy, Mom, it hurts me, too. *Bad.*"

She rocked harder, but said nothing. The rhythmic squeak of the rocker filled the uncomfortable silence. If she could crawl into the woodwork, she would. Thoughts of Michelle drifted through her head. She wondered if their marital arguments had bothered her as much. Could that have something to do with why she ran away? That led to despair. A lump formed in Stephanie's throat. She forced her thoughts back to her son. No words came.

Stephen unpropped himself so he could lay down on the couch. He turned his face toward the back and stretched his arms alongside his slender body. Within minutes, he was asleep. She peeked over at him, covered him with the cotton throw, and tiptoed out of the den to Michael's office in the back of the house.

He was sitting at the computer with his back facing the doorway. He hadn't heard her approach. His tie was hanging, still knotted at the neck, over the brass lamp. His blue oxford shirt with the button-down collar, pressed crisp from the laundry (he wouldn't have it otherwise), was rolled up at the sleeves.

His right arm reached a little to the side, with his hand resting on the desk, cupped over a gadget with a cord. "It's called a mouse," he had informed her when he first set up the computer in his home office. To her way of thinking, 'mouse' hardly seemed an appropriate name for a shiny piece of plastic that made the bright-colored screen wink with the slightest touch of his finger.

He stared, mesmerized, at his computer screen. For several minutes, she stood silent, watching him and reminiscing about their relationship. For the first time in a while, she felt the urge to be close to him, to feel his arms holding her tight. She wished she could tell him so, but the threat of rejection held her back. He was too busy, she decided. She tiptoed away, unnoticed.

Michael leaned back in his chair, yawned and stretched his arms over his head. He was stiff from sitting in one position for so long. "This grant proposal could make or break our future," he said as he tapped his finger on the monitor. "Gotta be perfect."

A ray of afternoon sunlight glinted off the solid brass picture frame on top of his computer hutch, drawing his eyes to a family photo. He clasped his hands behind his head and stared at the four smiling faces. A deep sigh escaped. They'd had it taken soon after they'd gotten back together. Everyone looked pretty happy. Memories of that reunion came flooding back—Stephanie's tearful confession of setting up his humiliation, forgiveness on each of their parts, and a glorious night together. It had seemed like a second honeymoon. How surprised she had been when he served her breakfast in bed. He smiled now, remembering her radiant beauty. The rose from the garden had been the crowning touch. Now, even the idea of it seemed . . . well, silly.

Yet, part of him deep inside longed to rush into the kitchen, sweep Stephanie up in his arms and carry her off somewhere. Anywhere. Maybe to that mountain cabin in North Carolina. But why bother? She wasn't interested anymore. Worry consumed her every waking moment. If not the kids, then something else. He closed his eyes, hoping to chase away the charm of the past. It brought no respite. Image after image marched past his conscious mind, accompanied by mocking words, "Forget it, fool. Those days are gone forever."

It was true. Much in their lives had changed. Michelle had disappeared. Where, why or how, they had no idea. Would they ever see her again? And Stephen was disappearing, too, a little bit at a time. So imperceptibly, they could barely sense it happening. One thing Michael *could* feel—a hard shell forming around his heart. He had no desire to interfere with the process, either. It seemed the safest way to survive.

Only Caleb had figured out the deceptive nature of appearances. He broke through the shell. With great care, the determined old guy had peeled off layer after layer of scarred, encrusted pieces.

But what good did that do now? Caleb was dead. Anger arose in Michael's gut. He pounded his fist on the solid oak desktop, sending a sharp twinge through his arm up to the elbow. "And where is *God* when you need Him?" he demanded. *"Nowhere."*

Something drew his squinted eyes to the right of his monitor. There sat one of Dr. Dobson's books that a guy from church had given him months earlier. He hadn't read the first word. Gold foil letters of the title etched against a magenta background now seemed to beckon him in. *When God Doesn't Make Sense* sure struck a familiar chord. He fought a losing battle against picking it up. When he did, the pages fell open to two hundred forty-six, where his friend had left a leather book mark. The words, "747 airplanes," caught his attention enough to prompt him to read,

> . . . everything in life is temporary.
> That thought occurred to me one day when I was taking a commercial airline flight. We taxied out to the end of the runway and waited for clearance to take off. I looked out the window and saw the remains of two huge 747 airplanes sitting on the field. All the paint had been stripped off the fuselage and rust was spreading down from the top. The insides had been gutted and the windows were sealed. Then I saw a tiny bit of blue paint on the tail of one plane and realized these had been proud ships in the fleet of Pan American Airways.
> The empty hulks looked pitiful sitting out there alone, shorn of their beauty. For some reason, they reminded me of the poem entitled, "Little Boy Blue" by Eugene Field (1850-1895). The first stanza reads:
> *The little toy dog is covered with dust,*
> *But sturdy and staunch he stands*

And the little toy soldier is red with rust,
And his musket molds in his hands.
Time was when the little toy dog was new,
And the soldier was passing fair;
And that was the time when our Little Boy Blue
Kissed them and put them there.

I might have composed my own poem as I sat looking out the window:

Time was when these two airplanes were new
And they flew to great heights in the sky.
But now they are rusty, forgotten, and old
And they seem to be questioning, "Why?"

I imagined the day these magnificent craft were rolled out of the Boeing plant with shiny new enamel and the proud Pan Am insignia on their tails. They were christened with champagne amidst cheers and laughter. Then they were taken on their maiden voyages. Little boys and girls craned their necks skyward to watch these beautiful birds come in for a landing. What excitement they must have generated for passengers and crew.

Now, the company that owned them has gone bankrupt, and the planes are grounded forever. How could it happen in fewer than 20 years? Who would have thought these multimillion-dollar aircraft would come to such a quick and ignoble end?

As we taxied past the shells, I thought about the impermanence of everything that now looks so stable. Nothing lasts very long. And we are the ones who are passing through, on our way to another life of far greater significance.

To those who are hurting and discouraged at this time, I think it would be comforting to look forward to the time when the present trials will be a distant memory. A day of celebration is coming like nothing that has ever occurred in the history of mankind. The guest of honor on that morning will be one wearing a seamless robe, with eyes like flames of fire, and feet like fine brass. As we bow humbly before Him, a great voice will thunder from the heavens, saying:

Now the dwelling of God is with men, and he will live with them. They will be his people, and God himself will be with them and be their God. He will wipe every tear from their eyes. There will be no more death or mourning or crying or pain, for the old order of things has passed away. (Revelation 21:3-4)[10]

Michael closed the book, and almost in slow motion, set it back in its place on the hutch. He blinked over misty eyes, then swallowed hard. Maybe God cared more than He let on. At least heaven held promise of better days. He glanced back at the photo. He knew *he* cared more than anybody imagined.

He found himself wondering what Stephanie was up to. Maybe they could talk. That might help. He saved the document on his screen, exited the program and turned off the computer, then rolled back his steno chair. On leaden legs, he moved to the kitchen. No Steph. He checked the laundry room, the bedroom and finally, the den. There, he stopped in his tracks.

She was kneeling beside a sleeping Stephen, stroking his blond hair with utmost tenderness. Her lips were moving, but he could hear only whispers. A surge of jealousy caught him quite by surprise. How he missed the quiet moments he and his wife used to have together . . . she would run her fingers through *his* hair and

tell him how much she loved him . . . In an instant, he felt ridiculous—she was tending to their only son! At that moment, he felt grateful that no one could read his mind.

Unnoticed, he turned around to head back to his office. No sweat. He still had a pile of work to do, anyway. Halfway there, he stopped in the hall to look at some of the old family pictures.

Well, maybe he could try writing her a note and leaving it under her pillow . . .

In a groggy stupor, Stephanie rose from her knees. Her legs and feet tingled with pins and needles from being cramped in one position for so long. She had fallen asleep praying, with her head on Stephen's back.

It was time to start supper. First, she went into the bathroom to freshen up and winced at seeing the dark circles under her eyes. They got worse every day. She gingerly applied the under-eye cover cream and a bit of lipstick. Next stop, the bedroom to change her clothes. She sat on the edge of the bed to ponder what outfit didn't need ironing. The flashing red light from the answering machine on the nightstand caught her eye, indicating two calls had come in. When could the phone have rung twice without her knowing? She had been home all day. Of course, Michael wouldn't have heard. In order to shield himself from distractions, he had set it up so only his business line rang in the office.

She pressed the Play button. The long tone came on. A hang-up. The familiar, high-pitched beep announced the next message. A male voice with a heavy accent surprised her. She didn't know any foreigners, but she listened anyway. "Hello, madam," the man said, "My name is Joshua Lieben. My wife and I are trying to locate my father. According to our understanding, he lives here in the States. Caleb is his name."

A short pause followed before the answering machine cut off and reset itself. Caleb . . . it couldn't be the same guy. She pressed the save button and headed to get Michael. Stephen still slept on the couch. She stood at the doorway of her husband's office. He was staring at the computer, as intently as he had been the first time. "Michael . . ." she called across the room.

He spun around in his chair. "Hey. What's up?"

"Sorry to bother you, but will you come and listen to a message on the answering machine?"

"Hon, I was in the middle of something. Can it wait?"

"I think you'd want to hear it."

"Who? A client?"

"No. Some foreigner . . ." She stopped. "Just take a break and come listen."

They walked to the bedroom together. Michael pressed Play. His mouth dropped open at the mention of Caleb's name. When the message was finished, he played it again. *"Caleb's* son?" he asked aloud. He shook his head, as if to bring himself back to his senses. "Caleb never had a son."

"How do you know?"

"He would have mentioned him. We spent a lot of time together. He told me about his family, his wife, his past. Besides, if he had a son, why would he have . . ." Michael stopped short, then continued, ". . . willed his property to *me?*" His lips tightened at the potential consequences. He listened to the message a third time. "Sounds like a decent guy, though."

Stephanie agreed. "Yes, he does sound very nice. So polite."

"But he didn't leave his address or phone number or anything. Why would the guy not leave enough information, if he really wants to talk to us?" His irritation was starting to show.

"Maybe he's absent-minded," Stephanie offered.

Michael frowned. "You know what? I bet this stupid machine is still cutting off messages."

"We just got it back from the repair shop."

"For the second time."

"So, how can we tell?

"I'll try from my office line. See what happens."

He left and soon the phone was ringing in the bedroom. Stephanie let the machine pick it up. Michael's voice came on, "Hello, this is a test. Michael, here, trying to determine if our marvel of an answering machine is acting up again. I sure hope that man ca—" Michael heard an all-too-familiar click. He hurried back to the bedroom.

Stephanie crossed her arms and shook her head. "I hate to say it, but unless you stopped right in the middle of a sentence, it just cut you off."

"Great." He sat down on the edge of the bed and plopped back. "I can't believe it. We're minding our own business, trying to survive, when, out of the blue, we hear from a mysterious stranger who claims to be the son of my favorite person in the whole world. Not to mention the deceased owner of our property. And we have no way of knowing where this guy is—or what he wants. That's just splendid." He sighed deeply and rubbed his temples with both hands. "On second thought, he could be looking for another Caleb. Or maybe it's a prank."

Stephanie laid down beside him. "Michael, sometimes I wonder if someone has hatched a plot to drive us crazy."

Almost in spite of himself, he took her hand. "You know, I've wondered the same thing."

❧ *Fifteen* ❧

Early the next morning, Michael joined Eric Marcos for one of Eric's regular cycling excursions. Although he hadn't been on a bicycle in a long time, Michael had accepted the counselor's invitation without hesitation. Running once in a while kept him in decent shape, so he wasn't worried about lagging behind. Besides, there might be some time to talk along the way—without the clock ticking at ninety dollars an hour.

He certainly needed a break from the stress at home. They hadn't heard from Michelle in several weeks, despite their pursuit of every possible avenue. It *was* driving them crazy. As far as he was concerned, the family simply could not revolve their entire lives around whether or not she might try to make contact at any given moment. Stephanie disagreed. She glared at him as he headed out the door at 7:00 a.m., water bottle in hand. *"Somebody* has to stay here!"* she called after him, with a martyr-like tone and demeanor.

When Michael saw Eric decked out in full riding gear— padded bicycle shorts, helmet, sports sunglasses, even special shoes that locked onto his pedals—he felt very outclassed. Oh, well. His plain old running clothes and sneakers would have to do. He didn't

have time to make a regular habit of the sport. It would be hard to justify a big investment for a few hours' use now and then.

However, when he found himself huffing up on his squeaky 10-speed, he questioned his own practicality. Eric seemed to slice through the wind on his whisper-quiet, titanium racer, leaving him quite a distance behind. Then Eric had to slow down and wait for him to catch up. It was humiliating. Once he got into the rhythm of things on the open road, though, he didn't perform too badly, he decided.

The two of them maintained a steady pace, so there was no way to carry on much of a conversation. Not until they reached the half-way point and stopped for breakfast. Sitting at a little country diner, waiting for their order of bacon, eggs, and pancakes, Michael opened the conversation. "I had no idea there were such steep hills around Lake County."

"I didn't realize it, either," Eric said, "until recently. I think this part of the state is one of Florida's best-kept secrets. Gorgeous rolling countryside."

"You're right. I was contemplating a family bike-ride some-time, but they'd keel over after ten minutes on this terrain. Not that they'd *want* to go anywhere." He paused to wipe a bead of sweat off his brow with his napkin.

Eric nodded. "Speaking of family, what's going on?"

"Law enforcement keeps telling us not to give up. They say publicity can really help. You know, getting her picture out to as many places as possible. We've been doing that as best we can. We might have a chance to make a plea on TV this week and we're lay-ing out big bucks for some billboards." Michael shook his head and shrugged. His hand clenched into a fist.

Eric studied him from across the tiny table. "Try not to lose hope, pal. When things like this happen, the mental struggle is the worst." Michael met his encouraging look. "How is Stephanie holding up?" Eric asked.

"She's stretched tighter than a drum." Michael hesitated, then spoke. "We got an unusual phone call from the detective late last night."

"Oh?"

"Maybe nothing to get worked up over. Some truck driver and his wife happened to see one of the flyers at Peace Convalescent Home. The trucker's been getting physical therapy after an accident. They feel pretty confident that our Michelle is the person who rode with them as far as Washington, D.C."

"Really?"

"Yeah. A girl her age was hitchhiking on a dark country road just off Route 27 when they picked her up. Some weirdos had just tried to pull her into their car. According to the trucker couple, they literally rescued her."

"You're kidding."

"No, dead serious. I haven't told Stephanie that part, believe me. She'd be a worse basket case."

"Understandable. Hitchhiking! Man, what could Michelle have been thinking?"

"I have no idea. She was asking for trouble—if it was definitely her." Michael cleared his throat and took a long drink of ice water.

"You don't think it was?"

"I don't know, Eric." He sighed. "The date they gave the detective was, in fact, the same day she disappeared. And the girl did tell them her name was Michelle. She said she was in Florida on break and some friends left her stranded. Said she wanted to get back to her family in New York."

Eric tapped the table with his forefinger. "New York? Of course, she would have tried to avoid suspicion."

"Right. And get this. The people said they let her ride with them because they felt sorry for her. They figured she'd be safer with them than hitchhiking. They're Christians, I guess. Trying to do their good deed for the day."

"Amazing . . ."

"Yeah, it's all just too coincidental to believe."

"There's more?"

"Well . . . the clothes they remembered her wearing fit to a tee what she had on when she left for school that morning."

Astonished, Eric shook his head.

"The guy's wife—she drives the rig, too, if you can believe it—remembered the girl making a phone call at the truck stop and acting very close-mouthed about the whole thing. Michelle *did* call home from somewhere right around that same time, got mad, and hung up on me—remember?"

Again, a nod from Eric.

"Also, the guy said that during the trip, she used lots of big words. Seemed quite proud of her vocabulary. Told him she tutored a kid in English. And that she had a younger brother who was a hemophiliac with HIV."

"Good grief, Michael, how can you say the lead is 'maybe nothing!' The chances of someone else fitting that description are a million to one!"

A smiling waitress arrived and set several steaming plates in front of them. He sighed. "I know. I'm just afraid of getting our hopes up for nothing. Especially Stephanie. She can't take any more disappointment."

"I can understand that. When it comes to their kids in jeopardy, women tend to be pretty protective."

Michael spread a generous portion of butter on his pancakes, poured on some maple syrup, and replied, "Tell me about it."

Eric paused to say a quick grace, then cocked his head. "Have you had a chance to meet that couple, you know—to see if they're credible?"

"No. The detective took a statement from them right at the convalescent home." He swallowed some coffee and wiped his lips. "They have no idea what all is going on behind the scenes now."

"What?"

"Well, they *were* the last people to supposedly see our daughter, and as such . . ."

Eric set down his knife and fork. "What are you saying?"

He glanced around, then took a deep breath. "The detective suspects them of kidnapping."

"No way."

"Yes. They could be charged any day now. Since she was taken across state lines, the Feds will get involved. About twenty years ago, the guy got probation for robbery and possession of narcotics."

"Oh. That does throw it in a different light." He leaned back in his chair, then toward Michael. "But why would they come forward with information if they're guilty of foul play?"

Michael's eyes narrowed. "For the same reason that parents who commit murder call the police to report their child missing." His words fell to the table with a thud.

Eric nodded. "See what you mean. Does the detective know, though, that Michelle *told* you she was running away?"

"Yeah. But that doesn't mean she wasn't taken somewhere against her will after she left."

"I don't know. Something doesn't set right."

Michael poked at his homefries. "Frankly, I'm in favor of charges being filed. They said they dropped her off at a bus station in Washington, D.C., but nobody there remembers selling her a

ticket. Let a jury decide whether or not the couple is lying. If they were dense enough to tote a juvenile halfway across the country, somebody has to give 'em a wake-up call."

For several minutes, they kept quiet and focused on eating what turned out to be a superb breakfast. Finally, Eric broke the silence. "One thing is for sure, brother."

"What?"

It was his turn to look Michael straight in the eyes. "The only person who knows the truth . . . is Michelle."

Michael stopped chewing and gave him a slow, solemn nod.

🙐 🙐 🙐

To a casual observer, the cute young couple looked just like any of the other couples strolling hand in hand through the park. They kissed a lot, stopped to look at the same things, tossed a few coins into a juggler's cup, watched the in-line skaters. They even sat on the grass and laughed at the antics of the squirrels begging for handouts. They were having fun, and before either of them realized how much time had passed, it was almost dusk.

"Matt, shouldn't we look for another place to stay?" Michelle asked as she retied the shoelace on her right sneaker. "We don't have enough money to keep staying where we've been."

"What's the rush? We've got all night. The Big Apple never rolls up the sidewalks. Besides, before we get settled there's something I've gotta take care of."

Michelle, with a question in her eyes plain to see, fixed her gaze on him.

"It's nothing, really. Just a small matter I need to put to rest."

This time the look wasn't enough. "What? You're acting like it's a big secret or something." She reached across and wrapped her arm around his waist, snuggled her cheek up against his shoulder and stared into the distance. "I know we haven't known each other that long . . ."

"But?"

"Well, *you* asked me if we could be friends. We don't need any secrets between us—do we?"

Her childlike innocence drew Matt like a bee to honey. He pulled her to him and leaned down until the tip of his nose touched hers. He studied her up-turned face.

Michelle's breath caught. She wanted to stand up and put a stop to the turmoil his nearness caused, but her muscles seemed to turn to mush. His eyes sparkled. She wondered if he knew how he made her feel, and if he enjoyed it. The thought made her cheeks burn. Still, she only managed a sigh.

He solved her dilemma by leaning back and resting his weight on his outstretched arm. "You're right. We don't need secrets, but there is something I need to do before we find a place."

"Matt, you just s—"

"Shhh, my sweet little Ashley Nicole. Didn't we take care of special business for you this afternoon? You are now the proud owner of a genuine fake ID, thanks to me, right?"

She scrunched her lips and toyed with her ring. "Well, yeah."

"Okay, then. Trust me."

"It took you long enough to take me over there. We've been here for over two weeks. And I deserve to know what's going on."

He reached over and cupped her cheek with the palm of his hand. His fingers stroked her left earlobe. "I'll tell you all about it the moment I get back. I promise."

Michelle didn't like this sudden change of plans one bit, but she liked the thought of arguing even less. She had vowed long ago that she would never sound like her parents. And that left her little

choice. She shrugged. "Okay. If your mind's set, I won't try to talk you out of it. But please don't be gone too long."

"I won't. I promise. Now, don't worry. I'll be back before you know it." He stood up and held his hand out to her. She grabbed it and let him pull her to her feet. "You can't stay out here," he added. He knew how dangerous Central Park could be at night. He sure didn't want to tell her that, though. He might never get away to do his thing if she clung to him like a scared kitten. And he couldn't wait much longer. Scoring a sale would be too dangerous even for a pro like him. New areas were best explored with enough light to see who you were dealing with.

After he dropped Michelle off at an all-night café across the street and got her situated in a corner booth, Matt picked up his pace. He was proud of himself for thinking in advance to leave a twenty-dollar tip for the waitress. She'd better take good care of his girl. A small part of him worried about her safety. He liked her—a lot. But at the same time, he wondered about her loyalty. With that thought in mind, Matt felt justified in leaving her alone while he went out on his mission.

He patted his camera bag and walked faster. He had heard rumors of several areas in the Park where deals took place, hands down. He'd check those out first. It was still fairly early yet with fewer cops on the prowl, so he told himself everything would be all right. He could sell at least a few ounces of pot and have plenty of time to smoke some himself.

He was too smart to let himself get hooked on crack, though a guy could find it anywhere these days. Wouldn't think of trying to sell it, either. People got crazy as loons tryin' to get the stuff. A little reefer, that wouldn't hurt. Never mind that he had been in trouble once already for possession, or that his strong craving made demands on him every day.

Around a bend, along the playground and past the rink, he recognized the old dairy building at the edge of the big grassy area. He was getting close to the first possible option. He quickened his pace. In a few minutes, the numbers of people walking the paths thinned out significantly. Those remaining, or sitting on the rocks and scattered benches, seemed a seedier bunch.

Matt slowed as he started looking for signs of any drug business. He was not disappointed. After what he considered some astute bargaining—the whole transaction took less than two minutes—he stepped back onto the sidewalk, closed his camera bag and began making his way back to the café. But he couldn't wait. He fumbled around for some rolling papers. Not a single one left. He'd been so preoccupied with Michelle earlier, he'd forgotten to buy more. He couldn't let *that* happen again.

Stopping to beg a couple of papers from an old guy sitting on a bench who was trying to roll a cigarette from a pouch of smoking tobacco, Matt wasted no time rolling up a joint. He wasted even less time lighting it up and taking his first long hit, then another and another.

"Fantastic," he mumbled under his breath. Not enough to get a buzz, but it relaxed him. After looking up and down the path a ways and, seeing no one, he decided he might just as well smoke and walk. Didn't want to keep Michelle waiting too long. Though the effects of the marijuana made him a paranoid on occasion, tonight it lulled him into a false sense of security. He quit paying attention and turned down another bend in the path, the joint hanging from his lip. He never noticed the shelter set back from the walk, or the two police officers standing there watching the passersby. But they noticed him. And they smelled the smoke. No other invitation needed. In minutes, he found himself frisked, handcuffed, and under arrest. They confiscated his camera bag,

too, with his stash. Used in the commission of a felony, it was fair game. Maybe if he just had a couple of ounces instead of eight on him, the officers might have given him a break.

One of his last thoughts as the door to the squad car slammed behind him was of Michelle—his pretty little "Ashley Nicole." What would become of her? He dropped his head and sighed. He admitted to himself that she would have been better off if she had never met him, and better off now without him. But he was going to miss her a lot.

   🙎 🙎 🙎

Michelle took another sip of her soft drink. She wrinkled her nose and let go of the straw after barely a taste. This was her second glass, and it had gone the way of the first—diluted with melted ice to the point of tastelessness. She glanced at her watch, then bit her lip. Matt had been gone for at least an hour and a half. Where *was* he? Anger warred against fear within her tender emotions. She could not settle on either one. Her pride stung from sitting alone so long, waiting for his return. Before anger could settle in, she'd start worrying that something bad had happened to him. Yet she dared not dwell on that possibility. What would she do then? Where would she go? They had gotten so close. He treated her like she was special. Her eyes began to fill with tears.

She looked up and saw a very pretty young woman with lots of eye makeup approaching her booth. Probably several years older, her green eyes and glossy black hair made a shocking contrast to the white leather mini-skirt outfit and spiked heels she was wearing. The woman smiled at Michelle's quick appraisal of her appearance. "Hi," she offered. "Wonder if I could share your table. I need to get off my feet. These new shoes are killing me."

No wonder, Michelle thought. It was a miracle she could even walk in heels that high. "I guess it's okay," she answered. She nodded toward the waitress. "At least she can glare at someone besides me. She's starting to get on my nerves."

The woman let out a throaty chuckle as she slid into the opposite seat. "Be glad to take some of the heat. My name's Jazzy. Actually, it's Jasmine. Most everybody shortens it to Jazz or Jazzy."

"Oh. Well, I'm . . . Ashley. Ashley Nicole." They shook hands across the narrow table. She was glad for the company, but not enough to admit it to a stranger.

"Beautiful name, darlin'," Jazzy cooed. "Have you ordered?"

"No, I'm not hungry. I'm waiting for someone. He should be here any minute."

"So you're working already? You look a little young. Then again, girls your age do pretty good."

Michelle flinched and glanced toward the entrance.

"Hey, it's okay. Don't worry. I was probably about your age when I got started." Their gazes locked for an instant. Jazzy lit up a long thin cigarette and held it between perfectly manicured fingers. Her polished red nails looked at least two inches long.

Michelle let go the breath she'd been holding. She had no idea what this Jazzy was talking about, but she could tell her reference to "a little young" had nothing to do with turning her in to the authorities. "I'm not so young, and I'm not working. I'm waiting for a friend. Only he's real late."

"Why don't we get a bite to eat to pass the time?"

"I'm really not very hungry. . ."

"Oh, doll, they make a fabulous club sandwich here." Before Michelle could respond, the waitress had arrived, pad ready. Jazzy ordered the club sandwich and a Perrier® with lime for herself. With arched eyebrows, she encouraged, "The same? My treat."

Michelle gave a sheepish shrug. "If you insist. Thanks." The waitress took their order and made her way toward the kitchen. "I haven't eaten since this morning. Guess I should." She paused to sneak a glance at the front entrance. Still no Matt. "I'm getting worried that something may have happened," she reluctantly admitted. "He should've been back by now."

"Don't mean to pry," Jazzy began, "but have you known him long?" Michelle stared back without answering.

"Ah, that's okay. In my line of work, I've learned to be a skeptic. Guys'll promise you anything to get what they want. Then once they have it, they sing another tune."

"No, my boyfriend's different. We haven't really known each other that long, but I can tell." She hoped Jazzy couldn't sense her lack of confidence.

"I keep looking for my special guy. Haven't found him yet, Ashley Nicole . . . But I will. *Someday.*" Her eyes took on a faraway look for an instant. She shrugged her shoulders and sighed. "Anyway, they serve great food here." Her unexpected shy smile, when it appeared, made her seem much younger than she did at first. She chattered on for several minutes.

Michelle, encouraged by the show of sincerity, took a chance. "Matt and I have only been in the city a few weeks. It's different from where I came from. So big. And so many people. That's why I'm kinda worried about him." Now it was her turn for the faraway look and the shy smile.

"Oh, I'm sure he'll be here soon. A friend wouldn't just up and leave you. With so many weirdos out—" The waitress's arrival with their sandwiches cut short what more she might have said, but Michelle didn't mind. Jazzy's words unknowingly came too close to her own fears. Plates in place, neither made any effort to resume the topic. They chose instead to comment on the quality of the food and the glamorous spots Jazzy had seen over the last several years. No doubt about it, she had been around.

Their meal finished, Jazzy asked the question Michelle had been dreading, "What'll you do if he doesn't show up?"

"I-I'm not sure," she stammered. "I can't just leave. And I don't have anypl—" She caught herself. "We were planning on getting another room after he got back. He knows his way around the city pretty well. Now . . ." Her words faded into silence. Her glance darted again toward the entrance—no Matt—toward Jazzy, and then at her sandwich. She bit her bottom lip, not wanting to blurt out more than that.

Jazzy leaned toward her before speaking. "I've got a suggestion." Michelle looked up, hope kindled. "I'm staying with a friend not too far from here. We work together, and I think you'd like her. You could stay in our apartment for a few days until you decide what you wanna do."

"But what about Matt? I can't just leave. I might never see him again."

"Leave my address and phone number with the cashier up front. She could give it to him when he shows up."

Michelle dared not accept too quickly. It sounded almost *too* good. Then she saw the flaw. "There's so many people coming and going, he could walk right in, and nobody would recognize him."

"I'm sure he'll ask for you. Besides, they know me here." She winked. "I could call in a few favors. Believe me, they'll keep their eyes peeled for him." Michelle wanted to think it would be that easy. "Have a picture of him?" Jazzy added.

"Oh, yes. Just picked some up today. He set all the controls on his good camera and a tourist pushed the button for us." She dug around in her backpack for the photos, then handed them to Jazzy, whose eyes widened.

"Girl, these are gorgeous! What a hunk! No wonder you been waitin' . . ."

"Thanks. I kinda like him."

"Think you can part with a picture long enough to leave it with the cashier?"

"I guess so."

"Then you'll do it? You'll come with me?"

She hesitated. Jazzy seemed nice enough—was even buying her dinner on the first meeting. "Sure," she heard herself say. She slapped her palm on the table. "I can't believe you just walked in and offered me a—but what could have happened to Matt? I warned him!"

"It's all right. You don't need to tell me the details. I just hate to see a pretty girl like you stuck out on these streets with no place to go. You've gotta escape the madness." She chuckled and reached across to clasp Michelle's hand. "Come on, Ashley. Let's pay the bill and I'll show you where we're staying."

"You said it's not far from here?"

"Only a few blocks."

"Okay. And can we get the picture to your friends before we leave?"

"Absolutely."

That settled it for Michelle. "Let's go, then. Maybe I'll come back later to see if he shows up."

"Whatever you do is fine with me," Jazzy declared as she scooted out of the seat and strutted up to the register, curvy hips swaying. Michelle followed behind her, feeling a mixture of anxiety and relief. She also felt quite out-classed by Jazzy's appearance—kind of like a country bumpkin at a society ball. Suddenly, she had a strong urge to cry. She missed Matt something awful.

🙖 🙖 🙖

A week later, morning dragged on for Michael. After trying to get some work done, he'd gone for a long walk to clear his head from a horrendous nightmare about Michelle. He had awakened before dawn in a cold sweat with the smell and taste of fear all around him. His heart was pounding, and he couldn't catch his breath. Even the sheets were damp.

The walk helped little. He kept thinking about his daughter, worrying about all that could happen. Now that they had a clue in which direction she might have fled, he couldn't sit still any longer and wait for his nightmare to become a reality. He had to decide on a plan of action.

New York City, of all places! He exhaled through gritted teeth. If he ever got his hands on that child . . . He must have been in shock the night he first heard the news from the detective. It seemed even harder to comprehend this morning. *How could she do such a thing?* Just thinking of her there, wandering the streets alone, sent shudders through his body. What kind of creeps would she run into? This thought, more than anything else, convinced him he had to act. And in the back of his mind a plan was taking shape. But then there was a strong possibility she never made it that far. All they had to go on was an ex-convict's word that she said she was headed there from Washington. In truth, she could be dead in a ditch somewhere. Michael immediately forced that thought out of his mind.

Sometime during the mid-morning hours—he couldn't put his finger on the exact moment—he began to feel a definite urgency about going to New York. Maybe he just couldn't bear to sit around any longer twiddling his thumbs. Who knows? He was certain of only one thing—he had to do something! If he got there

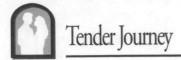

soon enough, he might be able to pick up her trail without too much difficulty. The more time that passed, the colder her trail, and the harder to track her down. Then he thought of Stephanie.

How would she react? She'd probably want to go with him, but one of them needed to stay and take care of Stephen. He almost decided to go back inside and talk to her about it. In fact, he got up from the stool where he was working and took three steps toward the door before he realized she had left the day before for Orlando. Stephen had late afternoon and evening appointments with two of his three doctors, so they had spent the night in a motel. They were supposed to be home any time.

He felt guilty more often than not whenever he thought of his son. Of course, he wasn't responsible for his present condition, but he *felt* responsible. He should have been more careful about that transfusion years ago, should have checked out the hospital's blood-screening policy, should have asked plenty of questions . . . Stephen had certainly done nothing to deserve an outright death sentence. Though he had not discussed his guilt feelings with anyone—Eric knew only about the undercurrent of anger—he never felt free of the lead weight hanging around his neck

His whole family was living in the shadow of a volcano, waiting for it to erupt again. Nowadays, he felt like running. Could that have inspired the urge to search for Michelle so far away? If he found her, maybe he could atone, at least in part, for some of his wrongs that had hurt Stephanie. Perhaps he could escape from the constant reminder of the past and put some distance between him and his feelings. Yes, if he could just find Michelle. Find her and convince her to come back home with him. A long shot, indeed.

Stephanie and Stephen arrived a few minutes after one o'clock. Michael had, by that time, called several airlines for prices on flights to New York City. Quite a bit higher than he would have liked, but he couldn't afford to wait thirty days. Contrary to popular opinion, even *he* wasn't that cheap. He hesitated before answering when Stephanie asked how his morning had gone. Why get her more upset? Instead, he squatted down in front of his son so they could look each other in the eyes. Everything else he had been worrying about faded in an instant. He reached out his hand and ruffled Stephen's curly hair. His eyes followed the path formed by his fingers. "How'd it go, big guy?" he asked.

"Okay." Stephen shrugged. "They say I'm . . ." He tilted his head to the side and looked up at the ceiling, then bit his top lip and inhaled deeply. " . . . holding my own." He breathed out. "Yeah, holding my own."

"Well, great." Michael squeezed his son's shoulder. Afraid to let Stephen know how much he agonized every time he went for an exam, Michael restrained the sigh of relief he felt at the good news. But when Stephen took a tentative step forward, he wrapped both arms around him and hugged him to his chest. Then, still hugging him, Michael lifted him up and spun him around in a circle several times. Their laughter eased the tension and restored a measure of peace. Even Stephanie joined in, free for a moment of the cloud of impending ruin.

Michael slowed his spinning. He timed it so that when he came to a halt and set Stephen back on the ground, Stephanie was directly in front of him. "Hi, hon," he said, a bit out of breath. Stephen turned his head around to get a better look at the two of them. "Everything go okay with the doctors?" he asked her.

"Da-ad," Stephen whined, "don't you believe me?"

"Of course. But I still want to hear from your mother."

"His T-cell count stayed the same," Stephanie interjected. "At least it didn't drop, but I was hoping it would have gone up. They're going to try him on a new drug. I forget the name."

He moved closer to Stephanie and put his arm around her shoulders. "Com'ere." He motioned his son over to his side. When Stephen complied, he clasped his shoulders and put his other arm around him. Together, they walked through the living room and out onto the porch. The three of them stood that way for several seconds without moving. Each had their own thoughts, and no one wanted to be the first to speak.

Stephen coughed, then wriggled out of the friendly, but unfamiliar, family embrace. He took a step, hesitated, stuffed his hands into his pants' pockets and strode to the far end of the porch. He leaned out over the railing. From there he could see the corner where the road twisted around the bend and dropped out of sight.

"Dad?"

"Yes, Son?"

"Think I'll ever see her again?"

Stephanie's face paled. Her fingers dug into Michael's arm, but he barely noticed. His attention was riveted on his young son.

"Why do you ask?"

"Don't be silly," Stephanie cut in. "Of course you'll see her, honey. She's—"

"Hold it," Michael cut in. "What brought all this about?" His own nightmare came flooding back, quickening his heartbeat a few notches.

Stephanie relented. She nodded and relaxed her grip.

Sensing her acceptance, however reluctant, he returned his gaze to Stephen, who stared at the porch floor. "What's up?"

"I miss her, Dad! And the teachers are always telling us not to get into any cars with strangers. People could be driving those cars who want to do bad things to kids. Then I think of Michelle . . ." He paused, slowly blinking. "What if one of 'em picks up my sister? She's my only one."

Michael breathed deep before answering. Those thoughts were tame compared to the ones that had crossed his mind more than once, but he had to show a strong front for his family. It would do no good for them to see how panicky he really felt. "We've just got to believe no one like that will come near her," he said. He tried to sound reassuring.

Stephen's head nodded his tentative agreement.

"It's not easy, huh?" Michael tilted his chin up to look at him.

"Nope." He hesitated a moment before continuing. "Maybe going to the doctor got me thinking. What if I wasn't doing so good? I mean . . . things can change, right? Why else do I have to keep going back all the time?"

It was Michael's turn to lower his gaze.

"What if I get lots worse before she comes home?" he pleaded. "I might never see her again." His voice broke on his last words. His chin quivered.

Stephanie could take it no longer. She slipped away from Michael's embrace, ran over to Stephen and held him to her. "It's okay, honey!" she exclaimed. "Somehow things will work out."

Michael came over and stood by them. He rested a hand on each of their shoulders. "Your mom's right. I've been doing some thinking this morning." He paused at length. Both Stephen and Stephanie glanced up, waiting. "Would it make you feel better if I went up North to look for her? I could pass out flyers, talk to people . . ." He braced himself for the onslaught from his wife he'd been dreading. It never came. Probably too surprised. She had considered him "unconcerned" before now. In a way, she was right. Reality had come crashing down on him that morning.

Stephen's fingers grasped his hand in a tight grip. Stephanie turned a puzzled, tear-streaked face to him.

"Would you, Dad? Would you please?" Stephen exclaimed.

Stephanie stared, wide-eyed, into Michael's eyes. The tenderness he saw rise to the surface surprised him. And the hope . . .

"I could be gone for quite a while. Who knows how long it could take to track her down?"

She hugged him. "I don't know what brought this about, but yes, Michael, *please try*! Anything might help."

Stephen released his hold on Michael's hand and raised both hands in the air. "Yay!" he shouted. His did his familiar hop-skip, waved his right arm in an arc and spun himself in a circle. "Go find her, Dad. You can do it. You and Jesus."

Michael chuckled. His son didn't get his spontaneous exuberance from him. He must have gotten it from his mother. She was the emotional one in the family. Whenever Stephen felt enthused about something, everyone within earshot knew about it.

"Let's not get too excited, son," he cautioned. "I haven't even left yet." He wouldn't want to calculate the odds against his success, and he didn't want Stephen to get his hopes up too high. Still, his son's confidence in him boosted his own waning faith. He stood a tad straighter as he motioned toward the porch swing. They walked over and sat down, he and Stephanie on the swing and Stephen on the steps in front of them. "So it's unanimous?" They nodded and set about making plans. Stephen begged to go along, but that was out of the question.

Later that evening, long after they'd put him to bed, Michael and Stephanie went back out to the porch swing. Michael had reserved a seat on an eight o'clock flight to LaGuardia Airport the next morning. It was the earliest he could conveniently get, unless he wanted to fly off that evening without a chance to prepare. He didn't, and Stephanie wouldn't stand for it. He would take enough decent clothes for a month. They would be clean, matched, and packed nice and neat, or he wouldn't go. That was just the way she did things, travel-wise. Her own purses and closets—quite another matter. Michael didn't dare bring up the inconsistency.

The only thing they hadn't done was spend some time alone together. No point trying to talk to her while she worked to get him ready. He had half her attention, at best. So he waited until they went back out on the porch. Trouble was, now that he was out here, he didn't know how to get the conversation steered in the right direction. That had happened to him more and more lately. They'd drifted so far apart. He wanted so much more from his last night with her. He intended something special, but after all the preparations, it was getting late. "Hon, you're quiet all of a sudden," he ventured. He put his arm around her and tried to pull her close.

She reacted by exhaling deeply and shrugging her shoulders. He waited. Nothing. "Is that it? I'm leaving tomorrow for who knows how long and all you can do is sigh and shrug?"

She sighed again. "No, I was just thinking about us. We feel so awkward with each other these days."

"Geez, Stephanie, I know that. How many times are you going to remind me?" He shook his head. Disgust contorted his features. "I get tired of hearing it over and over and over."

"Well, it's the truth."

"If that's all you can think to say, how about keeping your mouth *shut?*" He knew, even as the words escaped, that he'd made a mistake. A big one. It was too late to change it, and he felt suddenly too full of\ shame and resentment to apologize.

Stephanie turned her body to face him. The twin daggers in her eyes were outdone only by the razor-edged sharpness of her next words. "Don't try the poor-me routine with me. What do you think I've been doing all evening, except getting *you* ready? Did it ever occur to you to thank me?"

263

Michael only stared back at her, waiting for the torrent of words to dwindle enough for him to edge into the conversation.

"I didn't think so. You're too inconsiderate. You expect me to be the good little wife who waits on her husband hand-and-foot, yet you don't even notice when I do the million-and-one things that need doing. And now you get to run off to the glamour spot of the world. *By yourself,* no less! The least you could do is offer to help with some of this. But no! You hold off until I'm half-dead with exhaustion, then decide to try to get romantic. Well, fat chance." She folded her arms across her chest and scooted over to the far corner of the swing.

What she said was true. He had been hoping they could spend a few intimate moments together that evening, and he never once thought to help her so they could go to bed early. Before he could frame an apology, one that she'd accept, she continued.

"And do you know what really hurts? I *was* thinking of spending some time with you tonight. But not now! You just want to use me to meet your needs. Not only for cooking meals, ironing clothes, or keeping the kids out of your hair, but for sex—on the rare occasions when you feel so inclined. Well, let me tell you something. *I'm not interested!*"

With that she stood up and stomped back into the house.

Michael sat on the porch for some time afterwards, rehashing their argument. He couldn't decide whether to be mad at her or at himself for his own lack of tact. He knew he held some of the blame. If only he'd kept *his* mouth shut and let her defuse. But he hadn't. Now he was paying the price—sitting alone on a porch swing made for two. Stephanie was sleeping when he finally decided to go upstairs. He undressed and slipped into bed beside her. No sense trying to cuddle. She had her back to him. He flopped over on his other side and let out a deep sigh. Truthfully, they had both acted like a couple of selfish kids. He wondered what they could do to put a stop to the vicious cycle . . . In minutes, the only sound was the gentle breathing of two unhappy adults.

Morning found them still in dour spirits. They overslept and had to rush from the moment their feet touched the floor. It made a good excuse not to spend much time in earnest conversation. They limited it to the essentials:

"How much time do we have?"

"Do you have enough money?"

"Will you be all right with Stephen?"

"Call me when you get settled."

Neither brought up their argument of the night before. They pretended it never happened, except for the black cloud that hung over them. Breathless and tense, they raced around to finish last-minute details. They couldn't take a chance of his missing the plane on a nonrefundable ticket.

"Michael, please do find her," Stephanie entreated him just before the door to the airport shuttle closed behind him. Despite whatever differences existed between them, they both wanted Michelle back home.

Stephanie watched the van drive off until it turned the corner and disappeared. She stood a moment longer, staring at the now-empty stretch of road. That was how she felt. Empty. Deserted. By her husband, her children, and life. "Stop being silly," she told herself out loud. It made no difference. She'd lived without a sense of fulfillment for so long now, she felt exhausted and numb. And with that thought foremost in mind, she trudged back into the house.

❧ *Sixteen* ❧

ichael sat on the bed and surveyed the room he'd just rented at the Mayflower Hotel on Central Park West. Listed in his New York pocket guide as a moderately-priced, fine hotel, it turned out to be a tremendous deal for the price. Even had a refrigerator and serving pantry right in his room. Those would come in handy if his stay lasted very long.

He started out with a reservation for a week, hoping to make some serious headway by then. His choice landed him a spacious single room with a queen-sized bed and panoramic view of Central Park. For only twenty-one dollars more a night, how could he pass up a chance to enjoy one of the best spots in New York? He would need plenty of peaceful moments if he was to cope with the enormous task before him.

Further scrutiny of his room showed impeccable attention to detail and all the warmth of a grand old hotel. First class in every way. He really appreciated the high ceilings and walk-in closets; he could avoid the claustrophobic feelings he often got on the road. Stephanie would love the traditional cherry furniture (even if they were reproductions, no doubt), plush linens, and fine art prints.

And the lobby! She would flip over the huge nautical paintings in heavy gold frames, setting off a gold leaf ceiling, large bouquets of flowers and plush burgundy carpet. To her taste, exactly. He couldn't believe that he had happened upon a place so nice for not much over a hundred dollars a night. In upper Manhattan! He now understood its popularity with the media people, who had filmed several movies there. He could walk to Lincoln Center, the Met, and Carnegie Hall, in the rare event that he had a chance to enjoy himself. Classical music had always appealed to him, but he had never taken time to pursue it.

He flipped through the information pack, only to discover the hotel had a fully-equipped fitness center, complimentary coffee and newspapers in the morning, plus 24-hour voice mail for guests. The desk clerk must have told him about those amenities, but perhaps not. She was very busy when he checked in. She had mentioned the award-winning Conservatory Restaurant next door. He would be sure to try there first.

A sudden optimism flooded his soul. For a brief moment, he forgot the reason he had come to New York. Maybe the trip would turn out better than he expected. Someone certainly seemed to be smiling on him thus far. He hoped it was God.

"Ah, boy," he said, sighing long and loud. He said it again and fell back onto the bed, his arms spread wide, eyes closed. After ten or fifteen minutes in that prone position, he forced himself to sit up. He should get in gear. He hadn't come all the way from Florida to lounge around. Discarding one possible starting point after another, he felt immobilized. His only real hope lay in someone recognizing his daughter's picture. His suitcase contained thousands of flyers, and he intended to pass out as many as he could. That meant getting out on the street. Changing thought to action, he slipped his shoes back on.

He wanted to keep a record of every route he took, every person he spoke to and every place he left a flyer. "Man," he moaned, patting his jacket pocket for the leather organizer he always carried, but he came up empty. Must have left the thing on the airport shuttle—the last place he remembered having it. How could he be so absent-minded? It would involve major work to re-enter all those names and addresses in a new one, not to mention his to-do lists and many notes to himself. He would have to keep abreast of accounts to some extent while he was away. At least he had entered the info in the contact management software on his computer at home. Too bad he hadn't installed it on the laptop he brought along with him, though.

He'd have Stephanie express mail it to him right away. Of course, that meant instructing her over the phone how to copy a file onto a disk. A real picnic, there. The last time he tried long-distance to have her check something on his computer, it ended up a total disaster. Okay, so he got a *tad* impatient. She started sobbing and shouted into the mouthpiece, "You're trying to make me look like an idiot!" Then she hung up on him. He wasn't looking forward to the experience again.

Well, he had to have something temporary to jot notes down on when he went out. No telling how long it would take him to get to an office supply store. He scouted around. In decent hotel rooms, the maids usually placed note paper in a drawer or by the phone. There! He found several sheets of letterhead and envelopes in the top drawer of the desk. When he sorted through the items, a sheaf of papers folded in half and partially hidden beneath the room service menu came into view. Ever curious, and without thinking, he reached in to retrieve and unfold it.

On the front page he read in plain typewriter printing, *A Treatise Concerning Religious Affections.* Someone had penned in the upper right corner, Jonathan Edwards (mid 1700s). How odd! The time period fit in perfectly with the colonial setting of the hotel. A guest must have forgotten it, he supposed. Funny that the maids hadn't thrown it away. The person had highlighted several portions on each page. Quite the intellectual type. Michael couldn't remember reading anything by an eighteenth-century author since graduate school, but he felt compelled to peruse the marked passages now.

. . . Trials, above all other things, have a tendency to distinguish between true religion and false, and to cause the difference between them evidently to appear. Hence they are called by the name of trials, in the verse preceding the text (1 Peter 1:8), and innumerable other places. They try the faith and religion of professors, of what sort it is, as apparent gold is tried in the fire, and manifested, whether it be true gold or not . . .

And then, these trials not only manifest the truth of true religion, but they make its genuine beauty and amiableness remarkably to appear. True virtue never appears so lovely, as when it is most oppressed: and the divine excellency of real Christianity is never exhibited with such advantage, as when under the greatest trials. Then it is that true faith appears much more precious than gold; and upon this account, is found to praise, and honour, and glory . . .

Again, another benefit of such trials to true religion, is that they purify and increase it. They not only show the amiableness of true religion to the best advantage, but they tend to increase its beauty by establishing and confirming it; making it more lively and vigorous, and purifying it

269

from those things that obscured its lustre and glory. As gold that is tried in the fire is purged from its alloy, and all reminders of dross, and comes forth more beautiful; so true faith being tried as gold is tried in the fire, becomes more precious; and thus also is found unto praise, and honor, and glory.[11]

This was some heavy-duty, high-brow stuff for sure. Its owner must have been a theology student. Or maybe a well-read professional enduring some tough times. He skimmed back over the paragraphs he'd read. The words, trials and true religion, captured his attention. He hadn't considered the notion that his family was going through these ordeals as a test of faith. He shook his head. If so, he had failed miserably.

Maybe it wasn't too late. Lord knows, he could use some fine-tuning. Trials, huh? He vaguely remembered a verse from the book of Romans. He had studied and memorized it with Caleb. Something about all things working together for good to those who love the Lord . . .

No, he certainly didn't feel as zealous as during those too-short days with the sweet old guy. Far from it. But he still believed, didn't he? That admission brought relief to his weary features.

His stomach growled and gurgled suddenly. He toyed with the idea of grabbing a bite to eat at the Conservatory, then settled on it as a definite plan. Maybe a quick stroll around the Park afterward, a shower and an early bedtime. Good idea, instead of trying to go out now. He wanted to get a good start in the morning, pounding the pavement. He had a lot of ground to cover.

By 11:00 a.m. the next day, Michael had been traipsing around for hours. Every step he took heaped more discouragement onto his overloaded emotions. He'd abandoned Central Park long ago. How many times he thought he'd spotted his daughter, only to be disappointed! When he drew close enough to be sure, the resemblance faded. Only hope, painting a picture he desperately wanted to see. To make matters worse, he had left the bundle of flyers in a restaurant when he stopped for breakfast. Where was his mind lately? He was getting as bad as Stephanie. When he went back, they were gone. With any luck, the finder had enough sense not to toss them in the garbage. He had two copies with him, dirty and worn, folded up small enough to fit in his wallet. The remainder were stored back in his room. He decided to keep going. Might as well get a feel for the area as long as he was out.

He followed Broadway as it angled southwest through the theater district. Block after block, heading south through Midtown, he noticed the color of the neighborhoods shifted. It left him with the sensation of passing through a movie dreamscape. How many New Year's Eves had he watched the midnight celebration on TV? Now, walking past the very buildings lent a surrealistic cast to his mission. And the *crowds!*

He had no way of knowing that today the city had scheduled a free, open-air Broadway on Broadway production in Time's Square. He'd gotten into a taxi for the ride to lower Manhattan, but the traffic became so snarled, with streets barricaded for blocks around, that he'd gotten out in disgust and started walking again. Slow-going, still. At least he was making some progress and not fuming in traffic.

How could they do this in the middle of a workday? It made no sense. The crowds loved it, though. They were flocking in just to get a glimpse of the show taking place on the platform high above the street. And for those who couldn't get close enough to see, speakers blared from every corner for blocks. He felt like a

lone salmon swimming upstream, like the only human on earth making any attempt to get anywhere. Everybody else within sight seemed content to stay put. Not him. He had no time to waste. Now, he was a man on a mission.

His forward movement continued at an unbearably slow pace while he elbowed his way through the crowds. The numbers of people who turned out for the midday event exceeded his wildest imagination. Sure, he'd seen New York crowds on television. Being caught out among that teaming mass of humanity, searching for one young girl, seemed nothing short of impossible. The sheer folly of his task made him want to give up and go home. And it was only his first day.

It took him a while, but he managed to get through the crowds. The confetti ticker-tape celebration over, he started making better time. He took a two-block detour west through Bryant Park to check out any teenagers hanging around there. No luck. At noon, most of the people who were relaxing on benches looked like professionals from nearby office buildings.

Soon, he found himself heading south on Seventh Avenue. Why he hadn't chosen the famous Fifth Avenue, he didn't have a clue. He walked through the Garment District, with the famous Macy's on his left, stopped to check on the prices of a couple of suits on display there and in two small shops around the corner on the side street. He'd have to come back when he had more time. He could use a couple of new additions to his wardrobe. He passed Pennsylvania Station and a few blocks further, the Fashion Institute. From that point, he had clear sailing all the way to Greenwich Village.

Almost immediately, he sensed a major change in the atmosphere. Brown brick buildings looked older and more artsy, not nearly as glitzy as those in the brass-and-glass district earlier in his walk. Many of them sported bright-colored, hand-painted signs and store-front windows. Several he glanced at had something or other to do with gay/lesbian happenings. He winced. That brought no measure of comfort. He could not shake the thought that his little girl was out there in this.

He quickened his pace.

The sun overhead beat down relentlessly, and it was only early June. Though he'd taken back up his habits of running to stay in shape, the heat was taking its toll on him. *How much longer?* he wondered aloud. Besides the flyers, he'd forgotten to bring his travel guide. As long as the streets had numbers he could tell which direction he was going and about how much further he had to go. Here in Greenwich Village, the streets all had names. He did stop once for something cold to drink and as he showed the store clerk the flyer with Michelle's picture, Michael asked for the quickest route to the Statue of Liberty ferry.

"Straight ahead," came the curt reply.

No help there. He'd been doing the 'straight ahead' action for miles. He got back on foot. Block after block after block . . . "Gotta be running out of island soon," he mumbled as he took a long swallow of Gatorade®. "The place isn't *that* big." He wiped sweat from his forehead and continued on his trek. He saw a sign for the Holland Tunnel pointing to the right. Somewhere near Canal Street, Seventh Avenue turned into Varick and merged with West Broadway, so he followed that until it dead-ended. Now which way? The speed and volume of traffic had increased considerably.

The building directly in front of him, whatever the name, was immense. He crossed Vesey Street and turned right to walk alongside its base. After turning left, he understood—the World Trade Center, home of the tallest skyscrapers and some of most prestigious companies in the city. He stood in awe, staring at it, going

up and up and up into the sky. Suddenly, he imagined the lower section of steel and concrete caving in on itself. He shook his head. What a stupid thought.

If he remembered the map correctly, he had almost reached the Financial District and Wall Street, where shrewd investors earned fortunes every day. Speaking of fortunes, he made a mental note to call his stockbroker. He would have enjoyed a tour, but held himself in check. Stay focused. He had come to New York for one purpose: to look for Michelle. And she would not go to Wall Street. That was one place he could eliminate.

He showed the flyer to a corner policeman, who gave him directions to Battery Park. Yes, many young homeless congregated there. "It's still quite a few blocks away," he advised. "You'll run into some rough areas for walking. Better take a taxi."

Michael thanked him. For some reason, he preferred to stay on foot. He angled a bit to the west and passed the Oppenheimer Building. Then he went around Rector Park to the Esplanade along the waterfront and gave in to the call of the park benches situated on the walkway. He took a five minute breather before continuing around to Battery Place and finally, on over to Battery Park. It was four o'clock in the afternoon. He been moving steadily since early morning. Now that he had arrived, he didn't know which direction to start looking first.

From what he'd been told, many of the homeless would be out and about, doing whatever they did during the day. They wouldn't return until after dark, which was still several hours away. That's when he noticed the sign to his right. The last ferry to the Statue of Liberty would leave at four-thirty. Again not sure why, he made his way toward the ticket counter and bought a ticket. Of all places, he felt certain Michelle would go there. Ever since she was little, she had begged to see it.

Aside from showing the flyer to every clerk he could find, Michael spent the next hour and a half acting like a tourist. He walked around the grassy area at the base of the statue, and then went inside to view the historical museum. It was too late to make the trip up the winding steps to the crown, but he mildly enjoyed himself anyway. For a few minutes, he forgot his troubles. Much too soon, he heard an announcement that all visitors had to return to the docking area and board their respective ferries. Closing time.

Leaving the island, and watching the statue recede in the distance, he felt a deep melancholy tugging at him. He was proud to live in such a great country, yet he felt sad when he thought about how far America had drifted from her forefather's ideals. *"One Nation Under God,"* and *"In God We Trust,"* had no meaning anymore. They had become mere puppeted phrases during pledges and imprints on greenbacks. He couldn't help wondering how many of the country's problems stemmed from religious apathy. Who would have imagined that a nation founded by men and women risking life and limb to seek freedom of religion would end up banning public prayer? The very idea boggled his mind. He found himself wondering, too, if Michelle still cared about such things. In grade school and junior high, she loved American history. To tell the truth, he knew very few of her interests now. A new wave of guilt swept over him.

He felt a bump as the ferry docked, bringing him back from his thoughts. He reached over to make sure he had the flyer he was going to show around the Park. When they gave the signal to depart, he fell in with the crowd and made his way down the gangplank to shore.

He passed a table where vendors were selling mementos of Ellis Island and the Statue of Liberty. Souvenirs interested him little. With the approach of evening, the number of homeless staking out their claims on the choice camping spots had multiplied. Out in the crowd, someone playing a trumpet panhandled for his supper, or for whatever else he might crave to numb his pain. People, for the most part, ignored the fellow; in fact, as a rule, they ignored the homeless completely. They walked right past them and never turned their heads. Or if they did, they simply made a wider berth around them. He searched for the slightest signs of concern but could detect none.

Michael walked up and down the paths, looking into the faces of the few young girls he saw sitting on the grass or reclining against the base of some tree. He took out his single flyer and showed it to anyone who would give him the time of day. Nobody recognized her.

As Michael once again neared Bowling Green, he approached one of two foot patrolmen. He explained that he was looking for his daughter and that he had some flyers he'd like to get out. He didn't have them with him now, but . . .

The officer cautioned him to be careful. Many areas of New York had warnings against posting bills of any kind. Then he admitted that, if he just happened to see one or two of them around there with his daughter's picture on it, well . . . He'd let the next shift worry about them, unless, of course, they were too busy doing other things. In that case, who knows how long the things would stay up.

Michael thanked him and turned to go back into the Park.

"Hold it a moment," the officer called after him. "I've got a daughter, too. Let me have one in case we happen to run across anyone matching her description."

"Sure." Michael wrote down his hotel number and handed over the only extra flyer he had on him. "Thank you, again, sir. Thank you very much."

The officer wished him luck. Michael nodded, jotted a note in his organizer, and continued on back around to where he first entered the park. He lost count of the times he was asked by one or another of the vagrants for help. At first, he did give them some money. A little pocket change. Then a dollar or two, until he noticed that some of the faces started looking familiar. Angry that they were playing him for a fool, he quit doling out money. Two of them tried to intimidate him into renewing his charitable giving. When they saw he wasn't about to change his mind, they wandered back to wherever they'd set up camp and left him to his business.

He would have little success getting any worthwhile information from this bunch, he decided, but made a mental note of where he might post a few flyers if he came back down this far. A little discouraged, he realized how hungry he was, and how long of a walk lay ahead of him. Out of the question. His feet were killing him. Besides, it would be dark before he reached the hotel.

None of the buses he saw were heading uptown to where he wanted to go. The only taxi he managed to flag down told him he was heading to the lower east side. That left two choices: walk far enough north to where he could find a taxi or take the subway. An entrance less than fifteen feet from where he stood helped in his decision. Though a bit hesitant, he chose the subway.

Surprisingly, the entrance was well-lit, and business people of all races waited in line to get their tokens. He, too, paid his dollar and a quarter. Such a deal. He followed the clerk's directions to descend a couple of levels, look for signs and wait for the next train. He didn't stand there long before one pulled up. He got in and made his way toward the back of the car. It was crowded, standing room only. And right across from the door, stood a policeman.

He breathed a silent prayer of thanks. At least now he didn't have to worry about the crazies who rode the subway. Everyone sat quietly, waiting his turn to get off. Michael stood in the middle of the aisle holding onto one of the center poles. After three stops, he looked up just in time to see the back of the police officer's hat disappearing through the closing doors. A twinge of anxiety rose in his gut.

He tried to let himself sway back and forth, in time with the gentle rocking rhythm of the train on the tracks. Fatigue was setting in. His feet ached for all the walking, and the relaxing motion brought visions of a nice, comfortable bed. He let his eyes close for a few seconds. When he opened them, he had to blink to make sure he hadn't started dreaming. What a sight he saw at the other end of the car! He almost laughed, but thought better of it.

A fellow with very dark skin stood there, fitting a mouthpiece onto the neck of a beat-up alto saxophone. His hair hung in long braids, woven with purple and yellow ribbons. High on his forehead, he wore a bright green headband. The thing that struck Michael so funny was the way the guy had stuck two pencils—one on either side of his head—so they pointed up and out of his hair like a set of antennas. At the end of each pencil he had added extra large pencil erasers.

Again, Michael wanted to laugh, but didn't. Something about the guy made him uneasy. The feeling almost went away when the sax music started. He didn't sound half bad at first, playing some jazzy blues. Then he started an awful rendition of "Old McDonald Had a Farm." Squeaks and squawks on every other note. Honking noises that set your teeth on edge. Michael glanced at the people around him. Some shook their heads. Others, except for a slight tension in their features, gave no indication that anything out of the ordinary was taking place. They ignored the guy.

Perhaps that set him off. When he couldn't get any response, he stopped playing, let the sax dangle around his neck by its strap, and held a tennis ball container up in the air. "People, listen to me," he began in what he must have thought was an oratorical-sounding voice, "I been doin' real bad lately. Real bad. My finances ain't about nothin'. I don't have 'ny place to sleep, and I'm hungry. In other words, I'm lookin' for some green."

"Just what I need," Michael mumbled under his breath.

"Yes, isn't that the truth," said a slender oriental woman in a nurse's uniform standing next to him in the aisle. Her head shook from side to side. The deep fatigue he saw reflected in her dark brown eyes made him look away.

Meanwhile, the entertainer had begun another version of "Old McDonald," more horrible than the first. He came to an abrupt halt and picked up his tennis ball container. "This here's my offering basket. Now, we can do this easy, or we can do it hard, as hard as you wanna make it. It don't matter to me one bit." He let down the jar and held up his sax. "See this? I can play notes so beautiful they'll make you cry." He paused. "And I can do some playin' that will drive you insane. Stark-ravin' mad with just one note.

"Now . . ." and he took his time looking around the subway car, ". . . , if you put some green in the offering basket, I'll quit." He laughed. "Everybody will be happy. I'll have my money and you'll have your mind."

Michael listened to his spiel, trying to see if the guy had a screw loose, or if he was just running a scam. To his dismay, he couldn't tell. The woman in the nurse's uniform next to him was praying softly. He stared at her with his brows raised, wondering her opinion on the scenario. "You'd better start praying," she said. "It's the only thing that does any good." When he looked at her, she continued, "Go on, if you don't want trouble."

Tender Journey

Even as she finished speaking, they heard a commotion coming from the end of the car. Someone had jumped up—a young man wearing a white shirt and a designer print silk tie—and stormed over to confront the musician. "Why don't you *sit down* and *be quiet!*" he shouted. "I've been working hard all day. I'm tired, and I don't need this mess!"

Scowling, the braided saxophonist cocked his head. "Get back, y'hear? Don't you know *who I am?* I'm the Antenna Man, and this is my weapon. Now you *back up!*" he spat out, shaking his sax in a threatening manner.

The businessman reeled backward. He wasn't prepared for such bizarre behavior.

The Antenna Man saw his hesitation. That was all he needed. He took a step toward his confronter. "I tol' you 'bout this." He shook the sax again in his opponent's face. "I can drive you crazy with one note. *You* sit down and shut up. I've got the power, and if you know what's good for you, you'll sit down . . . *now!*"

Michael felt sorry for the poor guy facing the Antenna Man, and yet was annoyed with him at the same time. He should never have made a move if he wasn't prepared to follow through. It would only feed the sickness. That's exactly what happened.

For the next three stops, the guy ranted and raved about his tremendous power. Then he started announcing how, real soon, everybody could see him on television. He'd be on twice a week, and before long, the public could start buying stock in the Antenna Man. Michael could no longer keep a straight face. He stifled a chuckle.

"Don't laugh," the woman standing next to him half-scolded in a whisper. "You must pray."

He was ready to agree. While they were talking, the Antenna Man began making his way down the crowded aisle. Those closest to him reluctantly dropped something into his makeshift "offering basket." The rest averted their gazes, hoping they wouldn't find themselves eyeball-to-eyeball with him.

Michael glanced up.

The guy was at about six feet and still coming.

Closer and closer.

He wanted to look off in some other direction, but pride kept him looking straight ahead.

At about eighteen inches, the Antenna Man stared straight into his eyes with a crazed expression. Their gazes locked for an instant, sending a chill up and down Michael's spine.

He gripped the center pole with all his strength. Adrenaline flooded his muscles. His mouth went dry. His breath quickened. He was both afraid and ready, he hoped, for whatever was coming.

All the while, he heard the oriental woman praying. He strained to make out the words, but couldn't. No matter. God must have heard her.

The Antenna Man moved on, scrutinizing those around him as he walked. Suddenly, he burst into semi hysterical laughter. Then he turned his body sideways and slid past some people toward the door. While he was waiting, he kept himself occupied with a non-stop monologue about his supposed identity. "I am the great spirit!" he shouted. "I am spirit incarnate. I have all the power of the universe. You'll find out. Now, watch my power!"

The train rolled to a routine stop at the station. "Open sesame!" he commanded. When the doors opened and he stepped off onto the platform, nobody rushed to crown him. Instead, they breathed a collective sigh of relief.

Several minutes later, Michael relaxed his grip on the pole. His hand had begun to cramp, he'd had such a tight grasp on it. "Do you ride the subway often?" he dared to ask the prayer warrior.

"Yes. Every day, to and from work, for the last fourteen years."

"Does this kind of thing happen a lot?"

"More than I'd like," she replied with a resigned nod.

"How do you stand it?"

"I have no choice. So I pray before I get on, I pray while I'm riding, and I give thanks once I get off. I've been doing it so long, it's a habit." She turned full-face to him. "And it works, you know. I have never seen anybody hurt while I've been on."

"Oh, I'm a firm believer in prayer."

Her eyebrows drew together. "Then why weren't you *doing* it?" She paused, not really expecting an answer, but giving him a chance anyway. She inched her way toward the exit doors. When they opened at the next stop, just before she stepped through onto the platform, she turned around and reminded him with a brisk motion of her hand, "These days, you'd better pray, or you won't survive. You have seen nothing of the evil yet to come."

Michael stared at the floor long after the train resumed its journey. He understood what the woman meant. He also knew she was right. He'd been sending up a few hip-pocket, spoken-on-the-fly prayers. But she was talking about serious business. The kind of prayers that reach out and don't give up until they touch heaven. The way Caleb used to pray. No, a long time had passed since he'd been gripped by such fervor. Too long.

Still mulling over her warning, Michael got off at the 57th Street station. He walked the block and a half back to his room, not noticing anything unusual. He felt a renewed need to communicate with God, but didn't know how to break the ice. Just as he pushed open the door to his room, he had a flash of insight—he was afraid of prayer on that level. Much too intense, too intimate for him. When he got right down to it, he didn't want anyone to know his deepest, darkest secrets. Not even God.

With that admission still resounding in his head, he closed the door behind him, made his way over to the bed, and stretched out on his back. He was exhausted.

Maybe he should make an *effort* to pray, he decided. Where to begin? What to say first?

"God, I really want to find our daughter . . ." *As if He didn't know.*

"Stephen needs to be healed . . ." *Any dunce could figure that one out.*

"Stephanie and I have grown so far apart . . ." *Another no-brainer there.*

Nothing felt the least bit comfortable—like trying on a pair of somebody else's shoes.

He stared at the high ceiling for a long while and let himself reminisce about the day he stumbled upon Caleb at his Country Corner retreat. Somehow Caleb had helped him cross a threshold into a brand new world. Clearly, he no longer had access to that same place. At least, it didn't seem so. Why not? Why did he feel as if he didn't belong anymore? He wished he knew.

Just as he was drifting off to sleep, he sensed an inner urging to "give thanks."

For what? he wondered. Everything in their life was going as wrong as possible.

You could start with gratitude for protection on the subway . . .

Yes, he guessed he could do that much. He shivered when he remembered the Antenna Man. He mumbled a few quiet words as he rolled over onto his stomach. Within seconds, he was snoring.

❧ *Seventeen* ❧

As evening was coming on, the stream of people filing into Bryant Park on 42nd Street trickled down. Almost every folding chair was already taken, so several older women passed out blankets for more seating on the grass. Some of the homeless came for the free coffee and pastries. Some came to have a clean spot to perch on for a while. Many, in spite of their unfortunate circumstances, came to hear more about a God who could meet them right where they were. They had allowed a breath of hope into their souls, and it brightened their faces with new life. For others, no more than a faint spark flickered in the depths of deadened eyes, but they came, willing to listen.

The revival had only just begun. In fact, it started soon after a particular old foreign couple had wandered into the fledgling Mission Outreach Fellowship and offered their assistance. Yes, they would be thrilled to help with its ministry to the homeless, they had told the young pastor.

On the nights Joshua preached and shared his testimony, a transformation in the visitors became especially apparent. Within two weeks of the Liebens' arrival, the crowd at the church had outgrown the humble storefront room and had to be moved to whatever nearby location was available. Some evenings, that meant nothing more than an overgrown vacant lot strewn with broken beer bottles, rusty shopping carts, and stained mattresses. But by the time the guests arrived for the evening service, a handful of members from the tiny church had cut the knee-high weeds and picked up all the junk, piling it neatly in one corner of the lot. Tonight, they felt fortunate to meet in a nice park. Cloth-covered tables, laden with treats and beverages to be distributed after the service, stood along the edge of the grass.

Michael strolled up and scanned the shabby-looking folks in the crowd. He wondered what they were all waiting for. No doubt, nothing he would be interested in. He felt conspicuously out of place. He had awakened about forty-five minutes earlier from a nap after traipsing around most of the day, and decided to comb the area for a few hours at night. It couldn't hurt. An entirely different bunch might show up. That theory was proving true now. He had hit this same park the day before around noon and saw primarily business people like himself; now they were the homeless looking for a handout. Could Michelle be among them? Possibly. Though she had cleaned out her savings account before she left home, seven hundred dollars wouldn't go far in New York.

Trying to be discreet and not make the people feel like he was ogling them, he walked around both sides of the rows of chairs to get a glimpse of the faces from various angles, focusing on petite females with shoulder-length brown hair. Not one bore the slightest resemblance to his daughter. He gave up and decided to head further west down 42nd Street, maybe along Eighth Avenue. A rough area, there. His grip tightened around the pepper spray he had purchased that afternoon. He picked up his pace, moving further and further away from the park.

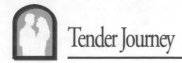

Several minutes later, a distinguished white-haired gentleman stood behind the podium on a small, square platform and began to speak. His compelling, enthusiastic voice and heavy German accent commanded instant attention.

"Good evening, everyone. Welcome to our humble tent meeting—without the tent." Several people laughed. When he smiled in response, his striking blue eyes smiled, too. "To Anna and me, a hovel would be a palace. Why? Because we are free. For almost a third of a century, we were held captive behind the abominable Berlin Wall. We stand here tonight, in the United States of America, because of our gracious God." A smattering of handclaps ran through the crowd. "Yes, give Him glory." He stood, left arm resting on the podium while his left hand protectively clasped his well-worn leather Bible

He raised his right hand, palm forward, to the eastern horizon. "You may have heard the wonderful news last November when the Berlin Wall was torn down. A twenty-eight-year reign of terror in our beloved Germany ended that day, and the healing has begun. It may take decades for our land to adjust to the changes. What you may not know, however, is that saints from around the world prayed for the Wall's demise from the very day it went up." A tear trickled freely down his lined face. "Anna and I, who count ourselves among those intercessors, had the privilege to witness the great victory! And tonight, thousands of miles away, we are taking part in another victory. We have the honor of telling you about our wonderful Savior."

Michelle sat tight-lipped and grimacing in the middle rear of the crowd. Barely a word had escaped her notice. Was this guy for real? He considered it a privilege to talk to a bunch of street bums? She wanted to get up and leave, but she couldn't move. Her muscles refused to obey. Her feet were killing her. Besides, she needed something to eat and they were giving out freebies—after they spoke their piece. To her dismay, the strong, clear voice continued.

". . . Anna and I arrived here just a little over three weeks ago. Oh, what a moment! All our lives we had dreamed of America. Even before the war, as teenagers in Germany, we longed to come here." His eyes searched the front row of seats for his wife. "How many years ago, Anna? Even before we married." He paused, the corners of his lips turned up in a smile just for his sweetheart.

"Then, the terrible era began. What a deviation from our inspired dreams of youth! Hitler's maniacal regime. World War II on our front doorstep. Persecution of God's chosen people, the Jews. Concentration camps with deplorable conditions and mass genocide. The Wall. How many millions died in the madness? Untold numbers. And for us, one stands out among them. Our only child, a daughter, Anja, was shot to death by a border guard in 1961.

"Yet, in the midst of our anguish, God was working to establish His plan for our lives. I crossed paths with a man I had heard mention of only in hushed, reverent tones. At the time, I thought the meeting coincidence, but God has no such thing in His vocabulary. He calls them 'divine appointments.'

"I heard the man speak and since that day, I have never been the same. One could sense beyond a doubt that he knew his God and loved Him with all of his heart. He had already been arrested once for his faith and sent to a concentration camp, but he went on living, loving and sharing the hope of God with his fellow prisoners, as well as with his captors.

"After his release, when I heard him, he had several opportunities to flee the country to escape persecution. Rather than take advantage of those opportunities, he chose to remain. Again, he was arrested for sharing the Gospel. Nothing could separate him

from the One he followed. Nothing could silence him. Not imprisonment. Not the murder of his family. Not even his own execution, for decades later, he yet speaks. This noble martyr, Dietrich Bonhoeffer, stayed faithful to the end. He not only wrote about *The Cost of Discipleship,* he died demonstrating it.

"I saw a power in Mr. Bonhoeffer's life that no amount of suffering could extinguish. Clearly, I did not possess the same spark. Soon after, I asked the Lord to consume me with the fire of His Holy Spirit. He has."

Joshua looked around the gathering. His gaze swept the dozens of faces, many of whom waited expectantly for his next words. They clapped their approval whenever he stopped talking for a moment. Little did he know that one young lady was resisting him with every ounce of strength she possessed. She crossed and recrossed her slender legs, revealing black textured panty hose with a seam running down the back. She made no attempt to pull down her tight, knit mini-skirt, but ran an impatient hand through her blond hair. Would the guy get it over with?

"Anna and I might have given up a number of times, just as some of you long to do." He paused. Slowly, he raised his right arm and pointed his finger out into the crowd. It swung to the left, then right, like a powerful searchlight before homing in on the middle section.

Michelle squirmed. The old codger was pointing right at her! Nah. Couldn't be. No way he could see her back there in the dim light. Besides, he had never seen her before. It sure seemed like he was pointing at her, though. She slouched down in her seat. Her thoughts betrayed her anxious state. Confusion threatened to engulf her. Why did she have to keep bumping into these religious fanatics? All she wanted was a clean place to sit down and something to eat. Joshua's next words irked her even more.

"'I am not sure that God particularly wants us to be happy,' proclaimed the late British author C.S. Lewis in one of his Oxford lectures. 'I think He wants us to *love* and *be loved*. He wants us to grow up! I suggest to you that it is because God loves us that He makes us the gift of suffering. Pain is God's megaphone to rouse a deaf world.' So, dear ones, I would exhort you to deny yourselves the luxury of self-pity. You are not the first human beings on earth to suffer, nor has your suffering been the most acute, by far.

"When life seems hopeless, when the problems you face appear so large that your broken heart cannot conceive of anything but disaster, defeat and despair, rejoice and be exceedingly glad, for your redemption draws nigh. A broken heart places you at the very source of the mighty, rushing eternal river of God Himself!" Those spear-pointed words transfixed his listeners, including Michelle. However, she did her best to ignore him and dug around in her backpack for a piece of gum. Everyone else seemed focused on the white-haired man on the small wooden platform. He paced slowly back and forth in front of the podium.

"God will not give up on you, no matter where you find your self at this moment. He created you in His image. Believe me when I say that your broken heart cannot compare to His. When He looks upon the millions of His creatures for whom He planned so many wonderful experiences, when He sees their lives ravaged by the enemy, do you not know that He weeps, as Jesus wept over Jerusalem?" His words grew in volume until they filled the park. "God is on your side—if you will let Him be. He *loves* you.

"'I avoid looking forward or backward and try to keep looking upward,' wrote Charlotte Brontë. Our Father in heaven specializes in the impossible. Rather, may I say, He literally *delights* in the impossible! Why? So that all men may be still and know that He alone is God. He will not despise you or laugh at you or turn you

away. Therefore, *never give up!*" A second longer Joshua's arm remained an inerrant beacon, pointing in Michelle's direction, before it lowered. Only then was she able to move, but the words kept resounding inside her head. *Never give up . . . never give up . . . Never give up.*

"Why not?" she wanted to stand up and scream at the idiot on the platform. She had nothing left to fight for. Everything she ever got was snatched away in a heartbeat, so why bother? Matt came into her life, made her fall in love with him and vanished without a trace. Jazzy dropped in out of nowhere, got her high a few times, set her up with a few clients who paid well and then, without a word, let her jealous roommate kick her out on the street.

Just then, Michael was passing by Bryant Park on his way back from scouting around. Head down, pace steady, he was lost in his thoughts. He needed a change from the neighborhoods he had been frequenting. Too seedy over on Eighth at night, pepper spray or no. Gave him the creeps. He walked faster. Suddenly, a booming voice saying, *"No, never give up!"* startled him out of his reverie. "You cannot know how close you could be to a breakthrough . . ." He glanced over in the direction of the sound and shook his head. Probably an old has-been preacher, talking to the same bunch of derelicts he saw earlier. He hurried on. Maybe a hot cappuccino and a fresh pastry at a Fifth Avenue café would do him good. He'd get a clean start in the morning.

Until that moment, he couldn't bring himself to admit that he'd been seriously considering giving up and going home. One false trail after another had sapped his waning faith and he'd been too proud to admit it . . . even to himself. Deep down, he despaired of seeing Michelle alive again, but the preacher's words acted like a catalyst. Funny. The guy reminded him a bit of Caleb. He sparked memories of the many talks they'd had together.

One could never see faith, he had learned. It was the unseen essential. Sure, you could see the results of faith in action, of perseverance in the face of total opposition. You could also see the results of doubt. And no wonder. Of all the varied ways they'd talked about to build faith, he'd done none of them. Or very few, at best. He thought back to that time when it looked like his marriage was history. God repaired what he and Stephanie had messed up. He really believed back then and acted on his faith. Not so lately. What to do about it, though? He walked faster.

Yes, a cinnamon cappuccino would hit the spot.

🐾 🐾 🐾

Michelle staggered over to the nearest bench in Central Park and plopped down. Her bloodshot brown eyes matched the sunken, dark circles underneath them. She had lost eight pounds already, and on her petite frame, that was a drastic change. She felt weak from hunger, but with no money, she did her best to ignore it. Nausea came in waves every few seconds. Her mouth felt like sandpaper.

Little did she care about her torn, filthy clothes, or her stringy, matted hair. Her pretty face and slender arms were bruised and scratched. Her skin, normally a beautiful smooth olive, had taken on a pale jaundiced color in contrast to the dozens of insect bites. Some had scabbed over, some were open, infected and angry red where she had scratched them.

She grabbed the bench and stiffened her arms to steady herself, but she could not stop the trembling. She needed some crack. Bad. If only she could get her hands on a beautiful white rock, everything would be okay. Then she would feel good enough to go look for a job. She had to have a real job.

 Tender Journey

Prostituting had advantages—good, fast pay and a certain power over men—but she doubted if she could handle it any more. Some of her "dates" were just too disgusting. And dangerous. The last guy got really weird on her. When she refused to comply, he dragged her into the bathroom, roughed her up and left her. She curled up in the bathtub, passing in and out of consciousness for several hours. Sometime later she'd crawled to the bed and slept until she awoke with a start. She hurt all over, but managed to walk as far as Central Park. How long she had been there or where she'd go, she had no idea. Maybe someone would feel sorry for her and offer her a rock. If only someone would . . .

She thought back to her first high on the stuff and smiled slightly. How good it felt! Like a taste of heaven. Like the first time with Matt. Like riding a magic carpet in the stratosphere, above the pain of life. If only she could ride the magic carpet forever, she would be happy. She would stop missing Matt so much. Why hadn't he come back to get her? If only she knew.

She wanted to forget about her parents being mad and her little brother dying and the guilt for resenting him and her boyfriend back home who had ditched her and all the perfect grades she used to have to get in school and worst of all, the sadness that ached deep in her gut since as far back as she could remember. She had to get a hit of crack. It had been too long. She needed relief. But no one came to rescue her. She started to cry. Soon, the salty tears had stained little paths on her dirty cheeks.

She was so tired. If she could just lay down on the bench for a nap. Just close her eyes for a few winks. That's all. She laid her head down, curled up and fell asleep.

A hand on Michelle's shoulder shook her over and over. Through a foggy cloud, she heard a woman's voice. With a foreign accent. "Miss, are you all right?" the voice was saying. "Miss? Wake up. We will not harm you."

Michelle closed her eyes tighter. She just wanted to sleep for days, months maybe. Couldn't this woman see she was tired? She rolled over on the hard bench and groaned. Every muscle in her body screamed against the wood. Her head hurt even worse.

She forced her eyes open and shielded them with her hands from the early morning sun so she could get a look at the source of the intrusion. An older woman with white hair was bending over her. A white-haired man stood beside the woman. When Michelle realized they wouldn't have any drugs, she whimpered and closed her eyes again.

The man spoke this time, with the same accent, but less obvious than the woman's. "Miss, it is dangerous for a young girl to be sleeping in the park by herself."

Why couldn't these people mind their own business and leave her alone? "I'm fine," she snapped. "Go away."

"Excuse me, miss, but you do not look fine," the man said. "You have cuts and bruises and you have been crying."

"I said, 'I'm fine.' Now, beat it!"

"We can see that you are very upset. My name is Joshua and this is my wife, Anna. We will not harm you."

Anna nodded. "Yes. We are Christians, concerned for your safety. Our pastor was beaten and robbed after a church service not long ago, so we know whereof we speak."

Michelle's mind locked onto the words, "Christians" and "church." She sat up like a shot. Her eyes narrowed. "I don't want anything to do with the likes of you!" she shouted. "You're all a bunch of *flaming hypocrites!* Now, leave me alone. *I mean it!*"

Joshua and Anna looked at each other helplessly and shook their heads. Anna sighed and spoke again. "All right, child, we will

not force our love on you. Nor will God." She took a flyer out of her purse and bent down to Michelle's level. "But in the event that you change your mind and wish to talk to someone, we will be happy to oblige you."

"Yes," Joshua added. "We will be volunteering at this ministry, at least for a season." He pointed to a picture on the flyer. Michelle turned her head away.

Anna placed the paper on top of her hands. "It is called *Safe Harbor,* a live-in program for young women who want a new start. We will make certain that someone there knows how to reach us, no matter where we are."

Joshua bent down and patted Michelle's arm. "God bless you, dear. We will pray for you."

Michelle jerked away from his hand, grabbed her backpack with her few personal belongings and spat out as she jumped to her feet, "Spare yourselves the trouble. You're wasting your time." With that, she threw the flyer at their feet, ran off and disappeared around the bend behind a clump of bushes.

Joshua and Anna sat down on the vacated bench. He leaned forward with his elbows on his knees and his hands folded in front of him. He stared at the grass beneath the bench and shook his head. Anna rubbed her hand in a soothing motion along his back. Neither said anything for a long while.

"Might we have made her yet more rebellious against the Lord?" she asked. "Perhaps we were too forceful."

"No, my love. We did what we thought was best. This morning we prayed for God to direct our path and to speak through us throughout the day. Did we not?" She gave him a hesitant nod. "And we were praying as we were strolling in the park before we saw her, were we not?"

"Yes . . ."

"Then, as you always tell me, 'We must have faith, regardless of the immediate results.' We planted tiny seeds in her heart and we made ourselves available to her. What more can we do?"

"I know, I know. But when I see the life of a young person wasted, I feel so sad." She raised her head and peered into the distance. Her eyes were glassy.

"I understand, my love—we feel somehow . . . responsible. Our Anja's life was cut off so early, and we could do nothing to prevent it. She had no choice. This girl *chooses* to throw her life away!" His face and neck reddened.

"Precisely!" Anna wiped a tear from the corner of her eye. "I find comfort in knowing that Anja died a noble death. At such a young age, she followed a deep compassion in her heart."

Looking up at the sky, he replied, "At least she is in heaven, dancing and singing praises to God."

Anna nodded. The thought comforted her further. "Joshua . . . that poor child we just met . . . who do you suppose she is?"

"A street urchin, no doubt. Every large city has them."

"I do not think so. She was wearing a very pretty ring. Did you see it on her right hand?"

"You know I never notice such details."

"Beautiful, it was. A pearl and three gemstones."

"How would she . . . ? Perhaps she stole it."

"Or, my love, maybe she comes from a proper family. Her parents could have given it to her as a gift."

"But why would she be sleeping on a park bench in such a condi—?" He stopped short and answered his own question. "Might she have run away from home?"

"Yes! I wonder why. She was rather angry about something."

"*Very* angry. Especially when you mentioned that we were 'Christians.' Did you notice that?"

"My goodness, yes. She sat up so quickly, I thought she would lunge at me. If she does have a home somewhere, her parents must be frantic. What should we do?"

"Try to find a policeman as soon as possible, I suppose. One has to be nearby."

She paused and frowned. "We do not know even her first name, nor anything about her."

"But God does, my precious. He knows every hair on her head." They joined hands while Joshua prayed, "Father, we thank You for the many opportunities You place in our path. We ask You to guide us regarding this young girl. You know why she is here and where she belongs. Keep her safe and use us, we pray, to do the right thing on her behalf, so that she would come to see how much You love her. In Jesus' name, Amen." After a quick hug, they took a few minutes to scout around the area for a policeman. Finding no one, they hurried back to the hotel to use the phone.

❧ *Eighteen* ❧

Dr. Eric Marcos mingled among the MarriageMaker class members, talking and laughing with them, until 7:00. Stephanie felt a little out of place being there by herself, but decided that she might as well go while Michael was in New York. She had really enjoyed the first class. It couldn't hurt to gain a few more survival tips. Besides, she needed to keep her mind occupied so she didn't lose it completely.

Eric took his place at the front and cleared his throat. "Let's begin with prayer, shall we?" He bowed his head, paused and took a deep breath. "Lord, we have gathered together again this evening to study Your roadmap for marriage. We admit that we simply cannot make our marriages work the way they should on our own. We make messes instead. Give us wisdom and teach us how to love one another, I pray. In Jesus' name, Amen."

"So, how is everyone this evening?" he asked.

A chorus of "good" and "fine" came back in response.

"Has everyone had a chance to talk about how you can implement what we discussed in the first class?" His eyes slowly took in those present. Most met his gaze, though some wore guilty smiles.

"Stephanie, it's good to have you. I respect your decision to come, even when Michael's away. We're standing with you."

She looked up, a shy smile greeting him. "Thanks."

Dr. Marcos must have read the apprehension so thinly veiled in her tentative answer, and to her relief, he turned his attention back to the class.

"Okay, let's start with a story. Forgive me if every detail isn't letter perfect, but you'll get the drift. One summer day, a man was lounging in his very own lawn chair in the backyard, relaxing and enjoying the gorgeous weather. Sunny and warm. A light breeze. Not a cloud in the sky. A picture-perfect day, with one exception. Our main man had been getting a little bored with the same old recreation routine.

"Suddenly, he had a brainstorm. He hurried over to the discount store, bought one hundred large balloons and rented a tank of helium. Can you guess what he did? He filled the balloons with helium and tied them to his lawn chair! He must have weighted it down, of course, until just the right moment, then . . . *lift-off!*

"With his cold six-pack beside him, he decided to float up just enough for a fun jaunt in the wild blue yonder. Anything to spice up a dull day. The next thing he knew, he was really airborne and climbing. Higher . . . higher . . . higher. A 747 happened to fly by. Can you imagine the pilot's radio transmission? 'Passed a man on a chaise lounge at 11,000 feet.' Well, from what I understand, a helicopter did finally rescue the guy. He was a bit embarrassed and quite chilly, but alive. His explanation went something like this, *'I just wanted something to do.'*

"The balloonist has plenty of company among thrill-seekers, doesn't he? Many marriage partners desperately long to feel the intoxicating 'high' they felt when they first met. Some of them resort to drastic measures to beat the blahs. Big spending. Drugs.

Affairs—whether physical or emotional. Even divorce. The experience usually costs them a whole lot more than a helicopter ride home. Why do they throw caution to the wind? In part, because they lose sight of where they're going and why. So, tonight, we will focus on the *purpose* of marriage.

"First, though, let's review from last week. Remember God's *plan,* his ideal goal for couples? Anybody?"

José raised his hand. "Oneness."

"Exactly," Eric assured him. "How about some other words for the concept that might be common today?" He looked expectantly to the others.

Stephanie volunteer, "Unity."

"Good synonym. Anybody else?"

Sean went next. "I have two: harmony and agreement. I sure want both with my fiancée—if I can ever get her to pick a wedding date before I'm too old and set in my ways. You probably have a hard time believing I'm the one who wants to settle down, but it's true." Several in the group smiled.

"I was going to mention 'agreement,' too," Barbara said. "Sean beat me to it." She paused. "I'd say fellowship. And togetherness."

"How about solidarity?" her husband Sid offered. "Or homogeneity, as opposed to heterogeneity." Stephanie glanced at him with a puzzled expression. Those sounded like answers Michael would come up with. Cerebral types—they were all alike.

"Interesting choices," Eric replied. "Who has another?"

Collette chimed in, "Just plain ol' closeness."

"Or compatibility," added her husband Paul.

"Intimacy," Bob and Charmaine contributed in unison. They looked at each other and laughed.

"More great ideas, everyone," Eric affirmed. "I'm sure we could define oneness in many more ways, but let's move on to the

purpose of that oneness. Why did God come up with marriage in the first place? Go ahead and ponder the topic for a few minutes, jot down as many ideas as you can and be ready to share a least one with the group, if you would." He paused to take a few swallows from a glass of water on the floor beside his chair. Everyone took pens from their pockets or purses. Pensive expressions filled the room.

"Okay, let's see what you came up with. Who wants to go first?" They looked around the semi-circle at each other. Nobody volunteered a word. Finally, Eric offered to start. "I believe one purpose for marriage is this: so we won't be alone! In Genesis two, eighteen, we read, *Then Lord God said, 'It is not good for the man to be alone; I will make him a helper suitable for him.'* I took that from the New American Standard Version in my Parallel Bible."

José's courage rose and he raised his hand. "To have children together in a strong family where they can grow up with a secure feeling."

Eric nodded his approval. "I agree, José. God encourages us to be fruitful and multiply—within His guidelines."

Charmaine's hand went up. "Somewhere in the Bible it talks about having somebody there to encourage you when you fall, but I don't know which verse . . ."

Maria came to her rescue. "It starts in Ecclesiastes four, nine. I know because we picked it for the pastor to read at our wedding." She gazed at José with a deep fondness. He squeezed her hand.

"Would you like to read it for us, Maria?" Eric asked.

She shrugged shyly, then shook her head. "I don't read English too good. Spanish, much better."

"Of course. Forgive me for being insensitive. Anybody?"

Sean volunteered, "I have it." He licked his lips, then began reading,

Two are better than one because they have a good return for their labor. For if either of them falls, the one will lift up his companion. But woe to the one who falls when there is not another to lift him up. Furthermore, if two lie down together they keep warm, but how can one be warm alone?

"Thanks, Sean. Which version were you quoting from?"

"The New American Standard."

"Okay. By the way, I see tucked in that passage at least one other purpose for having a partner. Maybe two."

Collette was quick to the draw. "Seems to me like it's referrin' to old-fashioned cuddlin'. Sure makes for good protection against cold nights."

Stephanie eyed her up and down, then sighed. Something about that woman irritated her.

Barbara cocked her head, as if debating. "It says they have a good return for their labor. In other words, a couple reaps blessing or prosperity, maybe, because four hands are stronger than two and two heads are better than one."

"That's a reasonable assumption." Eric nodded and crossed his arms. "God can take up the slack, though, for singles, if they ask."

Paul winked at Collette, then raised his hand. "You're all avoiding the biggie, so I'll just get it over with—sexual fulfillment." She elbowed him in the ribs, pretending embarrassment.

"You're absolutely right, Paul. Some Christians believe God created sex only for procreation, and they ignore a tremendous blessing He wants to bestow on them. Pleasure comes as a privilege of marriage. Between heterosexual, monogamous partners, I might add. Have we left out anybody who wants to share?" Nobody seemed to have more to say, so Eric continued, "Let's look at another passage of Scripture and see if we can detect other reasons

God has for putting folks together as one. If you would, turn to John, chapter seventeen, to a beautiful prayer of Jesus. Would somebody read verses twenty through the first part of twenty-three?" He waited for the rustle of pages to stop. Bob Harrington volunteered and stated he'd be reading from the King James.

"Neither pray I for these alone, but for them also which shall believe on me through their word; that they all may be one; as thou, Father, art in me, and I in thee, that they also may be one in us: that the world may believe that thou hast sent me. And the glory which thou gavest me I have given them: that they may be one, even as we are one: I in them, and thou in me, that they may be made perfect in one . . ."

Eric glanced around at the eager faces before him. Peace had taken up residence in the room. He spoke, his tone subdued, hesitant to interrupt the sweet presence.

Sid raised his hand. "Aren't you taking that out of context? I thought Jesus was praying specifically for His disciples in this passage."

"Good observation, Sid. He was. But, as Christians, we're also disciples today, called to make disciples of all nations. Thus, everything He said about 'being one' would apply even more so to married disciples, it seems to me. How can we be one with other believers if we have discord at home?"

An acquiescent nod came back from Sid. He looked a little sheepish, as if he regretted speaking before he had fully thought through his question. Eric sensed his discomfort and thanked him again for his concern about maintaining scriptural integrity. "From that same passage," he said, "can anyone find God's primary purpose for going to such lengths to establish unity among couples?"

Heads lowered over open Bibles. For a few seconds, no one said a word. "I'll give you a hint," he offered. "You won't find personal happiness in there."

Finally, a dark-skinned, weathered arm rose above the group as José quoted from the last half of verse twenty-one. His Spanish accent gave a staccato sound to his words, '*That the world . . . may believe . . . that thou hast sent me.*'" He paused. "Man, that makes me feel bad!"

"Why?" Eric's eyebrows rose.

"Because my motives for wanting a good marriage with Maria have been very selfish."

Eric nodded. "Can you explain?"

"Well, according to this verse, the reason God wants us to be super close is not just so we can live ever-after happily. That, too, yes, but as . . . how do you say . . . a by-product. He wants the world to see Jesus in us, so they will want to know Him, so they can be saved from eternity without Him!"

"José, that's fantastic!"

Paul gave a brief tap to his Bible. "I never saw that in there before. You did good, brother."

José beamed. Maria did, too. She reached her arm around his shoulder and gave him quick hug. Others in the group voiced their approval.

"Right here," Eric continued, "we have discovered God's real purpose for His plan. All the other reasons for marriage you mentioned earlier are good and right and important, but they pale in comparison to this one. In Matthew six, thirty-three, Jesus reminds us to '*Seek first His kingdom and His righteousness, and all these things shall be added unto you*' (NASB).

"Wouldn't it be great," he exclaimed, "now that we know the truth, if we could follow through? What joy we'd have! What a

breakthrough for the kingdom of God! Psalm one hundred thirty-three, verse one says, *Behold, how good and how pleasant it is for brothers to dwell together in unity!* Unfortunately, it's far easier said than done. In fact, gaining our 'promised land' often involves a battle of the most intense degree.

"For a clue as to why, let's go back in history a few thousand years to the original promised land—Canaan—described in Numbers thirteen, twenty-seven and eight. I'll read from the New International Version this time. No particular reason, other than variety of style.

> *They gave Moses this account: 'we went into the land to which you sent us, and it does flow with milk and honey! Here is its fruit. But the people who live there are powerful, and the cities are fortified and very large. We even saw descendants of Anak there . . .'*

"Aha! Obstacles in the way. Somebody else lived in the beautiful land God had promised to Abraham. Strong, giant-sized somebodies. They had no desire to leave. They enjoyed life in their prosperous, walled cities.

"Ten of the twelve Hebrew spies delivered an alarming report about the situation. In response, their discouraged countrymen begged to go back to slavery in Egypt, rather than claim their inheritance. As a result, the entire nation of Israel wandered for forty years in the wilderness until they died and their carcasses disintegrated in the hot desert sun. It's a wonder any of their children survived the ordeal.

"What an accurate symbolic description of a bad marriage! To those couples who plod through life together—or who finally divorce—marriage feels like a scorching wilderness by day and a blustery wasteland by night. Jackals and buzzards threaten to devour them. They stumble on in wounded weariness, with not a drop of hope in sight. Their children suffer even more. And to think those spouses stand on the very threshold of all the blessings of heaven. What a tragedy!"

Stephanie crossed her legs and picked at her fingernails, then doodled on her paper. Her abrasive argument with Michael the night before he left came charging back into her memory. She swallowed hard to push away the guilt that followed on its heels. Thankfully, Eric went on.

"Of the older generation of Israelites, only Joshua and Caleb ever entered the promised land. Why? At a crucial crossroads, they made the right choice. They saw the same giants as the other ten spies. No denial in their vocabulary. But they put the giants in perspective. Instead of focusing on problems, they focused on God.

"The same principle applies to our relationships. We can either fix our eyes on a flawed person, or on a perfect God. We can declare their defects or His promises. It's our choice. Without that decision, we cannot enter the kingdom of marital love any more than the Israelites could enter the promised land. We simply don't have it in us! Too many nasty giants stand between us and our goal. In other words, we have not only the MarriageMaker guiding us toward intimacy; we face an enemy driving us toward anarchy. Who might that be?"

Stephanie hesitated, then asked in a timid voice, "Satan?"

"Yes, the scoundrel. The marriagebreaker himself. He has a sole modis operandi—to steal, kill, and destroy what God has joined. However, we can't lay all the blame on Satan. We hold equal responsibility because we give him easy access in many areas. In fact, the way some of us go about our daily routines, we might as well be sending the devil and his crew embossed invitations—

'You are cordially invited to a home-wrecking party . . .' Drop in anytime. You're always welcome.

"Ridiculous, I know. But we do the very same thing by default. How? We insist on our own way instead of God's way. Selfish human nature acts like like a faulty alarm system that lets the marriagebreaker barge in unnoticed. While he's quietly at work, ransacking our relationships, oneness climbs out the back window. By the same token, the reverse holds true. When minute-by-minute, we ask the MarriageMaker to take over and fill our home with His awesome presence, we're safe. Then, the no-good bum has to hit the road! He cannot tolerate the Presence of God."

All of a sudden, Charmaine popped up from her seat, did a little hop, then sat back down. She waved her hand in the air and flipped through the pages of her Bible as fast as she could. "Oh, Eric, I think I just had a revelation."

"Go ahead! Must be good, as excited as you are."

"Okay. You know how you've been telling us the plan and purpose of marriage . . . oneness so others will come to know the Savior. Well, it seems like there's more, tied in with the very reason Jesus came to earth. I know I saw it in first John somewhere . . . hang on . . . yes, I found it! The second part of chapter three, verse eight, *The Son of God appeared for this purpose, that He might destroy the works of the devil.* Hallelujah! So, if He lives in us now, then that's our purpose too, as Christian couples. Right?"

Bob stared at her, wide-eyed. "Char, honey, that's incredible. You just reminded me of the Scripture we memorized last week, *Again I say unto you, That if two of you shall agree on earth as touching any thing that they shall ask, it shall be done for them of my Father which is in heaven.* We can do more good spiritually as a team. The kingdom of darkness won't stand a chance in our family if we get our act together."

Eric gave them a brief applause. "You guys have touched on a tremendous point." He looked around the room. "What do you all think?" Heads bobbed up and down in an enthusiastic show of support. Just then, as they were pondering the broad implications of such a revelation, Eric's pager sounded with several high-pitched beeps. He pressed the button to retrieve the message. Brows furrowed, he explained, "Gee, I'm sorry, gang. Got an emergency with a client. I'll have to let you guys go a little early tonight. Next week, we'll explore how to achieve our purpose in more depth when we talk about the *power* for marriage. Thanks for coming, everybody. You all contributed so much to the group. God bless you!" He paused, then after a few seconds, drew a card out of his jacket pocket. "Say, Bob, would you mind reading this aloud? I think it will provide good food for thought to send everybody home with." He handed the card to him and hurried out the door, briefcase in hand.

Bob glanced at Charmaine. "Hon, you can help me. Read every other verse—would you?"

"Okay." She smiled. "But you go first." He agreed and began.

LOVE takes time. It needs a history of giving and receiving, laughing and crying . . .

LOVE never promises instant gratification, only ultimate fulfillment.

LOVE means believing in someone, in something. It supposes a willingness to struggle, to work, to suffer, and to rejoice.

Satisfaction and ultimate fulfillment are by-products of dedicated LOVE. They belong only to those who can reach beyond themselves; to whom giving is more important than receiving.

LOVE is doing everything you can to help others build whatever dreams they have.

307

LOVE involves much careful and active listening. It is doing whatever needs to be done, and saving whatever will promote the other's happiness, security, and well-being. Sometimes, love hurts.

LOVE is on a constant journey to what others need. It must be attentive, caring, and open, both to what others say and to what others cannot say.

LOVE says no with empathy and great compassion.

LOVE is firm, but when needed it must be tender.

When others have tried and failed, love is the hand in yours in your moments of discouragement and disappointment.

LOVE is reliable.

LOVE is a choice and commitment to others' true and lasting happiness. It is dedicated to growth and fulfillment.

LOVE is not selfish.

LOVE sometimes fails for lack of wisdom or abundance of weakness, but it forgives, knowing the intentions are good.

LOVE does not attach conditions . . . Genuine love is always a free gift.

LOVE realizes and accepts that there will be disagreements and disturbing emotions . . .There may be times when miles lie between, but love is a commitment. It believes and endures all things.

LOVE encourages freedom of self. Love shares positive and negative reactions to warm and cold feelings.

LOVE, intimate love, will never reject others. It is the first to encourage and the last to condemn.

LOVE is a commitment to growth, happiness, and fulfillment of one another.[12]

Barb Upham

Bob finished the last phrase with a solemn tone. The group had grown very quiet. Stephanie watched him clasp Charmaine's hand and felt a twinge of envy. They led such a charmed life. Biting her lip, she picked up her purse. Her eyes were filling with tears again. She avoided looking at them or at any of the others. Too bad Michael couldn't be there. He needed to hear some of this stuff. How could she possibly explain to him over the phone all they had discussed in class?

She heard Bob ask if anyone would like to say a closing prayer. What if he called on her? She would cry, right there in front of everybody. To her relief, Sean volunteered first.

He changed positions in his chair and began, "Lord, we thank You so much for Dr. Marcos. Tonight please give him a special ability—an anointing of Your Holy Spirit—to help his client in crisis. Thank You for inspiring him to start this MarriageMaker class, and for allowing a single guy like me to attend. I may not be as ready for marriage as I thought." He took a deep breath. "My ideas of love have been so selfish. I cared more about making *me* happy than anything else. Forgive me, Lord. Forgive all of us. Help us to be more sensitive to one another's needs and teach us to love. Make us more like Jesus. In His name we pray, Amen."

Stephanie felt as if a huge dam behind her eyes was about to burst. Tears refused to be held back one moment longer. She leaned forward with the heel of her hand pressing in on her chest to ease the ache, and she sobbed without control—a low, mournful wailing. What would people think? Thank heavens, Michael wasn't there to see her. He would croak! She wanted to crawl through the floor. But she could not stop crying.

The next thing she knew, people had gathered around her in a warm embrace, as their voices carried her away in holy prayer . . .

Tender Journey

❧ ❧ ❧

Before they had gone much farther down the Central Park path, Joshua slowed his pace. A thoughtful expression creased his features. He lowered his gaze, then came to a stop. When he looked up, he avoided Anna's unspoken questions. Instead, he studied the outcropping of granite a short distance away.

"What is it, love?" She reached out to take his hand.

"As we were walking, I felt a sudden terrible heaviness, rather like the weight of that large rock, settle upon my chest. How do they say . . . 'a dream-in-the-pipe'? That is what I must have had in Germany," he reluctantly admitted. "To find my father is beyond presumptuous. It is *preposterous.*" He shrugged and faced her.

She clasped his hand tighter, then turned and peered along the path. "Over there I see a bench. Come. Let us rest a moment." She started leading the way. When they reached it, Joshua sat and Anna stood before him. She reached forward, cradling his face between her hands. "My dear husband, why do you doubt? Do you think God would lead us this far only to abandon us in a large city where we have no close friends or family?" She shook her head from side to side. "Nein. We believed He gave you the desire to come here to search for him. He provided the ship on which we traveled. Difficulties we have encountered, yes, but you know He has not deserted us."

A tender smile brightened her weathered features and a sparkle glinted in her eyes. "Were you not the one who comforted me through the years of our marriage? Yes, my weary warrior. When I felt to give up was better, you gave me reasons to keep going." She let her hands drop and sat down next to him. He followed her every move with his eyes, and turned on the bench to face her once she was seated. The corners of his mouth turned up wistfully.

310

"But this is different, Anna. We are old now. Starting over does not bring the welcome challenge it once did." He stared into his wife's eyes. The sheen of unshed empathetic tears enhanced their sparkle. She was so soft-hearted. The simplest things could trigger those wells of tenderness. Sensitive to her moods, he reached out and laid his hand over her two smaller ones.

She lowered her gaze. "When I see you worried, I feel more afraid." He gave her hands a gentle squeeze. They sat in silence, not in any hurry. They knew the time to speak would soon return.

Peace came like the breeze, too gentle to pinpoint the exact moment of its arrival. They only knew that their hearts no longer ached. Anna looked up to find her husband's eyes waiting to meet hers. He drew her to him. She leaned forward and laid her head upon his shoulder.

He stroked her hair, saying, "Things have not gone as I had hoped, but God holds us closer than ever."

"Exactly. And, yes, we are older than yesterday, older than the day before, but withered geezers, by no means!" She lifted her brow from its resting place on his shoulder and gave him a playful wink. It was her turn to smile. "Consider, for example, the Old Testament Caleb. Compared to him we are mere adolescents, no?"

"True. Eighty-five, I believe he was when he conquered Mount Hebron."

"So, we, too, have a few bad giants to battle in our new land, I gather . . ."

Joshua wrapped her in his left arm and snuggled closer. "Yes, Anna, many of them. You were right. Old need not mean helpless. Bolder, wiser, and more mature, I do pray so." He drew a small, worn Bible out of his pocket and flipped back and forth through the Psalms. At last he stopped at the ninety-second Psalm. He read verses twelve through fourteen aloud,

Tender Journey

"The righteous shall flourish like the palm tree; he shall grow like a cedar in Lebanon. Those that be planted in the house of the Lord shall flourish in the courts of our God. They shall still bring forth fruit in old age; they shall be fat and flourishing; To show that the Lord is upright; he is my rock, and there is no unrighteousness in him.

"See there?" she cried. "Thank You, Father, for Your Word!"

Joshua straightened on the bench. He slapped his right knee with the open palm of his hand, then stood up to stretch his legs. "We, too, shall be fruitful. We shall take each step as it comes, and do so in the strength of the Lord."

"Hallelujah! The man I adore has returned to his senses." She paused for a few seconds. "My love," she said, "we have met so many souls with needs greater than our own. That lonely young girl, for instance. We have each other. We have our God." She grew silent and her eyes focused on something only she could see. "The girl has nothing, from what I observed. I feel, so—so *burdened*—for her. What else can we do?"

Joshua dropped to one knee in front of his wife. He leaned forward and grasped her hands between his, then bowed his head. "I hurt for her, as well, Anna, but we must use wisdom." His words slowed, and became firmer, more detached. "Somewhere, she has a family who will help her when she asks for it. We must be more careful about meddling where we do not belong."

She raised her head up with her brows furrowed and eyes squinted. "How can you speak so? I disagree. We should continue to look for her. Does your desire to prove your strength outweigh your obligation to extend mercy?"

His face fell. "Anna, Anna, you misunderstand me. I would love to help the young woman, but I do not want to do anything

312

to cause problems, either for us or for her. As you remember, she was very hostile. We could worsen a bad situation."

"Jo-shu-a," she dragged out the syllables, "my dear one, please forgive me for speaking to you with disrespect." She slipped her fingers from his grasp and caressed his cheek.

At her touch he lifted his eyes to hers. "No harm done."

"You are gracious. But what reasoning, pray tell, lies behind your strong opinion? Help me to understand."

For a minute neither of them spoke. Private thoughts engulfed them so completely that neither of them noticed the footsteps of an occasional passerby.

Joshua looked up from his kneeling position. "Not for lack of compassion do I caution against involving ourselves further with the young girl. No, it is because all my compassion is taken up with caring for you. After the beating and robbery of our pastor, I came to recognize anew our vulnerability. I made a vow then to protect you—with my very life, if necessary." He pounded his fist into the palm of his hand. "I never dreamed of putting you in danger to follow my whims. Now, our money continues to decrease and we have no idea where to go from here. Not even a clue to point us in the right direction." His lips tightened. "A lady of your caliber deserves better than this."

Anna looked away. Even after all their years together, she had never grown accustomed to the change in his eyes when he was upset. Like the ocean in a storm, they turned a dark steel blue. She knew he spoke the truth. He would stop at nothing to protect and provide for her. "Thank you, love, for the honor you give to me," she said. "However, I feel compelled to remind you that seldom do you 'follow whims.' And our funds have dwindled because we helped the pastor and his family in their time of need. We acted in agreement by the leading of the Holy Spirit, did we not?"

He frowned. "I suppose you are right—again. What has taken hold of me tonight that I would speak with such cowardice? I seem to have put on a pair of eyeglasses through which I see only the negative aspect of every situa—." He shook his head. "Of course! I detect the problem! How could I have failed to prepare?"

"For?"

"You know as well as I, dear one, this basic principle of ministry. 'After the mountain lies the valley.' You recall what happened during the service in Bryant Park, I am certain."

"Yes. Wonderful victories for the kingdom of God."

"Precisely. Dozens of desperate people on their knees, weeping before the Lord, delivered from darkness into light . . . Thus, Satan has launched a counterattack to intimidate us. If he can reach me, he often wins you, as well."

She nodded. "It is no coincidence, then, that you sound like depressed old Elijah under the juniper tree?"

"None at all. Bless you for standing strong in my weakness."

"I am grateful for a chance to tip the scales back in the other direction." She reached out and mussed his hair.

He surprised her by reaching out with both arms and encircling her waist. She let out a squeal when he pulled her to him then stood with her in his arms. He held her that way for some seconds, his head against her breast, her feet dangling at knee level on him. A girlish giggle popped out.

"Put me down, you great oaf," she scolded, as she pretended to struggle free from his grasp. "Someone will see us acting like—"

"Two teenagers," he finished for her. "Go ahead and laugh. But I take this point of view: If we are young enough to fight giants in private . . . we are young enough to be lovers in public."

Her eyes widened. "That was quite profound, I do believe."

Surprised by the compliment, Joshua thanked her and set her

down. At that moment, Anna saw a stranger standing perfectly still in the middle of the sidewalk, a short distance from them. Her breath caught. By instinct, she locked her arm tight around her husband's.

The man resumed his walk in their direction. Joshua cast a brief glance at him. Patting her hand, he said softly into her ear, "Fret not. He seems harmless enough." As they glanced up, the man had picked up his pace and was moving away toward another bend in the path. They could see only the back of him, head bowed low. "He has serious matters of his own to contend with, from the looks of him," Joshua added.

Her muscles relaxed. "Yes . . . as do we."

"Then we ought to ask God to show us what to do next." His eyes had lost their uncanny intensity of a few moments earlier, and their normal bright twinkle returned. "Would you care to offer our prayers, love?" he asked.

"I would be delighted."

"I sense that we should first intercede for that gentleman. How does that suit you?"

"Even before you began to speak the words, I was about to lift him up before the throne of grace."

"Good. That confirms it. We have both heard the same voice."

With a sigh, she stared at the beautiful evening sky. "And felt the same heartbeat."

He tightened his arm around her. "Yes, Anna . . . the eternal cry of heaven itself."

❧ *Nineteen* ❧

oping to unearth some kind of sign of his daughter's whereabouts, Michael had been out scouring the streets of New York again. Still no luck. Every false lead drained more out of him. Days turned into nights, and nights back into days. He woke up a couple of mornings feeling certain that this would be the day for a breakthough. He'd either find Michelle or meet someone who knew where she was staying. Not so. Each evening, he would face the dreaded phone call home to update and console a disappointed Stephanie and Stephen. They were depending on him to pull off a miracle. Disgusted himself with his lack of success, he often tossed and turned until the wee hours.

He fought hard and long against discouragement, but things were starting to get to him. He was no closer to locating her than he was two weeks ago. He felt a kind of quiet desperation growing within him, and he worried what would happen if it turned to rage. He couldn't afford to lose his cool here in the big city. Maybe it was already too late. Then he remembered the woman's words to him on the subway—pray. He would, if he could only believe it would do any good.

The city had lost much of its initial charm. It was starting to intimidate him. The sheer size and close proximity of the buildings, the squealing, honking traffic or the countless bizarre people roaming the streets at any given hour of the day or night, all of it was setting him on edge. The place had a pulse of its own. It felt alive, hungry and ready to devour whoever innocently, or not-so-innocently, gave it the chance. He did not like the feeling. The more he saw, the more he feared for Michelle's safety. How could she possibly survive in this twisted maze of steel and humanity?

But someone out there *had* to have seen her. He just had to find them. One clue. A trace was all he would need to get started.

These thoughts so occupied him that he never noticed his taxi pulling over in front of the hotel. He sat, lost in thought, until the cabby coughed and said, "That'll be nine bucks, twenty-five, Mac."

"Nine dollars? Isn't that a lot for a ride around the block?"

"Nah. And it's not the block. It's how many times ya go 'round that adds up. Twenty minutes you've had me makin' laps."

Michael hadn't noticed. He'd been miles away, thinking of things he wished he'd said and done, and of actions he wished he could somehow erase from the slate.

"Like I said," interrupted the cabby, "that adds up to nine bucks and twenty-five cents. I gotta get movin'."

Michael noticed the cabby staring in the rearview mirror, so he nodded and reached for his wallet. He pulled out a twenty-dollar bill, reached across the seat and handed it to him. "Where can a fella get a decent snack?" he asked, while he waited for his change. After a second's pause he added, "At a *reasonable* price, I mean." His effort at sarcasm fell on deaf ears. The driver just looked back over towards the hotel and tilted his head back so his chin pointed towards the far corner of the hotel.

317

"Take a right up there. There's an all night café. Price is right, and they serve the best cup of coffee a body could want." He half-reached back. "Here's your change."

Michael took a crumpled ten-dollar bill plus three quarters from him, opened the door and got out. "Thanks," he added as the cabby glared at him for not tipping. The cab sped away, horn blaring, into the evening traffic. He watched the tail lights fade in the distance before saying to no one in particular, "Guess I'll try that cup of coffee." He turned and strode in the direction the cabby had indicated.

A steady wave of people flowed along the sidewalk, but Michael no more noticed them than they did him. He blended in with the hustle and bustle of the crowd, like one of those purple-sailed man-of-war jellyfish the winds of chance blow across the dark surface of the ocean. And, like an unlucky sailor whose boat blows into a sandbar, he was forced to an abrupt halt. The person in front of him had stopped.

Something up ahead, some kind of commotion, created ripples in the stream of people. Michael couldn't see the cause. The crowd was too thick. What was going on?

The sea of people parted. The woman in front of him stepped aside and a young man came into view. Hair disheveled, sweat dripping down his forehead onto his open-necked, navy striped polo shirt, he forced his way along the crowded sidewalk. He did not apologize to any of the people he shouldered aside, and he kept turning his head and looking behind him. As he approached, Michael caught a glimpse of the man's eyes.

They bore a look of desperation, darting back and forth, first over the crowd in front of him and then scanning the buildings lining the sidewalk. Something didn't seem right. Michael couldn't tell what it was until the guy came closer. His pupils were dilated.

Red lines streaked the whites, as if he hadn't had a good night's sleep in weeks, or was showing the effects of drugs. By his jerky mannerisms, he exuded a certain furtiveness. His right hand kept clenching and unclenching in time to his strides. He kept his left hand buried in his pants' front pocket.

Before Michael could see any more, the people in front of him bunched so tightly together that he lost sight of the guy. When he could see again through the crowd, he had disappeared.

Michael wondered what the scenario was all about. Something wasn't right. That's when he spied the café sign. Not noticeable, just a little wooden rectangular thing sticking out from the front of the building. He would never have seen it, as distracted as he was, if he hadn't been standing practically right in front of it. He read the sign out loud, "Metro Café." Must be the place. He headed to the entrance.

"Hey, what's goin' on!" someone cried out.

Michael faced that direction. Two blue-suited police officers were making their way toward him. The crowd was such that it forced them to set aside casual manners for expediency's sake. "Police," they declared. "Police officers. Let us through, please."

Near the café entrance the crowd thinned and the officers gained some breathing space. "Are you sure he went in here?" the shorter asked his taller partner.

"Positive. He cut right in front of . . . yeah, there he is . . ." The officer nodded toward Michael. "Right in front of that guy." He looked at Michael. "You saw him, didn't you? A guy in a dark blue and white shirt." Michael opened his mouth. The officer asked again, "He went in here, didn't he? Come on, tell us, but do it quick. We don't want this fish to get away."

Michael licked his lips, getting ready to speak, but the tall officer interrupted him again. "Forget it." He turned to his partner.

"Come on, we're wasting time out here. The creep could slip out the back way before we ever get inside."

"Right," his partner agreed. They entered the café together.

Michael watched, amazed. Just seconds before he'd been ready for something to eat. Now, he didn't know whether to follow the officers or go back to the hotel. His curiosity turned the tables. He chose to stay. When he saw the way they split up, one going left and the other right, he knew he couldn't leave.

Having this little drama unfold in front of him started him worrying about Michelle again. Without knowing what the police were doing, or who they were after, he had already begun imagining the worst. Their only daughter was out there with—Lord, who *was* she out there with? He hoped God would protect her. He knew where she was and what she was doing. The million-dollar question was—would He keep her from harm?

He stepped further into the café. It took a second for his eyes to adjust to the brighter light, so he lost sight of the two officers. When he spied them, they were converging on one of the bar-type serving counters from opposite directions. On the second stool from the left sat the weirdo who'd caught his eye out on the sidewalk before the police showed up. As he suspected, they wanted that one. Rather than approach any closer, Michael stepped to the right of the door. He found a spot along the wall where he could watch the scene unfold.

An older man, who'd been sitting on the far left stool, saw the officer approaching from that side. He reached for his coffee mug and drained whatever little was left. He looked to his right and saw the other officer coming at him from that direction. That was all the confirmation he needed. He slid off the stool and eased away from the counter. Without a word, he made his way through the crowd and out the door, never once looking back.

The empty stool provided just the opportunity the police officer had hoped for. A couple sat just to the right of the young man, so the officer on that side, the taller of the two, had to stand just behind and slightly to the right of their quarry.

The shorter officer stepped up to the counter. A waitress approached, but he waved her away. From out of nowhere he produced his wallet—police identification and shield displayed—and held it over the counter, in front of the other fellow, so there was no way he could miss it.

"I'm Officer Seals." He nodded towards his partner. "This is Officer McCartney," he said as he flipped his wallet closed and put it back inside his pocket. "New York Police Department. You got any identification on you?"

The young man continued sitting as if hadn't heard a word. Others overheard enough to make them stop what they were doing. Some, including the couple to his immediate right, even turned to watch. Anything to break up the monotony went over in a big way in the early evening hours. A sticky situation only made the distraction that much more attractive. As long as it was someone *else's*.

"Did you hear me?" the officer continued. "I need to see your driver's license or some other ID."

The young man looked at him. His face still appeared flushed. Sweat ran in rivulets from his forehead and cheeks. His bloodshot eyes stared fixedly at Officer Seals. He made no attempt to produce any identification.

Officer Seals glanced at his partner. Officer McCartney nodded and leaned a bit closer to the guy. "You're leaving us no choice, you know that?" They waited for a response. Still nothing.

Officer McCartney unsnapped the strap over his handcuffs. Officer Seals got up from the stool. He turned to face the guy.

"Whatsa matter? You deaf or something? We gave you a verbal order to see some ID."

Roaring like a wounded bull, the guy exploded off his stool straight towards Officer Seals. He drove the top of his head into the officer's stomach, pushing him backwards onto and then over the end stool.

Officer McCartney made a move to cut off his escape, but before he could get in position, the guy spun like a wide receiver evading a tackler. He slipped away, snatched an abandoned cup of coffee from the counter, and threw it at him. Enough splashed in the officer's face to momentarily blind him. The guy wasted no time taking advantage of the opportunity. He bolted for the entrance.

The entire episode took only seconds. People in the café hadn't had time to react. They stood, gaping, at the sudden outburst of violence. Michael watched from his vantage point near the door. One officer lay on the floor at the end of the counter. He struggled to kick the chairs away enough to give him room to free his thirty-eight special from its holster. The other groped for a napkin with his right hand and wiped at his eyes with his left.

Their quarry sidestepped them both. He lowered his head and shoulders like a running back plowing through the line of scrimmage and raced toward the door.

Time seemed to stretch out for Michael. He could hear the noise of the crowd, but it seemed muted and far away. The beating of his heart seemed much louder and drawn out.

The guy coming his way looked like he was running in slow motion. Michael started to react.

Three steps away. Two steps. Michael dropped into a crouch. Only a stride separated them. An instant more, and the guy was abreast of him.

Now! He expelled his pent-up breath in a great whooshing sound and launched himself at the fugitive.

The guy never saw him coming. One minute he was bearing down on the exit, already tasting freedom. The next, he lay sprawled face down on the floor, tangled in a mass of table legs. He never even noticed Michael, let alone counted on getting blindsided by one of the customers.

Michael lay half atop the guy. Frantically, he tried to keep him pinned down long enough for the police officers to get involved. Things still moved in slow motion. Where were they, for Pete's sake? From behind him he heard a woman scream, "Look out, he's got a gun!" Other voices added to the wild cacophony.

"Get down, all of you."

"Is he crazy . . ."

"Freeze . . ."

"Stop, or I'll shoot!"

Then Michael felt hands on him, grasping his shoulder. Someone pulled on his belt loops. Still, he held on.

He heard the chink of metal behind and to his right side. Another person joined the fray, this one in a blue uniform. His quarry underneath him struggled to break free, so Michael dared not relax his hold. He heard that metallic clinking sound again and felt somebody moving around on his right side. He couldn't see who it was from his awkward position.

"Okay, that'll do it, sir. You can let go now."

Michael held on.

"Sir, he's not going anywhere. I've got the cuffs on him."

Only then did he relinquish his hold. He rolled onto his hip and started to push himself into a sitting position. This brought him face-to-face with the fleeing culprit. Inches apart, they locked gazes. Michael was appalled by what he saw, but he couldn't look

323

away. The face in front of him was a rigid mask. Hatred emanated from glaring eyes. Michael felt sure this dude would not hesitate to retaliate, given the chance.

Just then, without warning, the guy spit at him. A big wad of spittle struck Michael on the right cheek and sprayed across his lips. He gagged. He rolled away from the captive and wiped his face with the back of his hand. That's when he heard laughter.

Anger's intoxicating energy coursed through his veins like a rushing tide. It gave him renewed vigor. He leaped up from the floor, then bent forward at the waist. Both hands balled into fists. Color flushed his face, matching the red-hot rage threatening to consume him. So strong was the temptation to send his fists crashing into the jerk's ugly mug, he could already feel the gratifying crunch of bone on bone. That would get rid of the hideous smile.

The guy struggled against the cuffs. Both police officers had him pinned to the ground, but he continued kicking and rocking back and forth. Finally, they grabbed his right ankle, clamped one end of a second set of handcuffs around it, and then attached the other end to the chain between his hands.

Michael drew back to swing, then froze.

He couldn't bring himself to throw the punch. He'd never seen anyone bound that way. Though he was angry beyond words, he didn't want to be cruel. Yet, he felt like one of those old-fashioned pressure cookers his mother had used. He was fast approaching the bursting point, and had no outlet for the torrent of emotions only barely held in check.

Control. He could not lose his cool.

He forced himself to take a deep breath. He straightened up, put both hands on his hips and stretched his neck back until he stared straight up at the ceiling. Another deep breath. Hold for a three-count, then exhale.

There, he felt better. At least he stopped trembling and his heartbeat was slowing down a little. He heard conversation.

"You got your side, partner?"

"Just another second . . ."

"Good! One less creep walking the streets," said an onlooker.

While Michael watched, the officers lifted the guy off the floor and half-dragged, half-carried him out through the front door. He followed far enough behind to stay out of their way, but close enough to hear what they said. Before they'd gotten fully out, a second patrol car, lights flashing, pulled up to the curb.

The passenger door opened. A rookie-looking officer jumped out, with his pistol in the ready position. He surveyed the scene to make sure that everything was under control. Satisfied, he shoved the gun back into the holster.

"What've ya got?" He took note of the prisoner's trussed-up condition. "Looks like the gentleman didn't wanna cooperate."

The shorter of the original two officers shook his head in disgust. "Another slimeball pervert," he replied, as he and his partner deposited their catch next to the police cruiser.

It took a second before Michael realized what he had just heard. Another *what?* All the while, the guy did nothing more than grunt and groan.

The taller officer tapped Michael on the shoulder. "Sir, would you mind hanging around for a while? We'll need you to fill out a report about what happened."

Michael studied the criminal, still face down on the pavement. A crowd, attracted by the flashing lights, pressed in trying to get a closer inspection. "I guess so," he answered. "I can stay just a few more minutes."

The officer nodded his head once in affirmation and turned back to the work at hand.

The new arrival, with the shorter officer, released the handcuffs from the guy's legs. Without giving time for the circulation to return, they each grabbed an elbow and stood him upright. "Up against the car, and spread 'em." He inched toward the car and moved his legs apart a little. "I said, *Spread 'em!*"

He obeyed, pronto.

"That's a good boy. Now, lean your face against the roof." The guy did as he was told. He still hadn't said a word, just laid his forehead on the metal strip above the passenger door.

"Check him, Bill." the short officer told his taller partner. "See what he's carrying, if he's got any ID on him."

Bill did so, stepping behind the criminal. First, he used his right foot to kick the inside of the guys shoes. This forced his legs even wider apart. Then, he stood up and frisked him. When he came to the his right back pocket, he pulled out a wallet and tossed it to his partner. "Here, Shorty. See who we got this time." He continued on with the search, but didn't find any weapons.

Michael watched all this from his vantage point. The one called Shorty reached inside the car and used the radio to call off the information on the guy's driver's license. There followed a brief discussion which he could not follow.

While this went on, the other three officers (the driver of the second vehicle had by now gotten out to offer assistance), settled their captive in the back seat, and locked him in. From there, the taller officer, the one named Bill, came over to Michael. As he approached, he pulled out a little notebook from his top pocket and flipped it to a blank page.

"Hi. I'm Officer Bill McCartney. And you're . . .?" He let the question hang in the air.

He hesitated a moment before answering. "Michael Nastasis."

"You from around here?"

"Actually, no, sir. I'm from Florida. I've been here for a couple of weeks on . . . business."

Officer McCartney looked up from his pad of paper for the first time. He held the pencil poised, ready to write, but instead he looked at him from beneath his now-lowered brows. "Mind if I ask what kind?"

Michael realized he must have looked too uneasy, because the officer quickly qualified his line of questioning with, "No problem. I was just curious. You don't find many people around these parts who'll get involved in an arrest. What you did in there . . . ," he leaned his head towards the café, ". . . took guts." He chuckled and shook his head. "Kind of stupid, though."

"What do you mean?" His defensiveness showed.

"The guy could have been carrying a knife, a gun, or who knows what. You looked like a linebacker the way you tackled him on the run." He paused another minute and shook his head one more time. "You made a great hero, but he could have cut you in pieces and handed them back before anyone would have been able to help. We were across the room, remember."

Michael's features took on a faraway look, as if he were seeing the possibilities, now that the real danger had passed. The color drained from his face. He reached a hand out to the wall to steady himself. "I didn't think. I just reacted. Did what I'd have wanted someone to do for me."

"You were lucky. And thanks. You made our job a lot easier."

Michael, never one to accept a compliment gracefully, lowered his gaze to shoe level and nodded.

"Anyway," the officer continued. "We'd like you to fill out a statement about the events, as best you remember them."

"Not a problem." Michael paused a moment. "Say . . . what did he do that was so horrible?"

The officer didn't answer right away. Instead, he glanced around at the swelling crowds. He took a step closer. "Let's move over there where there's some room." He did so, and Michael followed, anticipating his response.

Instead, the officer started on another tack. "How often do you get to the city, Mr. . . . Nastasis?"

Taken a little off guard, Michael responded to his question with a question. "Why do you ask?"

"We may need you to appear as a witness if this goes to trial. Cases like this usually wind up with a plea bargain, but a few guys wanna fight. If that happens, you'll be subpoenaed to come in and testify." He stopped speaking and watched, as if gauging Michael's response, then explained, "Some people evade getting on the witness stand, for one reason or another, so the state has a harder time building a case."

"I see. Well, I don't visit New York often. In fact, if not for a particular situation, I wouldn't be here now."

"You mentioned you had business—"

"Yes. Personal business." Ashamed, he debated further explanation and cleared his throat. He opted to confess. "Our teenaged daughter ran away. She's been gone for several weeks, but we discovered that she took a bus here."

It was the officer's turn to lower his gaze. "Well, if you've got a lead, you're better off than most parents who've lost young girls."

"You don't think we'll find her, do you?" he asked. His tone wasn't defiant, just tense.

"Like I said," the officer continued, resuming his official demeanor but not making eye contact, "if you've got any kind of lead, you're better off than most."

"Our 'lead' is simply this: a truck driver and his wife said they dropped a girl off at a D.C. bus station who wanted to get back to family in New York. They're positive she was my daughter, only Michelle doesn't have any relatives in New York. Basically, that's about it."

Officer McCartney looked uneasy while he talked. Michael had no way of knowing his thoughts, but he recognized the poker face and read between the lines. The guy was avoiding telling him how fruitless he thought his mission was. No wonder. He did have little to go on. Michael imagined himself combing the streets as a shriveled old man, to no avail. After all, people disappeared there all the time. He had no doubt that the Big Apple could swallow them up in nothing flat. *Maybe* they would turn up again—in the morgue. Most probably disappeared without a trace. Why would Michelle be any different . . . ?

"So you would appear in court, then, if it comes to that?" The officer's question jarred him back to the present reality.

"Uh, yes, I'm sure I could, as long as I know far enough in advance." Officer McCartney acted surprised. He couldn't know, of course, how meticulous his witness was about doing the right thing. "I believe in civic duty," Michael explained.

Neither spoke for several minutes. Michael's gaze kept wandering over to the guy in the back of the patrol car. In a strange way, he felt sorry for him. After a short breather, he once again voiced his earlier question. "Okay, I said I'd be here for whatever comes of this. Now, tell me what it is he's supposed to have done."

"You sure you're ready—"

"Yes," Michael interrupted. Fear clawed its way through him, leaving a knot in place of his stomach. "I can handle it."

"Okay . . ." His tone was dubious. "Lots of pretty young girls come here to make it in the big time. Modeling. Acting. Whatever. When that doesn't pan out, they wind up, shall we say, in less respectable trades." He tried to cushion his words for Michael's

sake. "Certain men know that. They seek out the vulnerable ones and groom them over a period of time."

"*Groom* them? Just what does that mean?"

"Well, here in the city—and everywhere really—you've got guys who prey on young people. Little by little, they prepare them for exploitation and abuse."

"How?"

"Spot their unmet emotional needs, especially for male attention. Win their trust by giving 'em gifts. Favors. Drugs. This guy is an old pro at the game. He's watched so many hours of porno movies, they've lost their thrill. Now, he needs more danger, more challenge. He produces child pornography and promotes it via computer. Cyberporn, the industry is called. And it's booming."

"You're kidding! That's the most *disgusting* thing I've ever heard. He *is* a pervert." He swallowed hard. "Man, and I use the Internet for research in my office at home. I had no idea that kind of trash was available."

"Lot of people don't. Parents think if they monitor cable TV and the telephone, they've covered all the bases."

"Will the creeps just *grab* girls off the street?"

"The bolder ones. Our man hasn't gotten that brave. Most of them are very insecure, so they have to build themselves up before they make their move. He goes after the youngest and newest prostitutes, promises them drugs, and propositions them with more cash. Hookers aren't innocent, granted, but they'll be a lot less so when he's done with them. Once he gets the girls off in some dark, dingy corner he . . . rapes them."

Now Michael was really confused. "Wait a minute. If they're prostitutes—illegally—and go with him, how can it be rape?"

"Good question. First of all, many of them are under sixteen, which constitutes statutory rape, even if they do consent. But *he* goes further. Once he's got them alone, he tells 'em they won't get paid if they don't perform for the camera. He scares 'em with threats of what he'll do if they don't cooperate. Men like him can get help, though, if they want to. I've sat in on therapy groups."

For a moment, Michael felt pity. He forgot about his child. Then he remembered and panicked. "Oh, man! How many of these sickos are running around? *My daughter* is out there . . ." His voice trailed off and he stared into the distance, as if he'd see her walking down the sidewalk any minute and rush to protect her.

Officer McCartney did not try to offer any kind, conciliatory words. His years of experience had shown him they did little good. He waited, and when Michael turned back to him, he said, "I'm sure your case is listed in the NCIC. APBs out, as well?"

Michael nodded. "From what I understand, 'yes' to both." He paused. "Authorities have charged the trucker couple with kidnapping for taking a juvenile out of state without parental consent."

"Oh. Well, I don't know how much more help we can offer, but we'll do our best. You've certainly helped us. I'll speak to some friends down in the vice squads. Call in a few favors. Maybe they can put some extra manpower out there on the search."

Michael didn't know what to say. His thoughts were filled with visions of Michelle at the hands of some wild-eyed pervert. He wanted to be sick. "I do appreciate your offer," he managed. He took a step away from the policeman and started to turn away.

The officer reached out and clasped Michael around the upper arm. "Listen, it won't do any good to worry. We'll do whatever we can, honest. I've got a daughter of my own, and . . . *I'm sorry.*"

Michael's eyes glistened with unshed tears. "Thanks," he muttered. Then, in a softer voice, "I'm staying at the Mayflower." He reached back for his wallet and pulled out a business card. "Ask for me at the front desk. I'll fill out whatever papers you need. Now,

though, I've gotta go." He went to leave, but not before stopping to stare into the back seat of the cruiser for one last look at "the monster." He had never seen a pedophile up close. His head was down. Michael shuddered. If he had *his* way, he would have kicked the guy where he deserved it until he never woke up.

He strode along the sidewalk until, after another ten or eleven steps, he turned back to Officer McCartney and waved. "Keep in touch." He didn't really expect to hear another word.

For a long while, he walked the streets on autopilot, just going in whatever direction his feet happened to carry him. The night's events at the café seemed like a vague remembrance of a surrealistic dreamscape. He felt as if his head were stuffed full of cotton candy and detached from his body. His eyes darted into every nook and cranny along the way. Things didn't register, at least on a conscious level. They formed disjointed images flitting across the foggy screen of his mind. That is, until he found himself almost home, across the street from Central Park.

Something called to him from the wooded green. Not a live human voice, of course, just his insides tugging at him. *No way,* he thought. He'd heard all the stories of muggings and murders. He'd had all the excitement he could handle for one trip. He tried to walk away, but struggled to shake off the notion that he was supposed to go into the park.

Michael stood there trying to convince himself that he was only imagining things. Suddenly, he wanted nothing more than to go back to the hotel room, take a hot shower, and climb into his nice, cozy bed. Yes, that's what he'd do.

He would not call Stephanie tonight, either.

He couldn't *possibly* call her.

His own raw emotions would spew out and scare her witless. The men in white coats would be coming to take her away . . .

֎ ֎ ֎

The next morning, events at the café seemed even more remote. Had he dreamed the whole scenario? And Stephanie's late-night call. Had he dreamed that, too? No to both. He started to piece things together. Upset that she hadn't heard from him, she had awakened him after midnight out of a dead sleep and verbally pounced on him with both feet. When he begged off for not feeling good and promised that he would update her in the morning, she let him go.

From the moment he woke up, his stomach churned. He formulated what he would say, so as not to alarm her. The phone conversation went better than expected. He started with the good news—a New York cop had said he would get personally involved in trying to help them locate Michelle! That was far more than they'd had to date. "Why would the guy go out of his way to do that?" she wanted to know.

Well, he, Michael, had lent a hand in stopping a restaurant robbery in progress. No big deal. He didn't have to tell her the *whole* truth, he rationalized. Just enough to keep the wolves away from the door. To his surprise, she sounded a tad proud of him, and said she missed him. She then proceeded to fill him in on the MarriageMaker class. He did his best to sound interested when she tried to explain the purpose for marriage. In reality, he couldn't care less. He was obsessed with hitting the streets.

He trekked around all day and into evening, focusing his efforts on the Middle East Side, as far south as Gramercy Park. Now he found himself heading west on 42nd Street, toward Seventh Avenue. The sidewalks were crowded, and there was still plenty of traffic. Cars occasionally slowed down enough for an occupant to talk to one of the pretty young ladies walking by.

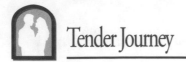

"Great," he said to himself. "Hookers already putting in an appearance." It would be worse on Eighth, with all the X-rated shows. He'd be sure to go further north before cutting over. Even here, the girls drew the attention of men out cruising. They seemed to attract one another like flies to flypaper. Michael's face reddened at the nasty image that flashed through his mind. What was the city doing to him?

He longed for a breath of fresh air. Not the exhaust fume mixture he'd been breathing, but clean, fresh country air. That left Central Park, the closest he could get. He took a last look around and set off toward uptown. He'd be at Columbus Circle within a half hour or so, he estimated. Once he got there, he looked both ways on the street, saw a break in traffic, and trotted across. The entrance to the park was only a few feet away. Again, he sensed the tug to go in. He had ignored the urge the night before.

At this hour, his favorite scenic oasis started losing its appeal. Anybody could be hiding in the off-the-main-path areas, waiting for some naive passerby to happen along. Yet, he felt compelled to press on. His imagination took off full tilt, conjuring up all sorts of dangers. Now that he'd started, though, his pride ensured perseverance. He mused about saying a prayer first. The thought was as far as he got.

He kept his eyes peeled, glancing from side to side of the walkway. It really wasn't spooky, he scolded himself, not this close to the south end. A few more minutes passed. The number of other walkers grew sparse. Shadows thickened and his imagination stepped up its assault. "I'm gettin' out of here," he told himself after one especially intimidating shadow. He started to backtrack, but before he could make any headway his conscience pricked him. Ever since his heroic feat in the café, he had turned into a coward! How could he leave if he was supposed to go on?

"Lord," he finally asked, "You don't want me to wander around here much longer, do You?" He didn't expect an answer. He wasn't disappointed.

Up ahead, the sidewalk made another turn to the left. He couldn't see around the bend, but he thought he heard voices. Without making a conscious decision to wait, his steps gradually slowed, then stopped. He wondered who on earth he would encounter this time. They couldn't be friendly. He told himself that was ridiculous. Thousands of normal people walked through the park every day and nothing happened to them. He shook his head. Disgust tinged his next words, uttered in a half-whisper, "Stop acting like a sissy."

Michael stood on the path, preoccupied with thoughts of his family. Then, as often happened lately, memories turned to bitter questions. *What had they done to deserve this situation? How could a loving God let it go on? Didn't He care about them at all?* In the meantime, voices drifted from around the bend in the sidewalk and suddenly fell quiet.

He shook himself free from his thoughts. He didn't want to let the dark catch him too deep in the park. Squaring his shoulders and standing straighter, he took a deep breath and resumed walking. His steps carried him into plain sight of . . . an *elderly* couple! When he saw them, he chuckled, half from relief, half from amusement. He couldn't help himself. The two were sitting on a park bench, so engrossed in an embrace that they never flinched at his approach.

Michael's strides slowed, despite his effort not to gawk at them. He couldn't see the man's features because his back was to him, but he noticed an abundance of white hair. From his position, Michael saw the man's left hand cradling her head and stroking her hair. Quite the Romeo, indeed!

335

They paused in their embrace. She opened her eyes, which sparkled even in the dim light when she gazed up into the man's face. There was no mistaking the look—rapt adoration. Could they possibly be husband and wife, acting in such a manner at their age? Seeing their moment of tenderness both embarrassed him and reminded him of Stephanie. He did miss her. He wondered if she would ever look at him with anything akin to the love displayed before him. Maybe his being away would rekindle the old spark. People used to tell him that "absence made the heart grow fonder." He hoped so. Well, he'd learn the truth soon enough. First, though, he needed to concentrate on Michelle.

No way would he let two potentially-senile senior citizens interfere with his mission to find his daughter. He quickened his pace and set his eyes for the next bend in the sidewalk, away from the couple altogether. He still had no idea why he was out there wandering through the park. Maybe he just needed the time to clear out the cobwebs. He couldn't help questioning what kind of help the police department would provide. He hadn't planned on Officer McCartney's generous offer, but he readily accepted his assistance. The way his luck had been running so far, he'd need all the help he could get.

Street lights had come on along the path, but for some reason, the atmosphere had grown heavier, more oppressive. When had he begun sweating so hard? He'd already soaked through the back of his T-shirt, causing it to stick to his skin.

"Why Lord?" he asked aloud. "Why won't You tell me *where* to look for her?" He stopped walking to stare up at the sky. Some stars were visible if he shielded his eyes from the lights of the city and looked straight up. "You're supposed to know everything. Why won't you help me find her?" He looked down and resumed his steps, but at a slower pace than before.

"I hate feeling helpless," he cried. "I hate *being* helpless. There's gotta be something I can do, but what? *What?* God, if You're out there . . . if You're half as good as Caleb used to claim, tell me what to do. *Please!*" He fell silent a moment. All he heard was the sound of his own footsteps. Either he had no ability to distinguish the Holy Spirit from all the other noises clamoring in his head, or the Lord had nothing to say.

Discouraged, he continued walking. The minutes passed uneventfully. Soon, he emerged a little over a block from where he entered. Not much had changed while he was wandering through Central Park. People were still strolling along the sidewalks. Something nagged at him. He'd seen for himself the limitless supply of attractive women with more on their minds than a pleasant chat. Plenty of people paid next-to-nothing for a few minutes in their willing arms. Why, then, would *anyone* prefer children? To save his soul, he couldn't begin to fathom it. Something major was wrong with the weirdos, in his opinion.

For whatever reason, they were out there in force. He was not so naive as to believe that the police had arrested the only guy in New York City who had that particular problem. No. He bet there were more of them than anyone realized. It scared the life out of him. Michelle had no idea that she had placed herself in such danger. Was he wasting precious time now, scouting around without a clue? He had barely scratched the surface of Manhattan, let alone the rest of the boroughs. Maybe that decent officer could give him more tips. He sure knew things about molesters. They prey on children who crave affection. Remembering that, Michael swallowed hard and shook his head. How often had he neglected his daughter over the years? He felt heartsick. Choking back tears, he turned in the direction of his hotel.

Yes, he *had* to find her! Or die trying.

337

❧ Twenty ❧

andy had succeeded in convincing Pastor Chip that the youth group could do *something* to raise reward money to help find Michelle. Every penny would go to Mr. Michael and Ms. Stephanie. One idea he'd heard about from a buddy at camp might work, Sandy told him. If it did, they could also use it to raise money for group trips in the future. Chip let him make a presentation to the kids at the regular meeting. His enthusiasm made up for a few nervous fumbles. To Sandy's great surprise, they cast a unanimous vote to give it a try.

"Guys, you need a catchy name," Chip advised them. "Then we'll do up some professional-looking graphics on the computer, and you'll be off and running." After a twenty-minute brainstorming session of jotting down every possible idea, they dubbed their endeavor, *"The Mighty Teens' Cleaning Machine."*

Each of them decided which odd jobs they would like to do on a Saturday or in their spare time—anything from mowing lawns, cleaning cars, washing windows, and weeding gardens to straightening up garages, painting, doing laundry, sewing, shopping, or babysitting. If they had a specialized skill of some kind not

338

on the list, they could make that available, too. One artistic boy offered to make signs for storefront windows. Sandy knew a lot about camping. He volunteered to clean and prepare equipment for people who didn't have time. The musician in the group would be glad to tutor young students struggling with piano lessons.

They intended to keep it fun. They wanted to reward effort and team spirit more than skill, so they decided it would be best to assign the same dollar-per-hour value to all the jobs. That way, no one would have to feel bad that their ability was less valuable to the cause than another's. Chip commended them for such a mature, thoughtful decision.

For several weeks, they had been selling coupons to church members to "hire" them for certain tasks during a specific time slot. (For example, Mrs. Cromden reserved Kevin to mow her lawn and weed her garden from 8:00-10.00 a.m.) When the kids completed their jobs, the "employer" would sign their work vouchers, write a check to the fund in their honor, and provide them with a ride to their next job site, if they needed it. Extra-special effort could be rewarded with a tip of any amount to beef up the fund. Many people who didn't need jobs done just donated money ahead of time for the youths' good intentions. The morale-booster helped a lot. In addition, the senior pastor offered to have the church match whatever they earned, and several wealthy businessmen agreed to do the same. Were the kids ever fired up!

Pastor Chip gave last-minute instructions. "Meet at the church by 7:00 a.m. to be ready to go to job sites by 7:30. Wear modest, comfortable clothes," he emphasized. "Bring water, sunscreen, hats, sunglasses, and bug spray for outside work, plus all tools—unless you've made prior arrangements."

Sandy left home on his bike at 6:30. He worked at breakneck speed for over ten hours, and took last-minute jobs from cus-

tomers who called the church office. By the end of the day, he had mowed and weeded two lawns, painted a picnic table and four chairs, washed one car, patched two tents, and cleaned the rust off more pieces of camping gear than he could count. He was so pooped, he could barely pedal home.

After a week of frenzied activity plus the matching grants, tips, and donations, they had amassed quite a sum. How much, would be kept secret for the time being.

🐾 🐾 🐾

Michelle plopped down on the cement stoop of an empty building on West Fifty-First Street. She was feeling worse by the day, although she had cleaned herself up a bit in a seedy motel room. An older hooker she had met made the offer and she had taken her up on it. She had to admit she felt a little better after a shower and washing her hair. The woman had even given her a pants outfit she had bought for her niece at a thrift store.

She folded her arms and laid them across her knees, then rested her head. No way would she cry.

"Young lady, move along!" barked a male voice.

She looked up and squinted. A cop.

"You can't sit there," he ordered again.

"Hey, man, give me a break. I just stopped for a minute."

"I'm sorry. No loitering. You could be arrested."

She knew big words, but that loitering one caught her by surprise. Whatever it was, it didn't sound good. And the last thing she needed was jail. Or for a cop to recognize her. Better to keep moving. She stood up, hiking her backpack onto her shoulders.

"Atta girl," the cop coaxed. His tone had softened. He started to leave, then turned around and pointed down the street. "By the way, Safe Harbor is not too far from here. Nice shelter if you want help." With that, he disappeared.

Michelle blanched at the word "shelter." Probably nothing more than a run-down flop house for women. The thought made her cringe. She hated to admit needing a handout, but she had few options left. Go back to turning tricks on the street. Too yucky and dangerous. Find a guy to take her in. No way. Her fiasco with Matt still stung too much to consider that possibility. Call home and ask her parents to come get her? *Out of the question.* She'd rather die first.

She mulled over the name. It sounded familiar. Why, though? She started to shuffle along in the direction the cop had pointed. Safe Harbor . . . Yeah, she could use someplace safe.

Suddenly, she remembered where she heard it before—from the old man and woman in the park! It had to be the same one. What had they told her? She wrinkled her forehead to think. She had been out of it that day. Something about being willing to talk to her if she ever needed it. Maybe they were there now! They had sure been nice enough, even when she treated them rotten. She quickened her pace.

When she reached the building bearing the sign she was look-ing for, she couldn't believe it. A *shelter?* It looked too homey for that. She stepped inside.

The woman at the reception desk gave her a warm greeting. "Hello, miss," she said. "Can we help you?"

Michelle cleared her throat. "Yes, ma'am. I'm looking for an old couple. The man has white hair. Hers is gray. They both talk with a foreign accent."

"I'm sorry, dear. Only women live in this building."

"No, I don't mean residents. They said they help out."

"Oh, I see."

341

Michelle glanced around. "Have you seen them here maybe?"

"An older couple, you said?"

She nodded.

"*I* haven't, but I just started as a volunteer myself. Do you know their names?"

"Uh . . . no. They told me, but I can't remember. All I know is, they had a foreign accent. The man had white hair. Hers was grayish, in an old-fashioned style, with a bun on top of her head. I met them in Central Park." She paused. "They gave me a flyer about a shelter, but I lost it somewhere."

The woman smiled. "They sound like nice people."

Michelle nodded again.

"Well, we do have a number of volunteers who help from time to time. Without their names, though, it would be hard to look up anything. Unless someone happens to recognize your description."

Her tone grew a little defensive. "But one of them *told* me that someone here would know how to reach them."

"Gosh, I'm sorry I don't. By the way, my name is Trish. And what's yours, hon?"

Michelle gave the name on her fake ID. "Ashley. Ashley Nicole Witherton."

"Well, let me see what I can find out for you, Ashley."

"Thanks." She sat down in one of the comfortable chairs. She looked up. Just then, two pregnant girls, obviously not much older than she, came through the door, talking and laughing. Michelle felt sorry for them. How stupid to get themselves knocked up! They should have used protection.

At last Trish returned. "I'm sorry, miss," she said. "Today's not my day. We've got a skeleton crew in the office and no one seems to know much. One guest says she remembers seeing a couple like that, but she doesn't have any idea how to reach them. The director might. Unfortunately, she's out of town at a conference. She'll be gone for a few more days."

Michelle's face fell. "Oh," was all she could muster. She had her hopes set on seeing the old couple *today.* Right now, as a matter of fact. Tomorrow she might change her mind.

A twinge of guilt pricked her heart. She remembered how rude she had been to them in the park, throwing down their flyer right in front of them. They were only trying to help her, a total stranger. Why had she treated them so bad? She didn't have a clue. She sighed and made up her mind right then that she would probably never see them again. If she did, they wouldn't give her the time of day. Case closed.

Trish must have noticed her disappointment. "Hon, you're welcome to stay here if you need a place," she offered. "There's no charge. We'll help you all we can."

Michelle frowned. She didn't relish the thought of living with a bunch of bag ladies. She swallowed hard and forced a smile. "No, thanks. I just wanted to see that couple. They seemed easy to talk to." She paused, then explained, "Besides, I have a good roommate. We rent a small place together not too far from here." She didn't even flinch at the lie. She rarely did anymore.

If Trish saw through it, she didn't let on. She smiled and replied, "Well, that's nice. A lot of girls would give their right arm to have a place of their own." She looked into Michelle's eyes. "I know I would have. Years ago, when I was selling my body to get drugs, I *wanted* to come clean. I really did. I just didn't believe there was a way out. Until I met Jesus. Now I'm married to a fantastic man and we have two beautiful childr—"

"Hey, lady, I gotta go," Michelle interrupted with a grimace. She turned on her heel and hurried out into the lonely streets of New York.

A half hour later, one of the other Safe Harbor volunteers brought Trish a flyer to post in the lobby. She set it down on the "mail to sort" pile stacked on her desk. After handling several phone calls and talking to a couple of residents, she took a minute to scan the flyer before putting it up. "MISSING CHILD," said the caption. Nothing out of the ordinary about that. Too many such appeals had crossed her desk in the short time she had been there. But *this* child . . . Startled, she stared hard at the photo of a young girl named "Michelle." Aside from the color and style of her hair, the pretty little face bore striking resemblance to the girl who had just come in. "Was Ashley her real name?" Trish wondered aloud. *She* certainly had enough aliases in *her* day. When she noticed a five thousand dollar reward was being offered for the missing child's safe return, she made a quick decision to report the incident. It was worth a try. She didn't need the money, but Safe Harbor could sure use it. New bedroom furnishings, better computer equipment for the office, a walk-in freezer . . . She picked up the phone to dial the toll-free number.

That evening, Michelle gritted her teeth and turned two tricks. The first client—she still couldn't bring herself to call them Johns—was pudgy and had long stringy hair pulled back in a pony tail. The second, skinny, with lots of pimples on his face and tattoos on his arms. She felt totally grossed out. To her delight, however, her third client, turned out to be a young medical sales rep in a white shirt and tie. He had marijuana with him and offered to share it with her. They got high together in his nice apartment on Fifty-Eighth Street, a block south of Central Park. He even invited her to move in for awhile. She could watch the place, keep it clean. She accepted without hesitation. Yes, her luck was turning around. Matt—wherever he was—could go fly a kite.

❧ ❧ ❧

Michael unlocked the door to his hotel room and fell back-wards on the bed. He loosened his tie, then pulled it off. He was exhausted, as usual. He had walked miles and miles over the last several days and handed out hundreds of flyers about Michelle. Tracking it all in his journal became impossible. He gave that up.

His normally-reserved nature had to be put on hold for the task at hand. Even after several weeks on search duty, he still found it more agonizing than anything he had ever done. Of course, he had grown more assertive since the café incident. He talked to everyone he ran into—shop owners, street vendors, students, con-struction workers, cabbies, joggers, business people. Countless times in the course of the day, he held up the flyer in the faces of total strangers and said, "Excuse me, I'm looking for my daughter. *Please,* have you seen this girl?" Many people ignored him com-pletely. Others frowned at him and continued on their way. Some took the flyer, glanced at it, shook their heads, and then studied him with a mixture of pity and shock, as if to say, "You must be crazy t'think you'll find her."

Not a single lead. Not a trace of hope. Nothing.

Now back in the seclusion of his room, he wanted to cry. His tear ducts forbade any release. He was numb. Humiliated. Just when he thought he was feeling as bad as possible, he remembered that he had promised Stephanie he would call her. The thought of having to tell her he had gotten nowhere *again* made his chest tighten. He rubbed his hands through his hair several times. She would probably cry—maybe even get hysterical. *God, please don't let her get upset,* he prayed.

He hoped she wouldn't mention it was his fault that Michelle was missing. "If you hadn't talked so mean to her on the phone

that night, she might have come home!" Stephanie had reminded him of it on numerous occasions. He found it hard to handle then. Now he couldn't bear it.

For forty-five minutes, he enjoyed the mercy of sleep.

He awoke to sound of the phone ringing. He was so disoriented, he felt like he was drugged. "Hello," he mumbled, still groggy.

"Mr. Nastasis, Officer McCartney."

The name or the voice didn't register. Desperately, Michael tried to collect his thoughts. Had he done something wrong? Posted flyers in unauthorized places? "Excuse me, I . . ."

The officer sensed his confusion and added, "You helped us out at the café."

"Café . . . I'm sorry, I was sleeping hard when you called."

"Remember? Pounced on the porno king we were after."

He sat up in bed and grabbed the phone base, almost pulling the cord from the wall. "Yes, yes, of course. And you offered to help me find my daughter. Do you have news?" his voice pleaded. He despised himself for the pitiful sound.

"Man, I don't want to get your hopes up. But I do owe you a favor, so I thought I'd call."

"What? What is it?" His voice had taken on an ultra-panicky rasp. He felt ridiculous.

"Oh, nothing bad but—"

"But *what?*" Michael interrupted.

"Nothing real solid, either."

Michael released a quick breath. "I'll take anything I can get."

"Well, it's kinda unusual, is all. A German couple in their sixties, who recently arrived in New York—he says he's a retired scientist—called the station to report they had met a young girl in Central Park. She sounds like she fits your daughter's description somewhat. Petite. Brown-eyed. About her age."

"You're kidding! They talked to her? How is she?" His words poured out in a gush of emotion.

"Now, Mr. Nastasis, don't jump the gun. Lots of stray kids hang around the city."

Silence on Michael's end of the line. He felt his hopes dashed. The urge to retaliate grew strong in him. "Then why did you get me all riled up, for Pete's sake, if you have no concrete answers?"

The officer bristled slightly at the sarcastic outburst. "Look, I was just tryin' to do you a favor. This isn't even my job."

He sighed. "I know. I'm sorry."

"Apology accepted."

"So, what did she look like? You didn't say what color hair."

"Short blond."

"Michelle has shoulder-length brown. Obviously, not her."

"Different hair does not rule out the girl they saw. Assuming your daughter does not want to be found, she might have tried to change her identity. Pretty common."

"Oh, yeah." To cover his sudden feelings of shame, Michael tried to make light of the situation. "Guess dye and scissors are easy to come by these days, huh?"

"Right. Anyway, I told the couple that a man, clean-cut and professional-looking, had come to New York searching for his daughter. For some reason, the old man got very animated when I said that, and asked if they could meet you right away. He left their name and number in case you want to speak with them. I wouldn't give them yours without your permission."

"Have they seen Michelle's picture?"

"I didn't ask. A buddy in the juvenile division took their call. He knew I had posted some flyers around the station, so he mentioned it when I ran into him at the coffee machine."

"You just *happened* to run into him?"

"Yes. As I said, I don't usually get involved in this end of the process. I'm a street cop, not a detective."

"So, in other words, he could have sat on that lead for who knows how long before somebody figured out—"

"Wait a minute. You gotta understand that detectives have pending cases coming out of their ears. They can't stop what they're doing to follow up on every single tip that comes in."

"True. Well, go ahead and give me the phone number." His tone came out a bit too commanding. He realized it, and had to apologize again.

"No problem. You're runnin' on a short fuse. I'd probably be worse if I were in your shoes." He read the information about the Liebens slowly, so Michael could jot it down.

"Thanks, Officer McCartney. I do appreciate this."

"Hey, call me Bill."

"Okay, Bill. I can't thank you enough. Guess we'll see what happens. Take it one day at a time.

"Right. Meanwhile, we're keeping our eyes open. Do as much as we can—with the manpower available, of course."

"Of course." They hung up after exchanging brief goodbyes. Michael sat on the bed for several minutes, staring out the window. He was having a hard time grasping the coincidences. He spoke aloud, as if the sound of his words would help convince him. "I'm here in New York and just happen to help with an arrest. Two Germans, fresh off the boat, just happen to see a girl alone in Central Park. For some reason, they have sense enough to call the police. Now they happen to want to meet me." He shook his head and scratched the back of his neck. He did remember crying out to God in total despair the other night. Could it be . . . ?

He stood and paced the floor several times. Fear fought to crush his sudden hope. Discouraging thoughts, one after the other, throbbed in his head. *You might as well not even bother calling those people. You actually believe some strangers ran into **your** daughter in a huge city like this? Get real! You'll only make a fool of yourself. The disappointment will make you feel worse than you do now. And you know Stephanie won't be able to take the letdown . . .*

On and on went the mental barrage.

He needed a shower, so before he did anything else, he'd take one. Maybe it would give him a fresh perspective.

Once he had dried off and put on his bathrobe, he sat down on the bed with his legs stretched out in front of him. The inner battle went on—take a chance or ignore the whole thing. He picked up the phone. What did he have to lose? Setting the clunky base on his lap, he dialed the number of the . . . what was the name? Lieben. He inhaled. It rang several times before the hotel operator answered. He gave her the room number the officer had mentioned. Then it dawned on him. They were staying right down the street and around the corner. That was too much. His heart pounded. Three rings. Four rings. Five rings. The operator came back on the line. "I'm sorry, sir. No one answers that extension. May I take a message?"

He hesitated. Would it be better to leave a message or call back? He couldn't make up his mind. The smallest decisions seemed major. He rubbed his palm on his thigh. The operator asked, "Sir, are you there?"

"Yes, ma'am, I'm sorry. I'll leave a message. My name is Michael Nastasis. N-a-s-t-a-s-i-s. Phone, 265-0060. They spoke with a young girl who might be our missing daughter. Please tell them I am anxious to meet them—at their convenience."

"Thank you, sir. Have a nice evening." She disconnected him.

Michael sat there, staring at the receiver with his mouth open. "After what I just told her, she says, 'have a nice evening'? That's it?

Well, I'll be—!" He slammed the receiver into the cradle. "How insensitive can people get?" One had to expect that sort of thing in New York, he guessed.

The phone rang again while it was still on his lap. He jumped, then picked it up. They were returning his call already. What perfect timing!

It turned out to be the hotel operator. Before he gave way to disappointment, she said, "Sir, I just wanted to apologize. What you told me didn't register until I disconnected. After answering these phones for hours straight, I go into automatic mode. Please forgive me. I do hope you find your daughter."

The woman's open display of concern stunned him. "Uh . . . thank you. Thank you very much."

"You're welcome. Good evening, sir."

"Yes. Good evening." He hung up the phone and leaned his head back against the wall. Again, he dozed.

He woke up with a start, then glanced quick at his watch. Stephanie. He hadn't called her yet! She would be worried, probably in bed already. He dialed their number. She picked it up on the first ring with a crisp, irritated "hello."

"Hey, it's me."

"Michael?"

"Of course it's Michael. Who else would say to you, 'It's me' at this hour?"

"Don't be petty. Why didn't you call earlier? Surely you haven't been out looking for Michelle until now."

"No, I fell asleep."

"Oh. Nice to know we're so important down here."

"Hon, it's not that. If you knew all I've been through the last few days, you'd understand."

"I've been through a lot today, too. Stephen's running a fever, the washing machine overflowed all over the floor, and we got an overdraft notice from the bank. Worst of all, here I sit, not being able to do a thing to help find Michelle. I have to wait for you to toss me a few crumbs."

He zeroed in. "An overdraft notice? How?"

"I have no idea."

"Steph, did you deposit that client's check I gave you? We needed the money in the account."

"I think I did."

"You mean you're not sure?"

"I'm pretty sure. I remember doing it the day after you left."

"You have the deposit slip, I hope?"

"I think it's in the checkbook." She exhaled loudly. "Listen, Michael, I've had it with your third degree. I'm doing the best I can. You should have made the deposit yourself before you left!"

"As if I had time. I barely made it to the airport as it was. Anyway, call the bank first thing in the morning and see if they have the deposit recorded. If they don't, you'll have to turn the house upside down. Find either the slip or that check. It's from a good client, and we cannot jeopardize the account by asking them to issue another one." He heard her sniffles loud and clear on the other end. His turn to sigh. "Why are you crying already? That's why I dread calling you."

"I can't help it. Sometimes you irk me. I feel like I could go crazy with all this stuff, and you're on my case about the stupid checkbook."

"I'm sorry, Steph. We're both under a lot of stress."

"Yes, we are. *You* remember that!" She went silent for a few seconds. "Well, I guess you don't have any good news, or you would have told me by now."

He remembered the call he was waiting for. "I may have some, but I don't know yet for sure."

"What does *that* mean?"

"Well, the police officer I helped that night called me. It seems that an older couple from Germany saw a young girl who matches Michelle's description somewhat." His tone was matter-of-fact, as if he were reporting a story on the news.

Stephanie gasped. "Somebody *saw* her? *Where?* Did they say whether she was okay?"

"Like I said, I don't know yet. I tried to call the number he gave me last night, but there was no answer. The people are staying at the Raddison Empire a few blocks away."

"Incredible. Oh, Michael, what if they *did* see her? That would be too much!"

"I know. But let's not get our hopes up until we know something more definite."

"Okay, I'll try."

"They may be calling right now and getting a busy signal. I better go." He thought of his son. "Give Stephen a big hug for me. Call the doctor if the fever isn't gone by tomorrow, okay?"

"I already have an appointment. What if it's serious? We really need another crisis right now."

"We've just got to believe it's nothing major. I'll call you as soon as I know more."

"Promise?"

"Promise." He paused. She sounded so vulnerable. Taking the plunge, he said, "Love you, Steph."

She hesitated. "I love you, too."

"Do you miss me?"

"Sometimes."

His heart dropped. "Just sometimes?"

"To be honest, I don't miss the tension between us. Or the arguments." She paused. "I'm sure you don't either."

"No . . . Think we can do better?"

"We can try. Promise you'll call ASAP?"

"I *promise*. Good night, hon." She had already said goodbye and hung up before he could say another word. He felt empty and alone. Without replacing the receiver, he got a dial tone and called the front desk to see if there were any messages for him. No, none had come in, the lady said. The light would be flashing on his phone, if so. He gave up and went to bed.

◦⟩ *Twenty-One* ⟨◦

Michael awoke the next morning at 5:30. He took another shower, read through two newspapers, and ordered breakfast from room service—anything to kill time until it would be late enough to try the German couple again. Why hadn't they returned his call? *They* were the ones who had asked to meet him. When he realized he still had time to waste, he retrieved the Gideon Bible from the nightstand drawer. He noticed it was the King James Version. The thought of bringing his Bible from home had not occurred to him. He flipped through the pages at random. Nothing caught his eye. He laid it back in the drawer. God seemed so far away, so disinterested in his family's plight.

But what about the coincidence with the police? With the foreigners? Maybe He was closer than it seemed. He thought again of Caleb and felt a twinge in his heart. The old bugger had him studying the Word in depth and praying several times a day. And *loving* it! Where had the love gone? Michael felt drier than an uprooted plant in the desert. Church eased things somewhat, but he and Stephanie only went on Sunday morning. Lately, not at all. Trying to make the other services cramped their schedule.

His conscience needled him. Or, could it be what Caleb used to call "conviction of the Holy Spirit"? Whatever, it annoyed him.

Eight o'clock came at last. He decided it was time. He dialed the hotel and asked for the couple's room number. It rang and rang. He couldn't believe it. He had missed them again! He put the phone gently back in its cradle, but it demanded all of his self-control. His insides churned and burned. He almost wished the cop had never called. The pie-in-the-sky tip was driving him crazy.

Where could they be? Maybe they were early-risers and had already left for a day of sightseeing. Just his luck. He had tried to be polite. Had waited to call them during decent hours, so he missed them altogether. Great. So much for etiquette.

In desperation, he placed his pillow on the floor beside the bed and got down on his knees. He felt awkward, unnatural, unwelcome. How long had it been? Months. At first, he didn't know what to say, so he said nothing. He took deep breaths, then waited some more. His lips would not move. He felt a sudden urge to take the Bible out of the drawer again. Without any great effort on his part, it fell open to Psalm Eighteen. After a long time of staring at ink on paper, he made himself read aloud, haltingly at first, then with more boldness:

I will love thee, O Lord, my strength. The Lord is my rock, and my fortress and my deliverer; my God, my strength, in whom I will trust; my buckler, and the horn of my salvation, and my high tower. I will call upon the Lord, who is worthy to be praised: so shall I be saved from mine enemies . . . He sent from above, he took me, he drew me out of many waters. He delivered me from my strong enemy, and from them which hated me: for they were too strong for me. They prevented me in the day of my calamity: but the Lord was my stay. He

brought me forth also into a large place; he delivered me, because he delighted in me . . . The Lord rewarded me according to my righteousness; according to the cleanness of my hands hath he recompensed me . . . With the merciful thou wilt show thyself merciful; with an upright man thou wilt show thyself upright; With the pure thou wilt show thyself pure; and with the froward thou wilt show thyself froward. For thou wilt save the afflicted people; but wilt bring down high looks. For thou wilt light my candle: the Lord my God will enlighten my darkness. For by thee have I run through a troop; and by my God have I leaped over a wall . . . As for God, his way is perfect: the word of the Lord is tried: he is a buckler to all those that trust in him. For who is God save the Lord? Or who is a rock save our God? It is God that girdeth me with strength, and maketh my way perfect.

A deeper crack formed in the concrete wall around Michael's heart. The torrent of pain he'd been holding back seeped through. He cried for only the second time since Michelle had vanished. He admitted fears he had been hiding from Stephanie—of *never* finding their daughter . . . or having to identify her cold, naked body on a slab in the morgue . . . or perhaps worst of all, he wasn't sure, seeing her curled up in a fetal position, brain-dead from drugs, while they visited her year after year in a nursing home. Any one of the alternatives sent terror through his veins. He thought of Stephen, but found no comfort there, either. His son's life would likewise be snuffed out by a vicious foe. He grabbed a pillow and pounded it with his fists. Again through clenched teeth and crying harder, he muttered, "God, I don't understand!"

Before long, another fear surfaced—finances. Would they lose everything he had worked so hard for? The family savings had dropped substantially, and the crises they faced showed no signs of letting up. Between his expenses in New York, the reward money, and Stephen's medical bills, the picture he imagined looked more than grim. In spite of his best intentions when he left Florida, he was getting little work done for clients. If he wasn't out pounding the pavement or dead tired, he had to fight to concentrate. He couldn't bill them for hours he wasn't putting in, of course. Less income was draining the coffers at an incredible rate.

Too, he feared Stephanie would break under the pressure. Would he end up visiting *her* in a psychiatric ward somewhere? Assuming she managed to keep her sanity, could their marriage ever bounce back? Would they experience the joy they had when they first reconciled? He sobbed wrenching heart-cries for help.

Minutes passed before Michael calmed. When he did, Psalm Eighteen drew him back. There, he gained insight he had missed the first time. Seldom had he been humble, merciful, upright, or pure all "prerequisites" to God's intervention in the battle against enemies. No, he didn't have a leg to stand on when it came to pleading for favors from heaven. Then again, who would?

He sat on the bed and picked up the scrap of paper with the phone number of the German couple. "Mr. and Mrs. Lieben," he read aloud to refresh his memory. The odds were a million-to-one against their knowing anything about Michelle, but maybe it *was* worth one last try. If he could catch a glimmer of hope! He dialed the number of the Raddison Empire and asked for the room number again. No answer. He was just about to hang up when the operator came back on the line. Her customary cheery response irked him. "Sir, no one is answering that extension. May I take a message for you?"

Michael started to snap at her, but clamped his mouth shut. Grouchiness wouldn't help. Besides, she had nothing to do with

his problems. "Thank you," he replied. "I did leave a message last night." Something prompted him to tell her more. "You know, it's strange. These people, supposedly senior citizens, aren't in their hotel room late at night or early in the morning. They don't even check their messages. And I'm returning *their* call to a police officer, who called me and said they were very anxious to talk to me."

He took a deep breath. "You see, I'm here in New York trying to find our teenaged daughter. This couple knew nothing about that fact, but they notified the police about meeting a young girl in Central Park. She happens to be about Michelle's age and size." He stopped short, suddenly hearing how disjointed and far-fetched his story sounded. He started to apologize.

She interrupted. "Sir, no need to explain. I would pursue every lead I could get my hands on." She paused. "I'm wondering . . . is it possible you have the *wrong* room number?"

He frowned and rubbed his forehead. "I don't know how. I'm sure I wrote the information down just as the officer gave it to me. But I guess anything's possible." He stifled mounting anxiety.

"What did you say their last name was?"

"Lieben. L-i-e-b-e-n."

"If you hold, sir, I'll check their registration." Michael's mouth went dry. He licked his lips and swallowed. After what seemed like forever, she came back on the line. "I have good news!" she exclaimed. "You did have the wrong number. The room you had was closed for repairs. I just rang the correct one and a gentleman answered. He said they have been awaiting your call."

"You're *kidding!* You spoke with the Liebens?"

"Yes. Mr. Lieben. Would you like me to put your call through? He did sound quite excited to hear from you."

Michael cleared his throat. He couldn't believe it. All that confusion for nothing! "Y-yes, ma'am," he stammered, "please do."

358

With that, the woman was gone. He had meant to thank her and get her name, but the ringing phone at the other end captured his full attention.

"Good morning to you, sir," said a rather chipper male voice.

"Uh, hello. I'm Michael Nastasis. Have I reached the party who notified the police about a young girl?"

"Why, yes, you have, indeed! We have been awaiting a reply and wondering the reason for the delay—"

"*You! I've* been trying since Officer McCartney called last night and getting no answer. I almost gave up. Somehow, he must have given me the wrong number. The operator discovered the mistake this morning."

"My goodness! Thankfully, you persisted, or we would have experienced further delay. As we speak, Anna is preparing our bags to vacate the room."

"Really?"

"Yes, we need to economize. The Westside YMCA will save us a large sum per day."

Michael's mouth dropped open. He exhaled. "Dear Lord . . . if I had slept later . . . or gone out for breakfast . . . or procrastinated, I could have missed you by a hair's breath! I might *never* have found you again."

"We would certainly have notified someone of the change."

"I'm sure you would have, but—" He paused to catch his breath. His heart was pounding suddenly. "From what I know of the YMCA, they don't even have phones in the rooms . . ."

"True. It is a bit more spartan than the hotel."

"Spartan is an understatement. They're usually in run-down neighborhoods. Don't they even have communal bathrooms?"

"Yes, but they offer private baths, as well. Anna and I chose the communal option for greater savings. However, the refurbished

historic building is situated on the west side of Central Park, at the corner of Sixty-Third Street, and is quite adequate, actually—"

"You don't say. I'm at The Mayflower on Central Park West." His heartbeat quickened again. "You'll be right down the street and I might never have known it. Do you realize that?"

"We are at the moment, also. The Empire is on 63rd at Broadway, directly across from Lincoln Center. As I said, sir, we would not have left without accurate forwarding information."

"Yes, but the way *my* luck goes, the person you gave the message to would have written it down wrong, lost it, or dropped dead first." He shook his head at the ramifications. "I might have missed a golden opportunity to narrow down the field to New York City." He swallowed. "Thus far, all we've known is that Michelle told a couple of total strangers she was headed here."

"Sir, I see your point now." His voice lowered. "And I am so sorry about your daughter. You must be quite worried."

"Very. We can hardly think about anything else."

"I can imagine so. You do have a photograph of her?"

"Of course. Everywhere I go, I have been handing out flyers with her picture and description."

"We have not seen such, but that is a fine idea." He paused and drew a quick breath, then exhaled. "Would it not be wonderful if the girl we encountered turns out to be your daughter?"

"That would be too good to be true."

"How can anything, as you say, be 'too good to be true'? We serve a *good God,* for whom nothing is impossible."

"You're believers?" he asked, amazed.

"Very much so. Anna and I have been praying for the child." Michael's eyebrows shot up. "You *have?*"

"Yes, we felt impressed to do so." Joshua cleared his throat. "Something was amiss, we realized, and we felt quite drawn to her, especially my Anna. We both sensed that the girl might well have run away from home."

"You did?" His eyes widened. *"How?"*

"A variety of ways." Joshua cleared his throat again and changed the subject. "Sir, could we not meet in person—perhaps in the lobby here? We will discuss the details then."

"That would be great. Just tell me when."

"Almost any time would suit us."

"How about in half an hour? Would that be too soon?" The urgency in his voice made him grimace.

"Let me check with my wife. One moment." Michael heard the sound of the receiver being covered, then muffled voices. A few seconds later, "Forty-five minutes will be more convenient for her, at about ten o'clock. How shall we recognize you?"

Michael hesitated and glanced in the mirror above the dresser. "Well, I'm six feet tall and have dark hair, going grey on the edges." He looked down. He hadn't even changed out of his bathrobe. Good thing the lady needed extra time. He cast a glance at his clothes hanging on the garment rack. "I'll probably be wearing a navy pin-striped shirt, khaki pants, and a navy sport coat. You?"

"I have white hair. I am of medium height for a man; Anna is quite small. She wears her grey hair drawn up from her face in a chignon. Our clothes . . . rather nondescript, I would say."

Michael smiled at the quaint picture he envisioned. "That should do it. I'll see you soon."

"Yes. We will be delighted. Sir, I regret to admit I have forgotten your name. Please forgive me."

"Nastasis. Call me Michael."

"Very well, Michael. And we are Joshua and Anna."

"Good. I'm looking forward to meeting you."

"Likewise. Good day, sir."

The receiver clicked in Michael's ear. As soon as he hung up, he hurried to get ready. He touched up his pants and shirt with the travel iron, ran a lint brush over his jacket, then dampened his hair, moussed it, and styled it with the blow-dryer. For the first time in a long while, he whistled and hummed.

Oh, what he'd give for a chance to call home with a genuine breakthrough! He could already hear their excitement and picture the joy on their faces.

Something good was about to happen. It *had* to.

Forty minutes later, Michael left his room, walked west on Sixty-First Street to Broadway, and angled over to Sixty-Third. He had no problem finding the attractive, canopied entrance of the Raddison Empire Hotel. He made his way into the lobby just before ten—late, in his opinion—and short of breath from rushing. So intent on his mission, he didn't allow himself more than a few seconds to admire the unique collection of shadow boxes depicting scenes from famous operas. He couldn't waste a single moment.

The elegant, old-world European decor of the lobby took him by surprise. He couldn't imagine anybody leaving there for a YMCA. That was like going from an executive home to a trailer. What could have happened to make such a move necessary? It was none of his business, he supposed, but it piqued his curiosity. His eyes scanned the people standing around, and those in line at the front desk. No older couples in sight who resembled the man's description on the phone.

He turned to his left. Across the room, beyond the oriental carpet and mahogany table bearing a bouquet of fresh flowers, he noticed an enormous tapestry on the wall, halfway up the curved staircase. At least ten feet wide, the woven work of craftsmanship had to be worth a fortune. His eyes travelled down the steps and back up, then stopped. Suddenly, he spotted them—a white-haired gentleman and a lady with gray hair pulled up into a bun. They were sitting on a scroll-armed bench on the landing of the stairway. Bathed in the warm light illuminating the tapestry above, they were half-facing each other, holding hands. Their heads were bowed, eyes closed. The incredible classic portrait stunned him. He sensed a certain holiness in the moment, making his breath catch. He felt torn between staring and turning the other way, and chose the former, with as much discretion as he could muster.

He decided he should wait until they looked up to make a move toward them. Their heads rose slightly, but instead of search-ing for any strangers, they gazed into each other's eyes. The man placed his arm around his wife and hugged her, then planted a light kiss on her forehead. She patted his cheek and snuggled in to receive his affection. The man rested his chin on her head. *Finally,* he glanced in Michael's direction. He smiled, gave a nod of acknowledgment, then gently patted his wife's hand. They stood up. He offered her his arm and they descended the stairs together with a quiet grace.

Michael moved toward them in long, quick strides. He held out his hand for a handshake and squeezed the man's hand firmly. Only then did he notice his eyes. Sparkling, crystal blue eyes with smile lines extending outward from the corners. Eyes reminiscent of something. Where had he seen the like before? He didn't know. "Mr. Lieben, pleased to meet you." His words sounded so mun-dane, almost ridiculous, considering the occasion. He glanced down at the petite woman seated at his side. "Mrs. Lieben, it's a pleasure to meet you, too." She smiled and nodded her head.

"Please, sir, address us as Joshua and Anna," said Mr. Lieben.

Michael hesitated. "If you insist. And I'm Michael Nastasis."

With the clumsy exchange of pleasantries over and done, his level of anxiety heightened. He looked back and forth at them. The moment of reckoning had arrived. His lips tensed. Palms started to sweat. "I suppose we might as well get right to the point." He unrolled the flyer he had rolled up tight in his left hand and held it up to show them. "By any chance, could this be the girl you saw?"

They took the paper in their hands and studied it carefully. Joshua furrowed his brows, then looked at Anna.

Michael's pulse raced. He had to remind himself to breathe. He swallowed hard.

The couple fidgeted a bit. Joshua, still studying the photo, said, "Your daughter is a very pretty child."

"Yes, Anna added. "Such beautiful hair and smile."

"Thank you." Michael's face fell. "You sound as if you didn't know that already. Does she look *anything* like the girl you met?"

"Somewhat," said Joshua. "Would you agree, love?"

She nodded, "Yes, they do favor one another.

Joshua continued to study the photo. "It is difficult to be absolutely certain."

Squinting, Michael asked, "What's hard about it? Either it was Michelle or it wasn't."

"The girl we met was faring quite poorly. She was thinner, in fact, very thin, with short, blond hair." He hesitated, and seemed to choose his words with care, ". . . and not so stylish. Her eyes were indeed large and brown, as I recall, but—"

"What was she doing when you saw her?"

Joshua took a deep breath and moistened his lips before answering. "Lying on a bench, fast asleep."

Michael's voice trembled. "In Central Park?"

They nodded. "We noticed her there alone. Her hair was matted and she had cuts and bruises in several places on her face. We stopped to offer our assistance. However, when she woke up, she became quite angry with us and ran away before we had a chance to talk at length. For those reasons, we notified the police." Almost apologizing, he added, "We did not know what else to do."

"No, no, you did the right thing. I'm just overwhelmed. And disappointed, I guess. I was counting on a definite, positive identification when you saw the picture."

Joshua nodded. "As were we." Anna tapped him on the arm. Michael waited while she whispered in Joshua's ear. Soon, the old man asked, "My wife just reminded me of something else she noticed. The girl was wearing a very nice ring of unusual design."

"Oh?"

"Yes. Anna, dear, please describe it for the gentleman."

"I will do my best." She displayed her right hand, palm down, fingers spread open. With her left index finger, she traced an outline on the fourth finger and said, "On a band of gold sat a single pearl. Coming out from the band, proceeding toward her knuckle were three thin, curved pieces of gold which formed three small, interlocking hearts. In the center apex of each heart rested a gemstone—an emerald, a ruby, and a small diamond."

"Does your daughter have one like that?" Joshua asked. "Oh, I hope for your sake that she does!"

Michael knit his eyebrows and cocked his head. He hadn't the faintest idea. It sounded expensive. Perhaps they had given her a ring for some special occasion, but what kind, he couldn't remember. Stephanie always shopped for gifts—extravagant ones. He blushed, admitting, "You know, I'm not sure. I could call my wife and ask her. Would you mind waiting?"

"Not at all," Joshua offered.

Relieved to have a moment to collect his composure, Michael walked quickly to a pay phone and dialed home with his calling

card. The answering machine came on. "Where on earth—? It's the middle of the morning!" He slammed down the receiver, angrier at himself for his ignorance than he was at Stephanie. For some reason, he tried again. She answered after one ring. "Where have you been?" he demanded, without even saying hello. "I just called and there was no answer."

"Pardon *me*. I was in the shower! By the time I got to the phone, it had stopped ringing. So don't get mad at me."

"Sorry, I'm on edge. It's very important. You won't believe what's happening. Waiting for me in this very hotel lobby is the German couple I told you about. They saw Michelle's picture and they both feel she resembles the girl they met. But it's hard to know for sure 'cause . . . well, kids change so fast. Anyway, Anna noticed a unique ring the girl was wearing, which could be our ace in the hole." He swallowed hard again. He could spit cotton. "Steph, by any chance, does Michelle have—"

Stephanie's gasp interrupted him. "A pearl with an emerald, ruby, and diamond, kind of separated from the pearl?"

"Exactly." Reality set in. "You mean she *does* have one?"

"Yes! Yes! *Yes!* Don't you remember?" She paused. "I had it custom-made. We gave it to her for Christmas last year."

"I thought so. Just wanted to be sure." The blatant lie slipped out with so little effort, he barely noticed.

Stephanie wasn't buying it. "Michael, come on. You never paid attention to those things and you know it. If you even remembered a big event, the kids considered themselves lucky." Her voice had a bitter edge.

He sighed. "Steph, please. Let's not go into that now, okay?"

"Sorry. I shouldn't have brought it up."

"That's right. We should be happy. This is our first major breakthrough. We didn't know for sure she was in New York City.

Now we find out that a petite girl with brown eyes and a ring just like hers was seen here just days ago. Think of it!"

"It is pretty amazing, I guess." She let out a sigh. "I'm afraid to get my hopes up, though, until one of us lays eyes on her and we know she's fine." She paused. "The couple who saw the girl, how did they say she looked? Was she okay?"

Michael ran his hands through his hair and rubbed the back of his neck. Why did she have to ask? "Well, she was thinner than the picture, which is to be expected. I'm sure she hasn't been dining gourmet-style like she did at home."

"You're trying to butter me up. What are you avoiding?"

"Nothing. It's just that she must have gotten her hair cut somewhere. And dyed." He stated the facts as quickly and unemotionally as he could.

"What?"

"You heard me. The girl had short, blond hair. But according to the officer, runaways often disguise their appearance."

"Oh." Dead silence, then sniffles. "Michael, do you realize what that means? She was *so miserable* at home that she would go to extremes to keep us from ever finding her . . ."

He hadn't considered that aspect. His heart sank. He could think of nothing appropriate to say, so he kept quiet. Stephanie went on, "Everybody loved Michelle's hair. She was proud of it, and spent hours taking care—"

"Let's *try* to look at the bright side," he interrupted. "Given the custom-made ring, it sounds like the girl was our daughter."

"Now you just have to find her again." Bigger sniffles.

"I know. But she can't have gone too far."

Stephanie sighed. "I hope not."

"Me, too." He glanced around. "Say, I almost forgot. The Liebens are waiting for me. I better go."

367

"Yes . . . you don't want to be rude." Her voice softened. "Michael, please thank them for me. Don't forget."

"I won't. You've got Stephen's appointment with the doctor this afternoon, so I'll call you later."

"Okay, bye." They both hung up at the same time. Why did he always feel so empty at the end of their conversations? He shook his head and decided to make a quick call to Officer McCartney. He wanted to update him so they wouldn't waste time hunting in the wrong direction. A receptionist at the police department took the message in a crisp, business-like manner. Michael felt that he may as well have delivered her the latest weather report.

Satisfied that he had fulfilled his responsibility, he headed back to find Joshua and Anna. There they were, up the stairs on the scroll bench, with their heads bowed. They sure did enough of that. They looked up just as he was about to squat down in front of them. "I'm sorry it took so long." He managed a smile and said, "Sounds like we've struck gold."

"Truly we have?" Joshua jumped up from the bench with his arms outstretched. "Oh, hallelujah! God has answered our prayers!"

Michael tried hard to echo his enthusiasm. "Yes, I double-checked with my wife," he said. "We gave Michelle a ring just like that for Christmas last year. It was custom-made."

"My goodness." Joshua slowly sat back down and put his arm around Anna, then stared at Michael. His blue eyes glistened.

Anna's face glowed with a quiet, peaceful smile. "How it warms our hearts to hear you are making progress!"

Their open display of emotion over the plight of complete strangers seemed nothing short of incredible. And yes, they *had* made progress. He decided to focus on that. He glanced at Joshua again. There was something so *familiar* about him. As he tried remembering where he might have seen him before, it struck him.

Caleb. In a split-second, memories flashed through his mind's eye. The old guy used to get so expressive when he was excited about something special God had done—just like Joshua when he jumped up from the bench. Michael studied this stranger-turned-friend across from him. White hair like Caleb's. The same light blue eyes with laugh lines at the corners. Even the smile. Less tan, taller and a little heavier. Not a mirror image, but now that he'd made the connection, the similarities were uncanny. Goose bumps sprang up on his arms. He rubbed his forearms briskly. Ridiculous. He wondered if he was hallucinating.

"Have you taken a chill?" Joshua asked.

He nodded. "No, I'm fine."

"All right, then. Do you suppose we should notify the police of our discovery?"

"Done. I called them right after I hung up with Stephanie."

Joshua smiled and winked. "Now, there is a man after my own heart. He does a job right."

Michael froze. Not only did the guy look like Caleb, get emotional like Caleb, and have his conscientious tendencies, he even *winked* like Caleb. Michael shook his head. He had been under way too much stress.

"Well, sir, we must be going now, in order to check out on time and get settled into our new quarters. Would you care to join us later for dinner?" Joshua asked. "Our treat."

"I'd love to. Maybe we could even take in a concert or a play. But only under one condition—if the bill is on me. We owe you at least that much for your trouble."

"You owe us nothing, Michael. We simply acted upon what we felt God was impressing us to do. And we are reaping the joy of obedience. Is that right, Anna?" He smiled at her.

Squeezing his arm, she replied, "Well-said, my love."

Joshua nodded once at him. "So . . . we shan't quibble over minor details. Rather, let us plan to celebrate a victory for you and our God!"

"I'll second that," Michael replied. He gave their hands a vigorous handshake and said goodbye. Funny, he felt better already.

🙣 🙣 🙣

The shadows lengthened as the last fading rays of sunshine glinted off the storefront windows. Rush hour traffic had finally begun to thin out. Men and women hurried along the sidewalk, visibly relieved that another day's work was past. Most seemed focused on their own forward progress, and rarely spared a glance to the left or the right. Those few who did paid scant attention to a young girl standing in the shadows of one of the doorways. To them, Michelle was just another one of the growing number of street kids. Certainly, none of the pedestrians cared about the pretty ring on her right hand, or the way she twirled it with her left thumb and index finger.

Though it was obvious that the girl could have used some small measure of kindness, nobody stopped for her. She'd given up expecting help from anyone since her salesman boyfriend traded her in on a new model. The rejection bothered her less than the shaking in her arms and hands she could no longer control. Lately, it had been getting unbearable. And she found herself having a hard time concentrating on any one thing too long.

At least her clothes were clean. Earlier that day, she had taken almost the last bit of change—it wouldn't buy much of anything else—and carried what she owned to the laundromat. It all fit into her backpack. She had on the outfit she ran away in, only now it didn't fit as well. The belt had to be cinched in just to keep the skirt where it belonged on her waist. Looking at herself in the cracked glass, she gave in and started feeling sorry for herself.

Thoughts of home suddenly filled her mind. The odd thing was, most were pleasant memories. All the bad times seemed less awful than they once had. At any rate, what mattered now was getting rid of the shakes. They had spread from her hands and arms to her torso. She could feel her stomach knotting, and already a slight flutter had begun in her legs.

Her eyes kept darting to her hands, to the ring her parents had given her. She remembered how proud she'd felt showing it to her friends. They "oohed" and "aahed" every time they saw it. A solitary pang of guilt found its way through to her quiescent conscience when she wondered how much it would bring, but she squelched the feeling into silence.

Yes, she could always trade the ring to Rocco for some of his super stash.

Decision followed close on the heels of a whim.

Her eyes strained into the dusk for a sign of the local pusher. It was still early. He usually did not make an appearance on the streets until well after dark, but tonight would be an exception. At least, Michelle hoped it would. For the moment, there was no sign of him. Only the thinning remnants of the working class coming home from their nine-to-fives. *Morons.*

She shivered again and crossed her arms. She clasped her hands onto her upper arms and hugged herself against the chill. Her eyes continued scanning the stream of pedestrians. It only took a few seconds for the faces to blend into one continuous mass. She no longer looked at people as people, having their own particular set of wants and needs. No. They mattered to her only to the degree that they could do something for her. This moment, what she needed was another rock.

Tender Journey

Michelle stepped out from her alcove and collided with a well-dressed businessman, probably hurrying home to his family. Jolted from his thoughts of the day's activities, he stumbled before catching himself. "Excuse me, young lady. You oughta watch where you're going."

"I was!" she said, trying to catch her balance, but fell back onto the cement steps anyway. Instinctively, she tried to rub the sharp pain from her tailbone.

He reached out his right hand to help her. He gave up when she cringed back, as if repulsed at the thought of touching him. He looked from her shocked face down to his hand, and let it drop at his side. "Miss, are you all right?"

"I'm fine . . ." Her voice trailed into silence. She lowered her gaze from his, staring at her shoes, then back at him.

He gave her outfit a cursory glance. No doubt he noticed it didn't fit as well as it should have, but he only nodded. "Well, then, I'll be on my way." He turned, shoved his hands back into his pants pockets, and strode down the sidewalk.

Michelle let out a sigh of relief. Controlling her trembling body while he was there took all the strength she had left. With him out of sight, she sat down and gave in to the shakes. She had to do something. Nothing would slow her down in her search for a good, quick high.

She hugged herself again, but to no avail. The shakes were only getting worse. And that Rocco? Never around when you needed him. When you didn't, you couldn't get rid of the creep.

Stomping her foot, she set off down the sidewalk to where she'd last seen him. She had to get something quick. As she walked, she twirled the ring. Boy, she sure hated to give up one of her favorite things. Every third or fourth step she'd slide it halfway off her finger. It slipped back and forth easily.

Michelle hovered around his usual hangout, but the infamous Rocco had yet to make his nightly appearance. Disappointment sent her reeling inside. Not enough to make her give up. She couldn't. Her need assumed monstrous proportions. Growing frantic, she suddenly lowered her head and fixed her eyes on the sidewalk, scanning from side to side. It had dawned on her that this area had seen thousands of drug deals. A few golden nuggets could have been left behind.

She grew more desperate with each step. People gave her a wide berth as they passed to either side. Every so often she'd stop to reach down and pick up, not a crumb of crack, but another shattered hope.

One young couple came abreast of her. "Look, honey," she heard the man saying to his girlfriend, "A chickenhead."

"What?"

"A crack addict." Michelle glanced up, then down as they passed. She heard him say, "Look at her. Like a scrawny chicken pecking around on the ground for food. Always looking for that last piece of rock." He laughed.

"Glad *I* wasn't dumb enough to get hooked on the stuff!" the girl exclaimed with a tisk as she linked arms with her partner and resumed walking.

Michelle continued, embarrassed that she'd been the butt of strangers' jokes. She supposed she deserved it, though. She had done the same to Hank, the trucker, when he mentioned his drugging days. Her only concern now? To find some crack. And that meant finding Rocco. Nothing else mattered. Not the people who looked at her out of the corners of their eyes as they walked past. Not what her parents would say about her swapping the ring they had given her. All she cared about was getting something to feed her craving—and to stop the shakes.

"Yo, little Nicky. I got what ya needs." A disembodied voice seemed to float through the air to Michelle, but she kept on with her self-appointed task, scouring the sidewalks for lost cocaine. "Yo, girl!" This time a figure accompanied the voice as a guy of twenty-something stepped from the shadowed alcove Michelle had just passed. "Git yer eyes off them empty cracks and take a peek at what the candyman's got for ya."

Recognition came slowly to Michelle, but when it did, she spun around and lurched towards what Rocco held cupped in his left hand. "It's all yours baby. Jus' pay the candyman his dues and it's *all yours.*"

Her eyes fastened on his hand. As desperately as she wanted what he held out to her, she hesitated. Rocco noticed. He pulled his hand back and stuffed the contents into his right front pocket. She gasped. "Whatsa matter, Nicky baby? Have a bad night?" He looked at her, at the hunger so evident in her eyes. She met his gaze for only an instant before looking away. "Ain't no freebies around here. You should know that by now."

She struggled not to stare at the pocket holding the precious drugs. She fought hard, and lost. A need far stronger than her willpower won out. She heard herself say, "I've got this ring . . ."

"What do I want wid a ring? I need cash, baby."

"B-but you can get cash for it," she stammered. "Here." She yanked the ring off her finger. Only for a second did his sullen eyes flicker to what she held out to him.

He reached out and grasped her upper arm. "Com'ere and let me take a closer look," he said, as he pulled her into the shadows.

Her heart skipped a beat. She gasped, "Hey, don't . . ."

"Shhh! Don't you be gettin funny wid me. I only want a closer look at what you're offerin'. Now shud-dup!" He took a tiny flashlight out of his pocket and turned it on with one hand.

She held her peace, hoping he would agree to take the ring and give her a good trade. She had no idea how much it was worth, but she bet quite a bit. After all, it had a pearl, a diamond, and . . . who knows what else? Maybe the price would carry her for several days. That would give her time to plan what she was going to do next. She held her breath while Rocco decided.

"What makes you think I want a ring like this, anyway?"

"I figured if you didn't, you might know someone who does."

"Ya did, huh?" He rolled the ring back and forth between his thumb and index finger. The tiny stones captured the light of the passing cars. "Maybe I can do something. Don't expect much."

Only then did Michelle release her breath. Her shoulders sagged, and she relaxed visibly, but the hunger never left her eyes. "What? How much can you give me?" Rocco fixed his gaze on her. The pupils looked like two deep pits, black as coal.

"It's gonna take me some time to get rid of this. And time is money." He looked away from Michelle, scanning the street in both directions. His right hand snaked into his front pocket. When he pulled it out, he clenched his hand into a fist and half held it out to her. "A fifty-cent piece." Michelle started to interrupt. Rocco gave her no chance. He cut right back. "Take it or leave it. It's the best I can do. *Nobody'll* give you that much."

Fifty dollars of crack. That was the biggest chunk she'd ever bought. She tried to mentally compare it with the five and ten dollar pieces she usually got. Fifty dollars should be enough for a while, she hoped.

Rocco withdrew his hand and put the drug back in his pocket. "Make up yer mind, Nicky. I got business to take care of." His voice took on a sweeter tone. "You know I've got what ya need. It'll take you straight to the sky." He brought his hand back out of his pocket and held it out to her, palm upward and fist half

375

unclenched. "Be a good girl. Get your candy while it lasts. You know it's super stuff from old Rocco."

Michelle stared hungrily, but made no move to take it.

Abruptly, the sweetness vanished. "*You*, little girl, are wasting my time. I'm an important businessman."

She hated when he called her little girl. Every time she'd come to him, he somehow managed to work it into their conversation. She'd never gotten up the courage to tell him, not that he'd stop even if she did ask. Besides, she was always too desperate by that point to make an issue out of anything.

"Last chance." He opened his fist all the way. Seeing the foil-wrapped packet pushed her over the edge. She stretched out her own hand and let him drop the packet into it. Trembling, she unwrapped the foil and peered at the white, rocklike contents. Her heart beat faster. She licked her lips to moisten them but her tongue had gone dry. Caught between the desire to break off a piece and smoke it right there on the sidewalk or to put it away until she could get under cover, she finally managed to re-wrap the packet. With a satisfied but still-hungry look, she made it disappear into her own skirt pocket. She handed him her ring and turned on her heel.

"Don't blow it all in one place, baby," Rocco called after her. His laugh, like the staccato yapping of a junkyard dog, rang in her ears as she traipsed along the sidewalk. She would have been humiliated to the max, had she not been so absorbed in finding a place to get high.

Soon . . . paradise.

❧ *Twenty-Two* ❧

ut of breath from pedaling hard on his bike, Sandy pulled up to the Youth Center twenty minutes early. Those times of fun and growth had become the highlight of his week. He loved Pastor Chip, who had a knack with teenagers. They respected his integrity, sense of humor, and love for them, but most of all, his relationship with the Lord. Everyone sensed a genuineness about him that ran deep. When Pastor Chip spoke, most of them listened, whether or not they took his advice.

Sandy paid particular attention—first, because Chip had become a father-figure to him and second, because what he heard lined up with principles Caleb had taught him while he was alive. Sandy was determined to live up to Caleb's standards, but the more he matured, the more he discovered how hard it really was. The concept of holiness had started to trouble him.

"Hi, Pastor," Sandy called as he walked into the center.

"Hey, Sandy, my man. How's it going?"

"Okay, I guess." He sighed.

"You're early, as usual."

"Yep. Thought I'd see if I can help ya set up."

"You're growing into a fine young man. Always willing to help. Caleb would have been proud of you. I sure am."

"Thanks. I do wanna serve God—with all my heart, but I ain't as good as you think." He paused and frowned, then sat down on the couch. "Pastor, can I talk to ya about somethin'?"

"Sure. Anytime."

"Well . . ." Sandy blushed. "Sometimes it gets awful hard to do the right thing. If I got m'self in the wrong place at the wrong time, I might ferget all about Jesus. Know what I mean?"

"I think I do. Temptation . . . right?"

He blushed again, then nodded with reluctance. "How d'ya deal with this stuff? Sometimes I feel so guilty about having bad thoughts, it eats me up inside."

Chip patted him on the back in a warm, father-to-son gesture. "Sandy, tempting thoughts will assault us as long as we're alive. Young men like you, on the threshold of adolescence, are very vulnerable. And with all the sexual freedom around today, it's tough. No doubt about it. But, you can do a lot to protect yourself against temptation."

"Like what?"

"We'll talk about that in group. As for guilt, the question is whether you *dwell* on those thoughts. Do you keep them around to mull over, or do you ask God's help as soon as you recognize them? That's the key. I'm sure you're not the only one struggling."

"The other kids act so cool, like they can handle anything."

"That could be a front. So take heart. God hasn't chalked you up as a failure. Just the fact that you're concerned means the Holy Spirit is working in your life."

Sandy sighed with relief. "Thanks. This has really been bothering me, and I feel funny talking about it to a lady, like Ma—if ya know what I mean."

Chip winked and smiled. "I do. Thanks for trusting me with your secret. How's your mom doing, anyway?"

"Better. Doc gave her new medicine."

"That's good to hear. Say, how about putting out the refreshments and the pillows for me while I go make some copies? The rest of the clan should be here soon."

"Sure thing, boss," Sandy said with a mock salute. He pulled the snacks from the grocery bags, ripped open the packages, and poured them each into separate bowls. Eight bottles of soda he lined up on the counter. He tore open the two bags of ice and dumped them into the cooler, then reached in the cupboard to find the plastic glasses left over from the previous week. Oversized pillows stacked in the corner soon found their way into the semi-circle, given Sandy's prompt attention to the cause.

Within minutes, the kids started wandering in, greeting Sandy and Pastor Chip. A couple of them headed right for the Ping-Pong table; others plopped down on the comfortable couches and chairs to claim their favorite spots. Two girls set their purses down on the cushions, then hurried over to study the giant picture collage on the wall and compare fond memories of their latest group trip. One boy turned on the VCR to play a Christian video.

At 7:10, Pastor Chip urged them to gather around. He opened in prayer. One of the boys, Paul, accompanied praise and worship on his acoustic guitar. A sweet presence filled the room as they sang, and their faces took on soft, relaxed expressions. After at least twenty minutes of basking in the Spirit, Pastor Chip opened the interactive part of the meeting by passing out a sheet on the discussion topic. The title, *Walking the Teenage Tightrope,* intrigued them, as his catchy titles always did.

Chip spoke first. "How many of you feel like you *are* walking a tightrope?" Every youth raised a hand. "So we've hit on a good

subject tonight. Who wants to get us started? Any takers?" He waited for one of them to answer.

Mark, a slender, dark-haired guy with glasses, raised his hand. "Yeah, I feel that way a lot. Like I'm walking on a skinny wire way up in mid-air—without a balancing pole. But that's not all. The wind is howling. Huge snakes with their ugly tongues flicking in and out are coiling on the ground below, waiting to nail me. One little slip and I'm history."

"Mark, what a tremendous description! Who agrees with him?" Most of the kids nodded.

"Okay then, what do the wind and snakes represent?"

Sandy spoke up. "Well, I think the wind is like the temptations that wanna blow us away. Snakes could mean the bad things that happen after that. Satan is waitin' to do us in when we fall."

"Very good. You guys are right on the mark—sort of." They scrunched up their faces and looked around at each other. "The winds of temptation do howl and the consequences of sin do await you. You're absolutely right about that. But—and hear me—you don't have to be walking a tightrope in the midst of them! You can if you want to." He paused, looking around at the faces so intent on his every word. "God will allow you to go through life that way because He gave you free will.

"Picture this. Let's say you're not a professional aerialist, just an average Joe. You're up on that tightrope, taking each step with utmost care. You've got both arms out for control. To your right and down, another amateur tightrope-walker struggles along. Suddenly, he starts teetering back and forth. He's losing his balance. He reaches up to grab your hand. You fight hard to keep your balance, but he's too heavy! Now you start to wobble, too. He grabs your hand tighter. You can't let go. He won't let go! He starts falling, falling, falling . . . And where are you? *Right with him.*

380

"That tightrope scene symbolizes trying to live the Christian life in your own strength. You'll be in for a pretty shaky experience. And if you get tangled up in a situation the Bible labels being 'unequally yoked,' it will be worse." He grinned and tilted his head. "That has nothing to do with having lopsided eggs for breakfast. I'm talking about what happens, for example, if you date unbelievers who think nothing of sex before marriage." He scrutinized the faces around him.

"I know some of you are. I'm also referring to making close friendships with kids using drugs. Some of you have done just that. You're doing the high-wire act, and one day, sure as shootin', the snakes below are gonna bite. By the way, beware of wolves in sheep's clothing. They *pretend* to love Jesus to get on your side. When you least expect it, they'll tear you to pieces.

"Now, don't feel like I'm picking on you; the same principle applies to adults like me. If we go into a business venture with an unbeliever—or worse, marry one—we set ourselves up to get pulled down. As with gravity, we're always pulled to lower ground, not higher. In other words, from the spiritual realm to the carnal.

"Let me show you what I mean. Everybody's who's sitting on this couch, could you get up for a minute? Mark, lie down there, and Sandy, lie down on the floor along the front of the couch. Mark, you try to pull Sandy up with you. Sandy, you try to pull Mark down on the floor. Let's see who wins." The two boys got into the fun of the game and the rest of the kids clapped and cheered. In less than thirty seconds, Sandy, the smaller and thinner one of the two, had pulled Mark onto the floor with him. The kids laughed and teased Mark about being a "wimp," then fell quiet as they took their seats. They understood Chip's example.

One girl, however, named Sherry, who was dating an older guy who hung around with a rough crowd, questioned him. "Yeah, I

hear what you're saying, but I thought the Bible says we're supposed to love everybody. Not be acting like we're better than they are. Sounds a little hypocritical to me."

Her attempt at sarcasm didn't fluster Chip. His tone remained upbeat and encouraging. "Sherry, you've raised a good point. God does call us to a humble attitude and to a loving ministry to unbelievers. *But* . . . He doesn't want us to be *yoked* to them. That means 'clamped together with,' like trying to put a sheep and an ox in the same wooden collar. Can you see the difference?"

She twirled her hair around her finger and blew a bubble with her gum. Finally, she admitted, "Maybe."

Kevin spoke up. "I sure know how easy it is to be deceived. I used to date a non-Christian girl I was super-attracted to, and justified it by telling myself, 'I can lead her to Jesus.' Believe me, it didn't work that way. *She* led *me*—and not anywhere near Jesus!" The kids laughed.

Pastor Chip nodded, thanked him and looked around at the group with a rather solemn expression, as if to say, "Are you listening?" He added, "Kevin's experience follows right along with the amateur tightrope-walker we were talking about. When somebody shakier than himself grabbed his hand and wouldn't let go, they both went down." Then Chip lightened up. "Okay, gang, enough about falling. I'd like to read from Second Samuel, Twenty-two, to see what we can do to *prevent* catastrophes,

As for God, his way is perfect; the word of the Lord is flawless. He is a shield for all who take refuge in him. For who is God, besides the Lord? And who is the Rock, except our God? It is God who arms me with strength and makes my way perfect. He makes my feet like the feet of a deer; he enables me to stand on the heights.

"Have you ever seen a deer or a goat leap around on rocky cliffs? What a thrill to watch! God gives those beautiful animals an astounding surefootedness that'll take your breath away. You know what? He gives Christians slip-resistant hooves, too. And we can plant our feet on solid rock, rather than on swinging tightropes. It's our choice. We will still face threatening conditions because God wants to lead us to 'the high places.' Steep cliffs, howling winds, bad weather, and wild creatures will come across our paths up there, but God transforms us into professional mountain climbers! We won't need the usual top-of-the-line equipment—good boots and helmets, lightweight clothes, sturdy nylon rope, aluminum chocks, and stirrup ladders. Instead, He places us in the indestructible harness of His Holy Spirit and hangs a safety net of forgiveness beneath us, just in case.

"But kids, there is a crucial element to understanding the victorious Christian life: *God will not force us into His harness!* He loves us enough to set us free to go with Him or not. We could say it like this: He waits until we 'give Him permission' to help, similar to the way a doctor requires a signature on a consent form before doing surgery. The doctor has the technical ability to do surgery without it, but he won't, no matter how critical the need. Of course, God could grab us by the collar if He wanted to and slap us into submission, but that's not His style. He waits to be invited." Nodding heads assured Pastor Chip that most of them were still with him.

Just then, Cindy Harrington raised her hand. "I was thinking about another analogy. Imagine sitting down to a big dinner with all the trimmings. A guest doesn't just dig into the food as soon as he feels the urge, if he's got any manners. He waits until the hostess sits down and picks up her fork. That's his cue. So, the Lord believes in etiquette, you could say. He is a gentleman."

Sherry, who had challenged Chip earlier, made a slight face at Cindy. "I'm not much into the highbrow stuff. Down home where I come from, we don't wait for anybody to pick up a fork. Mom just yells, 'Okay, y'all, *help yourselves!*' and we go runnin'."

Chip intervened. "You know, you girls are both right. The Holy Spirit is not snobbish, but He is a gentleman. He waits for a heartfelt invitation, no matter what personal style it's delivered with. Until we pray, 'Help yourself to my whole life, Lord, to every part of me,' He keeps His opinions to Himself."

Neil raised his hand. Chip urged him with a smile to go ahead and share. "Man, I'm still back on the harness idea, maybe 'cause I did some climbing a few weeks ago. But I have to confess. I've had it backwards. I've been trying to harness God—the Creator of the universe—for all the neat bennies I wanted from Him."

"I appreciate your insight, Neil," Chip said. "Don't feel alone. We're all guilty of trying to use Him. To collect material blessings, or even to acquire spiritual gifts. But when we 'take His yoke upon us,' we're saying, 'I'm Your child, Lord. I'm depending on You. I trust You.' And notice the difference between 'child-like' and 'childish.' None of us wants to act childish—immature and selfish. We do want to be *child-like*—dependent and trusting.

"Unfortunately, we all wander off, trying to do our own thing. We think we know more than God." He paused. "Or, then again, maybe I'm talking to the wrong group. None of you know anything about that. Right?" He chuckled and waited a moment for someone to take issue with him. There were no takers, only a few sheepish grins. He clapped his hands together. "Looks like that settles that. What do you say we review what we've covered so far: two opposite ways of approaching the Christian life. What was the word picture we used for the first?"

"Tightrope-walking," several youths answered at once.

"Right," Chip agreed. "Doing things in our own strength. And the alternative?"

"Mountain-climbing!" they chorused.

"Good! That's where God's strength comes into play. Why would we choose the second way?"

Sandy's hand went up. "Simple. 'Cuz God wants us to. It makes Him happy an' . . . shows Him we love Him." He paused. "I had another reason, but I los' it." His brow wrinkled. "Oh, now I 'member. Just 'cuz we oughta. The leastest thing can knock us off a skinny, wiggly wire in the air—'less we're in the circus."

Chip laughed. "Excellent, Sandy. Nothing can make us fall from the mountain if we're anchored in God's harness. From that secure position, we can even reach down and pull somebody else to safety. We can climb the highest peaks in His very steps. And oh, how fresh the air is up there, kids, how exhilarating . . .

"I was talking with a friend of mine earlier about one of those things that can make us tumble if we don't know how to deal with it. We mentioned the topic briefly at the beginning of class. The old 'bite-the-apple-it-won't-matter' trick. *Temptation.* It has been common to every man and woman since the Garden of Eden. We might as well face facts. Temptation will threaten us from time to time throughout our lives. Here's why.

"James one, thirteen refers to each person being *drawn away by his own lusts and enticed.* Are you ready for a bit of trivia? The expression, 'drawn away' is a hunting term meaning 'lured into a trap.' Enticed, a fishing term, means 'to catch with a yummy-looking bait.' Satan and his evil critters may bait the hook, yes, but our own lusts give us the urge to bite. *Which* things lure us depend on genetic weaknesses and past experiences. But, as Bible teacher John MacArthur has said, 'Our big problem is not the tempter without, but the traitor within.'" That brought moans and groans.

"Fortunately, we always have a way of escape." He paused. "Or, is it really necessary to run from lusts? Couldn't we charge out there, straight at the tormentor, strut our spiritual stuff, and defend our turf? Let's stop on that note and take a social break for fifteen minutes. Help yourselves to the goodies."

No moans or groans followed his last comment. They talked and laughed and munched and gulped right until the last second. Then Pastor Chip corralled them back to their seats. He put his hands in his pockets and strolled back and forth in front of them.

"Right before break," he said, "I asked you whether we should try to escape—that is, run from—lusts. Any opinions?"

Chris, a tall, muscular guy, volunteered. "Boss, I vote for charging ahead. I don't wanna be a chicken." Several other guys seconded him. Sandy kept quiet. The girls giggled and whispered among themselves.

"Okay, I'll give you my position. I'd like you to think back to when you were little tikes. I know it's hard to remember so long ago, but do your best. Did you ever have to contend with a town bully—to and from school, during class, out on the playground? One who showed up everywhere. You had no peace. He mocked you without mercy. Maybe he was older and bigger than you. I bet your mom and dad told you to show your fists and beat him to a pulp. Be a hero. Right? Wrong.

"No doubt, their instructions to you went something like this: 'If he comes after you, high-tail it out of there quick. Run to safety. Find a group of kids. Or a grown-up.' You see, parents know that some enemies are just too big and strong to take on any other way. God knows it, also, for He says in Second Timothy two, twenty-two, *Now flee from youthful lusts, and pursue righteousness, faith, love and peace, with those who call on the Lord from a pure heart.* The original Greek word for 'flee' means to run away, to vanish!

"We can't argue with the Word. If God says to high-tail it out of there when temptation shows up, do it. We already mentioned one safeguard to prevent the bully from getting too far with us. Anybody remember what it was?"

Denise, a petite redhead with a million freckles, answered in a soft, high-pitched voice that sounded like a question more than an answer, "No real close relationships with unbelievers?"

"That's right, Denise. Good. Who can think of another way to flee temptation?"

Paul, the one who had played guitar and led singing, volunteered, "Stay away from situations you can't handle. Like . . . don't go to parties and bars if you wanna stay sober. Don't go parking for hours if you wanna stay pure."

"Good, Paul. Avoid risky situations. Anybody else?"

Sandy spoke up. "Be careful what you think about. If a tempting thought hits your mind, don't jes' stand there and mull it over for a while—like a cow chewing her cud. Spit it out, cause sooner or later, you might jes' wanna go do it."

"Right on, Sandy. A Christian brother shared a secret with me that works for him. If he finds himself thinking about a woman in a way he shouldn't, he prays and pictures a cross on her forehead. That reminds him that he's been trespassing on God's property. She is a creation of the Almighty, not just a pretty female he has a right to fantasize about."

Chip stroked his chin. He grew more serious. "And let me add something crucial to your point, Sandy, regarding thought life. Be very careful to guard what goes into your eyes and ears. What you look at and listen to determines what your mind will dwell on. Pornography, everything from so-called 'soft porn' to hard-core, is deadly. Don't think one time with a magazine won't hurt you. Some people may have used that excuse when they tasted their

first sample, but they wound up poisoned from the side-effects of a potent addiction."

Eddie, a handsome, tanned blond with an athletic build he didn't mind showing off, cut in. "Hey, wait. My dad's left that stuff lying around the house since I was knee-high to a grasshopper, and he's fine. No big deal. Some of it's kinda . . . well, interesting. Dad says all men—unless they're dead—read it."

Chip's eyebrows rose. He took a deep breath and looked around. The kids stared at him, waiting to see what he would say.

"Lord, help!" Sandy prayed silently.

At last, Chip forged ahead. "Eddie, I'm sure your dad loves you very much and wants the best for you. I believe if he knew the danger of what he's doing—to you and to himself—he would never take the risk. I promise you, real men do not need pornography to find satisfaction." He swallowed. "I'd like to talk to you more about the issue. Could you see me after class, and maybe we can set up a time to get together?"

Eddie stared up at the ceiling, then lowered his eyes to meet Chip's sincere gaze. He hesitated, nodded, and answered in a somber tone, "I guess so."

"Great." He looked around the room. "Any other ideas for handling temptation?"

Connie, a chunky brunette with a pretty face, raised her hand, then put it down. Chip noticed and nodded to her with a "go ahead" gesture. She squirmed and fidgeted with her class ring, then shifted in her chair. "I don't know if this fits or not. I'm learning it in my diet class. But it has to do with temptation."

Chip smiled at her and nodded again. "I'm sure it could help us. These struggles fall in the same category—lusts of the flesh."

Gathering her courage, she continued, "Well . . . my leader says people turn to self-gratifying behavior because they need comfort. I do that with food. Instead of eating too much, I'm learning to deal with bad feelings. When I'm afraid or insecure or angry, food just seems like it will make me feel better, but it never does. I feel awful afterwards. I try to remember that before I binge. Only the Lord can fill up the empty places in my heart."

"Beautiful, Connie! Gosh, I appreciate your willingness to let us in on such a sensitive issue. What you shared will help all of us." He paused and tilted his head. "Folks, listen to what Connie said. She has been learning to address the painful emotions that make her seek comfort in something she thinks will satisfy, but doesn't. Could that same principle apply to winning the battle over sexual temptation?"

They stared at him with blank expressions. Nobody said a word. Sherry sighed, crossed her legs, and folded her arms across her chest.

Chip winked and continued, "You're mighty quiet all of a sudden, gang. I believe the exact same principle applies. You might think I'm off-base, but even mental health experts suggest that repressed emotions, especially anger, can cause serious struggles with lust. They call it addiction or dependency in modern circles. The longer those negative emotions go unresolved, the worse the temptation to find relief somewhere. Anywhere."

Sherry uncrossed her legs and sighed again. "Well, to be honest, I can't imagine going without lovin' until I'm married. That'll be a hundred years from now. If sex were bad for you, why did God make it so much fun? In my opinion, fooling around is okay, as long you care about somebody. And play it safe."

"Sherry, I can sure understand why you believe those things. I used to feel the same way when I was young and so did many of my friends. But I found out the truth. Just in time, thank the Lord. 'Safe sex,' as it's used today, is a myth. A deception. A lie! No

sex—except in marriage to a faithful, uninfected partner of the opposite sex is really safe. We can sum up sexual safety in a word you may or may not have heard, and one you probably won't like: abstinence. Doing without. God doesn't say you must do without forever and ever, but just until marriage.

Eddie looked at Sherry. They both shook their heads and smirked at each other.

Chip saw them, but ignored their attitude. "I bet you've all heard the expression, 'Absence makes the heart grow fonder.' When you can't see someone as much as you want to, you begin to appreciate the person even more. Often true, isn't it?" The kids nodded. He continued, "I have a better expression that you'll find even more true if you give it a chance: *abstinence* makes the heart grow fonder! Say it with me . . . 'abstinence makes the heart grow fonder.' Everyone except Sherry and Eddie repeated the clever phrase in unison.

"I have to admit," Chip said with a smile, "I can't take credit. I saw it on a bumper sticker from the Florida Chapter of Concerned Women for America. They also produced a paper with a subtitle that really grabbed my attention—*What Teens Don't Know May Kill Them . . . But Who Will Tell Them?* A short time later, a powerful message by Focus on the Family came across my desk, courtesy of a member of our church. It was entitled, *In Defense of a Little Virginity.* The next day at the bookstore, I saw a book by Josh McDowell called, *Why Wait?* I finally realized that God might be trying to tell me something. As your youth pastor who loves you guys, I should do my part to help you. I told Him I would.

"The late Francis Schaeffer, one of the great philosophers of our time, said something like this, 'Modern man has his feet firmly planted in thin air.' So true. He has no values, no absolutes. He denies the connection between the laws of God and what happens in life. Our society has shifted to a post-Christian era where people make decisions based on one thing—their wants.

"Because you're young, many of you believe you're impervious to harm. In my day, the consequences of sexual promiscuity were chlamydial infections, herpes, and gonorrhea. Today, you're toying with the skull and crossbones. AIDS is nothing to mess around with. To date, a positive diagnosis almost *guarantees* a painful death."

Without raising his hand, Eddie spoke up. "Pastor, where have you been? Didn't you ever hear of *con . . . dominiums?*" He grinned at his own pun. "You can buy 'em anywhere, no money down. Plus, the government and other groups pass out free ones."

"I wasn't born yesterday, strange as it may seem. But statistics prove that 'protective devices' can break, even in the rare event they're used properly and consistently. Did you know that the HIV virus is so teeny-tiny, it passes through holes visible only through an electron microscope? 'Condominiums,' as you call them, can trick you into a surprise of the worst kind."

With that, Eddie frowned and avoided eye contact.

"Kids, you may think I'm an old fuddy-duddy, but I'm not saying these things to make you look stupid or to cramp your style. I'm telling you because I care about you. So does God. One way He demonstrates His love is through His moral laws. If you're practicing premarital sex, you don't realize what damage you're doing to yourselves. Not only can you catch fatal diseases, you actually set yourself up for a lifetime of sorrow. Sin gives pleasure for a few moments, but never happiness, I guarantee it. Please don't settle for less than God's best!

"Sex outside of marriage alters the way you look at yourself and other people. Mutual respect and trust go out the window. Don't buy into the lie that on one fine wedding day, 'Presto!' you

will instantly trust a mate to remain faithful for a lifetime. How can you? You have no basis for believing that person will be able to resist sexual temptation. Why? *No track record.* I promise you, tempting opportunities will arise throughout your lives."

Sherry crossed her legs again. "Man, I never looked at it that way. My mom trusted my dad about as far as she could throw him. And he was suspicious of her every move. With good reasons, on both sides." She paused. "It's hard, though. Society expects certain things if you wanna move up the ladder."

"I'm not so sure, Sherry," Chip said. "Morality is enjoying renewed popularity in some segments of the business arena. A few head honchos of Fortune 500 companies—the biggies—are even scouting for young men and women with character. Above IQ, they want character. Above training, they want character. Above talent, they want character.

"These leaders have grown tired of hiring smart superstars who are headed down the primrose path to moral and emotional bankruptcy. Ironic. God has taught the same principles in His Word for thousands of years, but human beings have been acting as if He's a blithering idiot. Or, that He doesn't exist. Well, He does, and He knows what He's talking about. We are not our own, the Bible says. When we deviate from His instruction manual, *we* lose. And kids, you'll find a real jungle out there to get lost in." He cocked his head for several seconds. "By the way, what's the difference between a jungle and a garden? Anybody?"

Pat, a short, small-framed, studious young man, raised his hand. "A garden doesn't just happen by itself. A jungle does."

"Go on . . ."

"Well, in a garden, somebody has to plant seeds, usually in neat rows, for flowers or vegetables or fruit. Then he has to water and fertilize the seeds. And pull the weeds." He paused. "A jungle

392

grows wild, with everything planted at random. I guess it's kinda like a huge, overgrown garden."

"Great answer, Pat. In other words, we might say that a jungle is a garden out of control. Only wild animals live there. You often hear the business world referred to as a 'jungle,' a dangerous, dog-eat-dog, out-of-control place. Without restraint, any power—no matter how good—destroys. Take fire . . . wind . . . water.

"Now, what if we apply that principle to the natural desire for sexual pleasure? Love, as God planned it in marriage, blossoms into a beautiful garden. Lust, as Satan promotes it, turns loose a herd of beasts to devour you. The only trouble is, you won't realize you're stuck in a jungle until it's too late."

"Boy, Pastor," Sandy said with a fearful tone, "what if we don' wanna get ate up?"

Chip looked around and gave them a reassuring smile. "There is hope in Christ Jesus. Do you remember God's harness we talked about earlier tonight the one that will keep us sure-footed for mountain-climbing? The same Holy Spirit is quite a seasoned world traveler and tour guide. He not only knows mountains, He is familiar with jungles, inside and out. If we let Him buckle us up in His awesome 4-wheel-drive Jungle-Runner, He'll keep us safe and sound on the right path."

Cindy exclaimed, "That's really neat, Pastor Chip. You make stuff so easy to understand."

"Great. Just got the jungle idea from the Lord as we were going along. The key still is, though, will we give up our agenda for His? Will we *use* the tools—prayer, the Word, praise and worship, other believers—that He's tucked into our backpack? Let's close tonight with a short exercise for you to work on as a group. I'm going to pass out copies of *'The Teen Bill of Rights,'* which Focus on the Family referred to in the article about virginity. Originally, this

 Tender Journey

Teen Bill of Rights was printed in a brochure promoted by the federal Centers for Disease Control and the City of New York. Take one, please, and pass them on." He handed the stack of papers to a girl at the side of the room, then waited until he could see everyone had a copy. "Follow along with me as I read aloud:

> *I have the right to think for myself.*
> *I have the right to decide whether to have sex*
>   *and whom to have it with.*
> *I have the right to use protection when I have sex.*
> *I have the right to buy and use condoms.*
> *I have the right to express myself.*
> *I have the right to ask for help if I need it.*

His eyes met theirs. "Okay, here's what I'd like you to do. Let's analyze this *Bill of Rights* to see how it stacks up against God's Word. Wherever the statements do not agree, create an amended version that you think Jesus would sign His name to if He were here in person. Don't worry about making it sound too official. Just be sure to support the changes with as many Bible verses as possible from your reference list.

"I'll give you one hint to get you started. The word 'surrender' may be very helpful." He paused a second for the page-turning to stop. "Everybody understand the assignment?" Heads nodded. "All right then. Move your chairs into a circle and get started. I'll stop you in thirty minutes, so work as a team and work fast."

They scooted their chairs around until a visible circle emerged. Kevin volunteered to act as spokesperson. Heads bowed. They studied the mini-document again and then, point by point, back and forth, they hashed over the wording. Bibles opened. Pages rustled as they flipped to the Scripture references Chip had listed.

After thirty minutes sharp, Chip called, "Time! Let's hear what you've come up with." He rubbed his hands together briskly, in a show of great anticipation.

Kevin stood. He held the piece of paper by the top and bottom, then lifted it high, as if he were holding a scroll, and cleared his throat ceremoniously. "We, the undersigned members of the Body of Christ, being of sound bodies, sound minds and sound spirits, do hereby renounce the *Teen Bill of Rights.* We proclaim the *Teen Believer's Bill of Rights* to read as follows:

I surrender the right to think for myself. There is a way that seems right to a man, but in the end it leads to death (Proverbs 16:25). I will look to God's Word instead of my head, following Him in all my ways so that He will make my paths straight (Proverbs 3:6).

I surrender the right to decide whether to have sex, or whom to have it with, because my body is a temple of the Holy Spirit. I do not belong to myself. Jesus bought me for a high price (1 Corinthians 6:19-21.) God will give me the privilege of sex when I get married (1 Corinthians 7:1-7), so I will keep myself pure until then for Him and for my mate.

I surrender the right to buy and use condoms because I will not need a fake protection if I abstain from sex. Instead, I will run from sexual immorality and the evil desires young people have. I will run toward righteousness, faith, love and peace (1 Corinthians 6:18 and 2 Timothy 2:22). Since I am only a steward of God's money and not the owner, I will give back to Him at least ten percent of everything I receive and spend the rest on important things (Malachi 3:10).

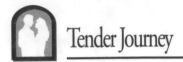

I surrender the right to express myself whenever and however I feel like it. Only a fool says everything on his mind; a wise person holds his tongue (Proverbs 29:11 and 10:19). I will ask God to control my tongue so that I don't set a whole forest on fire from one tiny spark (James 3:5).

I reserve the right to ask for help whenever I need it. I will read my Bible, ask for God's direction in prayer and ask my parents, my pastor and other people who love God for advice. There is wisdom in a multitude of counselors (Proverbs 24:6). God loves to give wisdom to all who ask (James 1:3).

The End

Kevin rolled up the paper and sat down. The kids clapped vigorously. Chip joined in, then jumped up and exclaimed, "You all did a tremendous job! I'd tip my hat to you—except I'm not wearing one." They laughed at his silly sense of humor. He added, "I mean it, guys. That was excellent!"

Kevin grinned and pointed to the rest of the kids. "We all worked together."

"I can tell, for sure." He tilted his head and wrinkled his brow. "This has so much good stuff, we should make a keepsake out of it. I could design an official-looking copy on the computer and print it out on parchment paper to look like a real Bill of Rights. You could sign it and post it wherever you want, as a reminder. If I did that, who would be interested?"

Everyone but Eddie raised their hands. He looked around at his peers, then scrunched his face, and raised his hand. "I'm outnumbered big time. Guess I'll grin and bear it."

"That's my man," Chip praised. "Now, it's between you and God." With another hearty round of applause and a sincere prayer, he dismissed the group. He encouraged them to hurry so as not to keep their parents waiting. "Bless you guys," he called after them. Within a few minutes, only he and Sandy were left. They quickly cleaned up the garbage from the refreshments and set the room in order. As usual, Chip offered to take Sandy home so he wouldn't have to ride his bike so late. When they were settled in the van, Sandy said, "I really liked class t'night, Pastor."

"Thanks. Did we answer those questions?"

"Yep, sure did. I'm a-climbin' the mountain. God's got me hooked up. He ain't—I mean isn't—gonna let me fall."

"Good man."

Sandy was quiet for a few minutes. "You know, I been thinkin' a lot 'bout somebody lately."

"Michelle, I know."

"Her, yeah. 'Course. But that Mr. Hank we met at the ther'py place. I liked him. Wonder if he can drive his truck yet."

Chip's mouth dropped open. He took a deep breath. "I didn't tell you? I thought I did."

"Tell me what?" Sandy asked, his tone anxious. "Somethin' wrong? He got worser?"

"Sandy, I—"

"Pastor, tell me! I jes' remembered a bad dream. He an' his wife was in these dark rooms—like little closets— cryin' an' cryin' . . ."

"You dreamed that? When?"

"Day b'fore yesterday. Woke me up."

Chip cleared his throat. "Wow . . . son, they were charged with kidnapping Michelle. They're both in jail, awaiting trial."

"Jail? That's the stupidest thing I ever heared!" He rubbed his hands back and forth through his hair several times.

A long sigh came from Chip's side of the van. He pulled into Sandy's yard. "I don't understand it all, either."

"Pastor, they love *Jesus!* I seen it with my own eyes. It was them who told the p'lice where she was runnin' to!"

"I know, Sandy. But sometimes people take us by surprise."

"You b'lieve they done an awful thing like that? Not me. Michelle runned away. She tol' Mr. Michael she was gonna do it!"

Chip turned on the overhead light. "As I said, I don't understand the whole situation. They did drive her out of state." He patted Sandy on the shoulder. "Gotta have faith in the criminal justice system. If Hank and Dot are innocent, it'll come out in the trial."

Sandy's eyes filled with tears. He rubbed his chest. "Man, then why do I feel so terrible? In my dream, they was cryin' . . . *hard.*"

"I'm sorry, big guy. I should have told you sooner."

"That wouldn't do no good. I'd still feel bad." He grabbed the handle and shoved open the door. Within seconds, he had pulled his bike out from the back. "Bye. An' thanks for the ride," he called with a profound sadness in his voice. He didn't turn around or wave like he usually did. "Lord," he prayed as he trudged toward the house, wheeling his old bike, "Let Hank an' Dot know You ain't abandoned 'em. Now we really hafta fin' that dumb Michelle. Please he'p Mr. Michael fin' her . . ."

All of a sudden, he remembered. It was *his* idea to take the flyer to the convalescent home that night. *He* had been the one to show it to Hank. He laid his bike in the dirt and charged into the house as fast as he could go. He was only trying to help! How could it turn into such a mess?

✣ Twenty-Three ✣

Startled out of a sound sleep, Stephanie awoke. The little red lights of the bedside clock glowed 2:15. What had awakened her? Maybe just a dream. She lay curled on her side for a while, arm wrapped around Michael's pillow, and floated in and out of a half-sleep. The only sound she heard was her own breathing.

She listened harder . . . There it was. She *had* heard a noise.

Her breath caught in her throat. She couldn't quite make out the sound, except that it was soft. Like something shuffling across a distant floor.

She lay quiet, straining to hear whatever it was again, and hoping that her imagination was just playing tricks on her. No. She heard it again.

A surge of adrenaline flooded her body. Every muscle quivered with tension. With Michael and Michelle gone, that left her and Stephen alone in the house. "Oh my God!" she whispered into the darkness.

A solid thump stunned her to silence. She bolted up to a sitting position. Her hands clenched into fists, pulling the bedclothes

tight around her chin. What was it? Silence. The space of two heartbeats passed. She heard a whimper, then a gasp, and she knew. *"Stephen!"* she shouted. At the same time she threw back the covers and bounded out of bed. She was running even as her feet hit the floor. Down the hall, around the corner into his bedroom. She turned on the light without slowing her pace but stopped dead in her tracks the instant her eyes adjusted. His bed was empty! Frantic now, she turned and ran back out into the hallway.

She looked to the right. No, he wouldn't be there. That was the way she'd come. She pivoted to the left, down the hall to Michelle's room. Maybe he wanted to sleep in her bed for some reason. No. Empty. She shivered and listened further, but all was silent. Where could he have gone?

The noise. There it was again. A soft cough, then—a groan. From downstairs toward the kitchen. Near the back door! The sound drew her like a moth to light. She turned and darted down the stairs. Through the house she ran. Her hand stabbed around in the dark and flicked on the kitchen light switch. For the second time that evening she stopped dead, her heart pounding.

Stephen was crumpled on the floor against the cupboard.

"Oh, honey!" she cried. She dropped down to her knees, not even pausing to pay attention to the sting of the hardwood floor. She reached out to cradle him in her arms.

He opened his eyes. Slowly, ever so slowly, he turned his head toward her.

"Sweetie, are you all right? Talk to mommy!" She rocked him back and forth. His chest rose and fell with each hasty breath.

He coughed again. She stared wide-eyed at each rhythmic motion as if the next breath would be his last.

He managed a faint smile. "Mom . . . m'okay." His raspy voice barely reached her ears.

"*What happened?*" she asked, as she slid her right hand from his shoulder to cup his face with her palm. She leaned her head closer to his mouth. From her new position, she noticed how he kept his palm pressed onto his side. Out of instinct, she reached down and tenderly tried to slide his hand out of the way to see what lay underneath his pajama top.

He winced when she tugged at his fingertips, but let her move his hand. Now, it was her turn to wince. Just below his left ribs, a large, deep purple bruise had begun to form. An injury on the left side could be more serious than on the right, she remembered.

"Oh, Stephen . . ." She tried to keep her voice steady, not giving an indication of the anxiety already gripping her. "We need to get ice on that right away."

"I'm okay, Mom," he said in a stronger voice. He used his right hand to try to prop himself to more of a sitting position.

She watched the way he hitched himself around. There was something he wasn't telling her. "Here," she offered, "let me help."

He heaved a sigh once he got settled. "I fell—pretty—hard." His words came in ragged, breathy gasps and his face grimaced in pain. "Heard noises—by the door. Glass broke." He pointed with his right arm. She looked where he pointed. At first she didn't see anything. A miniblind covered the window. But after a longer look, she detected shards of glass on the floor. Stephen let his arm drop. This time his breath caught from the pain in his side. He coughed and squirmed to get comfortable again. "Mom, before I could get scared I—yelled at the man."

"A *man?*" She thought her heart would grind to a halt at his words. "Someone was in the house?"

Stephen nodded. "I told him off. 'Jesus lives here,' I said. 'So *get out right now!*' He ran fast tryin' to escape. Knocked me against the counter. Something hurts pretty bad right here." He pushed

his finger on the tender spot and gasped at even that small amount of pressure. No doubt about it, he was hurt.

Stephanie knew she couldn't take time to worry about who had broken in or what they might have taken. Her son came first. What to do? In what order? Her mind drew a blank. You had to be so careful with hemophiliacs. She and Michael had meant to practice emergency measures, but they had never gotten around to it. Like so much else in their life . . .

"Don't move," she ordered. "I'll get some ice for that bruise." She stood up straight and took two steps back into the kitchen, but slowed her progress almost as soon as she'd begun. "On second thought, you'll be better on the couch." She paused only a second longer then turned around to face him. "Think you can get there if I help you?"

"I—" He moved, then bit his lip. "I guess so, Mom."

"You're going to be all right. Just take it easy. Here." She dropped down into a squat and put her arm behind his neck. The other hand she held out for him to take hold of. "Ready? Only as far as the den."

Stephen nodded his agreement.

"Okay. Upsy-daisy." Trying not to put too much strain on his left side, she pulled with her hand and supported his back with her arm. Together, they managed to get him standing and shuffled over to the couch. He sat down. His eyes went glassy from the force. That was enough to send Stephanie into a near panic. She grabbed for him. He waved his hand to let her know he was all right, then stretched out on the cotton throw.

Letting go of the breath she'd been holding, she dashed into the kitchen and grabbed one of the ice packs from the freezer. Thank the Lord for small conveniences. On the way back to the den, she squeezed the cloth-covered plastic into a moldable shape.

"Here, honey," she said and extended her arm towards him. Whatever else she'd intended to say was lost when she saw the pained expression on Stephen's face. She finished the two strides it took to bring her alongside the couch, then knelt, and lifted his hands. "Here. Hold this right where it hurts the most," she told him. She remembered to try to keep from showing how afraid she was, but the sight of the ugly bruise almost caused her to cry out. A small gasp escaped before she was able to prevent it. Beginning just above his bottom rib and on down almost the span of her hand, the skin was discolored already. She had to call for help. Immediately. First, she wrapped the throw around him to keep him warm.

"Sweetie, you rest here. And hold that ice pack in place." She headed straight for the telephone in the kitchen.

"Mom, I'm not goin' to the hospital, am I? *Please?*"

She turned around. Torn between her desire to keep him calm, and the very real possibility that every second's delay could further endanger him, she teetered on the brink. Common sense won out. "We can't take any chances. We'll let the experts decide when they get here." She paused another moment. Light from the lamp striking his eyes at an angle caused them to sparkle like they hadn't in awhile. Her own eyes misted over. "Now rest while I go call. Besides, I need to report the . . . break-in. Right?"

He nodded. She felt as if he were staring straight into her very soul, looking for a sign that everything would be okay. In a moment he let his gaze slide down to the bundle he was holding against his skin. "I just don't wanna be a baby."

She barely heard him, his words just above a whisper. It was enough, though. "Stephen," she said, "you're *far* from a baby. You are the bravest nine-year-old I've ever seen." He smiled. She turned and reached the phone in three quick strides. The light was

403

enough for her to locate the three critical numbers on the keypad. She punched 911, and waited. Only after the operator had picked up midway through the second ring did she realize she had been holding her breath.

The male voice on the other end of the line asked the nature of the emergency. Her own voice quivering, she told him about finding Stephen on the floor, badly bruised, and mentioned his hemophilia. He asked for the address. She stated the information in as brief, yet complete, a manner as she could manage. He assured her that a rescue unit would be on its way, and continued to pose other questions—the age of the victim and whether or not there were any special considerations the techs should be aware of before beginning treatment. Medication? Allergies? Contagious diseases?

She almost faltered on the last item, but chose to be honest. "HIV," she said. The words almost caught in her throat.

If the truth bothered him, he didn't let it show. "All right," he said, "are you on an extension near your son?"

"Not right next to him," she replied.

"Can you move as close as possible, please? I'd like you to monitor Stephen's vital signs, in case he needs something before the paramedics arrive." She switched to the cordless phone. When she picked it up and turned the phone on, he was right there with more questions and instructions.

His steady, unflappable voice had a soothing effect. If he wasn't too worried then she didn't need to be, either, she supposed. Of course, he wasn't there with them. He hadn't seen the huge bruise on Stephen's side. And it wasn't *his* son. No wonder he could stay so calm. Nevertheless, she felt a definite sense of peace settling over her while she walked back and forth, listening to him.

With as much intelligence as she could bring to bear in her fuzzy-headed state, Stephanie looked for the signs he wanted and answered his questions. He must have had a reason, but there were so many of them. Just about the time she started to get frustrated, she heard the doorbell and a loud knock. The sudden intrusion made her jump. "There's somebody here now," she exclaimed.

"That's the crew, ma'am. They just radioed in. They have arrived at your home." Before the operator could say anything more, Stephanie raced to the front door. In one move, she threw open the locks and opened it. They said hello as they picked up the stretcher and started to come in. She just stood there in shock, her mouth gaping. They looked like . . . she didn't know *what* they looked like, standing there in plastic goggles, masks, and gloves. Aliens? The one on the left had a name tag just above his pocket. *Jay,* it read. From the way he held the stretcher, she could see a patch on his upper right shoulder. She made out the words, *Emergency Medical Technician.*

The taller man, Bobby, had *Paramedic* stitched across his badge. "Ma'am," he said, "you did make a call to 911—correct?"

"Oh, excuse me. Yes, I did. I just didn't expect . . ." Her voice trailed off. She stepped aside to let them enter. As they passed in a rush, her eyes darted between their rubber-covered hands and the intimidating face gear. The scene reminded her of a science fiction movie. "He's in the den," she heard herself say as she led the way.

A low-level anger started to bubble inside. Gloves she could understand. Stephen had AIDS. But the rest seemed like overkill. It would scare the child out of his wits, poor thing. Before she could say a word, the paramedic, who introduced himself as Bobby Green, asked if she was doing okay. She didn't answer. He didn't appear to expect one. Jay positioned the stretcher next to the couch, loosened the straps, and fluffed up the pillow.

"Here, big guy," Bobby said to Stephen, "I hear you've been takin' on some wild tigers. Let's have a look at that bruise."

His steady voice soothed some of her anxieties. He really seemed to care. She had to trust him. But she still didn't have to like the armor they were wearing. After all, it was *her son* they were protecting themselves from. She didn't know what to do, so she resigned herself to watching. Even then, she missed the brief exchange between the two medical personnel.

"That's a good shiner," Bobby told Stephen. "You must have had a nasty bump. Feel any sharp pain in that area?"

"Not anymore," Stephen responded. "It's numb right now."

"How numb?" Bobby cast a concerned glance at his partner.

"Kinda like . . . at the dentist. I can sorta feel everything, but not like it's part of me." He moved his head slowly from side to side. "I can't explain."

"That's all right. You did fine." The two men had already maneuvered themselves into position. "We're going to move you now," Bobby continued.

He turned to Stephanie. "It'll be easier if we use the thing he's lying on to lift him."

"Of course," she said. She watched them grab hold of the throw and pondered the coincidence of it being right there, opened up on the couch, when Stephen first lay down. His eyes locked onto hers the minute they started lifting him. They never left as they transferred him in a half-slide, half-lift onto the stretcher. She tried to reassure him, but was afraid her faltering smile did little good. Again, she held her breath as they rolled him from the den and through the living room toward the front door.

Before they reached it, she was beside them, asking if she could ride along in the ambulance.

Stephen gave them a pleading look.

"Of course," Bobby said. "You can sit in the chair made especially for moms—assuming you don't get in the way." He smiled.

"I'll be good," she said, nodding. She reached out and opened the door. While they rolled past with the stretcher, she fumbled around in her purse for the keys. It took her a minute to find them. As usual, they were buried all the way at the bottom. And then, her hands were shaking so bad she didn't think she'd ever fit the key into the lock. By the time she did and ran to the ambulance, the rescue workers had Stephen inside. Bobby was hovering over him. He never even glanced up. His attention was totally focused on what he was doing.

As soon as EMT Jay saw her, he jumped outside to help. "Watch your step," he said, offering his hand. She crouched down, placed her feet on the step, and hoisted herself in.

"You can sit there," said Bobby, nodding toward a jumpseat behind the driver's seat, near Stephen's head. She felt relieved to be so near and not relegated to somewhere on the bench that ran along the length of the unit. She sat down, then leaned forward so she could be as close as possible. Jay closed the door behind her. Aside from a brief realization that he must be the driver, she didn't give him a second thought. Her eyes locked in on her son. Tears welled up. Reality was fast sinking in. This was serious business. Very serious. She rubbed her arms. She was trembling like a feeble, ninety-year-old woman.

"Look, Mom," Stephen said, breaking the spell of fear. A grin crept into his young features. "Up on the roof." He pointed.

Stephanie did as he asked. The ceiling was plastered with decals of teddy bears, dinosaurs, and all sorts of things that would hold a child's attention. "Pretty neat, huh?" She tried to smile.

"How many y'think are up there?" the paramedic asked him. "I bet you could come close."

He studied the arrangement for a few seconds. "Gee, I don't know. A whole bunch."

407

"The last I counted, there were thirty-nine. Jay, my main man there, does our interior decorating." He winked.

Stephanie couldn't help but smile.

"Wow, I wonder . . ." Stephen's words trailed off into silence, but his eyes stayed focused on the ceiling. He didn't seem to notice that the vehicle had started moving out onto the road. Stephanie's head turned toward the driver the moment she felt the first subtle lurch. She watched him talk into a radio. She heard the word, "transport." They rounded a corner. That brought her attention back to her son and to Bobby, the man attending to him. In his hand, he held a syringe with a long needle.

"What are you doing?" she demanded.

"A transfusion. Standard procedure for his type of injury."

"Why?" Her voice started climbing. A trace of hysteria tinged her tone. All their trouble had begun with one of those! Someone following "standard procedure." Before she realized it, she had leaped off her seat and was wrestling with the enemy for possession of a weapon. *Protect Stephen.* That single thought clouded reason. "Stop!" she cried. "He's been through enough!"

"Ma'am, please." Bobby's stern voice drew her attention back to the moment. "I'm trying to help your son.

Fear clawed at Stephanie. They were totally dependent on outside help. But this "helper" looked so odd, staring at her from behind his thick plastic goggles. Her throat tightened so she couldn't speak. She could only hope the blood had been screened.

"Mom . . ." Her son's voice, a little weaker, but his voice nevertheless, pierced the fog. "It's okay, Mom. I'm not afraid."

Tension drained from her. She felt too tired to hold her hand up any longer. Then she noticed why it was up in the air. She had a tight grip on the paramedic's arm. She let go. "I'm—I'm sorry. I don't know what got into me . . ." Her shoulders slumped.

"It's okay," Bobby said. "I understand. But I was going to have to get your attention myself." He felt around on Stephen's arm and addressed him. "My friend, I think I found a vein that'll cooperate. Let's get this thing going." Stephen let him maneuver his arm into a more accessible position. He swabbed it with something cool. "This won't hurt. Might sting just a bit."

Stephen nodded and sighed. He blinked, his mouth set into a grim line. He turned to stare into his mom's eyes. He had been poked more than a pin cushion. Still, he smiled weakly in return.

Stephanie grimaced, watching the paramedic insert the needle slowly into the vein and attach it to one of those hanging drip things. Once he appeared satisfied, he focused back on the monitor. It must have been while she was distracted with the equipment up front that Bobby had managed to get a blood pressure cuff on Stephen's arm and hooked him up to a heart monitor. He was quick. She didn't remember when. She just felt her own heart beating out of sync with the blips showing on the screen.

She gathered her courage. "How is he?"

"Vital signs look good so far . . ."

Stephanie waited, but only heard the beeping of the heart monitor. "You say that as if there might be more."

Bobby cleared his throat. "Your son is nine, you said?" She nodded, raising her eyebrows.

"Children his age are pretty strong. Their bodies fight hard to maintain balance, even when there's significant injury." He paused. "Although the machines paint a good picture, his body could be fooling us. Especially where there might be some internal bleeding. If we wait for his blood pressure to drop to a dangerous level, it might be too late. So we don't wait. That's why the drip." He paused. "Hemophilia has its own special circumstances—"

"I know," she cut in.

"So then you realize that a bruise to us is just a bruise. To your son, it could be fatal."

Stephanie gasped. "You mean he could be bleeding that bad inside right now and we wouldn't know it?"

"Yes. He's also bleeding from a small cut on his elbow. That's why we put him on the intravenous right away. Don't want to take any chances."

She rubbed Stephen's forehead. "How do you feel, honey?"

"Slee-py . . ."

She turned back to Bobby. The dials and gauges in front of him still held his attention. After another few seconds, he reached into one of the cabinets off to his right. He pulled out a plastic-covered package. She watched him set it on the stretcher within easy reach. Though her face mirrored the question in her heart, she kept silent. One thing she didn't want to do was distract him from giving the best care.

She had almost begun to relax when she noticed a change in one of the beeps. In an split-second, Bobby hunched over Stephen. He grabbed the package he had set on the stretcher, then tore open the plastic wrapper in one smooth move. With a flick of his wrist, he unrolled what looked like a small pair of pants. She couldn't help herself. "What are those?" she asked.

He started to reply, but halted in mid-syllable and made a "wait" gesture. "Get hold of dispatch," he commanded the driver. "May need to upgrade status. See what they think."

She heard the driver call back, "Roger, buddy."

The next few minutes passed as if in a dream.

She recognized only some of the phrases tossed back and forth between the two men. "Blood pressure dropping—shallow heartbeat—accelerating pulse."

Something was wrong.

Bobby grabbed the pants he'd just unfolded. He maneuvered Stephen so he could put them over his legs.

"Why are you . . . doing that . . . ?" she heard someone mumble. It took a second before she recognized the voice. Stephen's. She felt very alone. A bystander observing from a distance. Able to see every detail, yet unable to do a thing. She wanted to reach out to comfort him, but didn't trust herself to not get in the way again.

Stephen closed his eyes. His head lay back on the pillow, half turned to the side, as if he had fallen asleep. She had to keep herself from interfering. She laced her hands and clenched them together underneath her chin. Her elbows dug into the tops of her thighs. She barely noticed. Her eyes were glued to the scene playing out in front of her.

Bobby worked smoothly, but with no wasted motion. He finally got those funny-looking pants on Stephen. The driver called back to him to get on the phone. He did so, pronto. He spoke softly, yet fast, describing her son's symptoms to someone on the other end of the line. A doctor, maybe?

She closed her eyes and prayed under her breath. "Oh, Lord, don't let him—not yet, please!" Tears welled up and trickled from beneath her lids. "Give them wisdom. Guide their hands to do the right things . . ."

Nothing had changed when she opened her eyes. Stephen still lay on the stretcher, immobile, head to one side.

"Jesus," she whispered. "Jesus . . . Jesus . . . Jesus." Over and over she repeated the name.

Through blurred eyes, she watched. She almost wished she hadn't come along. To keep herself from getting queasy, she concentrated on the paramedic's face. His brow furrowed as he worked. His lips and jaw were tense, his eyes grave. Every now and then he'd say something into the cellular phone, pause, and nod.

411

 Tender Journey

Then he'd look at the monitor, squint, look at Stephen, and say something else into the phone. It seemed to go on forever.

Out of the blue, Stephanie felt a calm engulf her. It pushed aside the terrible fear. She took a deep breath—the first full one since she'd climbed into the ambulance. And then she saw why.

The technician's brow uncreased. He sighed in audible relief, leaned back, and rolled his shoulders to ease the tension. This time when he spoke into the telephone, she heard him say, "pressure stabilized." He set the phone back into the holder on the shelf.

"Does that mean he's going to be all right?"

His begoggled eyes met hers. "They'll give you a better idea at the hospital. We're almost there."

"Just tell me what you think," she pleaded.

"Your son still has internal bleeding somewhere, which caused his blood pressure to drop very low. The M.A.S.T. pants worked for now." When Stephanie only stared back with a slightly blank expression, he continued, "That stands for Military Anti-Shock Tights. They can be pressurized to restrict blood flow into the lower extremities. Helps keep the blood up where it's needed most—in the vital organs."

She wanted to ask if it was dangerous, slowing down blood to his legs and all, but she held back. She didn't know if she could handle the answer. Even thinking about potential side effects was too much. With great effort, she wrenched control of her wayward thoughts and focused on her son.

Stephen was staring at the animal stickers pasted all over the roof above his head. He looked so vulnerable. I.V. running into his arm. Heart monitor hooked up to his body. M.A.S.T. pants in place. But he did appear much more alert. He turned his head toward her. "I feel funny, Mom," he said. His voice, a barely-audible croak, shook her out of the fog that had closed in around her.

412

She turned to the paramedic, new questions written all over her face. He checked the instruments again and formed an okay sign with his thumb and forefinger. She breathed a sigh of relief.

Stephen's head moved a fraction. She reached out and clasped his hand in hers. "They're taking good care of you, sweetie. Don't worry." He let his head settle a little more into the pillow. He nodded as he did so.

"We're here, folks," called the driver.

Stephanie hadn't noticed the ambulance coming to a stop. Come to think of it, she had barely noticed it moving. Most of the trip seemed little more than a blur. She had no idea how long they'd been traveling. It seemed both an eternity and the briefest of moments. She wanted to say so much. To Stephen. To the super guys who had saved his life.

The back doors swung open. The driver latched them so they wouldn't close by accident. "Watch your step," he cautioned. "And be careful not to bump your head."

She remembered to duck, making sure she planted her foot securely on the step before putting all her weight on it. She glanced back to see how they were doing with Stephen. In an instant, they had the stretcher out of the ambulance and were rushing to wheel it through the emergency room doors. She had to run to keep up with them.

They delivered him into one of the smaller examining cubicles. Just before the curtain closed, he looked at her and smiled.

"Love you, Mom," he said in a whisper.

She grasped his hand again. Tears spilled from her eyes. "I love you, too, honey." She sniffed, and wiped a hand across her cheek to brush away the tears. "You're going to be all right . . . Promise."

"Excuse me, ma'am," one of the nurses said, "you'll have to wait outside."

Outside? She couldn't believe it. All of a sudden, fear gripped her again. She didn't want to leave him, as if he were somehow safer with her near.

"We'll take very good care of your son," the nurse added. "And you can help by letting us get started—unhindered—right away."

"I-I don't want to leave him," she stammered.

She shook her head "I know. But you can't stay in here. Hospital policy."

She felt another nurse pat her on her arm, just above the elbow. She gave Stephen's hand one last squeeze before taking a step back from the bed. The nurse inside the stall snapped the curtain all the way shut. Stephanie's last glimpse of Stephen was of him, lying there, surrounded by a cloud of white uniforms.

Someone guided her around a bend in the hallway and down to the reception desk. "I know you probably answered questions for 911, but there's some paperwork here you'll need to fill out for us." She stopped a few feet away from the reception desk and removed her hand from Stephanie's arm.

Stephanie finally turned to look at her escort. The woman was about her same age. Pretty. With auburn hair and freckles. She had the most compassionate expression she'd seen in ages. It made her feel like she had stepped into a hot bath. "You'll find telephones just down the hallway," the nurse added, "in case you need to call someone." She pointed at the desk. "And there are the papers. It's hard to concentrate now, I know. Do the best you can."

"Thanks. Will the ER staff know where I am when they need to get in touch with me?"

"Of course. I'll make sure of that myself—"

"And?" she interrupted.

"And they'll be out to talk to you the *minute* they know something." She paused. "Trust them. They're well-trained."

Stephanie nodded an "I'll be okay." She lowered her gaze to the floor, then looked up. The nurse was already heading back down to the emergency room. "Thank you," she called, and made her way over to the chair. One look at the clipboard full of papers launched her into another anxiety attack. Michael was the one who kept the records. She had to get in touch with him! With a sigh, she wondered why he was always gone when she needed him most. She fumbled around getting the hotel number out of her purse while she ran to the phone. Then her fingers shook so badly she kept punching the wrong keys. She tried several times. At last, she got through.

"Mayflower Hotel," announced a pleasant voice. "How may I direct your call?"

"Michael Nastasis. I don't remember his room number, but he's been there several weeks."

"Thank you. One moment please."

Hold? That was the *last* thing she wanted to do. "It's an emergency. Please hurry."

"Certainly."

Stephanie waited with bated breath while the long-distance call went through. Finally. One ring. Two rings. Three. Four. She sighed and shook her head from side to side.

Her hands gripped the receiver as if it were a life preserver. "Answer it, Michael," she whispered through clenched teeth. "I need you to *pick up that phone!*"

One more ring, then another. Her luck. Was he out looking for Michelle. She glanced at her watch. In the middle of the night?

She leaned against the wall and put a hand to her forehead. It rang two more times before she hung up. In a fog of frustration, she called back the hotel operator and reiterated about the situation at home. She needed to speak to Michael as soon as possible.

415

"Have him call that number at the hospital," she barked. "It's the emergency room." She hung up the phone hard.

She dreaded facing the maze that awaited her. Detailed paperwork you needed a doctorate to understand. Consent forms. Diagnosis. Prognosis. She wanted to run and hide. Oh, for a hug and someone to tell her everything would be okay. But no. As usual, she faced the tough stuff alone. And afraid. For all she knew, Michael was out having a night on the town. He had slipped before, hadn't he? Maybe *more* than once . . . She felt her cheeks burn with anger as she remembered. *Forget that right now,* she scolded herself. *You have more important matters to deal with.*

Further panic set in. Did she have the right insurance card with her? Michael had been looking into other companies to see if they could save on their premiums. Surely, he would have told her if he had switched. Surely, he would have given her the new information to keep in her purse. She thumbed through the thick stack of cards jammed in her wallet. Not a health insurance card in sight. From any company! Where *was* it?

Good heavens, would they even treat Stephen without proof? She didn't have a clue. Her blood started to boil. Michael was organized beyond belief in his business affairs. He probably alphabetized his paper clips! Why couldn't he have planned ahead where his family was concerned? He should have seen to it that she had everything she would need while he was away! And, to top it off, he had refused to spend the money for an out-of-state paging service. He would check his messages regularly at the hotel, he had assured her. Right.

At that moment, she was ready to strangle him. He was lucky he was a thousand miles away.

⋅❧ Twenty-Four ❧⋅

ichael sat on the edge of his bed, towel-drying his hair and wondering if today would be *the day.* He felt confident that a break was in the making. He looked at his watch. It was already . . . half past three in the morning! Anticipation had him wide awake. With special permission from the hotel night manager, he had gone for a long swim to try to relax. Too, he was also a bit disappointed that the Liebens had to cancel their dinner date. The wife—what was her name?—wasn't feeling good. Oh, well. Maybe they could reschedule. After the results of their first meeting, he was looking forward to getting to know them better.

Quiet expectancy filled him as he sat, rehashing the latest incredible lead—they had talked to a girl wearing his daughter's exact ring. It had to be her! Something was about to change, all right. Something important. He felt it in his gut. And what else but good news about Michelle? A positive breakthrough would make a fitting end to his escapades in the big city.

Thankfully, he did feel more tired after the swim and a shower. Maybe he could fall asleep. To encourage himself in that direction, he picked up the Bible and began reading from Psalm Forty-Six:

417

Tender Journey

God is our refuge and strength, a very present help in trouble. Therefore will not we fear, though the earth be removed, and though the mountains be carried into the midst of the seas; though the waters thereof roar and be troubled, though the mountains shake with the swelling thereof. Selah. There is a river, the streams whereof shall make glad the city of God, the holy place of the tabernacles of the most High. God is in the midst of her; she shall not be moved: God shall help her, and that right early (Psalm 46:1-5 KJV).

"Well, Lord," he mused aloud, "seems like we're finally coming *out* of trouble. I have to admit, it's about time." With that, he tossed his towel on the nightstand, shut off the light, and laid his head on the pillow. For four and a half hours, he slept like a baby.

As soon as he awoke at eight, he sprang into action getting ready. He intended to schedule a meeting with the detective ASAP. The ringing of the phone jarred him loose from his mental checklist. He had to push the damp towel off the phone to answer it. Funny, the message light was on. Somebody had called?

"Hello," he said. A pause, then, "Yes, this is Michael." He fell silent as he listened to the person on the other end of the line. His eyebrows went up. "Oh, Officer McCartney. Were you the one who left a message, by any chance? No?" He listened further, then asked, "So you've confirmed a report that a girl resembling Michelle was seen . . . *where?*" he continued without giving the man a chance to respond. "Do you have a street address? A landmark? Anything?" Another pause. "Nothing more definite?"

Michael's face fell while he digested what the officer was telling him. He reached out a hand to steady himself and settled back down on the bed. He let his head fall forward into his open palm and let the receiver slide a bit away from his ear.

"I'm sorry, Mr. Nastasis," Officer McCartney said. "We were unable to pin down exactly where. The people we spoke to weren't sure. Some had seen her on one street. Others on another. But with several separate sightings, we can be more confident that it *was* your daughter. She's still in the general area of midtown."

"Yes . . ." Michael answered. "And when did you say she was last seen?"

"The most recent was the day before yesterday."

"Why did you wait until now to tell me?"

"We only learned about this latest tip this morning. We had to confirm it to tie everything together. And you're the first to hear."

"Thanks. Say, I'm sorry for my impatience." Another pause. "Of all people, I should understand how things can pile up."

"Apology accepted."

"So, how do you *know* she keeps going back . . ." He swallowed hard ". . . to where the pushers and prostitutes hang out?" Blinking hard, he tried to erase the picture forming in his mind.

"We've got discreet ways, not always the most reliable. So we waited. Now we're sure." He cleared his throat. "Mr. Nastasis there's no easy way to say this, but it's got to be said. The girl gives every indication of being hooked on drugs. At the very least, she's been doing them regularly for awhile."

He took a deep breath and straightened himself on the bed. "All right. Thanks for the tip." His words came out clipped. Terse and to the point. He had been hoping against hope that she wouldn't touch the stuff. Time for a reality check. For the moment he would set aside feelings to focus on the immediate need. "You didn't say what kind." With luck, maybe only marijua—

"Cocaine. *Crack* cocaine—the cheapest and most addictive."

Michael felt a giant steel fist clamp itself around his heart. It was slowly squeezing the life out of him, tighter and tighter with

419

every word. He wanted to shriek in pain. But now was not the time. He had to think. Had to keep a cool head for a little longer. "Where do we go from here? You *must* be able to find out who she's buying the stuff from. If she keeps going back to the same source, couldn't we go and make him talk—"

"*We?* All we need is for her to catch a glimpse of you and take off running to another state. We've been lucky so far, but if she skips town, you may never see her again. You wanna risk that?"

"Hardly. But I can't just do nothing! I'm her father!"

"I know." He hesitated. "Look. I told you we'd help and we have. Don't make our job any harder than it is already. Your life is in jeopardy, too. Sometimes these things take a little while to work out. Sometimes they don't work out at all. Usually, by the time we find out what's going on, it's too late. The poor kid has overdosed or gotten herself killed. In your case, we've gotten some early breaks. Things look pretty positive. You're gonna have to trust us."

That was not what Michael wanted to hear. Every fiber of his being rebelled at the thought of sitting on his hands. The struggle flashed across his features, changing his face into several masks before settling into one of quiet determination. "I'll consider your approach," he relented. "But I don't like it."

"I can tell." The officer paused. "Look, if we didn't honestly think it was best, we wouldn't ask it of you. Most of us in the department have kids, too."

Michael took a deep breath. His white-knuckled fingers squeezed the receiver even tighter, but just for a second. He relaxed his grip in rhythm with his exhaling breath. "All right, all right. I said I'd do it your way."

"Good. And keep in mind," the officer continued, "that this is just for now. At some point, we may ask you to get more involved. Don't get your hopes up, though. It's too early to tell what kind of shape she'll be in when we nab her. Sometimes runaways feel more comfortable talking to strangers, for obvious reasons."

Michael's cheeks burned with silent shame. The truth was more than he could bear. He held his breath. If not for some occasional static on the line, it would seem he had hung up and left the officer to fend for himself.

After a moment, the man spoke. "I can only imagine how hard this is for you. We'll keep you posted on everything that happens. Are you planning to stay on at the same hotel?"

"I guess so. If Michelle is hanging around this part of town, that doesn't give me much cause to move somewhere else."

"No more personal search-and-destroy missions, though. Promise?"

"I *said . . . okay.*" A tinge of annoyance had crept into his tone. "What do you want me to do? Sign it in blood?"

Michael's sarcasm returned like a boomerang. "Let's hope that won't be necessary," Officer McCartney replied, his tone tense. After a few seconds, he apologized. Then he said goodbye and hung up.

Spine-deep chills gripped Michael, replaced by a churning resentment. Maybe law enforcement wanted full credit for pulling off her rescue. It would look better in their annual report.

He sat on the bed long after he'd placed the receiver back on its cradle. Anxious thoughts raced through his head, one after another so fast he could hardly catch a glimpse of one before another took its place. Deep in his chest, a dull ache throbbed with every beat of his heart.

The peace he'd felt while reading a few verses seemed now nothing more than a distant memory.

Fear—bitter-tasting—churned his stomach into knots.

His hands trembled. Oblivious to his own actions, he clutched

the Bible to his chest. He bowed his head, but the thoughts wouldn't go away. "Why, Lord, why?" was the only bit of heaven-ward conversation he could utter. His little girl . . . on drugs. Doing who-knows-what to get them. Where had he and Steph gone wrong raising her? Lord knows they tried.

The ring of the telephone startled him out of a deepening despondency. His ran a hand through his hair, wiped his palm on his trouser leg and picked up the receiver. "Hello."

"Beg your pardon, sir. Have I reached Mr. Michael Nastasis?"

Michael recognized the polite foreign accent right away. "Yes, Joshua. This is Michael. How are you?"

"Fine, fine. And you? Your voice sounds a bit strained."

He hesitated. "It's the weather. Been outside too much in the damp night air."

"Please be careful. You cannot take sick now."

"You've heard something I need to know?"

"I wish so. Since yesterday when we met I have been staying close to Anna."

"That's right. I forgot. Well, something's come up on this end. I've just had another phone call from the police. Michelle may have been spotted down around Forty-Sixth and Eighth." When Joshua failed to respond, Michael continued. "Where lots of weird stuff goes on." He couldn't bring himself to mention the details.

"We are very familiar with the area. Our church has a ministry to the homeless near there." Now it was Joshua's turn to be silent for a moment. "What further plans have you on her behalf?"

Michael snorted. "That's the catch. The officer made me promise I wouldn't get in the way and scare her off. Seems they fig-ure if she ran away from home, seeing me might send her running again." He paused. "I've *got* to do something, but the only thing I can do is pace. And it's killing me. I feel like a caged animal."

422

"In a small way, Anna and I share your angst. We can talk further over a meal. Please accept our invitation to lunch."

"Sure." Michael paused a moment. "Do you have anyplace in mind?"

"Perhaps the Carnegie Deli on Seventh Avenue. Not expensive, but tasty. Would you care to meet us there at eleven-thirty?"

Michael nodded. "That'll be great. I've heard their pastrami is the best in the city."

"Wonderful. We will enjoy some together. We look forward to seeing you then. Good-bye for now."

"Bye," he responded and hung up the phone. He got up off the bed and made his way to the bathroom. Leaning close to the mirror, he studied a cold sore forming in the corner of his mouth. It burned already. "Better get some ointment," he told himself, "or this one's gonna be a doozy." He started to unbutton his pajama top. Before he was half-finished, the telephone rang *again*. Quite the celebrity he was becoming. He considered letting the operator take a message, but changed his mind at the last second. He walked over to the bedside table to answer it. A good thing, too.

It was Stephanie. "Hi, hon," he said, faking an upbeat tone. "Guess what. I may have good news real soon. She's been spotted again—several times." He wasn't about to tell her where. It took a moment for him to realize how upset his wife was. She was trying to tell *him* something. They had a terrible connection.

"I can hardly hear you," he shouted. "What's up?"

"—pay phone at the hospital," came the muffled reply. Suddenly, the line cleared. She was sobbing. "Our son almost bled to death last night. I left several messages for you before I fell asleep in his room." Silence. "Oh, no!" she gasped. "I can't remember if I told 911 about the burglary . . ."

Tender Journey

By eleven forty-five, Michael was sitting across from Joshua and Anna in the Carnegie Deli. His designer luggage was piled up beside him. With tears in his eyes, he told them about the phone call from Stephanie. "My son's almost out of danger, thank God. But they both need me at home. On top of everything else, they were burglarized last night. That's how Stephen got hurt."

"My goodness! Surely, you could have cancelled our engagement today," Joshua said.

"I couldn't *not* show up. You don't have a phone in your room and I didn't know if you would get the message in time."

"Even so, we would have understood in such an emergency."

"I know." He paused. "But I didn't want to go back to Florida without a chance to see you again."

Joshua folded his hands. "You are leaving when?" He raised his white eyebrows over incredible blue eyes.

"Two o'clock this afternoon from LaGuardia. It was the first available flight," Michael explained. "I feel like a total heel that I didn't find out about Stephen before now. Supposedly, Steph couldn't reach me last night. I must have been out exercising to relax. I didn't notice the message light, either, for some stupid reason. You should have seen me this morning, tearing around the hotel room like a maniac, grabbing my stuff, and throwing it into suitcases. I tell you, it's as if I'm being yanked apart by two huge pairs of invisible hands. One's got my head. The other's got my heart. They're tugging and twisting away."

Anna said nothing, but her expression spoke volumes. Joshua reached across the table and patted Michael's hand. "Do what you must do as a husband and father. Anna and I will help if you tell us what you need."

Michael looked from one to the other. Compassion flowed from both of them. Though he'd only recently met the couple, he felt drawn to them. He was sure they could be trusted as much as a mom and dad. "I don't know what to even ask for," he said, shaking his head. "Our life is so out of control. It seems that when we come close to a breakthrough in one area, all hell breaks loose in another! I hate to leave New York, now that there's finally some hope. But how can I *not* go? My house isn't safe and my son has suffered injuries because of it. Plus who knows *what* else . . ." He wiped his damp eyes with his napkin. "I'm being forced to choose between my kids! Do you realize that?"

Anna bowed her head, as if she didn't want to embarrass him by seeing him cry. He appreciated it. He had enough shame to deal with. Joshua grasped his hand tighter and never took his eyes away. When he spoke, his kind words cut through the fog of Michael's confusion to speak peace into his heart. "Forget not that our God is there. He cares. In fact, He may have made the difficult decision for you. Just this morning, did the officer not issue firm instructions to step back and let them supervise the search?"

Surprised, Michael gave him a reluctant nod. "I resented it, big time. Felt like they were trying to steal all the glory."

"Perhaps God Himself was at work in disguise. He used an angel *and* a donkey to block the path of Balaam."

"So you think I'm doing the right thing." He sighed.

"Yes, Michael. Return home—not only to your son, but to your wife. Her needs must come before those of your children. God provided her to you first. Without her, you would not have your children."

"I never thought of it that way. But she doesn't put *me* first. They're her prime concern. By comparison, I could drop dead. As long as the kids are okay, she's happy as a clam."

Joshua gazed at Anna. "I remember after Anja's death, I struggled with those same feelings. Maternal instinct runs to the core."

As Michael rubbed his thumb around in the condensation on his water glass, he ventured to ask, "Who was Anja?"

"The only child God ever gave to us," Joshua replied. "She was growing into a beautiful young woman." He squinted and fiddled with his napkin. "A border guard shot her just after the Wall was erected in 1961."

"Forty-five she would be if she were still alive," Anna added. "A mother herself. We might even be grandparents . . ."

Michael's mouth opened. He shook his head. "I'm sorry. I had no idea. You've been through as much as we have."

Anna nodded. "Thus, we understand. Grief consumed me after she was taken. Nothing else mattered for nigh on a year. Joshua mourned as well, though differently. He tried to draw comfort from me. In my anguish, I often turned him away."

Joshua squeezed her hand. "Those were difficult times, indeed, love. But we made a valiant recovery!" He put his arm around her shoulder. "We have enjoyed a full life. Not by accident, mind you. Long and hard we toiled in our little vineyard, watering, adding nutrients, planting seeds, pulling weeds. Years later, we are reaping a sweet harvest."

"You certainly seem more content than most." Michael toyed with his fork and ran his fingers through his hair. "You know, I've wondered why you showed such concern for our daughter, a total stranger. It's because you lost your own, huh?"

Joshua's crystal blue eyes met his. "In part. Anja had barely turned sixteen when she died."

"Michelle will be sixteen soon." He gulped. "Lord have mercy, I just had an awful, sinking feeling."

"Oh?"

"What if the real reason our paths crossed . . ." He paused to lick his lips. ". . . is so you and Anna can help us cope with the loss of our children. Michelle . . . *and* Stephen. Through you, He might be trying to cushion the blows we've got to look forward to. Nice of Him to be so thoughtful." He grimaced.

"No doubt our meeting took place by divine appointment. We do not yet understand why. However, joy could result just as well."

Michael shrugged. "Guess I'm learning to expect the worst. How does the old saying go? 'Blessed are they who expect nothing, for they shall not be disappointed.'"

Smiling, Joshua said, "Clever, certainly, your adage. But does the thought line up with Scripture? Jeremiah Twenty-Nine, Eleven reminds us, *'For I know the plans that I have for you,' declares the Lord, 'plans for welfare and not for calamity to give you a future and a hope'* (NASB).

"I need hope, that's for sure."

Joshua's features took on a grave intensity. "As do we, Michael. As do we." His blue eyes locked onto Michael's dark brown ones. "Son, I give you my solemn word. As long as Anna and I live in the city of New York—provided the police feel we would not hinder their efforts—we will continue to distribute your bulletins and search for your daughter."

"You *will?* Gosh, I don't know how to thank you."

"Nonsense. The honor is ours."

Michael paused. "By the way, what do *you* two need hope for?"

With a nod, Joshua replied, "To find my father. But that story, my good man, must wait for another day. I fear the plane could well depart without you!"

Michael glanced at his watch. Fifty-five minutes until take-off! He gobbled down a few more bites, said a brief farewell, and, luggage in hand, hurried to hail a cab to the airport.

❧ *Twenty-Five* ❧

From outside her makeshift cardboard shelter in the park, whimpering sounds awoke Michelle later that night. Half asleep, she crawled out to see the source of noise. Nah, it couldn't be. But it *was!* A *puppy!* "Here, boy . . . here, boy!" she called softly. A fluffball of fur bounded into her arms and licked her with wild abandon. The full moon overhead cast enough light to reveal a few details. It was a little female. She held her closer. No collar, no tag. A stray? Must be her lucky day! Beneath the thick beige coat, she felt ribs protruding from the skinny chest. She looked again at the cute face. Unmistakably, a yellow Lab.

The puppy whimpered some more and snuggled in under Michelle's chin. With one hand, she held the animal and with the other, she smoothed out the dirty, torn quilt she had scavenged from a dumpster—the same place she had found the large cardboard box she had made home. She lay down on her side, tucking the puppy against her chest. "You're mine now," she whispered into the warm coat. "What should I name you?" She concentrated as hard as her foggy brain would allow. "I know. *'Angel!'*" As Michelle petted her and rubbed her ears, Angel let out a long, contented sigh and fell asleep. For the first time in weeks, Michelle did the same. No wonder. The long walk on Eighth Avenue had seemed like forever.

The next morning, she sat on a rock next to her cardboard house. Litter of every kind was strewn around her legs and feet. She bemoaned her fate and the loss of muscle tone in her body. How skinny she was getting, except for the slightly-rounded belly. At least it was barely noticeable under her baggy clothes. Could she *possibly* be pregnant? She shuddered at the awful thought.

In her lap she cuddled the puppy, not more than eight weeks old, who kept trying to nurse on her finger. "You hungry, little girl?" she cooed, rubbing her face into the soft, golden fur. At the sound of Michelle's voice and the feel of her skin, Angel's tail started to wag, thumping on her arm. "I wish I had somethin' for ya, baby, but I don't. Can't remember when *I* last ate. Not that I care." Angel licked her hand again, as if to say, "I'm okay if I got you." Michelle held her up, nose to nose. In response, she received an exuberant tongue-lapping all over her face that made her giggle with delight. She hadn't laughed in a long time.

The sound of a truck engine drew her eyes away from her new four-legged companion. About a block down Transverse Road, closer to the famous Belvedere Castle, parked a long van with *"MercyMobile"* printed across it. A woman stepped out. Within seconds, people were lining up at the door. Michelle squinted and stared for several minutes. *Food!* "Angel, look at that! Freebies. Maybe they'll give me somethin' for you, baby."

She got up from her crouched position on the curb and ambled down the street toward the truck. The line forming in front of it grew by the minute. Bums were creeping out of the woodwork! She petted the puppy's head and tried to run-walk, saying as she bounced along, "Hang, on, girl, hang, on." As fast as

she could, she raced to the back of the line. What if there was nothing left? When her turn finally came at the window, she closed her eyes and heaved a sigh of relief. She looked up. Kindness in the older woman's face greeted her, so much so that she could barely stand to look at her. She glanced instead at the ground, then at Angel, and asked, "Would you please have some scraps for my puppy?"

"I believe we could arrange that. But how about you, child?"

"Whatever."

She handed Michelle two brown bags and made a playful "shh" sign with her finger. "We cannot feed every animal, of course," she half-whispered, "but here is some for both of you."

"Thanks," Michelle replied with a tight smile, and snatched the bags out of her hand.

"You are most welcome." The woman looked at her intently, glanced away, then tilted her head and seemed to study her again. "Miss, I-I . . . have something else for you. Would you mind waiting here for a moment?"

"Guess not." Michelle's eyes darted around, then came to rest on the woman, who was acting very nervous all of a sudden.

"Good. I will return presently." With that, she was gone.

In preparation for the delay, Michelle shifted her weight onto her other foot and cradled Angel in her arms like a baby, cooing at her and nuzzling her soft fur.

Back inside the truck, Anna rushed over to Joshua, who was busy unloading supplies from cardboard boxes. She was almost hyperventilating. "My love—I believe that young girl—is standing right outside!"

"Calm yourself, Anna. What girl?"

"For heaven's sake! The one whose father—we met for lunch!"

"Michael's daughter? *Truly?*"

"Sh-h-h!" Her voice lowered to a whisper. "Yes, love. I feel quite certain. She bears striking resemblance to the child in the pictures—as well as to the girl we met in the park."

"Glory to God!" Joshua exclaimed. Then he remembered what the police had told Michael. His face clouded over. "How is she?"

"Thin enough to blow away in the wind. Only for her animal did she request any food. I gave her a supply for the two of them. I told her I might have something else for her, but I fibbed so I could come speak to you. We have so waited for this moment. Whatever should we do next?"

"Call the police."

"My goodness, how? She will become suspicious if I try to delay her with silly conversation."

"Just try to occupy her long enough for the officers to arrive."

"Would you come out with me? *Please . . .*"

"That might alarm her. You go, Anna. I have full confidence in you. I will pray and search for a phone."

She did as Joshua urged her to do. On her way, she picked up another bag of food—the one she had set aside for her and Joshua.

"Miss, please forgive me for the delay," Anna said as soon as she stood back in front of Michelle.

Michelle frowned. "No problem."

"I gathered extra supplies for you to take with you." Anna held out the bag in her hand.

She grabbed it and mumbled, "Nobody treats me nice. Why you, lady?"

"Because of Je—" Anna stopped in mid-sentence. She paused to take a deep breath. "Because I believe you need a friend. And you do resemble a girl my husband and I befriended in Central Park not so long ago."

She responded with a puzzled smirk. "I do?"

431

"Yes, indeed. The girl we spoke to had to leave suddenly before we had much time to chat. Imagine our surprise when we learned that someone of her age had inquired about us at a shelter. We felt sorry to have missed her."

Michelle stared at Anna. She studied her hair pulled back in an old-fashioned bun, as if to say, "Now, why would *I* be looking for a couple of old fogies like you?

Meeting her with a direct gaze, Anna continued, "The volunteer at the shelter said the girl gave her name as 'Ashley.' Would that be you, child? We only want to help you."

"I go by Ashley someti—, I mean . . . yes, my name's Ashley Nicole Witherton. Right, Angel?" She petted the dog vigorously.

"Oh. That is your real name, then." Michelle looked away. Anna swallowed hard and clasped her hands. "Or would it perchance be . . . Michelle?" In an instant, Anna regretted her question, but she could not retract it. The damage had been done.

The petite teen's eyebrows drew together over two narrowing eyes. "Why would you pick *that* ugly name? I *hate* it." Her tone was strident, demanding.

Anna recoiled. No, things were not going the least bit well. And Joshua said he had full confidence in her! In the most casual tone she could muster, she replied, "No reason in particular." By now her hands were quivering. Her mouth felt desert-dry. Silently, she prayed that Joshua had reached the police. Oh, where *were* they? She watched a fearful expression, the look of a hunted rabbit, steal across the girl's face.

"Lady, who *are* you, anyway?" came the next harsh question.

"Anna Lieben. My husband and I volunteer here."

"No. Not your name. I wanna know why—out of a million names in the entire universe—you picked 'Michelle.'"

"Mere speculation."

"You think I'm stupid enough to believe that? You must be nuts. Or senile." With those words, Michelle pressed the puppy to her chest and bolted through the new crowd of homeless people gathered around the truck.

Anna shouted after her, "Child, please stay!" She made a move to pursue, but thought better of it and rushed inside the truck. There she bumped into Joshua, who was just returning from his mission. Her face contorted with pain and shock. "Surely it was Michelle," she cried. "When I inquired about her name, she grew very angry and fled!"

"Which way did she go?" Joshua asked. Anna pointed to the north, toward Belvedere Castle.

"Fear not, love. Two officers will come at once with the dogs. They will find her."

"Must they pursue her like a criminal? She is but a child."

"No longer, Anna. Runaways require every kind of intervention." Visibly softened, he paused. "To help them, they must be caught—before they throw away their entire lives!"

The sound of squealing tires and slamming car doors captured their attention. "Men in uniform," Anna murmured, stifling a gasp, "armed . . . with attack dogs . . ."

"All is well," Joshua reassured her. "This is far different from the pursuit of defectors at home. We intend to help her." He stepped over to talk with the officers and pointed in the direction Michelle had gone. Shaking his head, he walked back to Anna as the officers fanned out through the crowd.

Her eyebrows rose. "What is it? You seem disheartened."

"We have nothing belonging to her. The dogs follow best the particular scent on a person's garments. Or, if she is carrying drugs on her person, they can track that scent, as well."

"In which case she would be arrested, would she not?"

"I assume so. We did not have time to discuss all the details of the situation."

"And if she has no illegal substances?"

"It will be most difficult to find her—unless they happen to spy her on foot out in the open."

She sighed. "Why did I not have sense enough to secure something of hers?"

In slow motion, Joshua replied, "No, do not burden yourself with guilt. What training have either of us in such matters?"

Anna shook her head. Her eyes filled with large tears. "None, but how can we tell Michael and his wife . . . that their lost child escaped from right in front of me? Tell me *how?* They will consider me an *utter half-wit!* And I *am!*" She started to cry.

"You are no such thing, Anna. You did your best. How could you predict what would prompt the girl's flight?"

"I could not. But I could have chosen another topic of conversation! The weather. The sights of New York. I might have asked about her puppy. One could detect her obvious fondness for little Angel. Anything on earth but her real name!" Anna balled up her hands at her sides and stomped one foot. "Herr Lieben, did I not ask you to go with me? If you had been less stubborn, you might very well have caught her, and we would not find ourselves in this most *dreadful* predicament!" Sparks flew from her eyes.

Joshua had not heard her address him in such an accusatory tone in many years. The pain of it sent a searing shock wave across his features. His lips parted to speak, but he said nothing. Taking a deep breath, then another, and closing his eyes, he encircled her in his arms. She cried as he stroked her hair. They stood that way for several minutes. Finally, she whispered, "Will you forgive me for letting my temper fly?"

"I have forgiven you already. You were afraid."

"Yes. I felt so helpless . . ." Her voice trailed off. "In an odd sort of way, I was trying to save Anja. They robbed her of life and I could do nothing to stop it."

"I understand, love. This situation has opened wounds we thought had healed long ago."

She hugged him again. "Deep wounds. How I wish to spare this child's parents from such grief." She wiped her eyes.

Reluctantly, Joshua went to make the call to Michael, who answered the phone on the second ring. Joshua explained the situation and poured out apologies on Anna's behalf. Michael acted gracious, but failed to mask the disappointment in his voice. He did remember to thank them both. "Believe me," he said, "it means a lot just to know somebody cares enough to *try* to help."

That statement brought a frown to Joshua's brow. "Of course we care—very much. So do many others, I am certain."

Michael sighed. "It's hard to tell. Right after she disappeared, we had some support. Friends helped look for her, handed out flyers, made a few calls. Now they avoid us like the plague. Never hear from any of 'em. Probably afraid our bad luck'll rub off."

"Or perhaps they fear speaking out of turn. No one wishes to cause you more sorrow for their bumbling."

"Maybe. I sure appreciate your call, though."

"In spite of the disappointing update?"

"Yes. Somehow, it helps to know that Michelle's not alone in New York. Even if her buddy is just a dog."

"Anna could see how much she adores the creature. She named her 'Angel,' a very appropriate title."

"Angel? You don't say . . ."

"I believe so. Yes."

"Oh, let's hope that's a good omen. You know, Joshua, she nagged me to get another dog after we had to put Ebony to sleep.

Guess I kinda blew her off," Michael added, his voice cracking. "I wish I had it to do over now . . ."

A long silence crept in. Joshua cleared his throat. "Each of us has regrets, my friend. And your son? How is he faring?"

"Stabilized at the moment. We're not out of the woods yet, but he is doing better. He's home."

"What wonderful news! We will pray yet more fervently for complete healing."

"Thanks. We need all the help we can get."

"And with God, you have all the help you need." Joshua's voice grew more animated. "Do you realize that Michelle's fondness for Angel could cause her to seek aid again? Anna said she asked for food, not for herself, but for the dog!"

"She did? That means it *was* our daughter you ran into." Michael sniffed. "Ever since the kid was a toddler, she'd give her food away to animals. Steph and I have torn our hair out trying to get her to eat. I swear she survives on air."

Joshua smiled. "Incidentally, how are the two of you doing?"

"Okay, I guess. Been going to counseling, which helps. We're learning about the importance of 'letting go.'"

"So soon you have abandoned the fight then?"

"No. It just means we're learning to accept the fact that if and when we do get her home, we can't force her to recover from drug addiction. The counselor says we could enroll her in the best treatment program in the nation, but unless she really *wants* to get well, it won't stick worth beans."

"I see. At any rate, Anna and I vow to continue the search with renewed vigor. Time is of the essence."

"You and Anna have done more than enough, really. Maybe we should let law enforcement handle it the way they see fit. They sure gave *me* the old heave-ho." He paused. "Say, why don't you

436

come stay with us for a while? It's beautiful here in Florida. We have plenty of room . . ."

"My heavens! Your generous offer takes me quite by surprise." He took a deep breath and exhaled with a loud sigh.

"So then . . . you'll come?"

"Allow me to give Anna the respect of discussing the plan with her. She does the same for me, which has served us well through the years—" He stopped short. "Goodness. My coin supply will soon be exhausted. Would you care to pray before we disconnect?"

"Uh, yeah, that'd be fine."

Joshua changed the receiver to the other ear, bowed his head and closed his eyes. After several seconds of silence, he began, "Oh, Father, in the mighty and holy name of Jesus, we intercede for young Michelle. Thank you for keeping Your loving arms around her and your most powerful angels encamping about her! May she arrive home safely at the earliest possible moment. And Lord, lead her into a brand new relationship with You, whatever the cost. Encourage her dear family during this most distressing time. We depend on Your tender care, for we believe—*despite all appearances to the contrary*—that you love us beyond comprehension. In the name of Jesus Christ, our Redeemer and Lord, Amen."

"Amen," Michael croaked. "Thanks." He wiped a tear from his eye. "Boy, it's weird. I'm *so* anxious to have you in Florida. How do you think you'll get here?"

"I cannot say at the moment. We will advise you soon."

"You might try the train to Orlando. Good way to relax and see the east coast of America."

"What a brilliant idea! Orlando is the destination, you say?"

"Yeah, I think that's the closest train station. Actually, we're in the country near Howie-in-the-Hills, about fifty miles from there. We'd be glad to pick you up wherever."

"Howie-in-the-Hills, eh? It sounds delightful. Anna adores quaint country villages."

"She'll love it here. And nearby Mt. Dora is pretty neat, too."

"In Orlando lives the world-famous mouse character?"

"He sure does. Maybe we'll take you to meet him one day. Stephen's wanted to go, but with Michelle gone it seemed, well—"

"No need to explain. I understand. As soon as we confirm a schedule, I will phone you."

"Great. We'll pick you up, no matter what the hour. In case we're not in, leave a message on the answering machine."

Joshua chuckled. "The last of those devices I conversed with took a notion to destroy my message altogether, I fear. We have not heard a return word from a soul."

"Yeah. They go on the fritz at the worst times. Ours was out of commission, but it's been working fine lately." He paused. "Hang on, let me give you my calling card number."

"That is what?"

"You can make calls from any phone by just punching in my number."

"My goodness, that is too much to expect. We have barely become acquainted."

"I trust you. It'll be a lot easier for you than bothering with change." Michael read the access code from his card and explained how to proceed from there.

"How kind of you!" Joshua exclaimed. "We joyfully anticipate meeting your wife and son." They exchanged warm goodbyes.

Joshua hung up and hurried back to the *MercyMobile* where Anna was waiting. "Your delay has worried me so," she exclaimed. "Was he awfully disgruntled with us?"

"No, love. Merely grateful for our effort on their behalf. He invited us to stay with them in Florida—"

"And abandon the search in New York? Pray tell, have you both gone mad?"

"Nein! He feels that you and I have done enough for now. The police have the case well under control." He grinned. "Think of this, Anna—how much more readily they can identify the child with a puppy in her arms!"

His grin was contagious. With a giggle, she said, "Oh, *yes!* That had not occurred to me."

"Nor to me, until the moment I said it." He gave her a big hug.

"For what duration did Michael propose we stay?"

"He did not specify. You have doubts, then, about the trip?"

"Not if you feel it is right. You have talked with him far more than I. I trust your judgment."

"It does seem that the Lord has provided the next step of our journey. We could not stay forever at the YMCA and we have no further leads here about my father. Moreover, we have an opportunity to see America which may never arise again."

"True." She tilted her head. "How will we travel?"

"Michael suggested the train. We could enjoy some highlights of the Eastern Seaboard."

Anna clasped her hands. "Oh, Joshua, trains are my favorite! I always wanted to go on such a trip at home."

"I know. And I regret that we never did." He hugged her again. Just then, the next volunteer showed up to man the truck, so Joshua seized the opportunity to hail a taxi to Penn Station.

Once there, they made arrangements in person for the trip. They found the Amtrak clerk quite helpful and thanked her for the fifteen percent "senior citizen" discount offer. When she showed them the guide with the cities the train would pass through, they couldn't decide whether to leave in the morning or evening.

They both felt torn. Should they reserve their daylight through-the-window sightseeing hours for historic Philadelphia and Washington D.C. or the charming cities of Charleston and Savannah? "A hard choice, indeed,"Anna said, shaking her head.

"The south would provide greater contrast to our native land," Joshua noted. That settled it. They would leave the following evening for the twenty-two-hour trip. Joshua called Michael to notify him that they would arrive on the Silver Meteor at 4:23 in the afternoon in Orlando—not the next day, but in two days. Michael displayed an unusual amount of enthusiasm. Their late afternoon arrival time would be perfect, he assured them. He could get a good day's work done beforehand.

✥ *Twenty-Six* ✥

When Michael hung up with Joshua, his heavy heart felt lighter than it had in months. Anticipation of happy times put a sudden spring in his step. Yes, he felt good. Almost as good as he did on Friday afternoons a few years ago. Back then, he was counting the hours until his weekend father-and-son visits with old Caleb. Bless his heart.

Buoyed by an unexplained hope for the future, he offered to take the family to dinner at Church Street Station after they picked up Joshua and Anna. Stephen was elated, both at planning an evening out and at the idea of having company in the guest room. He missed Michelle. Sleeping upstairs by himself was "icky." Michael teased him about being a big man now that he was nine.

Although Stephanie had always enjoyed strolling through the restored historic section of Orlando, she was not the least bit elated with the rest of idea. The prospect of two houseguests for an undetermined length of time elicited a cool response from her. "You could have discussed it with me first," she snapped. "The house is a mess. I've got enough on my mind without having to entertain a couple of old foreigners we don't know from Adam!"

441

Michael's defenses rose up in a flash. "Wait a minute. I thought you're the altruistic one in the family. This couple has done more than any of our so-called friends to help us find Michelle. Don't you think we owe them something?"

"I never met them. I don't feel as involved as you do."

He stopped and frowned. "What difference does *that* make? You looked like a zombie one day from crying your eyes out over a missing child you never met!"

"That's different. I was sensing the pain of the parents—"

"Well, give me a little credit, huh? I'm not a social moron." He tapped his index finger on his chest. "Maybe *I* 'sense' the Liebens need to come here for a rest."

Putting her hands on her hips, Stephanie retorted, "Since when have we made our home into a retreat for strangers?"

"Now that you mention it, it *was* a retreat when Caleb was alive. I happened upon the Country Corner during his off season. And if Caleb hadn't willed me this property, we wouldn't have such a nice place to offer."

Stephanie looked down. "Guess you're right." Her misty eyes met Michael's. "I'll try to be a good hostess."

"Thanks. Sorry I got harsh with you. It just means a lot to me. I don't know why. Joshua reminds me so much of Caleb in a lot of ways, I guess. Same white hair, same light blue eyes, lots of insight about stuff . . ."

Stephanie's voice lowered. "Michael, I hope you're not expecting more from Joshua than he can deliver. He's *not* Caleb."

"I know." He sighed. "There'll never be another one. But in the short time I spent with Josh, I just liked him, that's all. And his wife, too. They're neat people. You'll see. They've been through tough times themselves. Their only child was killed as a teenager and they spent most of their adult years behind the Iron Curtain."

She folded her arms. "So why'd they come to the United States anyway?"

"You know, I'm not sure . . ." He paused for a moment. "Now that I think about it, every time we talked we discussed my problems—Michelle, Stephen, the effects on you and me, et cetera. I didn't act very concerned about their situation, to tell the truth. They do some kind of street ministry in New York. Feed the homeless and stuff. Officer McCartney mentioned that Joshua was a retired scientist, fresh off the boat from Germany. But as to *why* they came in the first place . . . "

Michael ran his fingers through his hair. "Hey, I just remembered something else. Right before I had to rush off to the airport for home—I almost missed my plane—Joshua made a subtle reference to needing hope. When it dawned on me to ask him why, he replied, 'to find my father.' Said it was 'a story for another day.'"

Stephanie shrugged. "We'll find out soon enough. One of those missing persons sagas. Sounds intriguing."

"Sure does." Michael stopped short and frowned, then tilted his head. His eyes widened. He started pacing back and forth. "My gosh, I just had the weirdest thought." He rubbed the goosebumps on his arms. "Seems so far-fetched, I can't even say it." He burst out laughing.

"For Pete's sake, Michael, tell me."

"Okay, here goes. Remember the day a foreigner left a message on our answering machine and it got cut off? He was looking for his father. That man sounded exactly like Joshua. Polite. Formal speaking style. German accent. Well, Joshua *himself* just told me he left a message on some machine, but nobody ever called him back." Michael shook his head. "In the message, the father's name was . . . yes . . . *Caleb!* I'm sure of it." He gasped. "Steph, what if it is my Caleb? I'll have to be the one to tell Josh his dad is dead!"

Tender Journey

That day and the next flew by in a whirlwind for Joshua and Anna. In between packing, they did a quick sightseeing tour of New York City. At the Statue of Liberty, they got carried away and misjudged the time. They had to rush back to their room to finish gathering up their belongings. Anna could not make up her mind about which clothes they should wear for the twenty-two-hour ride. She wanted them both to arrive looking "respectable" to their new hosts.

Joshua laughed, urging her to hurry along or they would surely miss the train. "They will not care in the least how we dress," he teased.

"Perhaps not. However, I do." She picked out the garments least likely to wrinkle and laid them out on the bed. Compared to the high fashions she had been seeing displayed in the store windows of New York, she suddenly felt "dowdy" in her somber colors and dated styles. She told Joshua so. He gave her a warm hug, assuring her that to him, with or without clothes, she was a perfect beauty. He reminded her how God clothed the lilies of the field and the birds of the air more gloriously than King Solomon.

"Thank you for the lesson disguised as a compliment," she said, and proceeded to remind him that most women like to look nice. Especially when meeting others for the first time.

Smiling, he patted her head. In a mock patronizing tone, he proclaimed, "How fortunate that we gentlemen concern ourselves with more significant matters!"

She wrinkled her nose and tisked. "Never will you convince me of such nonsense. Men seek a favorable impression, too."

He winked. "Of course we do. Why else would we discuss our professions at the first opportunity? Ah, yes. The need to impress others is universal. It stems from the carnal nature rather than from the spirit, I suppose. Man looks at the outward appearance. God looks at the heart."

"So I am carnal, then, for caring how we dress?"

He shook his head. "If you were to make an idol of it, I would speak up. No. I believe you care most about the condition of your heart. Besides, I am as guilty as you in numerous areas."

"Thank heavens," she exclaimed. "If you were any more spiritual, I fear you would *float* to Florida!" He laughed, which caused her to launch into a soulful drama. "Imagine the sad scenario, love. There I sit, alone and lonely in the confines of my train berth, whilst you drift along on gossamer wings outside my window . . ." She paused for effect. "But . . . we would only need one ticket." They laughed until their sides ached. Finally, she grew serious, quizzing him further about the invitation. "Are you quite certain Michael asked his wife if she also wished us to come?"

Joshua had no idea. Anna's eyebrows rose. "What if Stephanie does not want company right now?" she cried. "How dreadful! She will feel under obligation to hurry about, tidying up the house, buying groceries, readying the guest room . . ."

"No, Michael will tell her that we are not fancy folks."

Anna shook her head and tisked again. "How little you understand women! After so many years as a married man . . ." She gave his cheek a playful pinch and he responded in kind.

"Women can scarcely be understood! However, I do make it my business to know a few things about you, my dear."

"Yes, you do, I must admit. And I love you for it."

"If not for the Lord, remember, I would be an insensitive brute. Hopelessly so. Thank Him, not me."

They embraced one last time in the simple YMCA room that had become their home-away-from-home. Joshua stacked their

445

suitcases on a cart he had borrowed from the front desk, wheeled it out into the hall, and locked the door. As he was checking out, the clerk informed him of a message that she hadn't had time to post on the board. She handed him a folded piece of paper with the name of their pastor's wife. Frowning, Joshua showed it to Anna. His brows raised. He sighed and tightened his jaw as he led the way to the phone.

છ છ છ

Right before dinner, Stephanie remembered that their third MarriageMaker class started at seven o'clock that night. It had been postponed twice due to Eric's bouts with the flu. In a panic, she called the babysitter, who agreed to be there at six-forty. When she told Michael, he flipped. He'd assumed the classes had finished while he was in New York. No, he didn't feel like going anywhere. He intended to do some organizing before the Liebens arrived and also wanted to plan how and when to broach the subject of Caleb to Joshua. But it was the last class and the babysitter was probably on her way already, Stephanie argued. That really irked him. In the middle of their "discussion," Stephen slunk off to his room.

They gave each other the ultra silent treatment most of the way to Eric's office. Michael drove faster than usual, tailgated the cars in front of him and braked hard at stoplights. She sat in her seat with her right hand gripping the armrest and her lips pressed taut together. She squinted her eyes to hold back tears. Finally, she could stand it no longer. She blurted out, "You're driving like a maniac because you know it upsets me."

"Let me drive, will you!"

"You know it scares me when you drive like this. I don't appreciate it one bit."

446

"You don't, huh? Well, tough. I'm the one with 'safe driver' on my license, not you. How do you like them apples?"

"The state doesn't have to ride with you. And right now, you're driving bad. On purpose. Are you trying to get back at me?"

"For what? Being an airhead? Forgetting important appointments on a regular basis? Ruining schedules at the last minute? Nah, why would I be mad about *that!*"

She sniffled. "Just admit that you didn't want to go to counseling or the MarriageMaker class. You did it to appease me. So now you make life miserable before we go. It never fails."

"I make *you* miserable? Hah! I think you have things a little backwards. You have been driving me crazy for months. I can hardly stand it, you get so upset at the drop of a hat. All you care about is the kids—Michelle this and Stephen that."

"Is that so?"

"Yes, and I'm tired of it. You ignore one major fact: we cannot do anything for either of them." Fear, masked by anger, broke through his voice. Stephanie heard only the anger.

Her eyes filled with tears. She fought them with everything in her. She wasn't about to give him the satisfaction of seeing her cry again. "Is that why you never act tender anymore? I can't remember the last time you wanted to be with me."

"As I recall, *you* were the one who filed for divorce." Sarcasm ripped through his words.

"That was several years ago! So now the real truth comes out. You said you forgave me that first night we got back together. Obviously, you didn't mean it if you're bringing it up!"

"I *did* forgive you! I just mentioned it because you said I never want to be with you. I'm to blame for all our problems."

"I'm not saying that and you know it. Yes, I filed, but you may as well have. You know you care more about your work than me.

Always have." With a huff, she added, "Besides, as you recall, I never went through with the divorce."

"What do you want, a medal of honor? You almost destroyed me by what you *did* do. Maybe I need to refresh your memory— papers served right after I got the Golden Eagle Award. Newspaper headlines." His voice grew louder. *"Restraining order . . ."* You humiliated me, big time. If it hadn't been for meeting Caleb, I don't know what I would've done."

"I acted out of hurt. You said you understood that. You had destroyed me slowly for years! Putting me down. Calling me names. Like 'airhead.' Withdrawing from me, emotionally, physi- cally—in every way."

"Me? What about you? You act pretty disinterested yourself. Right before we go to bed or even worse, *in* bed, you bring up how worried you are about everything."

"Maybe I need to talk. You might not, but I do, or I'll explode from the stress! I don't have any idea of the best time to talk to you. Whenever I come up with turns out to be the *wrong* time."

"At least we agree on that point. How do you expect me to get 'romantic,' as you put it? When you sulk or try to rehash the chaos in our life, it doesn't give me the least bit of desire to be close to you." He paused and half-glared at her while he spat out, "And when was the last time you really enjoyed sex, anyway? Half the time, you act like you're bored to death. Since this stuff with the kids, you've even cried when we're together! Before, during, and after. *Don't* think I didn't notice, because I *did!* How do you think that makes *me* feel?"

"Michael, I'm s—"

"You complain that I don't pursue you anymore. Let's turn the tables. When was the last time you pursued me?"

"I don't remember, but—"

"You don't remember because it's been ages. I suppose you expect *me* to take all the responsibility for our sex life. Well, I refuse!"

"Can't you at least say 'love life' instead? It sounds nicer. And no, I don't expect you to take all the responsibility. But the man *should* be the leader—in every area. Spiritually most of all. That might help me feel more secure."

Michael pulled into Dr. Marcos' parking lot at five after seven and squealed the tires as he turned into a parking spot. A number of cars were already there. He scowled. "You know how I despise walking in late. If you hadn't taken so long getting ready and tried to pick a fight the whole way here—"

"*Me?* I rushed around like a nut. You're the one who tried to get me upset and make me feel guilty. So I forgot a minor detail. Big deal. So I worry about the kids! I'm human. *Any* woman with her only two children in jeopardy would be falling apart." She stopped and exhaled loud and hard. "Yeah. Some father *you* are. I think you resent your own children for cramping your sched—"

"*How dare you!*" he shouted. He threw open the car door, lunged out, and slammed the door shut. Within a few seconds, he was halfway to the entrance to Eric's office. Stephanie sat in the front seat for a moment trying to pull herself together. She wanted to slug him. She glanced in the visor mirror to check her makeup. Then she stepped out of the car, slammed her door equally as hard, and headed for the door far behind him. "He'll probably go in without me, just out of spite," she muttered, and ran to catch up. She wanted no one to know they had been fighting, especially before MarriageMaker class.

When they made their way into the room, everyone was already seated in a semi-circle. Michael gave a quick nod of his head in acknowledgment and she managed a fake smile. In spite of

their preoccupation with what had just taken place between them, neither missed hearing Eric's introduction. They sat down in the only two remaining seats, but as far apart as possible. If Eric noticed, he didn't let on. He paused to give them a cheery greeting as they were getting settled. "Hey, Michael and Stephanie. Glad you're with us." Without wasting another moment, he prepared to share a story. They both hoped it would ease the wall of anger between them. "So let's take off once again," Eric said, "on our journey to the land of marital bliss. Pastor and author Chuck Swindoll relates a funny tale on his tape entitled, *'Escape Route for Anxiety Addicts.'*" He glanced down at his paper. "It goes like this:"

A woman lost her husband several months ago. She was lonely and needed someone to talk to. She went to a pet store, told her friend at the pet store about her loneliness, and the pet store owner says, 'Well, I got a great parrot. Let me sell you this parrot. Very expensive parrot. The parrot'll talk your arm off.' So she puts the parrot in a big cage, takes it home and hangs it in the kitchen. It doesn't say a word. One week later she comes back to the store and they say to her, 'How's the parrot?'

'Doesn't say a word.'

The store owner says, 'Well, did ya buy a mirror?'

She said, 'Uh . . . no.'

He said, 'Ya gotta have a mirror. A parrot needs a mirror, and when he sees himself in a mirror, he'll start talking. It'll just kinda prompt him.' So she buys this expensive mirror and hangs it in the cage. A week passes. She comes back—down in the mouth. 'The parrot doesn't talk.'

'Well, did you buy a ladder?'

She says, 'No, I didn't buy a ladder.'

He says, 'You gotta have a ladder. A parrot has to walk up and down, feel comfortable, looks in the mirror, and starts talking. It's only natural.' So she buys the ladder, puts it in the cage, and she waits.

She comes back a week later. She says, 'The bird still doesn't talk.'

He says, 'Well, did you buy a swing?'

She says, 'No, I didn't buy a swing!'

He says, "Ya gotta have a swing. Walks up and down, looks at himself in the mirror, swings a little, starts feeling casual, and he just starts talking.' She gets the swing, puts it in the cage.

A week passes and she comes storming in the store. The guy says, 'Ooh . . . what's wrong?'

She says, 'He died!'

'He *died?* Well, did he say anything before he died?'

She says, 'Yeah, he had one sentence. He said, "Don't they have any *food* down at that store?"'13

Eric could barely finish the punch line before he burst out laughing. His glee caught on, and soon everyone in the class was at least grinning. They waited for the moral of the story they knew would come soon. It did.

"We laugh because we're so much like that silly woman. In the loneliness of our human condition, we seek something, anything, to take away our bone-deep blues. We decide, 'Aha, marriage will do the trick!' After the ceremony, we spend an emotional fortune chasing after fancy mirrors, ladders, and swings to make the relationship work. All to no avail. We're miserable. Our partner is miserable. Neither of us get our real needs met and the marriage drops dead anyway. What went wrong? *We neglected the basics.*

"So tonight, let's talk about the *power* for marriage. Before we go any further, would you pray with me?" Eric closed his Bible and bowed his head. Everyone in the group did the same.

"Lord, thank You for the gift of laughter. How we need more merry-heart medicine to soothe our wounds! We ask You to make Your Word come alive for us tonight and throughout the rest of our lives. From the foundation of the earth, marriage was Your idea. Thank you for revealing Your blueprint to us. For truly, You alone—Father, Son, and Holy Spirit—are *the MarriageMaker.* In Jesus' name I pray, Amen." He opened up his Bible and looked around the room.

"What if there were a way to heat up our 'love quotient' without sizzling our souls in the process?" He scanned the group and smiled. There was a mischievous spark in his eyes. "Then again, I might be talking to the wrong group. I bet your relationships are as cozy warm as you can stand them . . ."

Michael folded his arms across his chest. He maintained a poker face, hoping Eric wouldn't notice him. Stephanie slunk down in her chair. They both heaved a sigh of relief when his gaze fell on Bob and Charmaine Harrington. She glanced at her husband. He stole a quick look at her. They smiled. Colette Chartier put her hand over her mouth and stifled a grin while Paul put his arm around her shoulder. The Latin couple, José and Maria Juarez, clasped hands. Sid and Barbara Brenner stared straight ahead. He cleared his throat.

Eric must have sensed the tension in the air. To loosen things up, he moved over to Sean, the single guy, and pretended to rough up his styled Afro-American hair, then shook his index finger at him in a playful gesture. "You're the exception here, my bachelor friend. My best advice to you is, 'Keep the heat turned down. Wa-a-ay down. Better yet—for now, think *arctic.*"

452

Sean laughed out loud and nodded. He pretended to shiver, then rubbed his arms, and made his teeth chatter. "How's that?"

"Perfect, Sean, perfect! Of course, after the wedding, you and your future bride will have to thaw out. Don't be surprised if that process takes longer than you think. Many Christian couples have a hard time making the transition from, 'No, we better not' to, 'Now we've got God's blessing!'" Even Michael and Stephanie managed a smile on that one. Eric really had a knack for addressing touchy issues.

He moved back to the center of the semi-circle. "I'd better quit fooling around. Marriage is a serious subject in God's eyes and worthy of our most diligent effort." He paused. "Let's delve right into our topic. So far, we discussed the divine *plan* for marriage in session one—*what* it should be like—and the second week, God's *purpose* for marriage. *Why* did He think of the idea in the first place? Tonight, in our third and final session, we're going to look at the *power* for marriage. *How* can we keep our relationships running in tip-top shape over the long haul?

"In the next ten minutes, write down as many points as you can think of—things you've read, heard from someone else or discovered yourself—about how to fuel a marriage. Each of you do your list on your own, please, and when you're done, I'll go around the group at random. Those of you who would like to, can share. Hope you all will."

He reached over to a table behind him to pick up a stack of papers. "Here's a blank *'Marriage Power-Boosters'* form, numbered from one to a hundred, for you to fill in and keep. You have plenty of room to list your own points, plus enough to write down what your classmates say tonight and things you may think of in the future." He glanced around the room. "Anybody need a pen?" No one nodded. "Okay, think fast."

Heads bowed. Stephanie stared at the front wall for several minutes, then picked up her purse, and fished for a pen. Michael swung sideways in his chair away from her and pulled his Mont Blanc out of his shirt pocket. With his paper laid across his Bible for support, he tried to think of something clever. Nothing would come. How could he think about improving their marriage? He was still fuming. Before either of them had written more than one item each, Eric called, *"Time!"*

Three hands went up, Colette's first. Eric called on her. "Tenderness," she said without hesitation. "Treat your loved ones in a kind, gentle way, not mean."

Eric nodded his agreement. "You're so right. The Bible says in Ephesians, *Be kind and compassionate to one another.*"

Colette's husband, Paul, went next. "I chose respect. When my wife looks up to me and acts like she admires me, I feel loved. I want to love her better in return."

"Very important point, Paul. Men need respect from their wives perhaps more than anything else. God made them that way. At the end of Ephesians five, the great passage on marriage, the Apostle Paul tells wives to reverence their husbands. Of course, that follows his command for husbands to love their wives as Christ loves the church. So don't get too smug, men." Eric winked and smiled. "Author and speaker Gary Smalley uses the term 'honoring' those we love—holding them in high esteem, as we would a valuable treasure. In other words, treat them as if they're special, because they are. Who else has a power tip to share?"

Maria Juarez raised her hand. "To me, love means giving to others, and doing for others, even if it costs us something. Love is actions, not just feelings. John 3:16 says, *God so loved the world that He gave His only begotten Son.* That shows us He did something specific and it cost Him very much."

"Great answer, Maria. The Greek word in the New Testament for God's kind of love is *agape*. You're talking about an unselfish love, a willingness to make sacrifices for the benefit of another person." She nodded. Eric added, "Sometimes agape love hurts."

José crossed his legs and piped up, "Maria knows, for sure. She married to me, so she have had very much practice. Back in my more wilder days, I hurted her a lot." He picked at the sole of his dirty tennis shoe where it was pulling away from the fabric. "Love, to us, is sticking with someone through theen and theek—like God does."

José's Latino accent, shabby appearance, and backward quotation touched Stephanie's heart. She tilted her head to study his tanned, weathered face. She sighed when she thought of his attitude toward his wife. Eric nodded approvingly. "You appreciate your wife, José. It shows and God approves. I have a favorite word for the concept you're bringing up. *Commitment.* Many mates don't have a clue what sticking with someone means. Or if they do, they don't act like it. Commitment to the Lord keeps us going when romance runs out."

Michael rubbed the back of his neck to ease the mounting tension. He had no urge to share anything with the group, and wondered if Stephanie did. He refused to look at her.

Eric paused, then raised his eyebrows. "Who wants to go next? Tell us what you think will give a marriage the power to succeed."

Bob Harrington raised his hand. "You've gotta plan time just for each other. Charmaine and I are both so busy, me at the office and her with the kids and volunteer work, that if we don't block off specific times, we never get around to us. Before we know it, a month or two has flown by and we haven't so much as talked in any depth. Even romance takes pre-planning in our household or it never gets squeezed in."

"Excellent point, Bob. For many people, busyness is a kind of emotional anesthesia to numb the pain of an empty life. I know that's not the case with you and Charmaine. You simply operate at the standard pace today. Dr. Dobson, founder of Focus on the Family, says that busyness alone destroys many marriages. Mates have no energy left for a quality relationship." He paused.

Sean raised his hand. "It's kind of like waiting until the end of a pay period to save money. You *want* to do it, but there's never enough left if you don't set some aside the minute you get your paycheck. That's along with the ten percent for the Lord, of course." He frowned and glanced around. "You need the discipline to work out a financial plan together. I've watched money worries destroy so many of my married friends. They ended up divorced, or at the least, hating each other. I've asked the Lord to never let that happen to me."

"And I pray it doesn't, Sean. You're certainly laying some solid groundwork now."

"I'm trying. You know, it seems to me that a couple of sports concepts can apply, too." He sat up and uncrossed his muscle-bound legs. "I've done some reading about the importance of balancing *exertion* with *recovery*. Researchers believe we all need adequate stress to perform at a peak level. But we've got to compensate with sufficient rest and play. 'Pacing' during the exertion phase helps, too. You can't run a marathon at one hundred-yard-dash speed. You've gotta adjust for the long haul."

Eric nodded. "You've competed in enough sporting events to know what you're talking about. I do believe what you're saying applies to marriage—or any endeavor, for that matter. Excellent points, Sean." His eyes scanned the group.

"Who wants to go next? Tell us something you think would power-up marriages."

Michael raised up from his slouched position and tucked his feet under his chair. He decided he may as well offer before Eric put him on the spot. Better to be on the offensive. He glanced at Stephanie for the first time since they arrived. She was picking a piece of lint from her skirt. He shrugged his shoulders, then raised his hand. "Sean mentioned the balance between exertion and rest. I think another balance is crucial—the one between going apart versus coming together. We've all seen two people who cling to each other everywhere they go. Literally. They look like Siamese twins. I don't think that's healthy. Men need to do things with men and women with women, as they did in the bygone days. The men met at the general store to swap hunting stories while the women made quilts at church."

Eric nodded. "Good point, Michael. I wouldn't have thought of that, but you're right about allowing spaces in togetherness. Sometimes absence does make the heart grow fonder. Although you don't want to use distance to avoid solving problems. The length and frequency of those seasons apart will probably vary from couple to couple. Opinions?"

"Oh, sure," Paul interjected. "Each couple needs to compromise on what works best for them. Take us, for instance. Since I left my position as sales manager and started my own business at home, Colette and I see a lot more of each other. She attends a women's Bible study, volunteers at the kids' schools, and plays tennis with a girlfriend. I attend a men's fellowship when I can and go to a fitness center with a buddy. We appreciate our time together more, and don't get overdosed on each other."

Eric nodded. "Good. Somebody else? Let's keep those power-boosters coming."

Sid raised his hand. "Learn to deal with misunderstandings and differences. Little stuff always pops up to create friction

457

between Barbara and me. It doesn't take much, even though we love each other. Like tonight, on our way here. We ran into an old man who needed directions. I gave them in a pretty concise manner and thought I had more than done my duty. Not Barbara. She wanted to go out of our way to lead him to his destination so he wouldn't get lost. But that would have made us late for class. To her, I was heartless. I thought she was being irresponsible."

"Sid, that's a great example. God created men and women so different! The trendy unisex concept doesn't hold water, no matter how hard society blurs dress codes and haircuts. Men usually think in a logical fashion. They strive to 'conquer' goals, however small. Women *feel* more and want to build relationships along the way. They love to 'smell the flowers,' as the old saying goes. And in addition to the challenge of gender, each human being looks at life through a unique set of personality glasses. Without a conscious effort on both sides to understand—and to look through the other person's lenses—we're in for an exhausting trip."

Sid's wife, Barbara, raised her hand. "Boy, do I ever need to watch stuff like . . . choice of words. Tone of voice. Body language. When I start getting critical, demanding, or whiny with Sid, forget it. He responds negatively every time."

Eric nodded. "Ah yes, speaking of the power for marriage, you've stumbled upon the potential ticket to the grand prize. The tongue! But that unruly critter'll get us in a fine fix at the blink of an eye." He looked straight at Barbara. "So you're saying that, after living with Sid for so many years, you know pretty well what will rub him wrong?"

"Oh, yeah. In fact, I could predict it with near one-hundred-percent accuracy."

"Okay, I'm going to ask you a personal question. You can plead the Fifth Amendment if you want. Do you ever go ahead and say what you want anyway? In other words, do you push Sid's buttons on purpose?"

She grimaced and raised her eyebrows. "Guess I do."

"Sid, how about you? Guilty of the same?"

Sid tilted his head and barely nodded.

"Good. You're honest. Let's stop right here for a moment to read from James, chapter three. Sid, would you do the honors?"

He took a deep breath and leafed through his Bible until he reached the right page. "I have the Amplified version, so it might take a while. That all right?"

"Fine with me. Continue through verse ten, if you would." Michael let out a deep sigh, sat up, then leaned back. He and Stephanie had already gone through that passage in a counseling appointment with Eric.

Sid cleared his throat, adjusted his wire-rimmed glasses, and began reading:

> *Not many of you should become teachers [self-constituted censors and reprovers of others], my brethren, for you know that we [teachers] will be judged by a higher standard and with greater severity [than other people]—Thus we assume the greater accountability and the more condemnation. For we all often stumble and fall and offend in many things. And if any one does not offend in speech—never says the wrong things— he is a fully developed character and a perfect man, able to control his whole body and to curb his entire nature. If we set bits in the horses' mouths to make them obey us, we can turn their whole bodies about. Likewise look at the ships, though they are so great and driven by rough winds, they are steered by a very small rudder wherever the impulse of the helmsman determines. Even so the tongue is a little member, and it can*

boast of great things. See how much wood or how great a forest a tiny spark can set ablaze! And the tongue [is] a fire. [The tongue is a] world of wickedness set among our members, contaminating and depraving the whole body and setting on fire the wheel of birth—the cycle of man's nature—being itself ignited by hell (Gehenna). For every kind of beast and bird, of reptile and sea animal, can be tamed and has been tamed by human genius (nature). But the human tongue can be tamed by no man. It is (an undisciplined, irreconcilable) restless evil, full of death-bringing poison. With it we bless the Lord and Father, and with it we curse men who were made in God's likeness! Out of the same mouth come forth blessing and cursing. These things, my brethren, ought not to be so.

Eric nodded at Sid, thanked him, and added, "For emphasis, let me read again, slowly, the second half of verse two and . . . hang on, let me find it . . . the first half of verse eight."

And if any one does not offend in speech—never says the wrong things—he is a fully developed character and a perfect man, able to control his whole body and to curb his entire nature. . . But the human tongue can be tamed by no man.

"Who here in the class has tamed the lion? Could I see your hands?" He waited. "Join the circus! We all say things we shouldn't to each other. That junk comes from the old nature. Every one of us will contend with it until we draw our last breath." Eric looked down for a second and then at each member of the class. "God won't let us off the hook. He expects us to be *quick to hear, slow to speak, slow to anger,* as James one says. That doesn't mean we should avoid frank discussions, either, though.

460

"One couple told me recently that they've been married for thirty years without an argument. Not even a minor disagreement! I would guess that 1) they were fibbing 2) they ate tranquilizers for breakfast or 3) *one* partner never voiced opinions. That poor soul must be churning inside with resentment. Unfulfilled expectations take their toll over time.

"Folks, every marriage requires, on a regular basis, what some experts call '*loving* confrontation.' It may seem like an absurd paradox, but it's not. Constructive communication—using explanatory 'I think/this makes me feel' phrases instead of accusatory 'you did/you never' words—exposes the offending issues. At the appropriate time and place, mind you. For example, if you need to remove a painful splinter from your finger, you go at it when you have a sterilized needle, disinfectant, and a bandage at hand.

"We would do well to have as much respect for our mates as our pinkies. In that case, we wouldn't dredge up painful stuff when our mate is running out the door to an important meeting. Nor at the table in front of children." He smiled. "Nor would we broach a touchy subject in bed as we're preparing for the special date we've planned all week. Save those moments for tender blessings."

Suddenly, he clapped three times, punched the air with his fist and exclaimed, "So then, a marathon marriage is fueled by everything we've mentioned and much more," he assured them. "You guys really did a great job contributing. We could probably compile a list ten feet long, just within this small class. And you have proved my hunch to a tee: we all have a very good concept of love in theory. In practice, not so hot." He paused and looked each member in the eyes. "*Why?* And where do we get the power to change? I'll give you a hint. Nobody has mentioned it yet.

"Let me tell you another story to illustrate my point. Some friends of mine decided they wanted a dog. They already had a cat

461

and a lovebird, but they felt a void in their home without a dog. Over a period of months, they traipsed in and out of pet stores, even answered an ad for American Eskimo puppies. None of those would do. Cute, but too frisky for their mild-mannered cat.

"Late one Friday night at a pet store, a gorgeous, pure-white Bichon puppy stole their hearts. He was small, quiet, gentle. And the best snuggler in the world. A silky-haired masterpiece of canine perfection. Only one problem. He cost over five hundred dollars. They knew they couldn't afford such an extravagance. She cried as they handed him back to the clerk.

"The next day they called the Humane Society to ask if any small dogs had been donated. 'Wish we had some,' he answered. 'Get lots of calls for 'em.'

"'Not a single small one, even full-grown, huh?'

"He paused a minute. 'Well, we did get in one a couple days ago, but he's in pretty rough shape.'

"They could hardly wait until that afternoon. They drove way out in the country to meet little Fluffy. When they saw the scrawny nine-pound mutt, compassion surged. He was a mess! And that was *after* several baths by a volunteer. What should have been soft, white fur was matted and rust-colored from flea infestation. They'd bite. He'd scratch—until he bled. His teeth, what few he had left, had turned brown from a build-up of tartar. Many were loose. His breath . . . well, you can imagine. He cowered and trembled in the back of a cage big enough for a St. Bernard.

"As soon as my friends stepped inside the cage, he inched over, nuzzled, and whined to be held. 'Please don't get your hopes up,' the manager cautioned. 'Probably has heart worms. Treatment's hard on dogs, so we usually put 'em to sleep.'

"My friends left discouraged that day, but couldn't stop thinking about the little fellow. They fought against naming him, just in case he couldn't be adopted. To no avail. The scruffy old mutt named Fluffy had already become Mr. Scruffums to them.

"The next week, they got permission to take him to their own vet for inspection. 'Heart worm test negative!' came the official verdict. Mr. Scruffums—alias Scruffy—was theirs to keep. For free! All he needed was neutering and dental work and housebreaking and grooming and heartworm pills and ear drops and tapeworm medicine and a flea control program . . . Within two weeks, they had invested a near fortune.

"Now, what if *you* discovered an unwanted dog in such bad shape? Could you walk on by? Let's say money were no object. Let's say you had room at home and access to the best veterinary care. Unlimited visits. I don't believe a single one of you could refuse to give that hurting creature what he needed. Yet—*and listen carefully here, class*—what we would do for an animal, we won't do for our mates! We withhold what they need to thrive when we have it within our power to give. Free of charge. Worse still, we dole out daily poison that brings further harm.

"At the altar we acquire, not perfect specimens, but 'shelter rejects.' 'Scratch-and-dent' merchandise. Let's face it: we're *all* a mess in one way or another! God says so in His Word. Mr. and Mrs. Scruffums, every one of us, whether camouflaged or not—and some of us do that quite well. So the real power for marriage starts with facing the truth. We each see ourselves for who we are: sinners rescued by grace. Patients who need healing. Orphans crying for love.

Now for the good news. As Christians, we have unlimited access to that potent medicine. Genuine love is by far the most therapeutic agent ever created. Says the MarriageMaker—alias, the Great Physician—'If love doesn't solve the problem, increase the dose.' Can we dispense it without Him? Not on your life."

Eric paused to take a drink of water, then continued. "You see, only God is love. His very nature demonstrates perfect, unconditional, sacrificial love. Our human nature demonstrates a counterfeit: imperfect, conditional, selfish."

Maria raised her hand. "José and me, we invited the Lord to change our home. It's much better now. But how can we show our friends and family they need Him, too, before it's too late?"

"Mainly, by example," Eric replied. "Let them see the changes in you. If they seek your advice, you might ask them if the atmosphere in their home is what they had in mind when they married. Galatians five, nineteen, through the first part of verse twenty-one describes what life is like without the MarriageMaker in charge." He waited. "Maria, would you read for us?" She flipped through her *Living Bible,* crossed her legs at the ankles, and began:

But when you follow your own wrong inclinations your lives will produce these evil results: impure thoughts, eagerness for lustful pleasure, idolatry, spiritism (that is, encouraging the activity of demons), hatred and fighting, jealousy and anger, constant effort to get the best for yourself, complaints and criticisms, the feeling that everyone else is wrong except those in your own little group—and there will be wrong doctrine, envy, murder, drunkenness, wild parties, and all that sort of thing.

Eric added after she was finished, "Not too appealing, huh? When the marriagebreaker has his way, we reap that kind of rotten harvest. Who will read the next two verses?" He looked around. "Paul, how about you, brother?"

Paul nodded and bent over his NIV Bible to read. *"But the fruit of the Spirit is love, joy, peace, patience, kindness, goodness, faithfulness, gentleness and self-control. Against such things there is no law."*

Eric thanked them both and continued. "Ahh . . . quite a difference. By inspecting the fruit—not only the visible kind, but the stuff in those hidden crevices of the heart—we can know who's in charge. God in His wisdom provides us with a 'testing kit.' If He, the MarriageMaker, is tending the orchard, the wholesome variety results: *love, joy, peace, patience, kindness, goodness, faithfulness, gentleness and self-control.* In fact, let me pause right here and show you an illustration a friend drew for me."

He opened a portable file box on the table behind him, removed a transparency, and placed it on the surface of the overhead projector. When he flipped the switch, the fan motor purred and a full-color drawing of a fruit tree came to life. He used his pen to point out various things as he talked. "Notice this: a few pieces of fruit are tied on with string—to branches half-broken off from the trunk. That's what we could call *fake* fruit. It has no taste, no nourishment, no life. At a casual glance, it looks pretty good."

Pausing, he surveyed the class members. "I would guess that some couples in our church keep their marriages polished to red-apple gloss in public, but in private . . . quite another story. They may fool people. They may even fool themselves. The omniscient Lord knows the truth, and He wants the real thing." Several people squirmed, including Michael and Stephanie.

"God's ideal for us looks more like this." He stopped to point at the illustration. "These genuine fruits come from branches attached to the trunk. Remember the promised land of the Old Testament? It was *loaded* with luscious fruit—clusters of grapes so heavy, two men had to carry them on poles resting on their shoulders. What rich symbolism! By His Spirit, He wants to fill the homes of His children with that kind of blessing!

"From this point, let's go on a treasure hunt. The promised land contained more goodies than fruit. In Exodus three, verse

eight, the Lord described the promised land to Moses as a spacious land *flowing with milk and honey.* It must have been a gorgeous place.

"Stay with me, everybody. This is super. Turn to the romantic love poem for husbands and wives, Song of Solomon. In chapter four, verse eleven, we read, *Thy lips, O my spouse, drop as the honeycomb; honey and milk are under thy tongue* . . . Then in five, one, *I have eaten my honeycomb with my honey; I have drunk my wine with my milk* . . . Amazing! The same visual imagery as the promised land! If married life should be filled with sweetness like that, why on earth does it taste so bitter for countless multitudes? Well, remember the poor, pampered parrot who died of starvation? He had everything but what he needed. Marriages will likewise keel over without proper food. Let's dig deeper.

"Now for the pièce de résistance. Interestingly enough, God uses the same two terms, *milk* and *honey,* to describe *His Word.* It provides the delightful taste of honey and the complete nourishment of mother's milk. That's in Psalm nineteen and First Peter two, if you want to check on me.

"However, there's one more outstanding aspect about the sweet stuff in the promised land . . ." He stopped. "No, let me give you a chance to figure it out. Who knows?" Colette tugged at her skirt and waved her hand with enthusiasm. Eric nodded for her to go ahead. Michael grimaced at her, as if she could do little more than embarrass herself.

"The milk and honey *flowed* . . ." she exclaimed.

"Yes. Very observant, Colette! The verb in Hebrew means 'to flow freely, as water, to overflow, to gush out.' Put two and two together, applying those principles to marriage. Wherever the Spirit-sweetened Word of God is allowed to go unrestricted, you'll find the promised land. Scanty, isolated pockets of Bible verses will not do. We need a virtual river of Word-filled prayer, flowing and reaching into every single aspect of the relationship between a man and a woman. Thereby, we will hear the Creator whisper to us His eternal 'call to Eden.' That very name, by the way, means 'delight, pleasure.' It may take a while for you to really digest the depth of what I'm saying. That's okay. But please, folks, don't let the beauty God intended for His children elude you. You're standing at the gate! Whether or not you enter in and possess the land as your own is your decision. God has done His part.

"In closing, let's see if we can highlight what we've learned in all our classes. Remember the MarriageMaker's ultimate *plan* for marriage we studied the first week?"

"Unity," José called out. "Like Jesus with the Father and the Holy Spirit."

"Good! *Oneness.* His primary *purpose* for that degree of unity?"

Charmaine hesitated, then raised her hand. "So the whole world can see who Jesus is—through us."

"Right. *Witness,* in other words. And where does the super *power* come from to get the job done?"

"The Word and prayer," Bob added.

Eric gave one more nod. "Exactly. *Worship,* we could call it. *Oneness . . . witness . . . worship.* In fact, let's do that together before we dismiss." He asked them to join hands. They sang a chorus and prayed before he invited them to meet for brief fellowship at an all-night restaurant. Everybody planned to go but Michael and Stephanie. They said their goodbyes before heading right home. In the car, they offered tentative apologies to each other for the fight before class and promised to try to do better. A peck on the cheek and a quick hug followed.

❧ Twenty-Seven ❧

ater that evening, Michael was chomping on microwave popcorn while listening to the late news. "Stephanie!" he shouted. "Com'ere!" His face was ashen by the time she reached the den with an armload of clothes to fold.

She took one look at him. "What's wrong?"

"You won't believe it." He shook his head back and forth.

"What? Please don't make me pull the facts out of you."

He pointed at the TV and bowed his head. "There was a bad train wreck at around eight o'clock tonight."

She stared at the piles of twisted metal on the screen and cars dangling off a bridge spanning a deep river gorge. One had caught on the rocks of the gorge walls; several were almost submerged in the water below. With a shudder, she looked back at Michael.

He spoke, his voice barely a whisper, "According to the report, everyone was injured or killed. It was the train . . . Joshua and Anna were on."

"No."

He nodded slowly. "Yes. The Silver Meteor."

"Are you *sure?*"

"Yeah." He sighed long and deep. "It's the one. There are only two Amtrak passenger trains a day from New York. Terrorism is suspected." He buried his face in his hands. "My God, this can't be happening. Not with everything else."

"Michael, I'm so sorry." She sat down beside him on the couch and put her arm around his back.

Finally, he spoke again. "Stephen was really looking forward to having them here . . ."

"I know."

"The poor kid is going to think all there is to life is tragedy."

"It does seem that way sometimes." She paused. "I'm sorry I was so negative when you told me they were coming. Now I feel like a heel."

"It's okay. Forget it."

"But I feel awful for saying those things. That stuff Eric said in class is coming back to haunt me."

"Don't let it," he retorted. "You had nothing to do with the wreck. *I'm* the one who told them to take the train." The edge on his voice sharpened. "Then again, *God* might be sparing them the disappointment of Caleb's death. Which is more than He did for me." He stood up. The chill in his voice made her shiver.

"Why don't you try to find out something more definite?" she urged. "Joshua and Anna could be among the survivors."

He gazed at her, a steel-gray sorrow peering out from his eyes. "Steph, I don't want to deal with it right now. Let's just go to bed." He sounded full of despair, as if this time life had beaten him lower than his ability to rise.

The next morning, he awoke at five o'clock after fighting insomnia most of night. His head was pounding. He eased out of bed to the kitchen, made a pot of coffee, and went to sit in the

study for the first time in months. It had been Caleb's favorite place in the house. He sipped his coffee and stared, dazed, at the incredible collection of books on the shelves around him.

Caleb's well-used Bible was still lying, untouched since his death, on the library table. Michael opened it, but the words blurred on the page. He slapped it shut and broke down, crying like a baby. He just couldn't take any more bad news. None. Stretching out on the loveseat with the Bible in his arms, he fell back asleep.

He awoke to the phone ringing at seven. He had slept in an awkward position with his head on Caleb's Bible. Rubbing his neck, he managed a hoarse, groggy, "Hello."

"Good morning," came a familiar voice on the other end.

Michael shook his head to clear the cobwebs. "Who *is* this?"

"Have you forgotten so soon? Joshua, here."

The wreck flashed across Michael's memory. "*Joshua Lieben?* You mean . . . you didn't take the train last night!"

"No. An urgent message delayed us. Our pastor's wife was taken to the hospital."

Michael's volume jumped several levels. "For Pete's sake, why didn't you tell us as soon as your plans changed?"

"It was quite late when we felt confident enough to leave. I assumed we had ample time to notify you of the adjustment, as we were not due in until this evening." He stopped. "You sound so agitated. Whatever is wrong?"

"You're alive . . ."

"Of course we are. Why do you say such a thing as this?"

"Brother, *that train had a wreck!*"

"No. The one Anna and I were scheduled to take?"

"*Yes.* It was a bad one—about eight o'clock last night. We heard it on the late news."

"Good heavens. We had no idea." Joshua paused to catch his breath. "To think I was concerned about the extra expense for the change of ticket . . . I am thoroughly ashamed of myself."

"*You?* I assumed the worst and had a terrible night! I was the one who recommended the train, remember."

"Michael, my sincerest apologies. The possibility of such an outcome never occurred to me, or I would have phoned you immediately. I simply did not want to bother you at that hour."

"Right. Thanks." Michael clipped his words short. "Well, I'm glad you're okay. So we'll see you when?"

"Tomorrow afternoon at the same time, if that meets with your approval."

"We'll be there."

"Again, I am terribly sorry for any worry we caused you."

"No problem. Man, I'm just glad you're okay."

❧ ❧ ❧

Joshua and Anna arrived at the station in Orlando right on schedule the next afternoon. The reunion turned out much better than Michael expected. If Stephanie still felt reluctant to have company, she hid it well. She played the ideal hostess, making Joshua and Anna feel welcome, and helped to point out famous sights as he drove around the city. He wanted to kiss her for it. Of course, playing tour guide for the Liebens wouldn't overtax anybody a whole lot. They were enthralled by everything they saw. Lake Eola Park—sporting a walking path, sumptuous flower beds, two-seater swan paddleboats, and an open-air concert—delighted them the most.

When they got back in the car, Stephen rode in the back seat with the guests. He took to them so easily—and they to him. It

almost seemed as if they were his grandparents. Clearly, they had a way with children. Michael remembered glancing in the rear-view mirror at the three of them. He found himself smiling inside, amazed that things were going so right for a change. It was the most fun the Nastasis family had had in ages. They all ate until they were stuffed, strolled around Church Street Station until well after dark, and finally headed back to the parking lot at 9:30, tired, but content. No sooner had the car started moving than Stephen fell asleep with his head leaning on Anna's arm.

Once all his passengers had dozed off, Michael settled into the drive on the turnpike and reflected on the last five hours. Yes, he was positive now. Beyond a shadow of a doubt, Joshua was Caleb's son. The resemblance in every way seemed obvious beyond belief. He'd had to try extra hard to keep from staring a hole through him during dinner, and found himself daydreaming about scenarios from the past with his beloved mentor.

Michael now pondered the awesome task before him. When should he broach the subject? How? Wait to see if *Joshua* brought it up? What if he didn't? Just as well. No sense ruining their stay. But how could he just let the poor man go on, hoping against silent hope to find his father? Watch him making a fool of himself writing letters, making phone calls to strangers? It'd be terrible if he discovered the truth through somebody else.

No, Michael had to get Caleb's death out in the open as soon as possible. It was the only fair thing to do. If there were ever sad news about Michelle to hear, *he* would want to know. He would not want anybody withholding it from him for any reason. He could take it like a man. Michael struggled to swallow over the lump in his throat. They would talk at the first opportunity. How he dreaded that moment!

🐦 🐦 🐦

Weeks came and went with no further news from New York about Michelle. To make matters worse, Officer McCartney had resigned from the police department and no one offered to explain why. It was a devastating blow. Would anyone else on the force care as much? Doubtful. At least some center for missing kids was getting involved. Their only other consolation came from the growing bond with the Liebens. Even Stephanie and Anna got along famously. They puttered around the house and yard doing who knows what women could find to do for hours on end. Fine with Michael. It kept her busy. She had less time to nag him.

For some reason, though, he could not bring himself to talk to Joshua about Caleb. Every day he intended to, but something would always stop him. Instead, he walked around with a gnawing feeling of guilt in the pit of his stomach. At night, he slept fitfully and woke up with his jaw clenched.

Stephanie confronted him about living a lie. Once, she went so far as to accuse him of being afraid and jealous. Of what? Michael demanded to know. She suspected he was afraid that Joshua might try to claim his rightful inheritance of the property and jealous of the competition for a place as Caleb's favorite "son." *Ridiculous,* Michael proclaimed. Caleb was dead! And besides, if Joshua ever wanted anything of his father's, he could have it.

Early one Saturday morning, the two men climbed into the Lexus to head for Clermont. At least Michael had a reasonable excuse to get away from the house. He needed to pick up some supplies—a refill cartridge for his fax machine, blank computer disks, and a contact management software program for keeping better track of his clients. Joshua seemed pleased to be invited to go along for the ride. Little did he know. It was *D-day.*

473

Tender Journey

Joshua had no idea anything was up. He displayed his customary delight over little things along the way. In the few seconds at a stop sign, he pointed out a fawn lying in the grass with her legs tucked under her and a butterfly on her nose. Aside from blinking her huge brown eyes once, she didn't even flinch, he noted.

"You are rather quiet today, Michael," he said after several miles of silence.

"Sorry, guess I am. If you've got something you want to talk about, I'm all ears."

"Well . . . I was pondering a quote by Dr. Albert Schweitzer. I daresay I haven't been living up to it of late."

"That I find hard to believe. You have this one memorized, too, I suppose."

"Yes. But I must confess I rediscovered it in one of my journals this morning."

"Ol' Doc was a pretty good guy. Go ahead and tell me." He breathed a sigh of relief that the conversation was taking a side-jaunt for a while. He wasn't ready for the biggie. Not just yet.

Joshua rubbed his hands on his pantslegs, then half-turned in his seat to face Michael while he recited,

> *It is not enough merely to exist. It's not enough to say, "I'm earning enough to support my family. I do my work well. I'm a good father, husband, churchgoer." That is all very well. But you must do something more. Seek always to do some good, somewhere. Every man has to seek his own way to realize his true worth. You must give some time to your fellow man. Even if it's a little thing, do something for those who need help, something for which you get no pay but the privilege of doing it. For remember, you don't live in a world all your own. Your brothers are here, too.*

474

"There's some food for thought there," Michael admitted. "Tell me, though, how do you memorize so much?"

"A tutor coached me. Then, during the war, I further trained myself to forget the trivial and remember the important. It has served me well ever since. Philippians 4:8 says it better than I:

'Finally, brethren, whatsoever things are true, whatsoever things are honest, whatsoever things are just, whatsoever things are pure, whatsoever things are lovely, whatsoever things are of good report; if there be any virtue, and if there be any praise, think on these things.'"

"Josh, you *are* amazing. Just like Ca—" Michael caught himself in the nick of time. "This old friend of mine was always coming up with a gold nugget he had stashed away in his memory bank." Michael turned right onto route 561 from 455, set the cruise control, and glanced at his riding partner. "So how long have you kept a journal?"

"Forty-six years—since the war."

"You're kidding. Every day?"

"Most days, I would say. I try to jot a few notes."

"That's the history of a generation in there, buddy."

"Bits and pieces, yes. But I write not for historical purposes."

Michael frowned. "Why, then?"

"To record my spiritual journey. It helps to keep me honest." With that, Michael winced. Joshua continued, "I wish to know if I have matured over the years and learned from my mistakes."

A sigh came from the driver's side. "Yeah . . ."

Joshua pointed ahead and to the left where a faded, tattered American flag was blowing in the breeze alongside a well-manicured house. "Do you see the flag there, my friend? I hate to say

so, but that disgraceful specimen represents the United States rather well these days." His mood turned pensive. He furrowed his brow and shook his head as he stared out the window. "I have only been here a short while, and already I love this great land as my own. But I have deep concern for her."

"Why?" Michael asked, as he rounded a curve.

"For many years I have studied history," Joshua answered, his voice tinged with sadness. "America shows signs of an 'end state.'"

"Which is?"

"A civilization nearing extinction."

This time Joshua had gone too far. Michael scrunched his face. His surprise, with a hint of ridicule, seeped through his words. "What kind of a gloom-and-doom forecast is that? Militarily, America has the most advanced technology in the world. Economically, we've had our problems, yes. But we're by far as bad off as some countries! Take yours, for one."

"On that front, you win, 'hands down,' as you say."

"And the recession has shown signs of turning around . . ."

"Perhaps. Morally, however, America is almost bankrupt! Throughout history, any civilization which discarded moral values brought about its own demise." Joshua punctured his words with bold hand gestures, as if he were an orator behind a podium.

"Citizens must agree among themselves," he continued, "to abide by a strong moral code—not only for the welfare of individuals and families, but for the welfare of their nation. Relativism, on the other hand, refuses to accept any absolutes. It believes truth to be a chameleon, changeable with the situation and the persons involved. That idea fosters chaos. It makes a people insecure, nonproductive, and self-indulgent." He paused to catch his breath.

His soapbox speech caught Michael off-guard. "Wow, what got *you* so fired up?"

"I suppose the problem is fresh on my mind due to the visit we paid to our pastor before we left the city. He had complications from the beating. Not a soul stopped to help him, Michael! They stared at him and passed on by. We saw other abominable things there in New York, such as I cannot put into words. And I read and watch the news, as well. My heart breaks. Since I was a lad, I have had a tender spot inside for Amer—"

Michael interrupted, pounding his fist on the steering wheel, "Me, too. I've always had a strong patriotic streak. You know what worries *me?* The drift toward statism."

"Forgive me. I am not familiar with that term."

"The belief that government should take care of every human need. The state makes a terrible provider. You'd think communism would have taught us that!" He pointed at Joshua with his index finger and continued, "Government should encourage citizens to be innovative. Self-supporting. And what you said about lack of productivity—I couldn't agree more. The work ethic has almost vanished. There's very little motivation, no accountability . . . many people won't do a lick of hard work if they don't see an immediate payoff. It's not right!" Michael's face had reddened with the force of emotion he was venting.

Joshua lowered his voice. "True. Of course, strong character must be nurtured from a young age." He paused, placing his index finger on his temple. "Per your suggestion, I took the liberty of borrowing your copy of *Reader's Digest* and brought it with me. Interestingly enough, there is an article within about building strong leadership qualities in children."

"Oh?"

"Yes. Let me see . . . what were those three R's? In here this morning I saw them somewhere." He turned to the *Contents* and flipped to the right page.

"When I was growing up," Michael interjected, "'they were Reading, Writing, and 'Rithmatic."

Joshua shook his head, "No, more important than those. Listen, here they are: *respectful* (those who try to understand and abide by the rules); *resourceful* (those who keep trying or who try new ideas when there's a setback); *responsible* (those who face up to the consequences of their actions). Teaching such traits could help to turn the tide. Do you think so?"

"Maybe." Michael fell silent as he thought of how disrespectful and irresponsible his daughter had become. Had they fostered those habits in some way? He sighed. "Fixing one's own family is easier said than done."

Joshua put his hand on his shoulder. "My friend, please forgive me. I should have been more sensitive as to my choice of topics."

"No, it's okay. I've gotta try to forget the past and focus on the future." With an affirming nod to emphasize his decision, Michael pulled into a parking space. Joshua said he preferred to wait in the car. Fifteen minutes later, Michael returned with a bagful of supplies and a sly smile on his face. "I just had an idea, Josh, of a place I *know* you'll enjoy." He turned the keys in the ignition. "S'pose the girls can spare us for a few hours?"

Joshua winked. "And why not?"

"Good. My feelings exactly." They bantered back and forth about current affairs the whole rest of the drive. With each passing moment, Michael's resolve to get around to 'the Caleb issue' weakened. He and Joshua were having too much fun. Soon they were parked in front of a white, pillared building with a life-sized statue of Abraham Lincoln at the entrance.

"Whatever is this!" Joshua exclaimed, his blue eyes sparkling.

"You'll see. Come on in." Giving him a fond pat on the back, Michael led the way into the *White House in Miniature* museum.

❦ ❦ ❦

The midmorning sun warmed the back porch where the two women sat in wicker chairs with bright-colored cushions. For a long time, Stephanie and Anna worked in silence. Each was concentrating on the task in front of her. Anna's small wire-rimmed reading glasses graced the end of her tiny nose as she bent over a project in her lap like one on a mission. With slender, nimble fingers, she threaded a large needle with heavy thread. Then she picked up Joshua's brown sock and stretched it over an egg-shaped object she held in her right hand by the handle.

Stephanie glanced up from her reading just in time to notice Anna pull the sock down over the wooden contraption. The care Anna showed reminded her of Michael when he covered his golf clubs. Her curiosity was piqued. "Anna, what are you doing?"

Smiling, Anna turned and peered over her glasses. She raised her eyebrows in surprise. "You do not know?"

Stephanie shook her head. "I've never seen anything like that gadget. What's it for?"

Anna held up what now looked to be a sock-on-a-stick, along with her needle and thread. Stephanie noticed a hole in the heel of the sock, revealing the smooth, maple-colored wood underneath. "I place it inside Joshua's socks," Anna explained, "in order to repair them. From walking so far, they have holes."

Stephanie wrinkled her nose and squinted. "You *mend* Joshua's socks? How quaint! We just throw ours out and buy new ones. Mending hardly seems worth the trouble."

"Ya, but in Berlin, we learned to be thrifty. There may not be any new socks on the shelves when you want to buy them. Or, there may not be any money in the pocket when you do see them. Better to wear socks with holes mended . . . than feet with no

socks!" She laughed, then winked at Stephanie, and pointed her needle and thread at her. "Furthermore, Joshua feels my love for him when I mend his belongings myself."

Stephanie cleared her throat. "Reminds me of a book I read called *The Five Love Languages*."

"Oh? How so?"

"Well, the author said if you want people to know you love them, you speak their language. Some like you to *do* things for them. Other people need words . . . you know, compliments and encouragement, and others prefer touch, quality time, or gifts. Sounds like Joshua fits in the first category."

"Yes, 'tis true. When I do small kindnesses for my husband, his blue eyes glisten like the fjords of Norway. How can one count the cost of a treasure such as that? Tell me, child, how?"

Stephanie looked away and stared at the pond in the distance. She felt a lump rising in her throat as she tried to remember when she wanted to do something just to please Michael. Or he for her. A little teary-eyed, she glanced back at Anna. "You and Joshua really love each other, don't you?"

"Very much. Over forty-five years married we have been. It seems like yesterday. We have seen terrible suffering, but together? Untold joy."

"I wish I could say that. Michael and I have been drifting further and further apart. And the worst of it is, we feel totally helpless to change it."

"You are Christians, no?" Anna asked, with raised brows.

She sighed. "Sure. Sometimes I wonder, though."

"Can you not pray any time you wish in America? How can you be helpless, child, when you can talk freely to your Father in heaven who loves you? *God is your refuge and strength, **an ever-present help in trouble**.*"

Stephanie looked down and picked at a ragged edge on her thumbnail. She chewed on the outer corner of her bottom lip as her eyes filled with the tears she tried to stifle. "Anna, to tell the truth, I don't find much help from God anymore. I'm like the young widow in First Samuel who gave birth to a son on her deathbed—and named him Ichabod. What a name! *Ichabod. 'The glory of the Lord has departed from us,'* all right. That's how I feel. Like God has deserted my family, lock, stock, and barrel."

Anna lifted her glasses back up on her nose. "It merely appears so. He promised He will never leave you or forsake you. At any moment, prayer opens the door to Him again."

"Prayer is the toughest thing in the world for me sometimes."

"*Toughest?* I do not understand what that means in such a context. Meat can be tough, yes." She chuckled. "And in East Berlin, it was the toughest of all—if you could ever find a morsel in which to place your teeth."

Stephanie managed a half-smile, then proceeded to explain, "'Tough can also mean . . . 'hard to accomplish,' as in a task. I meant that prayer doesn't come easy to me." She paused. "In fact, if I'm honest, I would rather do anything else. And this 'praying at all times' idea bothers me to the max. I know the Bible says it in numerous places, but who can do it? Be realistic. Who on *earth* can pray non-stop? I feel like I'm talking to the walls, or to myself. I don't know which is worse. These days, I can't concentrate on a simple task right in front of me for more than five minutes, let alone talk for hours on end to somebody I can't see."

"I understand. Long ago, I found it easier to read, to put money in the plate, to do 'service' for the Master . . . even easier to go as a missionary far away. I had not developed the habit of prayer; my life reflected spiritual idleness. Joshua taught me that a calm inner spirit requires discipline—of schedule, of body, of

481

mind, of heart—and all discipline is difficult at the first. As great athletes train their bodies, so must we be trained to seek God."

"Oh." She frowned. "I always thought it was supposed to be easy. Like falling off a log . . ."

"Not for most persons. The very act requires humble dependence on the Holy Spirit, which we resist nail and tooth. Outside of prayer, we believe we are in command. In prayer, we realize we are not. That fact causes folks great distress."

Touched by Anna's backwards expression, yet puzzled a bit by her wisdom, Stephanie stopped to ponder what she was saying. She squinted. "So then prayer is kind of like a child eating his Brussels sprouts. He doesn't like them, but he's gotta eat 'em anyway 'cause they're good for him."

That set Anna to giggling so hard she had to put her sock-mending on her lap to dab her eyes. "No, no, no! One should enjoy listening and talking to the Lord. I count it a great privilege."

Stephanie raised her eyebrows. "You do?"

"Of course. Joshua and I discovered this secret together."

"No wonder! Michael won't pray with me at all. He knows how much we both need it, but he finds every excuse imaginable. If he ever does devotions at all anymore, he does them alone. It hurts me."

"I know, dear. Try to overlook his aloofness. Some people struggle to express themselves. Women generally find it easier to speak their minds than men. Do you not think so? Surely, they have a more natural ability to build relationships. And prayer is just that—a relationship of love and intimacy."

"As far as I can tell, Michael doesn't want either, with me *or* God. Like most men, he's too 'busy' with his projects. I refuse to pester him about it anymore." She grabbed the book in her lap with both hands and slapped it against her leg. "I give up!"

"Ah . . . I see." Anna returned to her mending for a short minute. Then she began in a softer tone. "Child, it is far better to lead by gentle example than to prod with the sharp stick of many words. Go on about God's business yourself. Thereby, *you* will change and your husband will change also when he observes your new ways."

Stephanie put her left hand on her hip. "Wait a minute. The Bible says *men* should be spiritual leaders in the home."

Anna nodded. "That is the divine ideal, yes. But they often fall short of the mark, as do we in our role. Thus, if you want your husband to rise to his rightful position, you had best not tell him how to behave. Let the Lord Himself command his attention. Proverbs says, *It is better to dwell in the wilderness, than with a contentious and an angry woman* (21:19)."

"*Men* can be very 'contentious' too, you know."

With a wink, Anna added, "Yes. But the Creator knows how we wives revel in pointing the finger. 'You did this. You did not do that. You ought to have done this. You ought not to have done that.' What happens then? Male pride—ego, do you say—takes offense and we find we have taken a long, hard journey to nowhere. Our message falls on deaf ears. An enormous wall has formed."

"Michael and I sure do have one between us."

Anna gazed into her eyes. "For more than three decades, an impenetrable barrier stood strong in my country. Even that wall came down, did it not? Nothing is too hard for our God."

"I wish I could believe that." Stephanie paused for a long while, then came back with restrained hostility. "Well, when the Lord finally 'commands my husband's attention,' he'll wish he had listened sooner." Her tone took on a sharp edge.

Anna looked down, busying herself with darning Joshua's socks. She tugged on her needle and thread at a faster pace.

 Tender Journey

Without looking at Stephanie, she asked, "Child, you sound as if you would be pleased if Michael suffers a bit. Pray tell, do I detect unforgiveness in your heart?"

"Well, when we first got back together after our separation, he acted like the Lord was the most important thing to him. It didn't last long. I used to really resent him for that. Plus, he cheated on me once—or maybe more—when he was out of town."

"I regret very much that you have endured such pain." Anna's voice softened further. "However . . . this is difficult for me to say, but I believe you may have bitterness toward Michael. Try to forgive him, with the Lord's help."

"I have."

"Perhaps. I am not convinced. Unforgiveness hinders your ability to pray at all—by yourself or with him. Daily, you must eliminate those bad emotions that arise between you. If you do not take care, those hindrances will block the passageways to your heart altogether. So great will be the damage, your relationship will require serious treatment—"

Stephanie smirked. "Yeah, like *bypass* surgery."

"Or a transplant of heart, to be more exact! Please do not allow the sun go down on your wrath."

"I'll try, Anna. But I feel afraid of getting close to him again. I don't want to take that chance."

"I understand your fear." She paused to take a deep breath. "Long ago . . . rather early in our marriage, I hurt Joshua very much. I fell into adultery while he was away on an extended scientific project."

Stephanie gasped. *"You? An affair?"*

"Yes. I am ashamed to admit it."

"I can't even imagine. You of all people. What did Joshua do—ask for a divorce?"

484

"No. He listened while I repented and cried. He offered me forgiveness. But he would not draw me close to him again for many years. In turn, my heart grew hardened toward him. How we were tormented! Such terrible loneliness we felt!" Her green eyes grew moist from the memories.

Stephanie shifted in her seat and set her book on the ground beside her chair. "So how did you get where you are now?"

"You are certain you wish to hear?"

"Well, not if it's too personal . . ."

"No, no. The grace of God intervened. He helped us to see that later or sooner, we both would sin. In ways large or small, obvious or hidden." Anna replaced the mended sock with another one full of holes. Her eyes met Stephanie's. "When Anja died, we came to realize that this life passes too quickly to stay angry. In the wink of an eye, either of us could stand before our Maker."

Stephanie got up, then smoothed her slacks. "Hopefully, not before lunch. I'm starving." Smiling, she glanced at her watch. "The guys should be home soon. In fact, they left hours ago. I wonder where those two characters are . . ." She excused herself and headed for the kitchen to make sandwiches.

A few minutes later, the car honked out front. Within thirty seconds, Joshua and Michael were almost sprinting around the side of the house to the back porch. They were all smiles. "Hello, sweetheart!" Joshua called to Anna as he pulled on the screen door.

"Where's Steph?" asked Michael, holding up a small bag.

"Inside preparing lunch. I'll go find—"

"That's okay. I'll get her." He hurried off, present in hand.

Joshua threw his arms around Anna. "Michael and I visited the most remarkable exhibit I have ever seen. Oh, I cannot wait to see your expression when I take you there!" He handed her his parcel. It was so heavy, she almost dropped it.

"Whatever have you done, you silly man! Today is no special occasion."

"Au contraire, mon amie. Every day with you is a very special occasion. Open your present."

She peeked inside and closed the bag quick, then reopened it and pulled out a large, hardcover book. She glanced up at Joshua before flipping through it, page by colored page. Her eyes grew wider the more she looked. She shook her head back and forth in awe. "This cannot be. A tiny replica of the very White House in Washington?"

Joshua nodded enthusiastically. "Exact. A one-inch-to-one-foot scale model, including the most minute detail of every single room! Decor, oil paintings, working lights . . . Everything."

"Goodness! How can such a feat be possible?"

"Through the dedication of one man and his family. They desired to give a gift to their country. I tell you, Anna, the crafts-manship was magnificent to behold. It took more than thirty years and hundreds of thousands of hours to complete."

She glanced up at him. "You were able to view it?"

"Yes. Just a few miles away in the town of Clermont! I suppose we should have waited to invite you ladies along, and Stephen, too, but Michael and I became engaged in a lively political discus-sion and . . . it just seemed the appropriate thing to do at the moment. Now it seems rather selfish on our part."

Anna motioned with her hands. "No, no, love. Fret not. You men deserve a nice outing now and then."

"Thank you, love." Joshua embraced her again, then stopped short. "I nearly forgot to share with you what touched my heart so. Come with me." He led her over to the porch swing, brushed off the seat for her with his hand, and sat down beside her. "As you know, George Washington was the first President of the United

States. However, he only assisted in designing the White House. He never lived there. The second President—a John Quincy Adams—did, and wrote a message to his wife on the first full day of their residence. It is now carved in the fireplace mantel of the State Dining Room." Joshua flipped to the last page of the book's introduction, reading aloud, "*I pray heaven to bestow the best of blessings on this house, and on all that shall hereafter inhabit it. May none but honest and wise men ever rule under this roof!*"[14]

Anna clapped her hands in glee. "Oh, hallelujah!"

"My sentiments precisely," he replied. He took her hand and bowed his head. "We would add to those immortal words, Mr. Adams, that we stand in agreement with your decree. May your vision come to pass in full measure, not only in the grand old building which belongs to all Americans, but in this, the beautiful home of our new friends . . . and in every home far and near throughout the earth. For as King David prayed in his last song,

> *He that ruleth over men must be just, ruling in the fear of God. And he shall be as the light of the morning, when the sun riseth, even a morning without clouds; as the tender grass springing out of the earth by clear shining after rain.*
> *2 Samuel 23:3,4*

"Oh, Lord God, send revival, we do pray! In Jesus' name. Amen and amen."

❧ Twenty-Eight ❧

When Michael, Stephanie, and Stephen pulled into the church parking lot that Sunday morning just in time for the second service, it was drizzling. Surprisingly, for such a dreary day, the lot was full. Joshua and Anna had stayed home only because she had awakened with a headache. Now the gray sky hung like a pall over everyone in the car. In a subdued voice, Stephanie noted the long walk in the rain and asked if Michael could please drop her and Stephen off under the overhang.

Remembering her ungrateful response to his souvenir gift from the day before, he barked at her about always finding something to complain about. "You think I like getting wet any more than you do? No. We can all walk together as a family." He shoved open his door, stepped out right into a mud puddle and soaked the bottom of his pants' legs. A curse word almost passed his lips but he caught himself. Stephanie stifled a grimace.

He shook his feet and stepped carefully around the puddle to Stephen's door on the back passenger side. Once Stephen was out on dry pavement, he moved to open Stephanie's door and offered a half-hearted hand to help her. She retorted, "I can get out myself, thank you." In response, he glared at her and tapped his fingers on the car roof while she proceeded to rummage around under her seat for something.

She reared up to face him, demanding, *"Why* couldn't you leave the big umbrella in the car like I asked you to? No—you had to go on one of your neatness binges. Now we're going to freeze in the air conditioning . . . We'll be lucky if we don't catch pneumonia!" Without a word, he grabbed Stephen's hand and made a mad dash for shelter just before it started pouring, leaving her to follow behind as fast as she could run in her dress pumps.

Once in the entrance to the sanctuary, they stood there fuming silently while they waited for an usher. All of them were busy seating other latecomers, and someone was already making announcements from the podium. Michael hated walking in anywhere late. He started to scope out the room for a seat himself when he felt a tap on his shoulder. He turned around. Sandy Hawkins stood behind him with a big smile on his face and his hand held out for a handshake. Sandy seemed to get taller and lankier every time they met. The kid was barely in his teens, but he looked much more mature than that. "Mornin', Mr. and Mrs. Nastasis," he offered.

"Hi," Michael forced himself to reply, with barely a hint of friendliness.

Sandy bent at the waist to shake Stephen's hand and said, "Mornin' big guy. You're lookin' *mighty fine* there in them fancy threads—I mean—those fancy threads."

Stephen smiled. "Mom got 'em for me." The light blue shirt with his spiffy navy sport jacket made his eyes even bluer and set off his lightly tanned face.

Sandy looked back at Michael and Stephanie. "Hey, you guys wanna see somethin' neat? Meet ya here after service."

Michael glanced at Stephanie, who raised her eyebrows and shrugged her shoulders. He kicked himself inside. Why had he even consulted her? She couldn't turn Sandy down if her life depended on it. Something about him tugged on her heart-strings every time. Maybe it was his poorly-cut red hair that refused to stay in place or his pale face loaded with freckles.

Maybe it was his clothes, always a size too big or too small and out of style. Michael recognized the suit as one of his own that he hadn't worn in years. Sandy's unironed dress shirt and tie—also several years out of style and mismatched—added to his pitiful appearance. She answered, "Sure, we'll be glad to," before Michael could even nod weakly. He was in no mood for socializing.

An usher finally greeted them and indicated a seat to the right, about half-way up. Without acknowledging Sandy again, they disappeared into the crowd.

The time of praise and worship passed for them almost without notice. They had forgotten their Bibles, and the ones in the pew were in use, so they half-listened to the Scripture being read— something about giving thanks in all circumstances. They sat, numbed. Nothing penetrated. Stephen, meanwhile, doodled pictures in his notebook of well-kept houses and sad-faced people.

Michael was hoping Pastor Fontaine's message of the day would spark something inside him that would keep him going for another week. Ever since he attended the first service with Caleb years before, he had looked forward to hearing his pastor preach. He thought back to that time, then pushed the memory away. He could almost hear Caleb's voice singing in his rich baritone and see his crystal blue eyes winking at him. Lord, how he missed the old guy! If only he had already told Joshua the truth . . .

Pastor Fontaine's voice jolted him from his reverie. "Friends, today marks the beginning of Missions Week, with a theme of,

'*You Can Touch the World.*' Actually, every day should find us fulfilling Jesus' Great Commission to 'go into all the world and
preach the gospel,' shouldn't it? But this week, we give *special
emphasis* to this very important aspect of our faith and honor those
who have laid down their lives for Jesus. As we've been announcing
for some time, a number of exciting events will take place. Be sure
to take a program for all the details.

"Our guest today is Rebecca Atallah, a missionary to Egypt for
over ten years. A friend of mine met her during a recent trip there.
Her testimony so inspired him that he encouraged me to invite her
here to speak. Would you help me give Rebecca a warm Crestview
welcome?"

Michael groaned inwardly as the congregation applauded. He
shifted in his seat, crossed his legs, and sighed. Why couldn't *Pastor*
be preaching? One of his practical messages would sure do a lot to
pull him out of the cloud of unnamed anxiety that was settling
over him. The last thing he wanted to hear about was the misfortunes of the Third World. As far as he could see, his family had
enough misfortunes in the *first* world—their own.

A couple of other people in the congregation must have felt
the same way, but were bold enough to take action. They left
before the woman even started speaking. Michael didn't want to be
that rude. While he was pondering his alternatives, Rebecca
what's-her-name stepped to the microphone. "Thank you very
much, Pastor Fontaine," she said, "for giving me an opportunity to
speak to your people. And God bless each of you, for receiving me
in Christian love today." He grimaced and toyed with the church
newsletter rolled up in his palm.

Rebecca continued, "Some of you might be wondering why
on earth anyone would choose to go to a forsaken Egyptian village.
'Furthermore,' you ask, 'what does that have to do with me?' To

491

answer both questions, I would like to tell you a story about an ordinary man and the humble people he grew to love as his own family. Most importantly, I believe you will gain a new appreciation for your God. May you come to trust Him more than ever in the calamities you face in your own families. He does make the impossible possible."

Clearing her throat, the missionary reached under the podium for a drink of water. Michael took the opportunity to glance at Stephanie with raised eyebrows. She ignored him. Well, maybe the message had something for them, after all. He decided to listen.

"The story began eighteen years ago in Egypt when a layman, lovingly known today as, 'Father Simon,' did a simple act of Christian obedience. He led his garbage boy to Jesus. The young lad found such joy in his new faith that he begged Father Simon, 'Please, sir, would you come and tell my family about Jesus?' So up to the boy's village he went.

"When Father Simon first arrived, he was not a 'father' at all, but a printer by trade. To the residents of the village, however, he soon became a VIP. Through Father Simon's loving heart, this once hopeless people became filled with hope. When I explain their plight, you will understand why.

"You see, the garbage collection system in Egypt is unlike that of the West. Your government generally provides pickup service and pays laborers a good wage for the messy job. In my country, the very poorest families do it. These 'garbage people,' as they are called, live apart from the rest of society—in seven ghetto-like villages—and there, they care for the refuse of a whole nation. I personally met Father Simon in one of those villages where I work. It is the largest one with about seventeen thousand inhabitants.

"Men, women, and children collect garbage each day from everyone's flats or houses throughout the land. I suppose that in itself is not so unusual, but they take the garbage back to their villages and into the only place available—their homes—where they sort it by hand into different piles. Being quite a thrifty group, they feed the biodegradable material to their livestock.

"Nobody in Egypt likes the garbage people. Naturally, when they wear the same clothes they've worn every day working in garbage for the last many years, they smell quite bad. Egyptian society looks down on them with great disdain, even though they provide a most valuable service. They live in utter shame on the lowest rung of the social totem pole.

"When Father Simon first came to the village, these outcasts felt no love except from other garbage collectors next door. They had no hope of a better life. They had no running water, no electricity, no roads, no services of any kind—neither churches nor schools nor clinics nor doctors. Everyone lived in tiny huts built out of scraps of tin scavenged from piles of garbage. Utter despair permeated the town, as the citizens had nothing to live for. Men would go out at night and spend their meager piastros, or pennies, on alcohol and drugs to dull their pain.

"Eighteen years ago, very few of these people had ever heard the Gospel. That was before Father Simon! They received the good news from him with open arms. As he discovered their receptiveness, he was soon making the trek every week to lead them in Bible study. The work grew more and more and in a very short time, many had accepted the Lord as their Savior. How happy they were to have the Gospel of Jesus Christ in their village!

"About a year or two after the first conversions, a growing group of believers in the village realized they needed a church. They approached the Patriarch of the Coptic Orthodox denomination, by far the largest in Egypt. Not only did they ask for the structure, they wanted the layman they called 'Father Simon' to

become their priest. Meanwhile, he had received a vision from the Lord that confirmed he should stay in the village as its spiritual leader. Miraculously, the Patriarch agreed to ordain Father Simon into the ministry—even though he had never attended a day of seminary—and everyone rejoiced. Build a church, they did!

"Then one day Father Simon said to his wife, "These people desperately need to learn to read. How else can they ever read the Bible?" She agreed. Together, they started the first school and, for many years, the only school. The first generation children were studying there when I arrived at the village almost 11 years ago.

"I had the privilege of watching an incredible transformation take place in the garbage people. As they responded to the Gospel, the Lord changed their hearts and their motivation. They now had a reason to live. They knew they were loved. They knew Jesus had a plan for them. The men, instead of carousing and drinking at night, started staying home. They took care of their families and saved their pennies. As a result, the whole appearance of the garbage village changed.

"The people started changing mentally and intellectually as well. They treated their families better and had a new desire to provide an education for their children. Whereas before, no one in the large, extended families could read or write, they decided to send one or two of their children to school. What a great sacrifice that was! They really needed everyone at home to help with the collection and sorting of garbage.

"Other services, such as small medical clinics, began to spring up with the help of outside funding. What a blessing! In the former generation, the infant mortality rate was about 40 percent. That means almost half of the children died of malnutrition and disease before the age of 5. As I visit families in the village today, I find most of them alive and healthy.

"Father Simon and later, Sister Emmanuel, even managed to persuade the government to provide electricity, sewage, and running water for the garbage people. It was indeed a challenge to convince the authorities that our village of seventeen thousand should receive what was commonplace for other cities, but the benefits to our citizens far outweighed the effort.

"In former days, the people used to do almost everything in the courtyard. They sorted garbage and stored it there until recycling time, fed and boarded their animals, and in the same courtyard, cooked, ate, and bathed their children. Sister Emmanuel taught them to separate their business from their personal lives as much as possible. Now if they must handle garbage in the home, they do so on the ground floor and live on the second floor! This one concept has greatly reduced the spread of disease.

"When I arrived at the village eleven years ago, I'd say two-thirds of the population were still living in tiny tin shacks; today, not more than ten to twenty percent. They live in durable, comfortable stone homes.

"Two lone cars parked in the village in those days—mine and Father Simon's. In fact, the road was so bad, I used to park way below the village and walk twenty minutes up the hill to get there. Now the road has improved, again with the help of the government, but primarily through the intervention of Father Simon and Sister Emmanuel. Today, cars come and go, as well as trucks hauling products for recycling. Fewer people must carry loads back and forth on donkey carts. Even taxis travel between the village and the rest of Cairo. So much change in just 11 short years!

"A friend of mine, Lila Kamel, came with me the very first day. We both felt God had called us to volunteer there and together, we began a new adventure. 'Lord,' we prayed, 'please show us what we can do to help.' We hadn't the slightest idea where to start.

 Tender Journey

Although I am a social worker by trade, and Lila has since gone on to earn her doctorate degree in development, neither of us had ever done that kind of missions work before.

"God showed us, step by step. He opened our eyes to an immediate need—a *church* school. Still very disorganized, with only two classes, untrained teachers, very few materials, and no school building (they met in the church balcony), we had our work cut out for us. Again, with the help of a few outside contributions, Father Simon built the school and Lila and I helped train the teachers. We all worked for many years to establish the program. To this day, teachers live in the garbage village, but they do have some education. They understand both the art of teaching and the unique background of their students. This has contributed to their success.

"From the beginning, I devoted myself to making Christian education the foundation of the school. One day each week serves as a kind of Sunday school, where we teach children the Bible. Through the use of audiovisual aids and songs about Jesus, they learn to express their faith in child-like ways. We also show them how to have fun. They do handicrafts and sports—two activities they had never experienced. It was so hard for them to play in the village because they cut their feet on the garbage piled all around. Now they enjoy their own separate playground!

"We then progressed into other areas. I began doing medical visits to the most destitute women and children. Today, teams of native women and girls go with me. A doctor has trained them in basic health care, first aid, and counseling about vaccinations and birth control, while I assist with on-going training and visitation.

"My friend, Lila, did not sit still, either. She went on to build a factory where the women and girls receive training in the use of looms. Their skillful hands weave recycled cloth, donated by large clothing manufacturers, into oven mitts, purses, rugs, and quilts. Beautiful patchwork creations have arrived on the scene of late.

"All these outward changes have come about in the village because Jesus is changing people on the inside. Very few outside groups have had anything to do with the process. Yes, a bit of funding helps and, of course, Father Simon and a few other volunteers have played a part. But most of all, the people themselves wanted to change their situation. They began wanting to live fuller lives because they had fuller hearts. Hearts filled with hope! They realized God had intended them not to be animals, but creatures who reflect the image and imprint of God.

"It fascinates me to see the results just from the first generation of children who learned to read and write in our little church school. They took the Bible back to their families and shared the Gospel with them. Whatever printed materials the children received—whether about heaven or hygiene—they read it at home to their whole extended families. Missionaries in miniature they were. As the children grew up, they also became the first trained leaders in their church.

"One could not have imagined that this fellowship would grow into a community of about 3000 believers. The members themselves run the church for the most part. So often, missionaries remain in charge for a long time, but not here. The garbage people build the churches, do all the teaching and run the social and medical programs. They lead, teach Sunday School, train young men to become deacons, and organize ministry to the poor. (The church has many widows and desperately poor people on their rolls whom they help on a monthly basis.)

Almost 100 percent of these laborers are the grown children from the church school when Lila and I arrived 11 years ago. What a thrill! When I see these girls grown up into young wives

and mothers, my heart leaps for joy. God is raising up eager and able women who want to serve Him by establishing Christian homes.

"Yes, I have learned a great deal from the garbage people—probably more than they have learned from me. As I visit the women, many of whom are still very poor, I would expect to find them depressed. Discouraged. Complaining. Unhappy. They should be that way, it would seem to us, because they live in such grim conditions.

"Many of these women spend every waking hour of every day with all their children hanging on them and needing to be fed while they sift through piles of strangers' stinky garbage. I can assure you that, unlike the West, Egyptians do not put the stuff in nice, clean plastic bags, sorted ahead of time according to dry or wet, bottles or cans, and so forth. No, everything is thrown into one receptacle. That means our villagers constantly cut their hands on broken glass, and must still handle all kinds of waste. You can imagine the implications.

"I literally have to wade through piles to get into the hovels they call home. But when I enter the room—and they often have one room per family—I find people who are not desperate, not in despair, not complaining. I find big smiles. To my greeting of, 'How are you today?' they answer, 'I'm just fine—thank the Lord.' When I ask women who have lost several children how they were able to cope, they say, 'It was very hard, but God was with me. He stood right beside me.' Often they add, 'The priest, his wife, and the church helped me, too.'

"Instead of complaining, instead of wailing and bemoaning their fate, these women praise God. With enthusiasm! Of course, this isn't always the case, but more often than not. Many of them are still desperately poor. Some haven't yet been able to change their outward situation as much as the others, but Jesus lives in their hearts. His light shines in their simple homes. Oh, you can see and feel it! I'm often amazed to find that, after wading through garbage, I have stepped into an immaculate, tidy room. They have the desire to make what little they have reflect the glory of God.

"The garbage people have discovered a wonderful secret few of us in the West have learned. I have, only because I have lived among them for so long. External circumstances do not make us happy or sad. How we *react* and who's standing beside us when we're going through rough times makes the difference. What is inside, or rather I should say, *Who* is inside, gives us joy and peace and hope. He enables us to live through terrible anguish as sane, healthy persons. Incidentally, I see very few signs of mental illness or psychological problems in the village. We need more medical doctors, but not many psychologists. This never ceases to amaze us missionaries.

"Yes, the transformation in the garbage village challenges me to the utmost. It goes against everything my husband and I learned as social workers. Our education taught us to change people's situations to help them to live better, so they can 'go up in the world.' In my casework in the States, for example, I would strive to help my clients get well, gain better insurance coverage—anything to help them manage their diseases or medical problems. Then, as their circumstances improved, I hoped they would have the motivation to change their inner attitudes. Of course, that rarely happens. Jesus said it wouldn't in Mark seven, fifteen). He said, *There is nothing outside the man which going into him can defile him, but the things which proceed out of the man are what defile the man.*

"If you would, ponder something for a moment. We could state Jesus' words in the opposite way—nothing that goes into a person makes him better (save the Scriptures); it's what comes out.

And what comes out has to be from what's *in* him. At best, Jesus lives in his heart, giving him a new life that flows out to others.

"From this miracle within individuals, I have seen an entire village undergo a transformation socially, physically, mentally, and academically. These people changed their outside circumstances because their insides—their hearts, their minds, their attitudes, their motivations—were changed. How? By the presence of the Holy Spirit dwelling in them.

"You see, the Lord uses the meek and not necessarily the wise to improve society. How easy to become overeducated, ineffective servants! Father Simon had little formal training. He didn't go to seminary. I'm sure he never even went to college. He doesn't have any great theories. He *does* believe in the supreme importance of the Gospel. He believes people need to be saved. They need to commit their lives to Jesus Christ and make Him Lord as well as Savior. To that end he busied himself during those first few years before he started tackling social problems. This truth continues to challenge me in my work in the garbage village.

"Father Simon didn't know when he started evangelizing the village that the presence of the Holy Spirit in their midst would alter the entire social fabric. He had no idea. He simply obeyed the Word and preached the Gospel! God took care of the rest.

"Has the Lord finished performing miracles among the dear garbage people? By no means. Now He is even working through them to reach far outside their borders! No one would ever have dreamed such a thing. He led the church to discover buried treasure, in a sense, right within her own land. Not silver or gold. Not oil or anything that would bring material wealth. What, then, you might wonder, did they find? I'll tell you. They discovered a large number of natural caves, some quite small, some huge, which had been used centuries ago and buried ever since. At first glance, one might overlook the value of their quarry. But we can't forget one important point: the ingenious nature of the garbage people. Out of necessity, they were quite accustomed to making something special from nothing.

"They proceeded to design a large underground retreat center. The smaller caves became kitchens, conference rooms, and dining areas, while the larger ones were transformed into meeting halls, even a three-thousand-seat auditorium. Not only can they serve their own village and the Coptic Orthodox Church, but many Christians from all over Cairo and greater parts of Egypt!

"Every Thursday night, believers stream in to take part in Bible studies and song services. Thousands of people from every walk of life gather to hear the Word of God and to worship and praise in Arabic until the very walls reverberate with joy. Praise the Lord! How well He has cared for His humble garbage people! He has performed a miracle for all to behold, and as the Bible promises, He will complete His work until Jesus returns to take us home.

"Through my beloved Egyptian saints, God has proved His Word true in First Corinthians one, twenty-seven to twenty-nine:

> *But God chose the foolish things of the world to shame the wise; God chose the weak things of the world to shame the strong. He chose the lowly things of this world and the despised things—and the things that are not—to nullify the things that are, so that no one may boast before him.*

Rebecca paused for a several seconds, nodded her head once to indicate she had finished and said quietly, "Thank you all. You have been a most gracious audience."

A hush descended over the congregation. They did not applaud. Somehow, to do so would spoil the sacred moment.

Many wiped their eyes; others bowed their heads. Michael and Stephanie watched Pastor Fontaine climb the steps to the pulpit. He asked the worship band to play softly, then addressed his flock with a somber tone.

"Beloved, God has spoken to me loud and clear through our sister's testimony, convicting me of a spirit of ingratitude. I enjoy so many blessings in America that I've grown fat and sassy. And proud. How often I need to be reminded of the way the rest of the world lives! How about you? Humility keeps us appreciative of one primary thing: His saving grace through Jesus Christ. Oh, let us never forget the huge gap between us and God, as well as our common ground with every other human being. The garbage people have humble, thankful hearts, don't they? As a result, the Holy Spirit fills them to overflowing with joy.

"If any of you need to get on your knees before the Lord and ask Him to do a new work in you, please feel free to come down to the altar." He waited for several minutes as dozens of people moved toward the front. As many as could find room knelt. The rest remained standing. Soon, hundreds of all ages were there, Sandy among them. Michael saw him standing at the back of the group, to the right side. He was crying.

Pastor Fontaine spoke again, "I sense that God is calling some of you to the mission field today. Hallelujah! Maybe He has been nudging you for years, but you have never responded. You know who you are. Listen to that still, small voice deep in your heart. Don't worry about the details of when or where or how. Simply say, 'Lord, here I am, send me.'" The pastor took his hankie out of his pants pocket and wiped his eyes. "Tell the Lord that you trust Him with all the details of your life . . ."

He turned to the worship leader and asked if the group could play a song by the late Keith Greene, then explained his request to the congregation. "From the time Keith was born again until he was killed in a plane crash, his soul burned for foreign missions. His gripping music lives on to stir us into action."

Pastor Chip, the youth minister, noticed Sandy crying. He got up from the front pew where he was sitting. He stood behind Sandy, placed his hands gently on the boy's shoulders, and began to pray. Sandy cried harder.

Pastor Fontaine caught a glimpse of the two, his younger colleague and the man-in-the-making who was always willing to help wherever he was needed. Pastor asked from the pulpit, "Sandy, is God doing something special in you?"

Sandy nodded, his head still bowed. He brushed the tears from his eyes, but they kept coming, harder than ever. Pastor Chip handed him a tissue. He blew his nose.

Pastor Fontaine prayed aloud, "Thank you, Father, for the calling You have placed on young Sandy's life." His volume increased. "Oh, God, I pray that you will anoint him mightily with Your Holy Spirit for the work You have for him to do, a work that You have ordained since the foundation of the earth. Thank You, Lord, that he is listening. Thank You, Lord, that he is responding. Thank You for his humble, tender heart, so very precious in Your sight!" Pastor's voice broke. He had to pause to calm the wave of emotion sweeping over him. His hankie came back out of his pocket. He stood speechless for a long moment, swallowing hard. At last, he asked, "Sandy, please come up here and tell us what God is doing in your life today. Would you, son?"

Sandy stood, numb, with his head bowed. Pastor Chip gave his arm a squeeze and whispered something in his ear. Slowly, very slowly, Sandy made his way through the crowd, up the steps to the podium, his eyes glued on Pastor Fontaine all the while. His face, neck and ears were crimson under the mass of freckles.

The pastor helped him get situated to speak into the microphone, something Sandy had never done before. His thin body visibly trembled beneath his baggy hand-me-down suit. When he began to speak, his voice cracked once. He cleared his throat and tried again. "After hearin' about the garbage people, I feel sad 'n glad all at once. Sad 'cause God showed me how I get t'feelin' sorry for myself lotsa times. I don' have no dad—I mean a dad, and most of the other kids do. He died when I was pretty young.

"An' my ma has MS, as some of you know. She can't say nothin' ever, or do nothin' but sit in her wheelchair and get weaker all the time. She can't even come t'church much anymore. In my mind, I complain and whine 'bout that an' a buncha other stuff. Like that we're so poor. I don' have nice, modern-type clothes, so I look weird compared to the other kids. I ride an old, clunker bike everywhere an' have t'park it next to all the bright, shiny racin' bikes with contraptions all over 'em.

"I can't read as good as the other kids, neither. I used to think I was dumb. Now the teachers say I jes' have what they call a learnin' disability. So I feel sorry for myself about *that* sometimes. Nobody knows I been feelin' that way 'cause I smile a lot, but inside it hurts. I feel 'shamed.

"God showed me today that He knows an' understands an' loves me, but He wants me to do better. Much better. He wants me to give up all that sulkin' I do in private 'an 'just trust Him,' as my friend Caleb used t'say. I reckon that sulkin' is the opposite of thankin'—lookin' in instead of lookin' up. He wants me t' look up.

"When I listened to the nice lady tell about the garbage people who are *lots* poorer than Ma 'n I, and they praise God anyway, I felt real guilty. I sure don't have to walk through garbage all day and cut my feet like they do. I don' have to stay home from school to help pick through the stinky junk from mornin' 'til night. I get t'go to a clean place 'n learn, even if it's harder for me. Even if I hate homework. Compared to the garbage people, Ma 'n me live like reg'lar royalty in our little old house.

He took a deep breath. "But I guess all I've talked about so far is feelin' sad hearin' the missionary lady. I felt real glad at the same time. She gave me hope like I haven't had much since Caleb died. You 'member him, don't ya? See, way down in my heart, I always wanted God to use me for somethin' special, like say a missionary. I never told nobody that, 'cept for Caleb Johannsen.

"Most people'd think it was stupid. They'd think, 'Sandy Hawkins? Why, he ain't nothin.' He can't learn no other language. He can't even speak his own too good.' So I can sure understan' how bad the garbage people felt bein' lowest on the totem' pole, an' I figure, if God can use *them* to do His work, as down 'n out as they was—I mean, as they were—He can use me, too! He must have a plan for me. Maybe even t'be a missionary far away. Or here real close. I don't care. I love Jesus so much, either one'd be *jes' fine* with me."

Almost before he finished his last words, Sandy moved from behind the microphone, down the steps, and through the crowd at the altar. His face turned bright red again. He searched for Pastor Chip like a chased rabbit for a hole in the ground. Their eyes met and Chip motioned for him to come sit by him.

A few scattered claps pierced the silence, then a few more, until the whole congregation was applauding and cheering. They rose to their feet in a standing ovation. Sandy almost crawled under the pew. He knitted his eyebrows, bit his fingernail, and squinted at Chip. He had no idea what to do.

Pastor Fontaine had been clapping along. He stopped to speak into the microphone. "Let's give God thanks and praise, for He has spoken to us in a mighty way. And the Lord would say to you,

Tender Journey

Sandy, as he did through Paul to Timothy in First Timothy Four, twelve, *Don't let anyone look down on you because you are young, but set an example for the believers in speech, in life, in love and in purity.* You have indeed set an example for us all. From what I understand, the Lord may already be using you. Isn't that right, Chip?" He looked at Pastor Chip, who nodded. "Brother, why don't you come and tell us about what the youth have been up to lately? Those of you at the altar will probably want to take your seats. You know how Pastor Chip can get when he talks about 'his kids.'"

Chip smiled at Pastor Fontaine's teasing. He straightened his tie and shifted his jacket. He patted Sandy on the knee, then stood up to head to the microphone. Once there, his voice became enthusiastic. "Thanks, Pastor. I'll let the little jab about my long-windedness slide this time. Seriously, I welcome the opportunity to let everyone know what a great group I work with.

"A few months ago, the kids decided to visit the sick and shut-ins. When Sandy first brought up the idea in youth meeting, the other kids weren't too enthused. But after they went one time, they loved it. They really had fun together and felt needed. Once a week, they've gone to hospitals, nursing homes, and private residences, anywhere with somebody who could use a dose of good cheer. It's quite a thing to see. They sing, play the guitar, do skits, read to the patients, or just listen. Some of the kids have even brought their pets to liven things up—where we could get approval, of course. Now, *that* was a sight!

"Another important project Sandy brought to our attention was to distribute flyers about Michelle Nastasis, and to raise more reward money for anyone who provides information leading to her safe return. Some of you may not know that the teenage daughter of a couple in our congregation, Michael and Stephanie Nastasis, disappeared awhile ago. To raise funds, the kids have done chores such as washing cars, mowing lawns, and cleaning. Then they rode around the area on their bikes to post more flyers. I see those neon orange papers everywhere I go."

Pastor Fontaine rubbed Chip on the back. "That's wonderful, just wonderful. Any leads?"

"From what I understand, a girl thought to be her was last seen in New York City, but as yet, she hasn't been found. Local law enforcement is working with the New York Police Department and the National Center for Missing and Exploited Children. Their phone numbers are listed on the flyer, as well as our church office number. We keep praying for a breakthrough."

Michael tightened his lips and clenched his teeth. The family had been trying to *go on* with life as much as possible! Besides, it was humiliating to be in such a position in front of the whole church. What would people think of them? Probably that he and Stephanie must be bad parents to be in such a predicament.

Part of him wanted to lash out for the invasion of their privacy and the imagined criticism. Part of him wanted to weep with gratitude that somebody cared. He showed no emotion. He leaned forward and clasped his hands around one knee. Sensing Stephanie glancing over at him, he stared straight ahead. He heard her take a deep breath, probably to fight back tears. It seemed most of her energy was taken up that way. But maybe there was hope. Greed for the reward money might motivate somebody who knew *something* new to come forward.

He heard Pastor Fontaine mention their names. "Michael and Stephanie, if you're with us today, would you come up and let us pray for you?" They looked at each other at the same time. Michael hated going to the front, but she raised her eyebrows as if to ask if it was okay with him. He shrugged his shoulders. "May as well," he whispered. "Can't hurt now."

Tender Journey

Stephen had fallen asleep with his head on Stephanie's arm. She carefully laid him down on the pew so as not to wake him. He'd had a fitful night. He didn't even stir.

Michael pulled his crisp white cuffs out from the sleeves of his suitcoat. Stephanie smoothed the back of her silk dress. At the last second, she grabbed a couple tissues from her purse. Michael offered his arm to her and they walked down the aisle looking poised and elegant. The pastor summoned the elders of the church to gather around to lay hands on them. The whole congregation joined hands across the aisles. Pastor Fontaine prayed first, then Chip, and the microphone was passed to one of the elders.

The last man, an older, balding gentleman prayed with great intensity. "Oh, Father, grant us a good report on this matter of a missing child. Give Michael and Stephanie and the law enforcement people wisdom every step of the way—who to talk to, where to go, what leads to pursue. Let not a single action be wasted from confusion or strife, but let every step be ordered and established by You. If anyone knows anything, I pray that Your Holy Spirit would prompt that person to notify the authorities soon.

"Precious Lord, give Michael and Stephanie peace, as only You can—freedom from fear, anxiety, and sickness of heart. In Your name, we bind the enemy in this situation. We render Satan powerless by the blood of the Lamb and the word of our testimony. We pray a hedge of angelic protection around Michelle. And Father, please send someone across her path to minister to her, wherever she is. We place her in Your loving care. In the powerful name of Jesus, Amen."

Michael opened his eyes. He shook his head to lessen the light, dizzy feeling. Stephanie breathed deeply. "Thank you all," she whispered. Michael nodded in agreement. The tiny hint of a smile emerged on both faces. They relaxed. It showed on their features.

They walked back to their seats as Pastor Fontaine went to recheck his notes and situate his Bible. "I prepared a message for today," he said, "but I feel impressed to simply give you a sneak preview." He paused to grasp each side of the pulpit with his hands. "We interrupt this program to bring you an emergency broadcast. A nasty criminal is on the loose in our area. He has taken up residence and is holding lives hostage by the scores. The thug's name? *Fear.*

"Interestingly, *the fear of the **Lord** is the beginning of wisdom and knowledge of the holy is understanding*—says Proverbs nine, ten). My message concerns how to capture the fear-*thief*—fear of man, of circumstances, of the future, of the devil. If you think politicians have declared war on crime, just wait. I am declaring war on fear. There's one difference, however. We can win *our* war.

"Throughout the Bible, the Lord provides us hundreds of commands—some say exactly 365, one for every day, though I have never counted them—to fear not, worry not, be anxious for nothing. In light of terror-producing situations such as Michael and Stephanie face in this very hour, and many of you also, how can God make such preposterous statements? He would seem to insult the intelligence of those of us in crisis. Perhaps the Ancient of Days has grown senile over the eons of eternity. Maybe He thinks He created hollow tin men instead of real people with tender hearts, shattered with grief and pain.

"No, beloved. Our gracious God, who is the same yesterday, today, and tomorrow, has not grown the least bit senile. He understands our frame and knows we are dust. But . . . God also knows Himself. Let me repeat that. *God knows Himself!* He does not suffer from an identity crisis or an insecurity complex. God never wrings His hands. He never bites His fingernails. He knows *who* He is . . . and *why* He is . . . and *where* He is going.

509

"Most comforting of all, He wants *us* to know who He is and why He is and where He's going. He wants us to know *Him* so we can find relief from the thief. To aid us in learning how to do that, it might help to study an institution familiar with such matters—a police department. Imagine the best possible kind. What would it be like?

"No doubt, at the top sits a strong man with high principles and deep concern for his men, as well as for the citizens of his community. He does not tolerate bribery, favoritism, brutality, or any such thing in his department. His officers know the law and take great care to abide by it themselves. The chief has trained them to be tough and tender warriors who love their comrades enough to die for them if necessary. But these officers are unusual. They love not only their fellow teammates. Like their chief, they hate crime and love criminals. They understand the difference.

"This ideal police department is well-run—organized, efficient, up-to-date. All instructions are clear and fair. The equipment—from dispatch down to every squad car—is of the highest quality and in proper working order. At a moment's notice, any man in the field can contact headquarters via his two-way radio. Assistance will come rushing to his side from all directions.

"No officer works in isolation. Although every man faces danger, he does not live in constant anxiety. If he does, he will have to step down from the force. No, these officers are cautious, but courageous. The academy trained them well.

"Beloved here with me today . . . heaven is our academy and headquarters. Jesus is our Chief. We, his officers. Do you suppose He will leave us stranded in the line of duty? Never!

"He provides the handcuffs of faith to immobilize the enemy. He has given us clear marching orders and a powerful weapon—His Word. His state-of-the-art Holy Spirit dispatch system never bogs down or malfunctions. His two-way radio, unlimited by time or space, is always open. It's called *prayer.* David Jeremiah says of this wonderful resource, 'Worry puts the world in the context of our needs, but prayer puts our needs in the context of God's greatness.' What a whole new perspective on problems!

"So, saints, with all the help we have at our disposal—our faith in Jesus Christ, His Holy Spirit at work through His Word and our prayers—the old thief doesn't stand a chance in our neck of the woods. *Cast all your cares upon Him, for He cares for you,* first Peter five, seven, tells us. All our cares! That means we can throw the joy bandit in the klink whenever he gets out of hand. Chief Jesus handed us the keys almost two thousand years ago. One question remains. Will we use them?

"Let us close in prayer. 'Heavenly Father, thank You for sending Jesus to prove to us beyond a shadow of a doubt that You love us very much. Help us, I pray, to use the tools you have provided to cope with our fears. Let them not steal one more precious moment until His return. In Jesus' name, Amen.'"

The worship ensemble led the congregation in a last chorus before Pastor Fontaine dismissed the service while Michael shook Stephen to wake him. He had slept through the whole thing, but that wasn't unusual these days. They gave him a few minutes to acclimate himself. He rubbed his eyes, yawned, and stretched his arms out in front of him.

A number of people stopped by to offer sympathy and to say they would pray for Michelle's safety. Michael nodded his tight-lipped thanks. Little did the well-wishers know of the battle their comments incited inside him. His loathing of helplessness made him want to shout at them to go away. Stephanie, however, acted gracious and told them she appreciated their concern. Once done with being polite, they waited in line to leave the church.

Sure enough, Sandy was waiting in the lobby where he said he would be. Michael found himself surprisingly relieved to see him. At least he wouldn't have to face any more ingratiating strangers. He shook Sandy's hand and patted him on the shoulder. "Great job, there, kiddo. You spoke like a pro."

"You sure did," Stephanie added.

Sandy's face lit up. "You really mean it? I didn't act too weird?"

"Not at all," Michael assured him. "They gave you a standing ovation, knucklehead."

Blushing, he replied, "But after I sat down, I 'membered all my stupid mistakes. Then it was too late."

"You did perfect, Sandy," Stephanie said, hugging him. "Nobody in the church could have done it better. Now what was it you wanted to show us, hon? We've got to be getting home for dinner with our company."

"Oh." Disappointed, he paused. "Well, Pastor Chip kinda spilled the beans already. I was jes' excited to show you this." He handed them a photocopy of a bank statement. "Us kids tried to help the reward fund is all . . ."

They glanced at the paper. Almost five thousand dollars had been placed in an escrow account for Michelle.

❧ Twenty-Nine ❧

The drive home from church passed too quickly for Michael. In his gut, he knew now was the time to face *his* fears head-on and tell Joshua about Caleb. His pulse quickened when it struck him that, had Joshua been in the service, he would have heard the name by accident from Sandy! No, Michael couldn't let that happen. He had put it off way too long. It had to come from his own mouth. And yet, he dreaded being the bearer of bad news. Stephanie noted his distracted state as she walked through the front door he held open for her. Stephen, then he, followed her into the house.

"Hello, folks," Joshua greeted them. "How was the service?"

"Pretty good," Stephanie replied. "A missionary told her story and a young neighbor boy was called up to speak. Then pastor gave a short analogy about fear."

"Yeah, sorry you missed it," Michael said, though his heart and thoughts had drifted elsewhere. He loosened his tie.

Stephanie set her purse down on the couch. "How's Anna?"

"Much better, thank you. She is resting since our quiet time."

"I won't bother her, then."

513

"No, it will be fine. She told me she wished to see you when you returned."

"Oh, good." She put her arm over Stephen's shoulder. "As soon as I get a snack for the champ, here, I'll go in and see if Anna needs anything." Guiding Stephen toward the kitchen, she added, "Come on, sweetie. Let's see what we can dig up for you."

Michael sighed. It would have been nice if she had also asked *him* if he wanted anything. He watched them walk away, then asked Joshua, "How about you and me taking a little stroll out back? There's something I've been meaning to talk to you about."

Joshua's eyebrows rose at the last phrase. He smoothed the wrinkles in his pants as he stood up. "Lead on, my friend. It sounds important."

Michael nodded, but maintained his silence until they had turned the corner near Caleb's old pottery shop. With every step he took, the uneasiness mounted. A metallic taste of fear began to creep into his mouth. His entire body felt rigid by the time he stood in front of the door. It was ridiculous. "I haven't brought you back here before now for a number of reasons. Guess it's time, though . . ." He reached out, grasped the rusting latch, and pulled. The door opened with a loud creak. "Sorry. Been meaning to take care of that since C—" Again, he caught himself.

"I will see to the task for you. A drop of oil in the right spot and all will be like new." Joshua's wink and warm smile did the trick for Michael. His tension began to melt.

He stepped inside. A musty smell greeted his nostrils. After fumbling for the light switch to the right, he turned on the light. His breath caught in his throat at the unobstructed view of the room's interior. Dozens of pieces of pottery sat on the shelves in various stages of completion, exactly as Caleb had left them before his accident. They looked like still-life ghosts from the past.

Michael chastised himself for not getting around to cleaning out the unfinished projects. He'd told himself over and over that someday he'd do it. Someday had never arrived. "Come on in," he urged his guest. "I'll tell you a little of the history of this place." Joshua did so, the door closing behind him. "A very special man worked in here. It was he who first told me about Jesus." He fell silent. It seemed like yesterday.

Joshua waited for him to continue, using the few moments to study his surroundings. "You must be quite fond of him."

"Very." Michael closed his eyes for a few seconds, crossed his arms, and shook his bowed head. "Rather, I *was* fond of him. He passed away about four years ago. Fell off a ladder while he was painting a neighbor's house."

"Oh . . . I am so sorry."

"Yeah. Me, too." With that, he finished undoing the knot in his tie and unbuttoned his collar.

"You miss him, I gather . . ."

"A lot. This room reminds me so much of him. We had many talks in here." Tears welled up in Michael's eyes, uninvited. "I can almost hear him speaking. Funny, he had a way of making the Bible come alive to me more than anyone before or since. This shop, for instance, he transformed into an interactive lesson on . . . let me think . . . trusting God. You know—clay vessels being reshaped at the hands of a Master Potter." He motioned toward the potter's wheel.

Nodding, Joshua studied the wheel. "He sounds like someone full of wisdom. With a man such as that, one could barely spend too much time."

Michael pulled the tie loose and draped it around his neck. "That's how I felt. So I met him out here every weekend for months during my separation from Stephanie. See, I ended up

here on a fluke when I was—" He stopped short. He turned to face the older man and looked directly into the blue eyes so like those of his mentor. "Yes, *searching . . .*" He swallowed once. His gaze never wavered from that of his new-found friend. He took a deep breath and reached out to clasp Joshua's shoulder. *"Your* search . . . may be over, as well."

Joshua's brow furrowed. "Over? I do not understand."

Michael almost choked on the lump in his throat. "Joshua, there's no easy way to say what I have to tell you. Believe me, I've wracked my brain trying to think of one."

"Good heavens, what is it, Michael?"

He balled his hands into fists and inhaled again. "I can't tell you." His voice grew raspy with emotion.

"Please. You must."

Exhaling, he said, "Well . . . the father you came to America to find . . ." He waved his arm to encompass the room ". . . and the man I came to love . . . I believe they were one and the same!"

"The *same person?*"

"Yes." He paused long. "By the name of . . . Caleb."

For the first time since Michael had met him, Joshua seemed shaken. "Caleb. Not Jo . . . Johannsen, perchance?" he murmured.

Michael gasped, then nodded. "That's him! *Caleb Johannsen!*"

"I see . . . he is dead then." The corners of Joshua's mouth quivered. Tears glistened in his eyes. "Allow me to sit down for a moment. Have you somepla—?"

"Sure. Let me get the stuff off this stool." He put actions to words and cleared a spot.

Joshua slid onto it immediately. "I . . . am at a loss. All these years, waiting. Hoping. Over? It is too great a shock."

Michael longed to comfort his friend, but he didn't want to make matters worse so he held his peace. He did stand behind him and put both hands on his shoulders. He could feel a tremor coursing through the muscles beneath his hands. Without needing to see Joshua's face, he knew he was weeping. Michael had a sudden desire to flee to the end of the earth, yet he dared not move an inch. Finally, he croaked, "I'm sorry. Lord knows I didn't want to be the one to tell you. I put it off as as long as I could."

"Of course." Joshua's head lowered.

"If it offers any consolation, Caleb was special to everyone, not just to me. In fact, today in church a boy from down the road told the whole congregation what an impact he made on his life."

"That is wonderful." Joshua's shoulders heaved a slow sigh. "It hurts just the same, I must admit. You all had the opportunity to grow to love him . . . I had hoped to do likewise. Now it is impossible." A sob escaped. "I will never feel his embrace, never hear him say, 'I am proud of you, son . . .'"

Michael couldn't remain afar from Joshua's grief a second longer. He rushed around from behind the stool and crouched in front of him. When he saw tears trickling down the lined face, his heart melted. Another dam broke. The pain from old wounds he had pent up inside came bursting forth.

For one of the few times in his adult life, he took an emotional risk. He stood and gently pulled Joshua to his feet. With no thought to what anyone would think, he drew Joshua to him and hugged him. Unashamedly, they wept—one for the loss of the father he would never meet, the other, for the loss of his closest friend, confidante, and mentor too soon taken from him.

Grief ran its course . . . for a season. Sorrow would need more than moments to heal, but they had taken the first steps. "Joshua," Michael said, holding him at arm's length, "for what it's worth, I promise to do my best to tell you about him." He paused. "He was so full of life, so full of God. And you remind me of him. In fact,

517

that was my first clue." Looking straight into those familiar crystal blue eyes streaked red from crying, Michael declared, "Take my word for it. Caleb would be more than proud to have you for a son. He would be honored. I am convinced he must not have known or he would have combed the world to find you."

"I was told that he had no idea. He and my mother were teenagers. They were not allowed to see one another again."

"Bless his heart." Michael shook his head, finishing with the trace of a smile. "Even Caleb . . . had a skeleton in his closet."

Joshua smiled back. Rubbing his eyes with the tips of his fingers, he replied, "As do we all. Many of them."

Michael cleared his throat. He suddenly remembered something that raised his spirits a notch. "Guess what just dawned on me. The guy made a tape before he died! Want to listen to it?"

Seconds passed while Joshua digested what he was saying. "Do you mean . . . hear the sound of his voice?"

Michael nodded.

"Oh, *yes!*" Joshua paused. "But may we save it for later? First I need to be alone with my Anna. And with my Savior. If not for them, I would not have mustered the courage to come this far."

"Sure," Michael said, with a shrug. "Well . . . I'll meet you in the study whenever you're ready."

"Wonderful. Allow us a couple of hours, if you would." He walked over to the potter's wheel, stared at it long and hard, then picked up a dusty, cracked pitcher and rubbed his hands over the cool surface. He pressed it close to his heart. "I have much for which to give thanks, you know."

That statement stunned Michael. His eyes widened. *"Thanks?* You're dealing with the disappointment of a lifetime and you wanna go tell God how much you appreciate it?" He folded his arms. "That's a bit extreme, if you ask me."

"It may seem so. My heart aches, yes. Down way deep like a bad tooth. But at least I needn't wonder any longer whether he went to heaven. You, my friend, have given me assurance that he knew Jesus as his Savior. Nothing matters more!" Michael kept strangely quiet while Joshua went on, "How grateful I am that God led us to America! I can put the entire matter to rest, at last." He stopped and tilted his head. "Think of the miracles required to bring us together from opposite sides of the glo—"

"Yeah, but it seems like God let you down. Why didn't He lead you here a few years earlier while Caleb was still alive, for Pete's sake?" Michael's tone turned stubborn, petulant.

Joshua's eyes met his. "I cannot answer for Him. His ways are not my ways. I know only that my God is faithful. He promises to work all things together for good for those who love Him." He paused. "Will I continue to believe in His lovingkindness when faced with temporary 'evidence' that He cares not? Will I continue to hold fast to the truth that He answers prayer when circumstances appear to call Him a liar? Will I continue to serve Him when He does not give *instant* reward to His servants? I do hope so. For I wish to bring joy to His heart."

Michael stood speechless.

Joshua followed suit a moment, then ventured to ask, "Would you care to hear one of my favorite Bible passages for times such as these?" Michael gave a hesitant nod. Teary-eyed and blinking often, Joshua began to quote from Habakkuk 3:17-19,

Although the fig tree shall not blossom, neither shall fruit be in the vines; the labour of the olive shall fail, and the fields shall yield no meat; the flock shall be cut off from the fold, and there shall be no herd in the stalls: Yet I will rejoice in the Lord, I will joy in the God of my salvation. The Lord God is my

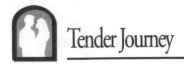

strength, and he will make my feet like hinds' feet, and he will make me to walk upon mine high places.

On that hopeful note, the two men strolled back toward the house as Joshua recounted the incredible events preceding their meeting. The fall of the Berlin Wall. His and Anna's arrival in New York City soon after Michelle's. Their encounter with her in the park and noticing such a detail as her ring. Notifying the authorities about her. Michael's act of heroism in the café and subsequent favor with those same authorities. The hotel operator giving Michael the correct number to his and Anna's room minutes before they were to check out . . .

"And somehow you reached *our* answering machine that one day," Michael added, a new enthusiasm to his tone. "You even got Caleb's first name out before it cut you off. I had no number to call you back, but eventually that, plus your distinctive accent, helped me put two and two together. Amazing." By the time they neared the back door, Michael sensed in himself a more positive attitude. "Josh," he asked, "do you think God brought you here for a reason other than Caleb?"

"Why, yes! To assist you in bringing your daughter home where she belongs," he replied with firm confidence. "That has been and will be the primary focus of our prayers."

Michael's conscience felt pricked. So like Caleb he was. More concerned about somebody else's welfare than his own . . . "Thanks," Michael whispered to him. "Please keep it up."

Joshua responded with a wink, a nod, and a warm pat on the arm, then headed into the house.

Michael considered following him in, but changed his mind and decided to go for a walk. He needed time to sort through his thoughts. Just as he neared the grape arbors, he heard a familiar voice—a panic-stricken voice—shouting, "*Mr. Michael . . . Mr. Michael!*" He whirled around. Sandy was pedaling up the driveway so hard, it seemed his old bike would fall apart under the strain. Perspiration poured down his reddened face and had soaked his hair. When he saw Michael, he dropped his bike and started running toward him almost before the bike hit the ground. "Please let me call Pastor Chip!" he cried. "*Ma's dead! Please . . .*" Then he burst into loud, wailing sobs.

Shocked, Michael made a gallant attempt to lend comfort. He expressed appropriate condolences, even reassurance for the future. He had however, expended the bulk of his sympathy quotient with Joshua. How much crisis care could one male dole out in a span of sixty minutes? "It's going to be okay, Sandy," he said, placing his arm across the boy's shoulders and leading him into the house.

Not a soul stirred. Stephanie must have gone upstairs with Stephen. Josh and Anna were probably in their bedroom "giving thanks." The idea sounded more ludicrous than ever. Try relating *that* theology to a newly-orphaned teen—within hours of his commitment to become a missionary, no less. Nice. God sure had strange ways of dealing with his choice servants.

He located the cordless phone and a box of tissues and handed them both to Sandy. "Do you know Chip's number?" he inquired. Sandy nodded while wiping the back of his arm under his nose. The pink designer tissues went untouched. Michael directed him into the den so he could have some privacy. "On second thought," he said, "better call 911."

Sandy gave him a hurt, confused look. "It's too *late* fer the hospital. She's gone." His eyes filled to the brim with fresh tears.

"An ambulance still comes, son, to take her b—" He had to stop there. The whole process hit too close to home. Was he sitting in on a dress rehearsal? He shivered.

Tender Journey

Fortunately, Chip answered when Sandy called. After their brief conversation, the boy hung up, looking much calmer. "He's comin' right out t'pick me up. He said I can stay fer as long as I want. An' he tol' me not to worry about stuff," Sandy added, "b'cuz 'my church fam'bly'll be there fer me.'"

"Well, that's good." Michael felt somewhat relieved to avoid the responsibility. After seconds of silence, he tried to make small talk and offered Sandy something to eat, which he declined.

"Can I wait here for Pastor Chip, though? It's kinda spooky at th' house by m'self."

"Of course," Michael assured him.

Sandy sat on the couch, leaned forward, and rested his skinny forearms on his knees. He stared downward, as if appraising his out-of-style dress shoes. They did look rather odd with white socks and blue jeans. He must have been in a hurry. After a long, slow sigh, he knitted his brows. "Know what, Mr. Michael?"

"What?"

"It's weird. I'm sad and glad at the same time—like I was when I was hearin' the missionary lady."

"Oh?"

"Yeah. Sad for me an' glad for ma." He sniffed. "She's with my pa . . . and Caleb . . . and the angels . . . and bes' of all, with Jesus. She don' hafta suffer no more, jes' settin' and watchin' life go by. Now, she's really livin'. I'm thankful for that." His weeping started again and subsided.

Michael moved to the couch beside him.

"After this mornin' at church, you can bet old Satan'll try t'wreck my faith. But I ain't gonna let him. No, sir-ee!"

"G-good for you, son," Michael encouraged, dumfounded.

Sandy grew thoughtful and bolder all of a sudden. "Yep. If Hank 'n Dot can keep praisin' God, so can I."

522

Michael tilted his head. The names were vaguely familiar. "Who are Hank and Dot?"

"You don' 'member?"

"Should I?"

"Sure. The folks what tol' the 'thorities about Michelle hitchin' a ride with 'em up north!"

"Oh. The ones in jail for kidnap—"

"That's them. Anyway, Pastor Chip took me t'visit Hank."

Stiffening visibly, Michael asked, "He did?"

"Yep. I begged him. You can *tell* Hank an' Dot love Jesus. They was only tryin' t'help Michelle. He 'n pastor 'n me had a good talk through the glass—'bout how sometimes b'lievers go through hard stuff that don' seem fair at the moment. But God uses it t'help other folks." Sandy sighed. "Hope He'll do that with me."

Michael was formulating a rebuttal when the doorbell rang. It was Chip. He greeted Sandy with a fatherly hug and expressed sincere thanks to Michael for being there for him. Within seconds, it seemed, they disappeared into Chip's van filled with family, leaving Michael feeling a little . . . upstaged? Oh, well, he'd finish his walk.

Grape arbors dotted the landscape. They bore no ripe clusters of fruit this year. Many looked shriveled from lack of irrigation. He felt comforted wandering through them, nevertheless. For over a half an hour, he strolled along the paths he had taken the day he arrived four years earlier. At last he stopped walking. He stooped over to tug a large, thorny weed away from where it had entwined itself around a vine. Rather, *the* vine. The very one Caleb had used to teach him about . . . yeah, dependence. Abiding and all that.

"Ouch!" he yelled, pricking his finger on a thorn. Comfort fled. Anger took its place. Then guilt. "Boy . . . I've let Caleb down," he mumbled, "in more ways than one. He's probably rolling over in his grave." Michael stood straight and stared up at the sky. "So You

 Tender Journey

think I've let You down too, huh? Well, the feeling's mutual."
Blinking hard, he continued, "Maybe I've really been mad at *You*
all this time! In fact, I *know* I have been. Thoroughly ticked off!
And I had a right to be! You took Caleb too soon when You could
have spared him. Not only that, You've dealt my family a *lousy*
hand we didn't deserve!" Red-faced, he went stomping through the
vineyard, swatting at plants, and yanking them out by the roots.

Suddenly—it hit him. He was acting like a spoiled brat.

Young Sandy had done it again! Brought him face-to-face with
his selfish, rotten heart.

And not just Sandy. He was surrounded! Look at Joshua. Here
was Caleb's own flesh and blood *thanking* God. He never even had
a chance to meet his dad, much less spend all those precious hours
in his presence . . .

Michael fell to his knees, then face-down in the dirt beside the
infamous vine. He felt like a total worm. "Lord, it's embarrassing!"
he cried. "Please forgive me. Help me get back on track. Close to
You again—like I was when Caleb was alive . . ." Hot tears of
remorse flowed into the parched soil beneath him.

Finally, he gained the courage to pray, "You know I haven't
done a very good job with my family, either. All the bitterness
that's somehow taken hold in my heart, Lord, do whatever you
have to. Just get it out. I hope it's not too late. In Jesus' name,
Amen."

❧ Thirty ❧

t was a gray, drizzly Thursday afternoon two weeks later when Michelle was caught stealing from an electronics store. The assistant manager immediately called the police. When they frisked her, they also found a rock of crack in her pocket that she didn't know she had.

Screaming for Angel at the top of her lungs, she was handcuffed and shoved into the paddy wagon. She gagged on the heavy smell of sweat, cigarettes, and alcohol permeating the closed-in vehicle. One of the other detainees seated on the bench told her in no uncertain terms to "shut up." He didn't want to hear it.

She was transported to the Midtown South precinct for routine paperwork, then on to Central Booking at Police Plaza, where they took her fingerprints, mug shots, and checked for priors and outstanding warrants. She gave her name as Ashley Nicole Witherton, age 18, address—"homeless."

From there, she joined other prisoners in the paddy wagon to court on Center Street, where she was arraigned before a judge. She had more fingerprints and another mug shot taken, this time with an official DOC number imprinted. Since she had no way of

raising bail, she was remanded back into police custody, leg-shackled onto a daisy chain with a group of inmates, and taken in a prison bus to Rikers Island. Heavily gated windows on board the blue, orange, and white vehicle allowed bare minimum visibility of Bowery Bay and La Guardia airport as they crossed the Buono Bridge.

She stole a few glimpses of the grim, hardened faces around her in the bus. As far as she could tell, most of them didn't seem the least bit agitated by the whole experience. It was incredible. She felt like something between a caged lion and a scared child.

When they got to the Rose M. Singer center for women, they were placed in holding cells. From there, they saw a doctor for a basic exam. "Where is your family?" he asked Michelle, in a foreign accent she could barely understand.

"Don't have one," she retorted, and lied about having lived on the streets for several years. She mentioned that she felt sick to her stomach a lot. He ordered a pregnancy test. Sure enough, it came out positive.

"You don't understand!" she shouted at him. "I'd rather *die* than have a baby!" She seemed so disturbed, he had her placed first in detox and from there, in a suicide watch cell. She refused to eat. Day and night, she worried about her dog and her future.

One day, a nice volunteer who introduced herself as Mary Catherine Thomas stopped by her cell to see if she would like anything to read.

"Yes, ma'am," answered a soft voice from behind the porthole.

"What kind do you like?"

"Mysteries or animal stories are okay."

The woman searched through the titles on the cart and pulled out *Old Yeller* and a Nancy Drew book. "Anything else I can do for you, miss?"

Michelle stared at her rubber flip-flops and cringed at the sight of her own filthy toenails. "Well, there is one thing. I'm worried about my puppy. I don't know what the cops did with Angel when they shoved me into the wagon." When she looked up, her eyes were filled with tears.

"I imagine they'd take her to the ASPCA."

"What's that?" she asked.

"The American Society for the Prevention of Cruelty to Animals. They'll find a good home for her." Michelle's distraught expression must have softened her. She hesitated, then added, "Tell you what. I'll see if I can find out from the arresting officer. Would that make you feel better?"

"Yes, ma'am."

"You don't have any family or friends you can call?"

"No, ma'am." She paused and looked up. "Some foreign lady and her husband tried to help me, but I ran. Wish I could talk to her now."

"Who is she?"

"Said her name was, 'Anna.' She was helping pass out food from this "Mercy" truck on the street."

"I'll see what I can do."

"If you find them, could you give 'em my address here?"

"I'll do my best. You take care, now . . ." She glanced at her clipboard ". . . Miss Witherton."

Michelle sighed and watched her walk away down the hall as far as she could see. She had zero faith that the woman would come through, but it was nice to have someone to talk to for a few minutes. Isolation was driving her stark-raving crazy.

The next afternoon, Mary Catherine came up to her cell with a piece of paper in her hand. "I found out both things for you. Your dog *was* taken to the ASPCA on 110th Street and is still

527

there. I asked that they hold her longer than the usual seven to ten days. They said they'd try, but wouldn't make any promises. The lady you met at the MercyMobile, a volunteer there, her name is Anna Lieben. She and her husband went to Florida for a—"

"Florida?" Michelle broke in.

"Yes, for a visit. The girl at the MercyMobile said the couple specifically asked that if a young girl named either 'Ashley' or 'Michelle' came looking for them, they were to give her the address and phone number where they'd be staying."

"They did?"

"Yes. You must have made quite an impression."

"I, uh . . ." Her thoughts were racing. "She probably felt sorry for me. Anyway, thanks for getting the info." She paused. "Did you tell the ASPCA where I'm at?"

"No. I figured that was your business. Although, to get anywhere, I did have to mention where I was calling from."

"Oh." Her face reddened.

Mary Catherine handed the folded paper to Michelle. "I had to get clearance to give this to you. We're not allowed to pass anything to inmates."

At the mention of "inmates" Michelle cringed. She managed to squeak out a quiet thanks.

Mary Catherine smiled and said, "Glad to do what I can." She studied Michelle's face one last time. "Honey, you sure look young. Kids under sixteen go to the juvenile center, not here to Rikers."

"I'm eighteen," she lied. "Just small for my age." But at this point, what else could she do? If they found out she had used a fake name and ID, she might get in even more trouble.

"Well, you take care," the woman urged. With that, she left.

Five minutes later, a guard came to unlock her cell door. "Movin' to a dorm now," he ordered. "Get your stuff." Michelle grabbed her book and jail-issued toothbrush, cup and regulation manual. The paper with Anna's address was still rolled up in her right hand. Under the guard's close scrutiny, she started to tremble and dropped the toothbrush. It bounced under the bed. He glared at her and told her to hurry up. She got down on her hands and knees to reach the toothbrush, then dropped the books and cup. Grinning, he asked, "Whatsa matter, kid? You nervous?"

She looked up at him, her jaw clenched, and fought tears with all her might. Not a word came out. She was learning already that was best.

He followed her down the catwalk, giving terse instructions as she went. A couple of women peering through the port holes in their cell doors whistled and yelled and called out obscenities as she passed by. Her whole body stiffened. Trying to force her legs to keep moving made her feel like a wooden soldier. It was all she could do to hang on to the few things in her hands.

Finally, the guard stopped in front of another heavy door and waited for the man inside the A station to buzz it open. Michelle stepped inside. Hearing the chilling echo as it clanged shut behind her sent shivers down her spine. Inside, the dormitory wasn't too bad. With rows of single beds, it looked like an army barracks she had seen in the movies. But the *noise!* A deafening chaos greeted her—radios blaring, women talking, yelling, laughing, and swearing. Two girls were giving each other the "high five" sign.

He led her to a bed against the back wall and indicated her locker alongside it. A heavy-set black woman with a head full of tiny braids and a large tattoo on her forearm peered over at her from the next bed.

"Hey," said the woman. "Name's Josie."

"Mine's Mich—Ashley."

"Alias, huh? Don't worry. I got some, too."

Some? Michelle wondered about that, but didn't respond. She took a deep breath as she placed all her worldly possessions inside the locker, then flopped onto the bed, and stretched out on her back. Carefully, she opened the paper Mary Catherine had given her, now a bit damp from clutching it so tight in her clammy hand. She smoothed out the wrinkles and studied the names—Joshua and Anna Lieben.

When she read the next several lines, she sat bolt upright. Her feet swung down to the floor, which bumped her knee on the edge of the metal locker on the way. She read the address again and rubbed her knee. Her breath quickened. Her heart pounded in her chest. It was her home address! *What was going on?*

"What's up, kid?" Josie asked. "Look like you seen a ghost."

Michelle stood up, still massaging the lump that was forming. She paced back and forth in front of the bed, alternately reading the paper and running her hands over her dirty, matted hair. "This is just too weird."

"What?"

She bit her lip. Could she trust Josie? She looked like a hard-core criminal. Besides, they'd just met. But she felt like she would burst if she didn't tell someone. She shook the paper hard and said, *"This.* I think somethin's tryin' to drive me nuts." She paced faster. Suddenly, she found herself admitting to Josie how she had run away, gotten hooked on crack, and met an old foreign couple who had tried to help her. "But I didn't even tell them my real name. And get this—now they're staying at my house!"

The whites of Josie's brown eyes grew bigger. "Man! That be *real* weird."

"They supposedly just came from Germany. How could they meet my parents in Florida?"

Josie shook her head.

She smirked. "My dad probably planted them just to catch me. I should've known he would stop at nothing!"

"If'n he did, mebbe it's 'cause he loves ya."

Her feet stopped pacing and she glared at Josie. "Fat chance. My dad just hates losing."

"That ain't so bad. Nobody comes lookin' for me anymore." Her eyes misted over. "They gave up."

"You been in jail before?"

"Yeah. Too many times t'count. Prison a coupla times."

"Prison? More than once?"

She nodded. "Looks like I be headin' back again, too. When ya can't pay for no big lawyer, y'always gets time. Plenty of it."

Michelle started pacing again. What'd Josie done to get in so much trouble? Better not get this old girl mad. She decided to change the subject. "I really need to talk to that Anna. She said they wanted to help me. Maybe she and her husband could get me outa this dump." She stopped short. "Long as I don't have to see my parents."

"What you got against goin' home, anyway? They beat ya?"

"Nah . . ." She stared at a spider making a web in the corner of the ceiling. "Just yell and nag a lot. Actually, there's somethin' else."

"What?"

Michelle eyed her suspiciously. "Let me put it this way: those stupid rubber things didn't do me any good. I'm pregnant."

Josie burst out laughing. "That all? The projects where I come from, lotsa girls ends up that way."

"Not in my family. It'll ruin the image—big time.

"They famous?"

"Nah. But my dad's got his own business. He's an engineer. They go to church on Sunday 'n stuff—I think they might be on some committee to help run the place by now."

"Uh-oh . . . Not lookin' good. Can't let socialite peoples find out their daughter ain't so perfect . . ."

"Right. If they find out, they'll kill me."

"Jus' for bein' pregnant?"

"Not only that . . . it gets worse." She chewed a hangnail on her third finger for awhile. "I don't know who the father is."

Josie whistled. "Ooh, girl, you been aroun' for such a youngin'. Hookin'?"

Michelle nodded. "And I'm in this dump b'cause I got caught . . . stealing. Couldn't make enough turning tricks! Too many young ones'll sell out for almost nothin.'"

"Bet you wanted some quick cash."

"Yeah. I needed to get high bad. Wouldn't ya know, I had a rock in my pocket the whole time! The cops found it."

"That be bad news, there."

Michelle paused to stare down the rows of beds. "Yeah, well, here I am. And pregnant, no less. Been thinkin' about an abortion. But they cost big."

"Girl, be glad you didn't go through with no 'bortion. I ain't been no lily white, but killin' my unborned chil' sixteen years ago been painin' me bad ever since."

"Why?" Michelle wrinkled her nose. "Nothin' more'n a bunch of cells. I learned in science class that it's not a real person 'til it comes out in the real world."

"You think so, huh? I got somethin' you oughta read."

"No thanks. School days are over for me."

"So was it a man or lady teacher what tol' you that a baby in the womb ain't a person?"

She shook her head. "Man. Professor type."

"Figures. I bet that chump never killed no baby livin' inside him. I has. An' it hurts fo' a long time."

Michelle paused to stare at Josie and digest the last statement. Josie leaned forward. "Y'know that lady with the cart?"

Michelle nodded and pointed to the paperback books she had given her.

"Well, she's been talkin' to me about the Bible. She says God gave us human beins' life from the very firs' moment we was just two specks comin' t'gether. She says He has a special plan for each person—even somebody like me. An' ya know what else the lady says?"

Michelle shrugged and pretended nonchalance.

"She says stuff like shame an' hurt an' bitterness down inside makes a body keep destroyin' hisself, 'long with any good he be wantin' t'do in life. Kinda t'prove he's as bad as he an' ever'body thinks he be."

"You're talking in circles, Josie."

"I ain't. But maybe it don't sound as plain as when she says it." She shifted positions on the bed. "Now, I ain't sayin' I b'lieved all the way yet, but somethin' tells me what she's says 'bout killin' babies is true. For a long time, I been havin' the nightmares and sorry feelins' t'prove it."

"Well, I'm not so sentimental. And I don't have much choice. I'm too young to get tied down with a kid."

"Mebbe. But some folks can't make no babies. They try 'n try 'n nothin' works. They be cryin' their eyes out over it. You can let yours be borned an' give it to somewheres that knows folks who be wantin' a baby."

"Just as long as my parents don't find out I'm pregnant. That's all I care about."

Josie crossed her ample arms. "You wanna end up like me—in an' outa prison 'til you be old an' wore out?"

She smirked. "Not really."

"Then wise up. A pretty thing like you'd get worked over good in the big joint. So you better get yo'self back home. Quick."

"You crazy? My dad will yell and my mom'll cry. From now 'til I croak, I'll hear, *'How could you do this to us?'*"

"I sees what ya mean." Josie grimaced and paused. "Well . . . why don't ya write those nice people stayin' wif your folks?"

"How can I? The jail makes us put our name on the outside of the envelope. My mom'd get suspicious even if she saw the fake name. She knows my writing."

Josie cocked her head. She studied the spider, who was dropping down from the ceiling on a strand of web. "How 'bout . . . if *I* write the envelope to those people? Inside, I could put a note of interduction. That way they would get yo' letter an' nobody else 'spects a thing."

"Josie, you're pretty smart."

"'Sperience—that's all."

Michelle thought for awhile, then knit her brows. "Wait. What good would that do? They're probably in cahoots together."

"Mebbe. On the other han', maybe those old folks'd run a little interference—if y'knows what I means."

Michelle smiled. "Yeah . . . maybe they would. I could use it."

That night, Josie decided to attend chapel service, for lack of anything better to do. She invited Michelle to go along, reminding her that the guests were supposed to come from a local church with music and skits. "Maybe even cookies, if we're lucky. It sure beats sittin' in here," she urged. Michelle declined with a flat, "I'll pass."

A guard came to gather up all the women going to chapel. Josie turned around to invite Michelle one last time, but she was already engrossed in a book. Instead, Josie tossed a folded piece of paper onto the foot of Michelle's bed. It went unnoticed. Or to be more accurate, ignored.

About an hour after Josie left, Mary Catherine stopped by with the cart of books. She seemed a little uneasy, as if she was having trouble finding the right words. She cleared her throat. "Ashley, the ASPCA returned my call."

Michelle sat up on her bed, clutching the side with her small, slender hands. "Don't tell me they gave Angel away already!"

"No . . ."

"Then what?"

"Well, she—"

"What?" She bolted to her feet.

"Got hit by a car."

"No! She did not!" Panic struck her tiny features.

Mary Catherine shook her head slowly. "It's true."

"Is she hurt bad?"

"She's unconscious. She has several broken bones and internal bleeding."

"They won't put her to sleep—will they?"

Mary Catherine shrugged and bit her top lip. "Treatment would be very expensive."

"No! Oh, please don't let them put her to sleep. *Please . . .*"

"I have no control over that. If I had the money, I would pay it myself." She placed her hand on Michelle's head and gave it a pat. "I'm very sorry, dear," she said, kindness filling her voice.

What good did that do? Slowly, Michelle turned away and shuffled over to her bed. With Mary Catherine still standing there, she crawled in, curled up on her side with her face to the wall, and pulled the covers over her head. Her muffled sobs drowned out the sound of the squeaky cart wheels as the woman moved on down through the dorm.

A while later, Josie came back from chapel service. "Ashley Nicole, wake up," she whispered. "I got somethin' t'tell ya." No movement. "It's 'portant." Josie started swaying and humming, "Amazing Grace." When she heard whimpers, she stopped, walked over to Michelle, and crouched down. "Whatsa matter, girl?"

Michelle shook her head and pulled the covers up further.

"What's up?"

After several minutes, Michelle turned over and peeked out from the covers. Her eyes were red and puffy underneath. In a nasal tone she answered, "Mary gave me bad news." She stopped to blow her nose. "My little dog got hit by a car."

"Didn't know you had no dog."

"Yeah. She came up to me in the park one night. I named her Angel." She sniffed long and loud.

"What a purty name."

"She was my best friend. I loved her so much . . . Mary said the cops took her to the ASPCA."

"So how'd she get hit?"

"I don't know. Somehow ran out in front of a car. She's not dead yet, but almost."

"Any hope?"

"Nah. My luck, they'll have to put her to sleep. I sure don't have any money."

"I'm sorry, girl."

"Stuff like this always happens to me. I finally find something that makes me happy and bam—it's gone! If there's a God, He must get a real kick out of knockin' the wind out of people."

"God ain't that way. I don' know much about the Bible, but I knows He loves people very much—'nuf to die for 'em. The devil's de one who likes to see folks hurtin'." She took a deep breath. "I was wantin' t'tell ya somethin', but firs' lemme show ya this poem

536

they gave us. A guy on death row in Texas s'pposively wrote it." She unfolded a piece of paper and handed it to Michelle to read:

"SCORNED, TORN, AND YET REBORN!!!"

"You spilled your milk, you rotten brat!"
Stepfather's slap was not a pat.
The angry words that spewed from his ire,
Hurt far worse than my hands in fire.
My tender buttocks black and blue,
Had been beaten with Stepfather's shoe.
Now my head hung low trying to disguise,
Tears that flowed from blackened eyes.
"You'll regret the day you were born!!!"
Stepfather's voice yelled with scorn.
"Now, get out of here and don't return,"
"Or I'll use my fists and then you'll learn!!!"
So with a sack of clothes and nothing more,
This child left out the front hall door.
Wounded and scared, I trudged the road,
My pitiful bag such an awesome load.
Just thirteen, 'Oh, such a fragile age?'
Yet just another chapter, another page.
From a life racked with pain and woe,
As far back as my thoughts would go.
I saw love as just another word,
It's demonstration had never occurred!
Remembering no hugs, no tender phrase,
No gentle or grateful words of praise.

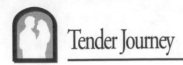
As thoughts drift through those fragile years,
John Moody kneels by his bunk in tears.
"Forgive me, Lord, for this rage inside,"
"It feels better to expel it before I die."
"Now with my soul battered to the bone,"
"I feel there is no way I can atone."
"How can I love, when I've suffered such hate?"
"And is eternal Hell my only fate?"
"They say I've killed of God's creation,"
"Yet our government kills as a Nation???"
"This leaves us all Lord so confused,"
"When we grow up in life so abused!"
"And Lord, I know, had I kept you in my life?"
"I would have conquered all my strife!"
"Please, if you hear a child cry into the night,"
"Woeful cries of pain, or scared cries of fright,"
"Please, Please, Dear Lord, go to it's aide,"
"For PEOPLE'S sins, I've known and and paid."
"And Please Lord, heal this heart so defiled,"
"Help me to mend from that broken child."
"Because in You there is a true FATHER'S LOVE,
"THAT EMBRACES ME WITH TENDER ARMS FROM ABOVE!!!"

WRITTEN BY JOHN GLENN MOODY, #933 /
ELLIS I UNIT / HUNTSVILLE, TEXAS / 77343
INSPIRED BY GOD!!![15]

Michelle sat up, stunned. She shook her head from side to side. "Wow. I never went through stuff like that."

Josie continued, *"I* did. The poem coulda been my story, 'cept addin' sex abuse to it."

"Really? You mean . . .?"

"Uh-huh. By the time I got to a foster fam'ly, I wasn't worth nothin'. I kept gettin' in trouble. At chapel t'night I gave in an' a'cepted Jesus as my Savior. Been runnin' all my life, but I fin'ly just got down on my knees an' did it. Man, it feels so *good!"*

Michelle stared at her quizzically. She did look different, somehow. Softer, maybe? Her brown eyes were shinier. Her mouth turned up at the corners. In fact, she could hardly stop smiling. Her white teeth gleamed in contrast to her chestnut-colored skin.

Josie paced in front of the bed. The sound of her tight jeans rubbing together accompanied her heavy steps. "Preacher t'night said God has His special ways of lettin' us get ourselves all boxed in a corner. Not 'cause He don't love us, but 'cause He do."

"How do you figure?"

"He be needin' t'break our pride enough t'get through to us with His love. See . . .you be boxed in, all right. B'sides bein' locked up, you got a hurt critter you loves real bad, an' no way t'help. You might could save yo' dog and yo'self— firs' by gettin' on yo' knees and secon', by callin' home."

"No way!"

"Then Angel gots no chance."

"Wait a minute. You don't have to put it like it's my fault!"

"I ain't. Just sayin' it be yo' choice."

"Yes, you're sayin' it's my fault!" She was shouting now. "You're tryin' to make me feel guilty. I feel bad enough already!" She propped herself back on her elbows.

"Am not tryin'-!"

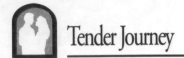

"You are, too! And I think it's pretty slimy . . ." She swung her legs around and dropped her feet to the floor. Her book fell off the bed, knocking over her full cup of water. She fished the book out of the puddle, then let the whole damp mess drop with a splat. Tears streamed down her cheeks and joined the puddle.

Josie stopped beside her. "Didn't mean t'hurt yo' feelins'. I was just tryin' t'keep ya from wastin' yo' life—like I has." She picked up the paperback Bible she had received that night and walked over to talk to another girl a few feet away who had one just like it. Soon the two of them were jabbering a mile a minute about the service.

Michelle followed the girls with her eyes, then plopped down on her bed, put her head in her hands, and cried harder. For a long time, she kept it up until she finally fell asleep . . . clutching her pillow under her arm like a teddy bear.

❧ *Thirty-One* ❧

The next morning before most of the dorm was awake, Josie's insistent voice jarred Michelle out of a light sleep. "Girl," she said, "you 'spect me t'b'lieve that mutt of yours jus' come up to you outa the clear blue? Sure you didn' steal 'er?"

Michelle nodded and yawned, rubbing her eyes. *"No way!* I was sleeping down by the pond in Central Park when I heard her whine. So I called to her and she came up and started licking me all over my face. She wasn't wearing a collar "

"Okay. If you says so." Josie winked.

"Wait. I wouldn't lie about that. As soon as I got back down under the blanket, she snuggled right up to me and fell asleep. We've been stuck together like glue ever since." She frowned. "Well, 'til I got sent here."

Frowning herself, Josie asked, "That dog didn' know you from Adam's house cat. How come she be trustin' you so much?"

Michelle stopped, tilted her head and said, "Don't know. Took a chance, I guess."

"An' you wouldn' hurt her for nothin', would ya?"

"That's a stupid question. 'Course not."

Josie maneuvered her heavy frame around to push herself off the bed. She paced back and forth, then turned to face Michelle straight on. "Well, I was thinkin' . . . Mebbe you oughta take a chance on God . . . like Angel did with you."

Michelle stared at the floor. She looked at the spider, who had crawled back into the center of her web. She caught a glimpse of her book, now wrinkled from getting wet the night before. Then she remembered Angel at the shelter—near dead, if she wasn't already. "Takin' a chance didn't do my dog much good," she answered quietly.

"Don' know 'bout that. Was she hungry when you found 'er?"

"Starvin'. She devoured everything in sight—including all my food."

"Did you play wif her an' give her hugs?"

Michelle tilted her head. Smiling a bit, she said, "Yeah, a bunch. Sometimes we rolled around in the grass for hours." She paused to think. "Why are you asking so many questions? Trying to make me feel bad again?"

"Nope. Makin' a point. Angel had a lot mo' than she had b'fo' she foun' you. You did d'bes' wif what you had. Well, preacher said God do d'bes' for us wif what He have, too. But He be havin' lots more. He owns everything in the whole worl'!" She started humming again and soon, *"He's Got the Whole World in His Hands"* broke forth in a rich, resonant voice. The melody seemed to just flow out of Josie—like a mountain stream tumbling up and down over weather-worn rocks.

Michelle sat up and leaned forward. She hadn't heard a voice like that in her whole life.

When Josie got to the verse about the "little bitty baby," she stopped to wipe her eyes. "I never knew fo' pos'tive if mine was a boy or girl, but I gots a feelin' she was a little girl."

"Why didn't you just have more kids if you like them so much? It's pretty simple."

"Nope, it ain't."

"How come?"

"Hurt m'self permanent."

"How?"

"Kilt her with a coat hanger . . ."

Michelle grimaced. *"Yuk! Shut up!"*

"You think them be hard words, girl? You musta not read that story. I put it on yo' bed b'fo' chapel."

"No, I didn't feel like it." She fished around among the covers, then spotted something on the floor next to the bed. "This?" she asked, as she came up holding two pieces of paper.

A nod indicated the affirmative. "Read it, starting wif the beginnin'. A nurse named Kathy done wrote it. I had to look up some words."

"Not me. I get straight A's in English."

"Oh." Josie looked down at her nails for a long moment. "It be easy fo' you then."

Slowly Michelle unfolded the paper. The title, *When Lilacs Bloomed,"* caught her attention. One of her favorite flowers . . .

The early morning sun was already warming the earth on a lovely spring day in 1973. The city of Rochester, New York, was preparing for its annual Lilac Festival, and the scent of hundreds of fragrant bushes filled the air. Birds chorused as background to my own humming as I walked across the park to the hospital.

I bubbled with anticipation of the day: I was scheduled to observe a Cesarean birth, and I smiled at the thought. A junior-year nursing student, I was spending my first week

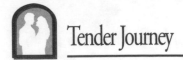

on a hospital maternity floor. Although I had already witnessed several births that week, the privilege of being present as a newborn drew its first breath left me amazed and
hungry for more.

Michelle set the paper down and stared at Josie. Her eyes narrowed. "I don't wanna read this."

"Read it anyway. You needs to."

"What? You can't make me!" Her hands sprung to her hips.

"Well, I'm a who' lot bigger than you, so I *could* make you.
But I won'." She stroked her chin. "I'd jus' quit watchin' out fo' yo'
little hide in here. An' if any of these dikes gets a hankerin' fo' you,
you be fendin fo' yo'sef, chil' . . ."

Michelle glanced around the dorm, back at Josie, back around
the room. She'd heard plenty of stories. With an aggravated sigh,
she took her hands off her hips and went back to reading.

Josie added, "Go to the very en'."

Michelle nodded.

Leaving the beauty of nature, I pushed open the door
to the hospital lobby. Here the sights, sounds, and smells
were different. The strong odor of antiseptic cleansers stung
my nostrils. Highly waxed floor tiles beamed. A voice
blared from a loudspeaker, paging a doctor.

I was reminded that I was entering a battlefield, a place
where a fierce fight against death and disease was waged
daily. Nowhere else, it seemed to me, was the essence of life
such a sacred trust. I felt proud to be part of such a noble
undertaking.

In the elevator, I stared down at my newly-polished
white nursing shoes and took deep, slow breaths to calm

my fluttery stomach. When the doors finally slid open, I checked in with my instructor, then headed for the dressing area; I didn't want to miss one moment of this exciting experience.

In the dressing room I stuffed my uniform into a locker and threw on a green cotton scrub dress. Drawing another deep breath, I hurried to the scrub room. There I struggled to tuck my hair into a paper cap and thoroughly washed my hands. Just as I was reaching for a sterile gown to cover my scrub dress, the head nurse entered the room and explained that there'd been a change: the Cesarean delivery had been canceled.

I tried hard not to let her see my disappointment, but my shoulders sagged.

"I'm sure you're disappointed," she observed, and then, brightening, added, "but there's an abortion that's just beginning. You could watch that."

Abortion? Somehow I had never considered the possibility of viewing an abortion! Since childhood I had attended church, and at an early age I committed myself to living by the principles God had set for me. I thought of myself as morally opposed to abortion in principle, but still something made it impossible for me to regard abortion as wrong in every instance.

Surely, I reasoned, there must be isolated instances where abortion is the best option. Simple curiosity, as well as my desire to be considered "open-minded," overcame any doubts I had, and I hastily agreed to observe the procedure.

I paused before the operating room door and squeezed my eyes shut. Then, composing myself, I slipped inside, where everything was in place and the procedure was about to begin.

The lights, the smells, the neat rows of instruments—it was all familiar. I reminded myself that this was a hospital operating room, not some back-alley 'clinic,' and that there was nothing sinister about it. This was possibly the very same operating room where I would have stood to watch the Cesarean birth.

From the foot of the operating table, I could see that the mother was already under the influence of the general anesthetic. She was about my age, and I began to fantasize about why she had decided on this abortion. Perhaps she'd been pressured by the father of the baby or by her parents. Maybe she was financially unable to care for a child, or perhaps it was just an inconvenient time for a pregnancy.

The low murmuring of the anesthesiologist, the O.R. nurse, and the physician interrupted my thoughts. I then focused on the procedure itself. Dilators of increasing diameter were gradually inserted into the cervix, or neck, of the uterus until it was stretched enough to insert the suction tube.

I watched with interest—it was all so clinical, so normal, so much like other surgeries I'd observed in the past. The medical personnel talked casually as they would during any procedure. My clenched fingers uncurled, and my rigid back muscles softened. I slowly relaxed and grew more comfortable.

The suction tube was connected to a bottle; inside the bottle a gauze bag dangled, waiting to catch the portions of tissue, which would be sent to the lab for routine examination after the procedure was completed.

Michelle looked up at Josie, who was staring hard at her. "I read plenty, thanks."

"No, you ain't. Remember our deal?"

"It's blackmail."

"No way. Nobody says I gots to watch out fo' you. I can change my min' any time I wants to."

Michelle heaved another exaggerated sigh and forced herself to continue reading. With the first sentence, she grimaced. Her breath caught.

When the suction machine was flipped on, its smooth whirring brought a flow of blood down the tube. Then I heard a soft "plop," and the physician muttered an obscenity as she realized that the gauze bag containing the tissue had somehow fallen into the blood at the bottom of the suction bottle.

In what seemed to be only minutes, the procedure was completed, the suction tube was removed, and the patient was ready to be wheeled to the recovery room.

One final task remained—the physician had to retrieve the bag of tissue from the suction bottle and have it sent to the pathology department. To ease the task, the physician and the O.R. nurse decided to dump the contents of the bottle onto an instrument tray.

As the physician's gloved fingers poked through the blood, I looked again at the young, unconscious woman and wondered how she'd feel when she awoke. Relieved? Ashamed? Frightened?

My thoughts were interrupted by the physician. "Oooh, look," she whispered, "I've never seen one come out like this before. Here, take a look!"

I stepped a bit closer, and she extended her bloody, gloved hand. Then I froze in horror as I saw what was cradled in her palm: a tiny body. This was not the "blob of tissue" that I expected to see after such an efficient, clinical procedure.

This was a fully formed, 12-week-old, *decapitated* fetus. Two tiny arms with the smallest fingers imaginable hung from thin shoulders. Two fragile legs dangled from the delicate torso. About 2 1/2 to 3 inches in length, this was a perfect miniature human body.

"I'm sure the head is here, too," the O.R. nurse spoke in animated tones, still examining the tangled contents of the gauze snare.

Sick waves of revulsion churned in my stomach, and I backed toward the operating room door. I knew, beyond any doubt, that what I'd witnessed had been the taking of a human life and that there could be no possible justification for it.

When I reached the safety of the dressing room, I stepped out of the scrub dress and fumbled with the buttons on my uniform. I felt numb. Dry-eyed, I sat down on the wooden bench and absently scuffed my feet together, noticing with interest that black lines now marred the shine on my white shoes. I'm not sure how many minutes passed before I mustered the strength to get up and walk to the maternity floor. The cries of newborn babies assaulted my ears, shrill and distorted. I stopped in front of the glass windows of the Special Care Nursery and gazed at the incredibly tiny infants, several of them barely four months older than the infant I'd just seen cradled in a bloody hand. Thousands of dollars were being spent to sustain their lives—why wasn't the life of that other infant just as important?

Eighteen years have passed since that spring day in Rochester, and I still like to think of myself as an "open-minded" person. But I'm absolutely certain of *this*—abortion involves the taking of a human life. That small, lifeless baby I gazed at, horrified, will never celebrate a birthday, walk in the park, smell the flowers or hear the birds. I've buried its memory for too long, and now I'm haunted by the thought of millions of tiny bodies being placed in specimen bottles and sent to pathology labs.

I've asked God to forgive me for remaining silent and to give me the courage to speak. He has, and in speaking I find a measure of peace. Now, at last, my tears flow freely, as I remember that day long ago when life was young and lilacs bloomed.[16]   —*Kathy Schriefer, R.N.*

Michelle laid the paper beside her on the bed. Her eyes were moist. She stared in the distance, then back at Josie. For a long moment, the two were silent. Then Josie spoke. "My youngin'd be 'bout yo' age right now, if she'd a been borned. Her name'd be Mandrika, Mandy for short. T'day was s'pposed t'be her birthday. Sometimes I sets t'wonderin' if she'd like singin' like I does. Singin' keeps from losin' my min' mos' of the time. I wonders if she be likin' t'bake homemade biscuits or pick wild gooseberries or chase butterflies. Would she be purty, wantin' t'dress up in lace an' play with baby dolls? Or would she wanna wear blue jeans and climb trees from mornin' til night . . . An' then I gets real sad." Josie's eyes filled with tears. A big one dropped on her T-shirt.

"Okay, okay! Stop! So maybe I'm convinced."

"Now you be talkin' some sense."

"I just don't understand how I can have a baby—especially in this dump."

"Call home."

"I can't. I'm too scared." Big tears welled up in her eyes again.

"Scared? Or 'shamed."

"Both. Humiliated would be more like it."

"Give it a try, girl. I knows they must be wantin' t'hear from ya real bad." She looked Michelle straight in the eyes. "Want me t'pray wif ya firs'?"

She sat motionless for a long time, then nodded slowly.

"Okay, grab yo' pillow." Josie reached over to her bed, pulled her pillow down and set it on the floor alongside Michelle's bed. With considerable effort, she knelt down on it and waited for her little friend to follow suit. They made quite a sight from behind—Josie's robust, dark-skinned frame next to Michelle's pale, scarecrow form.

When they were both situated with their hands folded on the bed, Josie began, "God, I don' know You too good yet, an' I don' much know how t'be talkin' to Somebody so big an' 'portant. But preacher said the Savior made a way for me to talk to You when He died on the cross. Thank You for Him. Thank You for lovin' me an' forgivin' me. I done throwed so much of my life away. I wish I hadn', but I did. So I'm here on the behalf of li'l Ashley here—or whatever her name is—"

"Michelle," interrupted a squeaky voice from beside her.

"I'm here on the behalf of Michelle. She be such a youngin', Lawd. She be 'shamed an' pregnant an' ascared to call home. An' b'sides, she gots a puppy she loves who's hurt bad. Help Angel get better somehow, please, an' let this chil's kinfolks a'cept her back." She stopped at the sound of sniffles and looked over at Michelle. "You be wantin' forgiveness, too?"

The small, bowed head nodded. A hand brushed away tears.
"You be wantin' Jesus as yo' Savior?"
Another slow nod and a sniffle.
"Then jus' ask. That be all I done."
There was a long silence before Michelle spoke. "God, I'm sorry I made such a mess of everything. I'm not so big as I thought." The sobs came quickly now. "I'm trying to stay off drugs and it feels awful. Please help me. I'm afraid to have this baby because it might be addicted or retarded or deformed and because my parents'll kill me and . . . because I just can't handle it!" She blew her nose. "I'm sorry for the bad stuff I've done. If Jesus can make me a new person, will You put Him in my heart . . . and please, if you can arrange it on the side, make my Angel better? Thank you very much. Amen."
An exuberant male voice behind her echoed, *"A-a-a-men!"* Startled, she turned around. An officer's brown eyes and smile shone bright against his dark skin as he passed by on his rounds. He sure was different from the mean one who had led her from the isolation cell.
She and Josie both crawled back into bed for a while longer before chow. They spent the rest of the day talking, going out for rec time, and attending a small Bible study group—at Josie's request. To Michelle's surprise, it turned out to be okay.
That evening, another guard came by. "Inmate Hicks," he said to Josie, "your name's up for the phone. Six minutes, remember."
"Yes, sir." Josie started to push herself off the bed, then looked at Michelle. "Jus' checkin' with my lawyer, if ya wanna call him that. Public 'fenders ain't never in." She paused. "Say, you be wantin' t'try home in my place? It's okay by me."
Michelle's eyes widened. Josie was offering to give up half of her daily ration of contact with the outside world, after waiting for

several hours. Amazing. But if she *did* take her up on the offer, who might answer the phone? What could she possibly say in six minutes? She felt immobilized. The next thing she knew, Josie was escorting her up to the one pay phone near the officer's station.

Her mouth felt like instant desert. She could barely swallow. Her palms were so sweaty that when she picked up the receiver, it slid away, banged against the wall and hung, dangling, by the metal-wrapped cord.

She tried again and managed to get her trembling fingers to stay steady long enough push the zero button for the operator. Somehow, the words came out, "I need to make a collect call . . ."

Josie stood nearby, with her ample arms folded across her chest and nodding. She flashed a thumbs up sign.

Michelle heard a woman's voice. "Nastasis residence, Anna speaking." The accent was unmistakable. She breathed a sigh of relief. Not her mom or dad, but an *ally!* Today must be her lucky day, she decided. She bit her lip as the operator informed Anna of a "collect call from Ashley" and asked whether she would accept the charges. Then she heard a loud clunk. Was it disconnected?

In her excitement, Anna dropped the phone. Joshua was standing nearby. She urged him over with a strong gesture and pointed to the fallen receiver. Her hands were trembling.

He retrieved it to his ear just as the operator repeated, "Collect call from Ashley. Would you accept the charges?"

"Yes, I will," he answered, motioning Anna back over to his side with animated gestures of his own.

After a brief silence, a timid voice said, "Hello . . ."

Joshua kept his tone as calm as he could. He didn't want to scare her away by appearing too anxious. "Good evening, Ashley. How have you been, dear?"

"Okay, I guess. By the way, my name is really Michelle."

"Yes, of course . . . Michelle."

"Tell me—are my parents standing right there?"

"No, no. We encouraged them to go out for their anniversary. Just Anna and I and Stephen are here. He is viewing a video on the television, I believe."

At the mention of her little brother, Michelle's voice cracked. "H-How is he?"

"Faring rather well, considering. He misses you terribly. Would you care to speak with him?"

"No, tell him 'hi' for me. I only have a few more minutes. Can I talk to Anna, too, please?"

"Of course. She would be delighted." He offered the phone to his wife.

"Good evening, Michelle, dear!" she exclaimed.

Michelle covered the receiver with her hand and took a deep breath first. "Oh. Guess you know my real name." She caught Josie's eye, who gave her another nod and a thumbs up sign. She spoke back into the phone, "Man, am I glad you guys are there and not my parents! I don't know what I'm going to do . . ."

"Whatever do you mean, dear? You should come home at the earliest possible moment."

"I can't."

"Why not? Your parents desperately want to see you."

"Believe me, they won't when they hear what I've got to say."

"Nothing could be so bad as—"

"Yes, it could."

"What, pray tell?"

Michelle cleared her throat. "I-I'm in jail in New York. And I have no idea yet when I'll get out." There. She said it.

Anna's eyes widened as she shook her head. "Oh, my!" she exclaimed. Joshua raised his eyebrows at her, but she couldn't utter a word. She went back on the phone to ask, "Are you all right?"

"Yeah, I'm okay. Except for a few major problems." Silence. "For starters . . . I'm pregnant."

"I see . . ." Anna shook her head again and fanned herself.

"Look, I've gotta go pretty soon. The guard'll be signaling and I can't afford to get written up."

"Of course not." Anna's voice already had an edge of apprehension. She had not forgotten how Michelle had slipped through their fingers twice already. At the moment, they had no address for her, no way of contacting her in return . . .

Michelle pulled a piece of scratch paper out of her pocket. "You guys said before you wanted to help me. I hate asking for anything, but I'm kind of desperate. See, I found this puppy—"

"Yes, I remember Angel."

"You *do?*" That Anna remembered her dog's name touched Michelle's heart. Tears threatened to push their way into her eyes for the umpteenth time that day.

Anna continued, "We met at the Mercy Mobile. For her I gave you an extra bag of food."

"Yeah, you did. She devoured it, too. Well, anyway, after I got arrested, the cops supposedly took her to the ASPCA shelter. Somehow she got hit by a car. She's there right now in bad condition." Michelle stopped for a breath. "So if there's *any* way you get some money to them—I think they're on 110th Street in East Harlem—maybe they would fix her up and not put her to sleep."

"Perhaps your parents—"

"No, please don't tell them anything yet. *Please.*"

"Michelle, we—" But the phone had clicked off.

Anna hung up and looked incredulously at her husband. "You will not believe what I have to tell you." She stood, shaking her head back and forth. "The long-lost Michelle, known also as Ashley Nicole, has landed herself in the jail of New York."

"I daresay that comes as no surprise."

"Love, she is expecting a baby! Michael and Stephanie will be devastated."

"But she is still alive, Anna! That alone is a miracle, is it not?"

A slight smile spread over Anna's lips and lit up her eyes. "Yes, I suppose so. Yet I feel so torn between sorrow and joy. I want to laugh and cry all at once."

"A true woman you are. But consider the positive side: this time, that silly child *cannot escape!*"

She giggled. "Yes . . . praise be to God!" She threw her arms around Joshua. He lifted her petite frame off the ground and twirled her around, then held her tight while he said a fervent prayer of thanks. When they finished, Anna asked him if he thought they should try to reach Michael and Stephanie.

He paused to weigh their options. "No, I vote that we allow them to enjoy the rest of their evening. What could they do for her at this hour?"

Anna agreed. "In a sense, though, I feel like a traitor to tell them at all. Michelle begged that I not mention a word." She sighed. "But if it were Anja, we would want to know, no matter what the circumstances." He nodded and wrapped his arms tighter around her, then led her over to the couch. There, they snuggled and reminisced before dozing off.

They both woke up when Michael and Stephanie wandered in at half past midnight. Joshua rubbed his eyes and the back of his neck. Anna rearranged her hair.

"Did you enjoy yourselves?" Joshua asked, yawning.

"Sure did," Michael assured him. Stephanie seconded with enthusiasm. They had gone to see an "oldies" double feature at the drive-in theatre—their two favorite movies when they were dating. Still holding hands, they both looked happier and more relaxed than they had in months. Michael even had a lipstick smudge on his neck, which delighted the older couple. Things seemed to be improving in the romance department. Whatever the reason for the change, it had their hearty approval.

Joshua raised his eyebrows when he caught Anna's eye. She responded with an inconspicuous "shh" sign and a wink.

The news about Michelle could *definitely* wait until morning.

❧ *Thirty-Two* ❧

Before dawn, Joshua and Anna arose, neither having slept very well. Their legitimate concerns about Michael and Stephanie's reaction to "the news" kept them tossing and turning all night. Joshua better understood Michael's apprehension regarding his father's death. He, too, hated to be the one to cause pain. Thus preoccupied, he had little time to grieve his own loss.

For almost two hours, he and Anna prayed and read the Bible as they snuggled together on propped-up pillows. Every Scripture they could find about encouragement . . . forgiveness . . . and hope, Anna jotted down in a worn journal. They knew they might soon need just the right medicine to soothe aching hearts.

At eight o'clock, Anna started brewing coffee and set the table while Joshua worked on a nice breakfast. As soon as the eggs were sizzling in the frying pan and the apple strudel rising in the oven, Anna knocked on the master bedroom door. She cracked it open ever so slightly. "Breakfast is served, dear ones," she called.

"We're awake," Michael answered. "Be out in a bit." A few minutes later, they wandered into the kitchen in their bathrobes. Stephanie yawned. Michael licked his lips. "With those smells

wafting through the house, we didn't stand a chance." He patted Joshua on the shoulder. "I didn't know you could cook like Caleb, too. You're a pretty versatile guy."

Stephanie cocked her head. "Yes, you are. To what do we owe this wonderful surprise?

Glancing over at her from the stove, Joshua smiled. "A feeble attempt to make your date last a wee bit longer."

"I'll go for that," Michael answered. "This is a feast!" He gave Stephanie a peck on the cheek. Groggy-eyed, they sat down at the table, sipped coffee, and nibbled on hot strudel while they related a few highlights of their evening out. They admitted it had been a much-needed boost for both of them.

"We surprised ourselves," Stephanie said as she glanced over at Michael, "that we can still have fun together." He nodded.

In turn, Joshua and Anna recollected some of the happy moments that had helped them survive the calamities they had faced over the years. Meanwhile, the entire foursome ate breakfast with plenty of gusto—amid profuse compliments to the head chef.

Then with utmost care, Joshua broached the crucial subject. "While you were away last night, we received an important phone call." He looked back and forth from Michael to Stephanie.

"From?" Michael asked, his tone casual. "That new prospect, I hope." He wiped his mouth with his napkin.

Joshua cleared his throat. He took a deep breath. "Not quite. We do have good news, however!" After a glance at Anna, he continued, "Other aspects, shall we say, are . . . less favorable." He took another sip of coffee as he lowered his gaze to the table, then up at the pair across from him. "Your daughter called."

Michael choked on his coffee. Wide-eyed, he and Stephanie both leaped in the air, leaning toward the older couple. *"Michelle?"* they cried, almost in unison.

He nodded enthusiastically. Anna joined him, adding, "Is it not wonderful?

Stephanie sat back down. "She . . . really called?"

"Yes, dear! And we can thank God that she is alive." Anna reached over to squeeze her hand.

Overcome, Michael sat down, too. "How is she?" He licked his lips, as if his mouth and throat were filled with sawdust.

Joshua's blue eyes softened towards his younger charge. "Considering her whereabouts of late, she sounded . . . very well."

Michael appeared ready to explode with emotion. "Guys, something tells me you're holding back. *Where* is she?" His tone was almost pleading, his eyes moist.

Joshua looked directly at the pair, first one, then the other. His voice barely above a whisper, he answered, "New York City." He cleared his throat again. "In the jail." He could almost feel the words dropping like hot lead in cold liquid. He winced.

Michael gripped the table. "Our daughter. In jail."

Stephanie stifled a moan and grabbed a handful of tissues on her way to the bedroom. Anna followed her to provide whatever comfort she could.

"I can't believe it." Michael shook his head back and forth. "But I don't know why I'm surprised. The police suspected drugs all along." He bolstered his courage enough to ask Joshua about the nature of the charges.

Joshua said he didn't know. He apologized and explained, "Son, we had a single goal in mind—to hold her on the line long enough to discover her whereabouts. She did say she had no idea of the length of her confinement. But both of us failed to ask why she was there. We should have done so, I suppose."

"Oh, it's okay. We'll find out soon enough." He clenched his jaw. "I can't wait."

"What is the next step?" Joshua asked. "As her parents, will you be able to sign for her release?"

Michael sighed. "I'm not sure how it works. I think we can at least post bond. Provided that a judge is convinced she'll show up for court."

"I see. No doubt, you will be relieved to see her home here safe and sound."

He nodded and wiped a tear from the corner of his eye. "That is the understatement of the year." He glanced back toward the bedroom where his wife had gone, then at the phone, now silent. "Was she disappointed we weren't home?"

That question caught Joshua off-guard. He was hoping the subject would never come up. How could he convey the truth and yet, not hurt further those who loved her? He paused, blinked hard and took another deep breath. "It is natural that she would feel anxious about your reunion—"

"Which means?"

"She asked Anna not to say a word just yet. But of course, we both felt that you and Stephanie should be the first to—"

"She did *what?* For Pete's sake, we're her parents!" Michael was shouting now. "After all we've been through! The mere thought of her humiliating us like that in front of you makes my blood boil!" He pounded the table with his fist. "I've got a notion to let her sit and stew in jail. She deserves it!" Thus said, he excused himself in a huff, not offering any explanation.

Joshua let out another deep sigh and set to work cleaning up the mess in the kitchen. It was the only mess he could clean up. Somehow, his and Anna's best intentions had gone awry.

He shook his head and made a decision then and there:

Michelle would tell her parents *herself* about the baby she was carrying. Then he began to pray.

🐞 🐞 🐞

Once in his office, Michael fumed and paced and shoved papers around on his desk. He studied the family portrait.

Michelle. *In jail!* It was downright disgusting.

He played with the computer and returned calls to a couple of clients. That didn't help. He still wanted to swear a blue streak and beat the tar out of something. Or somebody.

So much for his prayer in the vineyard about his bad attitude. His old self had returned with a vengeance. Part of the anger, he surmised, stemmed from pride. And jealousy. Their own daughter preferred to talk to near strangers more than to them! But Joshua deserved better treatment. The situation certainly wasn't his fault. He had his own grief about Caleb, to boot. Michael wandered back into the kitchen about a half hour later. Red-faced and sheepish-feeling, he admitted how sorry he was for his outburst.

Joshua acted as gracious as Caleb always had. He assured him that he understood. "The strain on you has been tremendous," he said. "No offense taken."

Michael mustered a grateful smile. "I appreciate that." He hesitated. "Josh, I really am relieved and happy that Michelle's still alive. But I'm furious with her at the same time. Besides getting herself in trouble, she makes *us* sound like ogres."

"I am not so sure that is the entire issue, my friend." He paused for a moment. "Let me show you something pertinent, if I may. Have you a Bible nearby?"

Michael rummaged through the mail on the counter, then checked on the desk. Stephanie had left her Amplified version there under a pile of newspapers. He sat down at the table and handed it to Joshua, who went straight to the third chapter of Genesis and began reading at verse eight:

561

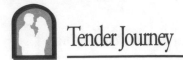

And they heard the sound of the Lord God walking in the garden in the cool of the day, and Adam and his wife hid themselves from the presence of the Lord God among the trees of the garden. But the Lord God called to Adam and said to him, Where are you? He said, I heard the sound of You [walking] in the garden, and I was afraid because I was naked; and I hid myself.

Joshua stopped reading. He looked at Michael. "Adam and Eve knew they had sinned against God. They ate fruit from the one forbidden tree. Notice in the last line that Adam confessed three feelings—*fear, shame,* and a *desire to hide* from the Lord. Is your daughter not reacting to you in a similar manner?"

Michael knit his brows and tilted his head. He remained thoughtful for quite awhile. Leaning his chin on his hands, he admitted, "Food for thought."

"I believe so. Children who rebel against their parents mirror humanity's rebellion against God, perhaps more than we would care to admit."

Michael frowned again.

Joshua's gaze softened. "Teenagers often show defiance in quite a visible manner—by their clothing . . . hair styles . . . loud music which we find intolerable . . . low grades . . . taking drugs . . . even by running away."

"You've got that right." Michael nodded.

"I suppose adults do resist God outwardly, as well. Many of us, however, have mastered the art of subtlety. No one but God Himself would know how far away from Him we have gone."

"You mean in the heart."

"Exactly. The place that, to God, matters most! The story of the prodigal son portrays this so well. He did turn against his father to a dreadful degree, squandering his entire inheritance on immorality in a faraway land. In contrast to his beastly behavior, his elder brother would seem the picture of obedience! Ah, he stayed home. He served. He worked hard in his father's fields. In fact, it was there he was laboring when his younger brother came limping back. But did any of his actions spring out of love? None. He would just as well have accompanied his brother and 'lived up' right along with him!"

Michael started to smile at Joshua's version of "lived it up." Instead, he questioned why he would make such a rash claim.

"See for yourself. How did he respond to the royal reception his father was planning? You will find it in Luke fifteen." Michael flipped to the page and handed the Bible to Joshua. He skimmed through the verses, stopping on verse twenty-eight:

But [the elder brother] was angry—with deep-seated wrath—and resolved not to go in. Then his father came out [and] began to plead with him. But he answered his father, Look! These many years I have served you, and I have never disobeyed your command. Yet you never gave me [so much as] a (little) kid, that I might revel and feast and be happy and make merry with my friends.

Michael made a steeple with his forefingers and leaned them against his chin. "Obviously, Michelle would be the prodigal . . ."

"I would say there are some definite similarities, yes."

"But our Stephen's not like the other brother. If I know him, he'd be the one planning a party for his sister."

They were both quiet for several minutes. Michael spoke. "I guess it applies to Steph and me?"

"Go on . . ."

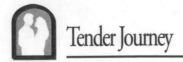

"Or maybe just to me. You're saying I have a choice to react like the brother or the father."

Joshua nodded. "Human nature will cause you to play the self-righteous one. You will resent your daughter because the consequences of her sin have been—and will be—so great. She has inconvenienced you and hurt you deeply. But the divine nature inside you will help you respond as did the forgiving father. If you draw upon the strength of Jesus Christ, you will seek to do whatever you can to restore her."

"Even if she has done much wrong."

"Yes. Even in the face of terrible sins. Why? Because the God we serve loves sinners—enough to die for them!" He thought for a moment. "Let me give you an analogy. A good fireman will do anything in his power to rescue someone from a burning building, will he not? No matter what kind of person is trapped inside, he will split open doors . . . smash windows . . . inhale smoke . . . and risk his very life. He seeks to rescue not only the innocent baby and the sweet, old woman, but the insolent punk who hurls insults at him for his efforts."

"It'd take a jerk to abuse somebody trying to save your life."

"But many children do the same to their parents." He paused for a long moment. "And Michael, we all do the same to God!"

"So you're drawing a comparison between our sins against Him and what our kids do to us."

"Precisely. Without an awareness of our own shortcomings, we will have neither the desire nor the ability to forgive them."

"Sounds like you're implying that, since parents are just as guilty—in God's eyes, that is—they should coddle their kids."

"Not at all, my friend. Discipline must be administered. God does so with us. He places parents in a position of authority for a reason. On many occasions, firmness is required."

Michael scratched his temple. "'Tough love,' I think is what Dr. Dobson calls it. He's the founder of *Focus on the Family.*"

"Yes. That term sounds accurate—a good balance. Parents bear an enormous responsibility before God to keep their own lives pure. Then and only then can they correct with grace rather than with spite." He paused, rubbing the leather cover of the Bible with his hand. "Our God does everything *in* love and *for* love."

"That is, when we've stopped doing wrong."

"Not necessarily. Remember that Christ died for us while we were yet sinners."

"Yeah, well, let's say Michelle comes home, does okay for awhile, then goes back to drugs. Again and again. I've heard horror stories about parents trying to keep their kids off the stuff!"

"'Tis true, you will not have any easy road. Addictions have tremendous power. But Jesus Christ has *all power.* And our Redeemer does not 'give up' on His children. Neither will you."

"How will we know, though, whether to be tough or tender with Michelle?"

"*He* will know what she needs at the moment. He will supply wisdom every step of the way, if you ask it of Him."

"We have. Well . . . not enough, I guess, huh?"

"You alone must answer that. You and your wife." He folded his hands. "Anna and I have learned to regard prayer as far more than a pastime. It has become our lifeline."

Michael's expression was solemn. "I hate to admit it, but I am afraid of the future. In fact, I'm scared stiff."

"I understand, son. Believe me, I do." Joshua placed his hand on Michael's arm.

Michael lowered his head. *Son . . .* Caleb always called him that. A big tear rolled down his cheek. "Stephanie's going to need me to be strong . . ."

Joshua looked him in the eyes, then grasped both of his forearms. "You shall be! Both of you can do all things—through Christ, who strengthens you."

Michael raised his eyebrows and sighed. "Man, it's gonna have to be Him, 'cause I'm a wimp at heart." A reassuring nod from Joshua took the edge off the fear.

Whether he wanted to or not, he would have to get busy making arrangements to get Michelle home. He decided he may as well start by trying to find out the number to the New York jail. He excused himself, and left Joshua reading the Bible at the kitchen table. On his way to the office, he peeked into the bedroom. Stephanie was curled up under the covers, sound asleep. She probably needed that more than anything. Anna was napping in the chair beside the bed. Or knowing her, she was praying up a storm.

After what seemed to be dozens of phone calls and hours caught on hold in voice mail systems ("inmate bail information, press one; travel information, press two . . ."), Michael discovered that Michelle—alias Ashley Nicole Witherton—was at the Rose M. Singer Center on Rikers Island. Just the name made his skin crawl. It reminded him of Alcatraz. A fortress where they kept career criminals so they could never escape. Shaken to the core, he called the attorney, then went to look for Joshua. He found him on the porch, nailing a loose floorboard. "Josh, you won't believe what I went through to get information on this child. Do you realize there are fourteen thousand people in jail on Riker's—and another five thousand throughout the rest of the city!"

"Nineteen thousand behind bars?"

"Yes. She should be at a juvenile center, but since she lied about her age, she's going the big time. Who knows what she'll run into? I don't dare tell Stephanie."

"No need to at this point. She would worry all the more." His brow furrowed. "Has Michelle stood in the presence of a judge as yet?"

"Once—for an arraignment. That's when they read her the charges, I think."

"They are . . .?"

"Possession of cocaine and grand theft." He rolled his eyes. "For stealing items of high value. I'm not sure of the amount. Otherwise, it would be petty theft. Unbelievable."

"I see. The next step, then?"

"I called an attorney friend of mine. He feels sure that we'll be able to get her released right away since she's a juvenile and hasn't been in trouble before."

"That is wonderful. Just wonderful!" All of a sudden, Anna threw open the porch door. She came rushing out. "Michael, it slipped my mind to tell you something so very important!"

"What, Anna? Tell me."

"I did intend to tell you last evening. Michelle said her puppy was hit by a car. A place for stray animals—I cannot recall the name now—has the dog. She pleaded with me to help save her life." Anna covered her mouth with her hands and gasped. "Oh, dear, what if it is too late? Do hurry!"

Michael's first reaction was to complain about the fortune they had already spent. Not to mention would have to spend in the near future. He glanced at Joshua. Their earlier conversation came back to him loud and clear. "So I bet you think this is a warm-up test of forgiveness."

Joshua winked. His crystal blue eyes sparkled. "God does provide such opportunities, on occasion."

He looked and acted so much like Caleb, it brought a lump to Michael's throat. "You know, your father once told me a quote by

Tender Journey

Mark Twain. I had forgotten about it, but it's coming back to me now. *'Forgiveness is the fragrance the violet sheds . . . on the heel that has crushed it.'* Guess this is a good chance to do that."

Anna exclaimed, "So, you will try to save Angel, then?"

"Do what I can. I know she loves animals."

Joshua gave his arm a squeeze. "Wise decision. It will help to reassure her of your love, despite her failures."

Anna added, "And build a bridge between you."

"Hope so. I have a feeling we'll need all the help we can get."

Joshua and Anna's eyes met. Little did Michael know how much.

The phone rang. It was the attorney. He had everything arranged, if they could just drop off a check for three thousand dollars for the retainer. Michelle could be released as soon as they could get to New York to pick her up—assuming they could get up another five thousand dollars bond. Michael swallowed hard when he thought about the additional dent to their savings account. But the five thousand would only be until her case was resolved, minus court costs. They could swing it. At least Michelle would be home and Stephanie would be ecstatic. For now, he'd let his wife sleep a little longer.

He went back to his office to make travel arrangements on his computer. When he punched in the credit card number for payment, he cringed. Even with discount airline fares, three round-trip tickets plus a one-way from New York cost a bundle. He did want Stephen to go along, though. Should he have invited Joshua and Anna? Probably. They were as responsible as anyone for her return. He went to ask Joshua. He declined, urging him to give his family time alone.

After Michael made the reservations, he started making calls to find Michelle's dog. That was no easy task. She had been moved from the ASPCA Manhattan shelter to the hospital on east 92nd Street. Amazingly, she was doing better, the clerk said. She had regained consciousness and was no longer bleeding internally. The vet had set two broken bones, treated multiple lacerations, and was continuing to administer antibiotics and anti-inflammatory drugs. The dog could be picked up whenever they were ready.

Dollars signs went flying across Michael's mental screen. "What is the bill?" he asked cautiously.

"Nothing, sir."

"You're doing it for free?"

"Not exactly. There's a note in the file—someone made an anonymous donation toward the animal's care."

"You're kidding."

"No. It's written right here."

"I-I don't know what to say."

"Sounds to me as if sombody's looking out for you."

"Yes . . . Yes, it does." He ran his fingers through his hair to gather his thoughts. "We'll be in to pick up the dog as soon as possible. We're flying in from Florida tomorrow." Whenever they could get there would be fine, she said.

Dazed, he hung up and sat for several minutes, staring out the window. His eyes spotted something he had never noticed before—a bird's nest in the big oak tree. Three gaping beaks poked out above the twigs. A bright-colored male was perched on the edge of the nest. One by one, he dropped food into each mouth. Michael's eyes grew misty. "Thanks, Lord," he whispered.

He went to tell Joshua and Anna the dog story. They just grinned and nodded. More prayers answered. Hallelujah!

The bedroom was his next stop. He awakened Stephanie with the good news. The three of them would be leaving early the next morning for New York. He also told her about the paid bill for the

dog. She shook her head in disbelief. Hand in hand, they went to Stephen's room to tell him they had found Michelle at last.

He bolted past them, down the hall to his sister's bedroom. They followed close behind, getting there just as he flung himself on her bed and grabbed her favorite teddy bear. He hugged it hard enough to squeeze the stuffings out of the poor old thing. "She's really coming home?" he asked warily, looking up at them through his long eyelashes glistening with tears.

They nodded. Michael filled him in on where she was, so he wouldn't feel afraid when they got to the jail. "She may not look or act the same as she did. She's been through a lot," Michael coached him. "But deep inside, she's our Michelle. We're going to have to work together as a team to get past this."

Stephen lowered his head, rocked her bear, and nodded. "I know, dad. You can count on me."

Stephanie gazed at her son—his ever-thinning frame poking out from his baggy pajamas and his streaked blond curls still tousled from sleep—promising his support. That did it for her. More tears.

Michael gave her hug and shed a few himself. "Do you realize," he said, "that our house is turning into the local waterworks? We should sell stock."

He didn't intend to be funny. But he smiled in spite of himself. Surprisingly, Stephanie smiled back. Then giggled. And giggled some more. Stephen, sensing a change in mood, whether or not he understood the reason for it, joined in. Soon, all three of them were laughing until their sides ached. It felt good.

❧ Thirty-Three ❧

lear, sunny skies greeted the Nastasis family when their plane landed at LaGuardia International Airport the next morning. Stephen's elation over the aerial view still had him talking. The friendly pilot had been nice enough to point out several landmarks—the Statue of Liberty, the World Trade Center, Wall Street, Shea Stadium, and Central Park—as they circled over the city. Neither Stephanie nor Stephen had realized how pretty New York was from the air. Far more than sterile skyscrapers and traffic-jammed streets, its large parks, lakes, bays, and islands formed a spectacular sight.

It took over an hour to pick up their baggage and rent a car. Michael almost went into shock at the cost of an economy model, but he saw no alternative. The rental agent gave him numerous tips about driving in the big city. "Keep your valuables locked in the trunk and don't act like tourists," she warned. She asked where they were headed, offering to give directions.

Too ashamed to admit the truth and unable to come up with an answer, Michael said, "We haven't decided yet." The agent raised her eyebrows in a dubious "if you say so" gesture.

571

From the map, they discovered that Rikers Island lay a stone's throw across the channel from the airport. "Look where we would have ended up if we had flown into Kennedy!" Michael exclaimed as he pointed to the huge area on the map. Eyes widened at the maze of fine black print separating the southeastern section from their destination near the middle.

"Man, that would have taken *forever*," Stephen murmured, shaking his head.

Under his breath, Michael thanked the Lord for the favor. In making the reservations himself, he had never even considered the location of the two airports.

Suddenly, Stephen tapped the palm of his hand with his fist. "Hey! I just had an idea . . ."

They both stared at him, waiting.

"How 'bout if we get the dog first? Then she can go with us when we see Michelle!"

Mom and Dad commended him. It *was* a great idea. Then they all sat on a bench and studied the map to figure out the best way to the ASPCA hospital at 441 East Ninety-Second Street. Unsure as to which north-south avenue would fall closest to 400 numbers, Michael asked the agent. "Between First and York," she answered, without so much as a glance from her computer screen.

He felt relieved that he had asked instead of assuming. The logical spot—between Fourth and Fifth Avenues—would have taken them out of the way. Stephanie made notes of the route so she could announce the turns to Michael once they got under way. He knew he would need every ounce of concentration to avoid getting sideswiped or mowed down. They would head west on Grand Central Parkway to the Brooklyn Queens Expressway, west on Northern Blvd, over the Queens Brooklyn Bridge and back east on Sixtieth to First Avenue, heading north to Ninety-Second.

Traffic crawled along at a bumper-to-bumper pace—or flew by like lightning. No in between. The incredibly narrow space between lanes had Stephanie on edge, gripping the armrest the whole way. It seemed to her that she could have joined hands with the driver of the next car over without so much as a slight stretch. To make matters worse, half of the drivers (especially the cabbies) ignored the lanes entirely. They made their own lanes. Michael considered the whole experience an immense challenge; Stephen found it fun. Stephanie did not appreciate it one bit. She asked if they could return the car at the earliest opportunity and take public transportation or walk. He agreed to consider the option.

Once at the shelter, it didn't take long to meet Angel. Stephen let out a squeal of delight at first glimpse. No wonder Michelle loved her! She was so cute, even with the shaved, stitched patches in her coat. They all decided it would be nice having a pet again to fill the empty spot Ebony had left behind.

Once they had cooed over Angel, they carried her back to the car for the drive to Rikers. Good thing mom had remembered to bring the essentials—collar, leash, food, and water dish. In spite of the white-bandaged splints on Angel's front and back right legs, she wriggled contentedly in the arms of whomever was holding her at the moment. She bestowed her gift of friendship, a generous tongue-lapping, on each member of the family, as if she knew exactly what they were up to, and was lending her wholehearted approval. Stephen snuggled next to her and soon fell asleep.

By the time they arrived at the jail, it was nearly one in the afternoon. Nothing could have prepared Michael and Stephanie for the actual experience. That their little Michelle was locked up in that enormous, foreboding place, did not seem possible. Glassy-eyed, they stared out the car windows. The sight of chain link fences topped with rolled razor wire; armed, uniformed guards,

and a line of female inmates shackled to a daisy chain, sent a cold chill through both of them. For several minutes, neither said a word.

Michael laid his head back on the headrest. "You know, Steph, I heard a saying a long time ago. I ignored it then, but a place like this sure makes you wonder."

Stephanie turned toward him. "What?"

"Well, if maybe it's true—that 'rules without relationship bring rebellion.' I mean, could that be part of the reason so many people wind up here?"

She shook her head. "I don't know. It's sad. When God sees people living like this, I bet it breaks His heart."

"By the way *my* heart feels, it must." Michael sighed. "All I ever did was make lots of rules for Michelle—'do this, don't do that'— and never had time for a relationship with her." He peered out at the razor wire and blinked hard to hold back tears. "Steph, I just had another awful thought."

Sniffling, she replied, "No thanks. I've got plenty of my own."

"What if Michelle really did get in this mess because of me? I don't think I could live with myself."

"Don't take all the blame. She's responsible for her actions. And besides, I did wrong, too. With Stephen sick, my own stuff going on . . ." She chewed on her upper lip. "I've never told you this, but the night before she ran away, I was in bed reading one of those novels I get so carried away with . . . you were in the bathroom . . . and she 'appeared' in the doorway. Just stood there in the shadows, not saying a word.

"She startled me at first. Said she couldn't sleep, so I asked her if she'd had a soda before bed, thinking it was the caffeine, or if she'd finished all her homework. You know how she worries about her grades. But maybe she was wanting to talk. If I had been more open to listen and not so preoccupied, she might have unloaded what was bothering her . . ." Stephanie buried her forehead in her hands. "You don't know how that has tormented me!"

Michael hung his head. "There's something I haven't told you, either, hon. The morning of the day she left, she showed up in my office, asking if we could get another dog. I was working on a proposal. I pretty much dismissed her with an indifferent, 'No, we can't-and-it's-not-up-for-discussion' attitude." He paused. "Worse yet, I made some smart comment about her being too busy with her boyfriend to take care of a dog, anyway. She had to remind me they broke up." His eyes met Stephanie's. "Maybe she wanted a dog so bad because she was lonely. Don't think all that hasn't come back to haunt *me.*"

Stephanie squeezed his hand. "I didn't tell you about my incident 'cause I was afraid you'd blame me for her leaving."

"Same here." He leaned over to hug her. "Guess we better stop that stuff, huh?"

She nodded and blew her nose. "I hope it's not too late, for Michelle's sake."

"Me too." He cupped her cheek in his hands. "I do love you, Steph. Will you forgive me for being such a jerk?"

"If you'll forgive me . . ."

"Deal." Michael took a deep breath, grabbed the cashier's check for the bond, and pushed open the car door, then headed for the building to stand in line in front of a bullet-proof window. The attorney had briefed him on what to expect.

Stephen woke up with the commotion, but Stephanie insisted he stay in the car with her. They tried to make time pass while they waited for the big moment. And wait they did. Each minute seemed like an hour. Stephen chewed his nails. He scribbled on his papers. He tapped his foot. He petted Angel. Stephanie fixed her

makeup and made an attempt to pray. Her heart felt like it would jump right out of her chest. She kept licking her lips and swallowing hard to stem the waves of nausea.

🙚 🙚 🙚

At three o'clock in the afternoon, all the inmates returned to sit on their beds for "count." It was the second major one of the day—first at seven a.m. and last, at eleven p.m., to make sure no one had escaped. When count cleared, Michelle lifted her mattress to pull out the jeans she had sandwiched between old newspapers. Josie had shown her how to dry her clothes that way after washing them in the little plastic tub under her bed. They came out stiff and a bit damp, but passable.

Suddenly, she froze in mid-action. "Josie," she exclaimed, "you wouldn't believe what just happened."

"What?"

"Well, I in my mind's eye, sort of, I saw my mom taking clothes out of the dryer . . . and handing them to me to fold. I could almost *feel* the soft, warm clothes against my skin and smell the scent of the dryer sheets. It was so real—"

The booming voice of a guard standing by her bed snapped her out of her reverie. "Witherton, pack 'em up!" he commanded. "You're goin' home."

She looked at him, wide-eyed. "What?"

"That's right. Somebody bonded you out."

She looked at a shocked Josie, who was grinning and flashing a thumbs up sign.

Michelle's own look of shock fell back on the guard. *"Home?"*

He nodded.

"Well . . . can I take a shower first?"

576

"Nope. Folks are waitin' outside and we need your bed." He paused to chuckle. "Just call it a 'come-as-you-are party.'" Josie stood up. Ignoring the guard's sneer, she shooed Michelle into immediate action.

It didn't take long to pull the few items out of her locker, once her trembling hands managed to open the stubborn combination lock. Grabbing her newly washed blue jeans and T-shirt, she ran to the bathroom to change.

She studied herself in the mirror for the first time in ages. *"Gross . . ."* she muttered. Everything felt too tight across her pouchy stomach and super baggy around her spindly legs. She kept the big T-shirt hanging loose to hide her tummy. Purple half-moons rimmed her big brown eyes. She didn't have a stitch of makeup to cover the dark circles, nor any blush to brighten up the drab color of her skin.

Her hair—worse yet. The dark brown roots had grown out several inches into the brassy blond dye she had used as a disguise. She had let her hair get so matted while she was living on the street, the jail "barber" had no alternative but to chop it off into a ragged boy cut. In her estimation, she looked a fright. But no time to fool around with it now.

She hurried back to her bed, then stopped to glance at Josie. It hit her. They would never see each other again. Somehow, it didn't seem fair. She was going home and Josie was going to prison. A lump started to form in Michelle's throat. She held out her hand, then decided to offer a hug instead. Her tiny arms couldn't begin to reach around Josie's broad back. "Take care," Michelle said quietly. "Thanks for being there—and for telling me what I needed to hear."

"Glad to. Stay clean."

"I'll try. If you give me your address, I'll write."

Josie jotted the information down on a piece of paper towel. "I won' be here too long. They be shippin' me out right after my sentencin', but I don' know where."

"Write me from your new place, then. I promise I'll write back."

"Got yo'self a deal, there. My mailbox be stayin' mighty empty." She looked away. "So long, girl."

"See ya." Michelle picked up her things and hurried to the officer's station to wait for an escort. What if it was her parents she'd be meeting outside? That thought made her stomach cramp enough to send her charging back into the bathroom.

Finally, the moment arrived. A guard in the control room pushed a button, the electronic door opened, and she walked out. *Free!* As simple as that. She remembered well the handcuffs and shackles and gated windows on the bus that had brought her to this awful place. Until seconds before, she was considered a serious threat to society. But no longer.

Amazing how money could make such a difference.

She saw her father off to the right side, standing alone with his hands in his pockets. He was staring right past her, still in the direction of the metal door. His face? Thinner, maybe. More gray hair above his ears than she remembered. His shoulders slouched and his eyes looked tired.

Dare she speak? She opened her mouth. Not a sound would come out. Not even a whisper. She walked up to him, lowered her head and managed three words, "Dad . . . it's me." Her eyes refused to meet his.

Michael looked down at the waif-like figure before him, the one who had called him "dad." He saw only the crown of a head with two-colored hair. If you could call the straw-like stuff, hair.

He inhaled deeply, held it for a few seconds, then breathed out slow and easy past the baseball-sized lump growing in his throat. With a gentle touch, he placed his forefinger under her chin and lifted her face. The pitiful child *was* his daughter. *"Michelle . . . my God, help us,"* he whispered. A hot poker of pain seared through his heart.

Her frightened eyes darted to the side, met his, then darted away again. She closed them. Big tears started to form at the sides and dripped down her thin cheeks. "I'm really sorry."

"Honey . . . I forgive you."

"I know I don't look very good." She was sobbing now.

He wrapped his arms around her bony frame, laid his head on top of hers, and cried. "You look beautiful to mc."

She shook her head. "You're just saying that."

"No. We've all missed you very much." Finally, he held her away at arm's length. "I mean that."

This time she let her eyes meet his. "You do?"

"Yes. I've realized some things while you were gone. During the brief times we spent together over the years, I did a lot of demanding. Not much listening. I'm sorry."

Shock filled her features. "I didn't know parents had to say they were sorry."

"Most of us don't know it, either." He cleared his throat. "So how about if we start over from here?"

She nodded and wiped away the tears with her hand.

He blew his nose on the hanky from his back pocket. "Guess we better go. There are folks outside who can't wait to see you."

Her face brightened a bit. "Mom and Stephen?"

He nodded.

"Anna and Joshua?

"Not telling. You'll see."

She slipped her arm around his forearm to steady herself. They walked outside into the sunshine and she sneezed several times from the glare. Her hands went up as a shield. "Gosh, the sun hurts," she said. Her eyelids clamped shut and refused to budge. Michael had to lead her toward the car where her mom and little brother sat, waiting.

When they were yet twenty feet away from the car, the doors swung open. Stephanie leaped out, shouting, *"It's Michelle!"*

Michael glanced over at his wayward daughter, who reacted with a nervous smile. Her eyes remained shut. She couldn't see her mother running toward her with arms outstretched. Nor her brother following close behind, carrying a puppy wearing splints.

"Hey, sis!" Stephen called. "We missed you . . ."

Stephanie gasped, then broke down.

The four of them locked in a tight embrace.

After what seemed like forever, Michael had to break loose. Stephen had set the dog on the ground and she was tickling his ankles. For some strange reason, she hadn't barked. Not a single whimper, not a peep. Michelle hadn't even noticed her.

Michael tugged at her shirt, told her to open her eyes, then pointed toward his feet and stepped back to allow room.

She looked down in the direction of his finger. At the sight of the familiar golden fur, now marked with stitched-up wounds, her mouth flew open. She let out a loud yell. *"Angel-l-l!"*

The next second, Angel was in her arms, licking her hands, her chin, her cheeks—anything within tongue's reach—using every ounce of energy she possessed. Michelle held her up high, twirled her around, and hugged her tight. "Oh, man, I sure love you, girl!" she cried. "I'm *so* glad you're alive!"

Suddenly, Michelle froze. She looked back and forth from one family member to the other. "P-please don't think I'm happier to see Angel than you. I'm just amazed she's even here because, well, Josie—"

Stephen shrugged. "That's okay. Dogs love without strings—kinda like God." The whole family stared at him, wide-eyed, for his latest tidbit of insight.

Nodding, Michelle paused and looked back in the direction of the door she had just been released from. "I can't explain everything right now, I guess . . . anyway, thanks so much for going through the trouble to get her for me."

Her dad broke in there. "You're welcome, honey. We had to have something to prove that *we* love you, too."

Michelle wiped her eyes again with her fingers and managed a smile. "I don't know why, but I'm sure glad you do."

❧ Thirty-Four ❧

inding a veterinary clinic to board Angel for a couple of days was easy. Michelle's distress over parting with her so soon turned out to be worse than Michael or Stephanie expected. It hurt them to see her so brokenhearted, but dogs and hotels didn't mix. Michael wondered if they shouldn't have waited until right before they were ready to leave New York to pick up Angel from the ASPCA. Stephen felt bad, too. He blamed himself for the idea. His disappointment straightened Michelle out in a hurry. She had to work extra hard to convince her brother it was worth it having her dog there with the rest of the family when she got out of . . . "Well . . . you know where," she said.

With the first crisis resolved, they headed for The Mayflower Hotel on Central Park West where Michael had stayed. On the way, Michelle pointed out the Convention and Visitor's Bureau. She had wandered in there during her "travels," though she never had money to visit any of the places advertised.

At Stephen's urging, they went in and found a baffling array of brochures on things to do and sights to see. He picked up one of each until both hands bulged. He admitted there wouldn't be enough time, but he could dream, couldn't he? Michelle kept busy glancing around the lobby, and commented about people "staring" at her—"as if she didn't belong." Stephanie tried to reassure her that wasn't so in the least.

A flyer on YMCA guest rooms caught Stephanie's eye. She opened it up and showed it to Michael. The Westside location was within a close walking distance, just down from Columbus Circle where they were. "Look here," she said to him, pointing to a photo. The refurbished historic building featured nice, clean rooms, the necessary comforts of an economy hotel, plus some of the best fitness facilities in the city. "It'd sure be less expensive for four of us. You'd *love* that, hon," she teased.

Her tone made Michael twinge a bit, as if she were implying he got tight-fisted when it came to his family. He held back a smart-alecky response. Something like, "Yeah, Steph, the way *you* spend money, we'd be broke if I didn't keep a close watch on things." To his utter amazement, he said he really appreciated her concern about the budget, and yes, the "Y" was a very nice place. Joshua and Anna had stayed there. However, he wasn't sure if it had double beds and he knew it didn't have phones in the rooms. "A telephone is mandatory for us. Besides," he added, "we need to celebrate Michelle's homecoming. Make it special."

Michelle lowered her head. "You don't have to do that, Dad. Honest. I look too awful to stay in some ritzy hotel—" Firmly, but with a new touch of gentleness he had lacked before, he insisted on sticking with his plan. After they got settled into the rooms he had reserved at The Mayflower (maritime decor and scenic view of Central Park appealed to all), they enjoyed a carryout Chinese meal, strolled around the park for an hour, and went to bed early. They were exhausted, but happy.

Early the next morning, they bought huge, fresh bagels smothered with cream cheese from a sidewalk vendor. That would suffice for breakfast. Without further hounding from Stephanie, Michael took Stephen with him to return the rental car. He'd had enough of the parking nightmare in Manhattan.

Meanwhile, Stephanie called around to find a hairdresser who specialized in corrective work. One man just had a cancellation, so she and Michelle hopped into a taxi, pronto. What a transformation he wrought in Michelle! After reconstructive conditioners, a return to her natural brunette color, and a professional cut and style, she looked almost like her old self, only thinner and more mature with short hair. Light makeup added the finishing touch. Michelle even cracked a tentative smile when she studied herself in the mirror. "Do I look okay, mom?" she asked, eyebrows raised.

Stephanie hugged her around the shoulders. "You look just precious, honey!"

Afterwards, they stopped at a boutique for a couple of casual outfits to tide her over until she got home. Stephanie noted that she seemed unusually nervous picking out clothes. She had always liked to shop. And where before she preferred a fitted, tailored style, now she kept zeroing in on "big and baggy." Never had Michelle been embarrassed about changing in front of her, either. Something was wrong.

In the middle of trying to pull on a pair of pants with an elastic waistband—she had always despised those—Michelle started to cry. News of the pregnancy came tumbling out, along with her fears about the baby's future and worst of all, what her dad would say. And no, she didn't know who the father was.

Stephanie could scarcely breathe as she listened. Her body went numb, but she hugged her daughter and expressed the whole family's support. They loved her. They would work it out.

Somehow. They had plenty of time to decide whether to give the baby up for adoption or raise it themselves. Then Stephanie took Michelle's thin hands in hers and said a little prayer.

At the end, she remembered something she had stuck in her wallet. She searched for it now. There it was, folded up behind her driver license. "Honey, listen to this poem Anna read to me when I wasn't doing too well. I think it's called, *'Do the Next Thing.'*

> From an old English parsonage down by the sea
> There came in the twilight a message for me;
> Its quaint Saxon legend, deeply engraven,
> Hath, as it seems to me, teaching from Heaven.
> And on through the hours the quiet words ring,
> Like a low inspiration: DO THE NEXT THING.
>
> Many a questioning, many a fear,
> Many a doubt, hath its quieting here.
> Moment by moment let down from Heaven,
> Time, opportunity, guidance, are given.
> Fear not tomorrows, Child of the King.
> Trust them with Jesus. DO THE NEXT THING.
>
> Do it immediately, do it with prayer;
> Do it reliantly, casting all care;
> Do it with reverence, tracing His hand
> Who placed it before thee with earnest command,
> Stayed on Omnipotence, safe 'neath His wing.
> Leave all resultings. DO THE NEXT THING.
>
> Looking to Jesus, ever serener,
> Working or suffering be thy demeanor.
> In His dear presence, the rest of His calm,
> The light of His countenance be thy psalm.
> Strong in His faithfulness, praise and sing!
> Then, as He beckons thee, DO THE NEXT THING."

"That's beautiful, Mom!" Michelle exclaimed. "You made it sound so pretty." She hesitated, then asked in a meek tone, "Speaking of 'the next thing' . . . can we please wait to tell dad and Stephen until we get back home?" Stephanie thought for a moment. She supposed that would be okay. They may as well try to have fun together for the next few days. They had to make up for a lot of lost time.

And fun, they had! So much lay within a short distance from the hotel. In Central Park, they took a horse-drawn carriage ride, strolled through the zoo, watched skateboarders, jugglers, and model yachts sailing on the pond. Michelle made a pointed effort to avoid bothering the homeless people. They were sitting and lying about, sleeping in the grass and on park benches. "Believe it or not, I was one, too," she whispered to her mom.

The four of them caught part of an outdoor concert at Lincoln Center, stopped at the Museum of Natural History for Michelle, and, at Stephen's request, the Hayden Planetarium. Stephanie really wanted to see the exhibit of rare Bibles at the American Bible Society headquarters, but they were running out of time.

They could only take in one more attraction, so they agreed on the Statue of Liberty. Taking a taxi as far as Greenwich Village, they walked the rest of the way down to Battery Park to catch the ferry to Liberty and Ellis Islands. They decided not to climb the steps to the crown. None of them could handle the three-hour wait on a narrow, winding staircase. Notwithstanding, it was the highlight of the trip.

After a supper of fantastic deep-dish pizza at an Italian restaurant and an hour relaxing in their rooms, they moseyed down to the pool. Michelle had shied away from her bathing suit, so she and Stephanie sat on the deck in shorts, dangling their feet in the water, while Michael and Stephen horsed around in the pool.

"Honey," Stephanie mused, "I haven't seen your brother this spunky in ages. Your coming home has really perked him up." Her comment brought out Michelle's prettiest smile and crowned the whole trip with a perfect finale. They would have to leave for Florida the following morning.

By ten o'clock that night, the kids made no more bedtime protests. Michael and Stephanie were alone now in the adjoining room, stretched out on the bed, reminiscing about the events of the last few months and watching TV. He dozed off first.

Stephanie pushed the on-off button on the remote when the movie ended at eleven. Little by little, her mind started to churn. Thoughts about the future—counseling, drug rehab, the baby that Michael knew nothing of yet—assaulted her head like wind-driven waves against a pier. She grew more anxious. She tried to think about something else—the sights they had enjoyed together, redecorating she planned to do at home, laundry waiting to be washed. Nothing helped.

Out of nowhere, she felt a terrible weight on her chest. It got heavier by the second, pressing her down onto the bed. She was engulfed in a sense of hopelessness beyond description. A feeling so bleak, so black and horrible that she closed her eyes tight to push it away . . .

It would not be pushed away.

Her thoughts worsened. Stephen's health would go spiraling downhill. Michelle would suffer repeated relapses and be sent to prison . . .

She and Michael would have to raise a grandchild alone.

Their life's savings would be drained dry.

They would lose the property to pay their debts.

She would crack up and spend years in recovery.

Stephen would die a lingering, painful death.

One after another, the fears grew bigger and more awful. Imagined scenarios loomed so real, she could have reached out and touched them. The weight pressed down heavier, giving an acute sensation that it would either crush her or make her chest explode from the pressure. She started to cry. She muzzled her face in her pillow to keep from waking Michael. From that point on, she drifted in and out of awareness . . .

He propped himself up on his elbows and rubbed his eyes. "Steph, what's the matter? I thought we had a great time together."

She rocked back and forth, crying harder, and began to moan soft and low. "Please, Lord, tell me we'll be okay. Please let me know I won't lose my mind. I really need to know. Oh, God, please help us. I'm *so afraid* . . ." Over and over and over.

In a calm voice he whispered, "It's okay, hon, we'll be okay. I promise." Taking her in his arms, he held her.

He spoke words of comfort again and again. To no avail.

He tried to pray.

She only cried harder, rocking and moaning about how awful life would be.

He became alarmed. She was acting hysterical.

It seemed as if she couldn't hear a word he said. Her cries increased in intensity until she was sobbing with a deeper sorrow than he had ever heard. If she got any worse, it could wake guests in other rooms.

His heart started pounding. His mouth went dry.

What on earth was going on? Was his wife having a nervous breakdown?

Maybe the stress had taken its terrible toll.

Should he call the front desk?

An ambulance? What?

What about the kids? Were they okay? He laid Stephanie back on the bed and checked their room. Sound asleep, both of them.

He hurried back to his wife. No change. She rocked and moaned and sobbed until she was choking on her tears.

Suddenly, it struck him: *call Joshua.*

He turned on the light by the bed. She didn't even react to the change in brightness.

Thank God he'd gone with his gut feeling to choose a place with a phone in the room! Had he actually heard the Holy Spirit for once in his life?

He dialed the number at home. It rang seven times. Joshua answered with a sleepy, but ever-polite greeting.

"Josh!" Michael cried. "Something's wrong with Stephanie!"

"She is ill?"

"I don't know. It's as if she's in another world or something. She's carrying on like a banshee about how scared she is. She won't respond to me at all. We had a great couple days, the best with the four of us in years and bam—"

Joshua cleared his throat. "A demonic attack."

Michael had heard about such matters, but had never put much stock in them. The subject seemed rather . . . well . . . silly.

"Attacks often precede or follow a victory," Joshua added. "And what better time? You have just received of heaven's blessings. Satan seeks to recover ground he has lost."

"So what do I do about it?"

"Pray, brother, *pray!*"

"I tried! She only got worse!

Joshua paused. "That simply means the devil fought back. Get busy. This time, lay your hands on your wife, ask the *Holy Spirit* to pray through you, and forge ahead."

"But I haven't done this heavy-duty stuff before . . ."

"What difference, my friend? No evil spirit has any authority in your midst. *You do,* in Jesus' name. Use it."

Michael felt ridiculous. "Honest. I don't have it in me to pray like that. You'd be better—"

"No, you can do this, Michael." Joshua's tone was firm. "If your wife or your children were bleeding to death, would you wring your hands because you are not a doctor?"

"Well, no . . ."

"Of course not. You would act on whatever knowledge you had. Do the same in the Spirit. You know the Scriptures. Proclaim them now to the enemy . . . and to Stephanie, as well."

"But I'm not some pastor. I'm just a man—"

"*Just* a man, you say? Nonsense! God Almighty has appointed you the king, prophet, and priest of your home. It is high time for you to rise to your position and do battle!"

Michael's cheeks burned. How dare he talk to him like a disobedient child!

A split second before Michael was ready to speak his mind, Joshua offered a sincere apology for having sounded a bit too stern. He explained that he got that way whenever he sensed the devil stirring up trouble where he did not belong.

"I find this devil business hard to swallow," Michael admitted.

"Why so? Did you not tell me," the older man asked gently, "that my father taught you to believe the Bible?"

"He did. But we didn't have a chance to get into this kind of stuff." Michael ran his hands through his hair. "Besides, even with what Caleb *did* teach me, I've grown pretty rusty."

Joshua chuckled and replied, "No matter. The oil of the Holy Spirit has loosened many a rusty part in my day."

With that, Michael's indignation vanished. He smiled a bit and thanked Joshua for the vote of confidence.

"Very well. I will disconnect now," Joshua murmured. "Rest assured that Anna and I will continue to intercede for all of you." He said a warm goodbye and hung up.

At the click of the phone, Michael glanced at Stephanie. After a brief respite, she was slipping back into the quicksand of despair. His own panic returned. He felt way out of his league. His simple prayer in the vineyard a few days earlier sounded like baby talk by comparison to what he needed now.

Still, he had already witnessed a couple of improvements from that short session. Mainly in himself—his temper, his patience level. Maybe there was hope for him yet. And certainly, Joshua wouldn't have left him stranded in an emergency. A glimmer of courage began to rise up within him. "Okay, Lord," he whispered, "guess it's You and me. I'm counting on You. Please help me pray for Steph. Holy Spirit, speak through me . . ."

Cradling Stephanie's head in his left hand, he lay down beside her and placed his right hand on her breastbone where she was complaining of an ache. His voice sounded timid at first, but quickly grew bolder than he expected:

"In the name of Jesus Christ, I take authority over this attack against my wife. The Word says the same power that raised Jesus from the dead lives in us. We do not fight against flesh and blood, but against principalities and powers and spiritual wickedness in high places . . ."

He stopped for a breath. He licked his lips. Verses and phrases he had never memorized were rolling off his tongue. "Thank You, Lord for Your protection. Whatever we bind on earth shall be bound in heaven. I bind up every single evil spirit sent to harm us. God has not given us a spirit of fear, but of *power* . . . *love* . . . and *a sound mind.* Now get out of here, Satan, in the name of Jesus Christ! You are not welcome in my family! *Go!*"

591

Tender Journey

Stephanie quieted down almost immediately. He marveled at how fast. It was the most miraculous thing he had ever seen! She said the painful heaviness on her chest left. The awful thoughts and feelings of dread vanished—like a vapor. She was left with a sweet peace, a safe feeling of being "wrapped in a warm blanket." From *his* prayers, no less! Incredible . . .

She shocked him further by asking if he would snuggle with her. He scooted over closer to hold her tight. "Boy," she whispered, "Everything seemed so hopeless, I wanted to die—" She stopped short. "See . . . there's a lot more to Michelle's coming home than you realize."

"What?" He raised his eyebrows, waiting.

"Michael, our daughter . . . is going to have a baby!"

His breath caught. "No. Tell me you're kidding."

"I wish I could. She blurted it out while we were shopping. I'm sorry. That's why I got so upset—"

He placed his index finger on her lips. "Steph, *I'm* the one who's sorry. You felt you had to bear it without me."

"But you always say I get too emotional."

"I know. I've been a pretty insensitive moron."

"You mean that?" She wiped away a few remaining tears.

"Yes. I'm starting to realize I've been part of the problem." Brushing her hair back from her face, he added, "I could have been a better husband and father. More caring, more involved. If I had, maybe we wouldn't be in this mess." She hugged him so hard he could scarcely breathe. They cuddled for a long while, ended up making love for the first time since Michelle ran away, and fell asleep in each other's arms. Could God really light a spark in the romance department? That was almost too much to ask.

The next morning before the kids awakened, Michael ordered room service so he and his wife could have breakfast in bed. Had they both not clearly remembered the demonic incident from the night before, they would not have believed it happened.

"Steph," Michael began as he sipped his coffee, "God has opened my eyes like never before. Satan has targeted families for destruction. If we don't wake up, we're gonna get creamed!"

Taking a slow bite of fresh fruit, she replied, "We already *have* been creamed."

"Right. And it's got to stop—now. We need a strategy."

"Offense or defense?"

"Both. We're in all-out war, I can tell you that. Against an invisible foe. And *he's* not playing games."

"War?"

"Yeah. *War.*" Michael climbed out of bed and paced back and forth. "I had a dream last night, hon. The devil knows just how to pit us against each other instead of against him. God has been working overtime to get our attention. Kind of like military leaders trying to convince civilians about a dictator's army."

She knit her brows. "So we've underestimated the enemy—"

"Yes. And *over*estimated ourselves. A lot of it's my fault. I should have been praying more—for you, me, and the kids. All these years, I've been letting us skip along on our merry way, mouthing a few 'hip-pocket' prayers here and there. Or, whenever I was in the mood, whipping through a quick verse on the fly. Man, it's so clear. We're facing a life-or-death situation!" He shook his head. "Michelle getting pregnant is the very thing that could destroy our family . . . but God's not going to let that happen. He'll help us turn it into a blessing."

They had to believe it wasn't too late.

That very day, they made a solemn covenant:

The Lord God would have first place in their home.

❧ *Epilogue* ❧

ramatic hues of purple, rose, and gold splashed across the darkening blue sky as the sun set once more. A stillness was settling in over the Nastasis home, punctuated only by a chorus of chirping crickets. The two couples had yet to move from their after-dinner spot on the front porch. Joshua and Anna sat on the wicker love seat, her head resting on his shoulder. Michael and Stephanie held hands on the swing and gently rocked back and forth. A friend of Michelle's had picked her up for a drug abuse meeting. Stephen was playing a game upstairs in his room.

In a quiet voice, Joshua broke the silence. "You two have been through a great deal of late. Now that life has returned somewhat to normal, do you have any plans?"

Stephanie shrugged and looked at Michael.

He hesitated, then replied, "Yes, one: recuperate."

Stephanie nodded. "We're both drained. In fact, I have never felt so tired in my life. We couldn't stand any more episodes like the ones we've had."

"I understand," Anna said. "After the initial shock of our Anja's death, I felt weary as you described for a year or more. How I needed a vacation! But our austere existence behind the Wall forbade such a luxury. In the early days of our marriage, however, we would travel to the mountains whenever time permitted . . ."

Joshua sighed, leaned his head back against the top of the loveseat and stared at the evening sky. "Ah, yes, my dear. I had long since forgotten those glorious days."

Anna smiled. "Those trips did us much good. We felt closer to God—and to each other—standing high atop one of His magnificent, snow-covered peaks. We could look out over white villages and bright blue lakes surrounding us on every side."

He nodded. "And remember how you loved King Ludwig's castle at Neuschwanstein?"

"Yes . . . so quaint it is! Stephanie, how you would adore it—nestled in the mountains like the setting of a fairy tale! But our favorite winter hideaway was Garmisch Partenkirchen in the Alps of Bavaria. By day, we would hike and ski until we could not take another step. By night, we would cozy up in front of the fireplace at the mountain house, sip hot drinks, play board games, and chat to our heart's content."

"And in general, become acquainted again." Joshua paused to cast a loving glance at his wife. "Anna, perhaps some time such as we had would help our new friends recover. Do you suppose?"

"Oh, yes. They would feel inside and out brand new." She gave Joshua another lazy snuggle.

Michael turned to Stephanie. Their eyes met and held for an instant. "We do know some people," he volunteered, "who have a cabin in North Carolina. The four of us could go. And take the kids!" Stephanie missed the mild teasing tone in his voice that accompanied the four-of-us-and-take-the-kids idea. She grasped the chain holding the porch swing, scooted over to the far edge of the seat, and frowned at him.

If Michael noticed, he didn't let on. He got up from the swing with a "be right back" gesture and added, "Gotta go get something important in the office."

Stephanie looked questioningly at Joshua and Anna, but they acted as in-the-dark as she was. Before they had time to discuss the matter, Michael had returned with a glossy white and navy blue folder in one hand and a video in the other. "Yep, we can all go to the mountains together. Michelle and Stephen will love it." He paused a moment for effect, then patted the brochure. *"But . . . only after Steph and I do what I have in mind!"* He sat down beside her and gave her a hug. "Just the two of us."

Joshua clapped to show his approval. "Brother, I was worried about you. I thought you had forgotten everything you have been learning." He hesitated. "Now, there is nothing wrong with the children. Anna and I adore their company. But you and Stephanie do need quality time alone."

Michael winked. "No argument on my part." He reached over and placed his right hand over Stephanie's left. "I don't want to get caught back up in the same old routine. It would be too easy." He moved closer to Stephanie and placed the folder, face down, across both of their laps. "I was a first-class dimwit in the husband cate-gory. However, I've been making major improvements." He turned to his wife. "Haven't I, Steph?"

She grimaced and shrugged. "Maybe."

"What?"

She giggled. "I'm teasing. You're doing much better. Hopefully, I'm doing better, too. But then—*I* didn't have as far to go . . ."

"You little squirt!" he exclaimed as he tickled her in the ribs. She burst out laughing, wriggled away, and pleaded with him to stop. He did, just in time to open up the white folder on her lap and take out a large brochure.

Stephanie's mouth opened when she saw the color photo of a tall ship under full sail. He read the title aloud, *"Star Clippers: Charting a Course to the Uncommon."*

Looking at Michael with pure astonishment, she exclaimed, "You're not serious."

"As serious as I can be. We're going to take a little jaunt into the wild blue yonder."

"That's too extrava—"

"Hush, my dear. Remember that biomedical stock I invested in a couple years ago? I cashed it in with a good return—better than I expected—so I'm spending the profit on you. After all you've been through, you deserve it."

She looked down again at the photo and took a deep breath. "I can't believe it. Ever since my daddy took me sailing when I was a little girl, I've wanted to go again. Oh, to feel the wind rushing past my face . . . to smell the fresh sea air . . . hear the call of the gulls . . ."

"Hon, you shared that wish with me years ago, but I never bothered to act on it. Too self-centered, I guess. I'd spend the money on office equipment in a heartbeat." He paused to pick at his fingernail. "Anyway, I chose this particular cruise line because we won't have to sit around and eat for twelve hours a day. We'll be able to lend the crew a hand, taking the wheel or hoisting the sails or whatever we want to do."

"You're kidding!"

"No. It's all in there."

She looked down at the glossy folder in her hands. "I never dreamed I'd ever go on a tall ship like this. They used to have these in the eighteen hundreds. Look at all those *gorgeous* white sails!"

He nodded and turned to the inside cover of the brochure. "Read this—out loud so Joshua and Anna can hear."

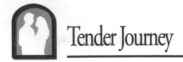

She held the paper at arm's length and began reading, with her own touch of dramatic flair:

> Standing on the deck of a four-masted tall ship, ready to weigh anchor, your pulse quickens as the captain issues a few brief commands to the crew. Suddenly, 36,000 square feet of billowing sails unfurl above you . . .

She stopped to pat her hand against her chest. "Thirty-six thousand square feet of white sails! Can you imagine what a sight that must be?"

He smiled, nodded, and motioned her to go on reading. She backed up a little ways and started again,

> . . . billowing sails unfurl above you as the ship begins to glide serenely out of the harbor into sparkling open seas. And you and your shipmates are traveling on the wings of the wind. To the one place on earth where the human spirit is still truly free—

Michael interrupted her at that point. "Granted, someone got a little carried away there."

Joshua nodded. "I was thinking the same. Sailing the vast ocean, as superb as it is, can never fill the tall order of setting the spirit free."

"We know Who can, though," Stephanie chimed in.

"Amen," Anna seconded.

Stephanie tilted her head and shrugged. "Guess the copywriter got caught up in the thrill of the moment. I know I will."

Michael patted her on the knee.

She crossed her legs and continued reading aloud,

Together, you will rediscover the natural wonders of the sea . . . You will sail on one of the two most remarkable and romantic vessels ever to grace the Atlantic Ocean, as well as the Caribbean and Mediterranean Seas . . . Welcome aboard. The adventure begins.

She set the brochure back on her lap. "This is incredible. You made reservations already?"

"Not yet. I thought about it, but decided you'd rather pick the date yourself."

She smiled. "You know me. Not too many surprises at once."

"That's what I figured. Besides, we have to choose our destination. Why don't we go watch the video? Maybe that'll help us decide." They went into the den and all four of them marveled over the breathtaking photography throughout.

When it was over, Michael turned to Stephanie. "So, my lady, what's your choice—the Caribbean or the Mediterranean?"

At the mention of faraway places, her face took on a worried expression. "But Michael, the kids. With all the extra care they need, that's too much to ask of someone, just so we can go zipping about on some yacht . . ." She shook her head. "I'd feel too guilty."

Joshua sat up straight. He removed his arm from around Anna's shoulders, leaned forward, and clasped his hands. "What if Anna and I were to volunteer our services? Surely we are good for more than furniture adornments."

Anna's head showed her agreement. "We would be delighted, if you could place your trust in us, of course."

"That wouldn't even be an issue. I was just thinking in case of emergency—"

Michael interjected, "Hon, I bet friends would lend them a hand if need be. We'll only be gone a week."

"Oh . . . A week. That might be okay. I had the notion of cruising for months."

He half-frowned, half-grinned. "Steph, hold on. You're not worth *that* much money!"

She poked him in the ribs with her elbow. "You better take that back right now!"

"I'll take it back under one condition—if you say, unequivocally, 'Yes, I promise to go and relax.'"

"Okay."

"Not good enough. Say, 'I promise to go and relax.'"

"Michael . . ." She made a face at him. "That's stupid."

He smirked. "I just want a commitment, lest you weasel out at the last minute."

"All right, I'll go. And try my best to relax."

"Close enough. I take back my earlier statement: you are worth the cost of a million cruises. In fact, you're worth more than anything."

"Except the Lord."

"Of course. He's gotta be numero uno." He stood up, pulled her off the sofa and twirled her around.

She looked him in the eyes. "You're really excited about this, aren't you?"

"Guess I am."

"It means a lot to me that you've been planning something so nice on your own. That's worth as much as the trip." She gave him a light kiss and soon, they were locked in a tender embrace.

Joshua picked up the Bible sitting at his side on the loveseat. He and Anna began reading quietly. When a familiar voice broke the silence again, they looked up.

Stephanie arranged her hair. "Better go get started on that kitchen," she said. "I left it a disaster area."

Anna got up from the loveseat and smoothed her dress. "I will help you—for I have in mind a surprise. Besides, I cherish our woman-to-woman talks." She tossed her head back a little for emphasis and glanced at Joshua and Michael with a twinkle in her green eyes. "Would you two gentlemen care to take a walk? Upon your return, my famous apple dessert will be served."

Michael winked at her. "*Now* you're talking, Anna."

Joshua stood up. "Michael and I will do the servant's honors tomorrow night. Agreed, brother?"

"Fine by me. Let's go enjoy the evening." They each gave their wives a quick hug and headed down the back steps.

Joshua rubbed his hands together. "Truthfully, I am glad the women took us off the hook."

Laughing, Michael asked, "Do you mean 'let us off the hook?' You *take* a phone off the hook."

"Oh, yes." Joshua repeated the tricky slang phrases several times to add them to his vocabulary.

"So why are you so happy about getting out of the dishes?"

"Ah . . . that superb sailing ship set me to deep thinking."

Michael waited for more. With the hint of a smile he replied, "Joshua, know what? You do the same thing Caleb used to do! He would make a statement that he knew would pique my curiosity to no end. Then, with a mischievous glint in those blue eyes, he'd delay the details to see if I was paying attention. It usually preceded an important point he wanted to make."

Joshua let out a soft sigh at the mention of the father he would never meet. "How strange . . . I do have in mind to say something of merit, I believe. And you say my father would act as I do?"

"Exactly. His eyes, the same piercing blue as yours, would sparkle and his mouth would curve up in half smile as he waited. He looked like a young boy with a secret."

601

Tender Journey

"As a matter of fact, I feel precisely so. What I was thinking is this: your ship might help us grasp some profound truths you and I have been discussing. After all, God must have a certain fondness for boats. He put Noah in an ark, did He not? Jesus invited His disciples into a rowboat. Perhaps He wants to place *us* in a clipper ship!" He paused. Michael's expression betrayed his confusion.

"The Lord is the captain of our ship, so to speak. He provides whatever equipment we, the crew, need to do our jobs until we arrive safely at our final port of call."

"Which is?"

"Heaven, son!"

"Interesting concept."

"But think of this, Michael: Our God is not only the captain. He is the shipbuilder. The navigator. The chief steward. And He even acts as a gourmet chef, serving up splendid meals en route if we will simply sit down at His table long enough to eat."

Michael thought about the implications of what Joshua was saying and nodded.

The older man leaned forward as they walked. "However, in an amazing sort of way . . . at the very same time . . . He is the *wind* that moves His vessel along! Remember—throughout the Bible, from Genesis to Revelation—the wind represents the Holy Spirit." He stopped, raised his eyes to the distance and exclaimed, "Oh, my! When I saw that ship gliding through the water with the ocean breezes filling her gleaming sails, it became so clear . . ."

"Yeah, now that you mention it . . . But if God handles all those jobs, it doesn't leave much for us to do."

"Au contraire, mon ami!"

Michael smiled at Joshua's cosmopolitan touch and pondered his point for a minute. "Well . . . I guess we should make sure we stay in the boat."

"Exactly. There we are safe. Just as Noah found protection from judgment and the disciples from the storm, so will we. Furthermore, we ought to stay with Him for the most important reason: so we can know Him. Respect Him. And love Him. Long journeys make for intimate chats and genuine relationships."

Michael's eyebrows went up. "I realize that's what God wants most. It's what I'm used to giving Him least."

Joshua nodded. "You wondered what is our part. You tell me."

"Well, now that you've got me going on this ship business . . . Let's see. We should definitely follow the route mapped out by the navigator . . . keep the equipment in good repair . . . and obey the captain's orders." He paused to stroke his chin. "If the wind represents the Holy Spirit, we'd better know which way the wind is blowing and how strong. Then we should set our sails in the right direction and hoist them to catch the draught."

"Right! Seasoned sailors understand one thing very well: they cannot change the course of nature to suit their fancy. They must learn to set the sails appropriately and 'go with the flow,' as you Americans say. If the wind does not blow, they do not go."

"True. And you're a poet and don't know it." He winked.

Smiling, Joshua added, "How far would that clipper ship move, with nothing but four bare masts poking high into the sky?"

"Not to the Caribbean, for sure."

"I dare say you and Stephanie would vacation in the harbor."

Michael cocked his head. "S'pose so."

"Although the boat on which you will travel, no doubt, has engines if the wind subsides." Joshua gave him a curious look.

"Sure. But the brochure says they depend on engine-power as little as possible. That's one reason I chose that company."

"Yes. And we would do well to follow suit in the spiritual realm. You see, we come equipped not only with 'sails,' but with

603

an 'engine.' Call that religious legalism, where one speeds through the motions on autopilot. Ritual may indeed keep us moving, but not necessarily to the correct harbor."

"I've been there. And ended up on the rocks."

"Have not we all? How difficult to choose the slower, quieter, more contemplative way of God. In days past, you know, sailors enjoyed no such engine-power option. They had to depend solely on their sails and the wind."

"Either that . . . or *row!*"

Joshua smiled. "Yes. Which would cause one to wear out in short order." He paused in thought for a few seconds, then added. "Surprisingly, many Christians live that way. They row when they could sail."

"Which translated means . . . ?"

"They depend on the flimsy oars of their own strength and burn out. They could be sailing under full power."

"I bet in the last few years Steph and I have done the virtual equivalent of three transatlantics, paddling like crazy in a rubber raft—with a slow leak! We're learning, I guess."

"As are Anna and I. Growth gives evidence of life."

"Yeah. Some of us just grow faster than others." He stopped to shake his head. "I'm tired of rowing myself half to death and still running aground. It's time to go under 'full power.'"

"You can, Michael!"

Michael broke in, "I know, I know—cut the engine, hoist the sails, wait for the wind. We've been trying. We're reading the Bible more together, which should help."

"That is very important. But there is more. You could read twenty-four hours a day, yet advance very little in matters of the Spirit." They walked on further and crested the hill that over-looked the pond, now swollen to a new height from recent rains.

Together, they descended to the edge. Joshua was the first to spot something small and white sticking up among the reeds.

As they drew closer, Michael could see what it was. "Will you look at that? Just like his mother." His tone grew sharp. "I've been talking to Stephen about putting his stuff away after he's done with it. These remote toys don't come cheap." He glanced at Joshua. Suddenly, he felt very sheepish about his short fuse. Besides, he had called Stephen into the house when it started to lightning the day before. "Sorry I got so critical," he confessed.

Joshua touched Michael's arm and made a "never mind" gesture with his left hand. His eyes lit up with delight as he pointed at the tiny sailboat. "Michael, I think the Lord has just given us something special."

"What?" His eyes wandered to the sailboat. He could detect nothing out of the ordinary.

"Take a careful look at that sail."

Michael shrugged. "A piece of old plastic stuck onto two perpendicular wooden sticks."

"Yes. Now think back to the clipper ship. Do you notice any differences?"

Michael stared off into the distance, then closed his eyes to remember the image on the video. "Size, obviously. Plus, it had a bunch of sails of different dimensions and shapes, instead of one. All white. And they were 'pöufy,' as Stephanie would s—" He stopped short. His mouth dropped open. "Joshua, I do believe I see it."

"What?"

"I see what you're getting at! If the Holy Spirit is the wind, our *hearts* are like sails. And we definitely need the clipper-ship variety to get anywhere."

"Why so?"

"I don't know if I can express it, but I'll give it the old college try. They have large surface areas exposed to the wind. When it blows, they get filled up and billowy . . ."

"Good. Go on."

"In other words, they're very pliable, for lack of a better word. The wind actually shapes them, whereas on this toy boat, the sail stays flat, no matter what. And stiff. Really more for show than anything."

"Very good observations, Michael! Quite astute." Joshua slapped him on the back in a complimentary gesture, the way Caleb used to do. "You have just described a tremendous picture of two kinds of believers. The first are very humble and flexible and receptive to the Lord. They respond with joyful ease to His commandments, as well as to His calling—whether He speaks through other people, through His Word, or by the whisper of His voice. Some Bible scholars use the term, 'submission.' Some, yield-edness, abiding, teachableness, surrender. 'Tis the same principle. The other group may demonstrate outward actions of Christianity 'for show-off,' but inside? A stiff-necked, unrepentant lot!"

"I probably fall into the latter category more often than not. I want to submit, but sometimes I don't like it one bit."

"Nor do I. But if we were to respond to His Holy Spirit with as much abandon as those beautiful sails do to the wind, oh what a difference in our lives!

Michael grew quiet. For several minutes, he didn't say a word. Finally he spoke. "I was just thinking how wind is everywhere—in and on and around the sails. And they, in the wind. You could barely separate the two."

"An unusually close relationship, yes, I would say. The Word and prayer —*with a yielded heart*—will do the same for us."

"Then we wouldn't have to row the hard way, huh?"

Joshua shook his head. "Storms will come, yes. But we will not face them alone." He took a last look at the toy sailboat stranded among the reeds. All of a sudden, he started humming, barely more than a whisper at first, then louder.

"What's that tune you're singing?" Michael asked.

"An American song taught to me by a teacher. I believe it's called, 'Row Your Boat.' I cannot remember the words, however."

"Oh, most of us learned it as a round when we were kids. Here you go:

> *Row, row, row your boat,*
> *Gently down the stream*
> *Merrily, merrily, merrily, merrily*
> *Life is but a dream.*"

"That is precisely it!" Joshua exclaimed.

"The words to that song bothered me as a child. I *wanted* life to be a dream. Unfortunately, it's the real deal."

"True. At any rate, new lyrics went floating through my head. Sometimes poems or songs come to me." Joshua tapped his head with his forefinger.

"Just like that?"

"Just like that."

"Well, let's hear it, Beethoven." Michael chuckled.

Joshua cleared his throat and with a half-kidding, half-serious face, sang,

> *Row, row, row your boat,*
> *Way out, on your own.*
> *You will tire, then expire,*
> *As you complain and moan.*

607

Michael burst out laughing. "Joshua, you are too much! You just made that up?"

He nodded. "Wait for the second verse:

Sail, sail, sail your boat
On the deep blue sea.
With the Holy Spirit's help—"

He stopped. "Fiddlesticks! I have no last line."

Michael laughed. *"Fiddlesticks?* Haven't heard that expression in ages. Last line or no, you are downright clever, my friend." He raised his eyebrows. "Sorry I can't help you there. A poet, I'm not."

"How do you know? Have you ever tried?"

"No . . ."

"Then say not, 'I can't.'"

They walked a little further around the pond.

Suddenly, Michael urged, "Okay, sing it again."

Joshua did and directed with his finger to the beat. When he came to the last line, he made an abrupt cut and shook his head. "Not there."

Michael raised his index finger. "I think I've got one. Do it one more time and I'll join in on the last line." Joshua began,

Row, row, row your boat.
Way out, on your own.
You will tire, then expire,
As you complain and moan.

Sail, sail, sail your boat
On the deep blue sea,
With the Holy Spirit's help . . .

Michael chimed in at just the right moment. Slightly off-key, slower, and with a melodramatic sustained last note, he crooned, *"Free . . . you'll . . . tru-ly . . . be-e-e-e-e!"*

Joshua clapped with all his might. "Bravo! Bravo! Just perfect!"

Out of breath, Michael exhaled with a loud burst. "I wouldn't go that far." He laughed again. "You're just like Caleb, you rascal. He would get me to do the craziest stuff. I would forget all about my image. I'm a stuffed-shirt at heart."

"That phrase I do not recognize."

"Another old expression. I don't know the exact meaning. Something like too serious, pretentious, no fun."

"Well, then! You need to discard that old stuffy shirt." Michael stifled another grin at Joshua's version.

"And is it not the Lord to have used both of us to accomplish His goal?" Joshua patted him on the shoulder.

Nodding, Michael replied, "Strength in numbers, I guess. Like the clipper ship. With all those sails, it moves a lot faster than a dinghy."

"Exactly! Likewise in prayer. One can send a thousand evil spirits to flight, but two can send ten thousand."

"Boy, don't I know it. I remember when I called you from New York. Your prayers worked, in spite of me." He tilted his head and raised his eyebrows. "That experience opened Steph's and my eyes to a whole new dimension. We're not very well-equipped."

"How long do you intend to wait?" Joshua winked at him.

"We're trying, honest. We've always had a hard time praying together. Mostly me, I guess. She wanted to, but I felt odd. Too . . . vulnerable baring my soul in front of her."

"Believe me, I understand. You feel less than a man, expressing your deepest needs and fears to a woman. It requires humility to surrender to the Lord in this area."

"Don't tell me I've gotta eat *more* 'humble pie.'" Michael made a sour face.

"It is good for you, so prepare thy fork and thine heart. There is another bitter, healing herb in the recipe, as well—forgiveness."

"We're working on that. But there's one thing Steph and I still haven't explored. Some prayer-with-intimacy idea . . . The concept was totally foreign to us," he added, "until we saw it mentioned in a pamphlet Eric sent called, *Transform Your Marriage.*"

Joshua raised his eyebrows. "Ah, yes. Anna discovered the piece on the coffee table. We both found it to be excellent reading. Blending physical and spiritual elements of marriage seems quite biblical to us."

"You're kidding. It's far-out, if you ask me." Michael rolled his eyes. "At first, to tell you the truth, the idea seemed beyond ridiculous. I don't know . . . like the two of us showing up at a rip-roarin' barn dance dressed in white tails and evening gown. Out of place for the occasion—if you know what I mean." He blushed, then broke into a grin.

Joshua chuckled at Michael's apt analogy. "Again, I do understand. Anna and I felt a bit awkward when we adopted the idea years ago. No more, though."

"You mean you've actually been . . . that way?"

"Why, yes. The more we studied God's intent for marriage in the Word—a picture of the holy relationship between Christ and His church—the more it made perfect sense to make a few changes. And to stop practicing our faith 'in compartments.' *Give thanks in all things,* saith the Lord. So we did."

Joshua paused to reflect, then smiled. "Today, we could not conceive of neglecting to ask God's blessings on one another. To do so during moments of special closeness is the most natural thing in the world! Using the opposite of your barn-dance analogy, if we were to approach one another otherwise, we would feel odd, as if, oh . . . how do you refer to an event where the men wear tuxedos?"

"Black tie?"

"Yes, yes. We would feel as if we were trying to attend a black tie affair in soiled dungarees and work boots. That would not be kosher, would it?"

"Guess not. Let me put it this way—we might be open."

"Good. No need to force the issue prematurely."

"Right. But after all we've seen God do, maybe He would . . . So, if and when we're ready, then what?"

Joshua cleared his throat. "In such a delicate area, I would not care to usurp the job of the Holy Spirit. He taught Anna and me. He can guide you also. Simply set aside ample time to spend together—an hour or two, at least. Read the Word, the pamphlet, and thank the Lord for the many ways you have been a gift to each other." He winked. "Good heavens! The two of you will have plenty of opportunity on the trip to go exploring."

"I know. That in itself bothers me a little." Michael had something on his mind, but he wasn't sure he wanted to bring it up. It was embarrassing. He decided to take a chance. "With all the stress, we've let intimacy slip away. I feel pretty clumsy getting back in the groove with Steph. Know what I mean?"

"I do. Most couples—Anna and I included—have experienced the same dilemma. I promise you that a more thankful, prayerful attitude will restore joy to your love life."

He kicked a stone side to side, then into the pond. "It will?"

"Yes. Make your vacation count for Jesus. Minister grace. Give instead of take." He paused and looked Michael straight in the eyes. His own blue eyes misted over. "My friend, the sailing cruise will end in a week. Only your closeness with the Lord will matter when all is said and done. He is coming soon!" His voice cracked.

He looked up at the sky and faced Michael again. "I heard wise advice long ago—live *every* moment in the light of eternity."

"We'll try. Honest, we will." He swallowed hard. "Say, Josh, talking about all this reminds me. That night on the phone from New York you referred to something about my position as a husband. I never heard it put quite the way you did."

"King, prophet, and priest, I assume. They are three primary roles of Jesus in the Church. I believe that He expects godly men to represent Him thus in the home."

"I never heard *that* theory before. Tell me more . . ."

Joshua's eyebrows raised this time. "My goodness. I would find difficulty to explain in an instant what the Lord has shown me throughout many years."

"Oh, just take a stab at it. I have started to understand one thing—how the devil pits husbands and wives against each other."

"Yes. As in my native land. While we Berliners slept in our beds, the Wall was erected *to divide what had formerly been one beautiful city.* Likewise, Satan sneaks into homes to build a wall of hatred between couples. When? While spiritually, they slumber!"

"So I can see we've gotta stay awake. Then tear the wall down. And keep it down." He took a long moment to ponder his point. "Move the wall from between us to *around* us, maybe?"

"Hallelujah, Michael! You hit the target! Of course, you need more than a wall. Nehemiah stirred the Israelites to rebuild around Jerusalem high *towers* and strong *gates,* as well. Interestingly, each of those structures represents a role of husbands, as I see it. Wall = king—one wise enough to rule his domain and strong enough to protect it. Tower = prophet—one who sees an enemy approaching far in the distance and sounds the warning. Gate = priest—one who guards access to a kingdom and who ministers to its citizens. He ushers in divine blessings and drives out the enemy's curses."

"Wow, Josh! I can't be the only one who needs to hear more of this. Maybe we could get a few men from church together for a retreat—Caleb loved those, you know—and we could go in depth on the subject."

Astonished, Joshua stammered, "Perhaps . . ."

"No, really, I'm serious."

"I know you are. It touches me to follow in the footsteps of my father." He brushed away a tear from the corner of his eye. "Anna and I wondered what God would have us do now. Oh, if we could prevent one family from going through the heartache so many endure, it would be a dream fulfilled!"

"Let's try it. Maybe even here. After all . . . the place belongs to you." He stopped short and looked into Joshua's blue eyes again.

"What are you saying?"

Michael inhaled, then cleared his throat. "We didn't buy this property. Caleb willed it to me, only because he thought he had no heir. If he had known about you, he would—"

Joshua interrupted him. "Hush. He must have regarded you as a son. You owe us nothing. Besides, what would Anna and I do with all of this?" Smiling, he made a broad sweep in the air. "No, my friend, you are the steward."

"Okay, okay. But you and Anna are welcome here as long as you want to stay."

"Thank you, Michael. And while the Lord yet has work for us to do, we will stay. Yes, the gathering of men concept appeals to me a great deal."

"Me, too, for some reason. It's funny. I've never been a groupie type." He paused, stared again at the toy sailboat, then started walking around the pond at a brisk pace. His older friend hurried to catch up. "Joshua," he exclaimed, "I just had a super idea!"

"Do tell me. I cannot wait another moment."

Michael grinned back at him, shaking his head. "It's incredible. I can visualize the perfect setting for hands-on lessons about sailing and fighting. St. Augustine. The oldest city in the United States."

"Yes, yes. Give me the details." Joshua's eyes glistened.

"Well, it's the coolest place to visit. Neat shops, narrow brick streets, outdoor cafes. Bed and breakfast inns all over the place. Beaches. A gorgeous harbor just begging for sailboats. Even an historic lighthouse. *And* St. Augustine serves as home to a famous national monument—one of the longest-standing military forts in the world, with a view to match any I've seen. Josh . . . are you ready . . . the Castillo de San Marcos has *walls, gates,* and *towers.*"

Joshua stomped his feet with glee. "You don't say!"

"I do say. Oh, man. Guys could really get into what you have to teach at a place like that. And I bet Eric, this counselor I know, would want to get involved, too."

"Wonderful! It would be much merrier with more men."

They both burst out laughing. "'The more, the merrier,' you mean?" Michael asked, holding his sides.

Joshua's head bobbed as he grew more serious. "But we cannot forget the ladies. They would feel slighted."

"True. They need their own agenda, though, don't you think? Maybe we could do something as couples when the men return home."

With a sly wink, Joshua whispered, "I have it. We will plan a special surprise ceremony to renew wedding vows. Our wives will know only to dress up in white finery and meet us at a certain time and place. Perhaps we could follow the ceremony with a banquet, a long candlelit walk, and a romantic rendezvous for each couple."

Michael let out a whistle. "You've figured out what makes women tick, haven't you, my man?"

"After a lifetime, I do believe I have."

"Well, I've gotten a thing or two through my thick skull, too. How about if the next day, say in the afternoon, we were to round up everybody's kids and do fun stuff as a group?"

"You are brilliant, Michael. Brilliant. Do you realize that, in one weekend, we would demonstrate the divine order for families? Godly husbands who love their wives and together, touch their children. But where shall this extravaganza take place? Not entirely at the city of the fort, I gather?"

Michael scratched his head and ran his fingers through his hair. "Who knows? I don't think so, though . . ."

"I see. You envision a scenario more akin to the following: 'knights-in-shining-armor' ride off into the sunset to hone their battle skills and ride back into town to court the ladies-in-waiting. Interesting. Very interesting."

"Yeah. Wait a minute. You know what? Just a few miles from here is the Mission Inn Resort. A gorgeous place. And a perfect setting for the grand finale. I'll take you by there tomorrow to see what you think." Joshua nodded his heartiest approval.

By then, their walk had taken them full circle to the house. As soon as they stepped inside, they were greeted by the pungent cinnamon aroma of Anna's dessert and "where-on-earth-have-you-been" questions from their wives. Michael and Joshua just gave each other playful winks as if to say, "Sorry, ladies—our secret."

A sudden bang of the front screen door interrupted their camaraderie. It was Michelle. In the next instant, Stephen came bounding down the steps. When everyone had converged in the den with a warm dessert in hand, Stephen scoped things out around him and demanded to know what was going on.

"Nothing. Why?" Michael asked.

"Looks like you guys been havin' a meeting. Makin' plans. Got a video out, notebooks, flyers . . ."

Michael and Stephanie looked at each other with a blank expression. "Your mom and I," Michael declared, "are going on a short vacation."

"Without us?" Michelle whined.

"Yes, just the two of us. We'll be gone for a week and Mr. and Mrs. Lieben will take care of you and Stephen."

Her head tilted to the side. "Oh. That won't be so bad."

"Yep, they're neat," Stephen piped in. "But where ya goin'?"

"On a big sailboat. Dad is treating me to a nice present."

Stephen frowned. "Boy, wish we could go."

Michelle's eyes narrowed. "Yeah, I don't think it's fair for you guys to go and not take us." Her tone had a sharp edge.

Michael took a firm stance. "Guys, it's very fair. We haven't taken a trip by ourselves in years. Moms and dads need to do that once in awhile. It'll help us be better parents. Trust me."

Stephanie's voice softened. "Besides, when we get back, guess what, kids! We're all going on a vacation together."

"Oh boy! Where?" Stephen rubbed his palms back and forth.

Michael thought fast. "How about North Carolina? We could stay in a real log cabin, go hiking in the mountains, roast hot dogs and marshmallows, go canoeing, and maybe ride an old-fashioned train where the track is *so steep,* it goes almost straight up and down."

"Wow! That sounds scary!" Stephen gave his dad a thumbs up.

"And if you both behave while Mom and I are away, we may let each of you bring a friend on the trip."

Michelle retorted, "That would make it bearable, at least."

Stephanie reached her arm around Michelle's shoulders. "I remember when I was your age. I thought going on vacation with the family was the worst thing on earth. But it usually turned out better than I expected. So don't give up on us yet, honey . . ."

One side of Michelle's mouth turned up in an apologetic smile. She let out a sigh. "Sorry I got sarcastic. I'm still workin' on some stuff. I don't know what I would do without you all. A lot of girls like me didn't have anybody who cared if they ever came home."

Michael reached over to squeeze her hand. "Well, we sure did, honey. You chose a hard road we never would have wanted for you, but we'll walk with you all the way."

"Thanks." She grew pensive for a moment. "Will I be able to go hiking? And canoeing?"

Stephanie patted her arm. "I don't see why not. Nowadays, they want you to stay active until the baby comes. We'll check with the doctor to be sure."

That seemed to encourage her, but only briefly. She looked down and then back up, glassy-eyed. "I guess I got snippy because I'm feeling pretty guilty. Sandy tracked me down on the way out of the twelve-step meeting." Big tears spilled onto her shirt.

"He told me that these two nice people, Hank and Dot, are going to prison. Dad—mom, nobody kidnapped me. Not even close! They saved my life. Honest! Some creepy guys were trying to pick me up on a dark country road. They stopped their truck just in time. Who knows where I'd be?

"I lied to them about my age and where I lived so they would take me with them! All they did was talk about Jesus! *I* was a real brat." She buried her face in her hands and sobbed. "Sandy said their new truck got repossessed since they've been in jail . . . Oh, please, we can't go *anywhere* until I get this mess straightened out!"

Shocked into grim silence, Michael stretched out his arms to gather his daughter and the rest of his family for a 'huddle hug.'

Those were happening much more often lately . . .

Joshua and Anna looked at each other and leaned their foreheads together. His crystal blue eyes glistened brighter than they had in years. "My dearest Anna," he murmured through a grin as broad as an old Cheshire cat, "For this little family in our midst, I do believe I see a glimmer of hope. Would you care to give me your view of the matter?"

Nodding slowly as her arms encircled his neck, she just smiled her most radiant smile. "But Herr Lieben," she whispered, "my humble opinion is also this. Truly, you are a prince among men. Oh, how I thank my God for sharing you with me . . ."

And all of heaven, weeping, rejoiced.

Tender Journey Love Notes
In chronological order of the story . . .
101 Dos and Don'ts
for Building Happy Homes

Pray! and . . .

1. Be careful of using personal entertainment as a way to avoid closeness with your spouse. Couples often do this at bedtime.
(Michael watched TV and thumbed through a tech magazine; Stephanie buried herself in a romance novel.)

2. Don't stifle natural feelings of desire. Do whatever you can—biblically, of course—to fan the flame.
(Michael and Stephanie couldn't help but notice each other's attractiveness, but ignored it, even hid it.)

3. Don't work yourself up into a bad attitude simply because he or she is busy doing something else at the moment.
(Michael and Stephanie both assumed the other wasn't interested, then turned away, hurt, and sealed their fate.)

4. Never speak with sarcasm in your voice, especially regarding something your spouse enjoys. Show love by trying to appreciate each other's unique interests.
(Stephanie gave Michael a snippy response about the international news. He chided her about her choice of reading material.)

5. Don't give in to sudden fits of temper.
(Michael got mad over a slight inconvenience—the apparent failure of the remote control— and took out his frustration on Stephanie.)

6. Beware of selfish preoccupation so you don't miss between-the-lines hints when a loved one needs you.
(Stephanie was too engrossed in her book to observe that Michelle's unusual late-night interruption might have indicated she had something on her mind.)

7. Do everything you can to preserve the bedroom as a quiet sanctuary of rest and refreshment. Avoid discussions of business or family problems there.
(Michael got excited about new consulting opportunities on the other side of the world when he should have been getting excited about his beautiful wife lying next to him.)

8. Don't place all the blame on your spouse for changes and problems in your relationship.
(Michael decided it was Stephanie's fault for how far apart they had grown rather than taking at least half of the responsibility.)

9. Be willing to forgive, with God's help, and continue to take reasonable, lifelong emotional risks.
(Stephanie resisted reaching out to Michael and getting close to him again because he had cheated on her.)

10. Focus on what you can do in the present and in the future to improve your relationship; don't dwell on "the way you were."
(Stephanie grew sad and resentful whenever she reminisced about how nice Michael used to treat her when they were dating. She forgot that she didn't treat him as well, either.)

11. Don't mentally rehearse your spouse's shortcomings over the last day, month, year, decade, etc.
(Stephanie became obsessed with Michael's workaholic tendencies and frequent absences from home. She could have learned to communicate with him constructively about the situation.)

12. Don't dwell on the times your spouse has hurt you. Move on.
(Michael rehashed Stephanie's set-up after the honors banquet over three years earlier and rekindled animosity.)

13. Let God show you in prayer whether you have truly forgiven someone for hurting you.
(Michael mistakenly believed he had forgiven Stephanie for the humiliating set-up.)

14. If you have been unfaithful, accept the fact that it might take a while for your spouse to forgive you and trust you again.
(Michael dismissed the depth of Stephanie's emotional pain and pushed her further away. He expected more of a "quick-fix.")

15. Don't assume your relationship is as good as it can be or even better than it was.
(Michael thought he and Stephanie were doing okay simply because they mentioned divorce less often.)

16. Realize that everyone deals with tragedy and grief differently.
(Michael felt angry and bitter about Stephen's AIDS and buried his pain in his work; Stephanie felt hopeless, depressed, and withdrawn. Neither tried to understand the other person.)

621

17. Talk about what's happening in your family right now; don't bury feelings or hide them from each other.
(Stephanie concluded that she couldn't talk to Michael about her grief over Stephen; Michael, that he needed to put up an "I can handle it" front, even when he felt powerless and afraid.)

18. Take as many family photos as you can afford so you can cherish them as you grow old together.
(The portrait of Michelle and Stephen taken right before he was diagnosed became a treasured family heirloom.)

19. Express to your spouse how he or she can help you cope.
(Stephanie needed more hugs, listening, and words of encouragement, and resented Michael for not providing them automatically.)

20. Don't tolerate long periods of abstinence from intimacy.
(Michael and Stephanie were both guilty of this and paid the price— it became harder and harder to feel comfortable with one another.)

21. Don't go to bed angry—never, ever, ever!
(Michael was mad about her seeming sexual indifference; she was angry about his skewed priorities, and they went to sleep fuming.)

22. Share significant life events together whenever possible.
(Side by side, Joshua and Anna witnessed the fall of the Berlin Wall.)

23. Treat each other with tenderness, even in public. It makes your spouse feel special.
(Joshua and Anna were comfortable enough with each other to embrace in the midst of a crowd— nonsexually, of course.)

24. Be honest about grief when it surfaces, but don't dwell too long on sad thoughts. Seek professional help for depression.
(Joshua and Anna briefly relived their daughter Anja's death.)

25. Help your loved ones to forgive their enemies.
(Joshua urged Anna to pray with him for the soldier who killed Anja.)

26. Be concerned and pray for what God wants to do beyond the confines of your own home.
(Joshua and Anna, having prayed for the fall of the Wall, gave joyful thanks when it finally happened.)

27. Express forgiveness in tangible ways.
(Anna gave her flowers to a reluctant border guard. He represented an enemy who had hurt her by knocking her to the ground that morning and by killing her daughter years ago.)

28. Praise your loved ones when they do something commendable and be specific about the reasons for your admiration.
(Joshua praised Anna for listening to the voice of the Holy Spirit.)

29. Plan activities during the holidays to create special meaning and memories for each member of the family.
(Because Stephanie hadn't bothered to solicit Michael's input about the social calendar, he simply "went through the motions" unfulfilled.)

30. Respect the fact that each person's physical, mental, and emotional clock ticks to a different beat.
(Michael loved to start work very early in the morning; Stephanie preferred to sleep in a bit later.)

31. Understand the strong correlation between a man's sense of fulfillment and his satisfaction with his career.
(Michael's disciplined, independent nature made him a good candidate to pursue the challenge of being a self-employed consultant. He did, and was happier in his work than he had been.)

32. Encourage one another to take up a hobby or a project to stimulate personal growth, but don't let your own interests infringe on the family's well-being.
(Michael developed a new awareness of nuclear waste and felt very motivated to do something about it— to the point of almost neglecting income-producing clients. This made Stephanie feel understandably insecure. Of course, she didn't affirm him for his innovative efforts as much as she could have.)

33. When a loved one wants to speak to you about something, give him or her your undivided attention, or ask if you can discuss the matter at another time when you can better concentrate.
(Michelle went to her dad to ask about getting a dog, a very important issue for her. He barely looked up from his computer long enough to acknowledge her presence, much less to search for the real reasons behind her request.)

34. Care enough about your family members to keep abreast of all that's going on in their lives from day to day.
(Michael had forgotten that Michelle had broken up with her boyfriend—an obvious sore point for a teenaged girl—and glossed over the blunder as if it were no big deal. He wounded her deeply by his insensitivity.)

35. Demonstrate support for your spouse's choice of profession. He or she must spend at least one-half of all waking hours there; you don't.
(In spite of her reservations about future financial instability, Stephanie did have an inspirational quote matted and framed for Michael's office when he went into business for himself.)

36. Don't attack your spouse as soon as he or she walks in the door, even if you're on edge about a problem.
(Stephanie set a negative tone for the evening by snapping at Michael before he could say a word. He had left his office with the intention of expressing appreciation for her thoughtfulness, but her attitude foiled his plan.)

37. If your spouse makes even the slightest effort to be affectionate, put your own agenda on hold and respond.
(After Michael went a step further to offer Stephanie a hug—one of his rarer, more sensitive moments—she ignored his effort and gave him a cutting comeback.)

38. Listen carefully to the emotions and body language behind your spouse's words and show appropriate concern.
(Michael launched right off into his own topic about a client without acknowledging Stephanie's distress about Michelle.)

39. Be available. Make it *easy* for your spouse to talk to you.
(With Stephanie standing right in front of him, Michael failed to look up from his newspaper. She had to ask to talk to him about something important and even then, he only peered over his newspaper at her.)

40. When your spouse has a "gut instinct" that something is wrong, don't lecture him or her. Take heed. Try to understand.
(Michael chided Stephanie for worrying about Michelle being several hours late, but her concerns were legitimate in our day and age.)

41. Pay attention to subtle changes in behavior of loved ones and address the underlying issue before it's too late.
(Stephen had noticed that his sister had been locking herself in her room and talking less since she had broken up with her boyfriend. Michelle's girlfriend, Cindy, also said she had been kind of standoffish. Neither Michael nor Stephanie had noticed a thing.)

42. Pitch in with chores around the house. Every member of the family should share the responsibility.
(Michael decided to be a "nice guy" and load the dishwasher, as if he were doing Stephanie a big favor instead of pulling his own weight.)

43. Don't allow yourself the luxury of critical thoughts about your spouse, simply because he or she has a different personality and habits than you do.
(Michael was compulsively neat, precise, and organized—he usually balanced the checkbook to the penny—and he looked down on Stephanie for what he considered "messiness.")

44. Don't throw away items belonging to your spouse without discussing the matter with him or her first. Children also deserve to understand why you feel something they cherish needs to go.
(When Michael found the quote about priorities which Stephanie had left in the checkbook, he scanned it and tossed it in the garbage without a second thought as to why she might have saved it.)

45. Make bedtime a special bonding time with your children. Talk, read stories, reassure them of your love, pray for them.
(Stephanie tucked Stephen in bed, and even though he had already fallen asleep, she spent a few precious moments with him.)

46. Appreciate the difference between men and women regarding the home and family.
(Stephanie knew every detail about Michelle—distinguishing marks, what she had worn to school, and the address of her former boyfriend. Michael felt helpless. Instead of seizing the opportunity to praise his wife, he allowed it to bruise his male ego. He mentally criticized Stephanie for having a good memory when she wanted one.)

47. If you want to help members of your family appreciate what they have, together help others in need—and do a quality job while you're at it.
(In spite of Caleb and Michael's fresh coat of paint a few years ago, Sandy and Maggie's house was falling in disrepair. Volunteers had replaced the steps, but hadn't used enough care to make them level. Surely in a large church, someone could have come to the aid of this invalid widow and her son.)

48. Be a mentor or role model to someone younger than you. Submit to an older, more mature person yourself, as well.
(Until his death, Caleb had taken Sandy under his wing and became a grandfather figure to him. Their relationship had a profound impact on Sandy—and on Michael, for a time.)

49. Be thoughtful. Offer to do tasks or errands for a loved one without their having to ask.

(Sandy, at thirteen, made sure his mother didn't need anything before he left for the Nastasis house for just a few minutes.)

50. **Show genuine concern for another family in crisis.**
(Sandy was quick to find out if Michelle was okay, then offered to get kids to help look for her and tried to pray with Michael about it.)

51. **Be willing to confront someone—humbly, and in love—about an area where you see negative changes taking place.**
(Sandy took a chance when he pointed out to Michael the decline in his desire for prayer since Caleb died. Michael resented the admonition, but Sandy did his part faithfully.)

52. **Pray for others whenever and wherever they need it.**
(Sandy didn't let Michael's reluctance stand in his way. As soon as he pedaled toward home, he started praying for the whole situation.)

53. **If one child requires extra attention due to disabilities or illness, go out of your way to make sure the other children don't feel guilty, unimportant, and unloved.**
(A major reason Michelle ran away was because she couldn't deal with the negative emotions building up inside her due to Stephen's AIDS.)

54. **Make every effort possible to have at least one parent attend school activities your child is involved in. If you're a single parent who has to work, express sincere regrets for your absence and try to make up for it another way.**
(Michelle had never forgotten all the important events her parents had missed. She felt rejected and neglected, causing her to resent everybody in the family.)

55. Provide your children an "open-door" atmosphere to come and talk to you about what's bothering them—no matter what it might be. This deep sense of trust comes from time spent together. They learn they can count on you to really listen.
(Whether true or not, Michelle felt she had no one to talk to about the maelstrom of emotions raging inside her.)

56. Teach your loved ones ways to avoid danger, as well ways as to protect themselves in case it comes.
(Whether or not Michael and Stephanie had ever tried to instill in Michelle the dangers of hitchhiking, she ignored them. Stephanie had, at least, given her a pepper spray to keep in her purse. Using it bought her enough time to get away until the truck arrived.)

57. Follow the wisdom of the Holy Spirit and be willing to serve as a modern-day good Samaritan. Be aware, however, that it may cost you something.
(Hank and Dot may have saved Michelle's life by stopping to rescue her on a dark country road. Little did they know they would pay such a high price for their kindness—arrest for kidnapping.)

58. Don't alienate those you're trying to reach when they're irrational. Hostility and a demanding tone of voice will only send them fleeing further.
(When Michelle called from the truck stop, Michael tried to regain control of a scary situation. His authoritarian style, which had worked well to keep her in line at home, had a boomerang effect now.)

59. Acknowledge the fact that others may be better qualified to handle a matter than you are. Let them do it.

(Michael rudely rebuffed his wife as an alternative spokesman, even when she begged to get his attention. Then, it was too late.)

60. If your spouse makes a mistake in judgment, don't rub salt in an open wound. Keep quiet.
(Stephanie pounced on Michael with both feet after Michelle hung up on him, never considering how terrible he might feel already.)

61. When you're angry, it's often better to hold your tongue and just walk away until you calm down.
(Michael recognized that he was furious—enough to slap his wife for what she had said—but somehow he had the presence of mind to leave the room first.)

62. Make personal sacrifices in order to surprise your spouse with something special.
(Joshua had secretly saved money for years to be able to take Anna on a vacation he knew she would enjoy, not just one that would appeal to him as a man.)

63. Do fun things together to keep the romance of your courtship days alive.
(Joshua and Anna stayed in a nice hotel, strolled arm-in-arm through pretty parks, went window-shopping, dressed up for an authentic madrigal dinner, and took a cruise. He treated her like a princess; she responded in kind.)

64. Don't give in to the temptation to spice up your relationship in unwholesome ways.
(Joshua and Anna had no intention of visiting the sleazy area of Hamburg; they didn't need that to stay attracted to one another.)

65. Assist your spouse in the small details of life, in order that he or she may accomplish a sought-after goal.
(Whenever Joshua had an idea to illustrate a biblical point he might teach on one day, Anna would get ready with paper and pen to take notes for him.)

66. Recognize that God is not a slave driver. While He surely wants us to work for the benefit of His kingdom, He allows us seasons of rest to enjoy the blessings of His kingdom.
(Anna began to feel guilty about their nice trip when she remembered that souls were dying. Joshua reassured her that he had struggled with the same questions and finally felt peace.)

67. Understand that God made husbands and wives to complement one another with different strengths and weaknesses.
(Joshua and Anna capitalized on this. They were always quick to voice their mutual admiration. Anna needed Joshua's ability to remember so many facts; he needed her to make him more gentle.)

68. If someone speaks to you in a condescending tone about your faith, don't retaliate. Simply state your case in love.
(Michelle made fun of the stickers Hank had pasted in the cab of his truck, as well as of the tapes his listened to while driving. He teased her a bit, but never took offense or got on the defensive.)

69. Recognize your own weaknesses, and listen to your spouse when he or she issues a warning of potential danger ahead.
(Dot reminded Hank in a light-hearted way to go easy on his teasing with Michelle. He received her comment in good humor, made a promise to keep it under control, and apologized when he slipped.)

70. Before you say "good night," always kiss your spouse and say, "I love you."
(Even before crawling into the sleeper behind the truck cab, Dot showed her fondness for Hank—in spite of their guest's presence.)

71. Listen to Christian music and messages whenever you have an opportunity. While driving is ideal, assuming your spouse is also a believer and doesn't mind. Respect his or her wishes, too.
(Hank and Dot played tapes all the time while they were driving truck cross-country. Hank admitted it helped to keep him drug- and alcohol-free after years of setbacks.)

72. Teach your children the consequences of right and wrong, but remember to set a good example yourself.
(Hank and Dot discovered the ineffectiveness of, "Don't do as I do; do as I say" parenting.)

73. Love your family members, "warts and all." No matter what, let them know you love and believe in them, even when you cannot condone their bad behavior or decisions.
(Hank and Dot made this a policy with their children and with each other.)

74. Don't ever resort to shouting-match arguments or periods of cold, silent treatment. Learn how to communicate in more constructive ways.
(Michelle pictured her home this way, and it contributed to her unhappiness there. It used to be a way of life in Hank and Dot's home until they started praying together.)

75. Don't blow things out of proportion.
(In Hank's words, he and Dot used to be able to "take an ice cube and make a whole winter out of it." It kept them in constant turmoil.)

76. Don't belittle those who struggle with substance abuse; insist they get the help they need. If necessary, seek professional help for yourself as a co-dependent so you know how to deal with the problem in a rational, tough-love, manner.
(Hank's family and friends gave up on him when he backslid; Dot hung in there and became part of the solution.)

77. Receive the love of the Savior into your heart. Only then can you love others.
(Hank tried to show Michelle that human beings can't love each other very well on their own because they're basically selfish.)

78. Develop a constant, personal relationship with the Savior, not just a ritual of church-going.
(Things improved in Hank's life when he started being obedient out of genuine love for the Lord. He didn't want to hurt Him anymore.)

79. Instead of an *accuser,* become an *intercessor* for those around you (one who stands in the gap—in prayer and out of prayer).
(The doctor on Hank's tape showed how the intercessor follows in the footsteps of Jesus; the accuser, in those of Satan. Through intercessors, sinners feel convicted of wrong, but forgiven; changed, but uplifted; challenged, but motivated to do better.)

80. Before you point out your loved one's faults, look hard at your own. Prayer enables you to see them more clearly.

Tender Journey

(The doctor on Hank's tape pointed out that we'll have less of a holier-than-thou attitude when we allow God to correct our faults first.)

81. Recognize the damage marital problems cause to children's emotions and encourage them to talk about it. Even if you and your spouse decide to reconcile after a separation or divorce, don't sweep the matter under the rug with the kids, as if nothing unusual has happened.

(Part of Michelle's unresolved anger toward her parents stemmed from their having gotten back together "out of the clear blue" while she and Stephen were away at camp. The change was too drastic for her to swallow. And, whereas Michael and Stephanie had treated each other disrespectfully for years in front of her—another no-no—they now insisted on her respect for the partner. Mixed signals!)

82. Don't take out on the children your frustration toward your spouse.

(Michael and Stephanie's second honeymoon period lasted a short time before they started arguing again. Michelle felt that she got most of the fallout because she was the healthy child in the family.)

83. Don't let one child's more pleasant personality cause you to show favoritism. Each child is unique.

(Michelle believed that her parents loved Stephen more because he was so sweet and she, so moody by nature. She was further convinced of a lie: that they secretly wished she had AIDS instead of Stephen.)

84. Be quick to do fun things your children will enjoy.

(Stephen had been begging for Michael to watch a football video with him for months, and Michael finally realized he couldn't put it off any longer. They had a brief, but pleasant time—father and son alone.)

85. Just because something has little value to you does not mean your spouse feels the same. Respect one another in this area.
(Michael made light of the glass bowl Stephanie had broken, but to her, it was a family heirloom she hoped to pass on to Michelle. This brought deep emotions to the surface for Stephanie.)

86. Don't give your spouse trite, placating observations or suggestions when he or she is upset. It only makes things worse.
(Michael was trying to be helpful when he told Stephanie everything was going to be okay with Michelle. In truth, he had no grounds for making such a claim. It seemed to her that either 1) he was refusing to comprehend the painful reality of the situation) 2) she was the only one suffering from the stress of it.)

87. Don't assume your spouse doesn't care about a crisis as much as you do, simply because he or she shows fewer feelings about it, or tries to keep busy.
(Stephanie unfairly criticized Michael for not being as concerned as she was about Michelle when he watched the football video with Stephen. He was just doing what she had been harping on him to do—spend more time with the kids. Also, it was his way of trying to cope with his own guilt and fear for their daughter.)

88. Remember that a soft answer turns away wrath, but a hard one kindles it.
(At first, Michael recognized the volatility of Stephanie's emotional state and held his peace, but a few seconds later, he made a smart comment about her worrying enough for both of them and stormed out of the room.)

 Tender Journey

89. Give money to those in need, but use wisdom about who, where, and when. Talk it over with your spouse first, too.
(Dot and Hank had discussed Michelle's plight while she was sleeping, prayed for her, and decided to give her a few dollars for the road.)

90. Drive carefully, especially when your loved ones are in the car. Don't add to their sense of stress; they should feel secure and comfortable with you at the wheel.
(Hank had earned a "safe driver" status which he worked hard to preserve. Michael, on the other hand, made Stephanie very nervous on the way to MarriageMaker class by venting his frustrations behind the wheel. He was insensitive to how afraid it made her.)

91. Never be abusive, emotionally or physically, to your spouse and children. If you recognize even the potential for this syndrome, get help! And, if you detect abuse in another family, *pray.* Call the authorities, if necessary. It could save someone's life.
(The mother Michelle overheard in the bus station had an obvious abuse problem. In a public rest room, her young son whimpered in fear. Matt had run away due to abuse from an alcoholic father.)

92. Show special understanding to your teens after relationship break-ups so they aren't as vulnerable to opposite-sex attention.
(When Michelle met Matt, she was an easy target—still in the throes of rejection from her boyfriend. Her parents could have reached out to her more to restore her damaged sense of self-worth.)

93. If you need outside marriage counseling, by all means get it! Seek personal referrals to a *Christian* professional, ideally to one whose fee is based on income so you can afford to attend.

(Michael dug in his heels at the very notion, as if it belittled him as a man somehow. In truth, they could really benefit from an objective person to teach them to better handle conflict using the Word of God. Stephanie knew friends who had found help from Dr. Marcos.)

94. Don't manipulate your spouse into doing what you want, no matter if your intentions are good or not. Give him or her time make a decision without pressure from you.
(Stephanie reminded Michael how unhappy she was, acted pitiful and helpless, and generally just kept badgering him about counseling until he gave in. Then, as a "reward" for his compliance, she sent him "I'm available" signals—which she rarely did. He resented her for it.)

95. Spend time alone with *God,* not just with your thoughts.
(Michael went out to take a walk in the moonlight and could have used the opportunity to pray about what was bothering him. Instead, he simply reminisced and pondered how frustrated and afraid he was, as well as how far away God seemed.)

96. Avoid the mind-set that you *deserve* to be happy. It can lead to self-indulgence. Commitment to the Lord brings lasting joy.
(The plaque on Dr. Marcos's wall reminded Michael of the ultimate goal of "recovery"/Christian growth: to destroy the idols in our hearts and make us more like children of God.)

97. Stir up your faith in the Word. Believe that God cares for you. If you ask, He *will* get involved in the details of your marriage and family situation.
(Dr. Marcos assured Michael and Stephanie that he had seen many couples—including him and his wife—come through tragedy stronger, better than before. It took asking for God's help.)

98. Be careful how and when you express anger to your spouse. However, don't hold it in and let it fester, either.
(Dr. Marcos explained that anger often stems from selfish motives, not righteous ones like those of Jesus with the moneychangers in the temple. He encouraged his clients to own up to what God already knew.)

99. Hone your communication skills throughout your lifetime.
(Dr. Marcos emphasized the power of constructive, productive communication—a two-way street of talking and listening, done on a regular basis, covering all topics important to the relationship. The tongue can be the most healing agent or destructive weapon a couple has, as the Scripture verse from James showed Michael and Stephanie.)

100. Acknowledge your interdependence on other human beings. Give thanks always to God— and to them—for the blessings they add to your life.
(Michael admitted to Dr. Marcos how much Caleb meant to him. Without his influence, he might not have become a Christian. However, Michael found it nearly impossible to acknowledge how much he needed his wife.)

101. Maintain an eternal perspective. This world is not our final destination; it is a training ground to make us more like Jesus!
(Michael and Stephanie were reminded in counseling of their heavenly citizenship. As such, they had the capacity to take into account the unseen elements in every difficult situation, and stay at peace.)

P.S. We found this many "dos and don'ts" in the first 115 pages of *Tender Journey.* See how many more you can find. Send them to us. Who knows—we may include them in the future . . .

Questions and Answers
About LOVE PRESS

Q. What is Love Press?

A. An outreach of *St. Luke's Cataract and Laser Institute* in Tarpon Springs, Florida, founded by Dr. Jim Gills. Because of his belief in ministering not only to the eye, but to the whole person, St. Luke's has been giving away his inspirational books since 1985. In 1990, Dr. Gills' ministry acquired the name, LOVE PRESS.

Purpose Statement

LOVE PRESS is a Christian publishing outreach dedicated to winning the world to Jesus Christ, one person at a time. Empowered by His Holy Spirit, we give away quality books and pamphlets that *instruct* readers toward a better grasp of Scripture, *encourage* them to greater triumph over trials, and *inspire* them to a deeper love of God, family, and fellow man. *(See also Statement of Faith following questions/answers.)*

Q. Why do you give your books away?

A. We strive to give everyone an equal opportunity to read our materials. Thousands of people—prisoners, shelter residents, addicts, the inner-city poor, single parents, the elderly, for example—do not have the means to purchase books, but they do need hope. LOVE PRESS has been there for them. Readers who *can* afford a financial gift will play a part in passing on spiritual blessings to others. We leave that decision between each person and God. The name we gave this method of distribution is:

LoveLines: The Honor Innovation™

 Tender Journey

Q. *Does Love Press make money for St. Luke's?*

A. Not at all! It is a major expense for St. Luke's. This renowned state-of-the-art eye care facility alone makes it possible for books to be written, designed, printed, and distributed. For example, total financial gifts received since 1990 would not come close to the cost of *printing Tender Journey* one time. There are seven other books, plus several pamphlets available. We value your prayers . . .

Q. *Why does Love Press produce such nice materials, if they're given away?*

A. In our commercialized society, people often assume that if something is free, it must not be worth very much. (They assume the same about God's gift of His Son.) However, we believe the messages within our pages have tremendous value to the reader, and we'd like to give that impression at first glance. So when you get a LOVE PRESS book, we do hope you have a sense that, indeed, you have received a gift. Tell us if you like it and pass it on!

Q. *If I send Love Press something I have written, will you publish it?*

A. We may quote a brief excerpt within one of our publications, but other than that, we do not publish outside materials. LOVE PRESS is simply an outreach of St. Luke's to share books written by Dr. Gills. If you truly desire to be published, here are a few tips: 1) Pray for guidance 2) Become a student of the art of writing 3) Read, read, read, including magazines for writers 4) Attend writer's conferences, such as *Write-to-Publish* in Wheaton, Illinois, or the *Florida Christian Writer's Conference* in Titusville 5) Study the current year's *Writer's Market* and any other books about free-lance writing, usually available at the public library.

Tender Journey: *A continuing story for our troubled times*

Q. *I called the Love Press number and got a recording. Why?*

A. We're sorry for the inconvenience. You reached the voice mail ordering line. We maintain a very small staff in order to be able to give books away. Please record your message or send it by fax so that a staff member may respond at the earliest possible moment. Thanks for your understanding!

Q. *I read a book by Love Press that I really enjoyed. How can I receive more?*

A. Just write, call, or fax:

LOVE PRESS
P.O. Box 5000
Tarpon Springs, Florida 34688-5000
(813) 938-2020, Ext. 2200
(800) 282-9905, Ext. 2200
(813) 372 3605 (fax)

Leave a clear message stating the titles, quantity, your complete name, address, zip code, and phone number. Spell out proper names, please, so we enter them correctly into the computer. Those ordering bulk quantities will be asked to complete a brief application form.

Special note to inmates: due to the incredible demand from you (we're thrilled!), we must now mail in bulk to your Chaplain's office, rather than to individuals. If you have already tried to find our books there without success, write and tell us.

Also, *please share your copies with others.*

LOVE PRESS
Statement of Faith

1. We believe in one eternal God, the great I AM of the Old and New Testaments of the Bible, who created all things. He expresses Himself as three persons—Father, Son, and Holy Spirit. He is at the same time imminent and transcendent, capable of dwelling within a born-again sinner and yet, holding the entire universe in balance.

2. We believe that the Bible is a Book among books, God's one true written unveiling of Himself to mankind. The Bible stands alone in its power to change a human life forever. Because God inspired the very words of the original manuscripts, they are alive, perfect, worthy of trust, and bear divine authority.

3. We believe that Jesus Christ is fully God, yet walked the earth as a man in His native land of Israel. He is God's unique Son, the only one like Him. He demonstrated this uniqueness in many ways—when He was born of a virgin, led a life free from sin, died by crucifixion in the place of all humanity who deserved it, rose up from a sealed tomb, and ascended into heaven before many witnesses. Seated now at the right hand of the Father, He prays for believers without ceasing. Though He once surrendered to humiliation and death, He will soon return for His Church as an all-powerful king.

4. We believe that the Holy Spirit is a person of the godhead, a member of the trinity as much as the Father and the Son. He convinces us of our sinfulness, draws us into firm faith in Jesus Christ as Savior and Lord, enables us to pray, worship, and understand Scripture, and empowers us to live out the commandments of God in the world.

5. We believe that God created man in His image, but He loved us enough to grant us free will. Because we chose sin rather than obedience, it caused a great gap to form between us and a holy God. There is nothing we can do to earn His love, to close the gap, to make ourselves worthy or acceptable to Him. Only the redeeming blood of Jesus Christ can restore the relationship between man and God forever. He is God's ultimate gift of love to mankind.

Dear Reader,

Did you enjoy this LOVE PRESS book? Dr. Jim Gills and HeartLight would love to hear from you! Please respond if this book has made an impact on you or someone you know. Your testimonies encourage us so much. Send correspondence in the postage-paid envelope provided inside the back cover, or to the address listed on page 641.

God bless every single one of you!

Endnotes

1. Ciardi, John. "Most Like An Arch This Marriage." Quoted in *Writer's Digest Magazine,* November, 1991, p. 16. Used by permission of The University of Arkansas Press, Fayetteville.

2. Word Perfect 5.1 Thesaurus. Synonyms for "tender." Ottawa, Canada: Corel Corporation.

3. Carter, Wanda Hope. "Secrets of Success." Mukilteo, WA: American Arts and Graphics, Inc.

4. Hayden, Sterling. *The Wanderer.* London: Longmans Group, Ltd, p. 24.

5. Tan, Paul Lee. *Encyclopedia of 7700 Illustrations.* Dallas: Bible Communications, Inc., p. 783, #3328.

6. Trafford, Abigail. *Crazy Time.* New York: Harper & Row, pp. 1-2, 4-7. Reprinted by permission of HarperCollins Publishers, Inc.

7. Stanley, Dr. Charles. Taped message, "Giving Thanks in All Things." Atlanta: In Touch Ministries.

8. Lotz, Anne Graham. "Angel Ministries: Newsletter of Anne Graham Lotz," Winter/Spring, 1994, p.3.

9. Yancey, Philip. *Disappointment With God.* Grand Rapids: The Zondervan Corporation, pp. 70-71.

10. Dobson, Dr. James. *When God Doesn't Make Sense.* Wheaton: Tyndale House Publishers, pp. 246-249. Used by permission of the author.

11. Edwards, Jonathan. *A Treatise Concerning Religious Affections.* Carlisle, PA: Banner of Truth Trust, pp 21-22.

12. Upham, Barb. "Love Means Believing in Someone." Boulder: Blue Mountain Arts.

13. Swindoll, Chuck. Taped message, "Escape Route for Anxiety Addicts." Used by permission of *Preaching Magazine*.

14. Buckland, Gail. *The White House in Miniature*. NY: W.W. Norton & Company, p. 13.

15. Moody, John Glenn. "Scorned, Torn, and Yet Reborn." Used by permission of the author.

16. Schriefer, Kathy. "When Lilacs Bloomed." Focus on the Family's *Brio* Magazine, November 1992, pp. 22-25. Used by permission of the author.

About the Authors

James P. Gills, M.D., is the founder and medical director of St. Luke's Cataract and Laser Institute in Tarpon Springs, Florida. Internationally respected as a cataract surgeon, he has performed more cataract extractions and lens implantations than anyone else in the world. He has pioneered many advancements in the field of ophthalmology that make cataract surgery safer and easier for patients.

Dr. Gills has published over ninety medical papers and contributed to six books. He is an active author on spiritual topics as well. He has been an avid student of the Bible for many years and has written a number of books about man's relationship with God. (See listing of titles and descriptions at the front.) *Tender Journey* is the sequel to his first novel entitled, *The Unseen Essential,* which has encouraged and delighted thousands of readers.

As an ultra-distance athlete, Dr. Gills has participated in a total of forty-six marathons, including nineteen of the famed Boston Marathon. He has competed in fourteen 100-mile mountain runs (he's one of only a few dozen people to complete all four major 100-mile mountain runs) and in three 200-mile runs through the rolling hills of Virginia. In addition, Dr. Gills has completed five Ironman Triathlons in Hawaii, as well as being the only person to complete six Double Ironman Triathlons in less than 30 hours. The Double Ironman consists of a 5.5-mile swim, a 224-mile bike ride, and a 52.4-mile run. His passion for fitness led him, along with his son, to write *Temple Maintenance,* in which he describes the importance of physical, mental, and spiritual conditioning. He received the 1990 *Amateur Athlete of the Year* award.

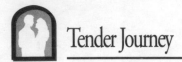 Tender Journey

Dr. Gills is a former member of the Board of Trustees of Trinity College and the national Board of Directors of the Fellowship of Christian Athletes. He is also recognized in the *Marquis Who's Who* and many other similar publications.

HeartLight is a writing and publishing management team based in Clearwater, Florida. They have accepted the love of God in Jesus Christ and seek to make Him known to the world . . .